GLORY
HOLE

GLORY HOLE

STEPHEN BEACHY

FC2

TUSCALOOSA

FC2 is an imprint of the University of Alabama Press
Inquiries about reproducing material from this work should be addressed to the
University of Alabama Press

Book Design: Publications Unit, Department of English, Illinois State University;
Director: Steve Halle, Production Assistant: Anya Malley
Cover design: Lou Robinson
Typeface: Baskerville

Library of Congress Cataloging-in-Publication Data.

Names: Beachy, Stephen, author.
Title: Glory hole / Stephen Beachy.
Description: Tuscaloosa, Alabama : FC2, [2017] | Description based on print
  version record and CIP data provided by publisher; resource not viewed.
Identifiers: LCCN 2017005463 (print) | LCCN 2017011970 (ebook) | ISBN
  9781573668736 (Ebook) | ISBN 9781573660624 (softcover)
Subjects: LCSH: Conspiracies--Fiction.
Classification: LCC PS3552.E128 (ebook) | LCC PS3552.E128 G58 2017 (print) |
  DDC 813/.54--dc23
LC record available at https://lccn.loc.gov/2017005463

For Johnny Ray Huston

I

This outward world is as a smoke or vaporous steam…breathed forth both out of the holy world and then also out of the dark world; and therefore it is terrible and lovely…for the pregnatress of time is a model or platform of the eternal pregnatress; and time coucheth in eternity; and it is nothing else, but that the eternity, in its wonderful birth and manifestation in its power and strength, doth thus behold itself, in a form or time.

—Jacob Boehme, *Mysterium Magnum*

1

ONCE, PHILIP GOT OFF THE BUS in a Montana town perched above the flatlands he'd just passed through. In the far distance, black and purple rain clouds had been pasted into the otherwise empty sky. The vapor trails hung down like chromosomes. This all happened a long time ago and nobody knows it. Might as well have dreamed it.

Once, Philip had a crush on a crazy. Roger, the crazy, was in love with Madonna, and had mailed her furniture, naked photos of himself, and dog shit once, and then, to apologize, he'd mailed her his thirty-page proof of the existence of God. He'd mixed words and numbers together with boisterous squiggles and indecipherable equations, all purporting to demonstrate an irrefutable divine truth: time and death, it all added up. Roger believed Madonna was into him, too, or that she was, at least, keeping tabs on him, sending her spies over Big Sur in airplanes and helicopters, and communicating with him through songs on the radio. Roger was handsome, with that childish magnetism that insane people sometimes have. Philip and Roger had both ended up in Big Sur because they'd been down to almost nothing. Separately, passing through, they'd seen the Help Wanted sign at the gas station. Roger had hit bottom in Oregon, living in a cabin in the woods and eating dog food, and was heading south toward LA to confront Madonna once and for all. Philip wasn't headed anywhere in particular at the time.

Now, Philip heads out the side door of his cottage, down the stairs to the basement. The past—it never goes away, until eventually it does. The world is full of different humans now, different sorts of thoughts, differently configured brains. The changes wrought on consciousness by volcanoes, by misinformation, by moving images and dark underground spaces...

Philip should have ducked into the basement, and he almost always remembers, but not today. The sound of his head colliding with the doorframe is shockingly loud. The pain is disorienting. He presses his fingers against the gummy blood clotting in his hair, and now here he is. Down below, dizzy and bleeding.

Down below, there are unopened boxes full of the books and artwork that Raymond's father left them when he died. The basement is unfinished, with naked Sheet rock and pink insulation shoved between planks here and there. The dirt floors of an adjacent crawlspace slope into dark corners. Philip's never actually seen a rat in there, but he knows they've passed through—maybe recently, maybe long ago. He's never seen the landlady either, who is rumored to be in Serbia, prosecuting war criminals. Mostly, the basement serves as a hydroponic garden. The grow lights buzz and the pumps of the aquafarms gurgle constantly. It's kind of soothing, but Philip sits down on a bucket now, hating the plants.

Upstairs the phone rings. After four rings, the machine gets it and Philip strains to identify the muted voice that drifts down. A voice through a cloud, he thinks. An angel from above. It's Howard.

The words could be coming from beneath the surface of a bathtub. It sounds like Howard's saying something about the Amish and a *shocking building* and then the phrase *hungry for God*. It sounds like *dreamers gurgling and protesting little boys* and it sounds like *big spenders sucking blood* and then again *hungry for* or maybe *angry with God*. The voice starts mumbling again, but then it says something like *inefficient in love*.

The urgency of Howard's tone suggests to Philip that he should rush upstairs and answer the phone. He hopes it isn't Howard who is either *hungry for* or *angry with* God. Howard's repressed anger is legendary; anger with doctors, anger with Daddy, with Mommy, with sixth grade teachers, with the Jehovah's Witnesses and other former coworkers who conspired against him for all those years, before his big breakdown, when he stopped repressing his anger and orchestrated a three- or four-day public tantrum that ended with something resembling a suicide attempt. His public pill-popping, his incoherent ranting, and his all too coherent threats got him fired, served with a restraining order, and eventually hospitalized when his building manager found him passed out on the floor of his room in the Tenderloin. Now, at sixty-one, he's on SSI and will never have to work another day in his life; he spends his days smoking weed, watching old movies, and listening to Judy Garland tapes, occasionally splurging on a masochistic hustler. He's never been happier. Of all the people Philip knows who have aggressively bottomed out, who have sunk as low as they could go, and then even lower, lower than they realized they could go, lower than they actually *could* go, sometimes repeatedly, only Howard made it work.

There's no natural light down here; the windows have been covered with blackout curtains. Rambling answering machine monologues are actually Howard's favorite mode of communication. Howard says something that sounds like *expert opinion* and something like *providing beef in my old age*. Philip's underneath the earth, receiving garbled transmissions from the Milky Way. What would we have to say to another species anyway? It would start out like phone sex, Philip's pretty sure, but quickly go awry. Either Howard hangs up or the machine cuts him off.

The changes wrought on consciousness by volcanoes, by misinformation, by moving images and dark underground spaces. Behold the skies, darkened with ash or satellite transmissions. In gloomy theaters or on tiny screens, with what rapture malnourished teenage boys would watch as rats gnawed a man to death. Basement laboratories, sewers teeming with biological life, constellations of flickering torches leading down.

The path through the bottom. For some reason Philip keeps thinking about Ted—Theodore, he corrects himself—scrubbing the floors of the video booths beneath the Nob Hill Theatre; when Ted was in Philip's writing workshop, back in the '90s, he wrote brutal memoir pieces about the obscure Beat poet he'd dated. Every time they had sex, according to Ted, the obscure Beat poet would say, *Yours is big, bigger than Kerouac's, but not like Neal Cassady's*.

Philip knows that when Ted's obscure Beat poet reminded Ted, every time they had sex, that he'd done it with both Jack Kerouac and Neal Cassady, he was surreptitiously placing himself in the great chain of visionaries who'd sucked each other's cocks. He was reminding Ted that no matter how bossy and unpleasant the obscure Beat poet was in bed, there was an esoteric benefit: Ted, too, was now firmly established in the great chain of visionaries who'd sucked each other's cocks, transmitting their occult wisdom through the ages in a kind of mystical osmosis. The osmosis led backward from Ted to the obscure Beat poet to Neal Cassady to the occultist Gavin Arthur to Edward Carpenter. From Edward Carpenter to Walt Whitman and probably on to Melville at least but Philip can't remember if Whitman actually sucked Abe Lincoln's cock or if Melville actually slept with Nathaniel Hawthorne, but he knows that Verlaine and Rimbaud are in there somewhere and that some obscure nineteenth century piece of ass supposedly leads from Whitman to Lord Byron and then back to da Vinci. And then all the way back to Plato and Socrates, supposedly, and further, in somebody's fevered imagination, either Ted's or the obscure Beat poet's, Philip can't remember. In somebody's fevered imagination the cocksucking visionaries were relentlessly leading the species up out of the primordial gruel and pits of primate excrement, up the back stairs and back into the main house, reestablishing some long-lost connection with something or other. In somebody's fevered imagination, the chain of cocksucking vision-aries dates back to the first she-male shaman bitch who painted bison on the cave wall, and back further even, to the first androgynous bonobo that picked up a pointy stick.

Before Philip gets a chance to play the messages and decode Howard's bulletin, Tony shows up at the door. Tony, a former opera singer, is always good for some drama. Tony used to drag Ralph up and down the stairs by his hair, consen-sually, when they were boyfriends and working out their issues together, in the '80s. Tony met Ralph shortly after he'd hit bottom himself, he tells Philip. Tony had eaten until he weighed five hundred pounds.

You should have seen me then, he says.

Five hundred pounds?

Five hundred, says Tony. I was living in Chicago, selling gourmet candy on the ground floor of the studio where Oprah shot her show. Oprah used to slink down, almost every day, wearing her shades, but she'd never say anything, just point at the candy. I had a girlfriend then, and I started smoking crack.

Maybe it was the drugs, but Tony always felt a strange kinship with Oprah, as she stood there, regal and ashamed, pointing at elaborate caramels and rasp-berry-filled truffles. At times Tony was convinced she was sending him messag-es telepathically. Her messages were elaborate and coded, but Tony understood the map she was drawing him of a journey involving fat and desire and per-formance and self-abnegation. She was communicating a deep understanding and revolutionary agenda concerning the sordid history of chocolate and the slave trade. They had become perfect mirrors for each other, Oprah and Tony, but she was the famous one.

On the machine, Howard tells of a tragedy that's all over the TV, a tragedy in an *Amish* schoolhouse, where a man showed up and started *shooting children*.

His version of events isn't even slightly chronological and focuses on the dumpy white guy whose *anger with God* drove him to pursue his *dream of molesting and murdering little boys*. Ten boys were shot in the Amish schoolhouse, he says, their *suspenders soaked in blood*. Howard says that the dumpy white guy never got over the death of his baby girl and that's why he was so *angry with God*. I guess he was *insufficiently loved*, says Howard. There's a long discussion of Howard's own anger with God, But Geez, he says. Enough already.

Howard's main point is that given his Amish heritage, Philip should see if he can exploit the situation, write about it, get paid—he suggests that the world will be clamoring for Philip's *expert opinion*. He suggests that maybe Philip can make enough money *to provide for me in my old age*.

They sit in the tiny backyard while Tony smokes the weed he's just bought. The wind blows mutilated clouds across the sky. The clouds seem damaged or ready to lose control, but nothing will come of it, that's a San Francisco sky. Lots of foreboding but nothing ever happens. Behind the house, the bottlebrush trees are in full bristly red bloom. The flowers look like the disposable brushes that Raymond buys to clean the toilet. The potted plants are hopeless. Raccoons or opossums steal every single tomato, every single orange, before it has a chance to ripen. Or maybe it's the rats; Bernal Hill is full of them.

Tony says that *every single schoolhouse shooter* has either been on antidepressants or recently gone off them.

You're making that up, says Philip.

I've never lied to you, Tony says, I want you to know that. He stands, and dramatically puts his hand on his heart, as if to convey his utter integrity. He looks hurt by the very thought that his integrity might be called into question.

That Tony is taking the opportunity to defend his constant and integral truthfulness, however, is completely absurd. He must know that his friends don't exactly *believe* anything he says—that they even harbor some doubts as to whether he'd *actually* been dating that guy who died on United Flight 93, back in August and September of 2001. Ralph has hazy memories of Tony mentioning some rugby-playing fellow, but in retrospect he's not sure if he first heard about the rugby-playing fellow before 9/11 or whether it was only afterward that Tony talked about him *as if he'd been talking about him for months*. The dead guy has since been declared *a gay hero*. Maybe Tony only tricked with him once, maybe he met him at a bar and had a conversation with him, a conversation that transformed Tony, for a moment, into a 9/11 widow. Surely Tony must realize, Philip thinks, that it is assumed by everyone who loves him that every story he tells is exaggerated, if not completely made up. Surely he understands that this is what is assumed to be Tony's style of self-presentation and self-understanding. *True for him*, as the therapists say. I've never ever lied to you, Tony says again, and I never would.

A squadron of jets thunders across the sky, momentarily drowning out the conversation. It's the Blue Angels, practicing for their annual air show. Tony gazes after the jets, hand still on his heart, using them as a kind of punctuation or transitional phrase.

People love an aura of authenticity, says Tony. They like it when something seems *true*.

Should I write about the Amish shooting? Philip asks. Should I pitch the story? Tony shrugs. Why not?

I can tell them my cultural knowledge and family name will get me special access, Philip says.

And will it?

Maybe. I mean I'm surely related to some of them, Philip says. I don't know.

Something rustles in the ivy, a small animal or a bird. For a moment the day seems busy with hidden life and meaning.

Have you heard of Huey Beauregard? Philip asks.

Tony has not.

Did you read that book by Armistead Maupin? asks Philip. *The Night Listener*? Tony shrugs.

Philip says that the true story it's based on is even more interesting.

A *true* story, says Tony.

Not just a *true* story, but an epic, Philip explains, in which several gay writers, baseball players, and other minor celebrities develop telephone relationships with a boy who was raped, beaten, and infected with HIV by his policeman father and his father's friends. An epic in which this boy gets his oddly titled memoir, *Between a Rock and a Hard Place*, published, although nobody has ever met the boy, only his adoptive mother. Various friends of the boy lose faith; they note how much his voice resembles that of his adoptive mother, and they begin to imagine that he doesn't even exist. Finally, after a definitive article clearly lays out the case that the boy is actually only an imaginary being dreamed up by this insane woman from New Jersey, the boy, offended by the lack of faith in his magical existence, disappears, only to reappear occasionally as a ghostly presence on various websites...

The jets fly back over the house, in the opposite direction and then curve westward, toward the ocean. Tony says something that sounds like *a juggler and enchanter*. Philip's head is throbbing again.

Just around the time that Anthony Godby Johnson disappeared, Philip says, this other boy popped up. Huey Beauregard. Same MO. A different set of gay writers leading to a different set of celebrities. Telephone calls and faxes but nobody ever meets the kid, until this weird munchkin starts getting photographed hidden behind fake beards and wigs. Same childhood of incredible abuse. Same stories of delayed puberty and mutant genitalia, because of the abuse.

But Huey Beauregard could be anyone, says Philip. Meanwhile, he's published a novel and a book of stories about his childhood of abuse. His heroin addiction, his AIDS, his Arkansas childhood with white trash monsters and his mother, who pimps him out in truck stops. My friend Felicia says that she knows for a fact the photo on his book jacket isn't really him. My friend Felicia says he was supposed to meet Sonya Brava in a park once but he never showed up. Felicia says that he claims he's agoraphobic because of the disfiguring Kaposi's on his face. At the same time, he was supposed to be working Polk Street.

Philip says, I used to live on Polk Street. Have I ever seen an androgynous little blond boy who looks anything like the munchkin in the magazines? Has anyone? It's probably the same insane woman in New Jersey who's concocted another fictional boy, says Philip. Felicia says that all of his cultural references are wrong. Like why would a boy born in 1982 be a fan of Suzanne Vega? Felicia says that Huey offered this young writer she knows money to impersonate him on his book tour. Huey's supposed to be this desperate kid who lives in a squat and hangs out with street kids and anarchists, but when the editor of *Roost* wanted him to find a squat for a spread in their magazine, he couldn't come up with it. An easy two grand for a couple thousand words. Felicia says that she's spoken to people who swear the voice that calls them on the phone sounds more like a woman. Why doesn't somebody investigate this travesty?

Why don't you investigate it?

For a moment Philip isn't sure if Tony really said that.

Tony says, You mean Felicia, Geordi's wife?

Philip says, My friend Felicia—she's kind of obsessed.

2

RAYMOND ARRIVES LATE, just as the training is getting underway, in a large conference room that looks like it might have once been a high school gymnasium. The roof seems too heavy for the walls, the whole structure in danger of buckling or collapsing in slow motion. Raymond squeezes in between a large white man in a crumpled suit jacket and a young, perky woman wearing boots and leg warmers under a denim skirt. Along with the nonjudgmental, almost conspiratorial smile the perky woman flashes him, the leg warmers and boots suggest that she is not a clinically trained Substance Abuse Counselor or an Abuse in Childhood Specialist or a Bereavement and Grief Counselor or an Art Therapist or Drama Therapist or Narrative Therapist or Intimacy Issues Specialist or End-of-Life Facilitator or HIV Benefits Counselor or Homeless Shelter Case Manager or Anger Management Specialist or Spiritual Crisis Manager or Gender Transitioning Issues Cofacilitator or Existential Therapist or Abstinence-Based Support Group Leader, like many of the members of the audience, who have come from agencies all over the Bay Area for this training on AIDS and Neurology, but like Raymond, an outreach worker of some sort, working in the streets. The trainer, a psychiatrist, a manic white man wearing a blue tie that he must think of as *bold* and *commanding*, paces a slightly elevated platform where Raymond imagines bleachers once sat, lecturing on the side effects of one particular HIV medication, the one that Philip was on for a while, but that had depressed Philip and filled his sleeping brain with horrible visions—interstellar airplane disasters, vicious black jellies with beaks, librarians running amok with machetes—or so he said. Raymond suspected Philip was exaggerating until one afternoon they went for a hike with Ralph in the crispy East Bay hills. It was hot and there was nothing much to recommend this hike except the view from the ridge, which was stunning enough, if overly familiar, but Philip just stopped hiking along the ridge and started sobbing. He couldn't feel pleasure anymore, he said. He couldn't live this way anymore, he said, with nightmares and no pleasure. Nightmares, fine, yes, he could deal with the interstellar airplane disasters and the murderous librarians and the cloud of death that would sometimes seem to be swallowing up the planet, he said, and even the weird feeling that persisted most mornings and into the afternoons that he was still dreaming, but that the dream was itself alive and tortured and conscious of itself as a dream, that it was *suffering from the daylight*. But he couldn't keep going this way, he couldn't even keep hiking along the ridge with the stunning but overly familiar view without some *fucking pleasure* or just the hope for pleasure *at the very least*.

So he stopped taking Sustiva and within twenty four hours he felt fine. Reborn, he said.

Years ago, when Raymond was a "troubled teen" and committed to a variety of sick institutions by his mother, other troubled teens would sometimes wake him up in the middle of the night and mutter to him about the blackening, the devastation, the cloud of death that was swallowing up the planet and its plants and animals and people. Raymond was subjected to legions of clueless mental health experts back then, none of whom helped him or understood him or even bestowed any sort of aura of benevolent care, as far as he can remember, but who all resembled in some vague, clinically trained, and nonjudgmental way, the large man with the hunchback and the crumpled suit jacket to his left and the perky young woman with the leg warmers and the denim skirt to his right and especially the trainer himself, with his bold, commanding blue tie, who has quickly segued from his description of the horrible side effects of HIV meds, not just the vivid dreams and feelings of unreality and depression, the deepest sort of depression progressing sometimes toward a numbing and belligerent despair, but also rashes and nausea and headaches and diarrhea, fatigue and vomiting and ringing in the ears, loss of appetite and suicidal thoughts, into a discussion of the efficacy and even necessity of prescribing more antidepressants to just about every client they might ever see, for any reason. Depression is serious business, he tells them, but this is not the dark ages. It's 2006!

The meeting is beginning to blur around the edges already, and Raymond is entering a timeless state in which this training is simply a continuation of a training he attended a few years ago on Sex Addiction. Effective treatments exist, the presenter says now, and yet there are so many clients still floundering out there in the wilderness without a proper diagnosis. The presenter of the Sex Addiction Training could have been this presenter's brother, his twin even, minus the bold blue tie, rubbing his hands together as he described the sex addicts who might become fixated on a particular blond boy, or who might become less productive at their jobs because of their constant need to cruise the Internet, searching for a particular blond boy, he kept repeating that phrase, *a particular blond boy*, *a particular blond boy*, and Raymond had noticed the people around him entering that phrase into their notebooks, *a particular blond boy*, just as the perky woman to his right is now scribbling notes into her notebook with rushed, extravagant handwriting, copying down the trainer's diamond-shaped diagram from the dry erase board with DEPRESSION in one corner connected to PSYCHOSOCIAL HISTORY in another and BIOCHEMISTRY *(genetic factors?)* written in the third corner leading to the uppermost point of the diamond: MEDICATION!!!

The perky woman is now circling the words *team-building* and *social monitoring skills* and *armoring* and the juxtaposition *Performance vs. Intimacy* while on his left the large man with the crumpled suit jacket occasionally jots down just a single word or phrase in his tiny notebook, never a word that has anything to do with the trainer's presentation, as far as Raymond can tell, he's just written the phrase *look within* and turns the page to write *in search of deep time*. There had been so many ways that sex addiction could become confused, hidden under other symptoms, *masked* by other secondary issues, and so could go undiagnosed, just as today the presenter with the bold blue tie discusses the degree to which depression can become confused, hidden under other symptoms, *masked* by other secondary issues, and so can go undiagnosed. The perky woman to his right writes *depression masked as "happiness"* and underlines it and the man to his left writes down the words ADMINISTER and SUPERVISE. Time, in this room, is expanding in elaborate loops, moving side to side, developing bottomless chasms. When Raymond was a troubled teen, committed to a variety of sick institutions and subjected to legions of clueless mental health experts, he was twice shot up with drugs that stopped the progress of time altogether and turned the universe into a tepid gray mush. It was only his grandmother who had saved him, who'd clung to his hand when she'd come to visit him in the crazy house and started weeping, restarting the progress of time with the sheer force of her empathy. *Just tell them what they want to hear*, his grandmother had whispered, *and don't worry about all that other mess*. The perky woman to his right now drops her pen and Raymond catches a glimpse of Isela just a few seats away, looking like her soul has left her body and is floating above the room, or even farther, circling over fishing boats on the Caribbean Sea perhaps or revisiting the streets of old Havana. The trainer with the bold blue tie tells the group that later in the day they'll be breaking down into small groups where they'll be sharing their own experiences, both clinical and personal, with the epidemic of depression.

At break, however, Isela pulls Raymond aside and tells him that Louie is dead.

Isela's caked under so much makeup she looks posthuman, radiating a garish intensity, surrounded by all the rest of them with their degrees and their social service drag.

I was with him at the end, she says, and he was smoking crystal like a motherfucker.

Isela's gravelly voice carried her over from Cuba during the Mariel boatlift, when she was a mere boy of seventeen or twenty-seven or forty-two, nobody knows how old Isela is, timeless perhaps, and Raymond imagines that even then her stubble was poking out from underneath the pancake, cosmetics melting and streaming down her face under the Caribbean sun, a flotilla of boats going nowhere, gulls circling overhead like vultures. The sea was as warm as a bathtub and pale green like glass. Many years later, on that same hot, glaring sea, Louie was on a cruise off the Florida coast with the same gulls circling and the same vat of cosmetics melting on some other woman's face, Louie's mother's face, Raymond saw a picture of her once, she looked like Louie in drag, but more haggard and twice as evil. The two of them, Louie and his mother, were handcuffed in front of the passengers they'd been playing wiffleball with just moments before, and extradited to California on drug charges.

Louie used to drive Raymond around the city, everyone in the Tenderloin knew him, everyone down at 16th and Mission. Finally Louie'd pull over somewhere and kick Raymond out, Get out of my truck, heifer. You're being mean, Raymond said. But I'm fulla sugar, too, Louie said. I's a nice bitch sometimes, and he smacked his lips in a kiss.

Louie relapsed, quit the outreach team, and started dealing speed, not necessarily in that order. Raymond would see him at dances in the middle of the night doing glorious, wicked moves, dressed sometimes all in red. He's the devil, Raymond realized one night on mushrooms, the devil from a black comedy.

You just get you some land with some water and grow your weed, Louie advised him once. Bury the money in the ground somewhere where they can't find it. They catch you, they send you away, you come back, the money's still there. Prison's not so bad, he said.

Why was it so easy to love the evil? The evil ones that were fulla sugar. Probably his childhood, Raymond decides in a vague way.

Louie, says Isela now. He always did have a bad heart.

Raymond's assumption for years now has been that Louie could easily, always, already be dead. As if Louie's ghost had appeared to him in a dream he then promptly forgot. Isela gives his arm an affectionate squeeze and excuses herself to go to the Ladies'.

Raymond steps out onto the sidewalk, where various therapists, outreach workers, and case managers are furiously smoking and ignoring each other. He strolls down the block, gazing in the windows of a mattress store and a nondescript bar, imagining that he could just keep going. The dead, at least Raymond's dead—how implicated they've all been in manufacturing their own random catastrophes. Raymond and his sister Mina spent so many days of their childhood huddled in their bleak Sunset tract home plotting ways to survive random catastrophe, a skill they learned from their mother, who'd spent her life working to fend off random catastrophe. It was probably their mother who instilled in Raymond the fondness he still has today for stories in which the will to live is instrumental in survival, stories in which a man's arms get hacked off by farm machinery, so he picks up the bleeding limbs with his teeth—both of them—and hurries several miles into town to get them sewn back on, or stories in which the sole survivors of a plane crash subsist by cannibalizing the dead, or the stories in Raymond's favorite book ever, *I Survived Rumbuli*, by one of only two survivors of the slaughter of 30,000 Jews in Latvia near the pits of the Rumbuli forest. Columns of Jews were being marched into the woods, forced to remove their coats and shoes. With gunshots in the distance, Frida Mikhelson threw herself on the ground with her face in the snow and played dead. Shoes landed on top of her, but she didn't move; soon she was covered with a pile of boots and shoes. More shots and then quiet. She lay in the cold puddle of melted snow until night, and then wrapped herself up in the blouses and scarves discarded by the now-murdered humans, then pulled her white nightshirt over top, to blend in with the snow, and crawled into the forest.

The point of these stories, for Raymond, is that death just might be an avoidable catastrophe, skillfully evaded by these protagonists, resourceful characters whose clear-headedness in their moments of crisis could be read as a justification for the years of their lives Raymond's mother and sister and at times Raymond himself had spent worrying about all the possible ways things could go wrong, imagining all the worst-case scenarios, so as to carefully avoid them.

The Blue Angels roar over Soma and the Mission District, buzz Bernal Heights, and then curve westward, toward the ocean. Every October it's the same. They've been doing it since he was a child out in the hideous Sunset Avenues, where he was hemmed in by the monolithic mental health facilities, and the squat, identical tract homes that now sell for a million dollars each. He used to kind of like it. He used to look forward to the virtuosity of the pilots he would imagine as handsome and brave and homosexually inclined, but now he just thinks of dead Afghani children, dead Iraqi children, dead Pakistani children.

After break, the trainer brings out a client, formerly homeless and now HIV-infected, and counsels him in front of the thirty people in the room. The formerly homeless man, a crack head, is supposed to be straight. He's trying to be coy about the details of transmission, but the psychiatrist with the bold blue tie is kind of obsessed. But *how* did you get it? he keeps asking him. *How?* After forcing the client to name a variety of sexual acts and drugs he's tried, the psychiatrist starts asking the client about his earliest sexual experience.

I was five, the client says. It was with my sister.

There are audible gasps.

Were you the abuser or the abused? the psychiatrist asks.

The client looks confused.

Did you abuse her or did she abuse you? the psychiatrist insists.

I was five, the client says, and she was six.

There is a pause in which the counselor looks at the audience and nods, as if at a matter of grave concern, or as if mimicking some sort of concern, or as if the client's statement has verified a particular suspicion, or maybe as if it's just a kind of tic, a nervous condition, a meaningless gesture he uses if he's ever at a brief loss for words. The psychiatrist moves the conversation on to the pleasures of unsafe sex, the drugs the client has most enjoyed, before getting into recovery, while having unsafe sex, and his many relapses. Once they are done, he excuses the client, and when the client is out of the room, he asks the audience, in a stage whisper, *Is he gone?* There are a few nods from the audience. The psychiatrist then begins talking about the *population* the client is from, how dearly that *population* values immediate gratification, how you couldn't expect a member of such a *population* to wear condoms, how, probably, it was his abusive childhood, devoid of real intimacy, that created in the client a need for the skin-to-skin contact he could only get through unsafe sex. The visible fervor with which the psychiatrist lays out his theories rapidly disintegrates the line between theory and pornography. Raymond looks around the room to see if this talk is making anyone else uncomfortable, maybe at least the other colored people, but everyone seems to be eating it up, leaning forward in their chairs and taking notes, except for Isela, of course, who is looking at her watch. Her watch, like her sunglasses, is so enormous that it verges on parody.

Raymond can't bear to return to the training after the afternoon break, so instead rides his bike back across town. When he gets home, Philip's up on the phone. While Raymond can't make out the actual words of whoever's on the line, the tone is audible, the intellectual speed, a verbal style that speaks of ambition and deadlines and one of Philip's schemes to make money. Those kinds of voices don't belong to anyone they know in San Francisco; it's "New York" on the line. Philip is listening intently now to the highly charged voice and scribbling down notes in a notebook, but pauses long enough to make eye contact with Raymond, a slightly manic eye contact that confirms Raymond's suspicions. Raymond goes into the bedroom and shuts the door.

Raymond needs to turn off his brain. He puts *Female Convict Scorpion* into the DVD player. Throughout the opening credits, Scorpion is thrashing around on the floor of the deepest dungeon, she's *under the jail*, as Raymond's grandmother would have said. When Raymond's grandmother advised him to avoid certain people, certain places, certain situations, it was generally so that he wouldn't end up, as other men she'd known had, *under the jail*. Scorpion's arms and legs are bound, but she has a spoon gripped in her teeth, rubbing it back and forth against the cold concrete floor, sharpening the tip. She has but one thing on her mind.

In the movie, some big prison official has come for a visit, and so they're bringing Scorpion up, for one hour, out of her dungeon underneath the jail. They'll regret it.

Philip pops his head in the door. I'll be right back, I have to take Leon some weed, I have to take Freddy some weed, he says, counting them on his fingers. One, two. And it looks like I'm going to Iowa to write about the Amish shooting, he says. Like, tomorrow or something. Before Raymond can respond, the phone rings again. Philip's chattering away, and then the next thing Raymond knows he hears the front door opening and then closing behind him.

3

BEING A PSYCHIC ALONE hasn't been paying Leon's bills, and so he's taken computer work. He's paid to spread rumors in chat rooms, to get people talking. About *Star Trek* cell phone rings, for example. *Have you heard about the new Star Trek cell rings?* It's changed the way he views chat room interactions, forever, he tells

Philip. For one thing, there's all kinds of bots out there, chatty little programs just jabbering away. Often, the only other people he can definitely identify as human are doing exactly what he is.

Philip likes the idea that maybe the actual people have turned their backs on these bleak virtual spaces and the machines and marketers are lost together in their own labyrinth trying to sell each other worthless products. Have you heard of Huey Beauregard? asks Philip.

Philip fills in the basics: former child prostitute, habitué of truck stops and meth labs, and now a mysterious wünderkind author, who barely shows his face. Felicia's former agent, Tristessa, Philip tells Leon, described Huey as an agoraphobic abuse victim who sat at his computer sending emails all day. But maybe he isn't exactly *sitting* at a computer, says Philip. Maybe he's already inside it. Maybe he's some kind of a *program*.

Just as he'd hoped, Leon has equally intricate theories—demonic entities, possession, beings from other planes. Philip likes to enter Leon's world; the apartment is so completely self-contained and always a pleasant temperature. Leon's calm, benevolent aura soothes him, even when Leon's discussing etheric monsters that feed off of human distress, and it's always cool and dark inside, with an enormous aquarium softly gurgling. There's also a huge-screen TV.

Despite Leon's belief that TVs are major doorways into psychic hell worlds, used as portals by all kinds of dark spirits who feed off the energy of hysteria and violence, Philip can always count on Leon to keep him up to date on the latest shooting or celebrity trial.

Next up: A closeted male star, deeply into Dianetics, is about to marry the mother of his child. *I've been shopping all day*, says his exhilarated bride-to-be. Leon believes the rumors that the star's bride-to-be was artificially inseminated with L. Ron Hubbard's sperm. They cut away from a saleswoman at one Paris shop saying, *She's so tall, but very thin, she fit into the sample sizes perfectly*, to the Amish shooting.

The opening shots of rolling Iowa countryside and laughing Amish children carrying their folksy, antiquated lunch pails home from school establish *the idyllic innocence that has been shattered*, says the newscaster, by this *shocking eruption of violence* where it was *least expected*.

East Liberty: some boarded-up shops. What was once a mechanic's shop, what was once a bar, what was once East Liberty Flowers and Such. Beyond that, the town consists of a lantern store, the town auction house, and a boarded-up edifice, formerly the East Liberty Home for Boys. The parking lot of the auction house, the town's only public space, is full of news vans and Harleys and families wearing sunglasses, just milling about. On the other side of the intersection is the usual shrine of stuffed animals, candles, and flowers, in memory of the dead boys. The schoolhouse itself is a boxy shack surrounded by yellow police tape and sheriff's deputies who keep the traffic moving, both the cars and the pedestrians who are already passing back and forth to gawk.

I'm going there, Philip says.

On screen, Amish women hide their faces from the cameras.

Why would you do that?

To write about it, Philip says. For a magazine.

But he knows that Leon's "why" isn't about surface explanations. Philip knows one sentence from a Paul Bowles story by heart. *It occurred to him that he ought to ask himself why he was doing this irrational thing, but he was intelligent enough to know that since he was doing it, it was not so important to probe for explanations at that moment.* That story didn't end well for the protagonist.

The newscaster says that the shooter told the children that if they did what he asked, nobody would be hurt, and he sent out the girls and the teachers. The shooter told them that he was angry with God because his own infant daughter had choked on a Christmas tree ornament, a tiny golden bell in the shape of an elf or a fairy—the early reports that it was an angel have been corrected.

There isn't any story there, Leon says. That story's over.

In a rambling note, the shooter claimed that he was haunted by the allegations of sexual abuse against the man who used to run the East Liberty Home for Boys. He claimed that all the talk of molested boys during the investigation infiltrated his dreams, destroyed his relationship with his wife, and left him obsessed with the idea of taking his revenge on God for the death of his infant daughter. He actually used the phrase "despoil His little lambs." He showed up with ropes, sexual lubricant, and a wedding dress. It is assumed he was intending to molest the boys, although nobody knows what the wedding dress was for. When the police showed up, he shot the boys and then himself.

The Amish, you know, Philip says. They get used. They're just an idea for most people, a joke. A joke about being pure and stupid and good.

Leon waits for Philip to elaborate.

I'm not interested in the killer, he says. It's the victims. My dad grew up there. They're like my family.

Leon says, You're interested in murdered children?

The newscaster says that the shooter was still alive when the EMTs arrived. He was rushed to the same hospital in Iowa City as the wounded boys. His wife refused to see him, refused to go inside the room where he was dying. If he croaked any final message on his way out, his fourteen-year-old son was the only one who heard it.

Leon says, The spirits of murdered children often get lost. They get stuck. There isn't really anything we can do for them, but they're dangerous.

Philip never asks Leon for advice or information about his future. Leon gets paid to do that, it's his job.

Maybe you don't need to go there, Leon says.

He mutes the TV.

I'm so ready to leave this plane, he says. For good.

For good?

I'm over the world of pain and punishment. The Satan-grid.

When Leon looks at the White House with his third eye, he sees a huge spaceship full of the nasty Grays hovering overhead, beaming down their mind-set of pain and punishment directly into the president's brain.

The Grays are not particularly evolved creatures, he says, they just have slightly more advanced technology than we do.

The Blue Angels fly directly overhead just now, as if to illustrate the concept of unevolved technology with their noisy antics.

What do you see when you look at Iraq with your third eye? Philip asks. What do you see when you look at Afghanistan?

Leon closes his eyes as if visualizing the mess even now. The bluest, most electric fish in his aquarium freezes for a moment, as if sharing Leon's concentration.

What has been unleashed is beyond even the sick games of the Grays, Leon says.

The psychic distress and torture thrills are leaking everywhere into the organism. They thought they could build this fantasy playground like a horror ride, Leon continues, and ship all the human boys and now the girls over to have some fun and play soldier and murder children and rape and blow things up. Boys will be boys and all that.

Who are *they*?

But it's leaking into everything, Leon says, it's in the water and in the clouds and in the brains of the boys, they ship them over and ship them back. The living earth isn't happy about it.

On the silent TV: generic agricultural images, gridded fields from above.

The Grays may have started it, but there are more serious players involved now, Leon says. Interdimensional stakes.

Now the killer's face fills the screen.

The Grays are, in fact, the least evolved members of another species, Leon says. The ones who were left behind when their more evolved fellows raptured on up to the next evolutionary dimension—to the Christ-grid.

He turns on the sound again.

A miracle of forgiveness, the newscaster is saying, as they cut from the still photo of the dumpy white guy who killed and wounded the children to a shot of a stern Amish man driving a horse and buggy and waving to one of his neighbors. Philip's suddenly overwhelmed with a dread of his people, their bonnets and bowl haircuts and ruthless theology.

Be careful out there, Leon says. He looks like he's about to elaborate on his warning—perhaps having sensed, from the dark energy whirling out of the TV portal, the angry discarnate entities wandering the countryside in search of receptive hosts—but thinks better of it. Leon's also leaving, he reminds Philip instead, for the Philippines. To see the psychic surgeons. The psychic surgeons remove weird particles of spiritual matter from people's bodies, cutting their chests open with just the power of their minds. They cure people of debilitating conditions, both physical and spiritual.

Are you sick? Philip asks. Are you feeling bad?

Oh Philip, Leon says.

He leaves it at that.

Freddy lives just a few blocks away from Leon, above Divisadero. His apartment's as cramped and overwrought as Leon's is cool and bubbly, but today Freddy's already stoned and in a contemplative mood.

He's just returned from the memorial service for a local poet, Joy Carter. According to Freddy, it was dreadful. Joy was a real complainer, and somebody had the brilliant idea to read one of her emails at the service. The poet who read the email delivered her petty grievances, modulating his pauses and creating a melodic rhythm out of thin air, as if these were sonnets for the ages. Maybe he was attempting to turn Joy Carter into a martyr for avant garde poetry and to transform her mourners into an enlightened elite. But all it really did, Freddy says, was remind us how annoying she could actually be.

Joy wrote gender-disrupting, meaning-destroying extravaganzas, book-length poem after book-length poem, she just cranked them out, typing nonstop during breaks from her receptionist job at the same nonprofit where Raymond works, The Golden Gate Free Healthcare Consortium. Her poems were based largely on her own dyslexic errors in reading and writing, expanded into nonstop roller coaster rides decimating the signifier, rewiring grammar, and resisting the production of meaning, or so Philip has been told.

Freddy blames the dreary memorial service on this younger generation. Having missed out on the nonstop memorial services of the '80s and early '90s, they lack perspective. Philip isn't sure if Freddy's including him in the parameters of *this younger generation* or not. After he's taken his bag but before he's paid for it, Freddy asks, Have you ever had a Marine?

Had?

I just had one last night, says Freddy. Butch little thing all ready to ship out to Iraq.

Philip decides not to mention that Raymond was enlisted when Philip met him in the early '90s. Raymond had wanted to get laid; he'd convinced himself that the military was the best place to find men who had sex with other men. Once he was *actually* getting laid, the Marines lost their appeal.

I had to tell him what I thought of Bush's filthy little war, Freddy says, but my pacifism just seemed to get him excited. I swear, he was getting off on my hypocrisy—a pacifist sucking a soldier's dick.

What, says Philip, we're supposed to *agree* with the people we have sex with?

Freddy glows, as if he's been forgiven. It's enough that we can be in the same room with them, isn't it? he says. Isn't that what *manners* are for?

It was *so hot*, he whispers. I'm going to have to write my congressman as penance. I'll write a handful of nasty antiwar letters to that monster Feinstein. Oh, let me show you the email he sent me.

While Freddy messes around with his computer, Philip wonders the exact same thing he wonders every time he sits in this overstuffed froufrou chair, waiting to get paid: What is Freddy's brother like? Freddy's twin brother, identical or fraternal, he's not sure, lives in San Francisco, but they hate each other, rarely speak, or so Philip's been told. Freddy has never once mentioned his brother, but his brother is a kind of legend, *the real poet*, people whisper behind Freddy's back. Somebody told Philip that Freddy's affair with an older poet had something to do with it—was it Robert Duncan? James Merrill? Either way, Freddy must be connected to the great chain of visionary cocksuckers himself. From Duncan to the abstract expressionist Robert de Niro Sr. to the occultist Harry Godwin and his Merchant Marine boyfriend Emil Opffer to Hart Crane and on back to Edward Carpenter, Walt Whitman, etc. Or else from Merrill to Greek poet Kimon Friar to occultist Hermann Specht and his Merchant Marine boyfriend Otto Müller to modernist painter Marsden Hartley or maybe Charles Demuth and on back to Carpenter, Whitman, and the bonobos. Freddy's twin published a poem or two in the '70s, but he turned his back on literature and the rumor is that Literature's loss is somehow tied to the feud, the psychological warfare between twin brothers, for some reason having to do with Freddy's mentor and lover—Duncan or Merrill or maybe even Harold Norse or Richard Howard.

Freddy's printer makes a shuddering whine as it spits out the email Freddy's so excited about. The legend of Freddy and his twin was circulating before Philip even knew Freddy or sold drugs to Freddy; Kathy Acker mentioned Freddy's brother the first time Philip ever met her. She declared the twin a genius. She had met him only once, in the run-down studio apartment in North Beach or the Haight where he lived and didn't write, but Kathy had said she'd never met anyone with such a keen…tactile intelligence? She claimed to have fucked him after he tortured her. Philip wasn't really sure why she'd make up such a story about someone he'd never even heard of, unless she was hoping the story would get back to her dear friend Freddy, for whatever complicated reason. But when he repeated the story to Lana Fontaine, she acted like he was a fool to believe anything out of Kathy Acker's mouth. She takes painkillers before her S&M scenes, said Lana—as if that was another lie, as if she was cheating—because pain was the truth and everything else was just play-acting.

Freddy explains that Joy Carter's premature death is being blamed on either the hormones, which as a transgender she'd been on for decades, or on some mysterious virus she picked up while sojourning in New Guinea. She'd gone to New Guinea to experience the glossolalia and gender fluidity of the non-Western mind, explains Freddy, but she'd been disappointed, he'd been told, even embittered, he had heard, by the degree to which the natives were both too Westernized and too blind to see her as a radiant example of resistance to the phallocentric signifier, a non-Western, postcolonial narrative like themselves. Insufficiently loved, he says, not just at home but abroad!

Freddy hands the email to Philip with a look of triumph on his face. It's littered with a patriotic vocabulary, but the subtext seems to be that the poor kid feels so mixed up about some guy he killed in a car accident—even though it wasn't technically his fault—that he has to get out of the country and shoot enough "things" that the dead guy in the car accident will no longer bug him so much. It's kind of devastating, actually.

Don't you just love men without the capacity for introspection? Freddy asks now. Like characters from Virgil. All action. Action equals character.

Philip's starting to feel like a hostage. Or like a whore himself, offering the bare minimum until he can get paid and go home. Was it Ted or was it Todd who dated Freddy and then cracked up a dinner party with tales of his sexual demands? Philip looks around at Freddy's bookshelves, which line every wall, crammed full to overflowing with books and journals and gay trinkets, brass candleholders with weird inscriptions in foreign alphabets and ivory-handled letter openers and bell jars. Ulrichs's *The Riddle of "Man-Manly" Love* next to Krafft-Ebing's *Psychopathia sexualis* and John Addington Symonds's *Soldatenliebe* (Does Freddy read German?) and Klaus von Verlag's *Warrior Eros: On the Ethical Superiority of Uranian Love* and Havelock Ellis's *Sexual Inversion*, cowritten with Symonds, and Magnus Hirschfeld's *The Sexual History of the World War*. He picks up Timothy d'Arch Smith's *Love in Earnest: Some Notes on the Lives and Writings of English Uranian Poets from 1889 to 1930* and opens to a well-worn poem by Horatio Forbes Brown:

> Dearest of all are soldiers, the young magnificent swordsmen;
> Be it the stalwart form of a dark eyed insolent guardsman
> Or a light haired hussar with the down new fledged on his smoothed lip…

Philip has long suspected that the mysterious magnetism between "the third sex" and military men that became explicit in the nineteenth century is part of an occult reality, probably evil, that he should try to understand. But since he campaigned Raymond into de-enlisting back in 1992—the only successful antiwar campaign he can think of—he's had zero interest in the minds of soldiers.

I'm off to Iowa, day after tomorrow, he says.

My condolences, says Freddy.

I'll be exploiting the Amish, says Philip.

What fun. Those studly farmboys.

Yes, but they're pacifists. Not your type.

All that sexual repression and guilty fervor can offer pleasures of its own, says Freddy.

Well, sure, says Philip.

It wasn't either Ted or Todd who dated Freddy, Philip remembers. It was Marcus Jones who'd dated him and Marcus's best friend, Anthony Glass, who'd told the story of Freddy's *imperious ass*, as Anthony had described it, before busting out with a full-on impersonation of Freddy bent over and slapping his own ass like a monkey in heat, going *Eee! Eee! Eee!* Marcus published a novel with Soft Skull, but now he's with a famous troop of pranksters who set up fake websites and pretend to be World Bank executives.

They're kind of my family, Philip says. My dad was Amish.

Really. I didn't know that. It explains so much.

How's that?

Oh, come now.

Have you ever actually met an Amish man? asks Philip.

No, but the one on that reality show is really hot. So gentle, but so severe at the same time.

What's that? *Amish in the City*?

No, no, a kind of spin-off, says Freddy. They put Amish kids in a Beverly Hills mansion with inner-city drug dealer kids…all these ghetto youth with their stylized hair and their underwear showing…it's a sort of bi-cultural competition, you know, the Amish kids end up going along on drive-bys and the ghetto kids have to milk cows.

Philip hopes this isn't really true, but feels suddenly lost. Once, he'd thought the dominant cultural values needed to be subverted. He'd even thought that was his job, as a writer. But values in general were unraveling at such an accelerated pace, parody had become impossible. That all of this spectacle was still in service to a nihilistic consumer culture of apocalyptic proportions was so universally understood, and shrugged off, that even mentioning that fact would seem shrill, earnest, hopelessly out-of-touch. When Marcus Jones's theater troop delivered fake press releases promoting slavery and environmental degradation, their corporate audiences clapped enthusiastically.

What do you think about Huey Beauregard? Philip asks.

Freddy bristles.

Why do you ask?

My friend Felicia doesn't believe he's real, says Philip. Felicia's kind of obsessed with him. You know Felicia?

What is she, a spoken-word poet or something?

Fiction, says Philip. She's like a surrealist.

Well clearly she's got an overactive imagination, says Freddy. Huey's real, all right. He's actually a friend of mine. A very good friend of mine.

Philip notes the strange shift, as an air of self-righteousness invades Freddy's otherwise completely amoral demeanor.

Have you met him? Philip asks.

Freddy looks offended.

Not in person, he says. He's horribly shy, as you might imagine. His face is covered with Kaposi's and other scars. Horrible, from the cigarettes. His mother.

Insufficiently loved, Philip wants to say, but Freddy's tone suggests that while the life and death of Joy Carter or the Marine trick are fair game, the suffering of Huey Beauregard is not.

By the way, says Philip. You know anyone who lives in a squat?

What, says Freddy, like some anarchist vegan huddling in an abandoned building?

Philip explains that *Roost*—that hip magazine of interiors—wants to feature the interior of a squat. They asked your friend Huey, Philip says. But when he didn't come up with it, I suggested Felicia to the editor, Tom Kruse.

Yes, Huey would be the one for that, says Freddy.

He doesn't tell Freddy that he'd suggested to Felicia that they create their own squat. Dress up his unfinished basement with debris and pose some random teen in the midst of it. Maybe decorate the walls with cheap Xeroxes of Sue Coe's paintings for that anarchist vegan flair. Over a period of six years Sue Coe went on a tour of slaughterhouses, all across America. Philip wanted to smuggle her illustrations of torture, debeaking, and slow, bloody deaths into the pages of *Roost*. Get Ralph to shoot the squat photos, since it would have to be done in a hurry—here today, gone tomorrow. So then, how could anyone fact-check it?

Freddy sighs. By this time on Saturday, he says, my dear little Marine will be on an airplane to Iraq.

Sue Coe not only drew what she saw, but kept a journal of her observations. *The blood comes gushing out, as if all living beings are soft containers, waiting to be pierced.* Freddy counts out Philip's bills. One, two. Crumples the money and presses the wad into Philip's waiting hand.

4

USUALLY, IT IS NIGHT. A few restless hours and then at some dark and nameless hour Raymond's eyes pop open for good. He checks the BBC news or Al Jazeera for the pictures that the American newspapers won't show, pictures of a one-armed Iraqi girl, pictures of a little Iraqi boy with his face smashed so badly he lost an eye and has difficulty breathing by himself, pictures of a despondent father with his child's corpse cradled in his arms, and after whipping himself into an enervating frenzy of horror, prints up a picture of a boy with his leg blown off by an American bomb, tapes it to the refrigerator, then rides his bike through the cold and drug-addled streets of the Mission out into the colder and practically deserted streets of the Avenues, as he's been doing for months when he can't sleep. Not the hideous Sunset Avenues of his childhood, where he was hemmed in by the monolithic mental health facilities, and the squat, identical tract homes that now sell for a million dollars each, but out past the scary Catholic university where his father went to school in the '60s, and into the Richmond District Avenues. Out there it's just Raymond and an occasional cop car and the ghostly blurs that flash through his peripheral vision, keeping pace with him for a moment before veering off toward the trees of Golden Gate Park. The ghostly blurs could be an image from one of his father's unpublished poems: the traces left on photon detectors, headlights on dark roads, or maybe just the Catholic phantoms haunting the dreams of a boy who'd aggressively abandoned religion and embraced the brave new world of science. Or maybe the ghostly blurs resemble the symptoms that Philip gets when a migraine is coming on, explosions of tiny lights and a dizzying radiance that Philip is always ready to weave into his hallucinogenic worldview. Is it a coincidence, Raymond wonders, that the two most important men in his life have both been writers and both been deformed in their childhoods by religious fanatics? Raymond was through Iowa briefly with Philip years ago, it was almost dark, *their headlights sliced the space and time*, as it said in one of his father's poems, and they parked beneath an old farmhouse that loomed Gothically above them on a hill and peered up the lane at the house where Philip's father had grown up and where Philip had spent so many hours during his deliriously uneventful childhood. A cop car passes and slows down several blocks ahead, and Raymond turns to the left to avoid it, off Cabrillo and toward Fulton. One ghostly blur follows to his right and another passes directly in front. The ghostly blurs are actually not images from a poem or hallucinatory mental fireworks— they are skinny white women, and they are jogging. Raymond remarked on this phenomena months ago to Philip, perplexed at the sheer number of ethereal women running through the city at some dark and nameless hour of the night. Well sure, Philip said, then paused briefly and said, They're anorexics. As if it was the most obvious thing in the world.

It is only at such odd hours, Raymond supposes, that the systematic production of certain life forms becomes so obvious—the way America is composed of little factories. A cop car passes in the opposite direction, slows, checking Raymond out. The cops in the Avenues never stop the obsessive, anorexic joggers, but they often stop Raymond, unable to imagine why someone of his description would be riding around at this hour in this neighborhood, unless to rape or rob the jogging anorexics or the other residents fast asleep inside their million-dollar bungalows, exactly the sort of situation Raymond's grandmother advised him to avoid so that he wouldn't end up, as other men she'd known had, *under the jail*. He turns right and right again, pedals quickly up and down the slight hills, back past the scary Catholic university. Raymond's father went to school there and Raymond went to a reading there once with Philip, and the poet who was reading turned out to be a man who'd given Raymond therapy, one of the legions of clueless mental health experts who saw him when he was a teen. The poet, Grover Bailey, had been one of the very worst. He'd given Raymond's mother therapy first and for two weeks she'd whispered his name in reverential tones, Grover, she'd say, Grover says I've never learned to really grieve, and then two weeks later she quit seeing him, and Raymond ended up under his care instead, at the Adolescent Day Treatment Center. Despite her own disenchantment, she believed Grover would be an appropriate role model for Raymond *as an African-American male*. What was Grover thinking as he gave Raymond the therapy he didn't want and couldn't use, his *mandatory* therapy, as Raymond fed him one lie after another, having vowed to never tell any therapist a single true statement? This proved to be a more difficult and complicated process than he'd guessed, but Raymond kept quiet for long stretches and Grover kept quiet; he was a quiet, fastidious little gay man whose shirts were always tucked into his perfectly crisp jeans. Was he then already a poet? Was he sitting there composing poems during those vast silences? Was he imagining a secret life for Raymond that could be implied by a few disjointed phrases and images, condensing the chaotic energy of an overgrown child into claustrophobic stanzas? Or was he questioning the wisdom of an aspiring poet giving the son of a failed poet *mandatory* therapy? As horny as he was in those days, constantly, Raymond hadn't even wanted to sleep with Grover. There was only one therapist in the whole place he'd wanted to sleep with, the very one who later declared that he was crazy. Probably just his countertransference, Philip said, when Raymond told him the story, the night after Grover Bailey's reading. Grover had read from a book-length poem in which women with straw hats were doing watercolors in gardens, ballerinas were swimming, nameless relations were eating flat mustard greens, and as he droned on, the idea that one could be both a poet and a therapist in America struck Raymond as the essence of a particular sickness at the heart of the national character. Although he was seething with rage, Raymond nodded off during the reading, lulled into a kind of half-sleep by the gardens, pools, and family picnics of the poem, only to be awoken toward the end when the poet took on a more urgent tone, and seemed to be exhorting his listeners to some sort of action, some sort of action was required because fathers abandoned their children. That was what Raymond took from the poem at least, but maybe he'd slept through the important parts.

He coasts around Buena Vista Park toward the Castro. Near the entrance to the park, a ghostly blur races past. He's pretty sure it's that mean girl he first met in eighth grade, Connie Cohen, but she doesn't make eye contact and Raymond doesn't want to talk to her either. The middle school he and Connie Cohen attended, out in the foggy Sunset Avenues, had been terrorized by the White Punks on Dope, a kind of gang who wore Derby jackets and Ben Davis pants before those things were ever hip, and steel-toed boots, and who smoked weed and scrawled swastikas all over the school and dressed up their racist worldview with some kind of alternative, bad-boy mystique, listening to Iron Maiden and AC/DC and Blue Oyster Cult, and although the whole thing seemed to be based on some twisted nostalgia for the Sunset District's rapidly vanishing Irish working class, as remembered through a glue-sniffing haze, somehow even Anthony Bello, a quiet Filipino kid with long, meticulously groomed and feathered hair, had managed to become a White Punk on Dope. Connie Cohen did poppers with those boys in math class one day, but then flirted with Raymond, a studious and well-mannered boy who was still then shocked and appalled. By the next week Connie wouldn't have anything more to do with the White Punks on Dope, however, and was cultivating a more bohemian circle of friends, a group that would enlarge to include Raymond by the ninth grade, when they were both at Lowell High, after the White Punks on Dope had dissolved in a haze of their own embarrassment and Raymond had started smoking weed and one day he'd done mushrooms and walked out of the school and seen an incandescent sentence spray-painted on a mailbox across the street IF YOU LIKE SCHOOL YOU'LL LOVE WORK and it was all over for Raymond in that moment, academically speaking, but for another semester or so he still attended ninth grade, more or less, and hung out with those hilarious girls who seemed destined for greatness as performance artists or professional party girls, such as Melinda, whose enormous head of fabulous red hair had captivated all the other rebels and bad kids so hypnotically that even after she'd shaved it off and declared herself a lesbian, like her older sister Suzie, the memory of the hair would lead dozens of ninth and tenth graders into endless coke-fueled parties in strange Victorian houses in what were to Raymond then the most exotic corners of San Francisco: the Haight, the Mission, and Noe Valley. Raymond, like his older sister Mina, had spent many days of his childhood huddled in their bleak Sunset tract home plotting ways to survive random catastrophe, but Raymond had discovered, by the time he was thirteen, that catastrophe carried its own kind of glamour and offered its own kind of pleasures, and he had begun to suspect that mere survival was an overrated goal. Melinda's sister Suzie does soundwork for Ralph sometimes these days, but back then she'd sit in the kitchen of those parties putting thick black eyeliner on and reading aloud from *Our Bodies, Ourselves*. It was after one of those parties that he'd been with Connie Cohen and this other girl Lu. They'd picked up this older guy, the sort of aimless, ex-military guy who seems sexy to ninth graders, but the older guy didn't want anything to do with Connie Cohen and Lu, he'd been mostly into Raymond. It was that weekend, in fact the very next day, that Raymond's mother committed him to the crazy house, the first time, where he was twice shot up with drugs that stopped the progress of time altogether and turned the universe into a tepid gray mush. Even after they let him out, an eternity later, Connie Cohen and Lu hadn't forgotten the slight and refused to speak to him. Connie Cohen told everyone he was gay. Nineteen eighty-three was not a good year for Raymond.

Now, at the top of the hill where Castro runs into 16th, Jonny Taser strolls nonchalantly with his companion at this dark and nameless hour as if it's the most dazzling noon. It occurs to Raymond that the odds of running into both Jonny Taser and Connie Cohen at this nameless hour must be cosmically tiny, akin to the odds of a universe developing that could support life. Jonny Taser was one of the original members of the outreach team, although nobody ever saw Jonny do any outreach. Jonny has always somehow managed to acquire groupies, like this one now, who just stands there with a placid smile as Jonny greets Raymond casually, asks if he's on his way down to the "fruit loop," the cruising area surrounding the rec center now named after that gay hero from United Flight 93.

Back in the day, Raymond would come into the office and Jonny Taser and Louie would be going at each other viciously, these two recovery queens tearing each other to shreds, but as if it was a joke, a joke that made everyone else in the room uncomfortable. Jonny Taser fed off the discomfort of others; the discomfort of others was like the anchor of his personality. Jonny Taser would be telling Louie that he saw Louie's mother at Fairy Lane, that she was *so horny she was eating dirt*, and he'd make this gesture with his hands, a devastating dirt-eating gesture so sick that Louie would, for once, have nothing to say. Louie claimed to be Peruvian, but Raymond had been told by Isela that he was just putting on airs, and in the middle of their battles Jonny Taser sometimes implied that Louie was just another middle-class Mexican boy enamored of the streets. If some of Louie's history was necessarily obscure, the details of where he'd acquired his street mouth were clear enough. But what about Jonny Taser, the child of Santa Cruz hippies, a Jewish gay-boy with a small frame and an enormous head, like an actor's? When the game had somehow lost its steam, Louie and Jonny Taser would make kissy faces and hug each other. You heard about Louie, right? says Raymond now on the 16th Street hill.

Louie used to drive Raymond around the city, sometimes Ralph was with them, gamely putting up with Louie's sexual harassment, sometimes Nick Gangway or Marcos, but never Jonny Taser, who refused to outreach with other people and somehow got away with it. Finally Louie'd pull over somewhere and kick Raymond out, Get out of my truck, heifer.

Louie always did have a bad heart, Jonny Taser says now, on the Castro Street hill, at whatever hour of the morning or night, the simplest explanation.

Was it AIDS or wasn't it?

Jonny shrugs.

I saw Todd the other day, Raymond says.

Lucky you, says Jonny Taser. I never run into Todd, only Ted.

He goes by Theodore now.

Right, says Jonny. *Ted*.

In their teens, both Todd and Ted dated old Beat poets, but Ted's was not the great sage that Todd dated, the old bard who'd made the transition from Beat to Hippie, into the mass media age and all of the canons, levitating military buildings and becoming a national treasure. Ted's old Beat was one of the rank and unshowered also-rans, a moderately respected purveyor of Sound-Body poems who was barely mentioned in Diane di Prima's autobiography, but mentioned prominently in each scathing indictment of the misogyny, neuroses, and abusive behaviors cataloged by a long list of surviving Beat wives, girlfriends, and abandoned children. When *Todd's* boyfriend loaned him out to a friend, it was to the crackly old granddaddy of postmodernism himself, the old junky legend holed up in his Kansas farmhouse. The old sorcerer hadn't had sex in a decade, and wouldn't again before he died, and so Todd felt that he'd at least earned a place in literary history. Todd was taken out to the barn, where they made paintings together with shotguns, paintings that would sell someday for tens of thousands of dollars, and he got to lie in the Orgone Box and pretend that his cosmic orgone energy was accumulating at a more rapid pace. When *Ted's* Beat loaned *Ted* out, it was to a Zen poet who ate nothing but grass, and whose body of work was entirely conceptual, a lifetime of silence. His silence had grown to include both his interactions with the boys that his more verbose Beat cronies would occasionally toss his way, and his occasional lectures at the Naropa Institute, where attentive students would sit uncomfortably for what seemed like hours, trying to glean the meaning of his smallest gesture. There was no Orgone Box, although the walk-in closet the poet lived in, lined with his own conceptual art pieces made out of jock straps and tinsel, mimicked the effect.

Upon arriving at the age when their relationships weren't technically rapes, both Todd and Ted moved on to transgressive novelists, but while Todd had captured the dark genius whose intricate tales of disemboweling boys had brought him a cult following, a growing reputation, and a leading role in a variety of sometimes incongruous avant-gardes, Ted's transgressive novelist was on a downward spiral from a summit that had involved publishing his cryptic and nonlinear stories, which all centered around images of diapering, in one collection put out by a small press that then immediately went bankrupt, and in a few late '80s anthologies. For a moment, both the transgressive novelists were perched in those same anthologies that packaged their experimental depictions of kinky sex, drugs, and Lower East Side living as forms of political protest, but by the time Todd and Ted had hooked up with them, Todd's transgressor was editing anthologies of his own, anthologies that never included *Ted's* boyfriend, who would call up and leave more and more pleading messages on the answering machine of Todd's boyfriend, knowing that Todd's boyfriend rarely left his house and always screened his calls.

Finally, both Todd and Ted struck out on their own. They both arrived in the city around 1993, where they moved in the circle of artists and writers whose orbit was defined by Kevin Killian's plays. They both hung out at Baby Judy's, and like everybody else that Raymond knew in San Francisco in the early '90s, they dabbled in sex work. Todd emerged from that trade with his dignity mostly intact; he bulked up and made the transition from a twinky boy-toy into a butch, tech-friendly gym rat, while Ted was still advertising himself as a straight nineteen-year-old skater or a bi-curious twenty-year-old college jock well into his thirties, leaving himself at the mercy of crueler and crueler johns who would make derisive comments about his receding hairline or say *Abercrombie and Fitch, please, Mary* before slamming the door in his face.

Todd co-created whimsical Internet animation during the boom years, and has now moved on to a career doing nothing in an Emeryville office building. Theoretically, he has three levels of supervision, but in reality he has none, and he's paid a healthy salary for acting busy. Ted is cleaning the muck off the floors of the Nob Hill Theatre. Todd is witty and intelligent, people like him. Ted is witty and intelligent in a way that irritates everyone he meets. As his prostitution run was reaching its inevitable end, he began reading people's auras for money, but his clients inevitably left feeling polluted and judged. Todd, on the other hand, gives tarot card readings full of welcome advice. One old guy who came to him, Todd told Raymond, had nothing much left in life but fisting. He grabbed Todd's arm during the card reading, just above the elbow. I could take it up to here, he told Todd. But not without drugs.

Tops like their bottoms on drugs, Todd said to Raymond. It's just like the ideal of housewives in the '50s, he said—the bottom is supposed to be insatiable and brainless, numbed into a state of perpetual compliance—like Ted, Todd said. But Todd had showed the old guy a future in the tarot cards, a future of expanded social possibilities, if he, too, would reach out and show an interest in others, as the tarot cards suggested. He reassured the old man that he was accepted, and went home alone. Ted would have fisted the old guy, for nothing more than a compliment. Ted was like all of Todd's worst impulses manifest as a real person. If Todd had become trapped in another dimension, a particularly unpleasant and cruel dimension, one of the nine Aztec underworlds perhaps, The Place of the Obsidian Wind or The Place Where People's Hearts Are Devoured, in that dimension Todd would have been Ted. Both Ted and Todd had been, for some time, although not in concert, roommates of Jonny Taser's.

His hygiene was disgusting, Jonny Taser is telling Raymond now. Ted had acquired a variety of nasty habits that Jonny blames on his years with the diaper queen transgressive novelist. The fact that he never washed his sheets—and I mean never, says Jonny Taser, not once during the three years he lived with me—wasn't the half of it. The sheets turned black, Ted developed rashes on his neck, and couldn't understand why. It's against Talmud, Jonny says.

Jonny's groupie nudges Jonny and something passes between them in silence. See ya later, Jonny says, and Raymond watches him stroll on into the night. Raymond coasts down the hill, around the fruit loop, and past the rec center named after the gay hero, and rides up again, backtracking to circle around the top of Buena Vista Park.

At the top of Buena Vista Park, the early risers walk their dogs and tweakers cruise in the bushes. It's cold and windy, but one of the cruising tweakers is shirtless, wearing nothing but turquoise blue shorts that seem to be made of the same material as a balloon. They're wrapped so tightly around the bubble butt, obviously the man's best feature, that in the dim morning light the cellophane blue booty floats like a disembodied head, weaving in and out of the trees, beckoning the tweakers to follow.

Watch your dogs, one of the other tweakers warns a woman with a cock-apoo. There's 4-inch beetles in this park, they'll crawl right in your dog's ass.

He's an old client, Davey. Davey looks like a caveman, with a square head and a wild shock of blond hair. Raymond's been chatting with him for years, here and there, in cruising grounds around the city, but he never seems to age.

Beautiful morning, Raymond tells him.

San Francisco, says Davey. A beautiful city full of ugly people.

Raymond has heard that one before; it's one of Davey's signature lines. Off to the side, a dorky, vaguely Latino kid wanders past. He's dressed himself up in the sullen masculinity that everyone his age is wearing these days, but he's not quite pulling it off. Saggy leisure wear with skulls and dollar bills. He's hovering around the edge of the cruising area as if he's just innocently wandered by, doesn't know what's up.

Raymond holds out his backpack full of condoms and lube.

They're free, he says.

No way! says the kid and grabs a handful. You like just give these away to be nice?

I'm an outreach worker, says Raymond. Do you know about safer sex?

Oh, I'm not into that, says the kid.

Up close his face conveys both cluelessness and brains. Like his features keep shifting or like he really doesn't know where the hell he is. A visitor from another planet having a hard time adjusting to Earth's heavy atmosphere.

There's at least five Sex Offenders who live next to this park, he tells Raymond.

Turns out he's from Utah, an ex-Mormon, which explains everything. He's definitely not gay, he says, but he's not, like, the opposite of gay either. It's just a phase anyway. His name is Melvin, he's almost nineteen and he lives in somebody's storage space in Oakland.

Is it a squat? asks Raymond.

It's at this apartment complex, Melvin explains. This guy has storage space in a garage and he lets me sleep there and keep my stuff there.

For free? asks Raymond.

Kind of.

So if you have a place to sleep, why are you in the park at the crack of dawn?

Melvin shakes his head in a lurid way, as if he's going limp, and his eyes roll back up into his head for a minute.

Long story, he says.

Sounds like a squat to me, says Raymond. You wanna be in a magazine?
No way! says Melvin.

Raymond gets Melvin's cell phone number to give to Felicia. The kid seems to have drifted into a kind of daze brought on by the thought of his impending fame.

Hey, he says finally. I have a question.

Shoot.

Is death real?

Is death real.

I mean I used to think…that it wouldn't make any sense.

You're asking my opinion.

I just thought that maybe…you know…you might have some insights. It's been kind of on my mind, Melvin says.

It's real, says Raymond.

Okay, never mind, says Melvin, and he wanders down the hill. Davey takes the opportunity to fill the gap in Raymond's personal space.

Davey tells Raymond he wants to get back into counseling. But I need to work with a man, he says. I have *huge* mother issues.

He makes a gesture with his hands to convey issues so enormous they would blot out the sun. Raymond loves these men, in a way, the gay men who've survived everything and gone on in the world, without hope or enthusiasm. *You wake up one morning and anything goes, and that's all right, too.* The cellophane blue booty emerges from the bushes down below, a phantom globe in the mist, and floats up toward Raymond, before disappearing back among the trees.

5

AND SO, EVERYTHING HAS ALREADY HAPPENED. The doorbell rings and, beyond it, the dim buzzing of noon. A buzzing like summer, like swimming pools loaded with chlorine.

It's Philip's oldest friend standing on the front porch, here for their lunch date. Bob Miller looks worse than Philip's ever seen him. Bob Miller has always been lanky and awkward. Now he's gaunt and unshaven, with a lurid abscess on the back of his hand. The sunlight is unforgiving. After a warmish hug, Bob greets Philip in his usual fawning manner—he tells him how much he loves his writing, how honored he is to be his friend.

Gosh, he says, I just really want to say how proud I am of you, Phil.

Bob Miller is the only person in the world who still calls Philip *Phil*. Bob Miller is the only non-Christian Philip has ever known who says *gosh* and *golly* without any apparent irony. A folksy contrast to the high-powered legal worlds he's moved through at Harvard, in Hollywood, in Paris, and in Silicon Valley.

Dottie, Bob's mother, was a spunky farm girl who married a Des Moines lawyer. When the lawyer, Gus Miller, impregnated his mistress, a mentally unstable woman who would kill herself a few years later, Dottie adopted the child and raised him as her own. This was Bob, but Dottie and Gus lied to him throughout his childhood. They didn't claim that Dottie was his biological mother, but that Gus was *not* his biological father; he was supposedly 100 percent adopted. People who didn't know better would remark that he looked like his father, and they all would laugh. It was a family joke—how funny that he, an adopted child, shared this resemblance with Dad. Bob Miller thought that the way an adopted son could come to resemble his father was the same way people started looking like their pets, and his laughter reflected this belief. It was nervous laughter, but sincere, the hilarity and terror provoked by the idea of biological mutation. His father's laughter, in retrospect, gives him the creeps. His mother's probably makes him want to die.

Dottie was into owls. Not the cold, ruthless night predators with enormous claws and sharp beaks that would swoop down on their prey in the darkness and devour them, but Disney owls, refrigerator magnets and ceramics, embroidered little bookworm owls. She resembled the owls she collected, cute and squat with big round glasses, and then one Christmas, when Philip and Bob were eleven, the Millers' house caught fire. The smoke ruined everything and so Bob and his parents moved into the Howard Johnson's Motor Lodge on the strip out past the mall, for a couple of months while the damage was being undone. Philip used to spend the night there with Bob; in the pool at the Howard Johnson's Motor Lodge, he and Bob were always swimming among strange men.

For thirty-six years their paths have crossed and recrossed, since they sat next to each other in Mrs. Parker's kindergarten.

Bob devoted his life to fulfilling his parents' dreams. For Dottie, he was a good boy, relentlessly polite, overbearingly nice. For Gus, he was a successful lawyer. It was an odd, even painful performance. During the dot-com years, Bob was on track to be a partner, with a gazillion-dollar salary, but since his father died, he's been discovering that the life of a high-powered lawyer never really suited him. Maybe he regrets having squandered his youth debating public policy, cramming for tests, and jumping through the hoops of Harvard Law School, while his peers were dropping in and out of school, dealing drugs, and living in bohemian squalor. Philip would like to think that Bob has simply decided to find himself, to figure something out, the delayed but necessary task of self-discovery. But he's kind of shrunken. With his weight loss, his bubbly eyes seem ghoulish. After fifteen minutes or so of his persistent obsequiousness, they can usually start back where they left off the last time, and have a real conversation—about Bob's creepy father, or the gay subtext in various Disney cartoons, or Bob's bitchy reports from the high school reunions back in Iowa. Except that Philip hasn't seen Bob in over a year, and so the obsequiousness lasts through the entire process of walking up to Cortlandt to find a restaurant, with the Blue Angels again shrieking overhead, and halfway through the process of eating the dumpy, poorly imagined crepes they're served for lunch. Bob grills him with a kind of contrived fascination about the Amish murders. So at least there were survivors? he asks.

Five boys were killed and five boys were wounded, Philip tells him.

And how do the Amish deal with something like this? Bob asks.

The most unusual thing about these killings, Philip says, is that nobody knows what the dead children looked like but the Amish themselves. The Amish don't take pictures.

Philip has seen only one picture of his father as a child, a class picture taken at his one-room school by his non-Amish teacher. More than half of the students at that school were his father's brothers and sisters and none of them looked happy to be posing for a picture. Riverside, Iowa, the future birthplace of Captain Kirk. Outside Riverside, Philip tells Bob, on a virtually unused country road, is East Liberty, the actual town of the shooting.

Gosh, Phil, so these kids don't have birthday pictures or anything?

There are no photographs anywhere, of any of the dead children, Philip says.

So will you stop in and see Jonas and Jolene? asks Bob.

He'll spend the night—tonight—at his parents' house. He's been grilling his father for the names of possible connections, cousins or acquaintances, who might be able to get him to the grieving families. His brother has given him a phone number for one of the ex-Amish members of an Iowa City band. Everybody's excited to be part of the investigation.

Bob asks how Raymond is doing. He was really sick, wasn't he?

He could have died, Philip says.

Bob says that Raymond must have a lot of fortitude.

Philip tells Bob that Raymond's favorite stories are those in which the will to live is instrumental in enabling survival. Raymond's favorite book, *I Survived Rumbuli*, was written by one of only two survivors of a massacre of 30,000 Jews in the Rumbuli forest.

Bob wants to know what happened to the only other survivor of Rumbuli. The one who didn't write the book.

When Bob excuses himself to use the restroom, Philip finds himself wondering what Bob is really doing in there. But he's no more drugged or erratic looking as he emerges, as far as Philip can tell. Bob wonders if Philip will cash a check from Dottie so Bob can buy some weed, and then interrupts himself to say there's something more important—the bridge. Bob tells Philip that he needs to tell him a story. It was almost a year ago now. Did I tell you about the bridge?

The way he says it, Philip feels like the whole conversation so far has been a mere prologue.

No, says Philip. We haven't seen each other.

Okay, says Bob, but instead he talks about Doris Day.

Once, Bob was just a boy on a trip out to California. His father insisted they splurge on lunch at a famous restaurant in Beverly Hills. Dottie was like: no way. She thought we'd look like the Beverly Hillbillies, Bob says and laughs. Philip is pretty sure that, in fact, they did look very much like the Beverly Hillbillies. In any case, they went to the restaurant, and there she was: Doris Day. Bob was so in awe that he didn't care what he or his family looked like. His own debased and humble aura, his family still reeking of an agricultural past, dusty with hard work and print dresses ordered from the Sears catalog—Bob probably loved the stark contrast with absolute glamour, a breathy and effortless radiance that shone all that much brighter for their abject Midwestern-ness, the generous and brilliant smile that Doris Day offered them as, with his father's encouragement, Bob went over to her table and asked for her autograph.

I think she's still alive, says Philip. Isn't she an animal rights activist?

Bob says that later he'd come to associate Doris Day with his biological mother, glamorous and slutty in a strangely wholesome way. A woman he met only once, he's pretty sure—*the lady with the green hair*. He was with his father and this strange lady at a motel, when Bob was maybe three or four. She was nice, but her hair was dyed and the chlorine in the motel pool turned it green. In his memory, she was always *the lady with the green hair*, and it wasn't until recently, since Bob's father's death, that he's put the pieces together and figured out that it must have been his mom. Memory's funny, Bob says. It's all a bit hazy, but he now has no doubt. Since his father's death, unfortunately, he can't verify his conclusion—Bob's the only survivor of the scene at the motel pool.

I have this whole mother/whore thing, he explains. I have this saintly mother, Dottie, and then I have this whore mother, my father's mistress.

The brain's funny, isn't it? says Philip.

For much of Bob's childhood, there was another mistress, another woman who called the house. She would tell his mother that his father had just left her, that he was on his way home now. Sometimes she wouldn't say anything at all. The phone would ring and his mother would become hysterical. His mother talked about this woman to Bob as if she was a witch, the embodiment of pure evil, and Bob hated her, of course, this woman who made his mother suffer, but he was also fascinated by her. She spoke to him only one time, when he answered the phone and she paused for the longest time, and then said, Tell your mother it's over. Her voice was sexy, illicit, out of control.

She was always in a nightgown, always putting on lipstick, always having sex with strange men. Whatever was supposed to be over, however, wasn't, not yet.

Strange men, Philip says. Like your father.

Like my father.

Outside, the parallel vapor trails of the Blue Angels are like claw marks across the sky. Something trying to claw its way *out* or claw its way *in*? As they leave the crepe restaurant, Bob reminds Philip to stop at the bank, cash that check, and then interrupts himself to return to the subject of *the bridge*.

It was a Friday night, about a year ago, and he'd had some other guy over at his apartment, he explains, some trick, who got up on the Internet and started inviting people over. He talked me into hosting an orgy, Bob explains, a little bit apologetic. He wants to make it clear that he isn't in the habit of hosting or even attending orgies. But one thing led to another, he says. In any case, several men came over, but when Bob woke up in the morning, only one of them was still there: John Garcia.

John Garcia was forty-two, he was manic-depressive, and they bonded rather intensely that morning. John Garcia was intent on explaining his life, especially his passion for *Don Quixote*. They spent the whole day together, and that afternoon Bob went with John Garcia to his house in San Jose. John Garcia wanted to show him his hot tub and his garden, he read to him passages from *Don Quixote*, and he played his favorite song for Bob, a requiem by Mozart. And gosh, says Bob, it was really beautiful and the way he talked about *Don Quixote* it was just so fascinating. You probably know it better than I do, Mr. Author and all, says Bob.

Philip shrugs.

I read it in college, he says.

Bob says, He wanted to talk all night and we just lost track of the time, listening to the music. John Garcia explained that he loved the requiem because it made death seem like it wasn't really so scary.

Bob had shared some things from his own life with this man, details about his biological mother and his adoption, the half brother he'd just recently met in Tampa, the *lady with the green hair*, but that hadn't really been the dynamic. The dynamic was John Garcia talking and talking—as if compelled to reveal himself in his entirety to me, Bob says. They had sex in the hot tub, but they'd agreed that at seven o'clock that evening John would take Bob to catch the train. Bob was supposed to go to this party in Fairfield or Vacaville that night.

Well actually, Bob says, it was another orgy.

So Bob's supposed to go to this orgy and John Garcia is supposed to drop Bob off, but they both putz around and miss the train; there isn't another one for an hour or maybe never. Bob calls his friends, the ones having the orgy, and they say it's fine for John Garcia to come along. John Garcia drives Bob there in his beat-up old car, it's like a Datsun 280Z or something, something low and sporty and ancient.

They cross the bridge to get there—not the Carquinez Bridge, but the one parallel to it, it's where 680 crosses the Bay, the delta, whatever you call it, out there by Martinez and Vallejo and Pittsburg, Bob Miller says. He takes several minutes to clarify the bridge's location and describe the way it overlooks some oil refineries on one side and a cute little town on the other, Bob thinks it's Benicia.

Bob tells Philip that at the party they kind of separated, he and John Garcia. John wasn't having the best time, it wasn't his sort of scene. It must have been Bob's sort of scene, because Bob tells Philip that he sucked *every dick in the room*.

John Garcia was acting strange, and Bob says that everybody who was at the party agrees that he acted strange. Kind of…obsessed.

John Garcia and Bob finally got together again around four o'clock in the morning. They had amazing sex, and then got ready to head back to John Garcia's place in San Jose. Where John Garcia's hot tub was waiting, where

Bob was envisioning a lazy Sunday morning of sex and weed and hot tubbing in John Garcia's beautiful garden. But before they can leave, John Garcia's desperate to check his email, he's kind of obnoxious about it, Bob says. Like interrupting the orgy host, who was really otherwise *occupied*, to find out how to get on his computer. It was like he had to take care of all kinds of unfinished business, Bob says, but he never did find a way at the party to check his email and so whatever business he had…

Something is sparkling at the edge of Philip's vision. Something's coming on.

On the way out of town Bob and John Garcia pass a gas station and Bob suggests they stop for gas. The tank looks from Bob's angle to be maybe a quarter full, but of course his angle, from the passenger's side, is pretty distorted. There's some complication about money, like they only have enough cash for the bridge toll—except there isn't a bridge toll, they're going south—or like who has a credit card and who doesn't, or maybe they're both so warm and cozy in the car that they can't quite imagine stopping at the gas station. Bob doesn't remember exactly, but he knows that despite all this discussion about stopping, they end up passing the gas station by.

Now, Philip and Bob stop at Philip's bank, only to discover that they won't cash Bob's check. There's an ATM down at the Safeway, Philip tells Bob, if you just want to get some money from your account.

Gosh, says Bob, what time is it?

He's late for some unspecified appointment downtown, the check doesn't matter, and he can get the weed another day. I'll come by when you're back from Iowa, says Bob. I need to finish my story.

Philip watches Bob scurry off after the bus, clutching a crumpled little transfer in his hand. Philip is light-headed. Everything—the filthy sidewalks, the pigeon shit, and the gleaming or rusty cars parked along the street—glows just a little too much, immersed in a sense of expectation. He knows what's happening, but he chooses to deny it for another moment. It dawns on Philip that Bob doesn't *have* any money in his account. It dawns on Philip that, other than the check from Dottie, that bus transfer may be the most valuable thing Bob owns.

As he stands there, watching the 24 Divisadero hobble away, the glow expands, an eruption of atomic flashes and sparkles. By the time he is heading back down the hill, he is dazzled, an entire side of his vision spattered with blinding lights. It's a migraine coming on. Back at home, he lies quietly on the bed with the curtains drawn, waiting for Raymond to come home to drive him to the airport.

It is primarily Bob's use of the word *need* that sticks in Philip's mind. I *need* to finish my story.

The year before, when Raymond was sick, the doctors prescribed him everything. They have a drawer full of every painkiller and anti-anxiety drug imaginable. Philip will pop a couple of Vicodins and fly through the clouds. If he has a window seat, the clouds will be entertaining enough, so distant, like a message from his own mind or from human history. The history of the brain's relationship to the sky. The history of Western metaphysics and nothingness. He'll be flying through it, and then he'll have dinner with his parents, sleep in his childhood bed, a 38-year-old mattress. In the morning, he'll drive to the dead boys.

But maybe the clouds will be too bright, like the world outside now. It isn't exactly that the light is painful, but that there always seems to be a brightness he can glimpse that would be painful if he looked at it head-on. Or it's the contrast that is painful and that threatens to hurl him into a world of pain. The contrast between the dimness in which he is immersed and some hideous brightness at the edges or between the dull light around him and a more severe darkness, the absolute blackness of certain doorways and basements.

6

AFTER DROPPING PHILIP OFF AT THE AIRPORT, Raymond meets Ralph at Fairy Lane, between the windmills in Golden Gate Park. Ralph looks good, despite himself. Playing tennis has kept him trim, and he wears faded work shirts that emphasize the pale blue of his eyes. With his hair closely cropped to de-emphasize the bald spot, he's successfully working a distinguished daddy thing, projecting an entirely false sense of self-assuredness, dignity, and financial security. Ralph thought he might find either a new leading man or a demanding top scurrying through the bushes here. From the shrubbery on either side of the main path, they can hear incomprehensible murmurs and yelps like animal noises, none of which seem to clearly emerge from the solitary figures perched enticingly along various paths.

There's nobody cruising here but homeless men and senior citizens, Ralph complains.

Raymond points out a couple of guys who probably aren't either homeless or retired, but neither of them is to Ralph's liking as either sex date or new star. In *Tinky Winky Rising*, Ralph cast his own boyfriend Hugo as a high school student who went from straightlaced, heterosexual A-student to murderous leader of a sociopathic queer gang in twenty-four hours of mayhem and debauchery after getting high on ginseng tea and watching *The Teletubbies*. Ralph killed off Hugo's character at the end of the first film, fortunately, since Hugo, the only one of the cast with professional ambitions, simply couldn't act. He had no presence, his movements were wooden, and his attempts to convey emotion came across as both hysterical and flat. In any case, Hugo has long since returned to Quebec to star in a French Canadian soap opera. The plot of *Tinky Winky Rising* is a little over-the-top for Raymond's taste, although it demonstrates the sort of trajectory he most enjoys in other people's lives, trajectories with huge peaks and huge valleys, rapid changes of fortune, such as Ralph's, from being dragged up and down the stairs by Tony during his years of student degradation at Berkeley to his recent stint as a highly paid producer in LA, from the period of unemployment and self-abuse that followed his years as an outreach worker to his trim, tennis-playing daddy persona, from his absolute low point, when he followed Hugo to Quebec, driving cross country in his old Volvo station wagon, to his glorious ascent as a porn director and neo-grind-house auteur.

Ooh, what about that one? Ralph says. Kind of like a blond version of Damien.

I don't know who Damien is, says Raymond.

You met him once, says Ralph. Maybe at the 17th Street Brigade office. He was homeless for a while? Had this really fucked-up childhood, mostly in a basement.

A former boyfriend. Damien was too disturbed to ever have anything you could really call a relationship—and was sexually aroused by radio static more than other human beings—but despite that fact he was with Tony for years, and later with Ralph and Ralph's girlfriend Sasha in a *ménage à tois*, and later just with Ralph.

The blond glances their way, but disappears among the trees.

Ralph tells Raymond that the first time he took acid, maybe fifteen or twenty years ago, he was with Damien in Damien's apartment in Berkeley. They were boyfriends at the time, if you could call it that, and they were just peaking, and then sirens started going off, red lights flashing. The authorities were shrieking through the neighborhood and they stopped right in front of Damien's building. Ralph thought they were coming for him, of course. In fact, the upstairs neighbor had had a heart attack. Ralph and Damien just cowered back into the deepest corner of the apartment, watching through the picture window that looked onto the back stairway as the paramedics clomped up and down the stairs. Up and down, up and down, a commotion that was unimaginable as a series of meaningful tasks and seemed more like a dramatic performance designed to reduce its audience—Ralph—to a state of utter dread. All that clomping back and forth was pointless. The man upstairs was dead. The paramedics finally loaded the corpse on a stretcher, but the stairs were so narrow, and there was such a tight corner leading down to the next floor, that the paramedics couldn't quite maneuver it. They tried various strategies and finally just set the corpse down, directly in front of Damien's picture window.

Ralph was trapped in the room—there was no other way out—staring at a corpse. Damien started strumming his guitar and humming nonsense words in an atonal, yet vaguely soothing drone. It helped for a minute, but then he stopped singing, tuned his radio to an empty frequency, and masturbated in the corner. Ralph decided that Damien was Life, but Ralph was frozen in between Life and Death, unable to break free into the reality of either one. It was all he could do to keep from calling his mother. Ralph thought that a stern femme like his mother might help him break free of Death's spell. Ralph thought that Life was a stern femme and Death a cynical butch. The paramedics were smoking cigarettes on one side of the window; he couldn't see them, but he could hear them casually chatting about this and that—strategies for dating emergency room nurses, for hatching reptile eggs, and for getting the corpse on its way, but with no urgency whatsoever. The trails of cigarette smoke that drifted lazily past the picture window took on the shapes of phantoms, of secret messages written in alien alphabets, of the erotic contortions of necrophiliacs. Fortunately, Ralph was rendered incapable of speech. He couldn't even crawl across the room to pick up the phone and dial.

The blond guy, who at least from a distance reminds Ralph of Damien, reemerges from a loopy trail.

Ralph shrugs and hurries after the blond, leaving Raymond alone on the main path with his backpack full of condoms. He supposes that Ralph is secretly hoping for an impossible synthesis—the two halves of his brain will be lulled into a superintuitive fugue state from which the perfect sex date and leading man will emerge. *A particular blond boy*. Or maybe two. More than anything,

Ralph loves to be paralyzed by the mutually exclusive demands of two dominating wills. A stern femme and a cynical butch.

Raymond, on the other hand, has spent his life trying to recover from the mutually exclusive demands of two dominating wills. His father loved light and air and austere, minimal spaces up above the world; his mother loved dark, comfy, ground-level flats with the curtains always drawn. His father was mean and optimistic and white, his mother was self-absorbed and pessimistic and black. His father was enamored of the future, insisting that natural selection worked for the best of all possible worlds, while his mother had firmly located the best of all possible worlds in the unrecoverable past. His father often insisted with an equally optimistic pigheadedness that there was nothing wrong with him, no matter how sick he was, while his mother traipsed back and forth to doctors for second and third opinions when she was perfectly well. Escaping the tyranny of that life-or-death struggle, their all-consuming egos and continual bickering, his father's poetry, his mother's endless complaining, his father's failure, his mother's poor choices, the broken dishes, the trips to Tahoe gone sour, even if Raymond's escape was only into the world of alternative therapies and HIV and trashy queens like Ralph and Louie and freaky writers and conceptual artists and scuba divers and street outreach...

Raymond sees somebody who looks vaguely familiar peeking out of the trees, vaguely familiar yet unrecognizable, like a character from a book. He's incredibly skinny and wearing a pair of dumpy sweatpants. Then Noel greets him, *Hey Raymond,* and it all snaps into place. Noel was an outreach worker for the Asian AIDS Project. Years ago—eight? nine?—back in the heyday of outreach, they worked together one night at a club, with Noel dressed in a traditional Filipino sari-like wrap and wearing an enormous straw basket on his head as a hat, full of condoms. Although he was kind of chubby then, he was elegant and glided like a supermodel through the club full of strobe lights and mineral smoke and glistening pecs. The men swarmed him. He was always stylish, with his black cashmere sweaters, and never would have been seen in public *back in the day* wearing some dumpy old sweatpants.

Noel gives Raymond a hug and apathetically fills him in on the past eight or nine years with a few basic facts: lost his outreach job, got hired at Project Concern, lost that job, tested positive, started doing meth. It's kind of empty here today, he says, as if that's the conclusion to his story.

Everyone's up on their computers these days, suggests Raymond.

Raymond feels that the imaginary world online has somehow supplanted the world he's from—a physical world, a world of actual bodies, actual sex. Raymond blames this frenzied shopping for the impossible on the dot-com years, which in Raymond's mind followed the same plot as *Invasion of the Body Snatchers*—the classic '70s *Invasion of the Body Snatchers*, with its dark and hopeless ending—the forces of the hive-mind win. Just like the dot-com years, a neutron bomb of gentrification that pushed half the people Raymond knew out of San Francisco.

Oh, no, Noel says. Sometimes it's really crowded here. People come here… in the middle of the night…in the dark. I'm kind of scared sometimes, he says, and he shrugs.

Raymond suggests that maybe meth isn't the best thing for Noel's immune system.

Some people are saying speed actually *kills* the HIV virus, Noel says.

The blond boy that Ralph was pursuing pops out of the bushes right next to them, flashes a look that's supposed to be seductive, and disappears into the trees on the other side of the main path. Up close, he doesn't seem to be a boy at all, but an aged gremlin with the lithe body and silky hairdo of a boy.

Did you hear about Louie? Raymond asks Noel, but Noel is gazing into the space where the blond disappeared.

It's nice to see you, baby, I'll see you around, he says, and chases after the blond.

On the other side, toward the soccer field, a guy in a dark hoodie is alternately making goo-goo eyes at Ralph, and looking down at some electronic device. Ralph seems unsure which way he should go. Noel and the blond quickly abandon each other, so Ralph scurries down the path in an effort to head off the blond.

Ralph was on the hiring committee that chose Raymond for his first outreach job in '93 or '94. The Western Addition outreach slot, the "black slot," had opened up after the queen who'd had it before—Charlie Adams, who actually refused to step foot in the Western Addition—sued the agency, 17th Street Brigade, for 40,000 dollars after the supervisor, Bobby Boatbridge, pulled a chair out from under him as he was about to sit down at a meeting about ways to improve outreach team morale. Bobby Boatbridge was an amazing dancer and an ex gangsta-gay, or so he claimed, and he was secretly, or not so secretly, fucking the Executive Director, Brian Hopkins. By the time Raymond was hired, the ED who was fucking Bobby Boatbridge had been replaced by another ED named Brian, Brian Burney, who was high on Valium and speed all the time and who went after Bobby Boatbridge and forced him out, because Charlie's lawsuit made them look bad, just as they were trying to negotiate a merger with another vast, AIDSy nonprofit, Operation Positivity, to form a superorganism, another kind of hive-mind, *efficiency and growth* were the buzz-words of the day, *efficiency and growth*, everybody said, *efficiency and growth*, autistic children self-stimulating with their meaningless magical chants, or not so meaningless perhaps, since three years later the merger finally went through and most of the outreach workers were let go, trashy and inappropriate queens were replaced through a series of layoffs and rehires with articulate and freshly scrubbed young people with boundaries and degrees.

The original outreach team had been the strangest constellation of recovering and inappropriate gay men. For one glorious moment, crackhead was an entry-level position in the world of San Francisco social services. So were ex-hustler, tranny prostitute, and prison bottom, and it actually *worked*, but a dozen years later, the most vicious and delusional crackheads have made their way into upper management with the rest of the sociopaths, and in the rank and file of the nonprofit world, everyone has their degree. The day Raymond first showed up for work, Louie had cornered Ralph behind the desk in the outreach office and was waving a buzzing vibrator at him. At 17th Street Brigade, sexual harassment verging on rape was tolerated, even encouraged, as long as it was done with a sense of humor. Everyone had sex with their supervisors behind closed doors or with their coworkers on the desk of the outreach office or with their clients at sex clubs and in cruising grounds or they took their clients home with them and did drugs with them or got angry with them and chased them out the door and down the front steps calling them names all the while. By Raymond's second day of work he was himself put on a hiring committee with Ralph, Louie, Jonny Taser, Nick Gangway, and Marcos, interviewing the three top candidates for their own Outreach Supervisor. The first candidate was an overly manicured and neatly packaged queen with nice muscles, muscles that Nick complimented during the interview, as it became obvious to everyone in the room that the two of them would be all over each other immediately after the interview, whether or not he got the job. The first candidate answered questions with more detail than was really appropriate, implying a history of intermittent steroid abuse and his own exhaustion with racist assumptions concerning his performance of black masculinity. He explicitly acknowledged an intricate psychology, a complex inner nothingness simplified through "overcompensation" into a clear focus on his pecs, his biceps, and his job performance at a series of more and more demanding positions, as measured by whatever abstract series of numbers determined by whatever series of judges—it didn't matter to him. His philosophical understanding of outreach was summarized as *the never-ending attempt to fill clients' infinite needs*, which, in combination with other statements made while sporting a nonsensical smile, posited the *streets* as a kind of bottomless pit, the future as an empty abstraction masking fundamental nothingness, and "supervision" as the sort of parasitic set of tasks that could only be considered meaningful by the supervisor himself. It was probably the most accurate response to their questions that afternoon, but hardly inspiring.

The second candidate said all the right things, but wore knee-high boots with heels and a suggestion of fur. He hadn't left the room but five seconds before Louie said, *Oh no, Miss Thing with her cha-cha boots, please girl*, and then Nick and Marcos chimed in, they all had the scoop from Yvette and Isela, the second candidate was into transgenders and took these social service jobs only so he could scam on all the TGs he'd meet through the agency.

The third candidate was Bill Broom. *Hire the cripple!* said Jonny Taser immediately upon his departure from the room, and although Nick championed the muscle queen, everybody else was unanimous for Bill Broom, who walked with a limp, had a bulging stomach that reminded them of Santa Claus, and who told them he was *in it for the long haul*. Within three months of his hire, he had taken all of his vacation time and quit.

During his brief reign, Bill Broom used Raymond's individual outreach supervision time one day to tell him the story, which he desperately needed to process, of *the little Arab* he'd picked up at the sex club over the weekend, who had, according to Bill Broom, managed to somehow sneak the condom off of Bill Broom's dick with his manipulative, hungry ass, while Bill was fucking him, so that Bill, who was HIV+, ended up coming inside him, which left him feeling raped by *the little Arab*, whose sneakiness and abject desire for unsafe sex left him flabbergasted and traumatized. The outreach workers all compared notes and discovered that he'd told the exact same implausible story to each of them during their individual supervision, differing only in a few minor details, but then Bill Broom was not only the boss, but a good friend of the Executive Director, Brian Burney, who was high on speed and Valium all the time, and in any case, before they knew it, both Bill Broom and Brian were gone, replaced by Joe Hay and Toby Newsom. In no time, outreach funding was lost and everyone was laid off.

Eventually, Raymond was rehired not by New Dog, but by the nonprofit that had served as the umbrella organization for the whole outreach operation, The Golden Gate Free Healthcare Consortium, although the free portion of the healthcare had been recently phased out in response to the financial restructuring necessitated by the Chief Financial Officer's embezzlement of funds, and in fact, healthcare in general was no longer seen as sufficiently sustaining the nonprofit's bottom line, so like New Dog, the GGFHC was more and more enmeshed in the business of addiction and recovery. The Founder, the brother of a woman who'd played a flamboyant villainess on one of those '60s gay-superhero TV shows, owned most of the buildings the organization utilized, which he rented out at an exorbitant rate to his own nonprofit, until the skyrocketing rents of the dot-com era made it more feasible to relocate the no-longer free healthcare services to less pricey neighborhoods and convert its former abode into condos.

It was years after his brief tenure as Outreach Supervisor that Bill Broom's face popped up in an advertising campaign, in brochures and on bus stops, for some immune-supporting protein drink that was supposed to magically rejuvenate people ravaged by AIDS. He was touting some product that in earlier days, before combination therapy, Raymond might have actually imbibed. What else had there been to do? There were only the alternative therapies, the miracle cures, the rumors of incredible T-cell boosts, and the sketchy science of immune system modulation. Raymond had actually scarred himself with one of those toxic liquids that was supposed to just bring on a minor rash, an allergic response that was to somehow recombobulate one's helper and suppressor cells. He and Philip both did the bitter melon enemas for years, stopping by the Filipino market South of Market once a week, even driving into LA when they were living in Santa Barbara, where bitter melon was in short supply, until they found out that the scientist who'd discovered the amazing healing properties of the acrid green juice owned a bitter melon farm up north. There was the noni juice, the aloe vera juice, the bottles and bottles of vitamins and antioxidants and mushrooms and herbs they'd shoplifted from every health store in town, the ginseng tea combined with AZT and d4T that made Raymond so agitated he tried to run Philip down with the pickup truck one afternoon, Ralph's inspiration for *Tinky Winky Rising*. None of those things had cured them, but who knows, really, if any of them helped? Raymond even attended a strange seminar once with Philip, maybe in '93 or '94, in the conference room of some downtown San Francisco hotel where they listened to a strange glowing white-haired man who was trying to peddle some kind of mineral treatment supposed to cure *everything*. His skin was the strangest color, he seemed radioactive or like one of the aliens from Metaluna in *This Island Earth*, horrifying, rather crab-like creatures who had disguised themselves as humanoids with incredibly high foreheads, shocking white hair, and the same sort of incandescent tan as the mineral doctor. Raymond and Philip sat at a long table for two hours with a dozen other desperate people watching the tan doctor break out strange charts and demonstrate incomprehensible experiments of electromagnetism with some wires and an aquarium full of soaking minerals, as he promised to fly each and every one of them to Salt Lake City, of all places, to undergo a week's worth of bio-electrical testing.

The guy with the hoodie crosses the path in front of Raymond, concentrating on his electronic device, where he seems to be mapping out the probability of sex dates in another dimension. Raymond's pretty sure he's more Ralph's type than the blond. The leader of the crab-like creatures from Metaluna insisted that several earth scientists be subjected to the Thought Transference Chamber in order to subjugate their free will so that they'd slave away for the Metalunans in pursuit of a technology that might save their doomed and frumpy race. The idiosyncratic paths of evolution had blessed at least one of the crab-people, Exeter, with a conscience that wouldn't allow him to degrade his fellow beings, and so he rescued the humans, as Metaluna was being destroyed. Raymond's father always insisted that natural selection worked for the best of all possible worlds. Raymond's father insisted with an equally optimistic pigheadedness that there was nothing wrong with him the doctors couldn't fix, so that as he languished for months in Alpharetta, with a lump on his cheek that the doctors had diagnosed as an infection, as they fed him six months of unnecessary antibiotics to treat this imaginary infection, he didn't listen to the advice of his girlfriend, whose distrust in Western medicine he considered a superstitious Chinese folk belief, or to his children, who insisted he get a second opinion, but sat around chewing his worthless pills until it became obvious even to his delusional doctors that it was a cancerous lump.

Raymond flew to Alpharetta to be with him during his misconceived and deadly treatment, and crawled down the permanently congested highways from the airport to the strange voidy nontown that resembled some suffocating absence from one of Raymond's worst mental institution nightmares. *Their headlights sliced the space and time*, as it said in his father's poem, but whether it was ten at night or nine in the morning, the cars were packed on an endless road that went from nowhere to nowhere. It was hot and smoggy in Alpharetta and there was absolutely nothing there, a contained and exterminated life energy that was also toxic, with hiking paths meandering alongside creeks poisoned with chemical waste, stinking from the waste, and a population that had been replaced by pods not recently, but seemingly decades, centuries, millennia before—although this was impossible, he knew, as this entire town had been constructed from the ground up just recently, it was a faux town constructed nowhere, never, for nobody, with its ridiculous name, Alpharetta, like some

'60s sci-fi dystopia, dreamed up by a psychopath for other psychopaths. There was nothing to do but shop, and nowhere to shop but these new nonmalls, malls that had been transformed so that they weren't malls anymore but just America, chain stores shimmering into the radioactive background hum, indistinguishable from that hum. Meanwhile, since the doctors had so obviously fucked up, they treated his father's actual cancer aggressively, too aggressively, inappropriately, it turned out, following his successful surgery with several rounds of intensive chemo, enough to kill a horse, they'd been told later, after it was all over, he shouldn't have had even one round of chemo since chemo was never effective for this particular type of cancer, was never to be used for this particular type of cancer, did nothing but create unnecessary suffering, and in this case pushed his father's weakened immune system over the edge, so that despite an initially amazing recovery, his whole system fell apart, his organs failed, and then one morning, when they least expected it, he was dead.

Ralph returns alone.

I'm fed up with the light ones, he says.

At one of their "Community Forums" at 17th Street Brigade, back in the day, they'd screened *Suddenly Last Summer* for a room full of addicts, recovering addicts, and homeless kids. They'd served pizza and sugary Food Bank pastries. In the movie, Sebastian, tired of trolling the beaches of Spain for cheap boys, declared he was "fed up with the dark ones" and "famished for blonds." By the time the street urchins were setting upon Sebastian with their knives and forks, one of the guys in recovery was giving Louie a blowjob in the supply closet.

You need to commit yourself to one option, Raymond advises Ralph.

It's about the journey, says Ralph. Not the destination.

Fine, says Raymond. Then commit yourself to the journey.

Ralph seems to be contemplating a defense. He might be considering passivity an act of will in its own way. Maybe he considers drifting where life takes him as the most reasonable way to live. Maybe he even imagines the loss of self in the dark woods of other people's desires as an answer to the culture's strident obsession with success, but in the end he says nothing.

I told you about Louie, didn't I? says Raymond.

Louie always did have a bad heart, says Ralph.

Who knew what Louie had? The last time Raymond saw Louie, maybe three years ago, it wasn't the hard, wicked Louie, it was a soft Louie, wearing enormous Michael Caine glasses and a sweater, paying house calls to sick friends, watering their plants. He was sweet to Raymond, *fulla sugar*, and he seemed healthy enough. Louie had a lover who'd died years ago, decades ago, before Raymond even knew him, the late '80s, when Raymond was still just recovering from his troubled teenage years and playing tennis with the cult kids in Berkeley. Louie never talked about his great tragedy, only vaguely implied an unfathomable loss in his wake; another AIDS widow, shoved into death's little waiting room at an early age, that vast, dimly lit foyer, an empty train rolling through another dimension, a ghost train passing through the land of the living while Louie wanders from car to car, plenty of beautiful scenery but not another human face, and the train just keeps moving. Across the rickety railroad bridge, across the great river, moving into unknown territory…Who knows? Maybe Louie thought that he could inspire *universal revulsion and terror* and so conquer his own loneliness. When did he move beyond even the fear of his own loneliness, when did it all become trite, except the smallest, most caring gestures, when did he reach that point where *what once was and what is and what will be* no longer matter, sad whispering spirits melt into animals from dreams and the faded family photos Raymond saw one day at Louie's house in the Excelsior, a barefoot Peruvian boy with a cane in 1911, an unidentified woman chasing her hat and laughing on a windy street in Mexico City in 1953, a group of miners with burnished, stoic faces, and Louie's mother in her youth, standing on a balcony looking disaffected, *supernaturally articulated lipstick, as if it had been applied with a razor blade*, and finally the lover, a little white guy, Kevin, wearing a scarf, almost preppy, totally conservative, they're on their way to an R.E.M. concert. He's still healthy in the photo, not yet a denizen of death's little waiting room, a room that grew until it encompassed the entire city of San Francisco, until it had covered the entire map, an infinite, all-encompassing mine shaft that Raymond stumbled into in 1991, 1992, still recovering from his troubled teenage years—*Be Here for the Cure*, the signs on the bus stops started to say, mean and optimistic, like Raymond's father, mean because so many of them wouldn't be anywhere for the cure, couldn't hang on, had already, more or less, let go…

It must have been AIDS, Raymond says.

A clown showed up at the hospital when his father was, unbeknownst to them all, dying, as if stepped forth from the hazy nightmare sidewalks of Alpharetta, clutching a bouquet of daisies and three red balloons. It must have been in the wrong room. Years earlier, Raymond and Philip had lived with Raymond's father for a couple of months after returning from Santa Barbara, where Raymond had tried out scuba diving school. Philip had hated Santa Barbara passionately; he'd worked as a page at the Santa Barbara library, where he'd had a run-in with the poet laureate of Carpinteria, and he began a novella, on the surface an account of the doomed love affair between a scuba diver and a murderous porn star, but in fact a dense tangle of words that Philip had convinced himself was an elaborate magical incantation, a curse he was placing on the city of Santa Barbara. He wouldn't really admit it, but Raymond knew he actually expected the city to slide into the ocean, and even years later when they were safely back in Northern California, when some crazed teenager declared himself the Angel of Death and ran over a group of pedestrians in Santa Barbara, Raymond recognized the mad gleam in Philip's eye and knew that he was secretly taking credit. By then Raymond had finally given up on all the careers he'd imagined would lift him beyond his troubled teenage years, all the classes and training programs, scuba diving, piano tuning, forest fire fighting, the Marines, tennis pro, sign language interpreter, all the toxic construction trades, pile-driving and iron-working and carpet-installing, every butch job in the world, Philip used to say. Raymond tried each one for a day or more, discarded it, sometimes returned for another try. Raymond knew how to get hired, especially for jobs he didn't really want.

Raymond's father had looked at that clown that showed up in the hospital that day with the daisies and the red balloons, and then looked away, as if it hadn't even registered, as if it was a hallucination or a harbinger of death that he needed to deny, and had turned back to Raymond and his sister Mina and managed to croak a few mean and dismissive things at them, a sign, they thought, of his recovery, and in fact he had become weller and weller, he'd had an amazing recovery, for a while. His surprising death broke Raymond's heart, but it had been broken before. His father's surprising death pushed his poor sister, however, over the edge, into a place of constant anxiety, self-flagellation, running over the same scenarios over and over again in her mind, the final days, the missed opportunities, the mean, cryptic comments, his sister, *la loca*. She'd probably never been exactly sane, colonized, as Raymond was, too, by the conflicting demands of their parents' voices. The two of them, as yin and yang as could be. Their father loved light and air and austere, minimal spaces up above the world; their mother loved dark, comfy, ground-level flats with the curtains always drawn. Escaping the tyranny of that life-or-death struggle, the broken dishes, the trips to Tahoe gone sour, even if Raymond's escape was only into the world of Ralph and Louie and Jonny Taser, of Isela and Noel, of Todd and even Ted, what light there was! What vision! Oh, to never be a child again, no matter what happens, to never be trapped in their dumpy house in the Avenues hemmed in by the monolithic mental health facilities, and the squat identical tract homes that now sell for a million dollars, a homogenous blur of meaningless architecture, built by sadistic robot architects to contain if not obliterate the magical world, the trees and the darkness, the loopy paths, the central esplanade, where Ralph is now paralyzed, between the bushes on one side and the other, the men on one side and the other, the guy with the hoodie seems to be down on his knees doing something to Noel, while the blond has hooked up with somebody who looks overdressed. The two of them are hard at something surely more predictable than it looks from the main path—from this perspective, they seem to be glomming on to each other, or trying to devour each other. It's almost like they're merging.

7

In Iowa, Philip's just missed the shooter's funeral. At the far end of a windy church parking lot, the shooter's widow and the son are just climbing into the backseat of a maroon sedan, then disappearing down one of these crooked roads with their police escort. A sheriff's deputy is perched nearby in a jeep, keeping watch over the shooter's grave.

The dirt in the cemetery is spongy and dry. There are no flowers at the unmarked grave, no clues, nothing to interpret but some anonymous, freshly scratched earth.

Philip knows already that there is no story here, but only mute horror, a fable that's buried itself in a hole, inside a barn or a hologram. Dust motes flit through the trapezoidal sunbeams that filter through cracks in the barn's façade or the hologram's warping edge.

Dead children. Puzzles that will never be solved, or that have already been solved. *He was a shy little boy and cried every morning when it was time to go to school.*

The rental car smells like formaldehyde. Philip can't make sense of the roads, none of which run in straight lines. He drives past the schoolhouse and the lingering crowds of tourists and then turns onto a road that veers through some trees, splits a couple of times, zigzags around, and expels him onto a straightaway, with the ghastly, abandoned structure of the East Liberty Home for Boys shimmering in the distance.

The Amish themselves have been hiding out from the press. It's too early or too late. Philip doesn't yet have addresses for the grieving families—New York is working on it. Meanwhile, he finds just one Amish man who will speak to him, the owner of the lantern store.

They chat across the counter of the store as the Amish man trims his fingernails with a small pocketknife. The conversation blurs around the edges, and Philip enters a timeless state in which this conversation is simply a continuation of every other conversation he has ever had with Amish men. The same conversation with a kind of hive-mind on the other end. Chores and theology and punishing gossip. God forbid you do something to get the people talking.

Soon it will be dark. Philip drives. The ruined orphanage always hovers there on the horizon.

The murders' aftermath is an agricultural and geometrical puzzle. Gold and crimson and beige fields. The solution will only emerge if he drives these nonsensical roads in exactly the right order. It isn't a mystery, but he's a detective. It's a biblical proverb, written in blood; that's the consensus.

A woman wearing an Amish bonnet and carrying a bucket is walking across a particularly beige field, toward the structure or mirage of the East Liberty Home for Boys.

Perhaps she's the mother of a murdered child.

Philip drives back the way he came, thinking he can circle around and head her off, if he keeps turning to the right. But once he's back into the trees, he loses sight of the faceless woman, and when the road splits, the right turn just leads down past a marshy zone, a spiffy non-Amish home with an SUV in the driveway, crosses a large creek or a small river, and back out into the daylight, but now the woman's nowhere in sight. The orphanage itself actually seems farther away. The road descends through another stand of trees, around a sharp curve in the wrong direction, and then up onto a hill from which the ruined structure now appears impossibly backward. The Amish woman is still walking directly away.

The entire landscape is an optical illusion. The mounds of hay are Van Gogh hallucinations. Philip parks the car on the shoulder, hops the measly barbed wire fence.

Slick muddy patches and actual puddles stand in depressed sections of the field. Philip's shoes cake with mud as he lumbers across it, dodging the cow patties. The brittle, stumpy remains of some crop poke aggressively out of the soggy earth, with dying wildflowers and clover in between the hard, broken stalks of whatever it was, creating an arabesque of burnished golds and reds intertwining the variegated earth tones, overlaid with the geometrical patterns of sowing and of reaping, and with hoof prints and boot prints.

It isn't the mud on his shoes or the smell of shit everywhere, but the way that he's suddenly reliving parts of his childhood he'd just as soon forget.

Years ago Philip read a book by a German, or maybe an Austrian, about an old man who wrote everything down, all the facts he wanted to remember. He covered all the walls of his home with these notes, clinging to the random arrangement of historical, biological, and geological facts. He lived alone and Philip's pretty sure he was dying. He's pretty sure the old man wandered off his property into a misty wood, following a path, maybe in the dark, down one side of a ravine and up the other. The walk was certainly catastrophic. Yes, the old man was dying, and he remembered descending a mountain once with his brother, getting stuck on a snowy ledge. The descent was impossible. He forgot why he'd ever wanted to keep track of the facts on his wall.

Memory is overrated, as far as Philip's concerned.

At the edge of the field is another barbed wire fence and then a thicket of briars and weeds. *Do Not Enter* and *No Trespassing* signs. There's a kind of a path that leads into the darkness and toward the ruined structure beyond, blocked by a chain and a prominent *Trespassers Will Be Persecuted* sign.

Soon it will be night. Philip knows that he will enter, because he always has. Or because it feels like this is the path that belongs to him. It is a path; people have created it. Entering is an essential aspect of Philip's mind, of his history, of his future, and this equation feels correct. Time and death, solve for x.

Maybe fifty yards through the brush, and he emerges into the fading light, revealing a kind of junkyard or sculpture garden in the clearing around the ruined structure. The rotting chassis of what may once have been an ambulance, with a variety of flags and graffiti stickers attached to it, toys and pieces of rusty metal soldered on for no discernible reason. There are springs and deflated tires in the yard, doll parts and machine parts configured into the shape of a robot corpse, its leg caught in a spiked metal trap. There's still a sign over the gap where the front door once stood: *East Liberty Home for Boys*, and underneath somebody has scrawled "abandon hope all yee who enter here" in paint the color of a moldy brick.

Inside, it's room after room covered with frayed wallpaper faded into inscrutable textures, crumbling walls, and once-beautiful wood floors now riddled with gaps. The floors are covered with broken beer bottles, rodent feces, cigarette butts, the abandoned nest of some animal, beer cans, condoms, shattered cell phone components, all the debris of the wayward youth who must now find shelter here. The vast Gothic structure has been gutted, more or less, but retains just enough of its institutional infrastructure—weird, chipped linoleum the color of rotted bones, fake wood paneling, popcorn ceilings—to be chilling. A brick fireplace is more or less intact and full of ashes and partially melted aluminum cans. It's like the site of a Sustiva nightmare Philip once had.

Or something dreamed up by some Eastern European or Latin American novelist in the latter half of the twentieth century. Agota Kristof or Gombrowicz. Fuentes, Donoso, or Rulfo. The novelist who came closest to imagining this haunted ruin was surely Antonio Garay Redozo, author of the lesser known but most fully realized gas-giant of them all, the 1200-page monstrosity *This Hideously Twirling Planet*. An orphanage on the Paraguayan-Brazilian border, deep in the jungle, where dozens of little boys are housed whose parents have been killed by one government or the other, with just one little girl, a blind albino who believes that she's a boy. After the orphanage burns down and the orphans flee into the jungle, they begin a series of strange transformations into animals, plants, and mermaids of the swampy rivers. The graffiti scrawled on the walls here, in chalky and neon layers, seems to form a kind of visual map of that novel, in fact, bestial figures, strange composite beings from genetically engineered futures, floating brains and stick-figures in flames and letters from alphabets that only rarely form coherent words. *Why are the children of darkness, the children of this world, more cunning than the children of light?*

A scratching noise comes from the next room. The dusty room leads to a back door, the rectangular gap glowing with daylight. Scrawled on the wall, a crowned cartoon figure that seems to be composed of foreign alphabets and bones, radiating like Aboriginal x-ray art, neither human or not. *Because they have the magical root of the original essence manifest in them.*

A haggard-looking boy in a gray hoodie is scratching some kind of message into the plaster of one wall with a small knife. He looks like he hasn't slept in days. He startles when he sees Philip and makes a move like he's about to run. It's okay, said Philip. I was looking for someone else. I just thought you were somebody else.

Whatever he was trying to inscribe is barely legible.

Are you okay? asks Philip.

Leave me alone.

Whatever you want, says Philip and peers out into the fading daylight. The woman with the bucket is nowhere to be seen. The large creek or small river is just back behind another stand of trees, and he can see why there's no road that leads here directly—a bridge used to connect the compound to the main road, but the bridge itself is in ruins.

After finishing his monstrous novel, Garay Redozo renounced literature and remembering and made his escape into a dismal Paraguayan hospital, where he worked as a nurse, tending the sick and the dying, until he, too, faded into oblivion. He'd wanted his writing to destroy itself as it pointed back toward the *equally fictitious reality* that provoked it, but it failed to live up to his expectations. As had, one imagines, life itself.

The boy is wearing black pants and hard shoes and a black shirt underneath his hoodie. He glares at Philip and then puts his hood up.

Philip wanders upstairs and back down, into the basement and down long hallways to vast other wings that have been partially demolished. The orphanage was once bequeathed vast sums of money, which they used for ambitious expansion projects, including a swimming pool down below that now resembles a tomb—until they were bankrupted by the wave of lawsuits from a stream of molested boys.

Up a rickety stairway is what was once an attic, but now, without a roof or two of its walls, is more like a deck. Philip takes a deep breath. Good Midwestern air, he thinks, although it feels just as modern as San Francisco air, just as greasy and irradiated, but warmer and with a smell of rotting dead leaves that would take him back to odd, detached moments from his own childhood, if he was willing to go.

From up here the landscape is variegated in the dusk, full of trees and color. This landscape suggests the presence of complex minds. Perhaps love hasn't died.

A clearing between the orphanage and the next farm over is actually a small cemetery. In San Francisco, they bury their dead in Colma, or burn them.

Maybe there's never been human love.

Everything that has happened here is still present. History is visible in the landscape now only as these ruins, these chicken scratches on the walls.

Philip wonders if there are places where the only authentically "human" activity is to hide. That is, the only authentic humans in such places must be hiding. Hiding from the rest of us, from themselves, from each other?

Philip's grandmother left behind a written record of her life, condensed from diaries. This record was over one hundred pages long and incredibly detailed about trips to the East Coast, people visited, beets canned; a lifetime of toil and hard times interspersed with fires, illnesses, childbirth, and delirium. At one point, three years pass in a single paragraph that begins, "In the summer of 1945 I had a nervous breakdown." Philip's father didn't remember much about his mother's *nervous breakdown*. She'd probably been given some tranquilizers, he said.

Philip's grandmother's funeral was held in the middle of winter in a freezing barn. An Amish funeral, the sermons were given in Pennsylvania Dutch, a language that Philip didn't understand. Occasionally, however, an English phrase would pop up, and jolt Philip out of his daydreams. *Victim of circumstance*, the minister said at one point. Shortly afterward, he said it again: *victim of circumstance*.

Something walks from the cemetery into the trees, toward the ruined bridge.

The woman in the bonnet. Philip hurries down the steps and through the room where the boy was scratching his message, now empty. Out the front door, he can't make anything out in the trees. It's difficult to find his way in the gloom, but a thin trail leads in the general direction of the bridge.

When he gets to the river or creek, however, there's nothing there. Rustling noises seem to come from all around, but the sound of the water confuses everything. And the echoes. He steps out onto the bridge. Most of the planks are sturdy enough, you just don't want to get too close to the edge. The water is cold and deep.

It occurs to him that this is a trap.

What happens is that two creatures start across the bridge, but only one makes it to the other side. It's an old story; it can be interpreted in any number of ways. In some versions they are swimming or floating on a raft.

The wind travels everywhere. But here, it is absolutely still, as if a circle around the old ruin defines a magical zone where the wind can't penetrate. Something gray is moving through the trees in the distance.

He moves toward it, back toward the clearing, but can't get any closer. It's just a shape, maintaining its distance. In front of the ruin, the boy in the hoodie leans against the wall, lights a cigarette. He smokes in silence for a few moments. He smokes quite naturally, as if he's been doing it for years. He doesn't look up as Philip emerges from the trees, but flicks his ash.

Is that a Russian flag? the boy asks.

He points at a little flag on the former ambulance, striped vertically red, white, and blue, next to a skull and crossbones.

I don't know, says Philip. It could be.

I don't think so, says the boy. I saw a Russian flag and I think it was different.

Philip shrugs.

I'm gonna get me a Russian flag, the boy says.

Philip asks what's so special about a Russian flag.

Because they were cool and they were fighting against the Nazis like we were, says the boy.

He stubs out his cigarette.

Who are you?

Who am I?

Are you the news?

The boy's skin is perfectly smooth and ghostly white and unblemished, with pale freckles.

Why do you say that?

I saw you before, the boy says.

Right, says Philip.

There is nothing interesting about the boy's face, except its haggardness. Probably his feelings are more complicated than the look on his face.

Kind of, he says. Kind of I'm the news.

Kind of.

But my dad grew up here.

The East Liberty Home for Boys?

No, not *here* here, says Philip.

The boy looks around, as if there might be somewhere else.

I mean the area, says Philip. I used to visit my grandma and grandpa around here.

The boy doesn't seem impressed. He's probably lived his whole life here—nothing Philip imagines could make himself belong.

As if he'd even want to—belong.

I'm writing a story, he says.

A story about the shooter, says the boy.

The idea of belonging oppressed Philip as a child. He'd thought he wanted to belong, but didn't, until he eventually realized that he'd just rather not.

A story about the kids, he says. A story about the Amish.

The boy spits.

I live in California now, Philip says.

Like on that show, the boy says.

Like a lot of shows. But not very much.

The boy looks at him directly for the first time.

You ever write shows?

No, not shows.

The boy looks away, and it seems as if he's thinking about something else, practicing a smile for a different occasion, or preparing to change his smile to a grimace at the appropriate time.

I was looking for an Amish woman, Philip says. Did you see her wandering around here?

Amish women don't come here, the boy says. It was probably a ghost.

This place is haunted?

The boy shrugs.

You ever write about a suicide? he asks.

You know somebody who killed themselves?

One.

He's thinking about that.

Or maybe two.

Two, that's a lot, says Philip. For somebody your age.

I think it's a lot for anyone.

The boy wants to impress him. Or maybe he really wants to talk about something that's bugging him. Philip tries to remember what you can say to a kid like this. It seems like he knew, once upon a time, or at least he thought he did.

You're right, he says. It's too much.

He can see something floating back toward the bridge.

Was it your family? Or friends?

Standing in the middle of the ruined bridge is the boy in the hoodie. Or a different boy in the same hoodie, since this one hasn't budged.

You can't marry a ghost, the boy says. Can you marry a ghost?

I don't know. If the ghost was into it, probably you could.

The boy on the bridge looks like a monk, with his hood up, gazing down at the surface of the small river or large creek as if in prayer.

I'd do it with a ghost.

You're just a kid. What are you, fifteen?

They could take over and change everything, the boy says.

The other one's perfectly still, gazing down at the water.

A lot of people wander around this place, the boy says. It's trouble if you don't be careful. I don't think all of them are real.

I'll be careful. You be careful, too. Of the real ones, especially.

I'm not scared.

The night has swallowed up everything. Philip doesn't have a flashlight.

You should be scared, the boy says.

Why me more than you?

You don't wanna die.

The thin trail, the path: the weeds are worn down by whatever has trampled on them to create a pale shimmer.

You don't either.

Maybe I'm a ghost, the boy says.

You don't look like a ghost.

Sometimes people can't tell. Sometimes ghosts can't tell.

Philip keeps his eye on the boy. He doesn't want to look at the bridge.

If I was a ghost, what would you do? the boy asks.

Same thing I'm doing now, I suppose.

You wouldn't try to catch me?

No, of course not.

Children like to run away, Philip remembers. They like to run away and to hide and to get found and to get caught.

You could make a lot of money from me.

I don't know about that.

If I was a ghost, I wouldn't let you marry me, the boy says.

Now there's nobody on the bridge.

You aren't old enough to get married, Philip says. Even if you're really dead.

The boy snorts. He seems to find that funny.

You like Wrath of God?

Wrath of God?

That band made of ex-Amish.

He compares them to someone or something that Philip has never heard of. At first he thinks it must be another band, but then suspects it's actually a kind of game, as the boy describes a kind of disintegration that seems to happen when an atomizing weapon is used to its full potential.

You know some Amish? Philip asks. Friends or family?

I know some, the boy says. I used to.

You didn't know any of those boys.

Not those boys. Other ones.

In *This Hideously Twirling Planet*, the blind girl could see the future, but not the past. She had no long-term memory, the price she'd paid for a prophetic vision she didn't really want.

Who did you know, Philip says. The suicide.

You know.

The boy flinches like he's about to be smacked and then he says, Enjoy your visit, sir, and hurries down the path through the trees and over the bridge.

Philip says, Wait a second.

In the dark, through the trees, it looks like there's two of them out there. For a second, but there's only one. And Philip lets that one disappear.

Inside, Philip lights a match and examines the boy's scratch marks. It looks like *Ftn blu LEGIT* or maybe *Ein bim LEGIT*. It's surrounded by graffiti dating back years, maybe decades, some of it surely scrawled by the orphans who were raised here. Skulls and owls.

Philip drives north. He drives for fifteen miles, allowing his thoughts to go where they will, forming a kind of phantom complexity that seems to be on the verge of something, as if it's almost just arrived. But it hasn't and it never will. He parks his rental car at the base of the old lane and peers up at the old farmhouse. The farmhouse, from this perspective, isn't different from his memories. It's pretty much exactly the same. *We must remember*, everyone always says. Because memory makes us human. Raymond remembers everything, and as far as Philip's concerned, he can have it. The bad old days of his troubled teen years, the good old days before the dot-com thing. Various chunks of Philip's own life that he can never quite recognize through the filter of Raymond's memory. Maybe "dying" wasn't the best way to spend your twenties after all.

In any case, forgetting is just as good. Why not forget this, for example, this farmhouse? It's out of the family now, so there's no risk he'll be recognized. A dog barks in the distance. He isn't sure what he's feeling; "nothing" most likely.

But it must be a deep sadness and a kind of resentment, he supposes, because he finds himself imagining a library composed only of the books that would have been written by those writers who died of AIDS, all those gay men and junkies and the rest, the ones who died in their 20s and 30s and 40s. The existential detective novel that would have been written by David Wojnarowicz, full of clues in burnt-out warehouses and cruisy truck stops; the epic of social realism that Bo Huston would have written, a work so dark and strange that nobody would actually understand it as realism; Reinaldo Arenas, without the perfect ending of AIDS to wrap his bitterness around, would have befriended Johnny Depp and written a surreal biography that critics would have hailed as the discovery of a new form; Severo Sarduy would have written a novel that Tony would never read, as a matter of principle, called *Mango, Guayabana, Cyanide*; Hervé Guibert would have written a novel called *The Unfinished* that would have opened, *When the dead are well cared for, they enter the earth and are happy*; Dambudzo Marechera would have perfected his attempt *to make himself into a skeleton in his own cupboard*; Yvonne Vera would have written a novel consisting of one

350-page sentence *without a subject*, about the rape and murder of a teenage girl in Zimbabwe; Nestor Perlongher would have fused his esoteric interests with the political radicalism of his earlier period to forge an entirely unprecedented approach to sexual identity and mystical masochism in a book of poems called *Rabid*; Bruce Chatwin would have written a memoir about his love affair with an imaginary gypsy in Antarctica; Sony Labou Tansi would have written a satirical novel about an African dictatorship ruled by an AIDS ghost; Essex Hemphill would have written a collection of sonnets about the life of racist poet Jim O'Bannon; Rick Jacobsen would have written a novel narrated collectively by all the boys Michael Jackson ever loved; Jamaica Kincaid's brother would have written his own memoir in which his sister barely figured; Steve Abbott would have written a sequel to *Holy Terror*; Sam D'Allessandro would have rewritten *Pinnochio*; Melvin Dixon would have rewritten *The Juniper Tree*; and what about Thomas Avena? Is Thomas still alive? Philip used to run into him every couple of years, on Polk Street or the edges of the Tenderloin, hobbling along on his cane, talking up the nutrient value of fried fish, plotting to escape from his rent-controlled Tenderloin studio once and for all for Mount Shasta or some foggy residence on the coast, talking shit about AIDS meds, accompanying Philip to the latest showing of Jerome Caja's paintings. But it's been years now and Philip fears the worst. He'd like to believe that Thomas finally made it to Mount Shasta, finally found a drug regimen he could stick to, but in October in the Midwest on a cold night, surrounded by the ghosts of Amish children and gazing up at the Gothic farmhouse where his father grew up, it just doesn't seem plausible. And what about all those gay and bisexual men, junkies and hemophiliacs who died, still prematurely, in their fifties, sixties, and seventies? Michel Foucault would have turned away from social theory and written a novella set in a gay dungeon; Isaac Asimov would have written a book of philosophy/psychology, the only category he was missing in the Dewey Decimal System, in which he would have formulated a rationalist and atheistic theory of knowledge as a sequence of tightly enclosed spaces harboring smaller and more tightly enclosed spaces, and the progression of the human mind deeper and deeper into these spaces as a descent into more and more sublime pleasures; James Merrill would have begun receiving transmissions directly from the future evolutionary forms hidden inside an active volcano and rendered their message in a poem in which each line represented a codon for one of the amino acids of the DNA, the poem itself forming a map for the crucial DNA mutation of a future form of life fluctuating in other dimensions as pure potential and trying desperately to emerge from human history, so as to give human history some sort of rationale, as prologue. A poor, distorted memory of pain, hunger, toil, loss, a kind of nonsensical yearning that could never be satisfied but that had continually tricked itself into believing it could. In the poem, this yearning itself would be a kind of transmission from the nonexistent forms pressing into the imaginal realms from the volcano, so that our dumb suffering forms would create a kind of culture. A chaotic soup, a bloody uncontrollable mess, out of which They would emerge and their luminous garden of eternal play and shadow; Arturo Islas, meanwhile, would have not only finished the third book of his trilogy, but would have written a novel in iambic pentameter (the sound of a limping man walking, or a young boy crippled by polio walking, himself walking), in which he would have imagined himself as an incarnation of the Aztec god Tezcatlipoca or Smoking Mirror, Lord of the Near and the Nigh, Night Wind, the Youth, the Enemy of Both Sides, Possessor of the Sky and Earth, the Keeper of Men, He by Whom We Live, He Whose Slaves We Are, etc.; Harold Brodkey would have written a 900-page book of "short shorts" about his homosexual love affairs; Thom Gunn would have written a collection of rhyming couplets about the old bar South of Market called *Good-bye Hole-in-the-Wall*; Waylon McClatchy would have composed a new translation of Rimbaud's *Le Bateau ivre* that would give off sparks and then disintegrate as it was being read. And why stop with the AIDS kids? This vast, Borgesian library could contain all the phantom manuscripts of the prematurely dead. Philip starts the rental car and pulls back onto the road. Had Joy Carter not been downed by the hormones or by the mysterious virus from New Guinea, she'd have become a student of dying languages and created an epic poem written in a particular dialect with no living speakers, not even herself. Raymond's father might have returned to poetry and written a book of haiku about China and nanotechnology. One of the dead Amish boys might have composed a hallucinated act of Amish terrorism in prose. There was some budding poet scrabbling for his dinner in some shanty-town beneath a garbage dump in Manila, killed at the age of eight when the mounds of garbage tumbled onto his entire community and wiped them out. The next Rimbaud joined up with the Shining Path at the age of twelve and died of cholera at the age of thirteen. One of the first great Afghani modernist poets was wiped out during his sister's wedding ceremony by an errant American missile. And what about Dania Dominguez, he wonders, as he drives back through the little town where his grandmother lived with her oldest daughter, after Philip's grandfather died. Dania Dominguez was a Dominican TG whose only published short story Philip had discovered in the back pages of a short-lived web journal that culled its material from the writing workshops of Bay Area prisons, juvenile detention centers, and homeless shelters. Philip didn't much read that sort of thing anymore, with the predictable hard luck stories and celebrations of outlaw romance. He'd only chanced upon Dania's story when it showed up for a mistyped web search. A baroque outpouring of the most beautifully ungrammatical sentences, a sort of stutter of clauses piled upon clauses, a collision of descriptions of drug highs and drug lows, elaborately tortured phrases about impossible family hells abandoned in the subtropical sun and about books stolen from the shelves of social service agencies. They were all Houses: Huckleberry House, Hospitality House, Guerrero House. The story ended ambiguously, with all of the plots dissipating or becoming utterly meaningless in the face of a clearly doomed escape attempt from a nameless House by a character who'd only but appeared in the next-to-last paragraph, but whose trajectory perfectly contained that of every other character in the story. Philip had already begun creating anthologies in his mind that he might labor over for years and that would serve as forums in which he could publish the work of Dania Dominguez next to that of Ascher/Straus, Stacey Levine, Alvin Lu, and Brendan Pelt, that lyrical diaper fetishist who used to date Ted. He was imagining elaborate scenarios in which he would liberate Dania Dominguez from her stunted literary halfway house and deliver her into the world of underappreciated geniuses, when he went to her bio and discovered that she had died at the age of twenty-three, before her story was even published. The anthology fantasy quickly morphed into one of discovering the lost journals of Dania Dominguez, scouring the storage shelves of various Houses where her duffel bag might still be sitting, to discover a heap of black-speckled notebooks, a mishmash of diary entries, unsent love letters, Spanish and English slang all jumbled together, and just enough brilliant little stories and monologues and prose poems to piece together a slim collection that would glow, radioactive, in the slush pile of every editor and agent in the world, catch fire, and burn a hole in their cold literary hearts with its incandescent joy and despair and naïve formal brilliance. It was just around that time that Philip was invited to attend the first Huey Beauregard reading by Ted, or maybe Todd, or maybe both Ted and Todd. It must have been Todd, whose ex, Benton Archer, had given Huey Beauregard his entrée into the literary world.

8

WHEN RAYMOND GETS HOME FROM OUTREACHING, there's a message from Howard on the machine. Howard loves to leave a message. He rambles on for several minutes about movie stars that Raymond's never heard of, about political movements from the '20s and '30s, and about a cute boy he's seen on the street, *He's gorgeous*, he says with a sigh, and even his sigh has a New York accent. And butch, he adds, *très* butch, and then the machine cuts him off. The only other message is from Dhoji, but after she yells *Philip Raymond pick up the phone! I know you guys are in there!* she just waits a few seconds and hangs up. Raymond heads out the side door and down the steps.

Raymond's father has been dead for almost two years now, but his things, the books and artwork he left to his son, remain in boxes in the basement. Raymond doesn't usually go down there—he's too tall, for one thing—but with Philip out of town he has no choice. Someone has to water the plants. The crawl space adjacent to the basement is creepy, and Raymond feels like something is watching him from the dark, something greasy and furtive and vicious, while the unopened boxes full of books and art make him feel not guilty exactly, but responsible, the recipient of an invitation from the dead he has yet to RSVP. Come join us here in the eternal nothing, that's the only invitation that ever comes from the dead, as far as Raymond's concerned, he refuses to believe in any ghosts, greasy or furtive or vicious, save the ghosts of memory. He would like to refuse memory's invitation as well, but after filling the hydroponic buckets to their optimal levels, the incessant gurgling as nonsensical as anything that memory or the dead might murmur, he carries two large boxes upstairs. He is, after all, the only living person in the house. The only functioning memory, a computer doesn't count. In the first box are books his father valued enough to keep until the end, *Contemporary Chinese Women Writers II*, which the back cover declares isn't "wound literature" like the first volume; *China's Avant Garde Fiction*, "filled with mirages, hallucinations, myths, mental puzzles, and the fantastic"; *In the Dark Hall*, a novel about an aristocratic Chinese boy's experience of the Cultural Revolution, "a lush and claustrophobic nightmare drawn with the precision of a scroll painting"; *The Embroidered Shoes* by Can Xue, who "possesses one of the most glorious, vivid, lyrical, elaborate, poignant, hellacious imaginations on the planet. She is the finest revolutionary Gothicist writing today and, as well, the true daughter of Kafka and Borges"; a novel by Yu Hua; a biography of Tz'u-his, the Empress Dowager of China; a history of the Manchus; Confucius's *The Doctrine of the Mean*; *Passions of the Cut Sleeve: The Male Homosexual Tradition in China*, which, using "literary, ethnographic and historical sources...demonstrates that male homosexuality was relatively open and tolerated through most of China's dynasties"; Ezra Pound's *The Chinese Written Character as a Medium for Poetry*; the charmingly illustrated *Foreign Devils: Westerners in the Far East, The Sixteenth Century to the Present Day*; several Sebald novels; and *She Who Is Alive*, a slim novel by Robert Harris, with a blurb on the back by Carla Harryman, "The reader plugs herself into the death drive dream of *She Who Is Alive* for a glide through the residual terror of the white part of the 20th c. Imaginary. She asks herself all along the way the disturbing question, 'Why do I love every minute of it?'" There are several popular science books about the forthcoming wonders of technology, computing, genetic engineering, and nanotechnology, the most interesting entitled *Hive Mind: 2020*; there's poetry by Yuan Mei; an autobiographical novel by former African child-soldier Chude Mbisi, *Graveyards of Memory*; a novel *Peking Man? Woman?* by Paul Chan Chuang Toledo Lin; poetry by Richard Wilbur, Denis Johnson, Isabella Gardener, and Gerard Manley Hopkins; Wilde's *De Profundis*; *Beyond Metaphor: The Theory of Tropes in Anthropology*; Levi Strauss's *Tristes Tropiques*; and *Berji Kristin: Tales from the Garbage Hills*, a novel by Latife Tekin about the slums of Istanbul, "ephemeral communities constructed from tin, cardboard and refuse torn down by the authorities each morning and rebuilt each night."

In the second box are photographs his father took, late in his life, when he'd abandoned poetry and devoted himself to images. As a photographer, he tended toward the abstract, the everyday made unrecognizable as pattern and line and shadow. There is no living flesh in these pictures. There are shadows on the smooth or rough plaster in the corner of a dim empty room; an old deflated tire embedded in cracked rectilinear pavement; the desiccated carcass of an animal, a deer perhaps, so silvery and flattened from decay that it seems to be a growth from the rough grasses where it lies; broken cement and partial footprints in ashy asphalt dust; a rusted bicycle corroded into a broken-down tunnel wall with the tunnel's lightened doorway barely visible in the far distance. There is a painting by his father's friend Julie; it used to hang in their squat tract home out in the hideous Sunset Avenues of Raymond's childhood, so many years ago. Julie was married to one of his father's teachers at the Writer's Workshop in Iowa City in the '60s; she was decadent and witty and so she and his father became fast friends, since his father was not only mean and optimistic, but decadent and witty, too, and sometimes a lot of fun. But while Julie was pregnant with her second child, her husband, the poet, Raymond's father's teacher, who despite his renown and his prestigious teaching gig had never graduated college, took an apartment in Chicago, ostensibly to attend classes at the University of Chicago. But another woman, a secretary in the English department, the woman the poet would marry next, started going up to Chicago with him, and as these things do, it all came out. In Julie's painting, entitled "To His Windy City Mistress," the hair on a woman's face, Raymond isn't sure if it's supposed to be the mistress or Julie, merges with the figure of a tiny pregnant woman, clearly Julie, preparing to push down a detonator, as in Roadrunner cartoons, to set off dynamite. The fuse takes the shape of a hand that dominates the foreground of the painting, suggesting *Talk to the Hand*, or whatever its equivalent was in the '60s, but maybe it's the hand of the mistress trying to shield itself from the inevitable, while the background is composed of scenes of lovers in Chicago, picnicking by the lake, strolling arm in arm, feeding ducks, a sort of montage, the cheesiness of the imagery playing off the tension created by the sparking fuse and the viewer's awareness of the inevitable, of the knowledge that in the world of the painting everything will be destroyed, obliterated, completely annihilated, in a fantastic scene of carnage born of the pregnant woman's rage, just as soon as the dynamite explodes.

II

There is nothing, no reality, but sensations. Ideas are sensations, but of things not placed in space and sometimes not even in time.

Logic, the place of ideas, is another kind of space.

Dreams are sensations with only two dimensions. Ideas are sensations with only one dimension. A line is an idea.

—Alvaro de Campos, *Notes on Sensationism*

1

WHEN GEORDI TOOK FELICIA TO THE TOWN IN MEXICO where his grandmother grew up, Felicia was surprised at how volcanic eruptions had produced such elegantly symmetrical forms and delicately shaded features in the landscape. Erosion had blurred the story as well. Where was she? Always the aftermath of something, always the middle of some process, always just now. Being a blonde in Mexico had exhausted her. Geordi kept going back past that house, where his grandmother grew up. It had been fixed up, and strangers lived there. Finally, Felicia dyed her hair black. Geordi looked at her sometimes like he didn't know her. For a while it was like Felicia was a different person, until Geordi got used to it, and she forgot for the most part, and then the natural color grew back.

At Huey Beauregard's website, there aren't many photos of the munchkin who sometimes appears in public, decked out in blond wigs and fake beards, but there are dozens of links to an endless array of reviews, celebrity acclamations of his universal appeal, and interviews. He claims to have lost his virginity in a truck stop restroom at the age of eight, dressed up like a girl, in exchange for twenty dollars that his mother spent on cigarettes and flip-flops.

The children from the adjoining apartment complex are shouting about all the usual things. Dispensing and withholding snacks, insulting each other's relatives and toileting habits, threatening to kill each other or kick each other in the nuts. Just outside, a girl begins beating a bush with a stick. She's about ten, and she beats the bush viciously, shaking her body in a frenzied motion and delivering a constant stream of invective. *I will fuck you up*, the little girl tells the bush.

The phone.

Hi, is this the magazine?

This is Felicia.

You called *me*!

It's some incredible magic that finds this boy on the phone with exactly *her*. It's the squat boy, Melvin.

Can we set up a time for me to see your place?

Right now, he says.

I'm not sure that's really possible.

I've been thinking about going to Salt Lake City.

Oh, don't do that, she says.

Really?

Stay right there, she says. Give me your address.

The little girl is still at it outside. She's accusing the bush of a variety of lies and infidelities. She matches the rhythm of her words to the rhythm of the beating, so that with each syllable the bush suffers anew. The poor girl is wearing herself out, and the poor bush is done for.

Things are kind of intense, Melvin says.

We can probably work around that. What's up?

Oh, it's nothing.

He lives in a garage behind a vast apartment complex near Lake Merritt in Oakland, in a storage compartment in the back. He gives her some incomprehensible directions. Then it's like something clicks on in his brain.

Where are you, anyway?

Felicia's house is compact, a Craftsman built in 1921. They're all over Berkeley, humble but detailed, constructed to last. Houses for workers. Felicia and Geordi have planted fruit trees in the back: an apricot, a pluot, a pear, two nectarines, two cherries, plums, peaches, and apples. No peaches, Geordi said, not the peaches, anything but peaches. As if he'd been traumatized by peaches, but he didn't really care. Blueberries. For the blueberries, Felicia has added iron sulfate to acidify the soil, cottonseed meal, peat moss as mulch. Felicia never thought she would own a home, not in Berkeley, not anywhere. She saw herself aging, but basically unchanged, alone, in a studio apartment, in some city. Not San Francisco, not Seattle, not New York. An imaginary American city, from a European novel.

Huey claims to live now in a "renovated squat" in the Western Addition. Huey claims to have sent faxes from public restrooms when he was homeless, with a fax machine a john gave him. His johns also gave him the books of the writers he eventually called up on the phone for advice. Benton Archer's novel *Undo*, for example. You'll like this transgressive literature, the john said, after sucking Huey's dick. Ah didn't even know what *trangressive* literature was, says Huey, but ah read *Undo* and ah was like *Whoa! Here's somebody as fucked up as ah am.*

When she was renting, Felicia was evicted once on her own, once with Geordi, and then again with Geordi. Then Geordi got a chunk of money from his father's estate. His father had believed in owning things, a little piece of land. He'd owned so little. She met him only once, in that little house outside of Bakersfield, where Geordi and his father sat around saying practically nothing to each other for eternity, and then shortly after that he was dead. In the mountains. In the snow.

Huey usually mentions all the writers who gave him his start, and always gives thanks to Dr. Bailey, at the Adolescent Day Treatment Center, who saved him from the streets. Sonya Brava went to clown school some years back, and told Felicia how they'd urged her to find her "inner clown." To take some few arbitrary characteristics and exaggerate them. Clown, writer, what's the difference, said Sonya Brava. The fact that Huey spells *transgressive* correctly when the john says it, but not in his own voice, is significant, Felicia decides.

The girl has stopped verbally abusing the bush and the silence is terrifying. She's swaggering away, stick in hand. She looks exhausted, disheveled, her braids come undone through her zeal, yet genuinely empowered. As if she's finally taken control of the relationship. The bush, however, may never recover. Felicia wonders if writing a book is maybe about a similar relationship to the world.

A space has opened up in the day. A change of plans, a reminder of what's real. Not much. The BART is swooshing through forlorn and depleted neighborhoods. Little houses tucked almost under the tracks, empty, rusting swing sets. Only the ghosts of children dead from lead poisoning would ever swing on those sets.

Televisions are running in the distance as they have been for all of time.

Felicia is seated in front of a pathological liar. The woman is on her cell phone, assuring somebody, quite convincingly, that she's just getting off the BART at a different station, in a different direction, where she is supposed to be meeting this person. You gonna see the train pulling up in a minute, she says, and I'll be coming down the stairs. I'm wearing yellow, she says. You gonna see me in a minute.

She is, in fact, wearing blue. The woman gets up on the phone again, assuring somebody else altogether that she is still at home, eating her breakfast.

There's a Celia Abad story—Felicia's favorite—where a woman rides a train, cradling a bundle that seems to be her baby. It's the title story from her collection, *My Tumor*. The woman's in a compartment with two men who smoke relentlessly. While the compartment fills with a thick, choking haze, the men discuss the psychological styles of different cities and different eras, the longing, in moments of weakness, for annihilation, the nature of inspiration, the pursuit of novelty, and the proliferation of suburbs built over ancient burial grounds, while the landscape rushes past, a blur of backyards and hanging laundry and hopeless little wooded areas where bodies are sometimes found of women raped, murdered, and strangled. The story just ends, but in the next story in the collection a little girl is playing in a backyard, hiding in between the sheets her exhausted mother has hung up to dry, a mother who receives strange men sometimes in the afternoon; a train rushes past; the faces in the window look like skeletons.

When she emerges from the tunnel, she has a Missed Call from Philip. In his message, Philip doesn't talk about the Amish at all. He says nothing about the dead children, the grieving parents, or the course of his investigation. He talks instead about his grandmother and Artaud—apparently he's sitting up in his motel room, reading their journals. According to Philip, they were simultaneously breaking down toward the end of the Second World War, and he wonders if Leonora Carrington was insane at precisely the same time. He seems to be on the verge of articulating a theory, but trails off.

She met Philip just before the dot-com years. They were both working with the at-risk youth, along with thirty other grossly underpaid young writers. They had endless meetings—the most gruesome meetings ever, Philip always said—and endless conversations about the supposedly intricate boundaries between themselves and the *populations* they served. They all cared. Robin Sullivan, a poet, cried at one meeting about how much she cared, not just about the troubled youth, but about her coworkers, too. Two years later she bought the house that Felicia was living in and evicted her.

The garage door is wide open, but Melvin is nowhere to be seen. The space has been partitioned with plywood and chicken wire. Bicycles and motorcycles and lawn mowers fill in the gaps between storage spaces and there's a girl, sitting in the middle of the garage, staring into space. She has black hair tied up in a ratty yet immaculately arranged purple scarf. Excuse me, Felicia says. Do you know a boy named Melvin?

Oh, says the girl. You're the magazine.

Her eyes never exactly register Felicia's presence, as if she's talking to her on a phone.

In a minute, she adds.

Nothing much seems to be happening except the conclusion to some thought or daydream. The flimsy door to the back corner storage space is wide open, and Felicia steps in to take a peek. The so-called squat. There's a sleeping bag and some blankets are shoved into a corner, some movie posters tacked onto the wall. *Suspiria* of all things, Aaliyah from *Queen of the Damned*. Sketches she assumes are Melvin's own, technically skilled but unimaginative Giger imitations, mutating life forms with brutal penises or hybrid genitalia. A machine that used to be a woman. The woman looks vaguely familiar, a déjà vu located in the future. Dirty clothes are strewn about with a hot plate and a long, frayed orange extension cord that looks like it's just itching to burn the entire complex to the ground.

Ralph arrives, wearing a pale T-shirt that brings out the spooky blue of his eyes. He's looking rumpled, but distinguished, like somebody's artsy yet academic daddy. Not like a director of horror and porn. She doesn't know him well. According to Philip, he likes to be bossed around. Kind of counter-intuitive for a film director, but Felicia suggests with her sternest mommy voice that Ralph take the pictures while Melvin's girlfriend drives Felicia to the hospital where Melvin has been admitted, and he obediently does as he's told.

Melvin's girlfriend's car is cold and smells like some small rodent crawled into the engine and died there. He thought he was having an OD, the girlfriend says, and she rolls her eyes.

She's appropriately suspicious of Felicia, even though she doesn't know where she's going, and Felicia does. I'm from *San Francisco*, she says.

It's like she's performing for an audience that doesn't include Felicia, but that is watching from exactly Felicia's perspective. As if Felicia is a camera or a window. She's just a girl. She pulls over once and closes her eyes, takes a few deep breaths.

I want *good* feelings, she says. Not *bad* feelings.

Once they get to the Emergency Room and locate Melvin behind a screen in a room that also serves as a kind of hallway, with six skinny beds lined up but no other patients, the girlfriend turns her back on Melvin and scrutinizes a complex machine tucked into the corner of the room, by the sink. Melvin looks nothing like he sounds. On the phone he sounds like a befuddled, stoner whiteboy. He's wearing a textured paper gown and bubbling over about all of his newfound life insights. He took some drug Felicia's never heard of, ordered it online—an "elixir," he calls it. It came on so fast, he says. After you were there on the phone, I was just cleaning, he explains. Felicia had told him not to change anything, and he panicked for a minute thinking that because he didn't follow the instructions, she wouldn't be interested. He totally wants to be photographed.

Actually, we won't be photographing you, Felicia says. Only the physical space.

She explains how one's context can be a kind of portrait. The way context reveals the set of assumptions that define a person, the way it creates a kind of outline.

Like the chalk around a dead body, says Melvin, and he seems at first totally alarmed by his own thought and then almost relieved by it. As if the idea of death is only scary at first glance.

His heart stopped beating. He couldn't hear it anymore at least. He'd never figure out the deal. He was dead and unenlightened. Maybe he was not dead but only dying—the times were getting all confused. Dying, dying. He dialed 911.

Bad idea, says Felicia.

I'm a Mormon, says Melvin.

Ex-Mormon, says the girlfriend.

The cops were just a bad idea. Salt Lake City is a bad idea. My mother is a bad idea, he says. My stepfather is the worst idea ever! Only his little brother is a good idea, a really complex and vulnerable idea.

He's kind of a weird little boy, Melvin whispers.

The affection that Felicia already feels for Melvin alarms her. It suggests that he must be a lost cause. That he must be somehow doomed.

A nurse comes in and quietly tells Melvin what she's about to do and then checks his vital signs. Melvin freezes like a statue. For a minute, Felicia thinks he's actually holding his breath. When the nurse leaves, he relaxes and says that doctors and nurses are the weirdest creatures with their funny little uniforms, it's like they're part of this game, it's like they're really children or murderers or ministering angels dressed up for some show, it's like a big elaborate sex game that gets all mixed up with people actually getting sick and dying.

He tells her his primary interest is in *ideas about the future*. The girlfriend rolls her eyes. Melvin acts like she isn't even there. He treats Felicia like a fairy godmother, on the other hand, a good omen.

It was kind of incongruous with my self-image, she tells Philip later. But we bonded nonetheless.

I always think of you as a good omen, says Philip.

She's sitting on a bench outside the Berkeley Bowl, watching its particularly aggressive grocery shoppers jousting with their carts.

Philip says, Before I forget. I saw Freddy before I left? Claims he's good friends with Huey Beauregard, says Huey's the real deal.

Has he met him?

Of course not.

Philip's eating at a diner in Coralville. The texture of the food, he says, is like the texture of a repressed memory. The waitress's opinion is that the Amish people are like saints and that the boys were like angels and the shooter's body should be dug up out of its tomb and left for the wild dogs.

Are there wild dogs around there?

That was what *I* asked. The waitress said that she has a Rottweiler what could do the trick but her dog's too good to chew on that bastard's bones.

In Iowa, it's drizzling, off and on. Plastic skeletons and witches hang forlornly around non-Amish homes. The town's quiet now, and cold; no more flowers or stuffed animals at the corner of Red Oak and Tulip, and only an empty field where the school's been demolished.

Are you getting your story?

I'd appreciate it if you not write a story. That's what the father of a wounded boy told me. He said there have been plenty of stories.

But they're talking to you.

A grandfather of two dead boys described his own psychological state as a hole with no bottom. The father of one of the dead boys told Philip it was a battle between good and evil in that school and good won—because the boys weren't molested before they were murdered.

The men will talk to him, not the women. The men won't let the women talk to him.

The thing is, I had my story, he says, but I blew it. I met the shooter's son.

So what happened?

I didn't realize it was him. I didn't even ask about the murders.

Then he recognized the face in one of the photos in *People*: The boy huddled stiffly next to his mother, the grieving widow, was the boy in the gray hoodie.

The shooter's son, that's the story here, not the faceless dead children, he says. Faceless dead children are just sad, nobody wants to hear it.

But he talked to you? Maybe you can find him again.

Except maybe Raymond, Philip says. Raymond can't get enough of faceless dead children.

According to Philip, Raymond collects photos of Iraqi children who've stepped on American land mines, photos of the lumpy tumors caused by our depleted uranium, articles about drone strikes that kill dozens of civilians. He's kind of obsessed.

People might care, Felicia tells him. I don't know. Maybe it isn't about whether you care or don't care.

What is there to say about a dead child? asks Philip. But a murderer's tormented son, that's America, that's the American story. *My Perverted Father Killed Children*.

Philip's been hanging out at the old orphanage, hoping the kid comes back.

It's late there, isn't it, Felicia says.

After hanging up, she feels vaguely empty. Not good, Zen empty, but the other kind. *Pushing upward in the empty city*. Maybe care is what she aspires to. Still, after so much time. It is not a word she uses lightly. Outside the Berkeley Bowl, a crazy, mildly whorish woman is having a conversation with the mango she just bought. The fog is coming in, shifting the mood. Felicia might like to be slutty. *Pushing upward in darkness*. She should call Geordi. Exchange her feeling of emptiness for the reassuring banalities of his day. His incredibly boring research, some new insights into an Arabic verb variant, maybe something a crazy librarian said or did to him in the stacks. In the UC Berkeley Library, Geordi often loses all sense of time.

Once, in the late '80s, in San Francisco, clowns waited at various stops along the route of the 38 Geary, individually or sometimes in twos. At every bus stop another clown would enter the bus, but without acknowledging the clowns who were already seated, so that the bus filled with clowns steadily and the other patrons became more and more anxious, until, at the sight of the next bus stop, another stranger with floppy shoes and a big red nose standing nonchalantly, they started panicking, screaming, beseeching the driver to *just keep going, don't stop, don't let it come aboard.*

Felicia might enjoy being a harbinger of evil circumstances.

An ice queen, that's how people usually think of her. It's why her husband's attracted to her; she's just like his cold, unloving mother, but not really. An ice queen with a heart of gold. A good mommy reminiscent of a bad mommy, it's so Hitchcock.

She would say *detached* and *self-contained.*

What Geordi needs, and what he got: a nurturer who only looks enough like an ice queen to excite him sexually, while giving him the compassion he never got, and desperately needs, to get over his childhood. A woman who cares.

Maybe it was a pose she used for something once, a mysterious aura, but now it's just who she is. A gentle, she hopes, and increasingly meditative hum around a self that is so pared down it is almost indistinguishable from the non-self it will inevitably become.

The Portuguese writer Fernando Pessoa developed a number of distinct *heteronyms*, alternate identities with distinct personalities—making up for his own felt lack of any personality whatsoever, he said. Alberto Caeiro, Ricardo Reis, Alvaro de Campos, and others, each with their own imaginary history and characteristics. Felicia has wondered if Huey Beauregard might be the result of some similar process. If Benton Archer, perhaps, after writing about messy teenage boys for so long, boys who wanted to be abused or murdered, had created an autonomous writing personality to embody such a boy's experience, and to free himself from the need to write perfectly sculpted sentences. To free himself to write badly. But Trey Bergman told her he was with Benton one day when Huey called Benton—and he could hear the weird, breathy voice on the other end of the phone. If Huey is somebody's poorly imagined alter personality, Trey told her, he isn't Benton's.

2

IN THE UC BERKELEY LIBRARY, Geordi often loses all sense of time. The Main Stacks are windowless and subterranean. There are strange knobby trees outside and everywhere but he might as well be lost in this forest of words. *Oh you wretches, you unfortunates, you pretenders to the truth, you falsifiers of knowledge—can you still bear to listen when it behooved you to be awake from the first?* Geordi isn't sure if the trance state he sometimes enters while contemplating his thesis qualifies as being awake or being asleep. The alphabet is like a kind of vegetation, like the bones of dead plants. *Regimes of Meaning: Signs and Their Dynamic Fields Within Medieval Arabic Cosmological Texts* grinds along toward its inevitable or perhaps unreachable conclusion. Chapter 7 is in good shape, but Chapter 6, "The Dynamic Verb Choices in the Variants of *The 8-Fold Garden of Space and Time*," is a mess.

Hours pass or maybe no time at all.

Another graduate student, Urszula Czaykowski, is circling Geordi's table in the Silent Study Area, waiting to pounce. She just wants to corner him and talk about her research.

The real author of *The 8-Fold Garden of Space and Time* hid behind intricately constructed masks and layers of untruth. Supposedly, he was an ancient sage. Supposedly, this wise man had hallucinated for thirty-two days and thirty-two nights and recorded his visions. The real author used an Arabic dialect found nowhere else, innovating and distorting vocabulary and grammatical forms to make it all seem foreign and old. The narrative occurred in a vague and distant place in a dreamtime without historical markers.

Do peaches grow in this place? Do airplanes fly overhead?

Urszula plops down on the table. Geordi, she whispers, do you agree that we are just a kind of percolating conscious foam growing at the edge of the void?

Geordi is still trying to formulate a response, when she answers her own question.

Everything here is still determined by the laws and philosophies of that nothingness, she says. We cannot yet escape it. Our only freedom is in relationship to that nothingness.

Urszula's like a nervous and willful little bird, hands always fluttering about her face. Her blond, almost wheat-colored hair has been chopped off in a way that suggests a catastrophic rip in the fabric of space and time. She's reinterpreting the life of an early-twentieth-century Polish modernist who wrote her books under a male pen name, who in fact lived, at times, as a man. In Warsaw, in Zurich, at Cambridge. She's reading from her notes, from the journals of the transgender modernist.

Geordi, she says. *Whatever happens in a space determines the meaning of that space.* This is 1921, you see what I'm saying?

A library is a space. A text is a space.

Geordi, she says, what do you think about this description? *The professor's mouth was shaped like the slot of a piggy bank.*

A piggy bank, says Geordi.

A song is a space, a book spread into the atmosphere, a public space, she says.

Yes, says Geordi. I guess so.

Geordi, she says. Am I frightening you?

She laughs before he can reassure her that she doesn't terrify him, no not at all.

At Cambridge, Urszula's Polish modernist always noticed the lonely figures of African students on campus, she tells him. Unlike the savage packs of whites, they sidled alone like he or she did.

A *mark of seclusion inscribed on their skin*, Urszula says, reading from her notes.

Geordi wonders if she's suggesting something about the scar on his own face; if she's identified him as a lonely modernist, too.

And what about you? she says. What is this you are reading?

He hands her the 1927 Mather translation of *The 8-Fold Garden of Space and Time*. English on one side, one of the Arabic variants on the other. An embossed gazelle that is particular to the Overlooked Treasures of the Orient series. A brief foreword acknowledges the existence of "several" different versions, and insists in two sentences that its choice to translate the major verb consistently as "take captive" is the only reasonable choice, unlike Burton's lazy and willfully lewd nineteenth-century translation that waffled between "violate" and "seize roughly." Mather was at the time an administrator for the British in Bahrain, still then a colony. Geordi doesn't care about the English translation, but it is his first look at this particular variant of the so-called original Arabic text.

Geordi explains that in the twelfth century, *The 8-Fold Garden of Space and*

Time was accepted as over a thousand years old. While a few delusional modern scholars still maintain it is a first-century work, originally written in Greek or Aramaic, most everyone now accepts that it originated in the Islamic world in the ninth century.

And this is because why? Urszula asks.

There are eight variants, he says. The differences are so complicated that it must have evolved for several generations by the eleventh century at least.

Ah, I see, says Urszula.

She sets it down dismissively.

And why do you care? she asks.

Geordi sighs.

I'm edging toward some new evidence about the transmission of ideas, he says. The evolution of the verb forms, and the…aura of meaning around these verbs…

You believe there is a secret hidden in the past, she says.

Geordi shakes his head. She reminds him of his mother, he's not sure why.

Do you believe they murdered a verb? she asks.

A studious young woman at the end of the table gives them a dirty look. They're too loud, it's all too loud.

The original crime, Urszula says. The childhood trauma.

The studious woman's texts, piled up preposterously high, suggest she plans to become an engineer.

Are you a closet Freudian? asks Urszula, and she laughs again. Why don't you come with me, Geordi, let's eat something.

You remind me of my mother, he says.

Your mother was a lesbian? she says. Or a blonde?

Of course not, Geordi says.

But in fact his mother was, for a while, a blonde. After she left his father, after they left the Central Valley and moved to Long Beach. The fakest blonde imaginable. A California girl, she used to say. She wanted to be a different person.

Geordi explains in his quietest voice that like so many cosmologies, *The 8-Fold Garden of Space and Time* begins with a primal division, built around two terms, the terms usually translated as "Space" and "Time." But each term exists on a continuum of meanings, including the text's most original image, the in- and ex-halations. The idea that they are opposites is not exactly true, or only partially true. The existence of good and evil in the universe is explained as a grammatical process, and so it is not surprising that the treatise itself would develop into eight major variants, each of which would use a different verb to convey the journey or captivity of the angel within the garden.

But why, Geordi, she says.

What do you mean *why*.

I remind you of your mother, she says. This was Freud's idea, too. The twentieth century's greatest quack-pot.

Quack-pot?

This is not correct, she says. I mean like a con artist, like a charlatan, what is the word?

Quack, I think, says Geordi. Just quack.

Yes, quack like a duck. Quack quack, quack quack, quack quack.

Geordi's mother wanted to be a different person. Not the one who was married to his father, not the one who worked in the fields. A less constrained person, a less Catholic person. And she was for a while, a different person.

I'm not a Freudian, says Geordi. I'm sorry. You're nothing like my mother, not really.

The secret crime is hidden in the past, Urszula says.

I'm a scholar, says Geordi. Like you.

She runs her fingers through her hair like she's invigorating an extension of her dendrites.

You're studying the past, too, Geordi says.

Yes, of course, she says. The past.

She stands up, and begins pacing, as if giving it serious thought.

I am trying to uncover a secret, too, she says.

The studious young engineer in the next cubby is nakedly scowling at her, but Urszula doesn't notice.

Yes, this is true, Urszula says. But the secret in this case is the presence of queer bodies, the suffering of queer bodies, and of queer resistance, of course. It isn't mystical. It's about uncovering stories that are important today, stories that have been removed, replaced, forgotten. Pasted over with the bland, smiling faces of heterosexuals in love.

Geordi is pretty sure that his own face doesn't qualify as either bland or smiling, no matter how much he loves his wife.

The Polish modernist's family had her committed to a mental institution, she says. You see what I'm saying?

Urszula sits back down on the table, next to the creepy globed lamp.

Freud, they were reading Freud in Poland, says Urszula. They were practicing his methods already in 1907. Seven years she spent in a string of mental clinics because she had chosen to live as a man. Until the First World War broke out, and they let her go.

They let her go, says Geordi. I'm glad they let her go.

Geordi, says Urszula. Come have dinner with me.

Oh, says Geordi. I have to finish what I'm doing.

It's your thesis, says Urszula. You will never finish what you are doing.

Not today, says Geordi. Another day.

He waits until she's gone. He waits some more. He's lost his train of thought and will never recover it. His academic training leads him to see ruptures, absences, and shifts in emphasis instead of smooth causal lines. This is what he believes about history, what he has been taught to believe. He ascends the circular stairway back up to level A, and heads out.

The fog has come in, and Geordi walks out the front door past the monument filled with names of Berkeley Builders, down the steps, and into the fog. He is walking into the fog to find his way, because he learned this long ago, that you walk directly into the fog where you cannot possibly see a thing, this is how you arrive somewhere. For many years, as he walked up and down those steps, he believed without much thought that the Berkeley Builders must be great architects or even thinkers of the past. Geordi walks on across the campus through the thick mist toward his car, a campus full of knobby trees and brainy kids, but he could be anywhere. It's cool and dreamy and so still. Figures emerge along paths like numbers in elaborate, shadowy equations. Of course, the Berkeley Builders are actually just rich people who have given the university enough money to list their names on a monument. This is most of what you need to know to understand how history has been created.

It's too late for a summer fog. It's more still than that, like the first fog of winter. Thick and low to the ground.

Geordi believes there is a secret hidden in the past. This is true.

His car is wet. He drives carefully, although without thinking about it. He has never yet killed anyone. Once, an orange cat darted in front of him, with another silvery cat just behind, chasing it. He was surprised by the speed of his own reflexes, surprised that he didn't kill either cat. The two cats formed a meaningful sequence: cause and effect. He was the representative of time and death, probably, but he didn't crush them, not that day. Geordi would prefer to make it through his time here without either creating or destroying life. Tonight, like every night, the Berkeley pedestrians march out into the dark crosswalks heroically, aggressively, without hesitation.

There is, in fact, a secret hidden in the past.

Every afternoon as a boy, at the hour when everyone was resting, Geordi would leave the fields and sneak through neighboring orchards to the wall outside the town where the graveyard extended endlessly beyond its gates, and the airport road stretched out like an invitation into the western sky.

Geordi mostly imagines his childhood now as a dream about that cemetery and those airport roads. He would set out on an aimless journey or immerse himself in adventures in the western sky. His childhood, a fantasy, is barely accessible, but stepping through to enter that cemetery, he was entering that place where his hidden desires—so hidden he's not sure he's ever known what they are—fused with the hidden desires of other men: fame and adventure in the places of the dead.

Geordi was a child prone to fevers. Once, he was resting under the trees and burning up while his parents and his two sisters picked the peaches. His father rarely spoke. Was he hiding in his silence or living a secret life there? Maybe Geordi simply could have gotten well quickly, but the idea of being sick thrilled him, and what thrilled him about it was that it would lead him into a world of visions and unreality. He set off for the cemetery but lost his way.

He should have kept to the main road from the beginning. Those wastes were inhabited only by wolves and silence and various reptiles and an open bus with no windows. He may have boarded the bus. The passengers, who sat opposite one another facing the center of the bus, exchanged nothing except for general remarks about the holes in the road. Geordi decided to occupy himself with something so as to drive away the hallucinations and began to sing an imaginary song to himself. *The road is precisely the road now before me. I began my first sea journey at the age of twelve.*

That was the last thing he remembered, or dreamed. What there was at the highest place was only darkness. When he woke up, the deep gash across his face was his only entrance to a mystery that he couldn't remember. He'd blacked out. He had passed through the enigma of boundless time, there in the darkness. Somewhere.

The tennis courts, where Geordi turns off Martin Luther King toward his little Craftsman house, are lit up like a supernova, brighter tonight because of the fog. It looks like the fog has collected on the courts, like a cloud come down to earth, imprisoned in a wire cage under the punitive lights. A child moves through the thick chowder of light, alone with its balls and its racquet. Perhaps it is doing something sporty, working on some skills, but its movements look more like modern dance. Just a lone dark shape moving nonsensically, with an odd spastic rhythm, immersed in a luminous haze brighter than astrophysics.

A spastic child turned into an abstraction.

It is *me*, thinks Geordi.

Which doesn't make sense, and yet it's absolutely true. Time and space are the same substance, a deranged zone where the psyche performs its shadows, its reservoir of psychic forces, its communicable diseases. Geordi's crawling down the side street, watching the creature perform its ritual when somebody or something thumps the car. Blam.

Already? he thinks, slamming on his brakes, sure somebody's dead. Something like a detached head is bouncing toward the gutter. But it's just a basketball, hurled from the midst of a rowdy group of children on their way to the courts. It's landed on his hood and then bounced off into the street. The children are laughing at him.

Later, Geordi's eating pasta and a red sauce with the fresh asparagus Felicia picked up at the Berkeley Bowl, and chatting about her surprising day: a boy on drugs, a so-called squat, a hospital visit.

When she's done talking about the interior decorating choices of her lost Mormon child, he tells her that he found a slightly different use of one of the major verb forms in the Mather translation's variant. He watches Felicia do her best to look like she cares. He tells her about Urszula's research instead.

The Polish modernist's family had her committed to a mental institution, he says.

Like Raymond, says Felicia.

I can't imagine Raymond dressed up as a woman.

No, no, it wasn't like that, says Felicia. Just makeup and glitter and singing in his room.

She tells him that Philip met the shooter's son. She goes off on a tangent about Huey Beauregard and what a fake he is. Now Geordi is doing his best to look like he cares. When they run out of other things to talk about, Felicia asks him if he has a favorite Nazi.

Then Geordi's sleeping restlessly. The next day he's back at the library and the next day again.

The ancient sage who supposedly wrote *The 8-Fold Garden of Space and Time* didn't really want to write down his overwhelming visions. The visions were like a wild river and his only "bridge"—or "life raft" or "perception" or maybe "awareness"—consisted of the words that flowed from his tiny pen. After being carried like so much flotsam down that river for thirty-two days and thirty-two nights, he supposedly used the pen to gouge a bloody mark on his own forehead.

A sign of what? For whom?

In the morning, while he's in the bedroom getting his papers together, Felicia pops her head in and says, The only thing scarier than the last twelve minutes of this film is the first ninety-eight minutes. Is that a logical sentence?

Geordi has to think about it.

The sentence is fine, he says. It just means that the scariest thing ever is the first ninety-eight minutes of the film. The second scariest thing ever is the last twelve minutes. It just seems off because—why make the ending less scary than the beginning?

At the library, as he's descending the circular stairway, he spots Urszula through the window to Level B, so keeps going and hides himself deep down on Level D. He postpones his research, thumbing through Mexican literary magazines from the '70s and '80s. He discovers a poem by Freddy's twin brother in both English and Spanish translation—the one Philip told him had tortured Kathy Acker.

He distracts himself comparing translations of Rimbaud. *When the world has been reduced to a single gloomy wood for our four astonished eyes,—. When the world shall have shrunk to a single dark woods for our four eyes' astonishment,—. When the world comes down to this one dark wood / Before our four astonished eyes… When the world shrinks down to one last gloomy woodland in your eyes and in mine and in the others… When the world is reduced to a single dark wood for our two pairs of dazzled eyes—*

On his way out of the library, he nearly walks into a blind man. The guy curses at him, a low growl, and Geordi's pretty sure he calls Geordi a bitch. Geordi decides not to apologize, not to let the man hear his voice. It's only after he's outside in the bright day that he thinks he should have stood up against the blind man's misogyny. If that's what it was. He's lost track of how the word *bitch* is evolving—has it lost its gender yet? As he's puzzling over this question, Urszula catches up to him. She's wearing boots with heels that make her taller than he is.

Blindness is like a practice for death, she says. Don't you think?

Blindness? he says.

Muteness, too, she says. Travel and reading and sex. Different ways to practice for death.

I'm not sure we need to practice, Geordi says.

Geordi, she says, you are hilarious. Much too nice, like Americans. If it was me, I might have murdered that nasty blind man.

Good thing it was me, says Geordi.

Geordi, she says, tell me if the English is right.

She's translated more of her Polish modernist's journals. Urszula has discovered that he or she wasn't actually enrolled in classes in Cambridge, although he or she behaved like she was. Urszula reads out loud as they walk past the cafés and restaurants toward downtown.

A great missionary has returned from his sojourn in the wilds of Australia to speechify in the church, she says.

Give a speech, says Geordi. You want to say "give a speech."

Yes, yes, says Urszula impatiently. Give a speech.

She continues reading an overly wordy passage in which the university police are glowering at the modernist in the church for "having no hymn book and not belonging to the song."

Not belonging to the song? says Geordi. Maybe *not singing along?*

I like *not belonging to the song*, says Urszula.

Okay, says Geordi.

The song is over, she continues. *The speaker begins. He talks of savage peoples, of great conversions, of how the fanatical barbarians must be forced with violence to accept the truth. An adherent of the brotherhood of plunder, he goes on about the perfection of England, the great benevolent mission it has spread to every corner of the earth, capturing spoils and slaves, the chosen nation. English civilization and English law he says over and over again, English civilization and English law…*

They've arrived at the BART station. Maybe there's a better word than "adherent," Geordi tells her.

Yes, it is too much like a bandage, she says. Thank you, Geordi.

He takes the BART toward the city.

When the train emerges from the tunnel to the West Oakland station, he can see smoke rising to the east. *Smoke always rises from the distant pond* in the Rimbaud poem. Or *The upland pond smokes continuously* or *The high pond fumes continually* or *Endless steam off the highland pond* or *The high pond is constantly steaming*. Is something burning or only misting?

Otherwise, the sky outside is perfectly clear. One little cirrus-like wisp that could be the last lingering remnant of morning fog blown in from the bay, or maybe just a smudge on the window. Before Geordi can make a definitive interpretation, they descend again, through the tunnel to San Francisco to another library to read Manfred Kropp's essay "A puzzle of old Arabic tenses and syntax: *The 8-Fold Garden of Space and Time*." At the library, hours pass or it could just as well be days or weeks.

While many scholars consider the author's use of tense lazy and disturbed, Kropp argues it is a rigorous attempt to create a text *pretending to exist outside of time*. By attributing his work to a vague, mythical time, the author might have been trying to free himself from contemporary restrictions. *The 8-Fold Garden of Space and Time* could certainly be considered heretical. It is rare that theologians and mystics of this period view the origins of evil as completely divine and eternal, for example. Within certain dense allegorical paragraphs, prohibitions seem to become doorways. Participating in prohibited erotic behavior, for example, is a path toward realization of the architecture of the garden itself. Without a law to ignore, the author wonders, how could freedom be manifest?

Geordi catches the bus to Divisadero and then catches the 24, which will take him all the way to Philip and Raymond's cottage in Bernal Heights.

The bus lurches and groans forever. When Geordi took Felicia to the town in Mexico where his grandmother grew up, she was fascinated by the volcanic landscape. Geordi could care less about geological processes. He had thought he shared with his wife this profound indifference to minerals, erosion, and especially the vast wasteland of prehistory, devoid of conscious life. Next thing he knew, she dyed her hair black. For a while it was like she was a different person, like she called forth different aspects of his own personality, like they now shared a strange new subset of interests and opinions. Geordi wanted to get a peek inside the house where his grandmother had grown up. The year he was scarred, he'd stayed there for two weeks with his grandmother and his great-aunt Consuela, who owned the house. Geordi had finally escaped. Even before they'd left his father, it was Geordi's mother who narrated the story of their lives. His sisters narrated their own versions, which sometimes undermined his mother's slant, but retained much of her emphasis on geography as salvation, social mobility, and failed romance. Consuela's house had dirt floors, an astonishing invention.

The sky is streaked with blurry wisps of cloud. When Geordi arrives at the little Bernal Heights cottage, there are two other guests already seated in the backyard. Raymond introduces one of them as "Philip's oldest friend" and the other as his "date," a word that makes both of them—not Raymond—crack up. He introduces Geordi as "a poet." They are here for the same reason as Geordi, he gathers. Purchasing weed.

Philip's oldest friend looks awful, pale and covered with sores, and seems somewhat unhinged. He's missing several teeth. B-movies from the '70s and '80s are the only interest Geordi's absolutely sure he and Raymond have in common, so he tells Raymond that he's planning a lecture on *The Dark Secret of Harvest Home*.

Have you seen *Female Convict Scorpion*? Raymond asks Geordi.

Geordi hasn't heard of it.

Hold on, I'll loan you the DVD.

As Raymond goes into the house, the old friend makes an ass-grabbing gesture behind Raymond's back, and then leers at Geordi as if he is in on the joke, as if he, too, must want to grab Raymond's ass.

What are you up to this morning? asks the date. Picking up some party supplies?

Actually, smoking helps me to concentrate, Geordi says.

Gotcha, says the date, and then he pantomimes fellatio.

Inside the house, the doorbell rings.

We're on our way to an orgy, the old friend tells Geordi. You wanna come?

The old friend does a weird little shuffle that seems suggestive of dancing, maybe sex, general "good times" in a loose and uninhibited body.

Not today, says Geordi. Work to do.

He shrugs, as in: you know, *work to do*. It's clear that these two haven't slept. It's clear that 3:00 in the afternoon is, in a different world, the morning of a night that has yet to end.

When Raymond returns, he's with Freddy and some young guy who seems vaguely attached to him.

Geordi darling, what a pleasant surprise, says Freddy.

You know each other, says Raymond, obviously relieved. Nobody introduces the young guy and Geordi doesn't ask.

Geordi explains to Raymond that Freddy read with Lana Fontaine just a few months ago at the reading series Geordi curates. Raymond has been to Geordi's reading series because Philip read there once.

Philip was on a double bill, Raymond tells Freddy, with a man who called his videos poems, his poems memoir, and his strumming on the ukulele vibrational interventions.

You know Nathan Lins, says Geordi to Freddy. I appreciate his willingness to embrace less traditional and less pleasing sound waves. I'm always impressed with the way he reinvents every physical space he enters as a contested zone of artistic meaning.

Let him win! says Freddy. He slaps his friend on the knee, and the guy doesn't even flinch. We should all surrender before his onslaught with that hateful ukulele.

Raymond says, The first time I met Lana Fontaine, over Thai food, probably in 1993, she asked Philip: Where'd you find him, Polk Street? As if I wasn't even there.

Geordi would rather not speak ill of Lana, whose rigorous dismantling of grammatical sense he admires.

Freddy's never been to this house before, he tells Geordi, but he has shingles—chicken pox for grown-ups—and he needs his weed. He shows them an ugly rash on one side of his back, painful-looking asymmetrical stripes, as if he's been clawed.

Whoa, freaky, says the old friend.

I suppose it means my immune system is shit, Freddy says.

The pain in his back was excruciating, like a particularly evil elf with pointy boots was kicking him in the side exactly every three seconds, he explains. Saint Nick's little companion Ruprecht who used to chase naughty children with his switch or maybe it was Goethe's Erlkönig come to give me a foretaste of death, he says. But definitely German, with a stylish little green vest and jacket, narrow at the waist, and those pointy fucking boots!

He sighs and relaxes into a chair.

I love painkillers, says Freddy. Painkillers, a glass of wine, and a little bit of weed and I'm happy as can be, he says. And a good fuck!

He slaps his friend on the knee and laughs at his own naughtiness.

He's a Marine, Freddy says. My second! he adds to Raymond in a stage whisper. *Soldiers whom Death, unflinching Lover, has sown / In our wasted furrows, to flourish again...*

Geordi discreetly examines the young Marine, who looks like he's performing the very idea of Marine. The idea of Marine is Death's prom date, he supposes. Is this what gay men like? What's the allure? His expression just suggests some kind of eternal, stoic waiting.

You wanna come to an orgy? the date asks Freddy.

Freddy doesn't seem to register the question. The speed freaks giggle among themselves.

Too bad Philip isn't here, I have so many stories to tell him, Freddy says.

Many people love to confess to Philip, says Raymond. Their evil thoughts, their affairs with thirteen-year-olds and married men. Technically, Philip's probably the accessory to a dozen crimes. Anthony Glass told Philip about a murder he supposedly committed once, by accident, in self-defense—with the little corkscrew appendage of a Swiss Army Knife.

Raymond says that his own father, a former Catholic, once told Philip that many years ago, when his thyroid condition was driving him insane, he'd stood in the kitchen chopping up some roast and imagined doing that to his own children. Chopping up Raymond and his sister Mina. In his own moral system, Raymond's father had told Philip, harming your own children was the worst thing you could do, and he knew that, but he just couldn't get the pictures, and Raymond supposes the urges, out of his mind.

How very Brothers Grimm, says Freddy.

Geordi doesn't mention that he, too, has told Philip things he's talked about with few other people and rather resents being lumped in with a bunch of lapsed Catholics.

Philip's a good listener, he says.

He lets people off the hook a little too easy, if you ask me, says Raymond.

And we *should* be let off the hook, says Freddy. For our behavior, at least, which is always inconsequential, if not for our poetry. Never for our poetry.

Raymond seems to still be pondering Lana's comment from 1993.

Philip's father read only James Michener, James Clavell, and Robert Ludlum, says Raymond. Philip claimed that the most literary book in the house was *Shogun*, and told Raymond that his mother read only C. S. Lewis, *Guideposts* magazine, and some book called *Mister God, This Is Anna*.

I love Jonas and Jolene, says Philip's oldest friend.

C. S. Lewis is more literary than *Shogun*, Freddy points out.

My mother actually read Genet, Raymond says. Not the novels, true, but the plays. On the other hand, my mother had me committed to a mental institution when I was only fifteen.

She must not have been paying very close attention to her reading, says Freddy.

Jolene was the most intellectual mother in the PTA, says the old friend. She was a Mennonite. She had ideas that didn't conform to the world's.

Jolene, says Raymond to Freddy and Geordi. Philip's mother.

Raymond says that he read *Our Lady of the Flowers* years later when he was sitting around the ironworkers union hiring hall waiting to get taken on as an apprentice. His grandmother would pick him up at the Oakland BART and drive him there by 6:30 in the morning, and he'd sit like some gentleman laborer from a Diego Rivera mural, improving himself through the reading of great literature, waiting for a job.

Genet hated men without consciences, says Freddy. He couldn't stand a man without empathy! They had to have consciously chosen evil, to have *overcome* their consciences.

Raymond excuses himself to fetch the weed. Freddy rubs his friend's thigh and seems to settle into a kind of contagious daydream. It is one of Freddy's poems, oddly enough, that most evokes Geordi's childhood, minus the gay content. In Freddy's poem, there are hotels and intersections of long straight roads and ancient squares and gardens. In Freddy's poem, as the poet approaches the public toilet, loneliness comes to mean a male homosexual and reality a naked penis. Arrows pierce the dead and arrows are memories. The human voice in the poem is blue.

The sky darkens outside. The sun has passed behind a hill or a building. The trippy light creates the impression that there will be many occasions for care and sorrow. When Raymond returns, Geordi pays immediately. Adrift, sometimes, it is only protocol that saves him.

When the world has been reduced to a single gloomy wood for our four astonished eyes, he says. To one beach for two faithful children—to one musical house for our pure harmony—I shall find you.

Could you repeat that? asks the Marine. He digs an index card out of his pocket, and as Geordi repeats the lines, he seems to be writing them down.

It's Rimbaud, Geordi says.

Have you had Huey Beauregard read yet? asks Freddy.

I was under the impression he doesn't appear in public, says Geordi.

Other people could read Huey's work for him, suggests Freddy. What about Todd?

He already read, says Geordi. He read from his children's book about an FTM dolphin, and from his memoir about his time with the Beat poets.

The Marine gazes at the index card as if evaluating a minor purchase, and then tucks it back into his pocket.

Todd's approach to the issue of ego was structurally foregrounded in a much more humorous and dynamic way than in Ted's memoir, for example, says Geordi.

You invited *Ted* to read? says Raymond.

He covered similar material from his own Beat memoir, says Geordi, ignoring the incredulous tone of Raymond's question, but highlighted issues of age discrimination and humiliation.

Ted? Who's Ted? asks Freddy.

I'm surprised if you never met him, says Geordi. He used to date Brendan Pelt?

He's Todd's evil twin, says Raymond.

The blood drains from Freddy's face. Geordi has never before witnessed such a literary display of emotion.

Twin? he says. Todd has a twin?

Not biologically, says Geordi. In a more Jungian sense.

It's the same thing, snaps Freddy. Precisely the same thing.

Geordi's afraid that if he doesn't get out now, he'll have to pretend he hasn't heard all the gossip about Freddy's *psychological warfare* with his more talented twin brother. So in the awkward silence that follows Freddy's hostile outburst, Geordi gets up to leave, making the moment itself slightly less awkward, but abandoning Raymond to the moments that will follow, alone with the tweakers, the Marine, and the freakish poet. But as Raymond walks Geordi toward the door, the phone rings and Raymond picks up. From the few words that drift his way, Geordi gathers that it's Philip.

After a minute, Raymond hands Geordi the phone.

Philip wants to say hello.

Hello, says Geordi.

Trespassers will be persecuted, says Philip. How's that for the title of a poem?

Are you trespassing? asks Geordi.

Not technically, not yet, says Philip. In a minute.

Geordi quietly tells him about Freddy's twin's poems.

Are they brilliant? asks Philip.

They do some interesting things with fissures and gaps, says Geordi.

After a long pause, Philip asks him to put Bob Miller, his oldest friend, on the phone.

Geordi doesn't want to risk conversation with the scary meth-heads again, and yet he returns to the backyard to convey the message. Before he can leave, a pipe of weed is passed his way, and he smokes. Raymond starts doing something vaguely baking oriented in the kitchen, which adjoins the backyard, and the date settles back into his chair and closes his eyes. Freddy is blissfully leaning against the Marine, and petting him like a dog. The voice of Bob Miller drifts in from the house. The bridge, he keeps saying something about the bridge. For some reason, Geordi imagines it as a bridge between an orchard and a cemetery, between the living and the dead.

In the cemetery in his childhood there was no bridge but there were oak trees covered with lichen. Orange and yellow organic textures that seemed like imprints of calligraphy over the equally weathered and imprinted bark. The trees were convoluted. Geordi had a fever. He went walking, he must have gotten lost. Geordi was left with a gash on his face and vague intuitions. The intuitions were prophetic and beyond language, but the impossible exists also within Ibn Arabi's *Fusus al-hikam*, Ibn Al farid's *Al Jamriya*, and of course, *The 8-Fold Garden of Space and Time*. *The only way forward is to annihilate all that's been written. In the future there will be no self and no future and no belief in the future. But it is also important to sleep in order to dream of the absence of time.*

He was just a boy, a feverish child. He went walking. He never came back.

3

FOR THE *ROOST* ARTICLE, Felicia would like to separate Melvin's things as much as possible from his own ideas about his things, and approach them as an archeologist might. On the other hand, the question of *Suspiria* keeps nagging at her. She pops her head into the bedroom where Geordi is getting dressed. The only thing scarier than the last twelve minutes of this film is the first ninety-eight minutes, she says. Is that a logical sentence? Geordi looks at her, uncomprehending. Sorry, she says.

It just seems off, Geordi finally says, because why make the ending less scary than the beginning?

Marriage lasts forever. Oh, certainly there are divorces, but Felicia doesn't want that. She wants to skip over to a different track from time to time, live a different life running parallel alongside the married one.

Melvin's in San Francisco, "doing some research," when Felicia calls him. Did you sleep in the city last night? asks Felicia.

I need to try that sometime, Melvin says.

He's never seen the movie, he tells her, but he likes the word. Suspiria, he says. Suspiria. He can't remember where he found the poster, maybe it was for sale on the street? She asks him what sort of research he's doing. Melvin isn't *from* outer space, he explains, he *is* outer space; he's both a message, and somehow at the same time the recipient of that message.

Consistently Felicia finds herself the most rational person in the conversations she's having. She wouldn't have seen that coming, fifteen, twenty years ago.

I might go somewhere new, Melvin says.

All by yourself?

That other thing wasn't working out, he says. There's, you know, compatibility issues.

So you aren't together anymore?

Not sure if I broke up with her or what, Melvin says. I don't have the time, I got things to figure out.

***

On the train, she reads Fernando Pessoa. She's often the most rational person in these relationships, too. Pessoa describes himself, in 1915, as a repressed sexual invert. *It stops in the mind. Yet always, in moments of meditating about myself, I have been uneasy. I have never been sure, nor am I yet, that this temperamental disposition could not one day go down into my body. I am not saying that I would then practice the sexuality that corresponds to the impulse, but the desire to do so would be enough to humiliate me.*

Felicia's riding to North Berkeley, to meet Sonya Brava. Sonya's first book of stories, *Muchacha Was a Sex Fiend*, was published by W(h)ere Woman Press. It was funny and hip and sexy enough to gain her a serious cult following and attract the attention of savvy agents and editors. Sonya sold her memoir, *Oblivion Highway*, to Knopf. Felicia wonders if that's why it's been over a year since she's seen her or if it's just the whole baby thing.

Felicia is most herself, she's pretty sure, when she is alone. When she is somewhere in between. When she has just lowered the book she's been reading and is gazing into the distance. At her reflection in a window. At nothing.

Eating is the best thing to do in Berkeley, and everybody here seems to be doing it all the time, feasting on delicate, organic pastries, gourmet cheese and crackers, hormone-free tostadas.

Sonya had shared Felicia's anti-baby position during the early years of their friendship, until she was overcome by her biological clock. Felicia and Sonya had both been bisexual and promiscuous in their younger days. They'd flirted, but become friends instead.

Sonya says that when she was pregnant, people would just come up to her. Like she was public property, just anyone felt it was okay to give her advice. You look so vulnerable, this one woman told her. A couple of them actually touched her belly. You're so small, another one said, does your doctor know?

The baby itself is a charmer, a well-behaved and sleepy little girl, just beyond blob. She's kind of humming in the stroller, a busy machine. Sonya hadn't wanted to know the baby's gender beforehand, but her mother assumed Sonya was keeping that knowledge from her out of spite.

The worst thing, Sonya says, is how they act like it's made me a different person. Like I've somehow rejoined the family. Like I'm not the black sheep dykey bitch poet that ran as fast out of fucking Modesto as I could. It makes me wanna, you know…tattoo the baby's scalp or something.

Felicia examines the little head, with only the wispiest hair to cover it.

You become a member of the world's biggest club, Sonya says. A club you never wanted to join.

Sonya wants Felicia's help. Dennis Cardona corralled her into editing this anthology, *Sexual Outlaws of the New Millennium*—I know, Sonya says, way too 1991—and it was all fine, she's almost there, really, but with the baby she just doesn't have any time. Basically, they just want my name on it, Sonya says, to appeal to, you know, my legion of sex-obsessed hipster fans. So Sonya suggested that they hire a co-editor, who would get half of her advance money, not much in any case, but something, and who could finish up the work. Which is where Felicia comes in.

It's not open submission, says Sonya. We have some unpublished work and we have some big names, so it's really just about finding quality work from a few more writers who aren't *totally* obscure.

What about Charles Scott? asks Felicia.

Charles Scott would be perfect. Do you know him?

He hit on me once, maybe ten years ago, when he read here. He was really drunk, he probably doesn't even remember me. He gave me his number then, but I never called him.

What, did he want you to beat him up? Punish him?

I'd imagine so.

I'd want to put Philip Yoder in, says Felicia.

Kinky straight sex is more what they want to focus on, says Sonya. Think Mary Gaitskill, Stephen Elliott.

He might have something less gay. Like something out of *The Limping Man*. Did you read *The Limping Man*?

The book was supposed to be two love stories put together. One gay, one straight. Ricky and Dhoji weren't exactly straight, but you know, says Felicia. Together they were.

Philip and Ricky and Dhoji were all connected through some gay hippies on Haight Street. Philip and Raymond lived there for a while, in one apartment in a house controlled by these gay hippies; somehow they'd had nowhere else to go during the dot-com years. Ricky had his messed-up American childhood: his father's suicide, his dysfunctional white trash hippie mother, his endless pendulum in and out of foster care. Sexually active by the age of seven and turning tricks by thirteen. He became the underage boyfriend of one of the medical marijuana gurus, not the one who ran for governor, she thinks, but the one who ran for the Senate against Dianne Feinstein? He was always seducing people and then betraying them, according to Philip, father figures mostly, but also friends, lovers, men, women...

Wait a minute, says Sonya. You didn't date this guy, did you?

I've never met him, says Felicia.

Felicia says, You're thinking of JJ.

In any case, Ricky eventually blackmailed the medical marijuana guru he slept with as a teen, to get the money to go to India. To get over a bad marriage, to find himself, to clear his head. In India he met Dhoji, a young Tibetan woman looking for a ticket out of her oppressive Dharamsala girls' school, where she was sewing handcrafted knickknacks for the Dalai Lama. Ricky promised to marry her but had to return to the States to get his divorce finalized from the other wife.

An epic's worth of separations and reunions for the two improbable lovers, says Felicia. Dhoji became a heroin addict for a while in Delhi. There's more to it than that—meat smuggling, robbery, prostitution—but the story ends with Dhoji's triumphant arrival in America as Ricky's wife. Or maybe it ends three years later, after two pregnancies and an endless series of fights, affairs, and failed money-making schemes, when Dhoji leaves Ricky, with her two toddlers and a suitcase, and shows up at Raymond and Philip's door.

But Philip started getting bored with the facts and it started getting more and more fictionalized. He started incorporating elements from the porn star/ scuba diver story, so that everything was happening underwater or on film and you couldn't tell the difference between the two.

The baby blinks up at them, incredibly alert, and makes gurgling sounds.

Felicia tosses out a few more names: William Vollman, Benton Archer, Waylon McClatchy. If you could get Vollman, it'd be fantastic, says Sonya. Benton has a certain crossover appeal, and Waylon has become big since he died.

She shrugs.

You'll figure it out, she says.

She says she needs to go to the restroom to breastfeed the baby.

Just do it here, says Felicia. It's Berkeley.

Oh, I know, says Sonya. But you know, no matter how discreet you are... Men just turn away, but I swear, every woman in the room feels compelled to give you a *look*. Sometimes a mild look of disapproval, but usually what's worse, a benevolent look of encouragement. Before you know it, some practicing midwife wraps her shawl a little more tightly around her shoulders and taps you gently on the shoulder…so gently, it's like a kitten…and offers pointers on your fucking technique.

I'll be right back, she says and the heels of her boots make a clacking sound as she winds her way to the back.

The last time Felicia was home, sitting across the table from her own mother, it suddenly struck her that her mother was like a rodent. The way she scurried around the house, the way she attacked Felicia offhandedly, as if from below.

It was in that same moment that Felicia fully understood how devastated she would be when her mother died. Inconsolable, she decided. And she got up and went outside into the muggy heat to escape from this presentiment of her own grief and from her vast and unsatisfying love for this woman, and it was the strangest thing. Her father was smoking a cigar and chasing ground squirrels around the yard, and paused, looked at Felicia, and said *Squinty-eyed rodents*. He began listing the poisons he'd dumped into their holes to kill them, Revenge, Mole-Tox, Rampage, Last Stop, Fumitoxin, and then the poisons he'd dumped on the lawn to kill the weeds, Roundup, Manage, Total Kill, Vantage, SedgeHammer, Weed-X. He told her that some new kind of beetle was on its way into the state to destroy all the ash trees. They would surely devour his own ash tree, he said. The only thing strong enough to kill that beetle, he guessed, would be DDT, but DDT wasn't legal anymore, he complained. His tree was doomed. She said nothing, she had long ago decided to say nothing. He'll die soon, she'd long thought, I'm just going to be nice to him.

They talked about her father's growing collection of quarters, quarters with the names of states on them. Every year the government issued four more, in the order that the states were admitted into the union, and he had them all, all the ones that had been issued so far. He didn't yet have Hawaii or Alaska or a handful of other latecomers, of course. He didn't like their holes, he said then about the squirrels, the holes worried him. When she was leaving, at the airport, her father gave her a handful of quarters with his own state's name embossed in them, so that she would take them back to California, circulate them in California.

Back from the restroom, both Sonya and the baby look bizarrely refreshed.

While she was pregnant, Sonya tells her, she became convinced that Mike was cheating on her. Normally she wouldn't have cared that much about some one-night stand. We're pretty much Don't Ask Don't Tell, she says. As long as it isn't, you know, serious. I had a few incidents, too. But it was mostly just with women, she says.

Which makes it less serious? says Felicia.

Sonya laughs. For Mike it does.

But I was in my eighth month, okay? I knew he was fucking around, I knew it, but I started getting paranoid he was fucking some guy. Some little blond boy, dressed as a girl. Oh, it's just what he'd go for. And you know, as a plumber he meets them all. Everyone's suddenly a freak when you handle their pipes. Everywhere he goes, Mike's the butchest daddy they've ever seen, and you know how he is, he gets *off* on it.

Felicia knows exactly how he is: she can't stand Sonya's husband.

I started searching his pockets, says Sonya. And checking the numbers on his cell phone, she says. But it's hopeless. He calls like twenty strangers with their shit backed up every single day. So I decided to follow him.

It was easy enough—the Mr. Rooter van was the easiest thing in the world to tail from a distance. She rented a car and followed him in disguise.

You're kidding, says Felicia. What kind of disguise?

I wasn't exactly thinking straight, says Sonya.

And?

I put my clown suit on, says Sonya. How else am I going to camouflage my pregnant belly?

Right, says Felicia. How else?

So. As Mike goes in and out of people's homes, Sonya watches him to make sure he carries his tools in with him, checks out the people who answer the door. At one apartment complex in North Oakland she actually walks around back, as if she's lost, looking for some misplaced child's birthday party, in order to get a look in the back window and make sure that Mike doesn't have somebody bent over the kitchen table. He doesn't, but then late in the day, just after five, he makes a suspicious stop at an office complex. Sonya's been at it all day and the fumes from the clown makeup are starting to get to her, it's all turning mildly hallucinatory. She parks in the loading zone out front, races inside to see the elevator light stop at the sixth floor. There are only two clients on the sixth floor, a real estate agent and a woman who offers some vague kind of consulting that sounds half mystical, half financial. In the elevator she's alone with a mother who looks exhausted and a child who looks terrified. On the sixth floor, the door is cracked to the financial mesmerist's consulting office and Sonya catches a glimpse of Mike entering some further chamber, toward the back. She steps inside. She can hear voices in the back, Mike, a woman, and the sound of water running. She catches a glimpse of herself in a faux Italian mirror hung on the wall underneath some ratty sage-like plant and freaks out. You know I'm a scary clown, says Sonya.

That was always the hardest part of clown school for her. Not embracing her inner clown and not acting out her inner clown and not dealing with other people's responses to her clown image, but actually seeing herself as the clown she had become, encountering her own clown image in the world, her manifestation as something troubling, monstrous, inappropriate—not to other people, that's easy, but to herself.

You sound like Geordi somehow, says Felicia.

Geordi would be a sweet, shy, melancholy clown, says Sonya. I'm a scary fucking clown. A nightmare, serial killer, sex monster clown.

Just as she says this, Geordi walks past the café with some woman. It always startles Felicia to see him out of context. The woman is in her thirties, blonde and dykey in a femme way. Geordi looks like he's being kidnapped.

Plus, Sonya continues, I can only just hear the sound of my own mouth-breathing drowning out all reason. That damn red nose suffocates me, I'm lost, and then I clearly hear the woman in the back say, That seems like an awful lot of money for something that small, and then I hear Mike being reasonable and explaining the costs of various little connectors and faucets or some bullshit as his voice gets louder, because they're obviously coming my way. The deal is not going down. This hypnotizing money lady is too cheap, she's going to keep getting more estimates, dragging more and more raggedy plumbers into the dark recesses of her narrow, airless space.

Sonya backs out of the office just as she sees Mike's reasonable face emerge from the airless back rooms. He looks up, startled by something, by her, the receding clown blur. What does he see? A garish pornographic smear? A waving flag, a child's toy? She presses the button for the elevator, but the light shows it's stuck on the lobby floor. She ducks into the real estate office, which is open, but empty. It's another sleek and terrible space, with big sliding glass doors that open onto one of those horrible little '70s balconies that make you think of Astroturf, looking out over the goose-shit pond of Lake Merritt. Inside there's only spare but elegant furnishings, a huge comfy leather sofa with home decorating magazines spread out on a coffee table in front of it, a chair or two. Except for a desk near the entrance cluttered with computer and papers, the rest of the room looks staged. She hears Mike's voice in the hall, and pulls the door shut behind her.

She can still hear Mike's voice, and the woman's petulant complaining voice, and then a cheery, faggy voice, and the door of the real estate office begins to open, but then abruptly stops as whoever it is chats some more. She ducks down behind the leather sofa and lies down in that space between the sofa and the sliding doors, remaining perfectly still. She can see the doorway reflected in the window, and the cheery real estate agent comes in, and sits at his desk, and she supposes that if he looked over in her direction, he'd be able to see a reflection in the sliding glass doors as well—the reflection of an evil clown crouched and waiting, but waiting for what?

Seeing myself like that, Sonya says, I was convinced that I wouldn't give birth to a human child.

A monster?

No, I was the monster, she says. It was like I knew I could only give birth to an object. Some object, I couldn't think of the word for it...something hard and round and smooth.

Hard and round?

Something...like a reflection.

Sonya closed her eyes as if that would make it all go away, and she heard the incessant clicking at the computer keyboard, on and on, he just kept clicking and clicking....

Oh shit, says Sonya, and she sticks a menu in front of her face.

What is it? asks Felicia.

Gloria Carrera, Sonya whispers. My editor at W(h)ereWoman Press. They owe me like 2000 dollars.

So why are *you* hiding? asks Felicia.

I really could use that money, says Sonya.

The baby's eyes pop open. Felicia supposes it's about to scream.

Gloria's crazy, says Sonya. I guess she always has been, but now she's just falling apart. It's not like she *has* the money, you know what I mean. And I don't think she spent it on crack, but she just...I don't know. Not even Victoria Cañada can get the money she's owed.

The editor doesn't look crazy. Not homeless and schizophrenic crazy, certainly. Not even Anna Kavan crazy or Leonora Carrington crazy or Janet Frame crazy. She's chatting with a silvery, bespectacled woman who looks impossibly brainy, like she's been mapping out postapocalyptic feminist societies for decades.

Ever since the controversy, you know, when she published the translations of Irma Carrasco, says Sonya. That dead fascist with those wonderful poems. I think it pushed her over the edge.

Sonya gazes at the menu in her hand, as if the answer to this karmic riddle is hidden somewhere in its descriptions of the vegan cheesecake or the organic flan. The baby starts to scream.

Melvin calls just then, but instead of speech, there's a kind of choking noise.

What is it? Melvin, are you okay?

It's my house! he says. It's like…

Felicia's having a déjà vu or something.

Burning, he says.

Now he sounds incredibly calm.

The garage is on fire?

The whole thing, says Melvin. It looks totally different. The structure, I mean. It's like you can really see the insides. It's like there's this skeleton that was always there. I always thought this would happen.

What do you mean by *this*?

All my stuff was in there, Melvin says.

Your *Suspiria* poster.

At least I have my sketchbook with me, Melvin says. But I lost a bunch of future life forms from higher-gravity scenarios.

Oh honey, I'm so sorry.

She can't tell if he's overcome with emotion or if she's projecting some sort of extreme vibration onto the silence.

Maybe I can find you another poster, says Felicia. Online.

I wonder if *she* did it, Melvin says.

Felicia says, Your girlfriend? Do you really think so?

Ex-girlfriend, he says. I don't have anywhere to go now. I mean, it's probably like a message or something. My friend Jared said I could stay with him.

That sounds like a good idea, says Felicia.

But he's in New York or something. I have like ten dollars and I'm running out of minutes on my phone.

Sonya is waving at Felicia in "good-bye" mode and backing toward the exit with the screaming baby in one arm, pulling the stroller with the other, contorting herself to face away from the table where Gloria Carrera is obliviously listening to the smart woman.

I better get out of here, Melvin says. Everybody's going to think I did it.

Felicia says, You were in San Francisco last night.

I know, I know, Melvin says, but it sounds like he's apologizing or confessing.

You didn't leave your hot plate running, did you? asks Felicia.

I just had some noodles, Melvin says. Hey, I'll call you back.

4

THERE'S A STENCH OF MANURE HERE and land that goes on flat as forever until it gets all tangled up and smashed looking in the vicinity of some river or creek. The same river or creek that runs past the East Liberty Home for Boys most likely. This is the Glick farm. Most days in Iowa, Philip pops a few Vicodin and makes a halfhearted visit to the home of the only one of the grieving families he hasn't yet spoken with—the Glicks seem to have left town, but he knocks on the front door and stands a minute, then knocks on the side door and stands a minute—and then drives around aimlessly, hoping to spot the boy in the gray hoodie.

Why is he here?

He was called to come, he tells them when they ask. Called by God, they think he means.

He could just go home now. They've all talked to him, pretty much, without saying anything surprising. A loud call from God. The Amish 9/11, the hole with no bottom. *Like a dream.*

The rain's let up today, and patches of light peek through, just enough to illuminate a dark ceiling of clouds.

He's found the entrance to the old orphanage from the road—a barely visible lane that ends at a barricade with a ditch along either side. There's enough space there to park your car, if you angle it into the ditch. You can sit there with the flies buzzing, make some calls.

When he calls Raymond, Bob Miller is there with some trick, picking up a bag, and Geordi, too. He talks to Raymond briefly, and then Geordi, and then Raymond puts Bob Miller on the line. Bob Miller finishes telling him the story. The story of the bridge.

Afterward, Philip sits in the car for a while.

Artaud: *Around this circle is a zone of moral abandonment in which no Indian would venture: it is told that birds who stray into this circle fall, and that pregnant women feel their embryos rot inside them.*

Grandma: *In the summer of 1942 we bought a farm east of Kalona and got possession of it the next spring. This was a place that needed lots of attention and tender loving care, so we had our work cut out for us to do. The farm was run down and didn't produce very well. Ben L. Yoder quotes Dad as saying the land was so bad it didn't produce good cockleburrs. The house and barn were old, but seemed fairly good, strong, and solid. We also had a chicken house, a small milk house, and a few small hog coops. That first spring we put up a machine and buggy shed, and also rearranged the house some to make it suitable to have church services when the time came.*

Artaud: *There is a history of the world in the circle of this dance, compressed between two suns, the one that sets and the one that rises.*

From the barricade you have to make your way through more overgrown weeds and brush, down a road with a chain across it, and through a huge gap in a crippled chain-link fence. Past more *Trespassers Will Be Persecuted* signs to the old bridge. At the bridge you have to ignore the *DANGER UNSOUND STRUC-TURE* notices and make your way across the least rotted boards.

Philip has a flashlight this time. The sun is setting already out there beyond the fields and the barns. At dusk the light inside this ruin is the light of eternity.

When Philip was a boy, Bob Miller was his best friend, a queer little only child born into a kind of madhouse of secrets and lies. They used to play in the abandoned brick factory back through the trees behind Bob Miller's house. The old brick factory was a wonderland of broken windows, crevices like mine shafts in the earth, a maze of partially collapsed walls, and doorways leading nowhere.

It's like Philip's always lived here, in this ruin.

His path and Bob's have crossed each other their whole lives. In the '80s, when Philip was hitchhiking through Washington DC, Bob was an intern for a Supreme Court Justice—one of the evil ones—and Philip slept on Bob's floor. Bob's parents were divorcing and Bob had just recently learned the secret of his birth. When Philip and Raymond were struggling in Santa Barbara, with Raymond in scuba diving school and Philip shelving the 600s at the library— cars and boat repairs and diet books—Bob came up from LA, where he was doing legal work for Disney, for Philip's reading at the Earthling Bookstore, and they had a bizarre dinner together afterward with Dottie's long-distance boy-friend, an old high school flame of hers—he'd lived in Japan and Saudi Arabia, he sculpted men's hands, and he'd retired to Montecito. At the reading, Philip read all of his passages that insulted Santa Barbara and its closet cases, the sort of thing he was liable to do back then. Later, Philip and Bob were neighbors in the Haight for a couple of years, while Bob was living with his Southern belle of a boyfriend, Dwight. After the breakup, Bob moved to Oakland and devoted himself to tracking down his half-brother, the son of the unstable woman who'd killed herself. Later, Bob would go on about his visits with this long-lost half-brother somewhere near Tampa. Philip had long thought of Bob Miller as his own evil twin; or maybe he was the evil twin and Bob was the good one, it didn't really matter. But Bob talked about his brother with the same goofy enthusiasm he talked about everything—overlooked local landmarks, forgotten minor celebrities, museums devoted to trivial historical incidents—always a booster in search of an underwhelming cause to celebrate.

Ftn blu LEGIT or maybe *Ein bim LEGIT*, scrawled by the shooter's son into the plaster. Two suicides, he said. His father and who else? Down and to the right it says, *Matt Loves*. Whoever Matt loved, the name has been worn away by time. The boys who were raised here and educated here are men now. Maybe they're dead, maybe they're in prison, maybe they're rich from the lawsuit money. Next to the shooter's son's message, Philip's been marking off his days among the Amish on the wall, as if he's in prison.

Artaud: *The dancer enters and leaves, and yet he does not leave the circle. He moves forward deliberately into evil. He immerses himself in it with a kind of terrible courage, in a rhythm which above the Dance seems to depict the Illness. And one seems to see him alternately emerging and disappearing in a movement which evokes one knows not what obscure tantalizations.*

Grandma: *In the summer of 1945, I had a nervous breakdown. I went to the doctor all fall and winter. One Sunday that winter Esther and one of the younger children stayed home with me. Esther got severe stomach pains and was very miserable so I wrote a note and sent the younger child to the neighbors to call the doctor. When the doctor came, Esther's pain was gone, but the doctor examined me and decided I needed to go to the hospital. Then on January 31, 1946, I had an operation. It was a very serious operation, and because of the loss of blood I needed blood transfusions. So Jonas Paul, who was just old enough to give, and Dad each gave a pint for me. I was in the hospital for ten days. They let me get out of bed only once before they sent me home.*

A rasping or scraping noise from the interior of the structure startles Philip. It's followed by a sound like something *scurrying* and then clear footsteps, slow and quiet at first, then hurrying away.

There is still enough daylight to see in *this* room, with its doorless doorway and empty windows, but farther in is darkness.

Hey. Is that you?

He stumbles down an endless, narrow hall lined with photographs of American presidents.

In a small room to the right, his light reveals a dark figure aiming a flashlight at him. Philip gasps in terror. It's his own reflection in the remaining shards of mirror hovering above the old sinks of the bathroom. He turns the faucet, and nothing trickles out.

Something scurries past in the hallway. His light catches the figure as it's turning a corner to reveal the boy in the hoodie.

Hey!

He hurries after him, around the corner, stops to listen. To his right, steps lead down into a basement. Something's breathing down there.

Hey, it's me, the news guy? I talked to you the other day.

Down the steps, slowly. The basement hallway is cooler, and moist. Narrower and curved with more doorways, oddly patched over with brickwork at places, as if certain rooms have been walled off for good. The walls are stained with dark splotches. One open doorway leads into an old storage room, still full of junk. Crates and boxes full of papers, manila envelopes, old maps, and insurance policies. Flies are buzzing back here in the dark. Thick, black, evil.

Why would there be flies?

When the shooter, on his deathbed, told his son that he had killed many boys, he might have claimed that it was the greatest moment of his life. Was his son envious?

Maybe his son wants to die.

Philip retreats into the hallway, follows it to its end: the old swimming pool, tiles now cracked or missing altogether. The figure is huddled on the edge, hooded, hugging itself.

Leave me the fuck alone.

Philip shines his light just to the side, so that it isn't blinding. It's a girl.

Turn that shit off.

Sorry.

A girl or maybe a woman. He can't see a thing now.

You can be alone if you want, he says.

Don't count on it.

The sound of her voice is intense in the vast, tiled darkness. Loud and echoey.

I'm looking for a kid, Philip says. He hangs out here sometimes.

There's somebody else in here, Philip thinks. Behind him or even farther down.

I don't know his name, he says, but he has a hoodie like yours.

Everybody has a hoodie. *You* have a fucking hoodie.

He wonders if she's been watching him. Tracking him.

It's gray. His hoodie is gray.

You aren't supposed to be here. It's not appropriate, dude.

You are?

I might as well own this shit, says the voice from the dark.

It isn't completely dark in here. His eyes are gradually adjusting.

My hoodie is gray, she says.

You're from here?

You're not.

Kind of, I am. My dad grew up here.

And?

Amish.

Maybe we're related, she says. Maybe you're my cousin.

You've got quite a mouth on you for an Amish girl.

Ex.

He's not sure if he believes her. There was some stripper, he remembers, the girlfriend of a reality show guy, who claimed to be ex-Amish, but wasn't.

I'm a Yoder, Philip says.

Everyone's a fucking Yoder.

Where'd you learn to talk that way?

Around, dude.

Around, Philip thinks. He's been there, he supposes. Where else is there, in the long run?

What do you want with the kid?

I'm a writer. I'm writing a story.

You're into that? Sickos and murder?

It's just journalism. I'm into elevating the conversation.

Her basic shape is coming into focus, but nothing from her face. He's probably just imagining that the area where her face should be is darker than the darkness.

The conversation about sickos and murder, she says.

It's not my usual thing.

What's your usual thing?

Fiction.

Vampires? That kinda stuff?

No vampires.

Too bad.

She flicks a lighter, a blazing little spark. For just a second the walls seem closer than he'd been imagining them, and she seems closer, too.

You're just another vulture, right? Circling round the dead boys.

Philip senses somebody behind him, flicks on the flashlight, and turns. Nothing there and the woman or girl hasn't moved.

Kind of nervous?

Philip turns off the light.

You know, one of those boys was my cousin.

One of the murdered boys.

Everybody's my cousin. A hundred and twelve.

A hundred and twelve?

How many first cousins I got. Everybody's always fucking pregnant. Everybody's always having a fucking baby.

She flicks the lighter again, and in its glow he can see her face, halfway in light and halfway in shadow. She lights a candle on the tiles beside her, and then another one.

What do you do in here?

I light candles.

What, some kind of ritual?

Kind of.

Pentagrams? Dark powers?

Satan, right.

Something metal, in and out of her hoodie pocket, flashes in the candlelight.

I'll leave you alone then.

That's what you think.

Philip mulls over the different ways he could interpret this statement, trying to settle on the least threatening version.

Maybe I can hook you up, she says.

I don't need any drugs.

You're probably a pervert.

Well, sure, says Philip. By the local standards, I suppose so.

She has the hollowed-out look of a tweaker, but maybe it's just the candlelight that makes her look like a decomposing corpse.

I'm going to turn on my light now. I'll point it away.

The beam of light doesn't make her look any better.

My cousin writes stories, she says.

Maybe I'll see you around, Philip says.

He backs toward the hallway slowly. She's fumbling in her hoodie pocket for something. He reaches the doorway and turns, hurries back down the hall and up the stairs, trying not to run, trying not to scream.

Out in the moonlight, nothing's quite as terrifying. Maybe just half as terrifying. The sky has cleared, and a cool breeze is rustling the trees. The robot sculpture, with its leg emerging from the animal trap, seems almost cheery, life-affirming, compared to his new acquaintance down below. He makes his way back toward the bridge and back through the trees, out to the lane where his parked rental car gleams darkly. He shines his light on it from a distance, to make sure nobody's crouched inside, waiting.

5

HOW DO YOU LIKE THE UNDERGROUND PRISON? the warden asks. Lonely enough to welcome even me? The warden will allow Scorpion to enjoy the sun, but for one day only. We'll treat you like a human just today, he says. Geordi scribbles that sentence—*We'll treat you like a human just today*—into his notebook. He's pretty sure he'll use it in a poem.

The warden says, I'll be leaving this prison. You'll grow old underground.

You can never go outside so I'll tell you the truth, the warden says. I hate you for ruining my eye. Nothing else matters. I'll drive you mad.

Up above, an important official is here to give the warden his promotion. Female convicts play horns and drums in an annoying military style.

Work hard and atone for your crimes, the official says to the inmates. Try to be a good citizen again.

Enter: Scorpion in chains.

Unable to stand, Scorpion falls to the ground.

Why do you stare at us like that? the official asks.

The warden says, She'll bite you. If she has enough strength left. Ha ha ha ha ha ha ha.

Everything has been leading up to this moment. Scorpion crouches waiting to strike…

Hours pass or days or weeks. The landline rings and the machine gets it. It's just Geordi's mother, warning about the dangers of identity theft.

Scorpion lunges at the warden's good eye with her sharpened spoon. Hits the lens of his mirrored shades, knocking them off to reveal the scarred hole—where Scorpion ruined his other eye, long ago. Maybe in a different film.

Musicians play warped carnival music. Mutant music. *We'll be wilder than Scorpion. Let's start a riot.*

The prison is unleashed.

Geordi stops it there and gathers his things. He feels like he's forgetting something.

There are days and there are nights, there are dreams and there is the dream. Across town, he lectures to his undergrads as if sleepwalking. Some of them are wearing cat whiskers or funny hats and he realizes that it's Halloween.

Afterwards, at the library, he researches the creation verb used in *The 8-Fold Garden of Space and Time*. The easiest translation is "hewed" or "crafted." The universe was hewed by sixty-four wondrous paths of wisdom and engraved in eight books. The Islamic world of the ninth century is a complex, haphazard cemetery. Crisscrossed by dry roads layered with footprints, leading through the surrounding orchards toward a western sky streaked with pink clouds. Every tombstone is a variant text. The powers of evil are the inhalations (a word that might also be translated as "western sky" or "abyss" or "hole") of the angel, the powers of good the exhalations (or "morning sun" or "celestial music" or "glory"), but given the bizarre and complex, almost yogic practices of breath control ascribed to the angel, it is never quite so straightforward and the intermingling of the in- and ex- halations forges a kind of vapor or alphabet of ridiculous complexity. The number of possible combinations within the text's system is infinite, because every entity—material, spiritual, high, low—is comprised of different combinations of in and ex halations. The angel is revealed as the basic structure of everything: a fiber, a pattern or mist, the walls of life and death.

From under the table, something pulls at Geordi's leg. A small child or a troll? There's nothing there, but then Urszula's plopped down on top of the table. She's discovered the most amazing things about her cross-dressing modernist.

Take a break, she says. Come along on a picnic.

I'm very busy right now, Geordi says.

Really? she says.

Geordi looks back at the text in front of him.

No, he says.

He follows her off campus to her car, which is parked a confusing distance away. First stop is The Dollar Tree Store on Shattuck. The Dollar Tree Store is inexplicably packed. It has the frenzied, jaded, "anything goes" quality of a Greyhound Station in Sacramento or Boston. Screaming children being dragged by their wrists, dazed speed freaks wandering through random configurations of Christmas wrapping paper and foam sandals and goldfish crackers. Fake flowers, cuddly bears, and soon-to-be-expired tuna. Nothing in the place costs more than a dollar. The whole city is shopping here today, but there are only two women working the registers. The alpha cashier is performing the very idea of The Dollar Tree Store. She's wearing cheap, plasticky oversized gold chains, incredibly fake eyelashes, and fake nails as long and curled as corn chips. Urszula is pondering a display of Halloween accessories in the front—skeleton garlands, glow-in-the-dark witches, and these plastic, blood-red goblets with embossed silver skulls.

Just what I needed, she says, picking up the goblets. Perfect for our little picnic.

Geordi wanders the carpeted aisles aimlessly. Unescorted children are grabbing things manically off the shelves. They seem equally up for grabs.

In the interminable checkout line, Urszula seems simultaneously at home and garishly out of place. Like a former Nazi hunting for bargains in a Paraguayan market, he thinks. She has three of the skull goblets, black napkins, and a package of hair dye. The woman on the package has hair exactly Geordi's color.

Excuse me, says Urszula to some guy who's wandered over from the other line. But we were here first.

It's all good, it's all good, says the old drunk. Those fuckers in the other line, they cut me. I'm gonna have to go home and get my Uzi and come back and shoot up the place. Ha ha ha ha.

That's not really funny these days, says Urszula.

Yeah, it's funny, says the old drunk. It's okay, she's my favorite checker anyway.

He waves his thumb toward the woman with the fake lashes and predatory nails. The mob just pulses and twitches in its liney formation and every thousand years everyone shuffles a few paces up. The family in front of him is stocking up on these fluorescent green sodas that look radioactive. The poor, thinks Geordi. How much time we spend waiting in lines. By the time they emerge, Geordi is dazed and inexplicably hungry. Urszula's car is cramped and littered with debris.

They speed toward the hills and then through the Caldecott tunnel. Years ago there was an accident, involving a gasoline truck, a school bus, and a drunk driver. Many people escaped but a few lost consciousness when the tunnel filled with smoke. They died in the fireball that followed.

As they emerge into the searing daylight east of the hills, Urszula chatters on. It's not just that Natasza, her modernist, took on this man's identity and called herself Grzegorz. It's not just that he or she traveled across Europe, that he or she met Huelsenbeck, Ball, Tzara, and Emmy Hennings at the Cabaret Voltaire. It isn't just that he or she had a sexual relationship with Hannah Hoch in Berlin in the '20s. It's not just that Urszula's modernist may have influenced not only Hoch but, indirectly, Duchamp and even Breton…

Geordi isn't sure why he's here. When they get to the 680 freeway, a flashing sign on an overpass informs them of an "Amber Alert"—a child has been abducted.

It isn't just that Urszula's modernist wrote a convoluted murder mystery in the form of a poem, she tells Geordi. It isn't just that the killer in the poem takes on the victim's identity. It isn't just that the detective and the reader both are left unable to interpret the murder and the poem.

Geordi tells Urszula that a poem attributed to al-Khali in praise of Lefty, his favorite singing Persian boy, asserts that although he has no idea what the boy's song means, and never will, since it exists as he is writing only in memory, he applauds the song out of love. Urszula isn't sure what Geordi's point is. The poem goes on to suggest that what he means by love is the "disintegration" of the heart, says Geordi.

Oh my god, says Urszula. It is just like that in the murder poem.

Geordi tells her that legends, perhaps instigated by the actual author of *The 8-Fold Garden of Space and Time*, explained that the sage who supposedly wrote it died prematurely, from mysterious convulsions, as punishment for revealing forbidden secrets before their time—thus enhancing the prestige of the teachings.

Yes, says Urszula. But what is your point?

Geordi shrugs. He's pretty sure he doesn't have or need a point.

Are you hungry? she asks. Grab a snack from the basket in back.

Geordi digs through its beautifully arranged fruit, cheese, crackers. He eats a grape but finds himself unable to continue. Urszula talks about poets he's never heard of—Milobedzka, Krynicki, Biloszewski. She describes them as eccentric introverts who burrow into the confined spaces of their poems. They shut themselves up in cramped little stanzas. She stops in downtown Pittsburg to get some wine. Urszula insists—you cannot have a picnic without wine. The downtown is empty of anything but the blazing sun. Urszula tells Geordi that Polish poems are received completely differently in America than at home. Here they are just this product that represents "history." Americans think they don't live in history anymore, she says, but they suffer this nostalgia for it.

And so they read the Poles for our deprivation, she says. Our despair, our black humor, our sense of "Literature."

They pass through Antioch. Bleak little houses with walled-off backyards where abducted children would be found. They cut south on a little road heading into brown and desolate hills. They've arrived at their destination: Black Diamond Mines Regional Park.

Black Diamond means coal. There were active mines here from the 1850s to the early 1900s.

I love it here, says Urszula. It is savage and like another planet.

The hills are giant hay mounds peppered with gnomish trees. Hazy clouds make it all seem like a candy landscape—a harsh, brittle candy. It's not so exotic for Geordi. It's familiar and hallucinatory, like the landscape east of his childhood. Dry and crackling and beaten down by the sun. They sit at a picnic table and Urszula eats delightful little sandwiches and cheeses that Geordi just politely nibbles. He's too hungry to eat, but Urszula eats ravenously and pours wine in their skull goblets. The sort of goblets that poison would be served in, he supposes. Somehow, he thinks, this has all happened before. It's as if he's replaying some dreadful scene, or that he's glimpsed this afternoon in nightmares: the afternoon of his death, or something very much like it.

Urszula has definite ideas about poetry. It isn't to be *merely* a collection of precious details and moments, she tells him. It isn't to be *merely* a chopped onion to provoke sentimental tears or to mourn the passing of the days, she says. It isn't to be *merely* a megaphone for the whiney egomaniac's petty complaints against life or the body or the emotions. It isn't to be *merely* a podium for self-promoting stylists. It isn't to be *merely* a bulletin board for well-meaning social appeals.

The wine tastes funny and Geordi's feeling very strange. He's pretty sure that he likes poems that do all of those things.

It isn't to be *merely* a voice for the voiceless, Urszula continues, or a lament about the impossible set to a catchy rhythm. It isn't to be *merely* an absurdist Frisbee tossed gleefully into the void. It isn't to be *merely* a game played with language at the expense of possible meanings. It isn't to be *merely* a technical if futile assault on the edifice of culture. It isn't to be *merely*…

Then what is it to be? asks Geordi finally, unable to take another sentence.

It is to be a Heraclitean mode of thinking, says Urszula.

A poem is a kind of murder, says Urszula. A poem is a sacrifice aimed not at the future but at the present. A poem is a resistance to ossified language and symbol systems that create a false, static sense of reality. A poem is a crack in the edifice of a centralized and petrified imagination. Evil, says Urszula, is a product of stale language. Language must boil and fluctuate. A poem must not be afraid to kill, she says.

I never knew you were a poet, says Geordi. Are you a poet?

I write novels, says Urszula. It's more or less the same thing.

She pours him another goblet of wine. The silver skull winks in the sunlight. Not a goblet, not really. It's just plastic.

The most centralized and hardened and dead metaphors are those of gender and of heterosexual relationship, says Urszula. They must be toyed with and either transformed or eliminated without mercy.

She talks about the political situation in Poland, which is very bad right now for gay people, horrible. Poland is ruled by evil twins, she tells him. They are telepathic with each other, and the only way to tell the difference between them is the mole on Lech's nose.

You're making this up, says Geordi.

You do not read the news, says Urszula.

They hate gay people, minorities, they let the mobs run around, the beatings, the murders, they look the other way. They were child stars in this movie *The Two Who Stole the Moon.*

They love Bush in Poland, Urszula tells him.

Geordi imagines vast winters full of potato patches and orphans. Urszula is gazing into the distance with her cruel, peasanty face. Her teeth are crooked. He knows nothing about the cold winters she's passed through.

There's nobody else out here, nobody but them.

She's onto her Polish modernist again. It's not just that the male identity Natasza ultimately took on seems to have belonged to an aspiring poet who she met in 1915 in Prague, when she was fresh out of the mental institution. It's not just that the aspiring poet died under mysterious circumstances…

It occurs to him that Urszula is not at all who he thinks she is. In fact, he doesn't know who he even thinks she is. He might have been abducted that day as a child. He might have been drugged.

He stands up, wobbling.

The lesbian community in *this* country, Urszula says. They don't realize how borderline pedophile and Republican they are.

Her non sequiturs are probably designed to distract him from her sinister intent. He wonders if she put something in the wine.

Come, she says. Let's go for a walk up the trail. You have to see this.

It's happening again, thinks Geordi. But he doesn't know what *it* is. In the nouns derived from the verb *ana*, there are no clear semantic grounds by which to distinguish between *an imprisoning captivity* and *an affecting preoccupation*. The two serve as metaphors for each other, but determining what is the metaphor for what, in terms of prisons and obsessions, is sometimes an impossible task. He knows better than to follow this woman, although it's probably too late.

Up the trail it is surprising and it is beautiful. A different kind of landscape, with skull-like rocks and animistic cliffsides from the American Southwest. Lichen on the rocks in organic patterns. Orange and yellow, textured like imprints of calligraphy over the equally weathered and intricate stones. Scat on the trails, almost black but with little red berries mixed in. What carnivorous creatures live here? They pass the entrance to an old mine, with the year 1930 engraved overhead. Urszula stops to rest on a bench. Geordi wanders up the trail on his own. *And then he followed a road.* You can see the oil refineries and the polluted delta in the distance. On the rocks, lovers have engraved their names. *Luis Loves Lupita.* Higher, higher up the trail. Those wind farms in the distance. Sandstone, smeared orange and red. Smooth. The hills from up here like woven wheat-colored mats with inlays of black fungus. Wheat-colored grasses mixed with darker patches, purplish, the color of shadows. What did he think earlier? *Giant hay mounds peppered with gnomish trees. Hazy clouds, a harsh, brittle candy.* If he survives the afternoon, he'll use the image in a poem. The poem will also be a murder mystery. The hills are shaped like women making love. Along the trail, the bright purpley red manzanita trees. Fleshy, with roots sticking out of the dusty textured hillsides like arterial veins in the hieroglyphic earth. Coulter pines. Something he thinks is called smoke bush.

They found the body of Geordi's father back among some trees. A trail through the mist and pines, off the highway. He was traveling over the mountains to Reno and had parked and walked up the trail, maybe in a daze. A little girl discovered the vague shape on the ground, bluer than the fresh snow that surrounded it. His father's corpse. He had a stroke, they said. Geordi believed his father had been dying, little by little, for years, but nobody had noticed. The birds had pecked out his eyes.

He wanders back down the hill. Urszula is smiling funny.

You love to think of yourself as lost little boy, don't you? she says.

Come, sit, she says and pats the bench.

Her topics all blur together. It isn't just that he or she died in a mental institution. It isn't just that skinheads are attacking gay rights marches. It isn't just that Poland is sliding into fascism. There's no sense to her woozy, brittle words. Geordi realizes that she's talking only to distract him and that she's going to kill him and take his identity. She'll dye her hair and go off into the world as a man. As Geordi. She'll publish poems or even novels. As Geordi. She is a killer and he is her victim.

He's not sure what the protocol is for such a situation.

Did you look in the mine? she asks. Come.

Probably manners aren't the appropriate response. She's leading him to his death and Geordi is just stumbling along beside her. The poison has made him so light-headed.

There are train tracks leading into a gaping doorway in the earth. A locked metal fence, but cold air rushes out of the mine. A lightbulb burns inside; maybe they give tours. The air blowing out smells…sulfurous? It's freezing. Geordi's dizzy. He's fainting and it's all the same thing. Fainting or dying. Murdered, abducted, poisoned, a poem. And it's okay to faint, he realizes as he's falling deep into the center of the earth. You just let go…It's okay to faint or to die, either way.

The moment of letting go is such bliss.

Between the tenth and twelfth centuries, *The 8-Fold Garden of Space and Time* was interpreted by rationalists and scientists. In the second half of the twelfth century, it was adapted by esoterics, mystics, and kabbalists.

Sometimes in dreams, a luminous writing appears, a hieroglyphic scripture that seems to represent all of the living and all of the dead.

His grandmother is about to tell him the secret—the thing that happened that day he set off for the cemetery. Where is she? She's huge. *Mija*, she says. *Mija*. Abuela, says Geordi. What are you talking about? You're a lesbian, *mija*, she tells him. Geordi looks down at his own vagina. What a relief. He's falling.

A fire breaks out of the secret depths of the lake and, blazing up, illuminates and beautifies the mountain.

Hours pass or days or weeks. Geordi is gazing up into the brightness that frames the placid face of Urszula Czaykowski.

Are you okay? she asks. You passed out.

She is just a darkness, surrounded by blinding light.

You look different, he says. Did you dye your hair already?

She helps him to his feet. We'd better get you home, she says. Here, come along.

Her face is enormous. They hobble down along the dizzying trail to the parking lot. She's opening the trunk, to shove him inside. But then it's just the picnic remains in there and he goes up front.

Just rest, she says. Don't worry, I am good driver. Where is it you live, Geordi?

He mumbles something and she says, It's not important. He has no strength. Whatever she put in the wine has sucked him dry of his essence. Of his manly power. No, she didn't put anything in the wine. They putter down the winding empty roads through the huge haystacks and the illimitable brightness. When he opens his eyes, they're crossing one of those bridges across the bay. He can't imagine why. He can't conceive of any geometry in which this isn't the wrong direction. But maybe that's the problem. The problem has always been his inability to perceive some fundamental geometry. All of the living and all of the dead.

He dozes off, remembering that he is a lesbian. Finally.

Urszula is chasing him through a funeral home that also serves as a kind of library. The walls are covered with lichen, but he knows that if he looks closely, it will turn into human hair. He knows that he's dreaming, but that's okay, too. You've always wanted to know horror, you inquisitive bitch, says the Polish modernist, so let's go. But they don't go anywhere at all.

When he wakes up again, Urszula's hand is in his pocket. She's taking out his wallet. The car is parked along some desolate road with no exit. It's twilight and they're in some strange wasteland of freeways and enormous trucks. An industrial nothingness so enormous that it seems they must have driven halfway across the country to find a place this desolate and empty. Everything here is huge, underpasses and buildings that look like canisters and just these booming trucks without drivers everywhere you look.

Where are we? he asks.

I took a wrong turn, Urszula says. It looks like I am maybe just a little bit lost.

She laughs in a way that makes no sense at all. She pops the trunk.

6

THE WOODS AROUND THE EAST LIBERTY HOME FOR BOYS are moist from the rain, rotten and wet like a lesion. In the daylight, however, the old ruin is barely terrifying. The flies are still buzzing in the old storage room, but it doesn't smell like anything's dead in there. Some melted wax around the swimming pool where the girl was sitting the other night, but no occult symbols or demonic incantations.

Upstairs, Philip scratches another mark beside the shooter's son's illegible scrawl. Another day in East Liberty.

But Philip isn't alone. He can hear somebody walking overhead.

He makes his way up to the next floor, wanders the halls, checking each of the desiccated rooms, with their frayed wallpaper, graffiti tags, and crumpled beer cans. Nothing, so he makes his way up to the former attic. It's cold in the open air and the brightness hurts his eyes. There's somebody in the little cemetery, mostly obscured, crouching next to a tombstone. There's something just beyond that looks almost like a bed. He hears footsteps beneath him.

He'd like to tell somebody: I give up.

But when he goes down a level, he sees a slight figure in a gray hoodie calmly walking away from him, toward the stairs that go farther down, to the ground floor. From behind, he can't tell if it's the shooter's son or that girl, so he just follows.

He catches up down below, where the boy is reading the messages on the wall. It isn't the shooter's son. This boy is younger, with darker hair. He looks well rested enough, but kind of stunned, as if he's still midway in a dream.

You're that writer, says the boy.

Yes, says Philip. Who are you?

Amos.

Amos. I'm Philip Yoder.

I know.

How would you know my name?

My cousin told me.

Your cousin. She's a woman?

She's a girl.

The girl I met the other night?

Amos says that he used to go to that school. He's thirteen years old.

I used to be Amish, but I got into rock and roll.

He's either small for his age or else Philip has lost his sense of how big a thirteen-year-old is supposed to be. He has black hair, blue eyes, a rounded, babyish build, although he isn't chubby. He's holding some papers in one hand, like a school report, and in the other a knife.

What are you going to do with that knife?

Inscription, that's all.

It's a much more serious-looking knife than the little penknife the shooter's son was using. Amos has a gentle, good-natured face, rounder than the shooter's son's. The shooter's son was easier to imagine acting out of misdirected rage.

Philip says, I guess your cousin probably told you I'm writing about the shooting.

My brother was shot, says Amos.

Oh.

His first thought is that Amos is lying, he's not sure why.

He asks him what family he's from. Amos doesn't respond and so Philip lists some possibilities. The Glicks? The Hostetlers? The Beachys?

You're writing a story, says Amos.

I'm writing for a magazine right now.

Amos is mangling his papers. Amos says that an author he likes is Borges and another one is Cesar Aira. He mispronounces both of their names.

I wanted to be an author, says Amos.

Amos explains to his assignment, or whatever it is, that at the old school, the Amish school, the teacher didn't like them to write about things that weren't true. They weren't to write anything that was only imaginary or that involved animals that could talk or stories about war or about magic. At the school he goes to now, in Des Moines, if he correctly spells all the week's spelling words, he gets to write a story using all of the words. Amos tells Philip that he's the best speller in the class. He used to raise a raccoon, but he had to leave it behind, on the farm. He used to sneak out sometimes at night and wander around the farm. Sometimes he walked beyond the farm all the way to this abandoned building where they used to do things to those dead boys.

It takes a second for Philip to remember that nothing was done to dead children at the old orphanage, but to the living, and so maybe two different events have merged in Amos's mind. Amos hands several sheets of paper to Philip. The pages are covered on both sides with a bland and uniform script—Courier, double-spaced. At the top of the first page is a list of words that have been crossed out. Hushed, luminous, bereaved, severe.

I am only a boy in a city full of trees, but every night I journey. While the other children of the city lie asleep and dreaming, I travel through the blue moonlight or the hushed, severe dark if there is no moon.

You wrote this?

Amos nods.

One of your brothers was shot?

Amos nods and then he says, I can't experience my mother's death.

When did your mother die?

She drove herself into a lake.

Oh, says Philip. I thought maybe Verna Yoder was your mother.

Verna is that rarest of things, an Amish single mother. Philip sat in her living room, while her son, one of the wounded boys, soaked his foot in a bucket.

They didn't find her for over a week, Amos says. Her body must have started to decay in that lake.

So Verna's not your mother.

It was probably all puffed up and bloated and maybe the fish ate at it some. I don't know, they wouldn't let me see her.

Yes, well, they probably didn't want to upset you. I'm not sure you need to experience your mother's death.

I don't like the smell of death, but I can bear it.

Amos smiles at the wrong moments and the smile is never directed at Philip, exactly.

I think of my mother as the Queen of Death. She wanted to kiss Jesus or some man for all eternity, I guess.

Well, says Philip. Okay.

She thought she could still breathe and kiss Jesus under water. She thought it was the real kind of baptism, and she didn't like her husband much.

He starts scratching at the wall with his knife. Chunks of plaster crumble to the floor.

The school I used to go to will be an all-girl school now that the boys are dead, Amos says.

He's looking directly at Philip now, while he stabs at the wall.

A school of the dead, he says. The Queen of Death allows everything to happen sometimes.

Did you have anyone to talk to?

Whatever makes her happy, Amos says.

Do you have anyone to talk to? Like a counselor at your school or something.

Humans call the forces of death, darkness, and chaos *hell*. But humans don't live in reality much.

Humans?

He looks at Philip sideways now, but as if he feels sorry for him.

I only make eye contact if I'm taking all my meds.

You aren't taking them now.

I'd rather live in reality. Rock and roll. Rock and roll is the closest thing to reality I know. We don't need the authorities, we just need honest information.

We? Who do you mean by we?

The shooter was hanging out too much with dead people. The dead just want the living to be dead, too. But only the dead can be dead.

Do you know that boy? The shooter's boy?

The dead control us too much. It's like time, I guess. You ever hear of a paperboy?

Amos explains that in the old days they used to send children out in the middle of the night to deliver newspapers but then men started taking them. His nonsensical smile as he says this should be creepy, Philip thinks. But probably only if you had believed in some idea of children instead of ever really listening. Amos says sometimes when he wandered the farm at night, they would catch him. Who would catch you? asks Philip.

A roaring sound from above, like a chainsaw, momentarily obliterates the possibility of further conversation.

What the fuck.

It's just Esther.

Esther's your cousin? The girl I met?

The girl who told me about you. I knew you'd come back.

How did you know that?

I get confused sometimes. God and the devil. Which one is it wants to keep things going like they are? Which one is it wants everything to end?

The machinery starts up again over their heads.

What is she doing up there?

Tearing down a wall.

I don't think that's safe.

Nothing that's fun or useful is safe, Amos says.

A horrible sound of machinery colliding and grinding a structure.

You're a smart kid, aren't you?

I'm the best speller in my class.

Philip goes out the back door to see if he can see what Esther's doing from the outside. Amos follows him and plops down in the grass. Esther appears at a broken window, wearing welder's goggles and her gray hoodie.

Don't worry about it, dude. It's under control.

She disappears. But instead of the noise of machinery, there's music. Some sort of death metal. Amos nods his head in rhythm, but as if in time to a different rhythm than the one the musicians are playing.

Within that rhythm, Amos tells Philip his story. Philip gathers that Amos was Amish when he was "a baby" and "a little boy" until his mother left the church to marry a man he refers to only as "him." This man, his stepfather, has been involved in various investigations, spiritual matters, and journeys by train, and is a dark force in the boy's life. After his mother killed herself, he was left under his care in a fantastic realm of murky lakes, evangelical ministries, and trash-filled basements called "the Ozarks." He returned to live with his Amish grandparents, until he left the church to pursue "rock and roll." He's been living with the members of his cousin's band, Wrath of God.

Dan Beachy is your cousin? I have his number.

Everybody has a number.

Philip shows him the picture of the shooter's son in *People*.

Oh yeah. That boy.

He starts offhandedly stabbing the dirt with his knife.

I'm pretty sure he's a ghost.

He's not a ghost, says Philip. He's the shooter's son.

I think he's coming from the future, Amos says.

He's here now. I just met him.

In the future, he'll be a ghost.

We'll all be ghosts. In the future.

He looks at the moist dirt that's sticking to the blade, wipes it off on his thumb and forefinger.

Did he know your mother?

How could he know my mother.

I don't know. Maybe you were friends.

Or enemies.

Philip gazes into the woods. Leon might say that this is just a network of shadows that imprisons reality. The world of pain and punishment. Nothingness turned into imaginary laws.

You know the boys, right? Philip says. The ones who were killed.

Somebody always has to die.

For a moment Philip feels like he's found a child he lost, in the woods, so long ago that he has no memory of it. Philip thinks he needs to tell Amos something. But he doesn't know what it is.

You seem like a nice man.

I don't know.

He looks directly at Philip, but says nothing.

He's here now, says Amos.

He points through the trees. Somebody or something turns and hurries away into the brush.

That was him? The shooter's son?

It's okay if you go after him.

Hey! Stop, I just wanna talk to you!

Wait for me here, he says to Amos.

Careful, Amos says. People drown in that river sometimes.

Philip runs into the trees. He doesn't see the boy anywhere, so he listens. Sticks cracking? The wind? Footsteps?

The path's a mess. On a path, always a path. Twists and turns and returns to somewhere you feel like you've already been.

A gloomy pilgrimage, going anywhere and nowhere. And then back to the source. You're constantly going to and from that place. You go out and discover your way. You return and the door's open for you. It's like breathing.

Philip smells cigarette smoke. The boy's a couple of yards away, leaning against a tree, puffing away.

You'll ruin your lungs, Philip says.

I don't care about my lungs.

You don't care about breathing.

He looks like he's been crying.

I'm not going to talk to you, the boy says.

Why not?

You know why.

Because of your father.

I'm not going to talk to you.

He pokes his cigarette at the air, at the sky or at a ghost.

My father had a knife.

Your father had a gun.

There was a package in the mail.

A package.

He tried to untie it but the knot was too much so he had to cut through the twine with his knife.

The boy won't look at Philip.

I knew he was going to do it. He was thinking about his crime like that.

Like opening a package.

Like cutting through a knot.

Now he looks at Philip.

What was in the package?

I think it was a bloody foot. I think they amputated and mutilated his son. It was either what was left of a foot or a baby.

His son. You're his son.

I went to see that band, you know. They played an all-ages show. But the other bands down there are so lame.

The sky is buzzing or the trees or flies or an exploding star in a distant galaxy.

Did your father tell you something?

He wouldn't read anymore, he had dreams.

Dreams?

They were bad.

Bad how?

He said to turn back.

What did that mean?

I'm going to disappear.

Don't do that.

Why.

He rips a brittle branch off the tree he's next to and cracks it in two.

Don't write about me, he says.

Possibilities are opening up and closing down. Philip can feel them like different branches in a network or web inside his mind, his life, inside time.

If you don't want me to.

Please.

The boy hurries off toward the bridge, and then starts running.

Back at the ruin, Amos is gone and Esther is on her way out.

Hey.

Yeah, what?

Where's Amos?

He had to go.

He's your cousin?

I have to watch out for him.

Seems like he needs somebody to do that.

She's smirking, but it doesn't seem to be a disagreement.

Happy fucking Halloween, she says.

I want to talk to him some more.

He'll be back.

He comes here a lot?

They want him back. Turn him into one of them.

Who's they?

The cult. The Amish. The family.

Philip digs in his back pocket and finds a motel receipt, writes his number on it, and hands it to her.

Have him give me a call. I've got his story.

He's got a whole bunch of stories. Like eight or nine stories.

She's already walking away, toward the woods.

He's a little freak, she says.

Philip assumes that's a compliment.

She says, What his mom did really messed him up.

Philip says, She drove into a lake.

Two times. Two different cars. The first car was still fucking down there when she drove into it the next time.

Her tone of voice suggests that she finds it ridiculous and yet admirable, in a way.

He'll be in touch, she says. I'm sure.

She shrugs and walks on, into the trees and toward the bridge.

He's alone now. The sun is setting. Earlier every day.

Later, the stars come out. It doesn't seem to have anything to do with Iowa at all, this sky.

The things Philip's learned, the places he's been. Deep beneath the earth. Intersected by fibers, rhizomes, roots, mineral skeletons, ghosts. Tremors rumble the planet's dreams and vibrate the phantom web attached to his own two eyes. The tremors are voices in the process of fading away. Do the voices come from above or from deep within the earth? They come from all around. They are the same, and they come from all around.

7

AH HEARD YER WORKIN ON A NEW ANTHOLOGY, the email says, *and since ah've always been a fan, I thought I'd let ya'all know that I have a story ah think'd be perfect fer the book. Jes let me know and ah'll send it on yer way. All the best, Huey Beauregard.*

Felicia's position is precarious. Poised so reasonably within the flimsy, conscious crust of matter. A troop of children passes by her window, dressed up like skeletons, witches, fairies, serial killers, pop stars, and prostitutes.

Melvin isn't exactly sure where he is, he tells Felicia. He's in some strange place in America, in the vicinity of New York. He thinks he can see New York in the distance, but people just look at him funny. He's staying in a little room behind a copy shop and a psychic's storefront, with his friend. The psychic is enormous and claims to be a gypsy and the friend is another ex-Mormon, one of the gay ones. Melvin says that Jared came to New York to be gay. Apparently, New York is the place to do that.

Felicia says that sometimes young people need to get away from the people who raised them in order to figure out who they are. Yeah, says Melvin, but it's like his whole deal, it's like all gay, all the time. It's like there's nothing else left over. He's always being gay or becoming gay or, like, furthering his evolution as a gay being. Rainbow pins and I'm Not Gay But My Boyfriend Is T-shirts, and gay magazines and gay beach reading and gay stickers and gay bars and a gay gym and he doesn't even go to the gym because he can't afford it and he doesn't really have a boyfriend and he doesn't even go to the beach because he burns. It's okay, it's just making Melvin kind of lonely. Even though Melvin considers himself a window through which the *species* is keeping an eye on this. He's going to learn things. Figure it all out. What's the deal? Anyway, the psychic's going to give Melvin a reading for free or in exchange for something she hasn't figured out. Melvin wonders if the magazine is out yet. God it's been so long, he says. It's actually been just two days since he left the Bay Area, Felicia points out. The psychic is pretty much on the same page as Melvin, he explains. Her grudge isn't against flesh and blood. It's against the so-called authorities of the universe.

Are you doing anything special for Halloween?

No way! he says. I forgot all about it. No wonder.

The voice is dazzled. As if, thinks Felicia, he's been wandering around in the middle of a costume party and only just figured it out this second. And yet the voice is like a warm ray of light just for her.

I'll be back there, Melvin says. Someday.

As if he's asking her to wait for him. Not like a lover would, but like some-body would wait for the door to the invisible world to be made plain. There are only dreams.

Brian Coe is a visual artist and the long-time boyfriend of Waylon McClatchy; he's returning her call from Barcelona, where it's the middle of the night. A squalid little studio with a great view, overlooking the streets where African prostitutes hang out. The studio's back door gives way to a rooftop which no-body else uses, effectively giving Brian an enormous deck. Brian is now sitting outside, in the dark, by the window, watching the tall, beautiful women call out to passersby.

Felicia helped Brian edit the Foreword to Waylon's collected poems, reissued after his death reinvigorated the market for his work, back in '97 or '98. She never cared much for Waylon's poetry. She'd loved his only novel, however, an artfully concise story about the narrator's relationships with the sad girlfriends of the hustlers he slept with. Krissy, Crissie, Adrian, and Cheyenne.

There were actually only three of those girls in real life, Brian tells her. They were all girlfriends of the same guy, who was nothing like the guys in the book. Lucky. Waylon couldn't stand to think too much about Lucky, who was proba-bly in love with him in some passive-aggressive way.

Waylon didn't want to be loved at that point, says Brian. He was already dealing with the idea of his own death in those days and it kind of eclipsed the notion of mutual dependency. He loved all of them, that's just how he was, you'd never guess it from his poems, but he really couldn't bear the idea that somebody else would miss him. No more painful good-byes.

Or maybe he didn't want anyone else's desires tying his spirit to the earth, suggests Felicia. He was ready to move on.

To become nothing.

That's not me, says Brian. I'll sit up in my coffin and cry *Love me love me love me* until the last shovelful of dirt is dumped on my head—but it makes sense for Waylon. But he couldn't help making people emotionally dependent on him, it was just his charm, who could resist it? When I came along, he thought he'd finally found the person who could be with him and then mourn him circumspectly, who could grieve and then carry on.

And did you?

Brian laughs.

You met me around that time, says Brian. What do you think?

You were carrying on, says Felicia.

Acting out more like it, says Brian. But yes, I carried on.

A group of trick-or-treaters is careening lethargically up the street and so Felicia shuts off her lights. Now she's the one sitting in the dark.

Waylon had brainwashed me enough, says Brian, that I actually thought I believed that I gave some sort of shit about Waylon's work and Waylon's legacy. That somehow his poems were a replacement for him.

The masked children pause in front of her house. Cannibals disguised as children. Demons, monsters, hungry ghosts.

I think Waylon would actually appreciate it, says Brian, if I peddled some long-lost McClatchy poems and spent the money on hustlers and drugs. He left enough garbage around. *Breakfast at the Porn Shoot*, that was one. He was always joking about it as the worst idea for a poem he'd ever had, but you know, it's still there. And then there's his epic poem, his secret life's work. It's basically a laundry list of all the guys he tricked with, but years before he died he decided it was too derivative of Tony Duvert. He didn't stop adding to it, though.

The group moves on, except for one Screaming Ghost who might be staring right at Felicia. It's impossible to tell.

I could write my own shitty poems and pass them off as Waylon's, if I wanted to.

If we could get something unpublished for the anthology, that would be amazing, Felicia says.

Brian says that a whole crew of scholars is always sniffing around. They've found pages of his epic poem in the archives, they think the world deserves it. The people have a right to know. An academic industry has sprouted from Waylon's corpse and then there's that hideous biographer, Jody Frost. Jody resents Brian horribly, can't understand how this vulgar barbarian has become guardian of the secret, unpublished work of the great master.

At the gate, the Screaming Ghost is still staring at Felicia, or staring at nothing. Wasn't Waylon one of Huey Beauregard's early supporters?

Oh, don't talk to me about that horrid little creature, says Brian.

Waylon was second, right after Benton Archer. Benton and Waylon were working on this collaboration with the artist Clyde Rosedale, you ever see that? A so-called children's book with stuffed animals? Bunnies get tortured and murdered, teddy bears are emaciated and dying from AIDS.

And then Benton hooks him up with this kid, this little genius, says Brian. Waylon's a sucker for that kind of shit. Next thing you know he's just always on the phone with this kid, who's always whining about how miserable he is, how his writing's no good, how fucked-up he is. You know, just fishing for sympathy, compliments, whatever it is. And Waylon's dying, but he's always up on the phone reassuring this kid that he's brilliant, that life will get better, that he shouldn't cut himself or find somebody to murder him.

Philip Yoder's convinced he's a fake, says Felicia. That he's really some forty-year-old woman, like in that Armistead Maupin book. He's kind of obsessed, actually.

He's some kind of con man, that's for sure, says Brian. You know he sent Waylon a picture of himself years ago. This cute little punk rock kid, perfect looking but with bad teeth, and Waylon's just creaming himself. That was his thing, you know. Handsome guys who wouldn't smile because they're too self-conscious about their mouths, full of teeth rotted out from all the refined sugar they were fed in their ghetto childhoods. Or trailer park childhood, in my case. And then Waylon would make them smile, he was so charming, and the guys would crack and grin and radiate this vulnerability with their dreadful teeth that would melt Waylon in turn. You'd never know it from his poems, but he was a real mommy at heart.

Oh, I can totally see it, says Felicia. His stanzas are like sad little orphans he's bathing and brushing their hair and sending them off to school.

Oh god, that's horrible, says Brian. It's exactly how he was.

The creature out front is shoving some candy in the Scream-hole of its mask.

According to Brian, Waylon couldn't love anyone, didn't have the capacity to love anyone, not in a romantic sense, an erotic way, who hadn't been just totally fucked over as a kid. Poverty, abuse, neglect. We were all sad little orphans in one way or another, he says.

But Waylon grew up rich, right?

His childhood was atrocious, too, says Brian. But the markers were less obvious. He couldn't love people like himself, maybe he couldn't love himself. But that sounds a little too easy, doesn't it? I think he did care for himself. I just don't think he found his own psychological makeup particularly sexy.

By the way, Brian says. The picture Huey sent Waylon? Looks nothing like that weird munchkin creature that's splashed all over *Vanity Fair* these days with Rosario Dawson and Debby Harry. Those perfect little teeth.

The picture on his book jacket isn't him either, says Felicia. It's a picture of some kid Benton Archer used to know.

Why doesn't somebody ask him where he got his dental work done when he was bouncing around all those truck stops and meth labs? Brian says.

Could he have known about Waylon's thing?

I don't know, says Brian. Maybe something Waylon said during one of their endless, endless fucking phone conversations. Or maybe he actually read the novel, you could probably figure it out.

The child crumples up the candy wrapper, drops it in Felicia's yard, and walks on.

I'll tell you, Brian says. When Huey found out that the pictures and other letters he wrote to Waylon had been put in Waylon's archives at UCLA, he got all bent out of shape. Waylon was almost gone at that point, but Huey was relentless, made Waylon write in a requirement that they could only be seen with Waylon's direct approval.

Like there's something in there he doesn't want anyone to know.

Maybe just those fake pictures, says Brian.

Or maybe something else, says Felicia. How does one get permission at this point?

Oh, that's easy, says Brian. From me.

In Felicia's favorite Anna Kavan story, the narrator is driving around in the fog and sees a group of long-haired teenagers *bobbing around in the fog like horrid Halloween pumpkins with candles inside.* She's on heroin and runs over one of the hippie-like creatures. Felicia's pretty sure the narrator's a woman, but maybe it never says. The police come and get her, but nothing seems real. Just masks and fog until the end when the distance and irreality begin to unravel and she wishes she could go back to the way it was, to feeling *like no more than a hole in space.* She wants to be nowhere *for as long as possible, preferably forever.*

The allotted time for children to beg for candy is over, but Felicia's still sitting in the dark, still on the phone. I'm dressed like June Cleaver, Sonya tells her. But I think it's too subtle.

My costume is entirely mental, says Felicia. I'm Celia Abad. I'm sitting in the dark, in that mental institution in upstate New York.

Hold on a second, says Sonya. The baby.

In Felicia's favorite Joy Williams story, a girl is getting a tan. Her name is Pammy. In the health spa, she is all by herself in a small room with a tanning bed, a long bronze, coffin-like apparatus. She is there under the ultraviolet lights. She has tested positive for tuberculosis, although she isn't ill. Under the lights, she thinks about many things: magic and Snow White, skating and delusion. The door opens. A man steps into the room and stares at her in silence. What? says Pammy. The figure closes the door without speaking.

At the moment, Felicia is the one who is cozy and blessed, surrounded by benevolent voices. Someday, she'll be the one who is hunted and wounded and cast into the dark.

Okay, Sonya says. What was I saying?

You're behind the sofa. You're down on the floor.

Right, she says. She had ducked into that sleek, horrible room so that Mike wouldn't see her. She could hear the voice of the mystical investment manager, so loud, horsey, and then the faggy real estate agent's voice, a sound like an inept pianist. And then he came into his office and Sonya hid. And the whole time I'm down there, she says, the faggy real estate agent is relentlessly clicking away at his computer.

Sonya had assumed his frenetic typing had to do with the pornography of real estate, posting and perusing listings, but the man's desires were far less sublimated than that. At a certain point, the relentless clicking stopped. She heard the man approach. She heard the man settle himself on the leather sofa she was hiding behind, but from the elaborate squooshing noises he made, it was clear he wasn't just sitting casually, looking at magazines or contemplating his commission. She lay perfectly still in the clown costume for what seemed like hours, as he occasionally jiggled or squooshed or even grunted or sighed, maybe it actually was hours, she began to think about the craziest things...

She remembered a dream her mother had told her about. Her mother had dreamed about a new mall west of town, it was supposed to be really grand. There was a little lake or something, a theater. She thought about a Chinese movie she'd recently seen about miners who would pick up these boys who needed work and then they'd murder the kids and stage phony accidents in the mines, collect the insurance money from the mining company. She thought about darkened sex mazes filled with men. She thought about women who were kidnapped and sold into marriages with disgusting men who wanted children and slaves, and she thought about women who were raped and then imprisoned or even stoned because they'd committed adultery and she thought about girls who were chained in the basement by their fathers and raped and impregnated and about paperboys who were kidnapped and turned into sex slaves by dumpy pizza delivery guys in Missouri towns. She began to feel oddly happy and at peace, there in her clown costume and unable to move. She thought about all the forms of slavery that still exist and that had ever existed and would continue to exist in every imaginable future until finally she heard someone come in. She could see the new guy's reflection in the window behind her, and it was the most terrifying thing she'd ever seen. He was wearing some sort of leather hockey mask, kind of *Silence of the Lambs*, kind of *Halloween*, and naked from the waist down. She stifled a scream, but leapt to her feet. The masked man stopped approaching, but the sight of the real estate agent—who was facedown on the leather sofa, naked, squirming in anticipation and with an oblivion pasted across his face that had to be drug-induced—immediately calmed her down. She had again become the most sinister person in the room, an uninvited witness to their choreographed scene. The masked man said something that sounded to Sonya like *You first*, and when the real estate agent registered her presence, he smiled at her as if she had stepped directly from his most avidly desired but least conscious sexual fantasy. Without missing a beat, she slapped the ass a few times, and grunted—she wasn't sure if they knew she was a woman—then motioned for the visibly excited masked man to take over, and slipped out the way she'd come in, through the front door.

Felicia has to admit that Sonya's ending is more entertaining than any of the more lonely possibilities she'd have dreamed up. The image of herself as a married woman makes her want to scream, and she tells Sonya so.

I hear you, says Sonya. Try being Mommy.

Outside, the street is empty. No little monsters in sight, just a vague sense of something lurking, some potential mayhem. Geordi should have been home hours ago.

It was the poet Joshua Clover who said to Felicia that the major function of artists in the late twentieth century was to drive up property values. When the house Felicia lived in, in San Francisco, went up for sale, so many years ago, the owner was asking for too much money. Felicia had never met the owner, but the real estate agent agreed that he was clueless and kind of greedy. He worked for the government, she said, but Felicia already knew that. It wasn't a bad situation. Felicia's roommates were an activist she'd had a few classes with at State and the activist's friend, who now worked in a bank. The banking girl stayed at her boyfriend's almost every night and the activist traveled a lot; her parents were rich. Felicia was left to deal with the real estate agent, an older woman named Carol O'Toole. Carol O'Toole had a glass eye and a scar on her face, like Geordi, although Felicia didn't know Geordi yet.

Felicia hadn't been frightened of her own solitude in those days, just slightly alarmed by what she was sometimes willing to risk in order to make the solitude more interesting.

Every weekend, Carol O'Toole would have an open house. Felicia would leave or just hang out reading or writing in some cranny while dozens of strangers traipsed in and out of her home. This went on for months.

Carol O'Toole had studied literature in college, which must have been in the late '60s or early '70s. She guessed that Carol O'Toole had experimented with drugs and written poetry and dreamed of living a bohemian life but, after a bad marriage or two, had settled into a life selling real estate. She got this idea from the wistful way that Carol talked about Felicia's possessions. There were so few of them and they were mostly books. This paucity struck Carol O'Toole as a kind of freedom and it made Carol O'Toole pine for her literary youth.

Fewer and fewer people showed up for the open houses the longer they went on, and so Carol O'Toole would sit around in Felicia's living room every Sunday afternoon from two to four and read Felicia's books. She gazed at the refrigerator magnets Felicia had arranged into cryptic word arrangements and she read the poem that Felicia had taped to her refrigerator then, and which she still has taped above her desk but rarely thinks about anymore, written by a fifth grade boy she had worked with. *Scared. Scared in a town*, it begins. One afternoon, Felicia found Carol O'Toole thumbing through Joseph Goebbels's awful novel *Michael* with a blank look on her face. As time went on, Carol O'Toole seemed to feel more and more comfortable hanging out there, and Felicia started to fear that she'd come home some Sunday evening, at 4:30 or even five, well after the time that Carol O'Toole should be long gone, and find her still there, passed out on the futon, having gorged herself on all the drugs, liquor, and poetry in the house. Carol O'Toole did find Felicia's first novel in the stacks one Sunday and asked Felicia all about it when she got home. It wasn't until several weeks later, however, that Carol O'Toole showed up with a copy of *Heart of Glass*, hot off the press, that she'd seen in the window of Modern Times. Felicia was appalled. It was one thing to have anonymous readers, friends, and even family members thumb through her unconscious. It was quite another to have this random woman who'd been intruding in her physical space now peering into her mental space as well. She felt somewhat raped. Felicia had never been raped, exactly, but she'd had a couple of experiences that were close enough, and so she felt completely justified in considering herself to have been *somewhat raped* by Carol O'Toole. Later, while the house was in escrow, Carol O'Toole gave Felicia several of her own poems to read. They were about avant-garde composers, starry nights, cruise boats, and the wonders of nature, and Carol O'Toole wanted Felicia's opinion. It was impossible for Felicia to read the naked longing in those poems and still feel *somewhat raped*, although technically, she thinks, the polite encouragement she'd felt compelled to offer constituted a continuation of that rape. And then Robin Sullivan, a poet and Felicia's former coworker, completed the purchase of the house and Felicia was evicted and never saw Carol O'Toole again.

When Philip hears about the archives in LA, he practically flips.

You have to go, he says.

Maybe over Christmas, Felicia says. We have to go down anyway to see Geordi's crazy mother and crazy sisters.

One sister's voice has become, in her forties, that of a chirping baby.

So when you talked to Raymond, Geordi wasn't there, Felicia says.

Is the library open all night? Philip asks. I bet he's still at the library. He's probably fallen into a particularly dense passage of *The 8-Fold Garden of Space and Time*.

But he's not answering his phone, she says.

He's fine, says Philip. Geordi can take care of himself.

Philip's back at his motel, lying down in the dark. He's not accustomed to speaking with people on the telephone so late at night. It's disorienting, he says, but in a good way.

For many years, Philip tells her, he assumed he'd die young; he got used to the idea. He had his priorities, the things he wanted to do, and he did them. Like so many others. Billy Bean, for example, went to Spain, to do a pilgrimage. It sounded awful to Philip, all that desperate camaraderie on the dusty roads, all the contrived epiphanies. Billy Bean had his epiphany: He wasn't going to die, as he'd planned. Combination therapy would keep him alive indefinitely, and *he didn't even have a 401(k).* Whenever Philip ran into him afterward, he would always say that *he didn't even have a 401(k).* Billy Bean was a couple of years older than Philip, and his T-cells were probably lower, so Philip didn't have the heart to tell him that he wasn't even sure what a 401(k) was.

Billy Bean left San Francisco shortly after that, to take a full-time job in an MFA program. Somewhere cold, somewhere full of big white people.

Felicia tells him that she bought Melvin a one-way ticket to New York. His place burned down. He thinks his girlfriend might have done it, she says. But I feel somehow...complicit.

Well, sure, says Philip. You wrote about it. Took pictures even, and then the space vanished. We all think the apocalypse comes from our own minds.

Which it does, says Felicia. It's just that Melvin...

A destroying angel, says Philip. He leaves catastrophe in his wake, the catastrophe that you were secretly yearning for.

You've never even met him.

I'm reading your mind.

No, she says. Not at all.

You're getting a little "mommy" with this, Philip says.

I know, Felicia says. It's just that I'm going to get almost 3000 dollars for this piece and it's all about him, about his interior decorating choices. And he has nothing.

I talked to my old friend Bob Miller yesterday, Philip says.

This is his introduction to a long, convoluted story in which Philip's old friend from kindergarten—they were in the Monday Red Row together—is doing meth and attending orgies, picks up a guy named John Garcia. They're supposed to go to this party in Fairfield or Suisun City, Philip tells her, and John Garcia is supposed to drop Bob off at some train station, but some force is holding them back, they don't really want to leave each other or maybe it's destiny.

Later John Garcia and Bob are speeding back toward San Jose to have sex, and probably do more speed, since how else would they be staying up night after night, sucking every dick in all of those different rooms?

On the way out of town they pass the gas station by.

Uh-oh, says Felicia, and Philip says, Right.

As they're crossing the bridge, Philip says, of course they run out of gas. There's no more power, the car is just coasting, slowing down, and so John Garcia pulls over into the right-hand lane and stops. There isn't a shoulder.

Uh-oh, says Felicia, and Philip says, Right.

Carol O'Toole's scar was much subtler than Geordi's, like a premonition.

Actually, says Philip. Never mind.

Never mind?

I'll tell you the story another time.

You're kidding.

He tells her she should write back to Huey. She should tell him if he meets her for coffee, they can discuss the possibility of including him. Act naïve, like she doesn't realize he never appears in public without his disguise.

Meanwhile, Philip has a story from a *true* genius, he tells her. Amos Yoder. According to Esther, there's seven or eight more.

Felicia has no idea who Esther is, or what he's talking about. He's changing the subject. Bob Miller's story, she thinks, doesn't end well. She thinks that it doesn't end well in a similar way to Geordi's story, if one thinks of Geordi's absence as a story. She tries not to freak out.

Who's Amos again? asks Felicia. The shooter's son?

It's like a fairy tale written from inside an Amish school or a prison or a mental institution, Philip says. Or like it keeps oscillating between different narrative horrors.

Are you sure that you didn't write this?

It's Courier. I use Times New Roman.

Philip, she says.

The shooter's son, I'm done with that, Philip says. He asked me not to write about him.

You saw him again.

He asked me, Philip says. But Amos. I think he's lying about everything. Or almost everything.

What's everything?

He says his brother was killed in the shooting, but it isn't possible. He isn't from any of those families.

Philip, she says.

But he did go to that school, he did know those boys. His cousin—I think she's his cousin—does weird rituals in the basement of the old orphanage. There's something down there, I think.

Philip, she says.

What?

In the pause that follows, she can sense the circuitous path of Philip's thoughts. It is clear enough, to Felicia at least, that the basement of the East Liberty Home for Boys has become a different zone of reality in Philip's mind.

Never mind, she says.

It's like Geordi, she thinks. He's looking for a place where the secret is buried. For Geordi it's the past, for Philip it's a basement. A hole in the ground or a hole in time. Everyone else there is already dead.

8

AFTER DRIVING THROUGH SEVERAL DESERTED, caustic portions of small thuggish cities, industrial areas with poor lighting, and past more than one clearly marked entrance back onto I-80, Urszula pulls over again. Geordi doesn't even bother to ask, but she tells him anyway—it's supposedly to consult her map, a battered, stained crinkle of paper. This map has been the pretext for all kinds of sinister maneuvers and so Geordi, in a burst of initiative, opens the door and runs into the night.

Behind him, towering above him, are freeways and traffic, on-ramps and vast apartmenty boxes towering above even those. He runs in the opposite direction into a world of fences and scattered, empty-seeming trucks and RVs keeping watch over a vast, unpeopled parking lot, and to the right a sort of bramble of blackberries. A wide path leads in the direction of the bay, but he hops one of the little fencey things, a small fence, more commemorative than adjudicating, and skirts the edges of a habitat for burrowing owls. He's still moving, more or less, toward the darkness and the sea.

The path just goes on and on. Urszula's running after him, it seems.

He passes a little beachy thing that veers off in the direction of something that might even be a racetrack, but keeps on down the path across a slender body of land that protrudes farther and farther into the bay. There's nobody around, nobody he can see, but a vague aura of clandestine populations back among the brambles and debris. He stops to catch his breath. *Geordi, Geordi, wait, come back.* She's got a flashlight, for god's sake.

She's scattering a creepy, intermittent light. Geordi always suspected somebody wanted to kill him. Or that somebody was waiting to chase him down with murderous intent, at least. To teach him a lesson that he could only learn through something resembling murder. He probably learned the lesson a long time ago, but he couldn't retain it.

He takes a smaller path to the right among the brambles and chunks of concrete, rebar, that tall yellowy plant that smells like licorice. There is a whole world back here. There are plasticky, tenty areas that seem to be inhabited. There is a lot of garbage and a vague stench of excrement: human, dog.

Is it the sound of the bay, waves somewhere crashing on some pathetic little cove, or is it just the roar of time? All of history, all of the living, all of the dead.

Smoke, smoke, smoke.

A small fire is discreetly grumbling up ahead next to a kind of canvas abode and a person sits there warming itself. A troll of some sort. And a dog, which barks furiously at Geordi, lunging and then falling back.

He's a friendly dog, says the troll. Don't mind him.

Could you…hold him back or something?

The troll speaks a few words to the beast, a thing that looks like a slightly more benevolent version of a pitbull, boxy and gnarled. It quiets and sits. Geordi is not a "dog person." Geordi finds their slavish devotion to their masters suspect, at least.

Lost your way? asks the old man.

Well, says Geordi. It's a long story.

It always is, says the old man. Pull up a seat.

He gestures toward some less raggedy chunks of concrete and overturned buckets.

Where am I? Geordi asks.

You really don't know? says the man.

Geordi weighs a few of the more obvious possibilities—he's already dead, he's dreaming or in a mental institution. He has inadvertently descended through a tunnel he didn't even notice into the underworld. He's lost his way in a dark wood about midway through his life's journey.

You're in the Albany Bulb, says the old man.

The Albany Bulb—it used to be a vast garbage dump, landfill, the place where construction debris was put, so nobody would notice it, tucked away along a less compelling shoreline. But it grew and it grew, a garbage dump protruding into the bay, and at some point it stopped being so unnoticeable and at some point—early '80s, the old guy thinks—they stopped using it as a garbage dump and closed it down and nature regained the upper hand. Trees and shrubs took root and animals came to live and eventually they turned it into a park.

So I'm in Albany? says Geordi. The little town with the desirable schools?

He's probably not even five miles from his house—how did he not know that this was here?

Do you *live* here? he asks the troll.

For the time being.

The old man laughs. He has no teeth.

His eyes light up and he leans forward, his tone changes—he speaks to Geordi now as he might speak to a companion, one of few or even an only companion, on a voyage to the most desolate regions of the Milky Way.

We're plotting the insurrection, he says.

The look on the old man's face is one that Geordi feels has sometimes belonged on his own. It had been sicklier when Geordi wore it. Now there are meandering circles of light scattering about the trail behind them.

Geordi, where are you?

Can you hide me? asks Geordi. In the…thing here that you live in?

The old man levitates a kind of flap that leads into an illuminated space larger than Geordi would have ever guessed, smelling of male and fur. It's a bit crowded inside. There are six of them, six old men conversing in a variety of languages, at least one of which is a variant of Arabic that has been out of use for centuries. One of them is explaining, in this dialect, that Abel is a word in Hebrew for vapor or breath. For the ephemeral, nothing. Abel is about dissipating or merging with the atmosphere, whereas Cain is about *acquiring*. The animal flesh. The men turn, gradually, so that it is like a kind of fluttering as their conversation dwindles—race of Cain, race of Cain, they are saying—and they are facing Geordi, smiling. The only difference between these fellows and the original troll is that, despite their grins, they seem tortured. They seem as if they've been indefinitely detained, disappeared, beaten, waterboarded, sleep-deprived, and viciously masturbated, frequently and recently.

Outside the tent, Urszula is now asking after him. She describes Geordi to the troll as *a little Mexican man*. Really? thinks Geordi. Is that the best she can do? She's saying he's about *so high* and he can imagine her holding a hand in the air. He listens to see if she'll mention the scar, but she lowers her voice. Inside the tent, the men begin describing the calamities and indignities they have suffered, at the hands of the authorities, in various languages. One of them starts blubbering. I've written it all down in my secret book, he says. Geordi's lost himself—a shadow, conversing with shadows, a dead man, the disappeared.

Noctilucent clouds.

Outside the tent, it sounds like Urszula is saying *a Heraclitean mode of thinking*. Is she talking about poetry again?

The sobbing old man thrusts his notebook into Geordi's lap.

Take it, he says. Take it with you and study it. I have it memorized anyway, but you can use it, you can use it to mobilize the insurrection, when the time is ripe, tonight, tomorrow…

Every insurrection is a part of the same insurrection, the man says. One insurrection spread out across space and time like music. Every insurrection shares a rhythm, a kind of vibration. Feel it. Feel it coming, feel it inside you, not someday, but right now…

Another one starts talking about crows. I've been walking all day, he says. I haven't sat down until just now. In Africa, the crows have white ties, he says. Bow ties, he says. Here they are all black. A crow is a person. It doesn't make sense. I've been walking all day.

She's gone now, says the guy who gave Geordi the notebook. All clear.

Outside the tent it's just the original old man, standing now, not bent exactly, but broken, nearly horizontal and propped up on his stick. The dog sniffs Geordi's crotch.

Geordi looks down at the notebook in his hand. It even has a title. The most probable translation would be *The Coming Revolution of the Lifeworld Against the Tyrants of Space and Time*. But an equally valid interpretation might be *The Foretold Escalation of Consciousness in the Face of Glory and Hell*. The old man points Geordi farther down the path. Geordi makes his way into the endless darkness, sloping downward toward the sea. He passes more tents, another barking dog, odd lights flickering in the brush. The path opens out, but guarding the sea is a dark figure. It's a womanish creature in a skirt, facing Geordi, arms raised in a gesture half welcome, half defiance next to the bay. Geordi approaches the dark figure slowly. She towers above him.

Geordi, calls Urszula from somewhere in the darkness. Geordi, please, I need to take you home.

The figure above him is both unmoving and kinetic. Arms raised, forever, in a gesture that includes him and yet that defies something he is a part of, something that has settled on top of him. She's incredible. A revolutionary matriarch. She's enormous.

Beyond her is the sea. She's a sculpture and she's made out of garbage.

III

I laughed for all the horrors I could imagine existing at that moment; for all the terrors and despairs and tortures and madnesses. I laughed to think of the strange things that were happening to human bodies all over the world. Some were feasting, some were locked in dungeon cells, some were copulating, some were singing, some were having babies, some were starving, some were weeping, some were having Turkish baths, and some were being torn to bits. I thought of the infinite number of postures, expressions, gestures and functions of the body; and these were the funniest thoughts of all.
—Denton Welch, *A Voice Through a Cloud*

1

JARED IS TAKING MELVIN on an endless journey through New York to see Ground Zero. A descent into the underground, warring tribes, and incomprehensible languages, all crushed beneath the mechanical functioning of an invisible empire—the subway's an old movie.

It's like an experience he's already had, countless times, and yet he totally hasn't.

Come on, Jared says. This is our stop.

Up above, Jared says, Stick with me. Trust me, you don't wanna get lost around here.

Where are we anyway?

It's a grid. You just have to orient yourself to the grid. There's the Avenues and the Streets...

Melvin tunes him out. A grid, no thank you. Utilities are for other people, along with schedules, personality tests, the weather. Scientists are holed up in their laboratories even now, breeding storms—among other suffering embryos. Melvin remembers a meadow once, with a storm threatening, the sky blue with black clouds towering into the upper atmosphere. The electricity in the air and the heightened visual field—it was all speaking to him. It was speaking about future life forms.

Jared wants to be the know-it-all in any case, so it's like Melvin's doing him a favor. Jared can be knowledgeable and virtuous, a martyr to the basic facts, and Melvin can get hopelessly lost. They've been playing the game since middle school.

…and the streets go from east to west…

Some burly little guy is blocking Melvin's way.

Hey baby, he says.

Baby?

The guy wiggles his eyebrows.

Share the wealth, baby.

Melvin feels brainier just walking these streets, but still not smart enough. Everything is open to interpretation.

You want…money?

Just let me have a taste, says the man.

He darts his tongue in and out of his mouth.

Okay, well, maybe another time, says Melvin and steps around the man to catch up with Jared, who has crossed his arms in exasperation.

I can't keep track of you every minute.

That dude totally wanted to rape me.

Jared rolls his eyes.

You're such a homophobe.

That's just stupid, Melvin says.

Jared walks on ahead, like he's too busy for this conversation. Too busy getting to a destination that doesn't matter anyway.

The only important question is how to feel as intense as existing already is. Sex is the easiest answer, after drugs, plus it's always on Melvin's mind anyway. The coolest thing about New York, Melvin thinks, other than the clouds, which are often silver, like the metallic ghosts that haunt the future, is that everybody here seems like a potential rapist. Really, they're all just so *fervent*.

Straight guys all think that every gay man in the world wants their ass, Jared says.

Was that guy gay?

We're in the West Village, dummy. Open your eyes. Look around.

Jared's doing that thing, where he pretends that his own highly specialized and recently acquired knowledge has elevated him into an intellectual sphere that renders Melvin relatively retarded. New York—as if he was born here, as if he's a genius at navigation because he knows the name of the neighborhood.

I'm not a homophobe, says Melvin. You oughta know that if anyone.

And just how should I know that?

Oh, come on.

Jared actually has his hands on his hips.

Getting your dick sucked doesn't make you some sort of champion of human rights. A lot of the biggest homophobes are total closet cases.

I'm not a closet case.

Oh, really? Then why are you here?

It's a detour, Melvin says.

Oh, nice.

You know what I mean. I don't know, there might even be a warrant. I'm on the lam.

So you're using me. Really nice.

He walks on ahead, without even looking back. This lasts for blocks. Melvin weighs the truth of the charges. Is he a closet case? No way. Is he using Jared? Possibly. Is he a homophobe?

I'm not using you, Melvin insists, when he finally catches up with him at a traffic light. And if I'm such a closet case...

The light changes.

Okay, so you're gay, great, finally, says Jared. Just like your little brother.

Don't talk about my little brother.

You two have both got the gay gene. Got it from your mom.

Oh, says Melvin, and you don't?

I'm not totally gay like you, Jared explains. I wasn't born gay, I just got molested and it confused my natural instincts.

For the rest of the journey, which is ridiculous, Melvin's picking through the evidence in his mind. He wonders if he was molested. He's heard that sometimes you could repress the memory—it comes back in dreams or in vague feelings or just unconventional desires. Bingo. It occurs to Melvin then that he's living with a false idea of himself. The idea he has of himself is based on the idea of himself he imagines in the minds of everyone who knows him. It's not exactly belief but a kind of hazy background noise—the idea that people are walking around out there thinking about him, with this particular idea of him, more or less true, but mostly just in the good ways—the essence of Melvin burnished into an affectionate haze and composed of his life story, the story he tells himself, at least, about his life, a story they've all memorized. Minus the porn he watches and the Sex Offenders he used to stalk and a few actual sex acts he's kept to himself and the bed wetting that started up after his mom's wedding. He could probably get rich if he could come up with a way to sell this fantasy to other people—some sort of program or website that would help everyone imagine that a blurry haze of friends was imagining them all the time. Sick.

More to the point is intensity? And awareness of intensity. Melvin is real, it's true. Slaves exist, working to make him tennis shoes. The shadow of a tree on a brick wall. A sense of stillness in the midst of all this commotion. A sense of motion, always, within the stillness. The sound of weeping from deep underground.

Look, Jared says. We're here.

Or maybe there is no point. The point is that there isn't one? Ground Zero is real. Chain-link fences and stalled construction, the beginnings of some sort of foundation. Melvin's not into foundations, in general. Terror exists and zero. Zero exists. Nothing exists, or doesn't it? It's crazy. It's madness. Silvery clouds and helicopters and forms and, in the middle of the forms, an idea: the letter Q.

The Q stands for Questioning, right? I told you I was Straight but Questioning, so how can I be closeted? I'm all up in the acronym.

Yes, says Jared. Words are a lot of fun, aren't they?

And I love my little brother, even if he is gay, so…

I think the Q stands for Queer.

Totally wrong. You don't even know your own acronym.

And you're way too old to be Questioning. Who hasn't figured out what they want sexually by the time they're like…fifteen?

No way. You're never too old to be Questioning.

Shhh, says Jared. Show some respect.

Jared stays all quiet, like he's just in awe or something. There's a bulldozer that isn't doing anything and some bald workers having lunch. Metal rods sticking up out of the earth. Melvin isn't feeling anything special. Ground Zero. He likes the phrase more than the location.

There's worse things in the universe than catastrophe and death, Melvin says.

Really? says Jared. Like what?

Melvin supposes that once something's immortal, it'll change the way it thinks, the reasons it even has to think.

Stasis. Stasis is totally worse.

People *died* here, Melvin. They're *dead*.

People died everywhere.

You can't overthink it like that.

Melvin's pretty sure this is a conversation he can win.

You have to *feel* it, says Jared. It's intense.

I can do whatever I want with my thoughts and my feelings, says Melvin. I mean, why's it intense? Hypothetically or devil's advocate or whatever? Dead, dead, dead, how many? Like 10,000 or something?

A lot, says Jared.

Okay, so death is intense. It's like number three after drugs and sex…

Number one. It's number one.

Fine, but why is 10,000 more intense than 1? Why is this spot holier than the In-N-Out Burger parking lot where my dad toppled over dead? Does something special happen when that many people die at one time? Does the membrane between life and death kind of waver with that many people passing through, does the portal open wider?

I can't even talk to you, says Jared. You're like…evil.

Membranes shimmering in the mist, in the breeze, silver clouds edged pink, and consciousness enters the clouds.

Evil, right. I'm like the opposite of evil.

That would be *good*. Are you *good*?

This world is totally like *The Matrix*, Melvin says. All our reactions, all the music and shit, they're all produced by the parent corporation. I'm not *supposed* to be sad, unless *somebody* wants me to be sad. Remember how everybody in Mrs. Shumway's class was acting all shocked and emotional and all those girls started crying and it was so fake! Everybody said so. *You* said so.

I was just a kid then. I didn't understand.

Why should Melvin weep? Somebody's already weeping, it or everything, a weeping underground. All the time. It just always is.

Anyway. Don't you think this country…*should* be attacked?

You're sick.

It took thousands of years to get rid of the kings. Finally, we had to chop off their heads, right? So how long will it take to get rid of Walmart and Applebee's?

Some places still have kings. And queens and beautiful princesses and handsome princes.

You're missing my point here.

Your stupid, evil point is just your privilege talking. What do you know about *real* violence?

Melvin says, Nigga please.

Jared rolls his eyes.

You learn that in California? What's with the thuggy pajamas anyway?

Give me a break. I'm Mexican, it's like my culture.

Mormon pajamas are your culture, but I don't see you wearing that shit.

Don't be a dumbass. Everything is *real* violence anyway. The threat of violence is exactly what violence *is*. Being born is violent, dying is violent, being hungry is violent, being monitored and watched, sex is violent…

Sex is not violent! It just isn't. It doesn't have to be, unless…

And don't forget about the hostage thing!

Once, when he was a kid, Melvin was researching the emperor penguin at the library in Salt Lake City, but a man with a bomb took hostages. A kindly librarian—she looked kind of like a man—led Melvin and several other kids into a secret room. The room was carpeted and the kids collapsed onto the brightly colored floor as if they'd been traveling for hours. One little boy was whimpering. Melvin didn't whimper but he didn't blame the kid for whimpering, but another older boy elbowed Melvin and pointed at the whimpering boy and giggled and then Melvin giggled back. When what he really wanted to do was hug the little boy and tell him it would all be all right, which was true, although he didn't really know that yet. It was exciting that somebody wanted to kill them, somebody so crazy that he was forcing the world to play by his rules, for a minute, rules that didn't make any sense. You thought there was one kind of world on TV and another one at the library, but it turned out they were one and the same. When the time was right, the librarian led them out the back door to freedom. There were police and a lot of other people, and the other people cheered. Eventually, they shot the crazy guy, who had started to draw straws for which hostage he'd kill first.

You need to get over how supposedly oppressed you are because you're a Mexican or a Latino or a Hispanic or whatever.

Everybody's wearing this, it's just the style. And I'll get over my ethnic heritage just as soon as you get over your gay pain, how's that. And the *mo*lest, whatever that was about.

Oh, okay, I forget, you win. You're a closet case and the only Mexican Mormon in the world and your dad died and you wreak havoc wherever you go and you got a nasty case of PTSD from your little hostage incident and then there's your undiagnosed bipolar disorder. Just saying. And everybody wants to have sex with you, which is just so sad, isn't it? So compared to all those people who had the building fall on top of them, you've suffered really a lot. Am I right?

A woman in a shawl is staring at them. Probably she's been listening in.

They're dead. That's the difference. I'm still here.

Yeah, too bad.

And fuck that bipolar shit. It's called moods. Human beings have them. Sometimes I'm happy and sometimes I'm sad. I'm an intense person, that's all.

You do all this stupid crazy shit, you call me out of the blue and fly across the country like a chicken with its head cut off. You tell me how much you want to see me and all that and how it feels so cosmically right for you to be with me and blah blah blah. Okay, fine. Then when you get here, you just sleep or sit around jerking off to that weird porn you like so much so that you don't have to think about your life.

How do you know what I jerk off to?

It's my computer, asshole.

And sleeping isn't a mental illness! It's called jet lag.

It's been the same since sixth grade, says Jared. Exactly the same.

Then you take the pill. You take it. You can live in their little medicated robot world all you want. And when did you ever cut the head off a chicken anyway? You've probably never even seen a chicken. I'll tell you about some *real* violence. Debbie used to butcher them right there in my kitchen, and you know what?

Debbie? Who's Debbie?

The shawl woman taps Melvin on the shoulder.

To escape the motion of *their* time, she says, we'll have to journey through a house of mirrors, a grotesque carnival spectacle, the machines that create the illusions of empire.

Excuse me?

Just remember, she says. It's the masters who are driven crazy by the dreams of the slaves.

Melvin says, That's a good point.

If this was your dream, what would it mean? That's the question.

She hands him a flyer full of 9/11 conspiracies. She smiles, a bit enigmatically for Melvin's taste.

I'll think about that. Thank you, ma'am.

On the way back to the other, less New Yorkish zone that Jared lives in, Jared ignores Melvin, messing around with his phone. Melvin peeks over.

Are you sending guys pictures of your ass again?

I've got a couple of them really going.

Hey, I wanna see, send it to me.

You've seen my ass, whatta you need a picture for.

A picture's different, right? Two different things. Ass and a picture of ass. I want the picture.

I thought your phone was out of minutes.

I've got just enough left for the ass. Come on, Jared—show me the ass.

Isn't that a little tame for you? Just a peaceful little ass?

Melvin starts chanting it—Show me the ASS, show me the ASS. Jared blushes and gives Melvin a little shove and it's a relief after all that bickering.

Jared says, You're the most cuddly terrorist in the world, you know that?

Melvin says, Do you think my little brother might have been molested? You suppose that's why he's turned out so gay?

I'm not sure he's *turned out* yet, Melvin. What is he, five?

You're the one who said he's a fag.

You don't get to use that word around me. He's gay. Or pre-gay or whatever.

Yeah, yeah, I know.

He's totally being oppressed, says Jared. That's what you should worry about—all the heteronormative assumptions he's being bombarded with. All the closeted Mormon bullshit.

The parent corporation, says Melvin. You see what I'm saying?

Of course I see what you're saying, says Jared, and it makes Melvin so happy that he gives him a hug.

Back at the little room Jared lives in, behind the copy shop and the psychic's storefront, however, Jared calls Melvin a cockteaser. The room has one window and a mattress and new carpet of the most inhuman texture. Squishy, grayish, smells like embalming chemicals. Jared's stuff: lumpy, twinkling piles of laundry, overly flesh colored, two books, posters of guys in their underwear, a mushy chair. He calls Melvin withholding, a sadist, cold, evil, and so on, like all he's been thinking this whole time they were out in the silvery light, contemplating historic catastrophes, is a list of horrible things to call Melvin. He keeps on and on like this until Melvin just pulls his dick out and says, Okay, I'm sorry, I didn't know it meant that much to you.

Jared's always going on about what an amazing cocksucker he is, but his teeth are too sharp and Melvin keeps grimacing. Jared's getting all huffy. You don't even look at me, he says. Melvin says, Is that what you're supposed to do? Jared's sighing and pouting and Melvin decides to just gaze at him kind of dreamily and see what happens next. He starts up again and Melvin keeps gazing. But at the same time he wonders if he's doing this because Jared made him feel bad or if he actually enjoys it. What is sex for anyway? To look at somebody so hard they become disgusting and then forgive them for that? He gets distracted by his own texture, his earth tones, this smooth plane of flesh, this firm mammalian thing that could totally arouse him if he forgets it's himself. Sticky and male and bejeweled. Jared's head bobbing on top of it, frantically looking up to remind himself, probably, that it's attached to Melvin. Aren't gays supposed to be different? Jared wants to pretend that there's nothing in Melvin's head except Jared, but Melvin's like: What could I be thinking about him? He likes Coldplay and Radiohead and the White Stripes, his mom still loves him even though he's gay, but his dad's just an asshole like everybody else's except stricter: no Cokes except Diet. Jared was always an aggressive Monopoly player during family night, he had a real knack for owning property. All Melvin ever wanted was a Get-out-of-jail-free card.

Sometimes after they had sex, Melvin's ex used to stare at him without saying anything. At first it was good, like naked perception and intensity, but then the longer it went on, the weirder it got, and he'd say, What? And she'd just keep on like she was looking at him hard enough to turn him ugly in her own mind, until he was nothing but a random configuration of stuff on the outside hiding weakness and stupidity on the inside. Her smile wasn't a smile of affection, it wasn't a smile from the blurry haze, the happiness that comes from blurriness, it wasn't even enigmatic, it was, what's the word, precise. It was contempt. Finally he'd jump up and knock something over, freaking out a little. Sorry, sorry, sorry, she said. She knew she was making him crazy. I'm fucked up, she said. It's part of it.

Sometimes at the dinner table his stepdad would do that. Something would slip out, just talk, kid talk, a word he wasn't supposed to say, a word he wasn't supposed to think, and Denny the fucking first would stop everything and put down his fork and just stare.

Melvin thought about murdering him sometimes. He tried to murder him magically. He thought about it so hard—one good tragic accident, why not? And freedom. If this was a dream, what would it mean? Probably al Qaeda was born from his own desires. Blow it all up, gas or irradiate the people with dirty bombs, crop dusters full of anthrax, or hijacked planes. Clear the ground, evolve *into* something. Punctuated equilibrium.

Jared just leaves without a word but later tells Melvin that Melvin has to leave the next day or as soon as possible. Melvin marches into the concrete hallway with the bathroom they share with the psychic and the copy shop and then through the psychic's back door and her special curtain. She's eating weird crunchy orange things from a plastic bag and watching a show where people are being showered with garbage. But there's money in the garbage, too, and they have to grab as much money as they can get out of the garbage.

What is it, dearie?

He's pretty sure New York was a mistake. He has unfinished business in the West. He was going through some difficult times back then.

She dims the light, caressing his hand, gazing into his eyes. He can see the appeal, but really. Madame What's-her-face warns that a conflagration is coming. Famines will occur and plagues. Right, says Melvin, but what about me?

Patience, my boy, she says. She's talking about the devil and his many guises and silent dreams, the error of his angels that they merged with the wisdom of the Knowledge Tree, their misbegotten attempt to change the order of the magic words that built heaven. She discusses pregnancies that might be brought to term through invisible secret symbols, through a reconciliation of the world with the world. Then she starts making vowel sounds. Next: Oh living water, oh child of the child, oh glorious name, oh existing one who sees the aeons, she says. Finally she gets to the point: many struggles, a long journey, loneliness, and hunger. Many will love him, he will find what he's seeking. Melvin wants more specifics about the journey.

She's seeing a large body of water. A frozen landscape but beyond that a place of mist.

One more thing, Melvin says. I'm worried about my brother.

He's in danger, but the danger will pass, she says. He's a special person, isn't he, she says. He attracts many loves.

He's only five.

Love knows no age, dearie, she explains.

Next: It's getting dark and Melvin is wandering the fervent little streets in the neighborhood. At the natural foods store he rips off a few dangling phone numbers from the Ride Board and keeps walking. He's pretty sure Jared's stuck in the present, or even the past. Melvin is ashamed of the fact that he used to believe in love. Love as it was always being sold to the general population, two people crawling through the muck of the world to gaze into each other's eyes. No, thank you. Back when he was a kid, Melvin used to disparage women who had sex only for pleasure, he used to disparage anyone as *shallow* who slept with people only because they had beautiful bodies. He's ashamed of how freely he tossed around the word *slut*. Melvin was looking for a girl that he could respect, a girl with intelligence, who would stay true to him, discuss philosophy with him, blah blah blah. If they weren't interested in what he had to say, he'd object that they were just trying to *use* him.

Now, the idea that someone would want to rape him blows him away. What the rapist will lack in beauty, it will make up for with strength, aggression, the sheer force of its desire and its will. Melvin hopes it'll use tools or something. Melvin walks past a gymnasium where a totally buffed woman is lifting huge weights, hair down to her waist and wearing a wife-beater and practically no breasts but huge muscles, and so Melvin is just walking back and forth past the window like he's so confused and helpless that anyone who wanted to could take advantage of him. Next: She flexes a muscle. She's only looking at her own reflection.

He takes the subway to the actual New York part of New York and walks some more and then wanders into a part of the park with lots of trees thinking he'll find a place to sleep. There's a few guys with serious gay rapist vibes wandering about. One of them gives him a hard stare, and then sidles up next to him.

Ever occur to you that whatever you do just sort of goes up in smoke when you die?

Melvin says, I'm not sure that's really true.

Sure it is. Good, bad, whatever. Poof.

Okay. And?

He grabs Melvin's crotch and starts rubbing, a little too hard.

Ow.

The pain of love is the deepest thing.

You're hurting me.

The night lasts forever.

I don't think we're really compatible in that way.

Believe in this, the man facing you. Right here, right now.

Melvin supposes that this painful rubbing, which he totally isn't into, is kind of like a rape. But not similar enough to make it worthwhile.

No means no, he says, and he hurries away.

He finds a more private spot in the bushes to figure something out. Maybe right now something is happening to his little brother, something that will change DJ, fuck up his brain, rearrange his chromosomes. The gay gene. It's lurking inside everyone, Melvin thinks. He realized that once, on drugs. And sometimes something happens to turn the volume up. He imagines genes as little radios tuned to whatever station. The problem is, the elite controllers and vampires are in charge of the FCC, metaphorically speaking. Melvin has trouble with metaphor, in general. He thinks he knows what it means and then he never quite does. The problem is, there's limits to what can be broadcast. That's where mutation comes in. The X-Men. Melvin's genes are tuned not to the gay gene exactly but to the Rape Me station, which is cool. The goal is intensity and cosmic knowledge. Exactly! The gay gene, on the other hand, is just this freaky little circuit or transmitter inside the body, which isn't just a secretion of the DNA, the body, not at all, you can't separate everything, one's the message and one's the alphabet or one's the radio and the other one's the atmosphere. The gay gene has an on or off switch, but sometimes it's stuck in the middle, isn't either on or off and the whole circuitry will go haywire. From individual bodies out into nations and economies, a whole system thrown off course, a ship that's been hijacked by pirates and veers into unknown crevices of space and time.

Nice. As the night wears on and the moon rises, the population in the bushes thins out and he's just standing there by himself when he hears the most disturbing commotion off beyond some trees, the shrieking or honking or gasping noises of a bird-like creature and a kind of thwacking and gargling sound. It's the most terrifying and horrible noise he's ever heard but he can't resist it. It seems to be all around him but more so through this patch of shrubs and he winds around on the path toward a clearing. Not twenty feet away is a coyote with a swan in its clutches. The swan seems to be, at least for the moment, alive, but then it clearly isn't, as feathers are flying everywhere, and blood. The coyote disappears into the trees.

Okay, so that was a little intense.

Alive! Force without personality.

Energy without shame. How do you disintegrate the empire from the inside? Maybe that's the point, the job at hand. How do you think something that isn't just the empire thinking for you? *Outside of the box.* We are the box or there is no box. There is nothing outside.

2

ALWAYS THE FRAMING. Leave out the modern building next door, the hybrid parked in the space out front. Ralph wants surfaces that convey desperate romance, the delicious follies of youth, the ravages of time. A suggestion of rubble and vacant lots, decrepit architecture halfway in ruins. He always wants the same things, if it's horror or it's porn.

We don't need to get artsy here, Tony insists. It's an action scene.

The owner of the liquor store, a former boyfriend of Tony's, has offered them use of the store next Sunday afternoon, when he usually closes. The building is stucco, crumbling. Textured like mud or human skin. A small window cracked just so, hairline fractures, asymmetrical spiderwebs. The gloomy window is perched in the beige, fleshy wall next to a torn poster: the unreal blue of an imaginary sky.

Inside, Neeraj is selling a child a bottle of lighter fluid.

Ralph says, We'll need to move the potato chip rack.

I'll worry about the set, says Tony. Set design is my department. You need to find us a star.

When he was young, Ralph liked to eat dirt with a spoon. Now, he's eating a sandwich. Neeraj is eating a sandwich, too.

I'm working on it, he says.

There's a limit to what we can film without a leading man, Tony says.

He's wearing huge aviator glasses, a huge red hat, and a huge red vest.

We can do the robbery, says Ralph. We can do the party scene. I'm shooting that porn for Sins Invalid this week anyway.

Ralph's ex-girlfriend Naomi helps run a nonprofit that celebrates artists with disabilities. They do performances around sexuality, embodiment, and the disabled body. Ralph's going to shoot some wheelchair S&M scenes for them, some medical play, some amputee adventures.

Tony says, Do we have enough extras for the party scene?

Chunk and Roman said they'd do it. Philip said he'd do it, I think he's coming back.

This reminds Tony that he needs some weed—at least an ounce. I need to de-stress, he says, from the conversation I just had with Victoria Cañada. Victoria Cañada, he repeats. The most *illustrious* writer my mother ever published.

Tony says that he refuses to read Victoria Cañada's work. As a matter of principle, Tony won't read anything about Latinos with the name of a tropical fruit in the title.

Victoria Cañada called to tell me how my mother really needs me, Tony says. Now that she seems to finally be breaking down.

Tony's mother's breakdown isn't violent or overtly suicidal, he assures Ralph. Tony's mother does, however, owe every writer she's ever published money. She's so mismanaged the accounts that even the recent death of her *second* most illustrious author can't push her into financial solvency. *Your flesh is the darkness of flowers*, wrote the second most illustrious author to a friend dying of AIDS. *Here death is born among flowers and the dead shall take root in the sky.*

The second most illustrious writer was a saint, according to Tony. But Victoria Cañada was getting on his nerves.

After having just moved out from his mother's house after two hellish years, Tony wasn't in the mood to hear about how *she* needed *him*. As tactfully as he could, Tony explains, he suggested that Victoria Cañada look after his mother, given that during the time his mother had nurtured the careers of her and a dozen other young, talented women of color, cleared a space for them, and thrust them onto the public stage, he had gone unparented. While Victoria Cañada's gritty vignettes had been given birth with utmost care, his stepfather had been masturbating in his face every day. Tony ate until he weighed five hundred pounds. Where was Mom? As tactfully as he could, Tony suggested to Victoria Cañada that he was over Mom and her breakdowns. As tactfully as he could, Tony suggested that the illustrious novelist take up a collection.

Ralph has heard most of this before. Tony's mother always struck Ralph as disinterested and self-involved, the sort of parent who might, really, be oblivious to the fact that her husband was jacking off in her child's face. But Ralph isn't sure.

Anyway, says Tony. Chunk and Roman and Philip don't constitute a *party*.

Chunk and Roman know a lot of people, says Ralph. How about you, Raj?

I'm not an actor.

Nobody else is an actor either.

No. I will not do this. Sorry.

Ralph observes Raj closely. Ralph will play the liquor store clerk in the film, with a fake-blood packet tucked under his shirt. He watches Raj chewing and becomes conscious of his own chewing, imagines how his mouth would appear to a spectator. The liquor store clerk could be eating this sandwich, he decides. Chewing has now become rehearsal. Ralph's distinguished daddy look will need to be rumpled a bit, hardened and embittered.

The botched robbery and the murder of the clerk will establish the lack of cohesion and leadership within the gang since the death of their leader (Hugo in the first film). But what about the clerk?

Neeraj, he says. What's your motivation?

My motivation?

What's your issue? Your inner conflict? What's the most difficult moment of your life?

For two years I was very sick, Neeraj says. More than two years.

He was running a fish and chips place with his wife and his sons. But he started to get headaches, dizzy spells, he was tired all the time. He went to the clinic, but nobody could figure out what was wrong. They tested his brain, they tried different kinds of pills. Nothing worked.

It got so I could barely keep us going, he says.

And then finally he went to the dentist with a pain. He didn't have insurance for dental care, but if it was an emergency, they would see him. They found an infection in his tooth. It had been there for years, a low-level infection—the hole behind his tooth was so rotten and full of pus that it had connected with the blood, the passageways going right up to his brain. It was dribbling pus into his blood and making him sick.

They couldn't numb him to pull the tooth, because when they tried to shoot the needle into his gum it was just mush. So they pulled the tooth anyway. The pain was incredible, but once it was over…within ten minutes he felt completely new. A different person. Reborn.

He smiles and shows Ralph the gap where the tooth used to be. He still doesn't have insurance or enough money to replace the tooth.

But who cares? he says. One tooth in exchange for my life, my life again.

Ralph considers his trip to Quebec five years ago, when he was chasing after Hugo, the low point of his own life. Lower even than his bad trip with Damien, when the EMTs set their dead body down in front of the picture window. That was at least a learning experience, he supposes, concisely packaged in an endless moment. The trip to Quebec, however, was an enduring catastrophe. He can't say he wasn't warned. Before he left, Philip sat down with him and told him he was about to ruin his life. His friends had had a conference, Raymond told him later, and Philip had been nominated to make the intervention. Ralph was giving up a rent-controlled apartment and a reasonably nondemanding job, a job that allowed him enough free time to film his own movies, Philip pointed out. He was abandoning these things in order to spend his entire savings driving in a barely functioning car to another *country*, where he'd be unable to work legally and would be financially dependent on a boyfriend who probably didn't even want him there. Sure, it was August, but winter would be here before he knew it. August is the worst time to travel across country, Philip insisted. You'll see only families on vacation, he said. Sick, abusive people, and their petty arguments will spill into every rest stop and diner and they might even drive into you head-on, in the midafternoon heat or even at dusk, as an answer to their own despair.

Despite his apocalyptic warnings, Philip had sold Ralph a quarter pound of weed. Ralph was going to drop it off for his old friend Vicente in Detroit, and make four hundred dollars of profit—money he'd need, he figured, to get established in Quebec. Established, said Philip, what does that even mean? Philip predicted that when Ralph came crawling back to his life, he wouldn't have enough money for a deposit on even the most revolting roommate situation. Philip pointed out that this would be the fourth time in his life that Ralph had followed boyfriends to exotic locales (Maui or Austin, Texas, or some communally owned Faerie land in Tennessee) with disastrous results in every case.

Ralph had just stared at Philip as if he'd wanted to strangle him. Because he had. He just wanted to get into the old Volvo with his things and his cat and the puppy and drive, and he didn't want to see this impulse as part of a larger pattern of behavior. The cat had become diabetic, required insulin shots twice a day. He'd had it for many years. The puppy he'd bought with Hugo, spontaneously, one afternoon when they were in the first throes of their affair. They'd run into a couple of shady queens who were selling the mutts out of the back of their pickup truck in the Castro. The puppy was cute and affectionate and so was Hugo back then, so it seemed like fate.

Ralph's radio barely received a signal (a crackhead had broken off the hollow antenna one night to use as a pipe), but as he drove across the vast emptiness toward Quebec, he would sometimes pick up meager transmissions. He slept at odd hours only when he needed to, napping at rest stops or dozing off in shady spots behind Burger Kings or Starbucks. Early in the morning or late into the night, as he drove through a brutal burning heat, through weird melting landscapes and past monstrous structures of wire and glass, with blinking lights on top, the radio would sometimes crackle alive and offer the most ridiculous songs and speech. It had been so long since he'd driven across America that he'd forgotten the country was blanketed with sound waves so surreal, so abject, and yet so oddly familiar, that they created only an odd expectancy, as if the punch line to an obscene and not very funny joke was imminent. When he lost the signal, the radio static would remind him of Damien, and he remembered other cross-country trips: in '86 with Jenny, his high school girlfriend, Tony and Damien's trip in '88 or '89, his own trip in '93 with Sasha and Damien, during the season of their *ménage à tois*. Wherever they went, Damien carried his own little radio, tuned in to a space between stations. Sasha was the best top ever and both Ralph and Damien had loved submitting to her elaborately orchestrated sex scenes in the most wildly inappropriate places. Freeway underpasses in Nevada, desert trails in Utah, rest stops in Nebraska, the deserted playgrounds of elementary schools in Iowa and Indiana and Ohio, because once she'd created the first jungle gym scene, none of them could resist. Damien got a little freaked out, not by the sex but by all that sky. Because of his childhood, locked in the basement, he would say. Ralph knew that he'd never actually been *locked* in the basement. His parents had converted the basement into a bedroom/den for Damien and his brother Troy, at their own request. Certainly their parents were strict. The boys were homeschooled and their dad didn't want them to play with most of the neighbor children, who he considered dirty and poor. Their mother rejected the ones who were left, calling them snobs with loose morals. This was exactly why the brothers wanted the basement: It had a side door into the backyard so they could sneak in or out, or sneak the neighbor boys in. Troy would read to the neighbor boys from the Marquis de Sade and suggest they act out the scenarios.

Technically Ralph doesn't "remember" Tony and Damien's cross-country trip in '88 or '89, when Tony and Damien rescued Troy from the loony bin, but after turning it into a screenplay, it's become more vivid to him than his own memories. Tony was dating Damien then, but Troy, always the more advanced of the two, had seduced Tony and created all kinds of plot complications, leading to Tony and Damien's redemptive scene of lovemaking in the cornfield as the "Un bel di" scene from the *Opera of the Night of Madame Butterfly* was thundering from the Opera Barn. Sometimes Ralph can't quite believe that he wasn't really there.

As he drove into the Midwest toward Quebec, Ralph plotted out other films, speaking into his tape recorder, creating a dialogue with an internal critic, a stern femme like Damien, or a cynical butch like Sasha, or both, two competing critics who would paralyze him with their mutually exclusive demands: More comedy! More horror! Somehow these imaginary conversations eventually converged into more or less coherent narratives full of elaborate plots with excruciating twists and turns. Sometimes the imaginary voice of Hugo would break in and demand that Ralph drive faster or more slowly, depending on his whim. Ralph thought his trip to see Hugo in 2001 would be like his trip with Sasha and Damien, an upbeat road movie, a farcical romantic comedy, but things more quickly and vehemently descended into noir than even Philip had predicted. His car broke down outside a small town in Illinois. The tow truck driver turned out to be the only mechanic in this town, which was basically a strip just off the Interstate. The heat was blazing, and Ralph checked into the only motel, a Days Inn or a Motel 6 run by a condescending Pakistani. He slept until after eleven the next day, when the maid knocked on the door. She was a white woman in her thirties with a mild aura of desperation, as if she'd lived in this furnace her whole life and was beginning to overcook. He assured her she didn't need to clean his room, it was all good. Before he left, he shoved the bag with the weed under the bed, where the cat was hiding, and then, as he was headed down the strip in the ninety-three- or ninety-four-degree heat, he thought better of it. Wouldn't such an obvious attempt at hiding the bag just call attention to the contents?

All of the businesses were on the right side of the road, with desolate, unused fields stretching off to the left. He passed a Kmart and then a bar that was housed in a trailer and then a kind of goose-and-gingham, matron-run restaurant, and then some empty space, and then he came to the four-way stop, with the mechanic on one corner and the sheriff's office/city hall on another. His poor Volvo was shoved into a back corner of the lot with all of its wiring ripped out and just hanging there, forlorn. The mechanic offered an odd explanation for the assault on the electrical system. It was a story about missed opportunities, failed marriages, and hypothetical monster mechanics in alternate universes. It seemed to Ralph the mechanic was somehow describing the actions that his evil twin would have taken, next to which his own could be understood as slightly more benevolent. The subtext was father issues. The mechanic assured Ralph that it was just a matter of ordering a couple of parts, which shouldn't be any problem to get in before day's end, and Ralph could be on his way by the next morning. Ralph, willfully optimistic, bought this preposterous story and walked back the way he came. He stopped at the motel room to get high, paid for another night, and then took the puppy for a walk in the opposite direction, under the freeway overpass, past a boxy house and a cattle gate and a field with a handful of cows and on to a little County Park neglected at the road's dead end, next to some railroad tracks that might have been out of use for decades. Or maybe not. A group of teenagers arrived at the park in a pickup truck and shuffled about, smoking cigarettes, staring at Ralph as if he was the most interesting thing that had happened in town all summer. He decided the weed was making him paranoid, but as the days crawled by and his parts didn't arrive, it became more and more obvious to him that this was in fact the case. Every morning every other inmate of the Days Inn or the Motel 6 woke and drove on toward their destination, never even bothering to take a dip in the pool, which was used only in the afternoons by unhealthy local teens and the younger children of the condescending manager. When he stepped into the bar in the trailer on the third day to get a soda and some water for the puppy, one of the patrons looked at him, as Ralph's eyes were still adjusting to the dark, and said, Oh, you're the guy from California. Ralph went and hid in his room for the rest of the day. Ralph's room was on the ground floor, overlooking a freshly paved asphalt parking lot that boiled in the ninety-five- or ninety-six-degree heat, releasing waves of pungent petroleum, but his bathroom window looked over the pool and the horrible shrieks of the swimmers invaded his dreams as he tried to nap sometimes during the relentless afternoons, because what else was there to do? If he tried to watch television, he began to feel like he'd fallen back into a nightmare he'd dreamed off and on throughout his entire childhood. Some days the maid would knock and suggest that she could spruce things up a bit and she'd wave her bottles of toxic chemicals and perfumed disinfecting sprays in his face. Every day he'd trudge down to the mechanic's, who would tell him that the parts still hadn't arrived. On the fifth or sixth day, when the temperature had risen to 97 or 98 degrees, and when Ralph's tone became perhaps just a little more insistent, the mechanic informed him, with no pretext whatsoever, that his little brother was the sheriff and the mayor of the town, and if he had a problem, he might want to talk to him, right across the street at the City Hall. *Flamingo Road* meets *Beyond the Forest*, thought Ralph. But more like *Beyond the Forest*, because there was no more powerful monster to attach himself to, as Joan Crawford had when the corrupt sheriff tried to run her out of town in *Flamingo Road*. No, he was doomed to die here, from a fever born of his own longing to escape. He'd be crawling on his hands and knees toward the train that could take him away, to Chicago, but he'd die as it pulled away, like poor Bette Davis in *Beyond the Forest*. That evening, as Ralph was eating the Thai food he had delivered every night from a restaurant two towns over, images of the murdered girlfriend of a congressman flashed across his screen, followed by pictures of people golfing, of suicide bombers in the Mideast, of a senator announcing his retirement, a vaguely porcine senator who had just had one of his own heart valves replaced with a pig's. Outside his room, the sun was still beating down. In *Beyond the Forest*, poor Bette Davis had to keep her shades pulled at night so that the bright lights from the lumber mill furnaces that churned day and night wouldn't keep her awake. Ralph found himself gasping for breath. He'd never broken out in a cold sweat before. He'd thought it was just a figure of speech. But here he was, in an air-conditioned room, with the shrieks of unwholesome teens drifting in from the pool at the back, sweating and cold. When he went out into the 98- or 99- degree heat for a walk with the puppy, across the blazing black asphalt and down the road, under the freeway overpass and past the cattle guard toward the little park, where two pickup trucks were already parked, he vaguely sensed that he was actually an experiment and that evil scientists or aliens were watching everything he did and taking notes. So many times, in years gone by, when Damien had become particularly animated in his paranoia, Ralph had worked to convince Damien that nobody was keeping tabs on him; he'd always listed the logistical difficulties of such a program, and he tried now to use those arguments against himself, but he kept hearing Damien's voice saying *Oh Ralph*. They'd both understood that whenever Damien said *Oh Ralph*, he was actually saying *Just because I was kept in a basement for most of my childhood doesn't mean I don't know more about how the world really works than you, you poor, naïve fool*. The pickup trucks belonged to the same kids he'd seen before, together with even more indistinguishable children, the same pimply, white, Midwestern faces, cynical faces, faces of kids who knew they lived in the most boring place in the world and were just waiting to escape; or faces of kids who weren't yet sure whether it was worse here than anywhere else; or faces of children who'd already concluded that every place in America was pretty much the same; or faces of kids who still lived in fear of the strange people and their ridiculous ways in other places, strangers who lived even just one or two towns over, where, according to their fathers, basic values were breaking down and a slightly lower standard of living turned the townspeople into thieves and scum, or where, according to their mothers, a slightly higher standard of living turned the townspeople into snobs and degenerates. There was nowhere else to go, really. Although Ralph hadn't yet spoken a word to any of these children, they knew the name of the puppy and they knew his name, too. They knew where he was from and they knew that he ate Thai food for dinner every night. I like that peanut sauce, one boy told him. It tastes like Captain Crunch.

On the eighth or ninth day, Ralph asked the mechanic, as tactfully as he could, how much he owed him only for the work he'd already done: ripping wires indiscriminately out of the car. The mechanic told him he'd need to tally it up, that he should call later and he'd give him a price, even though it was obvious, as Ralph spoke to him, that he had nothing else to do at the moment but read a true crime novel and let the women's golf games on the TV overhead wash over him.

Muted and green. Dykey and green. An unreal green. Greener and more electric than anything that should rightfully exist.

Ralph trudged back to the motel. Was he yielding to a form of blackmail exerted on him by his own personality? Ralph suspected he could become anyone for the sake of a pleasure he sought out instinctually, but sometimes rebelled against consciously: the pleasure of self-obliteration. On the ninth or tenth day, Ralph called the mechanic but there was never an answer. He imagined himself trudging down the road, past the Kmart and the bar and the goose-and-gingham restaurant, and past the empty space to the mechanic's. He went to the park with the puppy instead and this time there was nobody there, but he felt sure that he was being watched. That night he ordered three beers with his Thai food and drank them all down and then he slept. It was on that night that his phone rang at three a.m. and he dragged himself up out of vague dreams in which he was wearing an ankle monitor to answer it.

Hi, said a perky, oddly familiar woman's voice. Whatcha doin?

I was just sleeping, Ralph said. You woke me up.

Oh, said the woman. Well, we're just partying over here and thought you might wanna come by for a beer.

I think you have the wrong number, Ralph said.

She said, Isn't this room 117?

Ralph had to agree that it was.

This is the maid, she said. Remember, we saw each other around?

Ralph was at that moment convinced that, wherever she was, she could see the front door of his room and the heavy curtains over the window.

You're not doing anything else, she said.

If he peeked out from the curtains or walked into the parking lot, she would be following his every move. He knew he could obey her.

I'm just going to get some sleep, he told her.

But he couldn't sleep. In the dream she'd interrupted, he was on parole for something related to experimental drugs or illegal technologies. The ankle monitor, which looked like a garage door opener fastened to a hippie anklet, needed to be charged or he'd be in serious trouble, but he'd lost the charger. He'd left it behind, but where? Somewhere far away, impossibly far away.

By the time he crawled out of bed, the asphalt was already blazing and a group of teens was lazing around the pool in the back. It wasn't yet ten o'clock and it was 100 or 101 degrees. There was one girl who was maybe sixteen or seventeen and pregnant and then a couple of skinny boys. She was wearing a halter top and bikini bottom and they were wearing baggy denim shorts, and the girl looked him head-on and said, Oh, you're the guy Jamie called last night.

Jamie, said Ralph.

You know, said the girl. The maid.

We were there when she called, explained one of the boys.

Ralph went into the office and told the condescending manager he needed to rent a car. The car would be there within a half hour, he was told, and so Ralph went into his room and packed his few belongings in about five minutes and then sat and waited. He didn't want to even turn on the television, because he didn't want to take the time to turn it off once the car arrived. He sat on the bed and imagined nonexistence. He meditated on the void. He had fallen into eternity and realized that if anyone longed for anything, it was only oblivion. The territory short of oblivion was just boredom and the territory this side of boredom was terror and the territory this side of terror was absolute sadness and this side of absolute sadness was only the sort of mindless distraction that one would wake from every now and then into absolute sadness or terror. It was possible he was forgetting something here, but he didn't think so. No, oblivion was the real prize. Thousands of years later the car arrived and Ralph checked out and drove forty-five minutes to the next big town. He arranged to have the mechanic there go pick up his car with a tow truck, and he went back to the first mechanic and paid him the ridiculous amount of money he demanded and then he drove the rental car six hours straight to the suburb of Detroit and the crumbling house where his old friend Vicente was living with Vicente's sixty-two-year-old lover, Jack.

He was there for a week and a half. Every day Vicente would go to his job at the International School, where he worked as a teacher's aide, and Ralph would be left alone with Jack, who would watch soap operas and take pills and when he got bored sometimes he would come to the back patio, where Ralph might be speaking into his tape recorder, mapping out vague ideas for low-budget horror, and Jack would tell him about his life.

The first time Jack's parents had taken him to see a psychologist to be tested was when he was sixteen, he told Ralph. This would have been 1956 or 1957. His parents didn't want him to go to art school unless the doctor thought he was worth it, they told him. The psychologist suggested banking or sales, but when Jack was eighteen, he moved to the next state over and went to art school anyway. A few years later, his parents came to visit him and had him committed. It wasn't hard to do, if you were family and you could pay for it, not in the South. The state hospital cost only $38.50 a week. The police came to his job (he was working at a drugstore) and told him they weren't allowed to explain what they were doing or why and they handcuffed him and drove him through some lovely countryside down roads with very tall trees on either side, with feathery leaves, so the road was like a tunnel, and at the end of the tunnel was a sign that said *State Hospital*. Jack realized at that moment how troubled his parents must have been about his mental state, or at least his mother. He wasn't sure if his father cared or not. Jack had received a postcard from an old friend which his mother had read, and she'd confronted him, asking what sort of a man this friend was, what sort of a man would write, *There are many pretty boys on board ship but I keep my hands to myself*. Jack's brother had signed the commitment papers as well, the brother who was married, even though Jack had run into him at a gay party a few years earlier and his brother had asked him what he was doing there. Same thing as you, I suppose, Jack had told him. Jack told the doctor at the state hospital that he didn't think sex expression could be limited to just men or women and she told him that was an abnormal attitude and that was all. He got so bored in that hospital that one day he just walked out and went to live in a different nearby city. Then he moved up north and *apparently*, Jack said, which Ralph didn't understand at first, *apparently* he found a lover in New York and did odd jobs there until the art teacher from his hometown contacted him and told him he was retiring and moving to Panama, where sexual attitudes were more enlightened. He offered Jack his job, teaching art. Jack enjoyed the teaching, but soon enough his parents had him committed again. His parents didn't think he should be gay, and his doctors at this new hospital agreed. Once again he was handcuffed and driven out into the countryside and down a different road that looked almost exactly the same, a tunnel with tall trees on either side and feathery leaves and at the end of this road was a sign that said *Psychiatric Hospital*. It was a much pricier hospital, $342.50 a week.

The patients were both men and women, and time didn't work right in that hospital. Every one of them was receiving sodium pentathol and then electric shocks. You'd be in your pajamas usually, and then nothing. Jack could remember being shaved with an electric razor and realizing that he couldn't move and yet somehow he was being shaved, like an angel's hand was reaching down and shaving him. It certainly wasn't his own hand, unless he'd lost all sense of contact with his own limbs, and he wasn't sure which would be worse, to be shaving himself but as if he was two different people, or to be tied down and shaved by an angel. Jack underwent shock treatment at least fifteen or sixteen times. Often the orderlies would want him naked and ready to be examined and sometimes he'd hear other inmates screaming during their own shock treatments and that was the worst part. Everything else just sort of got obliterated with the treatments themselves, along with his entire memory of the months he'd lived in New York.

Finally the call came in to let Ralph know that the second mechanic had undone everything that the first mechanic had done and replaced the broken part and he could come back to Illinois and pick up his car. The radio worked fine in the rental car and so the drive back to Illinois flew past, with Ralph distracting himself with the hideous jingles and belligerent chatter of the American airwaves. In Illinois he paid almost all of the money he had left to the mechanic and the rental car company, including the profit he'd made on Vicente's weed, but successfully avoided coming anywhere near the small town with the Days Inn or the Motel 6 and in one direction the Kmart and the bar in the trailer and the goose-and-gingham restaurant and the empty space and the four-way stop with the mechanic's on one corner and the City Hall on another or, if you walked the other way, the freeway underpass and the little house and the cattle gate and a field with a handful of cows and the neglected park and the dead end and the railroad tracks. He turned right around and headed north, trying to make it to Detroit again to spend the night at Vicente and Jack's, but found himself nodding off north of Indianapolis and pulled off the highway to sleep in the back of the car. As he entered Michigan late the next morning, signs on the highway informed him that the Canadian border was closed, although they didn't say why. He assumed it had something to do with striking bridge workers, although he can't remember now why he would have thought such a thing. He arrived in Detroit to discover that Jack was eating ravenously and that America was under attack. Vicente was stuck at the International School because it had been surrounded by local law enforcement. They were under siege, either because the foreign students were under suspicion or to protect the foreign students from potential mob violence, it was never made clear. Not to Ralph at least. He watched TV nonstop for the rest of the day, thrilled by the enormous catastrophe, which seemed to somehow validate vague things that he believed. He wondered about the safety of the Pakistani manager back in that awful little town. Ralph could easily imagine a gang of the local teens, led by the maid, carrying pitchforks and torches and burning the Motel 6 or the Days Inn to the ground. He was at Jack and Vicente's for another week and a half, waiting for the border to reopen, and while Vicente went off to work, or took mental health days and then wandered aimlessly through areas of Detroit that resembled, he told Ralph later, what he thought Manhattan looked like after the attacks, Ralph sat around listening to Jack talk more about his poorly remembered life. One day in the mental institution a doctor said, This isn't a prison and I'm not your guard. Aren't you a citizen? A free man? I'll sign the papers and you can leave today, if you'd like. The doctors all liked to play games, Jack said, and if you noticed, they'd ask you if you knew what paranoia was. This doctor was smug; Jack had no idea what he was thinking, especially when he spoke. Jack had grown so tired of all the games. He was in no state to get out at that point anyway and it was around that time that he began to wonder if he'd ever had sex with his brother (the one who'd had him committed) but it became harder and harder to separate memories from the rest of it, the dreams or daydreams or the crazy thoughts from the drugs. But sometime later he was released to his mother's care. She showed him all of his Christmas letters and gifts from his friends in New York. He read the letters and discovered that he'd had a lover and he'd had many gay friends but he couldn't remember any of it. He wrote them back and told them where he'd been, but he didn't tell them that his memory of their faces, names, and the time they'd spent together had been obliterated. It was the strangest thing, he told Ralph. It was as if he was a ghost, say, who'd entered the afterlife and was having all of the trivialities peeled away, his whole life, which wouldn't matter anyway where he was headed. It was like he was spiraling farther and farther away but all of his loved ones were still sending him messages through a séance or a medium or some cheap fortune teller in Queens, and he could still hear the messages and send back some sort of reply, through a Ouija board perhaps, but none of it had any connection to the more and more vaporous entity he'd become. It didn't turn out that way, however, because after he told his mother that he thought it was perfectly normal to have sexual feelings for other men, she shouted at him, *You haven't changed!* She began weeping. *$6800 for nothing!* He wanted his mother's love so desperately and yet in that moment he wanted to strangle her or run her over with a truck. Instead, he went back to New York to meet all of his friends. He especially wanted to meet his lover, this man who'd written him all of these wonderful letters. He'd written about times they'd shared, dinner parties with witty and hideous guests, snow falling on the city in the middle of the night, figurative paintings, and horrible arguments that had come to seem hilarious in retrospect. The letters also made references that were indecipherable to Jack, to conversations and stories they'd shared, to connections which might become even deeper with time, to secret shames and pleasures, all of which was written about as if in some code, so that these conversations came to seem intimate and mystical and erotic to Jack, a blazing hearth that he could even return to, but then he wasn't sure how he'd recognize his lover. He didn't have to, of course. His lover recognized him. He slept with his lover and it was fine, but when he confessed to his lover several months later that he'd had no memory of him at all, his lover asked then how he could just sleep with him like that? It was like he felt he was being cheated on—because Jack was sleeping with a stranger. Jack told him that he must have done it before, so he just did it. A stranger, a stranger, what did that even mean? He was an electrical vapor, Jack wanted to say sometimes, and the rest of them were just meat. Or else everyone else was an angel and he was just a wooden boy. He thought it all would never end.

Sometimes he'd run into other people who recognized him and he'd have no idea who they were, so he'd just pretend. He became quite an actor, but he also suffered from horrible depressions for the next few years. For nine years after the treatments, he'd have these thoughts and never know if he'd be able to connect them or not or he'd be walking down the street in New York and suddenly not know where he was.

One day in 1971 it all changed. His thoughts began to connect again. Just as Jack said this, a man on the news said that the world had now become a fundamentally different kind of place. The future was more exciting now, because anything could happen, he implied. The horrible boredom of daily life had been thrown into question, and mass slaughter might erupt at any moment. A state of constant terror seemed like a pretty good idea to Ralph, and despite all of the trials he'd been through in that Days Inn or Motel 6, he now felt confident that he'd made the right decision and that Quebec was the best place in the world to relax with Hugo and watch the chaotic future unfold.

One day in 1972 or '73, Jack told him, a woman stopped him on the streets of New York and said, Sir! She grabbed him by the elbow and she asked if he would just stand with her for a few minutes and help her get her bearings. She wasn't sure where she was. Jack told her exactly where she was, which was in Lower Manhattan, not far from where they had, at the time, just recently razed some poor neighborhoods completely and evicted many residents and small business owners and constructed those horribly ugly towers, and she was so grateful. He walked with her through the neighborhood and asked her if she'd had shock treatment. He asked how long she'd been in the hospital, but she couldn't remember. It had been a very long time.

The border had reopened and Ralph was planning to leave the next morning, so that evening Vicente took Ralph out for a beer. Vicente told Ralph that he didn't love Jack anymore. In fact, as every day went by, he hated him more and more. Sometimes in his dreams he was beating him viciously. Ralph didn't know what to say to that, but he listened, which was all Vicente seemed to care about.

Crossing the border was complicated, but not ridiculously so. Ralph had imagined he'd be on some secret lists because of his subversive queer film projects or because of protests he'd attended in the '80s and early '90s, but it was no problem.

When he finally got to Quebec City, it was miserable. He wanted to move to Montreal, but Hugo wanted to stay near his mother. Quebec City was dreary and quaint and Hugo was cold. Hugo would leave every morning, in any case, to work on the soap opera, he claimed. Ralph would be alone in the charmless little studio with less and less desire to situate himself among the tourists in the neighborhood at some café. He had no money, no friends, and he didn't speak the language. Hugo insisted they spend every Sunday at his mother's house. She was a squat, hard woman who chain-smoked. The days grew darker and colder. By Christmas he wasn't getting out of bed until Hugo returned in the evening, and he'd sometimes forget to give the cat its insulin shots. Hugo was never in the mood to make love anymore and they quarreled about trivial things. In February, the cat died. In March, he borrowed the money from Sherry Mbeki to put a new battery in the Volvo and he swallowed his pride (he didn't have much left anyway) and called Philip and Raymond to ask if he could stay with them until he found a place, a job, whatever. They'd taken Dhoji and her two toddlers in after she'd left Ricky, so there was some precedent. Philip didn't even humiliate him, but told him a story about an androgynous virgin who fell into the hands of some robbers. Some of the robbers raped her and some seduced her with gifts. This was either a fable or an item from the news, Ralph couldn't follow it. Two weeks later Ralph left the dog, which wasn't at all cute anymore, with Hugo's mother. She didn't seem to care about such things. She'd had a child, Hugo's older brother, out of wedlock and had given him to her sister to raise. Ever since, she'd accept any stray, no matter how desolate or ugly. She smoked while Hugo said good-bye and Ralph got in the Volvo and drove back into America.

He'd heard so many horror stories about how Times Square had been cleaned up, purified of sleaze, Disneyfied, but there were still a few video arcades here and there, usually down in the basements of porn shops. In the cramped little space, all by himself, but surrounded by other cramped little spaces, where other men were holed up, he felt at home for the first time in months. He felt contained and embraced: All around him men were yearning for connection, for touch, for human contact. He didn't want to actually touch or connect with any of them, but the fact that they were out there, maybe connecting with each other, touching each other, or at least imagining touching each other, while actually watching porn in their cramped little booths, seemed like love to Ralph. As he watched the shoddy, plotless, poorly filmed and clichéd fuck scenes, all of the porn titles that Raymond had come up with over the years flashed through his mind like prophetic writing. *Rear Admiral*, *Bottomless Bottom, Ass Beast*. Actually that last one wasn't Raymond's, it came from an Allen Ginsberg poem. Why not? he thought. He had the equipment, he had the vision, he could easily enough recruit the talent. Distribution was the big issue, but the web had opened up all kinds of new avenues, he guessed, to evade the centralization of the giant porn corporations, with their relentless onslaught of shaved and muscled bimbos. He walked down Broadway pondering his future, with a variety of porn scenes running through his head, a mile a minute. It was as if he'd already filmed them or as if they already existed, in the atmosphere. Men, and sometimes women, and sometimes trannies, sucking and fucking in all the usual positions, and it seemed to Ralph in new positions as well. Positions that had never existed before, but that he would discover. He knew that this was improbable, a new configuration, and yet he was sure that it was coming. He imagined the new bodies and new genders and new positions of the future, abstractly, as he walked all the way downtown to visit the big hole in the ground where the towers had been. He had called Vicente to see if he could stay one night with them on the way back and Jack had answered and then given the phone to Vicente who said, Sure, stay as long as you want, but Ralph was now thinking it was so cold maybe he should take a more southern route through Atlanta or New Orleans and avoid the Midwest altogether.

Normalcy is relentless, thinks Ralph. Chaos and terror get turned into news hiccups and the whole social apparatus of numbing, mindless repetition inevitably turns delightful unpredictability into mass-produced despair. Back when he used to have Tony drag him up and down the stairs by his hair, for a while it seemed like he was touching some deep pit of pleasure, some primordial debasement and that he might transform himself completely. And then it just became routine.

Now, Tony is examining the reflection from the cooler doors, to figure out where to station the cameras. Neeraj has stepped out for a smoke.

If the lighting is right, we could even film part of the robbery as the reflection in the cooler door, Ralph suggests. A kind of warped mirror. You know.

Tony says, Don't be difficult.

It's my vision.

You've always needed a firm hand, Tony says.

The hole in Lower Manhattan was impressive, but difficult to actually see. Walkways and edifices had already been constructed so that Ralph had to circle and circle just to get in a position to see the empty space without paying a fee. There were souvenir books and T-shirts being hawked. Expansive lists of the dead. *The Portraits of Grief*, the book was called. A to Z, from Gordy Aamoth, whose golf game was improving, and who'd completed his biggest merger deal on September 10, to Igor Zukelman, who owned an ugly car with vanity plates in Ukrainian. Maybe some of these dead people had rich inner lives, but each obituary was given a pithy heading under the dead person's name. *From Lacrosse to Pool. Living Large, Playing Hard. A Poet of Bensonhurst. Pushing Jokes to the Limit.*

The Giving Gene. There weren't any titled *Party Bottom* or *Firegear Fetish* or *Stuck in a K-Hole.* Remains of terrorists had been identified and separated from the remains of the victims. Nobody wanted any evil dead cell tissue to be inadvertently memorialized.

One of the dead shared an interest in Charles Bukowski with his girlfriend. More recently, he'd set aside poetry and embraced photography, taking pictures of flowers and leaves. At twenty-five, he was experimenting with collages of found images and bottle caps. Ralph wanted evidence that for the dead, life had been a continuous revelation. It was magic unfolding. They were absolutely free and responsible for that freedom. One of them carefully pressed his clothes every night, and used special clippers to trim his mustache. His six-year-old son had leukemia. One man drove around in a purple car, listening to conservative commentators on the radio. His wife hoped the attack would influence the world, not to make it tougher, but a little more understanding. One fireman's fifteen-month-old daughter said *Dada* for the first time as the anxious family gathered around the television on September 11. One man created elaborate winter landscapes with ceramic figures in his basement every winter. He built miniature towns named for his daughters. *Behind them all was a dark blue night sky, lit up with electric stars.*

3

PHILIP WAKES WITH A START when the phone rings. It's absolutely dark, but his cell says three a.m. It isn't his cell that's ringing, however, it's the motel phone. It rings again, louder than would seem possible.

He gropes and manages to answer it, but there's only silence. His motel room is kind of like a premature burial. A click and the dial tone. He lies awake then in what feels like an endless darkness.

***

If there's nothing to keep you, where would you go? If your path has no real destination.

In Bob Miller's story, every action was loaded with a kind of prescient significance, as if John Garcia could sense his own future, or as if the future was reverse engineering John Garcia. The fact that John Garcia told Bob that his favorite music was a requiem, because it made death seem not so scary. The whole *Don Quixote* thing. The fact that John Garcia wasn't even supposed to go to the orgy with Bob, but that Bob missed his train. The fact that John Garcia had been desperate to check his email in the midst of the orgy, but somehow couldn't manage to do it.

Instead, John Garcia and Bob are speeding back toward San Jose.

On the way out of town they pass a gas station, and Bob suggests they stop for gas. They discuss the possibility endlessly, it seems, but maybe they don't have enough cash or maybe it's a cold night and it's warm inside the car, and so they don't stop. They pass the gas station by.

As they're crossing the bridge, of course they run out of gas. There's no more power, the car is just coasting, slowing down, and so John Garcia pulls over into the right-hand lane and stops. There isn't a shoulder on this bridge.

The Carquinez bridge, or not the Carquinez bridge but some bridge just like it. A parallel bridge, Philip can't keep them straight, what does it matter? It was I-80, or I-680. The car sits there and maybe the hazards are on or maybe they don't quite function. *If you don't change your life, you're going to die the death of Don Quixote,* John Garcia's therapist had told him.

John Garcia gets out to make his way along the skinny curb at the edge of the bridge to the emergency phone, and Bob sits there in the car. It doesn't occur to him, really, that it's dangerous to be sitting there—just that it's annoying. What is Bob thinking? What is rattling around his meth-addled brain? His biological mother, his dead father, his long-lost little half-brother? Every cock in the room he just left? A warm, cozy room, with Bob on his knees, first one, then another, while John Garcia keeps bugging the host to use his computer. On the bridge, after about five minutes, John Garcia comes back. Five minutes or one? Bob's sense of time is completely distorted. John Garcia hasn't even made it to the emergency phone, he's acting manic. Manic, Bob said. Twitchy and babbling and gesticulating wildly? He's a manic-depressive, a large part of the drama of his life, the life that he's supposedly in the midst of finally getting together, that he's just about to get together, so that he doesn't die the death of Don Quixote. Bob sets out to make the call instead and leaves John in the car. It's freezing, it's five a.m., the sun's maybe just starting to come up, or not yet up, but the sky's lightening. Bob turns back to get his jacket, finds John Garcia frantically trying to start the car. He just keeps turning the engine over, disturbed at the repeated clicking sound. Bob grabs his jacket and says, You know you don't have to do this. John Garcia says, Just let me do what I have to do, and Bob's like, Okay. He's on his own little trip, Bob decides, and Bob makes his way up the skinny curb toward the emergency phone. He walks for a few minutes and turns back to look. The whole sky is brightening now, it's this beautiful scene. He's at the top of the bridge. He can see everything, the bay or whatever you call it that far inland, the delta, the industrial refinery lights on one side, the cute little town of Benicia on the other. He can see the car sitting down there beneath him and this steady stream of interstate traffic streaming around the car as it approaches. The traffic is beautiful, a mass of sparkling lights, moving in a pattern, a pattern created by John Garcia's immobile car. One car isn't veering away.

It just keeps coming. It's big, like an SUV, and Bob's first thought is that it'll sideswipe the car and send John into the delta. He's wondering if John Garcia can swim, and thinking he probably can't.

It's all absolutely clear and almost slow motion, Bob Miller told Philip. Bob said it was like another type of time or another world had opened up in the middle of this one. It's like I'm swimming in a dream, Bob told Philip. The SUV just keeps coming until the very last minute. It doesn't even swerve. It smashes into John Garcia's car, and John Garcia's car is smashed completely and John Garcia is smashed completely. Bob is watching it like it's a movie, like it's something so far away that it has nothing to do with him.

Bob didn't talk about the aftermath. The cops and paramedics who surely arrived at the scene. He didn't mention the funeral. He'd read *Don Quixote* twice in the year since John Garcia's death. *But had the fortune in his age, To live a fool and die a sage.* Bob's interpretation of John Garcia now was as a sort of doomed spiritual messenger who'd offered him nuggets of spiritual wisdom. The golden rule, John Garcia had told Bob, meant that you had to do not only unto others as you'd have them do, but unto yourself. You had to treat yourself like an other who deserved to be treated well. Bob thought it was profound. It's not surprising that Bob felt a kind of destiny and meaning ebbing out of events, after spending the last twenty-four hours of the dead man's life with him, but Philip's kind of worried. Where is Bob tonight? It's hard to imagine. Hard to imagine that anywhere in the world it isn't just a dream of darkness. Nothing at all.

***

The next day, Philip drives past the Glick place, but doesn't bother to stop.

The intern in New York got him the shooter's address, but the family isn't living there anymore. Nobody could or would tell him where they'd gone.

He parks partially into the ditch in front of the barricade. Walks through the overgrown weeds and brush, down the road with the chain across it, and through the gap in the chain-link fence.

The chain-link fence: a flailing insect from outer space.

For the Aztecs, crossing through the underworld was complicated. A master would need not only food and clothing to fortify him for the journey, but his unfortunate servants, who were sacrificed on the same altar as his corpse. They'd also burn a reddish-colored dog, to help the master cross the subterranean river that blocked the path through the underworld.

Across the ruined bridge, through the trees to the ruined orphanage.

He makes his final mark on the wall, next to the shooter's son inscription, which already seems to be fading. Shrinking into the wall somehow, decaying. Philip has been here for twenty-three days.

A *sentence* is a period of time when you are in a particular place. You live within that space and that time. You live within the sentence.

Amos calls him. From Esther's phone.

It's not a good time, Amos says.

Oh, okay, says Philip. Are you busy?

There's nothing but a strange, distant beeping, like you used to hear on international calls.

It's my last day, Philip says. I'm leaving tomorrow early.

I can meet you after supper, Amos says.

The usual place? I'm there now.

The old building where they used to keep boys locked up.

Amos then says something Philip can't make out. It sounds like *alien weaving factory*.

Did you call me last night?

I wasn't around last night, Amos says. I was dreaming really crazy things.

Then he's either coughing or muttering. Then he's gone.

Philip's sitting in the rental car, parked in the darkness by the *No Trespassing* sign. The sun is long gone.

A figure moving across the bridge. He can't see her face; she's wearing a bonnet. She pauses in the center of the bridge, gazing down at the water.

In the water: nothing but a distorted reflection.

Something is moving from the cemetery toward her. Someone in a hoodie. Philip can't tell if they're speaking to each other.

Two people set out across the bridge. Only one makes it to the other side.

It's Amos. His lips are moving.

Artaud: *Insane asylums are conscious and premeditated repositories of black magic.*

In the distance, animals are drifting through the dark fields. Something is screaming or whistling, faintly, far away. A song or a cry of anguish, either way. When he emerges from the path, scattering a creepy, intermittent light from his flashlight, there's an equally creepy light emanating from the old orphanage, definitely real. A sort of mobile glow that suggests a haunting or a burning. As he gets closer, it settles into one place. Through a broken window, Philip can see that Amos already has a fire going in the old fireplace.

It begins to rain.

This is the real world and there's nobody else in it.

Amos sits poking the fire with a stick, a stack of typed pages next to him.

Are those for me? Philip asks.

Amos nods. Philip lays his jacket on the dusty floor and sits close enough to the fire to feel its heat.

Who were you talking to just now? On the bridge?

She won't talk to you, Amos says. She won't talk to anyone but me.

Is she your aunt?

She's in mourning. Her child is dead.

In the shooting?

She'll have something else instead.

Amos won't sit still.

An illusion, he says.

He paces, then sits, then paces again, telling Philip a lot of different facts and ideas and stories that jumble together and sometimes seem to incorporate the plots of recent popular movies, told as if Amos is himself the protagonist or the live audience or the director or all of these things simultaneously. Amos talks about his stepfather, the minister or celebrity or detective, and about his own guitar skills, and about H. P. Lovecraft, one of his favorite authors, whose work, according to Amos, isn't exactly fiction. He switches from subject to subject without any apparent reason, but continually circles back to several major

topics, so that when he finally trails into silence, two points have been empha-
sized: He's destined to be a rock star someday, and he's convinced that the
stories he's written are evil.

Your stories aren't evil, says Philip. They're just descriptive, and maybe what
they describe isn't always good.

Amos just frowns.

As Philip reads, the boy circles around him, outside the space of the fire's
illumination. After several minutes, Philip has to admit that the stories just
might be evil. Or that the boy might be possessed. If he's even the one who
wrote the stories, which Philip finds harder and harder to believe. They do
seem to match the boy's dissociative manner, his love of non sequiturs and his
preoccupations with martyrdom and guilt. In the bright firelight the words look
like they're composed of various layers. Like the words are three-dimensional,
or n-dimensional, extending into other worlds. It isn't just the brightness of the
fire—Philip's got that tingling at the edges of his vision, the precursors of the
auras and light-headedness he gets when a migraine's coming on. A few feet in
any direction is just darkness and Amos is somewhere within the dark. Philip
hears footsteps upstairs, directly overhead, but they echo like they're simultaneously emerging from the cellar. *The sky in our city is a permanent grey haze. It is not
unattractive or bleak, it is the color of a brain.* Philip wonders where Amos picked up
the British spelling of "grey."

Insane asylums without borders and moonlit barns and empty, haunted
one-room schoolhouses.

It's really raining now. A downpour of auras and meanings. Amos is back.

If you want, he says, I can ask her a question.

Just one?

One is probably enough. She sees things. The river's like her mirror. It's all
there.

Ask her where it's going, Philip says.

You know that already. Everybody knows that already.

Then ask her what it's for. I don't know that. Nobody knows that.

You stay here.

Amos pauses at the door and he's saying something, but his words are getting swallowed by the wind and the rain. It sounds like he's saying, *Nothing in the
words, nothing in the darkness.*

Wait, Philip says.

Amos disappears into the storm. Philip shines his light after him, but Amos
has reached a place in the trees that light can't reach. Maybe the realms of

Death have laws of physics that Philip doesn't understand. The flow of events in time might be dangerous and full of risks for a person or a species, for life itself. But maybe there's nothing really chaotic in the web of events, even though the process is complex and unpredictable.

A straight line can be a maze, like in that story by Borges. A single straight line that is invisible and endless. Philip cuts across the sculpture garden to the trees for cover from the rain. Shines his light at the bridge. The river is roaring with the storm runoff. Or maybe it's just the noise of the rain and the opposing winds that batter the bridge.

Two figures are intertwining on the bridge. The other one is no taller than Amos.

The light is exploding everywhere on the right side of Philip's vision. The air and the rain flicker, the rain is language, the atmosphere full of phantoms. One boy is on the right side, obscured by the flickering lights and auras, and one is on the left.

The bridge is an island in the river, obscured by mist and sheets of rain.

The hellish hurricane, which never rests, drives the spirits of the dead over the river with its wind. Mist from the river curls around a dead boy's mouth like a speech balloon.

The mutations of a hallucination are like the freakish mutations of the biological world. Of the various figures forming in the rain, many are dogs or human bodies with dogs' heads. It was said that the white dogs and the black dogs could not carry you over the river.

Lightning claws open the sky.

And when one of these dogs recognized his master, he came to throw himself into the water to carry his master across.

But the shooter's son is still on the bridge with Amos, and Amos is showing him a secret. Something bright as an apocalypse in Amos's hands explodes in the flashlight's beam. He's looking into it, a mirror. And then it looks like the boys are kissing.

Amos turns, looking at Philip, and then, as if underwater, falls to the rotten floor of the bridge. The shooter's son grabs his hips, roughly pulling him back, and seems to hump him with short, hard strokes. Somebody drops the mirror.

Philip closes his eyes.

Deliverance means Release. And then one boy falls as a dead body falls.

A splash in the river.

A narrow shadow glides across the surface. Philip seems to be looking at himself from outside of space. Flowing from one side toward the other, his body stuck on the rocks, then floundering, dislodging himself and carried into a deep pool between the bridge and the lip of the beach.

It's a trick. The trick is to cross to the other side.

The surface of the deep pool, the entire visible horizon, and even beyond, have been pulverized into swarming dots of light in a pulsating web of mist. It's a vast luminous nothingness. Philip crawls from the water, and collapses onto the muddy embankment. Turning over onto his back, he looks up at the clouds that roll, as if pushed, across the dark sky. The cosmos is losing its form, a vortex of meaningless and radiant specks in ceaseless transformation.

In the darkness, in the mist, the bridge is an island floating in the crater of a volcano. Philip is alone on the bridge. On the muddy embankment, it's a dead boy or a shadow, wet and shivering.

If he was just visiting this ruin, this town, his ancestral lands, this rotting bridge, Philip could have never understood the horror of this particular spot. There is nothing visible on either side of the bridge, only formless light and formless darkness and nobody can see where the river is going.

Dead strangers gather on the bank, waiting. Thousands of sullen shades, their resentment smoldering under the wet clouds.

They are all around him. Where else would they go?

It is only mist and rain that seem to be full of flashing lights because of the migraine coming on.

If there is still somewhere to go, hurry on.

There isn't.

Smoke-gray clouds form in endless chains with a thick edge, like steel lace-work. Philip turns slowly to look into the shadows of the forest behind him. Hanging by his neck from one of the trees is the shooter's son. Beneath the trees, the rental car, parked almost directly into the ditch at an oblique angle because of the steep slope. The boy is wearing a wedding dress. Between the hanged boy's legs is a bloody hole; beneath the hole hangs a small, black mass. Beneath the immense treetops that darken the air, past the two black windows that open out in the sidewall of the ruins. A flash of lightning illuminates the horror.

Just rain and shadows and an old rag caught in the dead branches of a con-voluted tree. Philip hasn't lost his mind, not yet. Still, he believes for no good reason that the appearance and disappearance of things may seem to occur at random, but isn't ever really senseless.

The river fades back into the map.

Amos is calling to him from the doorway to the old ruin. It sounds like he is saying, *Philip, save me from haphazard thoughts and images.*

***

Philip is back in the orphanage, sitting by the fire. The auras have faded, replaced by a dull pain.

It takes him time to get used to everyday reality again, to seeing a face: Amos, alone. A child he lost, in the woods, so long ago that he has no memory of it.

Philip thinks he loves this child, he's not sure why. Why this one and not the other.

Amos says, You wanted me to ask her what it's for.

He is lazily poking the fire with his stick, throws some more raggedy wood on the fire.

She says that, on the one hand, time is like a *project* and death is like a *goal*, Amos says. On the other hand, time is an *illusion* and death is just the *separation* of the elements that make up a human being on Earth's surface.

The fire is now truly blazing.

She says that the door to the invisible has to be made visible, Amos says. She says it's the only place left for us to go. But I think she has a little distorted view of things.

Amos, says Philip. Are you okay?

In her mind…, he says. It's like roundabout.

There wasn't a woman, Philip says. You were out there with that boy.

It was only me.

I thought I saw you.

Philip sets the manuscript down between them. Hundreds of white pages. Just a blank screen on which a boy with an overactive imagination can project his dreams.

I'm sorry, Philip says. I'm feeling kind of strange.

Amos says, Strange is the most accurate way to feel on *this* planet.

Amos picks up his manuscript and starts looking through it.

I carried him across, says Amos. I took him to the other side. But that was a long time ago.

It's like he's never read his own stories before but needs to find a clue hidden somewhere in that tangle of words.

We might as well be the same boy, he says.

He just keeps shuffling and scanning, shuffling and scanning, faster and faster. As if he doesn't have much time.

Could a human…give birth to…

He puts the manuscript down and looks at Philip, as if just now really registering his presence. As if just now realizing that someone else is real.

Amos talks then, with odd pauses and interruptions, about his desire to travel into space, far, far away. Amos mentions his father again, who was killed on the road when his buggy was smashed by a wayward SUV. It was a *hybrid*. Indirectly, Amos discusses the murder and the dead boys and the shooter and the schoolhouse, which in Amos's way of speaking sounds like a prison or a madhouse or an infinite cemetery under a starry sky.

Amos explains calmly and quite clearly that he is the one who made the murders happen. It's because of these stories that he wrote, which are magic. The stories became real. The shooter received them as a kind of transmission or a kind of writing in the atmosphere, which is why he also picked up the frequency of Amos's cousin's band. It isn't a coincidence, Amos explains, that the band is called Wrath of God and that the shooter told the boys, before he shot them, that he was *angry with God*.

Stories are evil, or at least the stories that Amos writes, which come directly from hell. Teams of miners have lost their maps, and are now busy searching for another route to haul words up from the caverns beneath the earth.

The only thing for Amos is to renounce his evil ways and go back to the church.

No, says Philip. You can't go back. You're not evil, the world isn't evil, none of this…

He gestures at the fire, the room around them, the old crumbling orphanage, the earth.

I mean, okay, it is, says Philip. Sure. Sure, the world is evil, but it's just the world. It's just what is.

Amos is clutching his face in his hands, as if trying to keep it from exploding into bits.

It's not your fault, says Philip.

Amos wails, although it sounds more like something inside of Amos than "Amos." The cry of an animal being butchered or the sound of an animal watching its children get butchered.

Amos dumps the stack of pages into the fire.

Sparks erupt and flutter to the floor, while Amos runs howling out of the building. Philip uses a stick to push the pages out of the fire, then stomps on them until they've more or less stopped burning and runs out after Amos. He can't see him in the dark, but can hear him running off across the muddy fields, still making weird noises.

The pages are smoldering. Philip brushes off the blackened edges and the cinders.

Philip stands in the center of the bridge. He can still hear the boy's wail, growing farther and farther away. The rain is letting up some. It's too dark to make out anything in the water below.

The burn pattern is odd—just a little browning around the edges but then a crater of charred blackness right through the middle. As if the manuscript landed on a hot coal that burnt a hole all the way through. Philip will read what's left tomorrow morning on the flight from Des Moines to Houston, and then while waiting for his connection in the Houston airport, and then on the final flight, with the planet beneath him spinning toward the west.

Now Philip drives up and down the roads, peering into the darkness. Sometimes he stops the car and listens.

4

THE MORNING OF MELVIN'S DEPARTURE, Jared's really nice to him and gives him a warm plate of fake bacon and toast. Melvin's arranged a ride to California with a young bald guy wearing sunglasses and with crooked teeth. Jared doesn't think that's a smart idea.

Who knows what kind of things these people are into.

I have to go somewhere, Melvin says. I have to do something.

When the car comes around and honks and a young bald guy wearing sunglasses is driving, it takes Melvin a minute to realize he's never met this guy before. Meanwhile, Jared bursts into tears. But he doesn't stop Melvin from getting his things together and walking out the door.

The guy in the car doesn't talk to him as they negotiate the city streets to the next stop, as if Melvin is just some sort of baggage. At the next stop another young bald guy with sunglasses gets in, he doesn't smile or talk, so Melvin can't tell if his teeth are crooked, but he isn't the original either. The original is the final stop, a stop that lasts hours, involves unexpected detours to coffee shops and pawn shops and mysterious apartments where somebody's former girlfriend may be storing somebody's former stuff, and telephone conversations with roommates of these former girlfriends and eventually probably with the former girlfriends themselves. Once they get on the highway, the three bald guys are gossiping about guys who are dorkier than them or so reckless as to be insane. They consider themselves to inhabit the perfect and only reasonable middle ground between the dorky and the reckless insane. They're talking about previous journeys, previous intoxications, and pets that have died. Sometimes they're talking on their cell phones and saying the exact same kinds of things and Melvin can only imagine them talking to other guys who are bald and wearing shades but then they get off the phone and laugh about the guys they were just talking to, who are either dorky or so reckless as to be insane.

Then it's just the sound of the wheels on the highway and the chatter of the bald ones. One of them breaks out the weed. Soon enough, everyone in the car is high. The guys view Melvin as a child, although he's only a few years younger than they are, he thinks, although behind those shades they might actually be older, they might be twenty two or they might be thirty eight, or some strange combination, different versions of the same person through time. And then he's so high that he realizes it's worse than that. Time is endless and they aren't talking to him because they think he's just garbage, they think he's a fag, they think he's a bitch, they think he's just afraid of everything and a liar. He's afraid to say anything and they despise the weak. Can you fall into a K-hole on weed? They're reading his body language, which is just all like: Rape me. They're robots, actually. They're laughing at him in another dimension. They just wanna humiliate him without even raping him, which is fine, because the last thing he wants to be raped by is a bunch of fucking robots! Melvin's heard that on a real ketamine trip, one converses with the secretive dead. The dead love to hang out with the living, but keep their agenda under wraps. Kind of like the robots.

Robot rape: No thank you. So he just curls up in the backseat and tries to sleep, because then it won't seem weird that he isn't saying anything or that he's only laughing at their lame jokes that aren't even jokes, but when they're laughing, he's laughing, because he doesn't want to seem like he's a snob, and better than them, or whatever, so he's laughing, but he knows they can tell that the laughter is just fake and that he's only laughing so that they don't turn on him and start making fun of him. The only thing worse, he thinks, than their secret contempt and snickering and texting, which is maybe even texting each other, he thinks, about the idea that he's a fag and a bitch who wants to get raped, is if they'd say it out loud. Next: Things are quieting down because everyone is asleep except the guy who's driving and Melvin, who's only pretending to sleep. Lights from other cars or streetlights on overpasses or UFOs swoop through the car in weird rhythms. At some point, whichever bald guy is driving pulls off the highway and into some rest stop and sleeps, even though it's cold as fuck and some mysterious zone maybe Indiana or close to Indiana, although Melvin isn't sleeping.

Weary travelers shuffle back and forth between the dark parking lot and the overly lit buildings, where a pay phone sits under a halo of light.

Babysitting Mormons is so boring, one voice complains. She lists a bunch of reasons, starting with the no-caffeine diet sodas and no cable TV. We don't need Showtime, another voice says. We can *be* the show. A voice on the TV is droning on about volcanoes, about carbon and steam, the ingredients for life.

The boyfriend does something to Katie to make her squeal.

Not in front of the kid, Katie says.

How else is he going to learn?

Katie switches the channel.

I can't hear another word about the fucking primordial soup.

On the new channel a man is saying, Mutual attraction and recognition of like by like: this law is exemplified in multiple variations throughout…

Ugh, says Katie and switches again. Something innocuous, people chasing down a killer.

I told you I always end up breaking up at the four-week mark, she says.

You don't have to.

No, but it's like a pattern. I start wondering—what am I doing this for?

Maybe you have intimacy issues.

Maybe I do.

Anyway, it isn't four weeks yet. So relax.

I'm relaxed.

You don't look relaxed.

If I start having a panic attack, I'll let you know.

She starts talking about a girl she met in the mental institution, Emma. Emma's always talking about how much everything *costs*, Emma won't eat anything that's *warm*, and Emma has serious daddy issues.

What's that about?

Oh, he raped her.

No way. Really?

Katie shrugs.

I know a ton of people who've been raped by their fathers.

A ton? Really? At that school you go to?

All over the place. My friend Gina was raped, my mom was raped, my step-mom was raped, that girl who sits next to me in social studies, what's her name.

By their dads? Or just raped?

No, not their dads I guess.

I wouldn't want to go to your high school.

You couldn't afford it anyway. Most of those kids are *rich* rich. Like my friend Devin? He has two refrigerators in his kitchen. Two refrigerators. It's hard to relate. There's like the rich kids and then there's the out-of-district kids, and all of us scholarship kids are just doing acid and going to rehab. But I have to be in a high school, I know that. And I totally get how you have to just be fake or whatever and make some friends and just get through it, but I need somebody to sit with.

You shouldn't break up with me. I'll sit with you whenever you want.

Katie seems to be considering this.

The kid creeps me out, says Katie.

The boyfriend says, He's a nice kid. He isn't any trouble.

I think he likes you, Katie says.

Of course he likes me, says the boyfriend. Everybody likes me.

It's the way he just sits there so quiet, listening to everything we say, says Katie. It's not normal. Maybe somebody dropped him on his head.

What, like this, says the boyfriend and leaps off the sofa, scoops DJ up, and holds him upside down over the zebra lamp. DJ doesn't scream—he's generally reserved about expressing his ecstasies and terrors. Maybe this wasn't always the case. When he sets DJ down, the boyfriend says, Why wouldn't you like me?

DJ asks him to carry him on his shoulders.

You're too big for that, says the boyfriend.

DJ doesn't know the boyfriend's name. They haven't been properly intro-duced.

Sit down, DJ, Katie says. I need to talk to you about something.

He does what he's told.

I know it's not your fault. I mean it isn't something you chose. But I have to tell you—being a Mormon is like the stupidest thing ever. I mean the Bible is stupid enough. But you guys, it's just like some schizophrenic wrote a book. It doesn't even make any sense.

The landline rings.

Let it go, says the boyfriend.

It's probably them, says Katie. If I don't answer by the fourth ring, the mom gets a panic attack. It's been an issue.

Hello, she says.

This is Katie, the babysitter, she says. They aren't home.

Yeah, he's here, she says.

I don't know, she says.

I guess so, she says.

She hands the phone to DJ.

It's for you.

DJ suspects that something quite unusual is always happening.

Pratt residence, he says.

The man who speaks to DJ is his older brother.

How are you doing?

Fine, says DJ.

I'm going to be in a magazine.

Can I read it? asks DJ.

It's kind of for grown-ups.

I'm five, DJ says.

I know, Melvin says. But you totally wouldn't be into it. It's just like…furniture and space. Your dad still got you on those pills?

The babysitter gave it to me.

DJ, listen for a second. What time is it there?

DJ doesn't know.

Should I ask the babysitter?

Never mind, says Melvin. Have you been doing okay?

Fine, says DJ.

He tells his brother that he's wearing his pajamas and he describes them for him: They're light blue and they have pictures of elephants on them.

Is anybody touching you? asks Melvin.

Katie is putting her hands down the back of her boyfriend's pants. It's very distracting.

I mean, you know, does your dad ever touch you or anything?

DJ can't hear anything very well.

Katie is staring at DJ like he's done something awful.

Hello, says DJ. Hello, who is it, are you there?

Listen, Melvin says. Maybe, I'm gonna come get you.

Okay, says DJ.

DJ says, I'm going to zap you with my brain.

He closes his eyes and concentrates all his mental power on his brother.

I just zapped you, he says. Could you feel it?

I totally could, Melvin says.

DJ says, We're going to Disneyland.

Melvin says, No way.

For Christmas, says DJ.

It sounds like somebody's knocking down a door, like the police are coming.

Shit, I gotta go. You be good, okay?

DJ hangs up the phone very carefully.

You know who that was? Katie asks.

Katie starts whispering to her boyfriend.

How many people? asks the boyfriend.

It looks to DJ like she's eating his ear.

Guys, too? asks the boyfriend.

He laughs and he says, I guess with a blindfold on, who can tell the difference.

Katie says, Guys are disgusting.

She scrutinizes DJ as if he's just reminded her of something she forgot.

Bedtime for you, she tells him.

He picks up his favorite astronaut to take with him to bed and waits to see what will happen. The boyfriend scoops him up again and carries him to bed. Katie comes behind and gives him his pill, a sip of water, orders him under the covers, and then turns out the light. She doesn't even smooth and tighten the covers.

Now DJ's alone in the dark. This is a different world where nobody is able to look for him, find him, or join him. The room looks out over some bushes and snow. DJ wonders if he could die. It has happened to other children. Not to his own mother's children. Supposedly, he could die and supposedly everyone does.

His plastic astronaut is blue and holding his helmet to his chest. His hair is cut short. DJ tucks him into his underwear, and the astronaut is held snug. DJ lies on his back, and then turns over onto his stomach, and then onto his back again. Pluto is the coldest planet in the world.

A face pops up and smashes against the window and DJ gasps.

It's only the babysitter's boyfriend, now laughing and making a funny face. He puts his finger to his lips and motions for DJ to come to the window. DJ takes the astronaut out of his butt and goes and listens to the boyfriend explain that he should unlock the window so he can come in. A man has never come in before, DJ decides. When a man comes inside, it's called a criminal and a stranger and it's a form of enchantment.

The stranger crawls through the window quietly and whispers, It's freezing out there, and then he says, Quiet, Squirt, Katie doesn't know where I'm at. He tucks DJ back in bed and smooths and tightens the covers. While the boyfriend sits on the edge of the bed, thinking, DJ puts the astronaut back in place. He thinks that he shouldn't have unlocked the window, because a kidnapper could come in. He's taking a journey in order to know enchantment. I'm gonna scare her, the boyfriend tells DJ. Okay, DJ says, and he holds very still while the boyfriend tiptoes out of the room.

DJ holds his breath and listens for the scream. But nobody ever screams. Out there in the living room, something strange is going on, but nobody ever screams in this house. Screaming is against the rules.

On the wall is a picture of the family. His dad is always watching, in theory. In the photo, DJ is practically a baby, but already he seems like there's something ticking away inside of him, something from outer space. His mom is kind of distracted and Melvin sort of hanging off the edge of the cluster like he's trying to wiggle his way out of the picture.

At some point at the rest stop the sun comes up.

The trip west is an endless series of mental perturbations and hypnagogic states that last more or less forever. A variety of substances that take the edge off or add several new edges. Meaningless towns and cities that could just as soon smolder, in ruins. Shoppers and merchants entwined in a vast retail plateau, killers set loose in the cosmos. *Pass me a soda, Bro.* What is consciousness for? The sodas are warm, the chips are stale. Melvin doodles in his sketchpad, genetic mutants from outlawed tribes, their brains soldered to currents of molten metal, and hopeless amputees with elaborate prosthetics. Usually people go, Hey, what're you drawing there, that's pretty freaky, and he's like, It's a future life form. Blood vessels replaced by mercury circuits and symbiotic fungi growing from their brows. The elaborate prosthetics have grafted nerve endings and serve several aggressive erotic functions. The guys just keep saying nothing at all, or like they ask each other about some girl they saw on Myspace, or some former girlfriend, and all the girls are too slutty or they're stuck-up frigid bitches. Sometimes the girls they date turn needy, which is like the emotional version of slutty, so the bald guys have to dump them. Or they turn into frigid bitches, confiscate the bald guys' stuff before telling them: Get lost.

Take a hit off this, Bro. The "Bro" is always ironic, but is the irony directed at the category of Bro's or more specifically the idea that Melvin could be a Bro?

Melvin considers telling them about his ex. Call her a bitch, should he call her a bitch? Colonized bitch. One of the guys is chopping up some Adderalls. Melvin's ex was a good person, there were just too many issues. She'd try to get him to take an Ativan and just lie around in some room with the fog on the window. She wanted to be satiated and dreaming. *Pass me the Celexa, Bro.* Time is freedom, but there isn't any left. The road is just one signpost after another, one scene that's already happened and it's all been mapped out. The same thing just keeps happening over and over again. This isn't even really a cross-country trip.

They stop in Iowa City; the bald guys wanna see this band.

It's crowded and people are drinking—the target audience—and it's dark enough but he feels incredibly lost until the music begins. The first song's pissed off and grandiose for the most part, with a lot of distortion and screaming, but there's a change in the middle with a few sad chords that make Melvin weepy. The jetlag, or carlag, he decides, is making him overly emotional, or maybe it's the fumes. There's a kid maybe twelve and he's wearing a straw hat and suspenders like some Amish kid from TV and the kid bounces up and down by himself at the edge of the crowd. When the music stops, the boy jams his hands in his pockets. A slightly older girl with skulls on her T-shirt comes over and talks right up in his face sometimes and the boy laughs. Then the music starts up again and it's like Melvin isn't alone. It's like you can get possessed by the music and just be forgetting you're a human, or like you can be more than that, more than just a person. Electric and full of weird cosmic juice—you're a guitar or a spaceship, the notes are trying to escape. The notes are expressing really complicated things that are like both human and not. Lonely and confused and too much for just one body, one time, one life. And then they're doing this angry song that's shifting in the middle and it's like the nights are cold, they're stars, they're spinning, it's the universe overhead and it's freezing in space. And Melvin's just starting to cry and he's shaking and bouncing up and down but the tears are streaming down his face. He's been away for such a long, long time. There hasn't been any place, he's too keyed up to sleep, maybe forever. And the music keeps ravaging him like that, and once when it stops, he sees that little boy just watching him cry. It isn't so bad being looked at like this, because music makes emotions belong to the group. The boy gives Melvin a hug.

This is my very last show, he says.

The way he says it, Melvin thinks this kid is going to die. Kill himself or something.

No, Melvin says. Don't do anything foolish.

You could stay awhile.

The boy says, Once you realize that happiness doesn't matter, it's all a lot better. Once you realize that saying things isn't the point.

Can I save you? I need to save you.

The boy shrugs.

Melvin says, Who are you? Are you a dream?

Same as you, says the boy. But I'm keeping my eyes open. I'm leaving this behind me—rock and roll.

The boy makes a gesture at the atmosphere. The bar is full of a haze from the cigarette smoke. The complex phantom beauty of shapes in the mist.

Keep your eyes open, says Melvin. I will if you will.

The boy reaches up a hand and touches the tears drying on Melvin's cheek. Melvin almost jumps back like he's been electrocuted, but then he doesn't. They're gazing, for a moment, at each other.

The boy says, I only make eye contact when I'm taking my meds.

Melvin says, Do you have a message for me? Or do I have a message for you?

The boy shrugs.

Messages are the problem, I think. I've got to go now. You won't see me again.

Next, a girl tries Melvin out. Has everyone been watching him cry? She says, You don't know what that does to me. She says, You could charge money for that. She thinks she's known him and she like senses they'll be together and he's like, That's really cool except I can't, you know, miss my ride, and she's like, You look just like the guy I totally wanna be with. Melvin says, You mean I'm him and you've found him or you mean there's this other guy and I look like him, and she just laughs and says, Don't be silly. He's like, That's totally cool, and she's like, Hold on just a second, and then she's back in the corner texting or something and next thing he knows she isn't there anymore and the music's starting again. The song's like a manifesto for poetic violence against every established order and convention. Then it's over and this old guy's standing next to him and he's drunk and he says, I wish I was like you. One of the bald guys is nudging Melvin and motioning for the door.

In the morning, the shape of clouds in the distance creates an optical illusion, like they're quickly receding, everything rushing away, and it's like plumes of smoke rising from the earth. The earth is aflame, burning. In the west: weapons, metal, killing.

Bro, wake and bake. Wake and bake. If Melvin ever hears the phrase *medicinal herbs* again, he thinks he'll stab someone. If anyone claims the constitution was printed on hemp paper or says that *the pursuit of happiness* was so obviously thought up by stoners. He has a job, that's all: Consciousness is job number one; sketching future life forms is job number two. He's been dealing with the postapocalyptic mutations and the refugees from genetic laboratories for a while now, but next he's trying to sketch some photon-based life forms.

The name of this road trip is Family Life. Flat places and time. Time and more time. Enough time to relive every humiliating thing, if you really wanted to. Everything dirty and useless about being a person. This road trip is Marriage. The prosthetic devices of the future amputees are suspiciously designed. Anybody who saw his sketch would understand what Melvin's thinking. *Pull over, Bro, I need to take a leak.* When the driver is addressed, the Bro is distinctly less ironic. The subtle display of their dicks within the flammable brush of the prairie is so monkey. Eee eee eee. Bands of male chimps hunt for little monkeys. They work themselves up in a frenzy. If they catch the monkey, they rip it limb from limb. Instead of sharing their inner experiences, they share the bloody dismembered carcass of the monkey. The blood of the monkeys transforms the chimps into monkeys of death. Meat makes emotions belong to the nation. Family Life is War.

Late that night they're getting a motel in Albuquerque with two beds and two of the bald guys are getting in one bed and the other guy's getting in the other bed and nobody's even mentioning the sleeping arrangements and Melvin's like: What the fuck? He's still high enough that he understands he's being given the choice of being a needy slut or else a stuck-up frigid bitch. He just curls up on the floor. Frigid bitch it is.

The guys decide to hang out in this town for a day and see the sights, whatever those are—sports bars? They just need a robot maintenance break. They're making battle plans. They want to conquer an imaginary territory and subjugate their lucid dreams. They're collecting souvenirs so they can relive the adventure forever. They leave him alone in the motel room with all kinds of drugs.

Melvin is over maleness, and femaleness, too. Another false choice obscuring the path to knowledge. The future belongs to a chick with a dick. The future belongs to a Sex Offender. The future is probably like one big Sex Offense.

A trip west never ends. Just keep walking. Out in the desert, along the edges of a ranch-type thing with jaggedy, electrified razor fencing like this zone where anything can happen. People who live surrounded by space are proprietous and crackly and capable of all manner of violent eccentricities. The clouds look like the particular life forms you'll get from the interbreeding of human and extraterrestrial stock. Bulbous and jellied. Easily streaked through with lightning and too smart for their own good. Melvin could see being impregnated by a female with a firm, fleshy tentacle. The warm mammal friction of human orifices would drive the aliens crazy with lust and she'd have to have Melvin's. Birds are haranguing him, as cold as they come. Bitch-ass birds. He's wandering past this ranch and this calf's sticking its head out of the electrified fence and it's kind of entangled in the fencing and stuck there and it's making this heartbreaking bleating sound and looking at Melvin with these weirdly cosmic and conscious eyes that are just like HELP ME HELP ME HELP ME but Melvin is just now too freaked out and he hears motors in the distance like some evil force is surveilling him and hurrying to accuse him of torturing the calf or to electrocute him on the fence and he's afraid that if he touches it he'll be electrocuted and maybe nailed to the fence forever. Doesn't anyone have something better to do with the atmosphere than turn it into a monstrous perceiving machine? I'm so sorry, he whispers to the calf, it just keeps looking at him HELP ME HELP ME HELP ME and so Melvin hurries away. A little farther down the road he sees this white horse that's rippling with texture and light and power and color and consciousness and flesh and just looking at him like I'm fucking beautiful and I see you looking at me and you see me seeing you looking at me and it's like everywhere he turns he's being watched by suffering or beautiful consciousness looking to be admired or relieved. Eye contact is madness. Madness, madness, madness. Are clouds secret whispering membranes? Are dust devils angelic orders? Out of some barn pops this Mexican boy carrying a bucket who smiles at Melvin in the same way as the horse and they say some words to each other that are just like *burble burble burble* and it seems to Melvin that they're just both totally in love with each other, they're both fucking beautiful and good-natured and rippling with freedom and consciousness and flesh and it seems like they might just sort of start touching each other right then and there going *burble burble burble* but then some aggro uncle or older brother or stepdad pops out of nowhere and starts screaming at the boy or maybe it's just his boss or even the white guy who owns the ranch, Melvin can't really tell, it's just like this horrible voice of shame and pain and the kid drops his head and scurries away.

Melvin used to want to stab Denny. Stab stab stab stab. It's so hot he takes some clothes off and sits down somewhere and drinks water and thinks about sobbing. Dangerous arrangements pervade everything. Everything. Robot rape leading to body parts in a plastic bag by the side of the road. This conscious-ness is brought to you by. This leisure time is sponsored by. This road trip is made possible by funding from chunks of bone blown to bits, scorched scraps of flesh, a jawbone with eleven teeth and part of a shirt with elaborate embroi-dery, all dumped near the military base in a plastic bag. Pretty soon everything will be looking at itself all the time, and torturing the parts of itself that create the most self-loathing. What is terror for? A steep learning curve. The differ-ence between terror and prison he ought to figure out before he ends up there. What is sex for? No difference, same difference, something like that. What is thinking for? Our core values. He puts his clothes back on before somebody shoots him naked. Naked, not what he meant. English is his dad's corpse. Dead Mexican daddy. Living white daddy. Is there a moral to this story? A win-win. The bottom line. Market placement. Bitch-ass words freaking in his brain. He can't get them out. *Burble burble burble.*

Back at the motel, the sleeping arrangements haven't changed.

Bro, we thought we lost you.

Love me. Keep me safe. Fluttering in the void.

The next day is a prolonged illness. Anorexic, dehydrated, bleeding out. In Barstow they stop for gas as the sun is going down and within fifteen seconds this skinny white woman is sniffing at their door. She just needs like five dollars, her husband left her she says, for a younger woman, ain't that a bitch. She's wearing tight black pants with a floral pattern up and down one leg and pink thongs with socks and a shirt that looks like it's made out of suede and her hair's tied back in a ponytail with a thick, pink rubber band, and when she repeats her story, as if nobody heard it the first time, and says, *ain't that a bitch*, the guys don't even reply. She can smell the human in the group and is on Melvin in five seconds while he's just trying to stretch his legs. She wonders if they're headed to LA, that's where she needs to go. She's got a job offer. She's got a career just waitin' out that way. Other hand, they could stick around right here. He's seriously entertaining the idea of calling the trip quits right here and now, how could it be any worse. Not to mention it would undo the fact of having a destination at all, which is kind of inherently unsatisfying. Who wants to get somewhere? The whole point is probably to never exactly arrive. If anything, the future should make space for people to never exactly arrive. So what's it gonna be? she's saying. You wanna party with me, get us a room? Her skin looks like crazy reptile leather that's been drying in the sun. Melvin hands her a warm soda from the backseat and she's still looking at him like she'd let him suck her own brains out for the last twenty dollars she smells in his pocket, while one of the robots is starting the car.

Melvin wakes up delirious hours later to find them crossing this bridge that arches over the water that must be some version of the Bay with these bright blinking oil refinery lights on the other side as the sun is going down over a romantic industrial wasteland. The driver says there's a short detour before they drop him off in Berkeley, they gotta stop at somebody's former girlfriend's place in San Rafael to pick up something that might be somebody's shit or somebody's drugs or who knows what and the guys who are driving are texting like mad. Eventually they're crossing another bridge low over the bay, which is full of islands, and past San Quentin Prison. There's an aura or electrical current in the atmosphere that keeps people's souls inside along with their bodies, he's pretty sure, and it's clear enough that he's never saved anybody, not even himself. Circling around and then into some dreary neighborhood waiting while somebody runs inside some crappy little house that looks like a meth house. It just suggests from its anonymous smallness and not overly decrepit wastedness a kind of lawless zone, and Melvin's sure at this point that the whole idea has been to deliver his delirious carcass to some serial killer in exchange for a soul for their fucking robot consciousness.

5

FELICIA IS CHATTING WITH DIANE MIDDLEMARCH. Diane's second novel, *Mademoiselle Q.*, was widely praised for its unflinching look at "erotic devastation," a description that Felicia prefers to the novel itself. But she respects Diane's work, and Diane is a name. Diane has agreed to send her a short piece for the anthology, and after they gossip a bit about other contributors, it occurs to Felicia that Diane might be somehow connected to Huey Beauregard.

Ugh, says Diane.

Ugh?

My ex-husband is the editor who first published Huey, Diane says.

According to Diane, while she was still married to Sylvester, Huey was introduced to Sylvester by Saul Torstenson, shortly after Sylvester began his affair with Mary Stringer. Sylvester and Mary formed an intense and probably pathological bond with Huey, she says, as if he was the illicit love child of their own affair. Their affair was quickly spiraling out of control, involving unwarranted six-figure book deals and booze-soaked weekends at every Writer's Conference from Breadloaf to Berlin. I always thought there was something fishy about that kid, says Diane, after he arranged to meet Saul in the park and instead some fat woman showed up.

A fat woman? Who was the fat woman?

His roommate, I think, says Diane. Or maybe she's in his band.

So Sylvester never met him in person?

Nobody ever met him in person, says Diane. Sylvester tried to surprise him once, at his squat in San Francisco. Turns out the address is a copy shop on Mission Street. The kid's got a PO box there.

But Sylvester did talk to him on the phone, says Felicia.

All the time, says Diane. All the fucking time.

When Felicia calls Benton Archer, she gets his voicemail and leaves a message. Every sexual outlaw of the new millennium, it seems, is somehow connected to Huey Beauregard. Next up, Sandra Holmes, who published a few of her memoir pieces about working as a lap dancer and being abused by her stepbrother in the same anthologies as Huey, tells Felicia that she met the munchkin figure once backstage at a reading, and became convinced that Huey was a young woman with her breasts taped down. Later when she heard he'd begun the process of gender transitioning, it made more sense. The hormones, you know.

Felicia scours Huey's website again, and then the website of his band. Huey's "bandmates" are wielding guitars and making pouty lips. Racer and Trauma. Clearly it isn't Racer playing the part of Huey in public, she's way too tall.

Trauma has long, dyed black hair but looks like a prom queen hiding out beneath a goth/punk surface. Trauma is an actress, and she plays *herself*, a naïve girl from West Virginia, on some new HBO series. Felicia wonders if she's seen her somewhere, or if it's just that she looks so much like so many porn actresses and pop stars that they all blur together, airbrushed balloons of flesh grown like genetically modified pumpkins in America. She compares her picture with

Huey's. That would be too easy, wouldn't it. But they have the same cheeks, the bewigged munchkin with no Adam's apple, raised in Arkansas truck stops, and the HBO starlet claiming to be a West Virginia gal. The website claims she's five-foot-five so if that's with heels, maybe she's really five-foot-two, which would be about right for the munchkin. But what about the mole by Huey's lip? Probably a mole can be faked.

But Felicia doesn't think it adds up. After a few more minutes of poking around, she has dispensed with the prom queen Trauma altogether. Trauma has been singing with Briar Patch for only a couple of years, replacing the previous singer, the *original* Trauma. It is the *original* Trauma who is supposedly Huey's roommate in their "renovated squat," along with Racer and with Trauma's little girl, Juno. It is the *original* Trauma who sometimes calls herself Jezebel and sometimes Emma Jo. In some stories she is the outreach worker who saved Huey from his life on the streets, and yet she occasionally speaks with a Slavic accent, according to more than one interviewer. A few more searches and there she is, hobnobbing with Meg Ryan and Cher at one of Huey's readings. The *original* Trauma is considerably more haggard and definitely more crazy-looking but, notes Felicia, not overweight at all. As Emma Jo, she is the author of several glowing reviews of Huey's books on Amazon. She in no way resembles the munchkin who pretends to be Huey.

The band's mailing address, through which one can order both their CDs and the opossum-penis-bone jewelry that Huey sells, is on Mission Street.

Geordi is in the other room, hard at work, in monkish silence. She pops her head in.

I'm going out for a bit. I'll pick up some Thai food, okay?

He grunts his assent. She drives across the bridge to the city.

The cosmology itself emerges intricately from the eight verb choices.

'anna: take prisoner or make a matter of concern

saqata: to fall out

naba: to befall

haraba: to flee

hada: to diverge

afficere: to do to, act on, influence, attack with a disease

al-mana: to be captive, be captivated, seize attention, emerge, reveal

rahima: to have mercy

Geordi's in the middle of an important line of thinking when the doorbell rings. The mysterious author or authors of *The 8-Fold Garden of Space and Time* have an obsession with what seem to be underground prisons, tyranny, and revolution, but which might also be construed as subterranean *concepts*, painful mental states, and laughter. If there are no clear semantic grounds by which to distinguish between *an imprisoning captivity* and *an affecting preoccupation*, why have translations of *The 8-Fold Garden of Space and Time* all rendered this particular verb form as *imprison*, when it could just as easily be *captivate*? Is there a subtle cue in the text he's missing? Such a simple and obvious shift would lead several key passages away from the typical Gnostic-influenced readings of time and matter as prisons and toward the more organic idea of the manifest creation as entertainment, an astounding or amusing tale, a distraction from fundamental horror, with the listeners willing participants in their own enchantment—not chained or enslaved victims of some evil demiurge.

The doorbell rings again.

It's been night already for hours. The boy at the door asks about Felicia, says, Oh you must be her *husband*, and then chatters on. The guys he rode here with didn't even wait to see if someone was home before they drove away.

The boy in the squat, he realizes, Felicia's boy, Felicia's squat, but she'd made the *visit*, as she'd called it, seem insignificant, far less catastrophic than it's clearly going to be. For one thing, Melvin has baggage, and he plops it down in the living room like it's going nowhere soon. For another thing, he talks a lot, he talks like he's been gagged for days and is talking to save his life. His face reminds Geordi of an older boy he used to pick peaches with, and who he'd held in the highest esteem, but who was often cruel to Geordi. Geordi's shyness elicited a charming protectiveness at times, but not always. The scar fascinated children, but also made them misread him. They thought that he was tough. If you translate the particular verse that Geordi has been gazing at for days as *you imprison my heart* instead of *you captivate my heart*, it's like the difference between being murdered or simply *fainting into the alphabet's embrace*. As the author of *The 8-Fold Garden of Space and Time* wrote, a thousand years ago.

Melvin's mannerisms strike Geordi as bizarrely and inappropriately erotic, and make Geordi immediately jealous of his relationship with Felicia. *My wife* should be home any minute, he tells Melvin. He brings Melvin a drink of lukewarm tap water. *My wife* will be happy to see you, he says.

Melvin says, I never know if I should trust my perceptions more or if I should like not trust them at all.

I'm just finishing up some work, Geordi says.

Melvin says, Sometimes I think my brain's only job is lying to my body about what it's going through.

The look on the freakish, yet carelessly handsome face rekindles the question that's just beneath the surface: merely *captivated* or actually *taken captive*?

I can't believe I made it.

Made it? says Geordi.

What sort of work are you *finishing up*? Melvin asks.

Verb forms.

Totally! New *life* forms need new *verb* forms.

These are old verb forms. Really old. Ancient.

Same difference.

Geordi's trying to imagine some way to make this conversation stop.

What now?

Maybe you should take a bath, says Geordi.

It's like I've decided something, something really important. I mean I'm actually here.

What do you mean by *here*?

The west side of the map. I crossed over from one side to the other!

You want to take a bath?

Mmmm, a bath.

Geordi tells the kid he ought to just clean up and relax until *his wife* gets home.

You could watch a movie, he adds.

He hands him the first DVD he can find and points him to the extra room, where the TV is.

A movie has the exact same job as my brain, Melvin says. It tells you you're somewhere you aren't. But I could probably turn my brain off for a minute.

The DVD is *Female Convict Scorpion: Jailhouse 41*.

The copy shop is run by an elderly Indian woman. Yes, she's met Huey. He's kept his PO box here for years. A very charming man, she says.

Pictures of a smiling swami are plastered above all her Xerox machines.

Really, says Felicia. You're the first person I've ever met who's actually seen him in person. He's very reclusive, very mysterious. Can you tell me what he looks like?

She describes him as a tall man in his 30s. Good hair. A very charming man, she repeats.

Felicia is sitting in a brightly lit Thai restaurant a few doors down, waiting for her take-out, when Benton Archer returns her call. Benton probes a bit about the anthology, then says he has a short piece he could probably give her.

Benton hasn't met Huey either, not really, he tells Felicia. Oh, he sort of met the little guy once, decked out in his fake beard and glasses, but it was kind of bizarre. This older woman who accompanied him—she had this Russian or East European accent and called herself Slavenka—was explaining to Huey who Benton was, as if they hadn't spent years and years talking intimately over the phone with each other, and then Huey quickly just kind of scurried away, unable to take the pressure of finally meeting his idol, the older woman explained. He's receptive to the idea that there might be something funny going on, but the idea that Huey doesn't really exist just isn't plausible. Hundreds, maybe thousands of hours he spent on the phone with that kid. A whole, complicated life history. It often occurred to him that Huey was a liar, perhaps pathological, that he wasn't precisely who he said he was, that some of his stories were exaggerated or untrue, but that comes with the territory, doesn't it? Life on the streets, foster care, abuse. How could he not be a mess? The one person who would have had to have spent significant face time with Huey is his therapist, Dr. Bailey, Benton says, who Huey always credits with saving him— Huey's even donated money to Dr. Bailey's mental health program.

This Slavenka woman, says Felicia. Was she overweight?

Benton doesn't think so, but he's not really sure. It's like he couldn't form a clear mental image of her. It's like she was blurry, or made of smoke.

Once, in the Central Valley, early in the evening, when Geordi was just a boy, the kids watched an older woman who owned one of the neighboring fields humming a little song to herself and surveying her possessions. They had decided that she was evil, because they coveted her fruit. They began making weird noises—like wild animals or shrieking spirits. At first she was angry— *Malcriados*, she yelled at them—but when she couldn't see them in the gloom, she became frightened and ran away, as if she was being chased. They hurried in and filled their pockets with oranges and almonds.

They were a gang of kids. That boy who looked like Melvin was the leader, the oldest, Gonzalo. It didn't occur to Geordi that if he didn't have friends his own age, there might be something wrong with him. They rode their bikes through the warmth of a summer evening that smelled like pesticides and hay. A little girl ahead of Geordi dropped a Valencia orange that hit the street with a thud and rolled into the gutter. They took refuge in a shed somewhere, as if that woman or the police might come out looking for the thieves.

In ones and twos, the other children left, until Geordi was alone with Gonzalo. He was proud that he was the last man out after dark, and yet slightly frightened of Gonzalo. Gonzalo kept peering through the holes in the boards of the shed, the gaps in between, to make sure nobody was out there watching them. The walls have eyes, he kept saying. The walls have eyes. For some reason, Geordi thought that he was going to show him dirty pictures or kiss him, but instead Gonzalo began slowly telling a story, a story that didn't seem outrageous at first, about his father, who'd been involved in secret military operations and moneymaking schemes, but became more and more convoluted until it eventually sucked Geordi's own father into its web. Geordi's father, a quiet man who worked hard, who picked fruit and didn't complain. When Gonzalo got to the climax of his story, in which Gonzalo's father was shot in the heart by Geordi's father, Geordi thought it must be a joke, and he laughed.

I'd appreciate it if you didn't laugh about my father's murder, Gonzalo said.

He was, it seemed, serious. His father had been murdered by Geordi's father. Because Geordi had never seen Gonzalo's father, and because it had all supposedly happened before Geordi was even born, there was no way to refute the story. Geordi became confused. He almost believed it, maybe he did believe it. The point of the story seemed to be that even though Gonzalo considered Geordi a good guy and a friend, there was a blood feud that couldn't be ignored. Geordi was going to have to die, or maybe just suffer so much that he'd wish that he was dead.

It was hot and dark in that shed and smelled of oranges, bitter almonds, and dust. Gonzalo's story grew more and more elaborate. Geordi's scar was involved, a clue or a piece of evidence, and the woman they'd frightened was involved, an accessory after the fact. Geordi was accused of secret communications with that woman, by means of a complicated code. Although Geordi knew he was innocent, he couldn't quite piece together the idea that Gonzalo might not actually believe his own story, that he had incorporated Geordi into a ridiculous lie. Geordi didn't understand children who lied. He had never learned how to lie. Gonzalo was telling Geordi that he would never leave the shed alive, for the fun of it perhaps. Finally he told him just to go, to hurry, before he changed his mind, as if he was giving him an undeserved reprieve out of the goodness of his heart.

It was never mentioned again. The story wasn't acknowledged to be a lie, even after Geordi met Gonzalo's father. Once, when they were lighting bottle rockets and Gonzalo wanted to shoot some of Geordi's, he did say, You owe me. You know why.

Later, when Geordi moved to Long Beach, Gonzalo was still back there. He saw him once or twice when they went back to visit, and he seemed even meaner and crazier looking, but still charismatic. His father killed himself, Geordi later heard.

Gonzalo used to wear a Navy uniform, he wanted to join the Navy.

Their refrigerator was full of sodas.

Geordi was hungry sometimes. Before they moved to Long Beach. Peaches made him ill.

He was hungry that day with Urszula, and yet he didn't eat. He must be crazy.

Maybe this was when Geordi realized there were things the adults weren't telling him. It didn't matter that Gonzalo's story was insane—it made the idea visceral, for a moment, that major events in the past weren't being openly discussed. This is probably when the idea first got lodged in his head that his father or his grandmother knew what had happened to him, what had scarred him. Not his mother. His mother was too self-absorbed to keep a secret.

It isn't until Melvin is ridiculously clean and perched in front of the television watching the movie that Felicia finally shows up with bags of take-out Thai.

Your squat boy is here, Geordi whispers. He's got luggage.

She seems to not understand, then composes herself, pops her head in the next room. Hey, she says. Melvin gives her an overly enthusiastic hug and more or less says that he's never been so happy to see another person.

Just relax and make yourself at home, she tells him. Did you have something to eat?

He says, I guess this movie makes me hungry.

He says, It's kind of like cartoons. Cartoons are totally important. They're the realms where future forms first manifest. Cartoons and alternative toys!

Hold on just a second, she says. You're a vegetarian, right?

She comes back out, gives Geordi a kind of bemused smile that doesn't seem at all appropriate, and begins arranging dinner on three plates, reserving more of the meat-free dishes for the boy.

You didn't tell me he was *staying* here, he whispers.

I know, I know. I guess there's been a misunderstanding.

A misunderstanding?

Let's just try to deal with it for the moment, okay?

A misunderstanding between who and who?

She takes the boy his food. While the boy makes gobbling noises, she's making up the futon in there with clean, crispy sheets and warm, fuzzy blankets and pillows. She's *mothering* him. Geordi isn't hungry. He's startled by his hatred for that horrible child. He could go out either the front or the back without passing through the room where the boy is chatting with his wife. He hears Melvin say, Did you ever write a book?

I'm going out to get some air, he declares, not even sure anybody's heard him. He's acting out, he knows that, and decides to just go with it. The air is just about exactly the same temperature outside as inside. It's cool, but too warm for November. The car is parked on the street out front, but as soon as he sits inside it, he's terrified of where he might go.

After his *fainting spell*, as he has come to think of it, or his *day with Urszula*. A day that seemed to promise horror and revelation, but left him instead with a notebook with hundreds of blank pages inside. Only a few pages had writing, but it must have been left out in the rain at some point, or dunked in water, until the writing became so smeared it was unreadable. The only message left in tact was the title, written in Arabic, and two sentences in English on the final page, written in pencil.

Felicia's showing Melvin this book she claims she wrote. It's called *Meatsicle*.

My stab at cyberpunk, fifteen years too late, she says, and laughs.

I'm totally into ideas about the future! Melvin tells her.

Honestly, the sci-fi stuff is pretty limited, it's just some sort of atmosphere.

She seems embarrassed to be talking about her writing.

Honestly, she says, I only really write about the present.

That's crazy, because I was just talking about the present with that guy.

That guy?

Your husband or whatever.

Felicia laughs, and looks around, as if Geordi might still be there, hiding.

I guess when you're writing, you have your own kind of present, she says. You have this awareness maybe, but a book is always read in the future. I mean someone will read it a year after you finished it or five years later or maybe when you're dead. But even if you're dead when they read it, even if you're just this voice from the grave, you never want it to be about the past or you know.

Not just the past, she says.

She has this faraway look like Melvin isn't even listening but he's listening like crazy. Melvin believes she's the most amazing and benevolent entity ever.

I'm totally gonna read this book, he says.

She says, Which is why I displace things in time, I think. In a poorly imagined future or in a dream, because I never want my reader to be like, oh, this is about how messed up things were back in 2006.

Melvin says, How fucked up things are right now.

But not only. I mean every day is the right day, too.

Unless…

She says, I know *the moment* is a horrible cliché and a kind of ontological impossibility. I know that, I do. But I guess I'm into taking care of it. To the best of my ability.

Melvin suspects that *ontological impossibility* is a description of his own life.

The moment becomes the past before you can even grasp it, usually. But you have to try. The past is just a subjective fantasy. Whether you're living inside the moment or looking at it from the outside…either way, you can take care of it, Felicia says. It doesn't have to be all hippie dippy.

But what about a book? Melvin asks. I mean…they seem so…

She seems to be really perceiving him now, and waiting for him to finish his sentence.

Overly…controlling?

You think so?

No, maybe that's not it, because I guess you can come and go as you please.

He stops, wondering where he got this phrase—*as you please*. Maybe from a book?

I mean you don't have advertisements and stuff either. That's a plus.

Come and go, exactly, she says. A book is like this tangled thing, that's like a person's mind. And you can walk right in and look around. It's totally different from a mind, of course, but it's kind of like a metaphor for a mind. What we do with our minds is we keep adding things, we keep perceiving things, we turn our thinking into this kind of gnarly movement. We know it will all be lost, simplified, dissolved when we die. What could be clearer than that? A complex something that dissolves into nothing. There isn't anything else, right?

I don't know. Maybe there is?

So you want your readers to dream into their own present. To vibrate. To wake up to the mystery of time. Something like that.

Wake up.

Time is like a fluid that memory and imagination create, a fluid you are always immersed in and that you can experience in multiple directions, but only now, in the present.

Like…everybody should be fondling each other and thinking stuff up, all the time!

Felicia blushes. Melvin's totally into that.

The mystery of time.

She looks like she's going to go on, but she says, It's late, you must be exhausted.

She'll pop in later and make sure he's all tucked in.

Felicia is standing alone in the dark living room, feeling especially conscious and alive, when Geordi comes in, looking either angry or freaked out. He begins whispering viciously, as if he's been rehearsing his anger, out there in the dark. He accuses her of keeping secrets. She should have been more forthcoming about the nature of "the boy," he keeps saying, never once mentioning Melvin by name.

Melvin's a nice kid, she says.

Shhhh.

He's just kind of kinetic, she says.

Geordi says, What do you mean kinetic?

Felicia says, Of, relating to, or produced by motion, you aren't familiar with the term?

His vicious whispering veers off in new directions—mean things she's said in the past, sexual experiences they've either had or read about, French theory.

Melvin's just a nice kid, she says, Melvin's not as much trouble as he seems.

Every time she says *Melvin*, Geordi says *shhhh*, guessing, probably correctly, that the sound of his own name will attract Melvin's attention. It actually sounds like Melvin's turned down the TV so he can listen to what they're saying. Felicia's pretty sure he's standing just on the other side of the door.

6

Freddy's Marine is reclining on Freddy's sofa in a way so reminiscent of one of Ralph's porns that Philip is momentarily disoriented. The guy's shirtless and wearing a Santa hat, a garish centerpiece that distorts the focus of Freddy's cramped and overwrought apartment. The overflowing bookshelves and gay trinkets and brass candleholders with weird inscriptions in foreign alphabets and ivory-handled letter openers and bell jars all seem to be in orbit around the musculature of his chest. Philip could swear he saw some war propaganda—some photo of *our boys* in Iraq—composed in exactly the same way. But now he can't quite suspend his disbelief enough for even the basic social conventions.

It isn't that he can't yet adjust, after spending twenty-three days in Iowa. He's delivering some weed; afterward, he'll be an extra in Ralph's movie. This is how it goes—you go somewhere, have experiences you don't understand, you meet people without clarifying a thing, and then it's over. His habits, his daily life, and his sense of self were all still here, just waiting to fill his days again. It's been surprisingly easy to just let them. It's just the half-naked Marine in the Santa hat that has left Philip speechless.

According to Freddy, this one even fucked Freddy while talking on the cell phone with his girlfriend, or at least while listening to his girlfriend chatter on, occasionally grunting at her or at Freddy, hard to know which. He'd have a distant expression on his face while Freddy straddled him, Freddy had said, and his seeming indifference to both the fact that his stiff cock was inside Freddy and to his girlfriend's observations, complaints, and future plans, excited Freddy to no end. Freddy's dream date, it has become clear to Philip, is to impale himself on a glacier. From Philip's vantage point in the overstuffed froufrou chair, the Marine's silence serves as a counterpoint to Freddy himself, fluttering and zigzagging frantically about the apartment, looking for something he's misplaced, forgetting what he's looking for, and complaining viciously about a poet Philip's never heard of who seems to have disrespected Freddy in some slightly public way. According to Freddy, the poet has never escaped from his own poetic convictions, which are derivative in any case, a pale imitation of poetic convictions from fifty years ago. He's repulsive, says Freddy. With all his talk about the holy word.

But you believe that, too, says Philip. In a sense.

Yes, but I'd never say it directly, says Freddy. And I'd never pretend that poetry makes me a good person. Oh…oh!

He shrieks and disappears into the tiny kitchen. Moments later he's pounding or kneading a lumpy bag of something on the kitchen counter. And then the phone rings. Freddy throws his hands in the air as if that's the last straw.

The machine will get it, he says. Oh god, Philip, you're a lifesaver, I need to get high.

A voice crackles into the apartment like an electrical storm, a voice Philip has heard before, in a nightmare he once had, or in the middle of a movie when he'd fallen asleep—a whispery, husky, overdone Southern voice. Freddy, it rasps, Freddy, are you there? Ah need to talk to you Freddy, it's real import-ant, can you pick up, doll?

And Freddy does.

Look, Huey, says Freddy, can I call you back? I'm all in a tizzy right now, and I...

Freddy falls into silence.

Amazing, thinks Philip. Amazing, the weird magical calm that comes over Freddy in the pause that follows. Amazing what that creature—whatever it is—has done with only its voice.

The conversation lumbers along, with Freddy barely speaking a word, but listening, rapt, occasionally offering some kind of comfort, assuring Huey that some celebrity really does love him. Philip thinks it's the tall ex-junky girlfriend of that superstar suicide, the woman who was raised by troubled Deadheads and who turned herself into a movie star. Or maybe it's Madonna.

No, Huey, no, says Freddy.

Maybe Philip's imagining the sudden chill in the room, but the Marine has goose bumps, too. Eavesdropping isn't very satisfying, however, when 90 per-cent of the conversation is barely audible, a sinuous hush and crackle.

She wants to be more myth than human being, Freddy is saying. She wants to embody immortality but she always just shows us time and death.

Hey, says Philip to the Marine. I'm Philip.

Danny, says the Marine.

Does this happen often? That this kid calls?

If he's calling, he's calling all the time, says Danny.

Philip studies Danny's face.

What are you thinking?

Excuse me?

I'm kind of stuck here, says Philip, until Freddy gets off the phone. And you're thinking something. I'm curious.

Danny smiles.

I don't think you really wanna know.

What? *Dangerous* thoughts?

He tosses Danny Freddy's bag of weed.

All real thinking is dangerous thinking, says Danny.

Aha, says Philip. Just as I suspected. You're a cynic, an adventurer, a man of the world. And how did you come to be here?

I have too much respect to discuss personal arrangements, says Danny.

He removes his Santa hat, as if to demonstrate his respect. Or as if to reveal his buzzed head, which is sexy in an abstract way.

You were in Iraq?

Afghanistan.

Huey, they're all like that, Freddy is saying.

Danny opens the baggie and sniffs Freddy's weed.

They don't know how to express their love, Freddy is saying. Bad behavior *is* love, for the famous.

Danny shakes his head.

What they show you on TV, Danny says. That isn't reality.

They've gotten very good at not showing reality, Philip says. You could probably say that's the genius of our culture.

Danny says, There's a lot of money being made.

All those weapons manufacturers and whatnot.

Computer companies, too, says Danny. Dell and HP. There's this mineral they're taking out of the country. They need it for the circuits.

What mineral?

I don't remember what it's called, it's greenish, it has a green part in it, they'd just tell us to move it from here to over there.

Danny fondles the Santa hat in a way that seems like it's supposed to project innocence, thoughtlessness.

Philip says, Dangerous thinking.

If you realize that all things change…, Danny says, but then he picks up a shirt that is draped over the chair behind him and digs a bunch of index cards from the pocket. He shuffles through them until he finds what he wants.

If you realize that all things change, there is nothing you will try to hold on to, he says. If you are not afraid of dying, there is nothing you cannot achieve.

Fair enough, says Philip.

Philip remembers the rainstorm, the mist on the river, the two boys on the bridge. One boy on the bridge or two boys on the bridge or zero boys, whatever it was.

That's Lao-tzu, says Danny.

You collect quotes, says Philip. Are they all of a military nature? Conflict, death, fear, impermanence?

I don't distinguish the martial so much from the nonmartial, says Danny.

Ooh, I like that. Everything is war.

Everything is tactics.

There is something about the way that Danny's face registers the process of thinking—clarifying that it is a physical task, involving the body's entire musculature—that makes Philip nostalgic for whole eras of history he never really lived through.

I'm curious in what sense you see yourself as a soldier, Philip says. I mean— is that you or is it just a performance?

How are you drawing your line between what's unreal and what isn't?

Philip wonders if Danny's mask is so entwined with his face that they've become the same thing. A male, a soldier. A killer for hire.

The unreal, says Philip, is an emanation or vapor created by a disturbance or a kind of wound in the primordial substance. It's accidental. The real is what's left when you peel those emanations away and peer into...whatever.

Danny says, You want to heal the disturbance.

Philip says, No, not at all. Without the disturbance...

Danny's eyes crinkle with intelligence, his sexiest gesture of the afternoon.

That peering is the whole point, Philip says. From time into eternity and from eternity into time. Many respected mystics would agree.

Danny nods.

The mind is like a bridge, right? Philip says. Too bad for us, we're stuck on the side full of death and dismemberment.

Danny says, The grass is always greener.

Philip wonders if he actually believes what he's been saying. If this was just a show, performers on one side, and audience on the other, performers as audience and audience as performers, then beauty would be enough. The musculature of Danny's chest, his buzzed head, his vulnerable lips, all that would be enough. But it isn't enough, is it?

I always have exactly sixty-four notecards, Danny explains. But they're always changing. I'm trading one out for another. I don't throw the old ones away, it isn't like that. I put them away. The sixty-four, those I keep on my person.

You use these to tell the future? asks Philip.

I use them to tell me about the present.

Philip knew somebody once who collected pictures of mushroom clouds. Philip had been shocked just how many different mushroom clouds there had been on the face of the earth, duly recorded from above. They were beautiful, awesome plumes of smoke, not always so mushroomy, surrounded by other clouds and by ocean or by desert. The Bikini atoll, New Mexico, Nevada, Eniwetak, Novaya Zemlya, Lop Nur, Christmas Island, Fangataufa, South Australia, Algeria. This guy believed that he could see faces in the atomic smoke. He believed these were demons who were revealing the unhappy future. He thought he could glean what they were telling him if he concentrated just a little bit harder.

Strategy is someone else's job, Danny says.

So you are a soldier, says Philip. Really and truly. Can I see?

Just keep them in order, says Danny.

The first card is Schopenhauer.

In endless space, countless luminous spheres, round each of which some dozen smaller illuminated ones revolve, hot at the core and covered over with a hard cold crust; on this crust a mouldy film has produced living and knowing beings: this is empirical truth, the real, the world.

He flips through—Cioran, Diogenes, Wittgenstein, Jesus. *Whoever has come to know the world has discovered a carcass, and whoever has discovered a carcass is worth more than the world.* Levi Strauss, Oscar Wilde, even Rimbaud. *When the world has been reduced to a single gloomy wood for our four astonished eyes. To one beach for two faithful children. To one musical house for our pure harmony—I shall find you.*

After Rimbaud, it's Clarice Lispector. Then Rilke. The series ends with Chuang Tse, Whitman, Heraclitus, Plotinus, Octavia Butler, and finally Martha Graham, the quote about vision.

I get it, says Philip.

Danny almost smiles.

You need Jacob Boehme, says Philip. I'm going to get you a quote from Jacob Boehme.

Freddy hangs up the phone. Philip expects Danny to stiffen somehow, but he doesn't. He looks relaxed and thoughtful in a kind of thoughtless way, as if they'd just been discussing the weather.

God, what a tornado that kid is, says Freddy.

But Freddy, too, seems perfectly calm.

I used to sub at the Adolescent Day Treatment Center, says Philip. Didn't Huey used to go there?

Yes, yes he did. That's where he first met Dr. Bailey, I believe.

Dr. Bailey? This is a real doctor?

Of course he's a real doctor, Freddy says. Once when Huey was a real mess, he got me in on this conference call with the guy. The doctor seemed like he had a real stick up his ass, but who knows? This is highly inappropriate, I remember Dr. Bailey saying. Which seemed ridiculous, given what poor Huey was going through at the time.

What was poor Huey going through at the time?

Freddy shrugs and then scowls at Philip.

I thought you didn't believe he existed.

Actually, it's Felicia who doesn't believe he exists, says Philip. Obviously you were on the phone with *someone*.

Oh, that woman, says Freddy. What did you say she writes?

Novels, Philip says. She writes novels.

Detective novels? Mysteries? Or little domestic dramas perhaps.

All of her books end with a woman alone, waiting, says Philip. Waiting, waiting for something…will it ever arrive? Impossible to say.

You're such a bitch, says Freddy.

But that's my favorite part, says Philip. I love those waiting women. I don't think there's anything wrong with telling the same story over and over again, in slightly different ways, from a slightly different angle, or even from the same angle but with a different…

He shrugs. Freddy plucks the bag of weed from Danny's lap and removes some ridiculously ornate yet elegant smoking implement from a drawer. And then he pays him.

Gotta run, Philip tells Freddy. I'm off to a film shoot.

Then he addresses Danny directly.

From the No to the Yes. Right?

The No *and* the Yes, Danny says. It's a sequence. But there isn't any *from*. And there isn't any *to*.

7

THE SOCIOPATHIC QUEER GANG dons their ski masks, and bursts into the store, toy guns in hand.

For a moment, Ralph ceases to exist and becomes the role: a terrified, but not completely surprised clerk, still eating his sandwich mechanically. The clerk is thinking: The need for life to devour other life is the most evil principle with which you could build a world. He remembers his tooth infection, his dizziness, the suicidal thoughts that came with it. Face to face with death, the clerk is having a silent realization: He's been living his life unnaturally, as if tranquilized. The clerk has always known that the distance between life and death is a flimsy sheet of cellophane. Death is spontaneous, magical, alive. Whatever. He lets out a little moan, like a wounded creature. He is finally opening his eyes to gaze into an everlasting abyss.

But the robbery is falling apart, not how it's supposed to, in an explosion of unplanned violence, but in an explosion of bad acting, forgotten lines, clumsy physical movements.

They do two more takes, neither to Tony's satisfaction.

Melvin borrows BART fare and tells Felicia he needs to take care of some urgent business. He knows he's causing trouble here. He's actually just going to walk the streets.

What sort of work do you do? she asks.

Work, says Melvin.

I just mean how do you usually make money?

Maybe I can do a focus group, he says.

A good focus group, sometimes they pay you a hundred bucks just to sit in a room with two-way mirrors, talking about some worthless product. But sometimes you have to lie about how much disposable income you have or what ethnicity you are or whatever. Your level of education or what kind of car you drive, because they want people who buy things with a little more regularity than Melvin.

Focus groups, says Felicia. You can live off of that?

Not really, says Melvin. But you know…

Felicia puts some minutes on his phone so that he can call her if he needs to.

She's the one who calls him, however, later, while he's walking up Haight Street. She asks him to do her a favor, pick up some weed from some writer guy. Melvin can meet him in the Western Addition, he's at a film shoot.

All these films you see on magazine covers and all that, Melvin says, they're all produced by the parent corporation.

This isn't that kind of movie, says Felicia. It's, you know. Indie.

They're all that kind of movie, says Melvin. Indie or whatever. We can't help it. But you have to be on the lookout for the messages from the *real* world, the *secret* world.

What about books? asks Felicia.

Totally, says Melvin. It's like a dream so complicated and just everything you

even think about that you can't even find your way out! They control everything and they're putting us asleep.

Felicia tells Melvin that he's probably right—whether you call the machine
global capitalism or the military entertainment complex or The Matrix. And
whether or not you think there's something outside of the dream or whether
you think the dream is everything there is.

In any case, she'll give him the ten dollars it'll save Geordi in BART fare
or bridge toll to pick up the weed. She gives him precise directions to find the
liquor store where they're filming, but tells him to call her if he gets lost. Philip
will be expecting him.

She's trying to make him feel useful and industrious, obviously. But he can
use the money to eat and maybe the writer guy'll get him high.

Felicia doesn't want him, that's clear. Or the husband, or whatever. But he
needs a room, a warm space, once in a while at least, to keep himself from
scattering into fragments.

At the liquor store, all kinds of people are milling about. A big guy is manning a camera outside, as a gang of freaks enters the store with their guns out.
Melvin weaves around the crowd, asking if anyone knows who Philip is.

Philip looks like he's just woken up, confused.

What's up? he says.

Are you the writer guy?

The writer guy?

Felicia sent me, he says.

Melvin, says Philip. Sorry, for a minute I forgot. You'll have to excuse me,
I'm feeling a little bit weird.

Totally, says Melvin.

Philip has this dazed look. He looks hungry, too, Melvin decides. Or it's like
something hungry is attached to him and he doesn't know it yet. Philip gives him
his bag of weed and they chat—about New York, about the exhilaration of having no possessions, about hallucinogens. Melvin tells Philip that during one of
his recent, overly intense drug experience, he realized that black holes must be
prisons for photon-based life forms. He wondered if the life forms were dreaming from within those prisons. He wondered if maybe we *are* those dreams.

Ralph tries it again. A terrified, but not completely surprised clerk, still eating
his sandwich, mechanically. Face to face with death.

Maybe it wouldn't be so bad if when you died, you became a puff of smoke.
A friendly ghost, just a mute bundle of gas without agency or a will of its own,

drifting cheerily here and there at the behest of the living and their desires. But one of the sociopathic gang members stumbles into the potato chip rack, sending little baggies tumbling to the floor.

Jesus Christ, says Tony. Cut!

Ralph wanders back outside for some air. He is immediately transfixed by the kid Philip's talking to. The face could be considered blunt, smashed even, a boxer's, but the dark googly eyes unsettle everything. The lips look like some stylized, futuristic sexual organ that's been lifted off another species and pasted there. Even when his face is perfectly still, the features seem to be in motion.

Philip is saying something about this hum he could hear, the sound of the earth turning in space. The molecular substructure of everything was superimposed over the night sky, he says. A pale, shining, transparent haze was elaborating itself, branching out in every direction from star to star. Every direction meant *infinity*, it meant directions that couldn't be perceived, directions that didn't yet exist. It meant that this transparent, cuneiform, rooting structure like light (but it wasn't light, Philip insists) had penetrated every possibility.

Sounds kind of scary and cancerous, the kid says.

No, says Philip. It only *is*.

The kid is explaining that the main thing for him is what comes out of the molecular substructure of everything, which he's convinced are *ideas about the future*. There's so many different ways for life to evolve and the best way, he explains, is probably photosynthesis, it's really spiritual, he says, for lack of a better word, to live off of light energy, he thinks, and that's the road to take that could eventually turn you into a photon-based life form, but in the meantime you'd have to be kind of wide and flat, like a pancake…

And that's not very sexy, says Philip.

Totally not, the kid has to agree, and then there's the vampire route, because blood is the most concentrated and easily digestible form of protein, so if you can live off straight blood, you can use less energy to develop your stomach and more to develop your brain…and your, you know…spiritual organs…

And live off the humans.

Totally, says the kid, and then he whispers, Sometimes I think they're a future life form and sometimes I think they already exist.

Yes, Philip says. They're called the rich.

The rich, says the kid. No, thank you.

Raymond rides up on his bike, and the kid looks at him with surprised recognition.

No way! You're the guy from the park.

Yeah, says Raymond. So what phase are you in these days?

The kid blushes.

It's complicated, he says.

It's Melvin, Ralph realizes. The invisible boy with the *Suspiria* poster.

What other types of post-humanity would you just as soon avoid? Philip asks him.

The global brain. Which is just like the empire with consciousness. No, thank you.

Yes, says Philip. Good boy.

Clones. Robots. Dead humans uploaded into machines.

Philip moseys over to Ralph and whispers, Felicia needs a place for Melvin to stay. You want him?

What's the catch? Ralph asks.

I don't know, says Philip. I just met him.

Just then Felicia shows up, and Melvin gives her a hug.

Melvin feels weird, all of a sudden. A contact high, but contact with what?

What are you doing here? he asks Felicia. It's crazy. It's like…a conspiracy theory.

I had business come up in the city, she says.

The idea that he's been surrounded by a group of people with ulterior motives is kind of thrilling, and he decides to just go with it.

Melvin, says Philip, I'd like you to meet Ralph. He's the director. He makes horror and he makes porn.

Have you ever acted? Ralph asks.

Melvin has to think about that one. Where do you draw the line, he isn't ever sure. He tells them he's devoting more of his time to trying to *break free* of the machinery of illusion.

Philip says to Melvin, I would never guess from your face the things that come out of your mouth.

Melvin gets tired of people who think he's dumb, but sometimes it's also exhausting when people think he's smart. This Philip has the look of somebody who knows something, some dreadful secret reserved for the privileged few.

So what are we here for? he asks. What *happened*?

What happened, Philip says.

Melvin's being perceived from multiple directions. When every part of itself can see what every other part is doing, the universe might collapse from its own boredom. That's when something more interesting might happen.

What do you *believe*?

I believe an angel got raped by an electrical storm, Philip says.

Raped? says Melvin.

What?

It makes Melvin kind of uncomfortable, being looked at in person, by all these old people, but at the same time it's what he likes best. Is that a shallow desire?

An electrical storm, says Melvin. Are you…?

He leans against Philip. *As if I'm dizzy*, he thinks.

And he is dizzy, he's always dizzy, but the moment passes, and he jumps back like he's been shocked.

It doesn't matter, Ralph says. I like working with amateurs.

Ralph explains the plot to his film, which is so complicated that Melvin can't quite follow it. Melvin's role would be instilling terror until the tables are turned.

I'm not sure I'd be so good at scaring people, Melvin says.

You don't have to scare anyone, says Ralph. The hardest part is when you have to look frightened, confused, you'd have to scream, maybe you get murdered. Can you scream?

What, like a bitch? asks Melvin.

Felicia makes a face.

I mean like some girl?

There's a lot of ways to scream.

Ralph says that he wants Melvin to be his new leading man.

What would I have to do?

No screaming, says Ralph.

I'd be more into the other kind, I think, says Melvin.

The other kind?

Is there money? asks Felicia. I'm just saying, because right now Melvin doesn't even have a place to stay.

There's no pay, but it doesn't take much time. We could work around your schedule.

I don't have a schedule.

And you could stay with me as long as you want, says Ralph.

But what about the porn?

Absolute silence follows this question.

It's mostly gay porn, says Ralph.

Melvin shrugs.

Are you bisexual? asks Ralph. Or what?

I consider myself straight, Melvin says. But you know, I'm just around.

You should probably try everything, Philip advises him. Everything consensual.

Consensual, Melvin says. That's kind of the problem.

Melvin tells them about back when he was in high school at this party and somebody had the idea to blindfold him and then this girl Julie sucked his dick and his gay friend Jared did it, too, to see if he could tell the difference. And he was like no, it was pretty much the same.

But it wasn't really my thing, Melvin says.

You didn't like being blindfolded?

No, says Melvin, that part was totally cool. It's just that I'm not so much into oral.

Ralph says, If you wanna be a porn star, you have to be my lead in the sequel to *Tinky Winky Rising*, too.

Fair's fair, says Philip.

Bisexual's fine, says Melvin. I'm not homophobic. Maybe I could be…

Everyone leans forward, into his pause, waiting for the next word.

Raped or something, says Melvin.

The collectivity seems to consider the merits of that possibility.

Maybe you could work the Mormon angle, suggests Raymond.

Sure, says Philip. The rape could be structured around a polygamous marriage.

He doesn't have the most classically Mormon features, says Ralph. I mean we could dress him up with the tie and the Bible before we rape him, but I'm still not sure he'll read as Mormon.

Safer to work the Latino angle, says Philip. You have a problem playing a grossly stereotyped immigrant laborer or street thug?

Raymond brainstorms porn star names. He wants to convey both "spicy" Latino and innocent boy next door in one name. Nacho Dynamite. A hint of danger, something explosive. Cody "the Bomb" Hernandez. Shorty Firecracker Lopez. Ralph is already laying out the visual language for the abduction. You really just need one establishing shot. A face at the window in a ski mask, or a van pulling up alongside Melvin as he walks by the side of the road…

I like the van idea. A retro, '70s van with an *Ass Gas or Grass* bumper sticker.

Wait a second, says Felicia. Just slow down here. Porn might seem like a lot of fun…

Don't get all maternal on us here.

He's a grown man.

Or something like that.

Film lasts forever, Felicia says. It might come back and haunt you.

Is that the best that you've got? Future orientation isn't going to go far with this kid, says Philip.

He winks at Melvin.

And nothing lasts forever. Not even footage of forced booty sex.

I'm never going back to the church, says Melvin.

That's not what I meant, says Felicia.

Places, places, Tony yells. He whisks the cast in the general direction of the store's entrance. He stops in front of Melvin, looks him up and down.

Who's the supermodel?

Melvin, says Ralph, I'd like you to meet the director's assistant. Tony. Tony, our new star.

Don't think of me as your director, says Tony. Think of it more as a collaboration.

Tony herds the gang onto the sidewalk.

The ugly things in Melvin's past—Mom's stupid marriage, his crazy girlfriend, and this whole trip to New York, Jared's abuse, and the whole terror train of a road trip—have been redeemed, kind of. He's going to be a star.

And you can live with me, Ralph says. I'll be completely at your disposal.

No way! says Melvin. And can I even use your phone? I'd use my own, but you know…I'm totally out of minutes.

The cameras roll. Ralph is once again opening his eyes to find himself face-to-face with everlasting darkness. He has fallen into eternity again and realized again that if anyone longs for anything, it's only oblivion. He lets out another little moan. So that's all it is. So this is death. What more?

Just as the gang is emerging once again from the open jaws of the liquor store, having finally acted out the fake robbery to Tony's satisfaction, the police show up—the real police, three cars squealing to a stop in front of the liquor store, guns quickly drawn, ordering the cast of the film to get down on the ground, hands in the air, somewhat contradictory commands that Raymond knows all too well.

Ralph, dripping with fake blood, puts his hands in the air, and Tony, still holding the camera, puts his hands in the air. Both of them try to explain the misunderstanding. Philip tries to explain the misunderstanding. Melvin and Felicia put their hands in the air. Raymond is slowly backing away, until a cop spots him, trains his rifle on him, and orders him down on the ground. His grandmother must be, just now, sitting up in her grave. Everyone is frantically distinguishing between the fake and the real, but the cops aren't having it. The police aren't interested in these fine distinctions, not yet, not today, and continue to treat every single person, blood-stained or not, like a monster they are just itching to kill.

8

DRIZZLE ALTERNATES WITH FOG. The city is hushed and muted; junkies are passed out on the sidewalks, dreaming. Everyone is sleepy, daydreaming, walking in their sleep. As November turns to December, everyone is dreaming the same sort of dream. They're all dreaming they are dead.

It's as if they've been hollowed out, as if they've been separated forever from the only thing they ever loved, before they even realized what it was.

There is music in the dream, but not time. Here is the dream: a barn on a dark road illuminated by electricity from the farthest reaches of space.

A star that can't live with the other stars moves back and forth, between the earth and the sky. In the farmhouse there's a basement and in the basement there's a solitary weaver sorting silk threads from some tangled mess and feeding them into his loom, operated by a kind of pedal, and underneath the pedal and the loom there's a trapdoor and everybody knows that underneath the trapdoor is a path to the only true home you've ever really known.

In December, even the animals dream that they no longer exist. Even the trees. The buildings dream of ruins. The computers dream of the scrapyards where Pakistani children pick through their radioactive guts for the valuable bits. The books dream of bonfires. The planet dreams of collapsed suns, and we all dream of the heat death of the universe. The ghosts dream, too. In December, only the ghosts dream that they're alive.

Wake up.

Do some outreach on Polk Street, drop off some condoms at the Nob Hill Theatre, and then the big rape. Come back home and bake the *tart tatin*. Raymond's day has been ordered, perhaps a little too neatly, but as he bikes across the Mission, crossing 18th Street, where he and Philip lived for two years without even a kitchen, it's like he's swimming across a vast sadness, a bottomless bowl, a submerged graveyard littered with ruins of the past and populated by the ghosts of memory. All of the people who were dying around them, too young, but older, for the most part, than Raymond himself.

Turner wasn't dying, but he was terrified of AIDS, rarely had sex and then only with most of his clothes still on. Turner was the type of person who wouldn't even take his clothes off at the gay beach, but would sit and draw. He drew sketches for his paintings, brilliant, corrosive paintings of bodybuilders, evil clowns, and Clubland vistas where muscle boys had lights streaming out of their nipples, the men Turner referred to contemptuously as *Pecapods*. But Turner was bright and talented and funny, he was skinny and he had bad skin, but soon enough he started doing steroids and going to the gym, and he became himself a Pecapod, a Pecapod with big muscles and even worse skin, and he started going to those clubs he supposedly felt superior to, and started doing speed. For a while Raymond would still run into Turner on the street or in a park and they could have a conversation. Turner would complain about Jerry Bloom perhaps, and their hatred for each other, roommates locked in a death embrace in their rent-controlled apartment, because neither of them could afford to leave. *Everyone thinks Jerry is so great,* Turner would hiss, but they didn't know about the ugly scenes that played out in Jerry's bedroom every other night, separated from Turner's bedroom only by paper-thin walls. Jerry was a boyfriend-beater, according to Turner, which Raymond found hard to believe, Jerry so wry and funny, a novelist, so socially awkward and ironically reserved, but then he'd also found it hard to believe that Bob Miller was a boyfriend-beater, when Bob Miller had confessed with a kind of false shame that he'd given Dwight, the Southern belle he used to live with, a fat lip. Years later, after Philip and Jerry did a reading, Raymond would meet this boyfriend of Jerry's that Jerry supposedly beat, a junkie mumbling incoherently over his Indian food, and it would make more sense. How annoying is it to be passing out at dinner after your boyfriend's reading? Raymond guessed then that maybe he was annoying because he wanted to be beaten. Bob's boyfriend Dwight, on the other hand, wasn't annoying at all, was difficult for Raymond to imagine anyone beating, or wanting to beat, so calm and reserved and polite, but then *he* left Bob shortly after the beating, while Jerry's boyfriend was always still just there. Anthony Gonzalez used to beat men for money, fasten them into a terrifying dental chair he'd found at the Goodwill. They'd pay to get tied up with telephone wire, a cavity search, or "just rape." Sometime in the mid-90s, Anthony Gonzalez started having some success in his art career, and he stopped beating men for money and also stopped returning Philip and Raymond's calls. Other people were reporting similar things, and so it was suggested, by Todd or Ted, by Lana Fontaine, that Anthony was getting a big head, was now too big for their little San Francisco scene. And then he moved to Prague. Years later, when he ran into Anthony walking down Valencia Street, Anthony told him that Raymond and Philip's relationship was so dysfunctional, it was too painful for him to watch; he had to cut himself off. You guys weren't that bad, Todd reassured Raymond. And anyway, Todd said, what human relationship isn't too painful to watch? What human being isn't poised precariously, waiting for just one more tragedy to push him over the edge? Turner, too, eventually plummeted, out of that unbearable roommate situation and into an even darker netherworld, became another one of those creatures riding a tweaker bike, who would scowl at you when you drove past, for some imaginary driving infraction, not even recognizing you, unable to perceive you as a figure from his previous, human life. There will always be one more tragedy if you need it, Raymond supposes, to push you over the edge, the edge is ever present, is, in fact, the basic situation, the deal, all edge all the time, *this place with only tight ropes / slick and greased like wrestling seals* was his father's line, too literal, Raymond always thought, but accurate enough, he thinks now, and in these cases the human being, such as his sister Mina, poised so precariously, becomes possessed by a relentless, obsessive, and uncontrollable *thinking*, and the people closest to her start calling her *la loca*, not to her face, of course, it was just a joke, he and Philip laughed every time they said it, *la loca*, but now it's just who she is, what she has become, lying awake at night, entertained and tortured by her own anxieties, all her stupid thoughts about the minutiae of the past, things she might have done differently, petty slights and resentments, mean, cryptic comments their father uttered in the hospital as he was dying, their mother's suggestion that Mina go spend some time with their mother's first lover, Beatnik Ronald, down in Belize, a fairly benign and offhanded suggestion that Mina analyzed for months. Mina's descent has accelerated since their father's death to the point that she sometimes imagines her landlord is breaking into her studio apartment to hide her loofah sponge, just to fuck with her, she said, and she's been lying awake at night, unable to sleep, obsessively running over the events of the past in her mind, relentlessly following her thoughts in endless, masochistic spirals, while listening to every noise from the couple who live overhead, imagining that they are in turn listening to every noise she might make, and so she'll barely breathe, huddled there all night long, listening and thinking about her present and about her past and even what lies ahead. About her present: the imaginary people who might be thinking badly about her. About the past: a series of random catastrophes she can undo and redo in infinite alternative universes. About the future: a series of random catastrophes only her anxiety can prevent.

Memory is a bowl in whose contents worms are breeding, wrote his father in one of the eight poems he ever had published, in a small quarterly out of Denver. The past is a festering soup, certainly, bottomless, no doubt. The sadness of the past is a disappointing meal. One day at the gay beach, while Turner, fully dressed, was sketching his evil, bodybuilding clowns, they were approached by an old hippie who hovered beside them, waving his own loofah sponge like a wand. He'd been recently transformed by a visit to the Iguazu Falls, he told them. Mysterious and unimaginable, he said. The roar. The mist. The old gay hippie would pause for so long between nouns that Raymond would think he'd drifted away, but then he would say something like *lost vapor* or *a prison of rain* and Raymond isn't sure why the memory of that particular phrase, *a prison of rain*, fills him with such vast sadness.

One rainy winter day, at another endless outreach meeting, Sharlene held forth on the particulars of her *personal history*. As Raymond bikes across the Mission toward the Tenderloin now, it occurs to him that Sharlene might pop up in the TL, walking across the street without looking, hobbling along on her cane, high as a kite. Sharlene was the worst of all his bosses. Sharlene was not a clinically trained Substance Abuse Counselor or an Abuse in Childhood Specialist or a Bereavement and Grief Counselor or an Art Therapist or Drama Therapist or Narrative Therapist or Intimacy Issues Specialist or End-of-Life Facilitator or HIV Benefits Counselor or Homeless Shelter Case Manager or Anger Management Specialist or Spiritual Crisis Manager or Gender Transitioning Issues Cofacilitator or Existential Therapist or Abstinence-Based Support Group Leader and yet somehow Sharlene had used her *life experience* to claw her way up the ladder along with a variety of other former crackheads who had risen to supervisory positions directly over Raymond's head, such as Vincent, her treacherous second-in-command. If you were someone like Vincent, you got your life together and surrendered your will to a higher power after waking up one morning wearing lipstick and a wig, unsure how you'd spent the past seventy-two hours, a mystery that would never be solved—although you'd stumble onto people once in a while who seemed to recognize you and called you "Julie." If you were someone like Sharlene, you did crack, you sold crack, you stole, some old woman stabbed you over drugs, you fell out a window, you hid in a garbage can, betrayed your own children, then went into recovery and got a job as a manager at The Golden Gate Free Healthcare Consortium, where you'd entertain the staff meetings that you ruled with an iron fist with the stories of your sordid past, including the betrayal of your own children, several separate complex dramas that would be alluded to repeatedly if never fully explained, all the while moving money from one contract to another, eliminating positions and consolidating budgets in a shell game that put more money in the hands of your friends and loyal subordinates, such as Vincent, who was probably kicking back some sort of percentage in exchange for his job. Sharlene was born into a nice middle-class family, grew up right there in the Haight with her leather jackets and her Black Panther hair, but then what happened? The '80s came along and she started living the life, dealing crack out of a hotel in downtown LA, until one day she did acid and freaked out on herself, all these skeletons were coming around knocking on her door. She couldn't even look at them, just reached her arm out the window with the baggies of rocks and her face turned away. It was like being holed up in a graveyard full of the hungry dead, she told Raymond and everyone else at the staff meeting one day, where Sharlene was wearing the pink fleece sweatpants that she favored and a black sleeveless vest that showed off the long scar on her arm, where she'd been slashed by that old woman over drugs, a kind of casual Friday meets dominatrix outfit, random elements from her aggressively frumpy, post-crackhead wardrobe intermingling with slimmer, edgier pieces that showed off the results of her gastric bypass surgery. Raymond was sandwiched in between Vincent, Sharlene's back-stabbing second-in-command, who was impeccably groomed, with his short, perfectly tamed natural and his gay secretary drag, sweaters and button-down collars, and a young perky woman who had some kind of degree and who wore soft, fuzzy sweaters with mannish slacks, a mode of self-presentation that blended the feminine and the masculine, the funky and the professional, in a way designed to provide special comfort and an aura of nonjudgmental listening to her particularly urban and sexually adventurous clientele, perhaps, or maybe she just wanted to express her own dissatisfaction with the categories of butch and femme and so even her hair was long and fluffy most everywhere but shaved close on one side and it had been dyed so many times that it didn't look real, it looked like a wig, and she wore startling lipstick and her name was actually Julie, as if the person Vincent had become during his mysterious blackout had materialized here at his side, a surprise guest appearance, the moment we've all been waiting for, ephemeral and transitory as that forgotten persona, since it was clear to everyone from the beginning, with her enthusiasm and her commitment, that Julie was only passing through, that she would exit at the first available opportunity for a higher-paying position at a slightly less dysfunctional nonprofit. Sharlene told them all at the meeting that day that her family didn't know what happened to their baby, meaning Sharlene, back when she was selling crack in LA—they always wanted Sharlene to stick to her *writing*. What Sharlene's *writing* consisted of, Raymond didn't even want to know. He could easily enough imagine her black speckled notebook shoved in Philip's drawer, with all of the other texts he's collected from insane people over the years, the same black speckled notebooks Raymond was given at the Adolescent Day Treatment Center so many years ago and at the lock-down ward before that, and before that even at the high school that he'd been assigned to after Lowell didn't work out, College Park High, where he was housed with other dropouts, teenage mothers, juvenile delinquents and retards, in classrooms presided over by the most rickety, the most jaded, the most bottom-of-the-barrel adults, while Raymond started experimenting with hunger, with sleeplessness and delirium, fasting he called it, at College Park High, the last time he personally ever wrote a story, the last time he ever would, a story about a hungry little boy. The existence of Sharlene's *writing* was one of those details that momentarily disintegrated the firm boundary Raymond liked to imagine between himself and Sharlene, along with the other revelation of that particular Outreach Meeting, which was that he'd been under Sharlene's thumb for close to a year before discovering that her father, not the responsible carpenter stepfather who wanted her to stick to her *writing*, but her biological father, was Beatnik Ronald, a name Raymond had been hearing for years. The fact that her biological father, Beatnik Ronald, was Raymond's mother's first lover, suggested in some disturbing way that he and Sharlene could have been siblings in an alternate universe, that they could have shared the same Family Dynamics Issues or Intimacy Issues or Bereavement and Grief Issues, they might have both suffered from the same Substance Issues and Codependency issues, the same Sex Addictions and Depressions and PTSD, that it might have been Raymond, not Sharlene, who was holed up in some cheap hotel in downtown LA. Knock knock knock came the undead zombies at

Sharlene's window, holding out their bony hands, grasping, grasping, why don't you come home and we'll enroll you in school, her stepfather would tell her, why don't you just write it all down in a book and forget it, her mother wanted to know. Sometime in the late '80s or early '90s, some ridiculous era, before or after Sharlene got that nasty scar on her arm, when some old woman cut her, before or after she jumped out of a three-story building to avoid being raped and destroyed one of her knees in the process. Was it before or after she hid in a garbage bin to get away from the cops, closed the top and curled up cozy as could be among the rotting fruit rinds and cigarette butts and soiled wrapping paper, one of her favorite stories, she made it sound like she'd been there forever, like she'd lived another life inside that Dumpster, a more contemplative life, the life of a mystic, meditating on the ten foul things, the festering corpse, the rancid corpse, the raggedy bones of the dead, meditating on her future life, her recovery and her relapse, meditating on her future career as nonprofit tyrant, hobbling along on that cane, limping through the halls of The Golden Gate Free Healthcare Consortium, loading up the GGFHC's storage closets with junk food snacks from the Food Bank she would ravenously consume herself or funnel to her formerly betrayed children, sitting Raymond at a desk with several months' worth of pointless forms to fill out, just to torture him, to drive him crazy, knowing full well that he had only been able to keep this job for a decade because it allowed him a sense of freedom, of mobility, a sense of flight from his childhood underneath the gray skies in the Sunset District in his depressing house with that hideous shag carpeting, where he was hemmed in by the squat, identical tract homes and the monolithic mental health facilities. Sharlene refused to replace Julie after she quit, insisting instead that Julie's share of the client contacts would have to be made up by Raymond, but whose share of the money under a variety of contracts would disappear into the shadows, like phantom money, dead money, a ghost of money that Sharlene had dreamed up in that Dumpster while she was meditating on how long and unnecessary life really is. But then Vincent called from work one afternoon, the day of the presidential election in 2004, and told Raymond that Sharlene had been fired for stealing money from a client. Vincent loved nothing more than being a tyrant's right-hand man, but he also enjoyed abandoning his former diva once she'd done herself in. Just after Vincent's call, the exit polls said Bush was losing, and Raymond grew giddy, like there was actual hope, like he'd been suffocating for years and had simply gotten used to it. But then, of course, the exit polls were wrong, or some other polls were wrong, election fraud blah blah blah, and the clownhead just kept bumbling along farther into the apocalypse, the sort of apocalypse that Sharlene might have dreamed up while she was hiding in that Dumpster from the cops, a cloud of death swallowing the people and the plants and the animals, Sharlene's little dream as she was cozying up next to the rotting wigs and half-empty bottles of nail polish and discarded underwear and stale potato chips and busted toys and used condoms and soiled wrapping paper in that Dumpster somewhere outside of some SRO or housing project in LA or maybe Dallas or maybe Oakland or San Luis Obispo, it could have been any-where on her tour of the world's ongoing devastation, Sharlene got around, Raymond thinks as he rides up Eddy, out of the TL and toward Polk Street. Raymond likes to keep abreast of the current developments in the ongoing dev-astation. Never mind the vanishing polar ice caps and rainforests, the rising seas and temperatures, and the impending extinction of most of the nonhuman spe-cies. Even the science magazines that used to be cheerleaders of technology and the military industrial complex have become excellent sources for signs of the more grotesque and less glamorous catastrophes. What else is there to talk about? The graveyard of garbage, for example, a kind of gyre of plastic in the middle of the Pacific, a dead zone two times the size of Texas. The vanishing groundwater in India, the towns in China that have come to be called "cancer towns." The overuse of fertilizer has depleted the earth of everything beneficial, poisoned the wetlands of the world, and run off into rivers and bays creating algae blooms that kill off all other life. Raymond is impressed by the fact that the genitalia and perineums of male babies all over the world have grown increas-ingly closer together, a result of the feminization caused by the effects of plastics, and he's impressed by the content of all that agricultural runoff, a miasma of hormone-tainted feces, afterbirths, and pesticide residue, and by the emergence of new, gelatinous growths in the manure pits of hog farms that trap methane and cause random catastrophic explosions. The borders between species and elements are breaking down, everywhere, across the entire planet, creating a bizarre toxic soup of radioactivity, genetic material, and cancerous cells. And every one of us still wants to feel special.

Nineteen-eighty-three was not a good year for Raymond, but neither was 1985, when Raymond was seventeen and committed by his mother for the second time, so that his own adolescence formed a kind of dead zone two times the size of Texas. He'd sit around in a circle with the other crazy boys in the dorm room late at night, taking turns confessing some secret or horrible thing they'd done. Raymond was the only one in the group who wouldn't admit that he'd "done things" with other guys, although in subtle ways he'd been "doing things" with most of his male friends since he was eleven and in quite explicit ways he'd "done things" with Roy, his tennis buddy. They'd done acid together, for one thing, and tripped out on the glowing yellow orb, slicing it through the air magically, they'd achieved an almost mystical choreography, they weren't competing anymore, they were collaborating in a graceful dance, they were alive in the moment, and one thing led to another, which was Roy's bedroom while his mom was still at work. Raymond wasn't so much into Roy, but there was no one else around during his solitary, aimless adolescence between the first trip to the crazy house and the second trip to the crazy house. In the crazy house, they shot him up with drugs that stopped time altogether and turned the universe into a tepid gray mush. *Just tell them what they want to hear,* his grandmother whispered to him, *and don't worry about all that other mess.* She was the only one who ever knew how to calm him down, she'd clap her hands three times to startle him sometimes from his overly complex and dramatic thought processes, clap clap clap, and she'd say *stop all that foolishness* and he would, more or less. He wonders if he might use the same technique with his sister as she whirls her brain around the neighbors' perceptions, their imaginary surveillance, the missing loofah sponge, their father's dying words, their mother's off-hand comment about Beatnik Ronald, her own fat thighs—clap clap clap—it's as if all of Mina's trite, relentless thoughts are a kind of prison, although that's surely a deceptive metaphor, what Raymond knows about prisons that aren't mental institutions he knows mostly from Genet and *Female Convict Scorpion. Prison's not so bad,* Louie used to say, but only, Raymond guesses, if you were ambivalent about *freedom* to begin with. Raymond is not, having been locked up twice, completely at the mercy of his guards and doctors, cast off from the free world and so knows for a fact that mental slavery and physical confinement are not at all the same thing, it's one thing to be trapped in holes of self-doubt or metaphorical cell blocks and quite another to be *under the jail,* so maybe his sister's repetitive, annoying, endless thoughts aren't a prison as much as they are a misguided attempt to break free, it's like they're running away from something, it's like they're trying to escape but they're trapped in a kind of maze, except they themselves, the very thoughts, are the bricks of the maze, are the maze itself, that's what she doesn't understand, it's not her pathetic life that's the problem, it's her pathetic thoughts, a mutating arabesque, but any turn of the wheel is only another kaleidoscopic dead end, forms trapped within forms, words hidden beneath the words, something struggling to get out and run amok, it's like she's been colonized by evil spirals that go nowhere, like the evil fungus that started taking over Raymond's own spine after he stopped thinking about HIV and bloodwork and meds for years and years and years. As if meningitis, a sometimes deadly inflammation of the membranes that protect and cover the brain, was a material manifestation of his sister's crazy thoughts, as if he was infected by her mental acrobatics, her pleasure, her torture, the mask over something else, some horror that's even worse than the endless galloping thoughts that lead nowhere, that reach no conclusions and merely serve as a kind of false face of language meant to hide the self from the self, meant to hide the real fears, the real monstrousness lurking at the heart of reality, unless even thoughts about the real horror of the food chain, even thoughts about the slow torture of the species, about the endless torture of Afghani detainees, of Iraqi detainees, the children killed by American bombs, even thoughts about the blackening, the devastation, the cloud of death swallowing up the planet and its plants and animals and people is itself a kind of hysterical mask over something even more horrific, more endless, more absolutely insane, or maybe not, Raymond thinks as he hits Polk Street and spots Howard, on the corner of Bush and Polk, chatting with a skeleton. The skeleton is wearing earmuffs and some sort of visor thing and gray sweatpants that hang off his bones like a tumor. Raymond knows this skeleton. It's Terry, who used to be a cheery, scooter-riding marijuana dealer and is now the AIDSiest motherfucker Raymond knows, diagnosed in 2002 or some ridiculous shit like that, way too late, when he must have been positive for years. There's no excuse, as far as Raymond's concerned, for not even getting tested until he was that far gone, although there was probably no excuse, he'll admit, when he himself stopped thinking about HIV and bloodwork and meds for years and years and years until the cryptococcal fungus had more or less taken over his spine, a pale, invisible haze elaborating itself, branching out in every direction from white cell to white cell, spreading vertically and neurologically in directions that couldn't be perceived, giving him debilitating headaches and nausea and bringing him to the brink of nonexistence, the closest he could go and still come back, which may be why he really doesn't want to see Terry today like some neon sign screaming DEATH DEATH DEATH.

Hi, Howard, hi, Terry, he manages in his sweetest voice. How's it going?

Howard is telling the story of Sammy Davis Jr. and Kim Novak's romance. According to Howard, Kim Novak was in love with Sammy and they were going to get married. But Harry Cohn, the head of Columbia Studios, was worried about the effects of a mixed marriage on the career of Novak, his million-dollar investment. So he put a contract out on Sammy, who then went to Frank Sinatra for help, and was told Frank's mob connections could protect him, but only in Vegas. Terry says that the way he hears it, they arranged for Sammy to be kidnapped for a few hours to scare some sense into him. Howard somehow transitions from this story to a story about his own colon. I don't have time to chat, says Raymond, gotta get to the big porn shoot. You guys should come. It's right up your alley, Howard—they're filming a kid getting raped. Not a blond, I'm afraid.

The word *blond* prompts Howard to share a memory, a blond boy whose dick he once sucked back in the Bronx. His skin was the color of milk, Howard says, and he presses his hand on his heart as if he's a Victorian lady about to faint. Terry turns the discussion of blond boys into a story about his own childhood back on some Indiana farm, about a birthday party gone bad, the evil parents who disowned him, their very own blond cherub, and cast him into the world to fend for himself. Raymond has heard all of this before. Terry was always self-absorbed, Raymond thinks, even before he was dying and weighed less than ninety pounds. Howard wonders if Philip ever tracked down the little blond boy he was looking for, but Raymond doesn't know what he's talking about. He brought a magazine over, *Vanity Fair*, I think, and showed me this boy dressed up in a wig and wondered if I'd ever seen him turning tricks on Polk Street, says Howard. Huey Beauregard, says Raymond. He doesn't want to hear it, so he gives the address of the porn shoot and starts up the Bush Street hill, while a line from his father's poem about death, *you'd think you'd have gotten used to it passing days in this cemetery*, makes him angry at his father, in denial, at Terry, in denial, at a whole range of other former friends and family members who made choices, each and every one of them, that led straight into the grave.

Raymond and his sister spent so many days of their childhood plotting ways to survive random catastrophe, a skill they learned from their mother, who'd spent her life working to fend off random catastrophe. But then the catastrophes so rarely proved to be random, it seemed, but carefully mapped out by the individuals themselves, the missing variable in the algebraic equations of people's lives, just as an exploding gelatinous growth in the manure pit of a hog farm is the missing variable in the algebraic equation of factory farming, just as the dead zone in the Pacific twice the size of Texas is one of the missing variables in the algebraic equation of the planetary dreamtime: the blackening, the devastation, the cloud of death swallowing up the planet and its plants and animals and people. It was just like that crazy boy at the Adolescent Day Treatment Center had murmured to him, so many years ago, in the middle of the night. His name was Stoney, of all things.

When they let Raymond out of the crazy house the second time, he got a job at Circuit City and threw himself into tennis, hit the balls around with

Roy, when Roy was around, and then in Berkeley with the children of that cult, *Ra's Lovers*. Ra was bow-legged and pervy, a trollish, vaguely Rasta, vaguely Manson type with an unappealing beard. He'd fathered a troop of tennis-playing boys, all named after some abstract principle. Wisdom was the oldest, and then Equality, Liberty, Victory, and the youngest, at least when Raymond knew them, was Bedazzlement. In the late '80s, they didn't even have the bus, just a camper shell parked near the Ashby BART, all of them wearing orange jumpsuits that looked like prison uniforms. Ra never fathered any girls, or maybe he gave them away. He had several wives, white women or Japanese women, who would wander around Berkeley selling incense. None of those boys ever talked about sex, all the sex belonged to their father, king of the camper shell. Were the boys gay, some or all of them? They seemed more *neutered* than gay, there was never any sexual tension with those boys, it was like thinking about them sexually would have caused them pain. The boys usually just talked about tennis, about Ivan Lendl, Yannick Noah, who they'd met in San Diego or Las Vegas, on tour, Martina Navritilova and her unnatural sexual practices, they talked shit about Jews, tried to get Raymond to smoke weed, which was a sacrament for them, and they used bee pollen, too. Liberty was a strange one, he had a deeply brainwashed quality and yet he seemed quirky and individualistic at the same time, he seemed somehow well-adjusted, and as much as he'd been force-fed tennis, indoctrinated daily with Ra's ritualistic and lethargic tennis instruction, Liberty was truly passionate about tennis, it seemed to suit his basic nature. Is it possible to have a basic nature if you've been raised by a pervert in a camper shell? Raymond had just come out of his own crazy period and didn't have as much self-esteem as Liberty, but they were mixed like he was and he thought they were so beautiful, along with all the garbage they'd been fed came a healthy dose of black pride and a healthy dose of self-love. But one day when he got to the tennis court, Victory was writing in a journal. Don't tell my brothers, he said, but he showed Raymond his poems. Maybe he knew that Raymond's father was a poet or maybe he just wanted an audience from a larger world, somebody who hadn't been raised in a camper shell, to see his poetry, which rhymed and extolled the basic principles of the cult, pitting the purity and innocence of misunderstood believers against the falsehood and insincerity of Babylon. It was sometime after this that Raymond found Liberty writing in a journal. The poems were more subversive, and included a variety of voices—unidentified, or identified as outcasts, poor people, the motherless—calling for or even demanding their freedom, which made Raymond curious and so he cornered Bedazzlement a few days later and asked if he wrote poetry, and Bedazzlement tried to evade the question—none of the boys had learned how to lie—but finally admitted that he did and a few days later he showed Raymond what he had. The meanings were more ambiguous than in his brothers' poems, with images of dark, tight spaces, both homey and terrifying, one-legged men obsessed with the need to sprint, and secrets revealed through the successful interpretation of the names of things.

Ra was impressed with Raymond's tennis and wanted him to drive around the state with them in their trailer, entering competitions, but even then Raymond had too much self-love to submit to such a thing. The past is a lake, bottomless, the sadness of the past, and is some sort of self-love the only kind of life raft? The Nob Hill Theatre raises the question of self-love, because Raymond hasn't been inside since his brief stint as a Boy in the Box back in '92 or '93. His brief stint as a Boy in the Box was disgusting and bizarre, even compared to his brief glimpses into Ra's murky camper shell, clouded with a foul and sticky incense haze. Raymond lasted only a half hour in the Box. He sat in his underwear in a weird see-through environment, like the one John Travolta lived in when he played a boy without an immune system, and just like in that movie, men could stick their hands in these latex gloves that protruded into the box and grope him. It was vaguely surgical and humiliating for everyone involved. The plastic gloves and even the whole plastic booth have probably by now made their way to the middle of the Pacific, he supposes. He's glad that he doesn't recognize anybody here now at the Nob Hill Theatre, asks the clerk if they could use some free condoms. The clerk waves him down the steps to the video arcade. The janitor will show you where the Free Basket is, he says.

Down below, Raymond doesn't recognize the janitor at first, as he's down on his knees scrubbing the floor of a video booth, a toxic halo of bleach haze shimmering about his head. The Savior descends into a cloud, puts on a garment of fire, and prostitutes himself with Nature. It's Ted.

Hey, Raymond, says Ted. A man in a neighboring booth cracks his door, masturbating with one hand and gesturing for Raymond to join him with the other. On the screen in there, anonymous cocks are entering anonymous orifices, but all the flesh is completely hairless and orangey. Ted, however, is puffy and drawn, as if bloated with his own nightmares.

Still working on your memoir? Raymond asks.

Oh, fuck that, says Ted. Memoir's so trendy these days, and you know, certain powerful people weren't too happy about the things I was writing. They were coming into my apartment at night, hiding my journals.

Powerful people? asks Raymond. Who, like that writer you used to date? The diaper queen?

Don't underestimate Brendan Pelt, says Ted.

Inside the booth, the channel changes as if it's on autopilot, and Raymond recognizes one of Ralph's films, *Finish That Ass, Marine*.

Not to mention You Know Who, says Ted.

You Know Who is certainly the Beat poet that Ted lived with so many years ago, the purveyor of Sound-Body poems, or maybe it's the Zen poet he hung out with in Boulder, in a walk-in closet lined with jock straps and tinsel. Raymond just nods.

So it's not technically a memoir anymore, Ted says. I've disguised the characters, changed the names and scenes, and nobody's caught on yet. It's disguised as a young adult fantasy novel, and it's set in this world where unicorns in their larval stage are these sort of amphibious brain sacs with more solid fleshy mounds protruding from what will become the third eye, and the mature unicorns prod the brain sacs to maturity by puncturing the flesh mounds repeatedly with their horns, and so the older poet unicorns mentor the brain sacs that emit a blue glow of pure poetic talent because poetry is the primary spiritual currency in this world and it's necessary for the old unicorn poets to mentor the brain sacs so that the poems can continue to spell out the time tracks that will lead their unicorn species toward a paradise outside of time.

Another video booth door has cracked open. Raymond can make out only an enormous eye and a fervent motion down below. In a quick, spastic movement Ted jangles his keys over his head and then claps three times, clap clap clap. Feed the meters, please, fellas, or move along. The video booth door slams shut.

So the old wise poets with the secret knowledge are trying to lead everyone out of time, Ted continues, but then sometimes they're real fucking assholes, the unicorn poets. So far it's constructed like a puzzle and nobody's identity is clear until you have all the interlocking pieces in place, and I'm saving that last piece of the puzzle until the final moment just before the book gets published, but once it's done, everybody will be able to decipher the code, one two three, and they'll know who the assholes are in this world which is just one world of many *anyway* and so-called imaginary worlds aren't any less real *anyway*, even scientists know that now.

Raymond spots the Free Box next to the stairs.

Sounds great, says Raymond. God, Ted, it's great to see you, but I've gotta go, I'm late for this porn shoot.

Theodore, Ted says. I go by Theodore now.

Raymond dumps the condoms out of his backpack and into the box.

Did you ever see *my* porn? asks Ted.

Raymond's not sure why the question disturbs him. Whether it was made in 1994 or 1997 or even last year, the film would have captured a less devastated Ted, a Ted who was always a mess, a self-absorbed monster, but kind of sweet, too, in an off way. The before/after quality is a little too heavy, as if porn really is a step on a downward slope, a path or a mirror, a descent into cockeyed imaginal realms like that part in Raymond's father's poem that goes, *for none of those who have worn the flesh will be saved or punished or spanked just the way they like it or invited to the orgy*, and it went on to describe the orgy, Raymond remembers, in a way that made sensual pleasure seem like a bizarre mutation, involving a vestigial cluster of feelers that went on expanding and contracting with a simulation of pleasure even after all the pleasure cells had been burned out.

What's the title? Raymond asks. I'll check it out.

The director loved my ass, says Ted. He said he'd never seen such a gorgeous, hungry ass.

Raymond starts backing toward the stairs.

Hey, you want your aura read? asks Ted. I'll give you a deal. Yours is looking a little cloudy, I'll tell you that much.

Raymond says, Hey, Ted, I'll see you around. He flees, up the stairs and down Nob Hill.

Five blocks away, in a "Lower Nob" basement studio that belongs to the rocker chick Suzie who does sound for Ralph, an enormous crowd has gathered around the brightly lit sofa where Melvin is to be raped. It's standing room only. Melvin is sitting on the sofa with a weird euphoric expression and the two rapists—some muscle queen friend of Chunk's from prison who used to work in a circus and some hard woman with dyed blond hair and huge tits that Ralph met through Suzie—are standing around smoking, looking bored, impatiently fondling their ski masks. Suzie is manning one of the cameras. Raymond knew her little sister during the brief time he spent in high school. Melinda, with her enormous head of fabulous red hair that had captivated all the other rebels and bad kids so hypnotically.

Philip is here and Felicia and Sonya Brava and even Geordi. Tony, Chunk, Roman. Howard managed to make it up the hill and Terry is propped in a corner like a hat rack. Suzie abandons her camera for a moment to say, Hello.

Cute kid, says Suzie.

Raymond says, You think?

Suzie thinks it's funny. He looks like a baby, but when she remembers being his age, younger than his age, it didn't seem like that at all. Suzie remembers a party when Raymond stayed over at their house when he was thirteen or fourteen. Raymond remembers how Suzie used to sit in the kitchen putting thick black eyeliner on and reading aloud from *Our Bodies, Ourselves*. Really? says Suzie. She wonders if Raymond's thinking of somebody else's older sister, some other lesbian rocker chick. In any case, she can't quite believe that it's been something like twenty-five years.

What have you been up to? asks Raymond.

For her day job, she tells Raymond, she shoots soft-core porn for this rapper in Oakland. It's all booty shots, these women shaking their asses at the camera to the rhythm of the music, ass after ass after ass. Sometimes Suzie sneaks the models around in luxury hotels in Miami and Vegas, for the glamorous backdrops these videos require.

What's Melinda up to? asks Raymond.

Suzie scowls.

Melinda's a druggie mess. She's probably technically schizophrenic and more or less homeless. She pops up at Suzie's house every couple of months, usually begging for pocket change. Suzie doesn't really want to talk about her sister, but it reminds her of a funny story.

You remember Connie Cohen? says Suzie. She used to hang out in your crowd.

Raymond didn't like Connie Cohen, who was slighted on one occasion, when the older guy she was trying to pick up was more into Raymond, he tells Suzie now, and so when Raymond came back from his first stay in the crazy house, she'd made his life a hell. Suzie didn't like her either. What a little snot, she says. Well, Melinda was good friends with Connie and has kept in touch with her—Connie's got a little girl now, almost a teen, and lives with her sister. But last time Melinda popped up, she couldn't stop ranting about Connie Cohen.

We're ready to roll! Ralph announces and a hush fills the studio.

Remind me to tell you afterward, says Suzie, and returns to her post.

Once it's all over, everyone seems dazed, or disappointed by the bisexual rape, except for Howard, who has his hand on his heart, like a Victorian lady about to faint. Melvin looks the most disappointed of all. Ralph is showing Melvin the footage, trying to convince him, it seems, that no matter what it *felt* like, for all practical purposes, it was a forceful and compelling rape.

On the Christmas after Raymond's father died, Raymond's mother took her children, Raymond and his sister Mina, into the kitchen, for her special gift, she'd said. His mother had told them she wasn't doing presents that year, for financial reasons, and yet for a moment Raymond actually imagined that he was about to receive something he'd always wanted, something mysterious, unimaginable even—he'd imagined that she'd broken down and gotten into the spirit of things after all. In the kitchen she offered her gift, however, nothing purchased with mere money. A gift of wisdom. She told them that they mustn't be afraid to be more successful than their father. He was a competitive man, she said, and so he didn't really want you to succeed. She suggested that he'd crushed them and turned them into failures. He treated you like shit up until the day he died—when you were giving everything you had to him, she told her children. The Christmas after he'd died. Her holiday gift to the family.

IV

...a hundred faces from the neon forest, sailors and hustlers and whores, where the sky is poisoned silver, beyond chainlink and the prison of the skull.

— William Gibson, *Neuromancer*

1

NOT A TRAVELER SO MUCH AS A POD, inhabited by a cultural injunction to be miserable. People go off here and there for the holidays and Felicia finds herself one of them, flying Oakland to Long Beach. She's trapped inside a vast machine, a psychological garbage chute of Botox ads, Christmas tree earrings, and before/after shots of celebrities who've had surgeries, addictions, or anorexia. But on her tiny TV screen, a documentary about santeria. *Deities flowed into each other, wore each other's masks, humans could either represent the deity or become the deity.* She switches it off, takes off her earphones. She isn't just inside the machine, she's a functioning part of it, too. Geordi is already asleep, slumped against the window.

Pontormo's diary is primarily a record of what he painted on the San Lorenzo mural day by day, what he ate, and how it made him feel. *On April 3 I did the legs from the knee down, the darkness and wind and the plaster made it very difficult; and at night I had 14 oz of bread, chicory and eggs.* He often upset his stomach, a problem he felt was related not only to what he ate, but to the weather. Half a kid goat's head, some wonderful fried pasta at Bronzino's, eggs, bread, lamb. *Friday I did the head with the rock that is underneath it, at night I had 9 oz of bread, an omelet and a salad, and I've been dizzy for awhile now.*

Felicia is never more at peace, never more herself, than when she is reading, or pausing in her reading, with Geordi asleep beside her. It's a short flight, and so the fall it might engender, into her own self—emptied of habits, vacated of context, returned to her most opaque and unsharable memories, with the shadow of the plane itself against the wisps of fog beneath her to the west—will be abbreviated. Out here there's no need to describe the surroundings because they are always the same. She has never met anyone on a plane. Only herself.

Geordi knows the names of clouds. When he is awake, he can distinguish the cirrus intortus from the cirrus fibratus, the cirrocumulus undulatus from the cumulus congestus, a nimbostratus praecipitatio from a mammatus, a mackerel sky from mares' tails. The ones that look like skeletal ribs, the ones that look like cotton writing, the ones that look like an ancient cracked parchment, the ones that look like a portal between the earth and the sky.

Pontormo was "underappreciated" after his death, until the tortured, melancholy, and kinetic bodies of his paintings were rediscovered by the tortured, melancholy, and kinetic twentieth century. He spent the last eleven years of his life painting the San Lorenzo fresco that was to be his masterwork: in the upper part the Creation, the fall, the sacrifice of Abel, the death of Cain. The lower walls depicted twin apocalypses: the flood with a mass of drowned bodies and the resurrection of the dead, a vast confusion at the end of time. Surrounded by suffocation and death, what was Noah saying to God? Why was everyone naked and deformed? A row of nudes formed a ladder from earth to paradise, and at the top Christ was surrounded by nude angels. Crowds of fleshy and ethereal beings all mashed together, one face or many crying in pain. The eyes of one tormented face meet the viewer's head-on.

He had the understanding which becomes a part of rootless children, of the difficulty of staying alive, how that grows from boredom into tension, then active solitude. But Pontormo took in an orphan of his own, raised the boy from the age of ten. Battista Naldini.

Felicia's reduced the story of her own childhood, her youth, to a paragraph; she was wild for a while, the paragraph begins. She's eroded it into a haiku. A few syllables for the women she slept with, married, masochistic, cruel. A few for the men. She's polished it like a few smooth fragments of phosphorescent bone. Not enough for a skeleton. They suggest a skeleton, perhaps. A feral, solitary creature. Wounded, getting over it.

***

Pontormo was born in 1493 or maybe '94. His father died when he was a small child and then his mother, his grandparents, and finally his younger sister when he was eighteen or nineteen. Vasari, whose *Lives of the Artists* provides most of what is known about Pontormo's life, couldn't figure out what Pontormo was up to. Even the evangelists were huddled nude in one corner with a book. The whole scene was absolutely full of nudes, *arranged, designed and colored with so much melancholy as to afford little pleasure to the observer*. It seemed to Vasari that Pontormo wanted to bewilder both himself and those who saw the work.

She's lived with Geordi for nine years, yet certain years of his life remain shadowy. His undergrad years in Boston, the years immediately after his mother left his father. He tells the same stories over and over again, maybe fifty, maybe a hundred. It isn't that he's hiding things. He doesn't mask his internal life to that degree, at least not from her. These are the stories that constitute his life. Various occasions when someone was attracted to him, several humiliations, a fight, a car accident, some funny stories about various "characters" he's known. A hundred and fifty stories, tops. And over and over, if not always out loud, the vague and mysterious story of the scar.

To stay alive, orphans fill their needs for food, sleep, and things to do, according to Pontormo's translator. *Their adolescence is maturity. Knowledge of what's past balances freedom to continue.* The descent has already begun, a human voice informs them. Geordi sits up, looking frightened.

Felicia has mapped out a chronology for the life of Huey Beauregard, based on interviews, bios, and information on the website. Born in 1981 in Arkansas. A specific town is never mentioned, although the word *Ozarks* is freely tossed about. At times he lives with his crazy mother and at times in foster homes. His foster parents invariably rape him. At times he lives with his Bible-beating "itinerant preacher" of a grandfather in a trailer park, who bathes him in lye. When he's with his mother, starting when he's seven, she dresses him as a girl and pimps him out of truck stops and cheap diners. She frequently abandons him for meth-head, pedophile boyfriends. The last time this happens, he strikes out on his own. Hits the streets of San Francisco in '91 or '92 where he turns tricks on Polk Street, gets addicted to heroin, and discovers he has AIDS. His johns expose him to the world of books, however, and Dr. Bailey encourages him to express himself through writing. Somewhere in there, his mother is dead.

His mother, who Felicia doesn't believe is real. Waylon McClatchy, a real person, dies for real in '97, so Huey must have been on the phone with him really, talking real talk, by at the latest '96. Huey's first short story is published in 1997, when he is sixteen, in an anthology edited by Bonnie Gold. *Salted Wounds: Memoirs from a World of Hurt.* At this point, he's been corresponding with Benton Archer for years already, it seems, and somewhere in there he is "saved from the streets" by Dr. Bailey. Around that time, he moves in with his bandmates, Racer and Trauma, although Huey has also described one of them as an outreach worker who saved him from the streets named Emma Jo. Are they lesbian lovers, Racer and Trauma? Is Huey sexually involved with either or both? Huey is friends by this time with Mary Stringer, Saul Torstenson, Brendan Pelt, and his agent is Jeremy Javits. His novel is published in 2000, his story collection in 2001. The first pictures of Huey, the creature behind the fake hair, don't appear until late in 2003. By now, he is being represented by Tristessa Carmichael and corresponding with rock stars and movie stars. In 2005, there are rumors of an affair with a European film star, daughter of a famous horror director; it is said that Huey may have fathered her child.

Pontormo was a lifelong bachelor and eccentric, a sad, fussy man with strange notions; he hated crowds, never went to feasts; he was so fearful of death that he never allowed it to be mentioned in his presence and avoided dead bodies. For Vasari, these are the stories that constitute Pontormo's life.

In the airport, the crowds of faces are tortured, melancholy, kinetic.

Geordi's sister Ramona is already here, at Geordi's mother's house, with her ex-boyfriend, Percy. Percy's camped out in the living room, leafing through magazines. Felicia gives him a polite smile and hurries deeper into the house to the guest bedroom to dump her luggage before he has the chance to say anything too creepy or awkward. The mother's up in her own bedroom, preparing herself, Felicia imagines, for some ostentatious display of indifference to her children. The other sister, Jessie, will drive up at the last moment from the gruesome San Diego suburb where she lives with a hypochondriac boyfriend who rarely leaves the house. Felicia can't imagine her doing anything in that San Diego suburb except watching TV and verbally abusing the hypochondriac, but apparently she has a job; she works with the elderly. This is what Felicia knows, pretty much. Ramona is bustling around the kitchen, cheery as can be. Do you need any help with anything? Felicia asks.

Ramona came home to live with her mother when she was in her mid-30s, after overly exhausting stints in several major cities, and has just recently managed to extricate herself into a studio in West Carson. She fills every environment she enters with a trite and oppressive chitchat, a veneer of cheeriness that obliterates everything in its path. At her receptionist's job, everyone believes she is twelve years younger than she actually is, a lie that has forced her to deform her entire life history, and that has involved her in an endless string of flirtations with men fifteen to twenty years younger than herself. In the meantime, her only actual intimacy has been her continuing relationship with Percy, the boyfriend she broke up with ten years ago, a mean and charmless man whose smugness is proportionate to his lack of success with the multimedia opera he's been working on for most of his life.

The Pontormo fresco that lives in Felicia's mind, full of melancholy, misshapen nude men intertwined in a cosmic fantasy of an inherently crushed and saddened eternity, isn't really plausible, she knows. She's most interested in stories of futility, however. Unfinished projects, journeys that go nowhere, meanings that never get revealed.

Percy was forced to stop working as a substitute teacher several years ago for giving a couple of ten-year-old girls hugs they found inappropriate and unnerving. What separates the work of Percy's lifetime, his *magnum opus*, the multimedia opera, never to be performed or appreciated by a single human being, from Pontormo's fresco, equally doomed to oblivion? Felicia is forced to pass Percy again on her way to the side door, which will take her out back, to the yard, where Geordi will soon join her, she imagines, sulking as a result of something his mother has said to him. About five minutes in, she's already desperate for fresh air.

Nowhere had Pontormo observed the order of the scene, measure, time, any rule, proportion, or perspective. Torsos with shoulders turned and sides done with great study and labor, but the torsos so large, the arms and legs so small, the heads lacking the grace his paintings were famous for. Vasari thought he tried to force nature too much. But perhaps Vasari was a jealous bitch; he'd been in direct competition with Pontormo, and might have been actively trying to destroy his posthumous reputation.

The rain has let up for a moment. Geordi seems oddly content, fussing with his mother's computer, which hasn't been working as she'd like. He's busy playing the role of the technologically competent son, and so Felicia begins a circuitous route from Geordi's mother's squashed little house east of downtown through Long Beach's more ghetto neighborhood toward the MoLAa. To what extent, she wonders, is she living as a prisoner of decisions she made at some point in the past? But she's pretty sure she had this thought before, and so all that's left is the more practical question of what to abandon.

It rains for a moment and then stops again. An obsessive-compulsive is picking cigarette butts and used Q-tips off the sidewalk, then hurling them down in slightly different locations. But he's dressed well enough, he seems entirely functional.

Southern California in the winter rain is the most desolate place on earth. But inside the MoLAa is another world. They're showing Tamayo's mixographs. Geordi would love these paintings, but his distaste for anything remotely sentimental about Mexican peasant culture won't allow him to even entertain the possibility. Random dust that was blowing across the earth got electrified, is how it looks. She'd thought her mind would disappear for her time in Long Beach. But here she is. Conscious and alive.

If you aren't looking for anything, every path is correct. Felicia takes a detour down the long thoroughfare that turns into the gay neighborhood: a few bars, a café, a handful of those troubling stores that sell a range of worthless trash items or *novelties*. The idea that anyone has ever bought a single one of these pendants, stickers, T-shirts, or balloons depresses Felicia and delights her with her energized repugnance for the world as she finds it.

The orphan loves the orphan, abuses the orphan. Maybe. Pontormo quarreled with his orphan until he went too far, cryptic moments of drama barely mentioned in the diaries among the endless references to Pontormo's bread and his torsos and his long fat turds. *Wednesday I had two eggs for supper, an endive salad, 14 oz of bread and dried figs and grapes. Thursday I had mutton, that was the night of the divisions.* The meaning of the last word is unclear, but it might have referred to Pontormo's big argument with Battista. The next day, December 13, 1555, he dined alone and started to manage on his own, as his adopted orphan had locked himself in his room. The boy would have been nineteen or maybe twenty years old.

***

In Felicia's favorite Jean Rhys story, a woman from the West Indies winds through a variety of unhappy housing situations in London, before ending up in jail because of an altercation with some hideous neighbors. In jail she hears a song, the song that was waiting for her, her whole life long. Back outside, she hums the song and a jazz musician catches it, turns it into his own thing, all wrong. But he gives her a little bit of money for having stolen her song, and she uses it to buy herself a new dress. A dusty pink dress.

2

IT'S CREEPY, WATCHING MELVIN'S tender little brain wrestling with a book. Lautréamont was right, Philip's pretty sure. Turn back! *The lethal fumes of this book shall dissolve his soul as water does sugar.* Philip sometimes opens up some tome he digested twenty years ago, at Melvin's age—*The Soft Machine, Gravity's Rainbow, A Thief's Journal,* or the book that Melvin's reading now with all of Philip's underlinings, from 1987 or 1988, still intact, Juan Goytisolo's *Landscapes After the Battle*—and discovers, with a feeling of some dread, that thoughts that have become so much a part of what he considers himself, thoughts he'd imagined he'd developed through a vigorous life of trial and error, had actually been *implanted* during his youth. So many wicked little pamphlets.

It's books, Philip's pretty sure, that convinced him the only way *out* was *down and out.* The path through the bottom. He's pretty sure he doesn't believe that anymore.

Maybe you shouldn't read while I'm driving, he says to Melvin. You'll get dizzy.

I'm already dizzy, says Melvin.

Come with me on a drug run, Philip had said. He figured the phrase *drug run* would capture Melvin's imagination, although he's not sure, come to think of it, if it's technically a drug run. He has to take Howard a bag.

Howard, who will never have to work another day in his life since his big breakdown; who spends his days smoking weed, watching old movies and listening to Judy Garland tapes, occasionally splurging on a masochistic hustler. The only one who bottomed out and actually made it work.

Melvin says, as if to himself, What is a book *for*?

Philip parks in front of The Gangway, one of the last surviving gay bars in the neighborhood. Half a miniature ship's hull hangs over the decrepit doorway, *SS Titanic*. A Christmas wreath on the door has seen better days. Nobody has ever opened the bar's blinds, because the clientele would surely turn to dust in the sunlight. Philip's crossed the threshold once or twice, but immediately turned back with the vague nausea you get from traveling in time. Philip tells Melvin that on the *Titanic*, they could have easily fit almost every single passenger onto the lifeboats, but they left many of the boats half empty. Drowning people screamed in the freezing water while the lifeboats scurried away. Of course, many of the rich survived, while very few of the lower deck passengers made it out alive.

Melvin's checking out some vaguely Islamic and occult-looking graffiti on the wall, composed of veiled, revolutionary women and esoteric calligraphy, partially covered over with posters for the latest end-of-the-world blockbuster.

The restaurant on the ground floor of Howard's apartment building has gone through many incarnations since Philip lived there, and is now something half Thai, half donut. Inside the restaurant two men are playing chess. Upstairs, Howard is nothing if not a gracious host—he has cleared the debris off of his two chairs and vacuumed up the mouse turds, although the television blares so that they must shout to be heard, until Howard finds the remote, which he misplaced during the cleaning.

They killed my Amish story, Philip tells Howard. All of that for nothing. Nothing?

A kill fee. But I'm afraid I won't be able to support you in your old age. Howard sighs.

But it's okay, says Philip. I was tired of thinking about how to make faceless murdered children fresh.

That reminds me, Howard says. I have something for you.

As he was tidying up, Howard came across a letter he never read, some sort of official notice from his place of employment two years ago. I'm kind of curious if there's anything in it I should know, he says. But I don't want to read it especially. He hands the envelope to Philip, then compliments Melvin on his perfect skin and asks him if he can take a look at his nipples.

This letter is in reference to and serves as documentation of your behavior at work during the dates indicated below. The morning of the twenty-fourth, your supervisor and other co-workers observed you walking around the work area with little apparent purpose but to disrupt other employees who were trying to work. You went from one cubicle to another and then finally went to the cubicle of Babette Donatello, your coworker whom you claim is the only person you feel you could trust. As you stood over her cubicle uninvited and unannounced, you said something to her which made her scream. She asked you to go away and then broke down and cried as a result. Everyone in the work area was then troubled and several employees rushed to her cubicle upon your leaving the area. Witnesses stated that you were constantly disrupting her and a nearby female coworker that morning. You publicly made reference to the female employees about certain aspects of your personal life and your disgruntled opinion about work. You then made an equally public comment that, "I JUST WANTED TO LET YOU KNOW THAT I WAS STILL ALIVE; I COULD NOT TAKE ENOUGH PILLS TO KILL MYSELF!"

Howard has said something to make Melvin laugh. No way! says Melvin. I wonder if that's even why we have them! In the past, the letter's author is describing a meeting with Howard and a Mr. Ramirez at approximately 10:15 a.m. on September 24. *While there, you immediately consumed several pills which you claimed were a prescribed medication by your doctor. As I began to discuss your behavior that morning, you interrupted me and raised your voice to the point where our voices could not be heard over yours. You took over the discussion and identified incidents in the past which made you feel frustrated with coworkers and management, issues which had little or nothing to do with this meeting. You complained of the girlie handwriting issue, a past event in which you behaved belligerently to a female coworker, resulting in an Informal Memo of Reprimand. You loudly said, "I DON'T TRUST ANYONE IN THIS OFFICE! I HAVE BEEN ISOLATED FROM EVERYONE ELSE!"*

And then Howard really turns on them.

"I DON'T TRUST YOU ANYMORE, YOU DECEITFUL LIAR! YOU ACTED TO BE MY FRIEND AND PRETENDED TO CARE FOR ME BUT YOU LIED ABOUT EVERY THING!"

Howard is now telling Melvin about how he met Philip so many years ago, about the sexual act Philip performed with him. At least Howard doesn't tell Melvin the paltry sum Philip received in exchange. Philip guesses he's trying to negotiate a similar deal with Melvin.

"Oh yeah, it's not okay for me to say and do things, but it's okay for everyone else...for Judy to fuck Lionel Murray...as she had been fucking Bill Crosley to get her way up!"

Why stop with the capital letters, Philip wonders. Howard took another capful of pills in front of them, just like he did with Philip later that evening.

He'd been calling and leaving more and more belligerent messages on the answering machine, accusing Philip of being a puritanical Mennonite prick for
not fronting him more weed. They took turns insulting each other and hanging
up on each other, but there was no way Philip could compete with Howard's
newfound scorched earth policy. Finally, Philip decided to just take him a bag
and be done with him. Once he got there and Howard downed the capful of
pills in front of him, Philip thought: *This is a cry for help.* But he wasn't in the
mood. A few days later Howard's building manager found Howard passed out
in his room with the door ajar and called an ambulance.

In the hospital, Howard dreamed of vast underground cities, he dreamed of
crying in his mother's lap, he dreamed of familiar buildings in the Bronx, long
since razed in reality, but which served as rest homes for the dead in the dream.
So many people he knew were there, just resting. Howard cried in front of the
hospital psychiatrist after relating these dreams. The good doctor wasn't especially interested. He was only trying to gauge Howard's suicidal intent. Was he
a threat to himself or others?

I am not a believer in God or a Jehovah witness so they all mock me and hate me here....
I am loud and talkative so they all hate me and are afraid of me.... I created a system that
allows one person to manage the control desk, but no one ever appreciated me for it.... Judy
Justice and Dan North always praised me, but never backed me up when it counted....

I've worked here for fifteen years, your manager Judy Justice and you, Tommy boy, the
smiling fool, know what I did for this office but nobody gives a damn!

Philip had accompanied Howard home from the hospital in a taxi. During
his breakdown he'd tossed papers and books and videos around, scrawled rants
directed at coworkers on cardboard boxes, and unplugged the refrigerator. His
apartment smelled. Philip was so over Howard and his infantile rages. But inside the smelly apartment, Howard apologized and even wept. Philip's always
been a sucker for tears of regret, although he's pretty sure he's never shed
them. How petty to wish away the very past that's led you where you're at. The
only past you have.

You then made your last threatening comment to Daniel Burns and loudly stated, "IF
YOU SEE ME WALKING DOWN THE STREET AND YOU WERE RIDING
IN YOUR CAR WITH YOUR WINDOW OPEN, I WISH YOU DROP DEAD."
Finally, as soon as the secured office lobby doors closed, you then turned and violently banged
on the doors, which was not only threatening, but extremely upsetting to all of the employees
in the office.

3

A CUP OF COFFEE AND A SANDWICH alone in the so-called arts district.

It feels like I've never been born, says the woman behind Felicia. That's what I feel like today.

Sonya Brava said something like that to Felicia once, with an even more despondent tone of voice. Sonya the extrovert would collapse from time to time, exhausted from her constant performance as a clown, a writer, a human being, but sometimes Felicia wondered if the collapse was also a kind of overdramatization. Sonya would sit in her pajamas and talk about suicide in a detached and slow and remote and impossibly quiet voice, as if she was receiving dictation from the most desolate moon of Neptune and relaying the simple facts. As if there was nobody else in the room. But there was, of course, somebody else in the room.

Felicia begins to count in her head the people she's known who've talked about suicide and those who've actually killed themselves, when a woman gently taps her shoulder.

Excuse me, she says. I'm wondering if I might photograph your sandwich.

The woman is wearing a bright, gauzy scarf and is emanating more good cheer than Felicia can process.

My sandwich?

It's for my website, says the woman. I post smiley faces on my website and invite others to do the same. Smiley faces that I find everywhere. They're all around us all the time. You see? There in the French bread of your sandwich? Two eyes and a big smile.

Felicia looks down at her rather forlorn sandwich, trying to make out the smiley face. The bubbles in the bread have in fact formed in such a way that a large half circle lies underneath two round spots.

Okay, says Felicia.

The woman photographs the occult smiley face from several directions and then gives Felicia her card, with the web address where she can find the picture of her smiley face along with thousands of others—sent in from smiley face hunters all over the world.

Felicia waits a moment or two and then wraps her sandwich in a napkin, hurries out of the café. Everything is closed or closing early, for the holiday.

Felicia hides away in the guest bedroom watching *Female Convict Scorpion*. She's so depressed that she dozes a bit. The window of the west-facing room is cracked, and traces of raindrops blow in, misting her face. None of the doors in Geordi's mother's house have locks.

Outside the bedroom is a garden way too tidy, with stones and overly groomed hedges. Tiny fractures in the stones like spiderwebs.

Seven women run across the sand of a bleak and enchanted landscape in matching gray prison robes. They descend the hill as if slowly collapsing downward. The village is buried in volcanic ash.

Dozes and wakes, dozes and wakes. The bedroom door is cracked and through it she can see her guide passing by. It's just Geordi careening down the hall. Is he limping? Blind? He's speaking to his grandmother on the phone. I'm coming to see you, he says. Granny is wrapped in a shawl somewhere in the Central Valley and the image on the screen flickers and pulses. The actresses are bluish and gray. Silvery faces of the dead emerging from long forgotten channels.

Pontormo's fresco at San Lorenzo was to rival the Sistine Chapel in its freakish glory. Not only was his great elaborate masterwork of ascending and descending nudes labored over for eleven long years of his life; not only did he die before it was completed; not only was it misunderstood and unappreciated after his death; but 180 years later, in 1738, it was whitewashed over, leaving no way to reconstruct it but through Vasari's hostile description and a few scattered drawings.

Felicia squints at the world of shadows and flickering dreams on the screen as if she could make something out. Ideas about the future. It sounds like Geordi's sobbing and he hangs up the phone. The women catch and club to death a dog, cook it over the fire. Eating the drumstick, Scorpion's nemesis catches Scorpion's stare.

Outside the guest bedroom, the sky becomes pink and then slowly gray as the streetlights flicker on down the avenue leading toward the port.

There's a goddess, you know, who sleeps for all of time. On a lotus leaf in the middle of an enormous pond, she dreams vast cycles of creation and destruction. Every so often a ripple in the pond disturbs her sleep, and she turns from her left side to her right side, or vice versa. A cosmos disintegrates, another one is born.

The end of July 1556, Battista left a note for Pontormo that said he wasn't coming back. Pontormo made no entries for the next month. Battista wasn't mentioned in the diary again. Pontormo died alone on New Year's Eve of that year, or New Year's Day of the next.

Still staring. Stop! I know I'm not a human but a beast. I killed my own kids with my hands. I hated their father for his unfaithfulness. I killed my two-year-old by drowning him.

*And the younger one…*She laughs maniacally. *Look, girls! The scar. I stabbed my unborn child to death!*

Roaring of flame. Wind blows the door open.

Women with torches walk through the wind. The wind blows out the flame. Strange light in the window, a blue glow. Shed collapses around an old ghost woman. Women's faces illuminated.

She's crazy, too.

Singing nonsense.

Has a knife.

We should have kept to the main road from the beginning. Having come this far, we begin to grasp who our hero really is…

She wakes then, as if after thousands and thousands of years. The streetlights have blinked and gone out again. The darkness is everywhere.

She stumbles up. Cold and angry, like she's just died. She doesn't give a fuck about any of this. Watch out. It's time for the Christmas festivities.

Female Convict Scorpion continues playing in an empty room. The singer is a ghost.

Women commit crimes because of men. Driven by love, hatred, and jealousy. Listen to my story of those seven sinful girls…

The first one hated her unfaithful husband so much that her hatred drove her to kill her children. The second one killed her lover after her lover killed her son. The third killed her lover's wife. The fourth sold herself to several men.

The fifth set fires. The sixth killed her own father after he tried to rape her. The seventh one...

Scorpion divides sticks. We know her story. She ties the sticks in bundles. Women make love by the flames.

The eighth is only the voice of the ghost itself.

4

THE THING ABOUT CHRISTMAS is that it's just making Melvin want to be raped more than ever. He's got Ralph's apartment to himself and nothing to do but watch it happening over and over again. He's gotta admit, he's pretty convincing. He keeps saying *Jesus fuck* in a way that seems totally real. The movie ends with the man and the woman dumping him out of their van. Melvin argued the last shot should have been the one where he's naked in the bushes along the side of the road with that *enigmatic* smile on his face. You're the muse, not the director, Ralph insisted.

Ralph's in Arizona, visiting some old parents. Bad idea. Melvin got so lonely he called up Jared in New York. It's just interesting to me, Jared said, that you keep living with gay men. Melvin could see where that was headed and made up a story to get off the phone. A story about a party he was going to, well not even a *party*, more like an *event*, a catastrophe, an *exhibition* involving bionic genitalia. *Half* the time I don't even know what you're *talking* about, said Jared. I'm learning Muay Thai kick-boxing, said Melvin and hung up the phone.

The last shot is the man and the woman smiling as they drive away from the scene of the crime, smiling in a way that isn't even slightly *enigmatic*. He starts again at the beginning.

Becoming an actor has skewed Melvin's relationships. Sometimes he'll tell lies like it's nothing at all. The movie opens with Melvin telling the guy who'll eventually rape him, *I'm not really into guys*. Ralph explained that there wasn't enough narrative tension if you were raping a gay. A lot of shots of the man's face and the woman's face, a lot of shots of the woman waving the dildo, and then strapping it on. God, Christmas lasts forever. There aren't any secret messages possible. You're just waiting and waiting until it's over.

He starts rummaging around, picking titles off Ralph's shelf, reading Ralph's emails. Ralph goes on and on to some guy named Vicente about *the irrational logic of all relationships* and sends cryptic questions to Philip about *Johnny Guitar*. He tells a girl named Sasha about the police raid on the film shoot. *I received a receipt for the items that were seized. Plastic black revolver toy w/6 inch barrel it said under Item #1. They also confiscated the fake eyeballs, I'm not sure why.* He explains to somebody named Roman his ideas about horror. *You have to be willing to kill anyone and everyone. You have to convince the audience that you just might go there. Get them involved with a decent, likable character and then slaughter him mercilessly. Murdering a child is always a good idea. An adorable child that everybody cares for—lead the child into hell and then abandon him there. Just as important, you must broadcast your intentions to torment and damage the child well before you actually do it.*

He says surprisingly little about Melvin. He does suggest to Tony dusting off the old *Opera Barn* screenplay and casting Melvin as Damien or more likely Troy. Describes Melvin as *charismatic*, that's good. But *dispassionate sexual demeanor?* And, *So far I've found ways to work around his serious limitations*; what does that mean?

Using close-ups from the porn might help camouflage his painful overacting; the stark realism of his discomfort and disappointment during the rape might also suggest his pain at the loss of his dead gang members.

Melvin gets up into the Internet rape porn instead painful ass rape videos latina tied and ass raped sports reporter with a sexy tight ass gets raped ass rape slave ass raping big tit mom hentai rape school rape asian rape man getting caught fucking a little asian babysitter young and cute teen getting fucked like a dog watch teen raped up the ass incest rape blue collar ass rape underage ass rape teen virgin ass rape porn sleeping hunk gets ass raped bisexual rape rape dream russian girl forced to fuck ass fucked bisexual guy in great MMF threesome slave is used naked and defenseless hardcore extreme bisexual rape interspecies male boy butt rape limp male owned rape of a male pig-bitch gay male raped by donkey mom raped in the kitchen woman shot dead and raped doctor rape patient boy raped by girls teen molested by roadworkers gang rape home invader rapes house husband forced boys prison rape arrested teen raped by police officer lesbian rape in the gym knifepoint rape rape of arab student anal rape after car breakdown it started as rape rape by 2 soldiers japanese gay boy rape group rape in a prison rooftop punishment she cheated and takes it rough from behind they gangfucked me in the locker room and I loved it asian guy gets raped hard stud in latex gets ass raped gay rape porn action rape in the forest daddy rapes young twinks blind fag gets raped straight scallylads raped hot hardcore bareback anal rape twink gets his ass raped with raw dick two military men caught a lad and want to rape him big muscle stud owns that tight little ass young boy brutally monsterfucked hard two tied trannies get hard raped by four ebony chaps hot brazilian ladyboy gets deep anal fuck brazilian burglars rape two shemales arab and black rape white boy israeli boys rape arab girls brutal soldiers afghan rape videos bacha bazi boys young arab boy rape girls raping boys pizza delivery boy rapes neighbor two boys rape sleeping granny mexican girl violated in the field big breast tranny gives guy doggy style rape two guys raped girl in front of boy black shemale rapes a college boy boy-breeder fucks mexican boy busty mom attacks sleeping mexican boy and fucks him hard straight men being raped shy latino straight boy fucked hard straight mexican guy stripped naked by his buds straight boy terrorized hard in the ass home depot day laborer fucked by huge uncut cock straight guys forced to ass-fuck twink in frat ritual hazing games with college guys impoverished hetero-sexual guys screwing group humiliates naked college guy dreamboy bondage terrorized twink sebastian penetrates and gets penetrated hot french brunette gets her ass raped hard anal rape at rented apartment french soldier fuck alge-rian girl french soldier fuck algerian boy french algerian thugs fucking on his knees poor little twink pounded surrender bitch dominique's strap-on vs white boy's virgin ass raw and rough tied up in the woods sweet torment roofied drift-er gets abused tied up in the cage arrest fantasy latino guy gets raped by two big dicks is this considered rape? forced bitch western girl get rape by asia man western girl get rape by asia man part 2 landlady rape brutal rape new girl-friend raped by police officers you shore got a purty mouth boy domestic vio-lence turns into rape horny men take down a cocky hustler at a busy sex arcade triple rape real doll rape porn outdoor rape porn couple rape girl together soldiers rape girl good old teen rape rape fantasy public bathroom rape date rape two guys rape girl at public toilet trailer park trash raped by intruder bride has twisted rape fantasy rape at karaoke bar schoolgirl raped by classmates rape by 2 soldiers two horny military men want to rape cute lad japanese sec-retary raped in the office teen girl raped at police station girl raped next to her boyfriend horny boy rapes nurse boy beaten for ransom money don't give that bitch a choice teachers rape little boy bitch in a box nun raped in church arab and slave dentist rapes patient while unconscious first choked then fucked bru-tal rape of a male whore by cruel mistress japanese wife raped by mental pa-tient japanese rape in prison model rape porn fuck sex tape amai liu raped with a huge sex toy suzi suzuki gangraped by black hoods latin boys in prison shower stranger raped my ass he fucked my tight ass in the county jail prison rape: inmates at large mischievous doctor takes his prison patients in gay violent bondage gym locker room holds twink prisoner guard enjoys having his cock sucked by the prisoners jail fun in south american prison prisoner gets banged in jail cell hung hottie gay rape porn best rape porn video you will see today daddy forced her to suck and fuck his friends twink forced to spread his ass for daddy father rape sons wife old dad forced rough sex with young daughter as punishment son rape mom until father at work drunk father forced daughter to suck and fuck brother forces sleeping sister for sex therapeutic sex and gay rape porn machofucker billy clay and gay rape fucking straight boy terrorized in his ass for the first time prison slave fuck prison bitch gets fucked basement prison holds men tied for the kinky fantasies of gay masters fucking prison style rampant prison thugs boynapped: anal assault airport security 4 airport security 5 tied cuffed and stuffed captive factory girls rape scene very hard rape policewoman rape scene young girl gets groped and forced into sex in a subway train shoplifting schoolgirls forced to sex dazed bimbo has cock forced up rear brazilian forced in kennel latina babe forced to fuck on gunpoint hot argentinean blonde sandra forced to fuck outdoors latino boy nailed humiliated by black guys lady force fuck his boy servant sneaker-boy forced fuck balaclavaed attack in the cellar young male busted on the roadside abuse and torture of a sexy hunk on your knees soldier! young army recruit learns a lesson tied up waiting for the fuck master stalker drugged girl and rapes her russian girl raped by repairman teaching a mormon missionary boy raped by creepy old man guy gets raped by two blonde whores junkie girl raped by drug dealers pregnant girl raped by doctors raped by spiderwebs raped by tentacles tattooed muscle guys rape a dude in the desert latino guy gets raped by two big dicks raw blindfolded boys take it in the ass and the mouth by a cop man with a sixpack gets his ass raped latina tranny brutally raped by masked robber slave's ass destroyed by fuck machine retro rape fantasy straight guy forcefully raped horny gay rapes in public a straight guy sage gets beatdown by antonio boy put sleeping pill into her drink and rapes her two crazy girls raped straight boy gets ass wrecked during gay massage force fucking a tight ass gay lad receives his clothes ripped and then is forced to fuck in extreme gay gang bang gorgeous forced entry military squad threesome fucking outdoors dude fucked in the ass by a leg amputee stump fucked 3 she fucks his ass with her amputee stump hot muscled stud forced into sizzling hot hardcore ass whacking frat house forced blowjob forced fuck teen hard teen gay boy tied with hands behind in the backroom is forced to suck cocks in group sex video gay boys get forced to do a threesome straight guys forced to ass fuck twink in frat ritual college teens forced into liking the dick old daddy forced hate twink sex twink forced to spread his ass for daddy gay forced into blowjob and hard anal straight lads forced to be gays gay jock forced his hard dick into studs tight ass horny blonde forced pool boy to fuck pledging teens forced to fuck and suck teen couple raped by another couple croatian crossdresser and his bitch wife angelica bella raped by three burglars crazy guy raped young girl black nasty tranny dominates bisexual asshole me and my bisexual slaves very disturbing bisexuals act russian girl raped by crazy guy brutal bandit beats and rapes hard his blonde tranny victim young cute boys in brutal action two guys one stump shemale soldiers pounding a latinos ass male amputee playing with stump dbk amputee fucking in the park legless guy cums amputee guy fucking on the sofa male amputee masturbates male amputee playing with stump sexy male amputee mexican amputee in masturbation 2 guys 1 stump hump the stump stump grinder erotic amputee stump massage hump the stump 2 stump fucked 3 daddy loves to abuse extreme twink hatefucking kidnap a men gang of men masked in cops bondage orgy straight guy coerced into having a good time straight guy get fucked hard as hell in his ass straight military dude barebacks a guy sleeping hunk gets ass raped straight studs butthole violated by the gay mafia his first ass violation innocent baseball jock gets violated by nasty coach gay boy violates roommates ass in his sleep dealer violates parole construction site violators my tight asshole brutally violated by a 200cm tall big man daddy violates young twink geneva convention violation tristian gets violated daddy loves to violate violated bound gagged guy violated in paint shop black daddy violated me amateur straight guys get violated boy ass gets red after whip used by pervert mistress spanks him hard torturing and making him suffer gas station rape 1: perverted discoveries sissy boy anal rape boy forces granny ass rape 12 year old boy gets raped by pit bull excited guy getting raped by dog women tied and raped by a dog old man getting ass raped by horse teen gets raped by crazy friend boy and girl raped by crazy couple dad anal raped teen friend for giving me alcohol raped a young mexican boy father rape son porn doc rape studious boy mexican boy gets caught jerking off twink raped in prison shower by big cock petite twink gets his little ass reamed latino ass rape video three rats rape daughter boys raped bride before wedding russian straight soldiers male rape porn sexy nurse raped by two soldier soldier rape arab us soldiers rape pretty redhaired woman during a battle in iraq soldiers savagely fuck and fist screaming woman soldier real rape video serbian soldiers rape real please rape me! volume 2 american soldiers captures vietnam girl captured female soldiers at vietnam war are brutally raped and killed after being fucked captured enemy woman horrible violated by soldiers soldiers rape skinny girl soldiers rape nurse american soldiers rape afghanistan girls soldier raped by cute chick us soldiers tortured and raped iraqi women russian army rape 1 arabian soldier gay porn rape video strong brunette soldier punished by boss in bondage brutal gay fuck raping an accused soldier a guard fucks his prisoner of war this interrogation goes a little too far! soldier gets fucked in the washroom soldiers don't accept no fucked by enemy soldiers queen gangbanged by soldiers young tchetchen sniper raped by russian spy captured and fucked by soldiers gay soldiers rape boy gay military ass fucking military punishment roman soldiers rape slave boy american soldiers rape muslim detainee with lightbulb public cafe shop boy tied by pervert gays and forced to deliver in bondage group sex in horny video chained muscle labor slaves str8 hung latino 18 yo minimum wage tire stacker goes gay for pay straight ex navy monster gay slave dressed just in ropes locked underground and trained in how to bondage sex tiny mexican getting his butthole wrecked in a short time str8 latino boys fuck each other straight latin boy gets his dick sucked good straight latin boy takes cock up the ass str8 latino boy penetrates himself bottom boy tops straight latin boy for first time str8 mexican landscaper lets me film him cumming straight mexican guy stripped naked by his buds old fat policeman abuse a latin twink straight cute mexican gets kidnapped mexican begs skinhead to breed his ass teaching a mormon missionary boy mormon boy gets fucked angel amputee cogida a ivan tattoo guy stumps and strokes his dick in his ass gives this guy a good feeling...

Finally Melvin checks out the local Sex Offenders site. Christmas is making him regress to his teenage years. He thought he'd hit the jackpot back then— pages and pages of people who liked to have sex with kids, with their pictures and addresses and everything. Megan's Law Rules, he thought. But he'd go hang out in front of their houses or walk back and forth until he got too bored and a couple of times he even knocked on the doors with some stupid excuse like he was selling something—newspaper subscriptions or chocolates or raffle tickets—but then once somebody wanted to buy a whole case of mint cookies and so he gave that up. He started just collecting money for charities he'd thought up like Needy African Children, Inc., or The Troubled Youth Foundation or Boys Will Be Boys or he'd just say that he couldn't find his way home or needed to use the phone or the bathroom. The Sex Offenders in Utah were so disgusting for the most part. Now here's one who lives just a few blocks away. Oral Copulation with Force, Violence, Etc. Not really his thing.

Melvin writes DJ a card with a picture of a Santa on it and a bunch of freaky-looking elves. Serious freaky, like some of the nanoforms, the hieroglyphic chattering DMT elves everyone always meets in hyperspace, not very Mormon. *I'll see you soon and we'll have lots of fun I promise* and then *XOXOXO Love, your only brother.* But that seems too gay and so he scribbles out the *X*'s and *O*'s.

He throws on his jacket and takes to the more-or-less deserted streets. Pagan winter solstice festival fine, longest night of the year, bonfires and human sacrifices, no problem. The whole spectacle and the whole depressing jingle jangle shit everywhere you go is just driving him crazy. The only message of Christmas: The human race is rotten, so let's have a group hug. Instead, the secret to existence should be hidden in Melvin's ass. Or at least somebody should believe that. Somebody should be driven half-mad by the idea and when he or she stares at Melvin's ass, he'll absolutely know the only way to touch the insane beautiful angel at the core of existence. Not in some halfhearted way.

He drops DJ's card in a mailbox. The 24 Divisadero comes groaning down the street and Melvin climbs aboard. Why not? It's just these cheery and depressed clusters of people carrying gifts and pies and bottles of champagne from one side of town to another.

There are more people on the street here, equally cheerful, some in drag, some in leather, but still it's all just like *Ho ho ho.* Melvin doesn't want a scene or a fantasy. And yet he knows that it won't really happen either without some sort of telepathy. A safe word, what's that? Isn't anybody plotting something? The anthropic principle, for example. An endless chain of ridiculous improbabilities so that one day in the heart of Mormon country the Melvin sperm would meet the Melvin egg just a month before Melvin's dad would topple over dead. Or not exactly topple. A mysterious accident. Maybe not mysterious for his dad, but for Melvin, because his mom only talks about it like some movie she slept through.

People close their blinds a lot. They don't want to see too much of the outside. Problem is, Melvin doesn't wanna be in there. He doesn't wanna be welcomed into any of those sites of ritual humiliation and loneliness, he wants to be circling outside in the dark, but just like—not the *only one* circling outside in the dark. Some rooms are lit up by twinkling lights or by televisions. He can see what's happening on the TV as if he was sitting right up in there with it. It's a cartoon where this big Santa Claus is spanking a naughty boy who looks kind of like DJ. A woman walks into the room, laughing. The little boy's crying in an overly dramatic way. The woman stops laughing when she sees Melvin not ten feet away, looking right at her.

***

Probably "human" is just a sad little cul-de-sac in the joyride of evolution. How about something less needy and self-conscious? Creatures with less painful self-awareness maybe, but still with the sensual *moment* of some so-called lower forms of life. Melvin's opposed to robots, in general, which is kind of like—going too far? Not to mention that they'd have to be programmed, with their so-called "artificial" intelligence, but even if they escaped the corny slogans, or even if somebody managed to program some compassion into them, it would still be the same basic conflict but encased in metal. Like: programming vs. freedom and imprisoned selves vs. cosmic wonder and all that business, not to mention that they'd probably be inflicting a lot of pain on whatever humans would be left over, and maybe we'd deserve it, because of what we do to all the so-called lower forms of life, but Melvin's still not into the idea of more flesh-torture at the hands of intelligent machines.

Cyborg sex, yes, mechanically enhanced flesh-fuck, you bet, but robot rape? No way. Down Valencia until he hits Market and then down Market Street to downtown. People are lined up already for the after-Christmas sales, which is kind of less horrible than Christmas itself, but he veers away. Death by trampling, the blurry, expectant faces. Who would miss this, but the dead themselves? Everybody waiting to shove clothes, CDs, electronics, leather furniture, and video games into every orifice. Reality's already virtual, who wants to escape into a fantasy begotten by a fantasy, a dream within a dream? Unless the two negatives equal a positive, if maybe everything's equally false and so real. He ends up in North Beach, finds an adult bookstore and video arcade that's open. Not a single patron has any rapist vibe so he just chats awhile with the other straight guy. He's in the middle of a run from Eureka down to Southern California but he decided to stop here for a minute because he does speed to drive his truck all night and all day, but when he's on speed, he says, it's like his whole body turns into a pussy, it just opens up for a fucking, and he's straight so he'd rather get fucked by a tranny, but it basically doesn't matter. Melvin apologizes and says, Sorry, I'm not compatible in that way. But they go into a booth together and watch some movies and the truck driver gets Melvin high on some kind of smokable powder and Melvin's watching this cock slide into a pussy and he realizes that it's just like the truck driver said and his whole body has turned into a pussy, which is different than wanting to get raped, there's the two feelings, one, of being a pussy, of being open and moist and receptive and in fact perfectly designed to accommodate some sort of alien penetration, and two, of this other need to be forced to do something against his will, and since his body is kind of opening up and turning into all these pinpricks of light, this infinite number of stars expanding outward from a place that was once a center but doesn't matter anymore, this veering away from each other of the two possibilities, one (being a pussy) and two (wanting to be raped), which would seem to be the same thing, but aren't, strikes him as central and probably metaphorical about the evolution of his ideas about the future and so he wants to draw some future life forms at the same time he wants to get raped at the same time he wants to get entered (as well as lovingly fondled, since he's now a pussy) at the same time he wants to save his little brother from being molested and turned gay and Mormon back there in Utah or in Disneyland and he's just watching this cock slide in and out of this pussy and then the money runs out and the screen goes blank and the truck driver says, I gotta go, I gotta get back on the road. Melvin says, Where are you going again? The trucker says San Bernadino, and Melvin says, Is that next to Disneyland? The truck driver asks him if he can get hard enough to fuck and Melvin's like, Sorry, I'm not compatible in that way. He says, But I can draw pretty good, I'll draw you a picture.

While they drive out of the city in this truck full of frozen fish, the calm yet fervent trucker tells him that he used to work as a Sanitation Engineer and as a Bereavement Counselor and for a while he was in Pest Control and so he talks at length about the difficulties in treating waste and the degree to which untreated sewage so often just ends up in oceans, lakes, and rivers, and he talks about different methods of treating termites and he talks about poisoning fish that various agencies and individuals don't like because maybe they aren't native species, and how first you have to kill every fish in the lake and how it takes years or maybe centuries for a body of water to get over that kind of mass poisoning and he talks about helping people get used to death and from time to time he looks over at Melvin's picture and Melvin tells him that his major influences are H. R. Geiger and Martin Ramirez and Joe Coleman and Daniel Martin Diaz and Pooch and the trucker says, That's pretty good but I thought you were going to draw me getting fucked, and so Melvin works that theme into his picture while at the same time trying to capture the trucker's look of calm fervency and the trucker's feeling of being a pussy and the trucker hits Highway 5 and starts checking out the drivers of the little cars that buzz around him, You can see everyone from up here, he says, and you'd be surprised at the things people do alone in their cars. He talks about what it's like to drive a truck and how right now, as Melvin can see, Highway 5 is covered by this cold layer of fog that he describes as tule fog and which he says transforms the Central Valley into the ugliest space on the face of the earth, it isn't that it's full of smelly cows and prisons and the small towns that supply prison guards and those who deal with beef, he says, but when it's cold with a layer of gray as far as the eye can see, so low it's like this icy ceiling, then there's nothing to even look at except this boring road and the boring gas stations. But they cruise along at a pretty good pace, and Melvin actually kind of likes the dystopian beauty of it, it's green enough and blurry. The time passes quickly in conversation about the trucker's various jobs and various marriages, and as they approach the Harris Ranch, the trucker rolls up his window and they both fall silent for a moment as they try to leave the sensory world, to withdraw into barely perceiving quietude and remain as unsmelling and unfeeling as possible while they drive for several miles past this endless series of cow pens full of more cows than Melvin has ever seen at one time before, all of them shitting and pissing and waiting to die, and then after a while they get to what the trucker calls the Grapevine, which just means, Melvin guesses, that it isn't flat and smelly anymore, it's like a mountain. The trucker says the Grapevine's a bitch to drive but it's a hell of a lot more interesting, and he starts checking out with more fervency the drivers of the little cars that buzz around them, and he says, What do you think about that guy? This older guy's driving a kind of nondescript blue car and Melvin says, I'm not sure what you mean, and the trucker says, He's a top, I bet he'd fuck us both, and Melvin says, How can you tell? The trucker says, I can tell. The trucker says, A lot of guys who are into truckers are bottoms, and so things don't work out, because most truckers are on speed, but you can tell when somebody's used to picking up truckers, they know what's up, and this guy clearly knows what's up. As it turns out, he's right. They all pull over at this rest stop, and the old guy and the truck driver talk and then the truck driver takes the old guy into the back, between the front seats and the refrigerated compartment for the frozen fish, where he has this bed fixed up, and Melvin wants to be polite, so he gets out of the truck and hangs around the rest stop while the trucker's getting fucked. Not even noon and he looks at maps and depressed clusters of family-like, post-Christmas humanity sulking and shivering. Faces melt in and out of the fog, muted with this sort of freezing and gloomy nothingness only a good rape would disperse.

For *Tinky Winky Rising 2*, Melvin suggested abusive cops and prison scenes and alternative dimensions that light can't get into. Only gravity. You can't film without light, Ralph pointed out, and said that it was harder to create a jail cell on film than you'd think without a budget.

When the old guy's done with the truck driver, he waves Melvin to come over and Melvin's thinking this guy has absolutely zero rapist vibe, he's like seventy years old and African American, and he's worn out by the truck driver anyway and seems more in the mood to just chat, That guy could go forever, he tells Melvin, he just never quits. The seventy-year-old is a graphic designer and he lives in LA but he drives the Grapevine just to find truckers, he's been doing this since the '70s. Melvin says he's on his way to Anaheim but the trucker's off to San Bernadino and the graphic designer says, Do you want to ride into the city with me?

Melvin climbs up into the truck to tell the truck driver good-bye, he thinks the trucker'll look different now that he's been fucked, satisfied, he thinks, or maybe a little bit of *ennui*, but he looks pretty much exactly the same, calmly fervent, and he's like, Nice to meet you, and puts the truck in gear and Melvin hops out. The speed with which the trucker says good-bye and drives away, checking out the little cars buzzing around the rest stop lot as he exits, feels kind of harsh to Melvin, like all this time they shared talking about sanitation and about beef and about becoming a pussy, is it really just like they didn't have any kind of bond at all? It's just the Christmas residue, Melvin supposes, his feeling of loneliness at the speed and, let's be honest, the indifference, with which he is abandoned by the trucker, but as he climbs into the graphic designer's car, he thinks he probably made the right decision to save his little brother, because if he'd just got off into the rape thing, back in San Francisco, sure, maybe he could have gotten raped but it would maybe be exactly like the trucker. On the other hand, this realization feels somehow at odds with his other discovery that the desire to be a pussy and the desire to be raped are two very different things, and yet he can't quite make sense of it, his brain's a little scrambled, from the drugs he did with the trucker, and so he's happy just to listen to the graphic designer as he drives him into the city. The designer tells him about his sexual experiences—about the '70s, which was an important time for the designer. He'd had some gay sex when he was in the army in the '50s and when he was in college in the '60s and when he first moved to LA, but he'd been in a relationship with a woman for five years, while Nixon was president. She knew that he was gay but she was one of those women who think gay men just haven't been fucked the right way by a woman. They were happy enough together for a while and he even helped her raise her little boy, but then after they split up, amicably, the designer says, her father didn't want him seeing the boy anymore, because of the gay thing. She wouldn't stand up to her father even though she didn't care that he was gay and she knew that he was like a father to her boy, more so than the biological father, who was never around. Years later he got a card from the boy, that was all, saying, Thanks for taking care of me when I was little. It hurt, he says, that that was all there was to it, apparently, and he cried then, he remembers now, at the loss of the little boy he'd once loved so much and who now didn't seem to care one way or another, as he hadn't cried during the time of the actual loss, which was in the '70s, after all, when he was in his thirties and without a lover or a child for the first time in five years. He'd go out every night, every single night, and he'd be thinking, wow, if he spent all the time working on his art that he spent cruising the bars and bathhouses and the highways between LA and the Grapevine, he'd be a fucking genius. It didn't matter, he was still out every night. Once, in the '70s, he picked up a taxi driver in traffic and he took the taxi driver home, set him down on the couch, and was about to suck his dick and this pistol fell out of the taxi driver's pocket and the graphic designer was like: What are you planning to do with *that*? And the taxi driver said, I wasn't sure that I could trust you, I just brought it for protection, and the designer said, Okay, well, why don't you set it over there, and then they got back to business. But, says the designer, it was really quite a shock, it was like Death had stepped into the room. Like another dimension had opened up, and Melvin says, Exactly. All that sex, he goes on, it was like a job, it was like revenge, it was like a misguided attempt at therapy to teach himself some lesson, and it did, he thinks, it did teach him about freedom and about the multiple paths of desire and the way that sex could be used for ego needs and the way that ego needs could be used for sex and then AIDS came along and he remembers the cover of *Newsweek* with the Gay Plague on the cover, in fact he still has that magazine, and he immediately stopped going out and stayed home for the next decade watching movies and working on his design skills and his posters and he became a much better designer.

As they get off the freeway Melvin explains that weapons are important in evolution and that viruses are important in evolution, well, microbes in general, and explains in detail the possible configurations of new cyborg weaponry and new cyborg viruses but then backs up to say that carbon-based evolution itself is kind of contrary to *real* evolution, to becoming a photon-based life form, the slow boat to transformation, he says, and breeding in general is just karma, and as the designer drives through Hollywood, there are huge posters of famous people that Melvin's never heard of with enormous lips and airbrushed skinny white women and reclining, voluptuous white men with big pecs. The designer drives up into Laurel Canyon, where he has this house, which is really bizarre, Melvin thinks, not because he has a house, because everybody lives someplace. But because the reality of this house, up along some winding roads lined with mailboxes on a hill with steep sides, is so different from the rest stop and the roads where the old guy picks up truckers, it's like they're two such totally different realities, that he never could have predicted one from the other, the world of his car and his truckers and I-5 and then the house, which has several levels just kind of dug into this cliff going up in the back and lots of windows and carpet and a television and movie posters, most of which were designed by the graphic designer himself, he explains to Melvin. He shows him some of his work, for *The Entity*, for example, with Barbara Hershey. Melvin asks what it's about, he likes that word, *entity*, because it suggests something less in a body, more photon-based, maybe an intelligent vapor or a gas and the designer says, Yes, it's just like that, except it's this invisible thing that rapes Barbara Hershey, repeatedly. She really had to act in that movie, says the graphic designer. Getting repeatedly raped by something invisible, that couldn't have been easy, and she's quite convincing, he says. In the movie, nobody believes her story. The men can't help her, her psychiatrist thinks it's about her incestuous feelings for her son, but of course, it isn't about that at all. It's about being raped by a real yet invisible entity. Finally the parapsychologists get involved and build an elaborate machine to trap and freeze the entity, but the entity just inhabits the machine and attacks Barbara Hershey with the machine itself.

Oh my god! says Melvin. That's exactly the problem with robots.

Melvin tells the designer that he draws, too, and he'll show him his stuff.

Actually, says the graphic designer, what I do isn't drawing. If I need something drawn, I hire someone to do it. I outsource the drawing. Design is more about the big picture, the *concept*.

I'm totally into that, says Melvin, and he'd show him his sketches, he says, but he left them in San Francisco, but he did some doodles on the way down, of the trucker who wanted to get fucked, and he shows them to the guy who says, Not bad, and then offers his critique.

Melvin needs to think about his arrangements, he tells him. About *hierarchy*. How do you make one idea stand out visually above the other ideas? In terms of the basic concept, he's got an interesting perspective, the graphic designer says, but he needs both thematic clarity and a way to develop his issues with a more original visual style.

Melvin says, You don't think I'm thematically clear.

The graphic designer just lets Melvin's lack of clarity fill up the silence.

What are you going to do in Anaheim anyway? asks the graphic designer.

I'm going to save my brother, Melvin says.

The graphic designer is dubious about salvation as a motif.

It's not a very original concept, he says.

5

A VOICE IS SAYING THAT THE HOTEL ROOM is boring. She lists a lot of reasons, starting with the pattern on the bedspread, which is so ugly it makes her faint. She suggests that maybe it would be okay to watch cable TV, just while they're here. A man is saying that HBO is not one of the ingredients of a godly life. It's basically porn. Shhh, says the woman's voice. I don't want you to wake him up. Somebody switches the channel, and a quiet voice is murmuring something that sounds like *my Mormony soup*.

So where did he come from? the man is saying.

I don't know, says the woman's voice. But he's already here, he says he's sitting at the Denny's.

Sitting at the Denny's, says the man. What's he doing sitting at the Denny's? It's just like him, he says. Sitting at the Denny's. Sitting at which Denny's? There's a Denny's just around the corner to the right and there's a Denny's just around the corner to the left and there's a Denny's straight down Katella Avenue. There's two more Denny's the other direction, other side of the freeway. That's five Denny's just that I know of, and knowing him, he doesn't know which one he's even at.

Shhh, says the woman's voice. I don't want you to wake him up.

He's already awake, can't you see that? asks the man. Just look at him, can't you see he's faking?

DJ loves hotel rooms. He never sleeps as perfectly, he never dreams as magically, as when he's in a hotel room. He's not sure he's ever been in a hotel room before, but he believes he has always secretly lived deep inside a hotel. It's true that he isn't exactly asleep, but he isn't faking either.

I suppose he's out of money, says the man. Isn't that why he's here?

The woman's voice whispers something far away.

I don't think it's the best idea, says the man. He's never been the responsible type and we don't know what he's been doing, we just don't know, he might even be on drugs.

He's sitting at the Denny's, says the woman's voice. He's drinking coffee.

Coffee, says the man. He didn't learn that in my house.

I would know if my boy is on drugs, says the woman's voice.

The woman's voice—it is his mom. DJ believes that once he was in a rage. He's heard the story at least, although he can't quite imagine it.

Whispering again, about people who go to Disneyland, looking for children to steal.

I could use a break, his mother is saying. I could do without The Mad Hatter again.

His father says something he doesn't understand. Then his mother touches DJ, so soft it is like a ghost. DJ, she says. Baby, it's time to wake up.

He opens his eyes.

His mother says, Wake up, we have a surprise.

His mother says, Here, let's get you your pill.

His father is standing at the window, looking out at the swimming pool. Is anybody swimming? Swimming pools are terrifying. He chews his Tegretol. His mother helps him out of his pajamas and into his clothes.

We're having breakfast at Denny's.

DJ's stomach hurts. Just a little bit.

Pancakes for you, says his dad.

Lots of pancakes, says his mom.

You know what the doctor said, says his dad.

It's Christmas, says his mom.

Christmas is over, says his dad. Christmas has been over.

We're on vacation, says his mom.

You know, says his dad.

He barely eats, says his mom. Look at him. Does he look obese to you? If anything, he's the opposite of obese.

His dad helps DJ on with his socks and his shoes, while his mom makes a call. She asks somebody which Denny's it's at. Is it on Harbor or Katella? Ask the waitress, she says. Okay, she says, we'll be there in maybe ten minutes.

They go down past the swimming pool, and nobody's swimming, and they get in the car and drive around the corner to the Denny's, and they park, and they get out and DJ's terrified, because that's what a surprise is: terror. Not to mention this place has the same name as his dad, which is DJ's name, too. But his mom and his dad look around inside the Denny's and then she says, It must be the one just up the street and his dad says, Why didn't you ask him for the address?

At the next Denny's, DJ feels weird. It's like they've moved—they got in the car and they drove, but they ended up in exactly the same place. A place that makes DJ feel weird.

Mommy, he says. My stomach hurts.

Oh, gosh, says his dad. Not again.

There's a stranger in the booth. It's his brother. DJ thinks he's going to faint. Melvin hugs him and Melvin hugs his mom and then Melvin shakes his dad's hand. They sit in the booth and look at the laminated menus and DJ starts bouncing up and down in the booth and his dad says, See, he's already getting overexcited, and his mom says, Baby, calm down, it's going to be a fun day today.

She says, After breakfast your brother's going to take you to Disneyland for the day and take you on all your favorite rides, he'll take you on the Mad Hatter and on the Jungle Cruise and all of it.

Just you and me, kid, says Melvin.

His dad starts talking to Melvin in a very serious way about his responsibilities and about no sodas and about how not to lose sight of him for even a minute and it's all very distracting. DJ empties a sugar packet into his ice water and stirs it, and since nobody is looking, he empties another packet and then another one and he stirs up the sugar water and takes a tiny sip.

So where did you come from? his dad asks Melvin. How did you get here?

Melvin lists the names of places that sound very far away and he tells his dad that he flew in on a plane, he wanted to surprise them for Christmas, and he's been making money with his new job—he's been driving trucks back there, he says, and he was in Pest Control for a while and he did a little bit of acting— so he flew in, and here he is and he knew that they'd be tired of Disneyland, because really, what grown-up isn't sick of Disneyland after a day, or so he's heard, although he doesn't really know, he's never been there. DJ's dad says, You have too been there, we took you the year after the wedding when I had that conference, and Melvin says, No, you left me with Aunt Becca and you went by yourself, and if you took some kid to Disneyland, it must have been Donny or one of your nephews because it sure wasn't me, and DJ's dad says, I don't think that's right, and he looks at DJ's mom with a puzzled kind of look, and so then DJ's mom says, Anyway, it doesn't matter, we're all here today and that's so wonderful that you have a good job. DJ takes another sip of his sugar water and then the pancakes come.

Afterward, in the Denny's parking lot, DJ's parents offer to drive them to the drop-off point, but Melvin says, It's right there, we can walk, good exercise, and DJ's dad frowns. People everywhere look confused, lost in a dream, they are all trying to get somewhere that you can't ever find. DJ's mom explains to Melvin all the things she's packed in DJ's backpack, a sweater in case it gets cold and some juice and a sandwich, because the drinks are so expensive inside Disneyland, and No sodas, she repeats, and DJ says, And I have my astronaut in there, and his mom says, Yes, he has the little blue man, and she gives Melvin a few dollars to buy him a hot dog, and she gives him the ride tickets, and she shows him DJ's pills and explains when they should be given and she says, So should we meet you right here, right here in this spot? That's okay, Melvin says, I'll just bring him back to the hotel, I know just where it's at. It's room 217, says DJ's dad and he says, Be back by seven o'clock. Sharp.

Melvin takes DJ's hand and they walk together to the stoplight where they can cross the street and then they walk on across an endless parking lot toward the entrance to the Magic Kingdom and already crowds of faces seem dangerous and excited in a disturbing way and even faces that are trapped inside making him feel ill and Melvin says, This is where you'd come to make a map of vulnerabilities in the hive-mind.

DJ says, I don't like the Haunted House.

DJ says, I don't want to go to the land with the bears.

Melvin looks back over his shoulder and he says, Don't worry, we aren't going to any of those places.

He says, Don't you think Disneyland kind of sucks?

Listen, Melvin tells him. He grabs DJ's hand and they start walking the opposite direction, back out toward the street. Melvin dials his cell phone and tells somebody that he needs to be picked up at Disneyland, right in front of Disneyland, and then he says, Well, fine, but I don't see them, and when he's done, he throws his cell phone in the trash.

That's how they trace you, he tells DJ. Cell phones. That's how people get caught.

6

In LA, while Geordi grabs a coffee by the bookstore on Vermont, Felicia calls Charles Scott. She tells Charles again how much she loves the piece he sent her for *Sexual Outlaws of the New Millennium*. He apologizes again for having come on to her so aggressively ten years ago. He doesn't really remember it, actually, just a drunken haze of lust that her name somehow still evokes. He'd love to see her, after all these years, but he's in some state of *deshabille*. The explanation for this is long and witty and confusing, involving medications and unhealthy relationships to money. Not to mention he's on deadline for the obituary he must now write for the splendid Lady Beatrice Cavanaugh Finch, dead just yesterday at ninety-four. Despite the positively criminal neglect she received from the American literary world, her historical novel *Diary of a Peg-boy* exerted a profound influence on Charles and on many of the most adventurous American writers of his generation. After several minutes of fascinating tangents about nineteenth-century presidents, and about two avant garde film actresses most famous in the '70s, it becomes clear to Felicia that trying to arrange a meeting with Charles would be preposterous and she excuses them both from this option as concisely as possible. I come down to LA quite a bit, actually, she says. Maybe next time around. She explains that her in-laws are in Long Beach and that she's been enduring another grim holiday. This provokes an audible shudder in Charles.

American holidays, says Charles. More unnecessary evidence that Americans live their lives as if they're already entombed.

Well, sure, says Felicia.

And Long Beach, he says. Don't get me started.

You get used to it, she says. We came up today to look through Waylon McClatchy's archives.

Whatever for?

It's not really about Waylon, she says.

It sounds like Charles is sipping something on the other end, maybe a morning martini.

Certainly Waylon's tepid life and writing don't merit more than one biography.

No, she says. It isn't really about Waylon.

Loud voices in the background of Charles's place—for some reason Felicia can't imagine it as anything but a hotel suite, with a balcony—interrupt them, as Charles begins cursing somebody out, and then returns to say, Sorry, I've got to deal with this beast, but if you're free later, give me a call.

As she drives across town, she tells Geordi that during her conversation with Charles Scott, she found herself saying *Well, sure*, realizing that *Well, sure* was something Philip always said, something she often hated.

Why would you hate *Well, sure?*

You can make some outrageous observation and he'll make it seem like the most obvious thing in the world, Felicia says. *Well, sure.*

When they get to UCLA, Geordi slides into the driver's seat of the rental car. Go to a museum, Felicia suggests. Or Book Soup. Check out that bookstore at Venice Beach. Just don't end up driving around all day.

Unlimited miles, says Geordi, but then he smiles in a way that's supposed to reassure her.

If you feel dizzy or faint, she says, pull over right away.

He glares at her.

I'll pick you up at five, he says.

Waylon's archives are tucked away on the third floor of this sedate and overly protected university building. A fussy young man takes several forms of ID from Felicia and insists she sign way too many pieces of paper, directs her into a tiny, windowless room, and then presents her with several fancy shoe boxes. The air-conditioning is on full blast.

The image of Waylon that gradually forms from these letters and unpublished drafts and scribbled journal entries is a strange one. Self-conscious and sanitized, not at all like the gossipy and unguarded man she met in the final years of his life. All of the correspondence, even the included emails, feel like they were written with history in mind. It's not that he has omitted any of his bad behavior. It's more like he's played it up in the most deliberate way to form a counter-narrative to the refined and polite public persona. It's all just a little too witty. A little too literary and quite a bit too centered on the famous. There are letters from John Ashbery, Michael Stipe, David Foster Wallace, James Merrill, even a letter from Celia Abad. She puts it aside. Even the pages from his epic poem don't feel like the draft of an unfinished poem. They feel like a polished version of something "unfinished" but designed to be read and debated by future historians.

She's quite sure that she's never written a letter or email with history in mind. It's a version of plastic surgery, it's how history is made.

Everything. She'd leave everything out.

History: Multiple paths tangling in elaborate networks through the gloomy forest. A pile of rubble, the polished fragments of bone. The story we have told.

Polished fragments of bone—she didn't used to think that way. She never would have used that image, she's pretty sure, before she met Geordi. Before his words, his phrases, his thoughts, became her own.

She never would have guessed that Waylon and Celia Abad had been in touch. Apparently Waylon contacted her first. *How gracious your kind words about my little scribbles,* she wrote him back.

Celia Abad writes about her family, about the murder of Magellan by a Filipino named Lalo Lalo, and about her health, which is better, she says. She discusses the work of the surrealists, of Henri Michaux, Anaïs Nin, Raymond Roussel, Jane Bowles. The only Filipino writer she mentions is Nick Joaquin. *I don't think of myself as having an imagination,* she writes. *When people talk about realism, I guess I don't know what they mean. What I write is realism for me.* She tells the story of Helen Ferguson as if Waylon would have no idea who she was; a young pale writer living out the sad destiny of a Helen Ferguson until in Helen's third novel, a young woman appears, adrift from her husband, searching for romance. The character's name is Ana Kavan, and shortly thereafter, Helen's is, too. Celia Abad always spells it *Ana* instead of *Anna*. Celia writes about *Ana* Kavan for pages. Celia doesn't pretend to be familiar with Waylon's work at all. She describes her surroundings in such an oblique way—a desk and some pear trees that don't fruit and views of the sky, some buildings on the horizon—but eventually the background clarifies, through subtle suggestion, into the mental institution where Throckmorton dumped her, and where she lived for the last several years until her death.

In Felicia's second favorite Celia Abad story, Celia's evil husband, Oliver Throckmorton, appears as an owl. The owl keeps appearing at the narrator's window with gifts, which at first seem marvelous: jewels and music boxes and delicate songbirds. By the middle of the story all of the gifts are decaying, releasing foul odors or, through complex series of events, introducing malevolent forces into the narrator's life. It's from her first book, before she began writing in English. Throckmorton translated the book himself, Felicia isn't sure if it was originally written in Spanish or Tagalog, in a collection titled *My Dream Autobiography*. After Celia's death, feminist scholars rediscovered her work, painted Throckmorton as a colonialist white male oppressor, and a new translation was brought out with the title *Autobiography of My Dreams*. Felicia prefers the second title but prefers Throckmorton's original translation. The narrator's positive spin on the devastation of her home at the end of her second favorite story, for example, contains more of Celia Abad's characteristic ambiguity and humor, whereas in the new translation, because of the simpler syntax, it just sounds like she's losing her mind.

In Waylon's journal, notes that seem to be from his "life" blur seamlessly into those for his only novel and into lines from his epic poem. How does a poet go about writing long-form narrative? At least on paper, Waylon doesn't wrestle with form at all. *If writing is a way to wander, editing is a way to erase one's self, one's embarrassing impulses, and to shape them into something refreshingly "not the self," as in travel,* he says.

She can't imagine that Waylon wrote that for himself, but that he wrote it for her. Or whoever he imagined would be in her situation, looking through his notebooks after he died.

The fragments from the epic poem list over two hundred guys, each given two or three lines, but they don't blur together. Each of them is incredibly distinct. There is something so precise about the details that it creates the sense of an impossibly vast world of idiosyncratic individuals. Here is the smile and here is the sordid décor and here is the arbitrary biographical detail. Here is the stiff or limp cock and here is the face, the belly, the teeth and here is the quote just before or after sex. And yet they are corporeal, complex, individual, suggesting an attitude toward sex that feels distinctly old-fashioned. You would suspect that Waylon believes in the soul. They are deluded and doomed and alive. Waylon got around. There is a boxer, a teenage bodybuilding champ, a bank robber, two different guys who believe they were abducted by aliens. There are two brothers that Waylon sleeps with separately, these two skinny Puerto Rican guys from the Bronx with huge cocks and bad teeth. Both of the brothers ask

Waylon or the narrator of the poem the same question, when he tells them he's a writer. *Is that hard work?* Waylon is touched.

In general, Waylon writes, *I don't care for people—at parties, over dinner, trying to impress me or waiting to be impressed. I don't really care for public faces or social life, and yet I can't save myself from my impeccable manners. I'm not even that interested in sex, really, but I like to have a man naked with me.*

One of the brothers had dated a famous married Marxist literary critic who was teaching at Yale, or *Jail,* as the brother pronounced it. Waylon also went to Yale and loves the mispronunciation so much that he repeats it, always spelled as "Jail," eight times in the epic poem.

The Huey material is neatly organized into its own little section: some early faxes he sent with messages scrawled in crayon proclaiming his great love and admiration for Waylon; a story he faxed about being whirled in a truck stop washing machine and then abandoned by his mother; a group of pictures he sent of himself and his punk rock, squatter friends. The boy in the pictures, supposedly Huey, is cute, with crooked teeth, but the grainy pictures and the styles of the punk rockers are totally early '80s—not 1994, when it was supposedly taken.

Felicia reads carefully and she takes notes. Writes down fax numbers and telephone numbers. They change constantly. There is a fax sent from a hospital in Seattle. There is a fax sent from Brooklyn, where Huey is supposedly hanging out with anarchists. Felicia writes down dates. Huey doesn't mention Trauma and Racer or their band Briar Patch until 1997 when suddenly he lives with them, although there's a mention of a band "of some really cool people he's been hanging out with" in '96, a band called Egregious Fuck. She tries to read the washing machine story carefully, for clues, but finds it almost impossible. Everything is overly explained, yet somehow still unclear. The actual mechanics of the truck stop and the laundry abandonment don't seem plausible, and yet there's nothing specific she can point to. It's as if the writer has never actually seen a washer or a dryer or a truck stop or a trashy mother, but is translating these details from a language (s)he barely understands.

The light in the tiny windowless room is dim and flickering. As if in a dream, the afternoon disappears.

By the time Felicia emerges into the permanently apocalyptic winter of LA, it will be dusk. Objects will be more stunning, more material, twisted in their fields. She'll remember a fragment from a Celia Abad story about a woman attached to a transparent fox by a small cord of light wrapped around her heart. It doesn't end well for the fox. She'll wonder what Melvin is doing, and for a moment she'll think of him as some freakish, beautiful creature like that doomed animal familiar.

Felicia will wait by the curb for Geordi to arrive. For some reason, she'll call Charles Scott. She has an excuse in mind, but as it turns out, she doesn't really need one.

You know why I was at Waylon's archives? It's the author Huey Beauregard. I'm convinced that he's a fake.

Oh yes, says Charles. I know the whole story.

The improbability of that sentence somehow won't startle Felicia.

According to Charles, a fat agoraphobic woman sits in her room all day writing the books and pretending to be Huey Beauregard while she sends her skinny sister out in public to play the part. He knows this because the fat agoraphobe's boyfriend is the godson of Drew Malone's wife or maybe it's the skinny sister's boyfriend. Drew is an old friend of Charles.

Drew Malone? says Felicia.

Charles is aghast that Felicia doesn't know who Drew Malone is, and he names Drew's several seminal experimental novels, what he would be known for in a *just* world. Since the world isn't just, he names the screenplays Drew wrote—after the experimental novels, he made the move to Hollywood and became a Buddhist.

The overweight, agoraphobic writer, says Felicia. Do you know her name?
He doesn't.

I assumed you did, says Charles. What then do you know?

Is it the bandmates? she asks. Is it Trauma and Racer?

That sounds right, says Charles. Email me later, would you? I have guests.

7

GEORDI MISSES FELICIA TERRIBLY ALREADY; without her he would be so lost. He's betraying her to spare her. Not horror, but maybe an overwrought idea of "Geordi," of what Geordi might do. Despite the odd, bubblegum pleasure that motion brings him today, north through the city to the 5. Onto the 5 and up toward the Grapevine. He has never thought of himself as a traveler. A *reader* and a *familiar road*, certainly. And yet he thinks of this as a "trip," which suggests meaningful signs, a distinct movement through various stages, a cohesive series of mental states, or a lesson. The actual relationship is only with himself—the "secret ordering principle," whether of the universe or his own mind, doesn't *need* him to do anything but pay attention. The form of a journey; the form of a poem; the form of a commentary on a partially corrupted text. The paragraphs of *The 8-Fold Garden of Space and Time* are only loosely connected to each other. There isn't an obvious structure. It's not exactly that in one half you get "the story" and in the second "commentary" on the "story." You sink into the depths of loneliness and maybe you never come out. Maybe that's just fine. One variant title could easily be interpreted more logically as *The 8-Fold Rising and Setting of Eternity*, one could easily be *The 8-Fold Breath and Wheezing*, one makes more sense as *The 8-Fold Musical Abyss*.

Pay attention.

He is attempting to distract himself from the purpose of his road trip—the irrational belief that he is poised to uncover "the secret" of his "missing time"—with the idea that the journey will offer its own unrelated instructions. You always find the thing when you stop looking.

The eight variant titles can be read as metaphors for the eight strata of the soul. Or vice versa. He pulls over at the rest stop across from where the plague rats are. The surrounding mountains are dusted with snow, and he's only just stepped out into the cold when he is set upon by a desiccated woman wearing tight black pants with a floral pattern up and down one leg and pink thongs with socks. A shirt that looks like it's made out of suede. The whole outfit maybe hasn't left her body in weeks. She just needs like five dollars or a ride, is he going anywhere near Barstow? Her husband left her, she says, for a younger woman, ain't that a bitch. She repeats her story, and repeats her request, for a five or a ride. She starts singing that old song, *I got five on it*, like they're old buddies and she's just clowning around, and then she falls quiet.

Los Angeles didn't work out, she says.

I'm going near Bakersfield, Geordi says. Sorry.

She says, Hey, it beats the Tejon Pass Northbound Safety Roadside Rest Area. You can drop me off anywhere, I'll head over on 58, my sister's in Mojave. Not my blood sister, but you know, more than blood, my soul sister.

She's curling herself into the car and Geordi's just allowing this to happen. An adventure, he reminds himself. She chatters on about her supposed ex-husband and various career prospects as they descend toward the valley and Geordi decides that this moment isn't dangerous, it's even kind of relaxing. The difficulty is going to arise when he tries to get rid of her. She'll never leave, he's pretty sure, without slitting Geordi's throat.

The woman's talking about cooking. I finally figured it out, she says. I mean, I'd have to read the instructions like a zillion times, but you know, some point I figured out you just gotta do what you're told. A recipe's like the law. Following the law, not really my thing, but I'm like, hey, why not give this a try? It was an unfamiliar symbol system, that's for damn sure. It's like some hieroglyphic code, deep Egyptian shit, time travel. Dice. Slice. Puree. What's the difference between grating and chopping, I needed to know. It's like I'm catching messages from the aliens here, but I'm just fixing a little lunch. Fixing a little lunch maybe wasn't in my genes. Dice. Slice. Puree.

When Geordi's on this road, he believes he's always been on this road. The 5 and then the 99. It's the same road either way. When they were kids and they were leaving the valley, for a vacation they always called it. Until one day his mother packed them up for good and said she couldn't take another minute in that horrible town with their father, who had no imagination. She wanted to live next to the ocean, she wanted to see the water from her window, she wanted culture and music and anything but those fields. His father stayed behind, without complaining.

It's good to weep for the dead, his travel companion is saying. Her hair's tied back in a ponytail with a thick rubber band. My Wade, she says, had that look about him from the day he was born, the very first day. Didn't quite belong to this world. Too good for this shit, that's for damn sure.

He's lost in her words and then the road, the snow, where is he? The familiar road isn't taking him anywhere meaningful or safe, it's taking him wherever.

It's good to weep for the dead, she repeats.

It doesn't look to Geordi like that face has cried for centuries. It looks so far beyond real grief, so far beyond even the kind of hope that could lead to real grief. Like its last tears evaporated around 1973 and the moisture from her heart followed. She's been hollowed out, he thinks, but then realizes he's been imagining her as an older woman, like all the women in his life. He tries to imagine her face less puckered up, with all its teeth. She's just a child, really, late twenties, early thirties.

What's wrong, sugar, your driving's getting a little erratic like, watch where you're going, ain't no hurry. Barstow can wait, and Bakersfield, too, for all that.

I need gas, Geordi says. They've just passed Mettler Station, but just up ahead is Grapevine Oil and the Freeway Express Mart. She glances at the gas gauge and he sees her skeptical look, so he says, Not gas exactly, but a gas station. I need to use the facilities.

You do whatever you gotta do, baby, she says. Just get us there in one piece or, well, however many pieces still with the…

She wiggles her fingers in a kind of expansive way

…élan vital, you know what I mean?

If he fainted while he was driving, he could probably trust her to grab the wheel and steer them to safety. He veers, rather dramatically and a little too fast, into the Grapevine Oil parking lot. He hurries into the men's room, which smells like the overpowering sweet and minty urinal cakes to the point that his eyes water. He isn't ready to die, not yet, not like this. He pulls money out of his pocket, a few wretched bills, as if he's discovered himself in a magic world, in possession of magic tokens. Magic because this paper is worthless, trash, a crumple of soiled tissue, but nobody else knows that.

Back out in the lot, Miss Thing is weakly smearing the windshield brush back and forth, as if she's earning her keep.

Thirsty? asks Geordi.

You bet, she says. Make mine a Diet.

Geordi waves a twenty at her, which she snatches with the instincts of a cheetah. Pick out what you want, he says. And get me some nuts, okay? I need to call my wife.

It's as if he's hypnotized her or used an evil spell. But she just stands there, looking at him. He takes out his cell phone and dials their home number, and as it goes to voicemail he says, Hi, honey, yeah, I'm almost there, just stopped in Mettler…

As soon as she walks into the store, Geordi starts the car and speeds back onto the 99. He doesn't look in the rearview mirror once.

So this is what it's like to be evil. To just say anything, with no relationship to the real world. It's great.

He has turned his back on society, on the human community. You can choose to do anything, really. It's just habit that keeps you enchanted. He might someday make his way back to what he thinks of as his life. A woman, his wife. A house, a thesis, a variety of social relationships, as flimsy as that money. A magic trick. Later, he'll accept the trick, return to it, sure. It can warm him a bit, the solid structures that will be there waiting for him.

Each strata of the soul has its own history, each wanders from body to body, from generation to generation, independent of the other parts. Each soul then is a meeting of elements with their own histories and experiences, a gathering or band liable to strange interconnections and fragmentations...

He is evil and alone with his crime. The world that he habitually accepts as somehow existing around him, whatever composite of memories and beliefs and images of landscapes he uses to fill in the gaps—it's still not cohering. But the idea of himself as a solitary criminal hurling through the void creates a counternarrative and joins him, somehow, to a bunch of dead poets.

Bakersfield then, and beyond, north toward that town, toward the fields where he picked peaches as a boy. A half hour through the dusty fields and nothing looks familiar. The sky isn't pink and ribboned with magical clouds in the west, it's just the searing emptiness he forgets as soon as he leaves this place, but that reasserts its unimaginable presence as soon as he returns. He drives haphazardly in search of the cemetery. He pulls over on the shoulder of a strange road that he's sure he's traveled, so long ago that it is only the "same road' in the most abstract sense, since the places it leads to and the places it comes from are populated by different structures, different people.

A fence. Grassy stuff blowing in the wind, he doesn't know its name. A layer of cirrus only in the far distance.

Geordi has the notebook with him that he received from one of the men in that tent. He reads the two legible sentences for the zillionth time: *Come on, let's run away, into the desert, with the icy stars and the emptiness of space overhead, where the incessant wind will obliterate any trace of our footsteps in the shifting sands. And they will never find us.*

Geordi abandoned a woman. Her fragility and hunger in the cold universe were more than he could bear. He hasn't eaten anything, and his hunger reminds him, more than the landscape, that he was once a child. He was a child who coveted sweets. There was a neighbor girl who played music for him. He was sometimes ill.

He was ill and alone and he wandered off. He got on the bus. He sang a little song. Not a real song, a translation. He was translating. It isn't his fault—he was just a child. Those people on the bus, it was the last time he belonged to anyone. Their thoughts: a phantom complexity. He assumed they knew him, assumed they knew his mother and father and sisters, knew where he belonged, in the same way that his grandmother did. But he wandered or was led astray and he awoke in the darkness at the top of the mountain. He is awake there still.

Why is he alone under this sky? He's about to cry for that child. But he turns around and drives back toward town.

His grandmother isn't surprised to see him. Sets him down and putzes about in the kitchen, to make him a sandwich, serve it on a plate with a Jarritos. She's fine, she's doing better, although she has some trouble getting around. Her knee's been causing her some pain.

I dreamed about your father, she says.

How was he?

He was wearing something Japanese. Like a little dress or something. He was afraid he'd been giving people the wrong idea, and he wanted them to see how the Japanese dress fit with his personality.

Geordi's grandmother limps just a little bit as she moves from one side of the little kitchen to the other, not the sort of limp his mother would use, exaggerated, for effect, but the most clandestine and effective limp possible. An honest and practical limp. She is smaller than she has ever been.

I guess anything makes sense in a dream.

You accept it, whatever happens. Just like this.

She makes a gesture. The room, the house, whatever. A moth flutters past, its wings vibrating the space. How has it survived into the winter? Is it one of the dead?

Abuelita, he says.

His father in the snow. The color caught the girl's eye. Bluish. There was a trail from the parking lot, but it didn't lead to the thing that had caught her eye. The woods were wet and rotting.

Was he blind? Geordi asks.

Blind?

Dad, was he blind?

I don't know. He didn't say. Wasn't important.

She is an old woman, she hasn't changed, but she is changing. She will be gone soon. It's worn her out. Everything. Her son, Geordi's father, the birds had eaten out his eyes. That town she lived in, the dirt floor. The gash on her grandson's face.

Abuelita, what happened to me?

What happened to you?

She's just his granny. What does it matter, the fantasies from the past? Something happened, or it didn't.

When the clock strikes two, she'll turn on her Mexican radio shows. She doesn't like the Spanish radio from Bakersfield. Aracely, next door, she fixed the antenna for her and so she can pick up her stations. It's coming in now, clear as rain.

8

A VOICE IS SAYING THAT second-generation robots aren't capable of evil unless they are programmed to do evil. But with a third-generation robot, the real-time simulation is creating something like a memory of the past and an anticipation of the future, so that robots can examine their own actions and behave differently based on their insights. This model can be built to take into account some aspects of the robot's own state: Is the battery charged? Is the engine running too hot? This is the beginning of self-awareness.

The other voice says, Fear, shame, and joy. But then what's the point?

The other voice—it's DJ's brother. DJ's at a motel again, but he isn't sure how he got here. He knows what it's called—the San Luis Obispo Motel 6. The voices keep talking about robots. It's distracting.

The first voice says, You are what we are calling a Biological Chauvinist.

Melvin says, No way. I just don't want to evolve the wrong life forms. Cyborgs, great. Vampire cows, no problem. Human/cat hybrids, human/squid hybrids, whatever weird new biological life form based on some freaky mutant mishmash of free-floating genetic material—all good.

Melvin and his friend Hakeem are inside the room but the door is open, airing it out. Hakeem doesn't like the way America smells inside its motel rooms. DJ is standing at the railing looking down into the cold parking lot. There are pine trees and a Dumpster and a barefoot woman in the night bending over a car, talking to somebody inside the darkness of the car. Another woman is talking to herself and walking her dog around the lot.

For me, who has this dream all my life of creating artificial intelligence, the answer is simple. The Artificial Intelligence must love Allah. It cannot be programmed to love Allah, but it can be programmed to understand all the knowledge of society and of the ethical values and from this the love of Allah follows.

Hakeem is taking off his shirt, which is very distracting, and then he goes into the bathroom and DJ can't see him, and Melvin sits on the sink in front of the mirror and keeps talking to him nonetheless. DJ is wearing a shirt that Hakeem bought him, with a little pirate boy on it, a peg leg, an eye patch, *Arg!* Melvin threw the other shirt away.

I guess we disagree about everything, Melvin says. I guess I don't know anything about Nigeria. Have you heard about the mice they're designing to self-destruct in a zillion different ways? They design them to get cancers or grow human ear tissue or whatever.

Hakeem is probably talking, but instead of his words, steam drifts out of the bathroom. Somewhere in the steam, there's a naked man.

I don't know, Melvin says. Maybe Allah's like…the opposite of the Empire, which is just like…not even necessary either.

Somewhere in the steam, there's a naked man. DJ's brother is guarding the steam.

But the only thing interesting to me is the zones in between the two bad choices, the places where new myths and new forms pop up. The cancer mice, the mice we torture, I'm totally against all that, but I think we could liberate them.

DJ has to get going, to get out of here. Either into the steam, where he would surely suffocate from pleasure, or in the opposite direction.

Free them from the lab. And then, who knows?

DJ hurries down the walkway past an open door where a woman is smoking on her bed. A stairway with gaps leads down into the parking lot like a bridge over an incredible chasm. Another woman is curled up on the stairs with her phone, hugging herself, cradling the phone. She seems to be crying. I'm just so confused, she tells somebody. He holds on tight to the railing as he makes his descent. He knows it's dangerous. He runs ahead toward the pine trees and the dog.

Hey, where are you going?

It's Melvin hanging over the railing at him.

I want to see the dog.

Okay, but don't go anywhere I can't see you.

He walks calmly toward the pine trees and the dog kind of barks and wags its tail and DJ freezes. The woman has a headset on and she's telling somebody, You gonna sell your baby for that, you powder-head bitch? Sell out everyone you know? Oh hello, Mr. Policeman, yeah, this is where all the crack houses are and this is where they sell the eight balls. Powder-head bitch.

DJ says hello to the dog and runs ahead past it and past the Dumpster toward the fence. Scandalous behavior, yes, but he knows the way. He knows the way, there's a forest. He runs ahead to the back fence where there's a missing plank. On the other side a gully and in one direction a parking lot full of RVs under lights, but if you follow the gully and avoid the shopping center and travel for a long time, you come to the woods. He knows the way. He's done this before.

Some garbage is blowing away through the night toward the freeway and a kind of troll creature is pushing a cart into the distance.

The trees are intricate and gnarled and covered with fur. The path is clear in the moonlight, like a movie. Is this what life is like? So beautiful and strange? He runs ahead through the trees. Twisted, gnarled, convoluted. Something with wings flaps overhead. It's cool in the trees. He forgets where this path goes, but maybe he's never been here before.

Love is hopelessness. The only love that matters is totally devoid of hope. The name of this level is Estrangement. The most important theme is that of Wandering.

The path through the forest turns one way and then another, and a smaller path disappears into the brambles to one side but he sticks to the wide path through the gnarled and knotted trees.

The heart must present itself alone before nothingness.

It's a clearing up ahead in the trees where the moonlight creates a kind of glow and what looks like…an enormous golden bed. DJ approaches tentatively, as if he's sneaking up on the bed, but he isn't frightened. There is somebody in the bed, somebody very old, but the bed is so high he must stand on his toes to see the wrinkled little face in its bonnet peering up at him from among all the blankets.

Finally, you're here, I say.

My face is white like a ghost's, but the eyes are black.

Is this your home? DJ asks.

Of course.

DJ looks around at the twisted trees and up at the enormous moon.

This is one of the largest reserves of old growth coastal oaks in the world, I say.

The trees go on forever in every direction, gnarled and hairy and full of bones.

I want to show you my friend, DJ says.

I'm your friend.

Yes.

The blanket is gold and purple and maroon with elaborate stitching in intricate patterns. Everything jumbled up together and yet figures remain distinct.

You've always been here, baby. You just forgot.

DJ remembers what happens next.

I'm going to die now, he says.

I shrug. The lines on my face are like the canyons on distant planets.

I mustn't speak to strangers, he tells me.

No, please, don't.

The lines on my face are like an old piece of paper with writing in a foreign language. The parchment scrunched up and torn. And all around my face, a pile of blankets with a hard mound in the center where the stomach should be.

Are you a man? DJ asks.

You're getting warm.

The trees are clawing at the sky. Everything is blue. It's cool in the forest, but not in an unpleasant way. He could travel in many directions, he's sure, but he might end up in circles. He might end up in distant lands.

I know you, DJ says.

Warmer, I say.

Maybe it's the most beautiful place in the world. But maybe not. He could stay here for a long time looking down at the crevices of my face. Just a little while longer.

Just a little while longer, I say. You'll listen to my voice.

Are you going to have a baby? DJ asks.

Well, I'm going to give birth.

On a table by the bed, a blue bottle and an empty goblet. And everywhere, the trees.

What's up in the trees?

It's a kind of lichen, I say.

It looks like bones, DJ says.

More like hair, I say. But perhaps what you're referring to are the actual skeletons I've hung directly overhead. With tiny skulls and tiny teeth. In the moonlight, the effect is quite terrible, don't you think?

It is difficult to tell what is the lichen and what is the bones, but he can see the faces peeking out either way. The holes where the eyes were and the terrible teeth.

Tiny bones, says DJ.

Yes, perhaps the bones of little boys just exactly your size.

I'm bigger than that.

Yes, I suppose you are.

I tilt my head and peer up at him in such a way that DJ thinks my head might fall clean off my neck.

It's funny, isn't it, I say, how two different creatures can see things so differently, even when they're looking at the same scene. We're utterly strange to each other. But then again, we aren't.

It's true, DJ supposes. True enough. Maybe everything that exists is just true enough—not overly true, but not garish and false either. Maybe he isn't quite big enough. Not big enough to contain all of his lusts—for a luminous nothingness and for a tender care.

I've been talking to you all along, but you probably didn't notice, I say.

I'm very thirsty, DJ says.

I know, poor baby. You all are, just so thirsty all the time.

I nod toward the bed table. The blue bottle and the empty goblet.

It's…

Yes, Midnight Blue 13. The quality of the glass is exquisite, and if you pick it up, turn it about in the moonlight, you'll see that the liquid inside is precisely the same color and gives off the most wonderful light.

DJ does as he's told.

I will tell you stories, I say. Some of them will be true.

Why?

There isn't ever only one reason to tell a particular story.

Is it poison?

Help yourself.

DJ pours just a little bit into the goblet, without spilling a drop.

You don't have to drink it, I say. You can just look deep inside it. What will it show you, I wonder.

It's blue.

You might see things not just as they seem to be, but for what they mean.

What do they mean? DJ asks.

He thinks that I seem to be breathing, or maybe it's crying.

The heart has to present itself alone before nothingness, I say. It has to beat alone in the darkness.

In his ears, DJ only hears his own heart.

It's a solo gig, I say.

He turns the glass in circles.

Careful not to drop it, I say. Broken glass is dangerous. You wouldn't want to ruin that pretty little face.

I'm a boy, DJ says.

Yes, of course.

DJ realizes he left the astronaut behind.

I have to go now.

Up to you.

I'll visit you again.

You'll visit me again.

DJ runs back through the trees, the way he came.

He knows the way back. It's easy enough, you just follow the path. Past all of these trees and the place where the owls were and a pile of feathers where it looks like some sort of very white bird might have been devoured by a wolf. And to the fence where the plank is missing and he squeezes right through into the parking lot of the San Luis Obispo Motel 6.

The moon is the same on either side of the fence. He's squinting at it when he bumps into a woman smoking, the woman with the dog.

You must be DJ, she says.

Yes, ma'am, says DJ.

What a polite little boy. Your brother's looking for you.

She makes a gesture with her thumb toward the tunnel in the building where the ice machine is.

What have you been up to, DJ? the woman asks

DJ says, Did you ever go to the neighbors where the bones are in the trees?

The woman says, Were you in the neighboring lot? You need to stay over here.

I know, says DJ. I was just playing.

The moon has almost reached the middle of the sky. There isn't any wind tonight at all.

V

You are walking along a road peacefully. You trip. You fall into blackness. That's the past—or perhaps the future. And you know that there is no past, no future, there is only this blackness, changing faintly, slowly, but always the same.

—Jean Rhys, *Good Morning, Midnight*

1

Danny sits in Freddy's dim apartment facing west—the most masculine direction—over a wintery hustle down below on Divisadero, in a kind of bloody twilight, reading Freddy's great work, so far, a book-length poem. Now that Danny's fucked him, Freddy's busy "composing." Freddy can't focus, he told Danny, until he's been fucked. He'll call for Danny at odd hours, desperate for inspiration. Danny respects people who make extreme demands from reality. Danny has theories about extreme demands from reality, but he keeps them to himself—it is in the nature he has chosen to keep things to himself. He's read the Greeks, but he doesn't tell Freddy this. Freddy's always quoting Rimbaud, sometimes in English, sometimes in French. While Freddy composes, on and on, Danny waits. Danny believes that gay men constitute a sort of occult society, similar to the brotherhood of warriors, with a similar metaphysical purpose. They harbor the male energy in its purest form, as destruction. They're like Christ.

Freddy quotes Rimbaud in the same way he gives Danny pages of his epic poem to read. He does it as if he's sending fireworks into the void. Danny is more than willing to represent that void.

Danny believes many things, yet he barely even speaks to himself, and this is his particular genius. Every fact or image or memory is a kind of burbling that in no way reduces the clarity of the stream. He understands a small fraction of what he reads, the Greeks or whoever, not because he isn't bright, but because he is a child with no real sense of history. His mother didn't speak about the past, which would have meant speaking about the man who impregnated her, and so Danny has rarely *felt* history as something composed of actual human activity—struggling, breathing, trembling, dying people—but has merely conceived of it as a *story* full of lessons. It is exactly the idea of history, however, the most masculine discipline, that feeds his sense of himself as a character without hopes or ambitions, serving a larger drama that effaces him. He has a good-sized, bland, attractive penis and his businesslike work ethic toward sticking it into others often leads to an almost hysterical devotion.

He isn't sure yet how he feels about that hysterical devotion. He prefers not to take it seriously. As for history, even his abstract ideas about its lessons are based on a hodgepodge of writings. Not much context. Hardly any knowledge about the cultures those writings came from. He's aware of the gaps in his own learning, but his idea of how to fill those gaps is random and voracious, effectively magical, without any system to guide him.

Similarly, the structure of Freddy's poem is intricate in appearance, but really quite simple. It's dressed up to shock and awe readers with a few simple tricks. The whole poem is structured around the number eight, like the *I Ching* or the DNA. Danny's a whiz at math, which he considers a pure male structure, like autism. So far he has identified only seven vectors, however. Vectors of the poem are constantly interrupted, to be taken up later according to a strict pattern. Danny's not sure if there's a name for the pattern or if Freddy invented it. A poem is a machine, sent into the future, Freddy said. His is designed to be consulted, like an oracle—it gives the future advice, Freddy said. You don't need to believe in anything, just the possibilities offered by chance. *A throw of the die will never abolish chance*, Freddy said, quoting somebody French who Danny had never heard of.

Danny thinks of himself as a conjunction of supermasculine vectors. All yang, no yin, the butchest show in town. He is so essentially butch his mother used to weep, for no reason, when he was a kid, overwhelmed by all that incomprehensible boy energy.

Once, in Afghanistan, as usual, they'd walked miles from the staging area through the unrelenting furnace. The sun was evil, something evil was always happening underneath it. Dubious procedures would often come to light underneath that sun. His mind was wandering—they'd been searching for insurgents.

Once, he contemplated the night sky with his mother.

She took him camping, because he was a boy, because she felt bad that nobody else would do it, but tents frustrated her and made her angry. He had known that the stars existed, but they'd never seemed like they had anything to do with us here, but suddenly he knew that he existed in time. Because for some reason, the stars had become real as the sun would become real, a giant furnace right there, just 93 million miles away, and so his mind was somewhere else as they hopped over a mud wall and headed down a path that skirted a town that seemed to be abandoned.

Gunfire erupted from every direction at once. Danny went one way and Danny went another, both of him transparent and wobbly, and neither one of him could remember what was real in that moment and what was not.

One vector of the poem concerns two twins, at least one of whom is evil. One vector of the poem concerns a woman with a lot of tattoos who is dying of breast cancer, it concerns AIDS and AIDS deaths, it's a kind of social history of San Francisco in the '80s and '90s. One vector concerns a phantom boy, a boy who dresses like a girl, a boy the poet is always comparing to Rimbaud. One vector concerns Danny intimately, for it is about the pleasures to be had in the arms of soldiers. There is a description of "alabaster biceps" which Danny considers to be his own. Danny isn't prejudiced, but his own whiteness is another source of pride. He considers the white race the most masculine race and a race with a sacred purpose: to devastate the face of the Earth. One vector of the poem is about Shahrazad, still spinning tales in the modern age in the face of apocalyptic forces. One vector of the poem is about the poet's own drug dealer, presented as the keeper of a kind of salon, where absinthe is drunk and pleasure seekers come to sit and wile away the hours with stories and other intoxicants. The word *wormwood* is used frequently in these sections. The seventh vector concerns a wandering woman. She's been struggling through Southern California wastelands, through art museums, airports, and large historical events, usually tragic. Danny believes she is in some sense "the soul."

Evil is a word for things that don't smell right. It's both real and it isn't. Danny followed the path around the edge of the abandoned town and Danny went straight down a narrow alley between mud walls into the middle of the town and in one direction he was evil and in one direction he was not. Space was rippling and cords of rippled transparency boinging rather silently through all of space and time.

Danny doesn't have any patience for those theories that posit constantly bifurcating universes and alternative selves. In this he is correct. Although time, an oddly one-directional dimension, is significantly more complex than the everyday human experience of it, it isn't *infinitely* complex. That would just be silly.

The wind. The terrible wind. The 120 Days of Wind. Sandstorms are a form of apocalyptic consciousness.

Always the jokes about butt-fucking. Jokes about bodily fluids and boy-fucking. The wind was a book dreamed by the Marquis de Sade.

Outside Freddy's apartment, the western sky is pink, even red.

The Blue Line from Chula Vista to downtown San Diego passed a vacant lot, where a solitary tree had escaped from a fairy tale. Danny rode the train with his mother, and the tree and the train ride were the same thing. Danny was a fastidious boy, clean, and he admired men in uniforms, who were like a large abstract father that he didn't need to deal with up close. He kept his distance from adults, unless they were ordering him around. He appreciated a good order, if it was delivered firmly and from a distance. The tree had been alive longer than he had, his mother told him so. It was always late in the afternoon, and the train and the lot were always bathed in an impossible brilliance. The light was like a radiating dust. You couldn't separate yourself from it or a boy's thoughts or a tree. It was not a showy tree, and Danny couldn't differentiate one type of tree from another, but surrounded by space it changed space. The space became real, a part of history.

One day, the tree was gone. Danny insisted they stop, but they were already past. He needed to examine the stump, to mourn for the tree, to experience his first true heartbreak. Not today, his mother said. The next time they went past, even the stump was gone.

He turns away from the bloody twilight and immerses himself again in the poem. The wandering woman is in conversation with Rimbaud, Mayakovsky, and James Merrill, in some sort of afterlife in which the dead are dependent on Ouija boards, not only to communicate with the living, but with each other as well. The messages the dead poets stutter out to each other concern their agenda for human history, an agenda that saddens the wandering woman. Danny admires Freddy's surprising use of enjambment. The woman with the tattoos who's been dying of breast cancer shows up on the scene and begins haranguing the dead male poets; two vectors have joined as one. Danny nods in silent admiration. He has to admit he didn't see that coming.

There is another ghost whose voice he can't place, offering a relentless critique of the manifest cosmos. After the final lines—*That human society is no more than a collective mental illness / that the building blocks of emerging life are morbid and psychotic*—Danny wants more. But now he must wait.

Danny's mother tried to hang herself when he was only eight. She didn't fasten the noose right or she didn't fall far enough, because her neck didn't break. She hung there, pissed off and astonished, and then started bouncing herself up and down like a yo-yo, trying to get it to work. The convulsions mesmerized him; then he cried and hugged her legs. She sighed and let herself down. You have to live, Mommy, he said. I just don't want to do it alone, she replied.

If Danny ever decides to tell Freddy a story, it'll be this one. He's sure it would end up in the poem, abstracted and immortalized. Doesn't matter. Danny belongs to eternity already—he sleeps in it and wakes in it, dreams in it and blurs into it and gains his only ephemeral clarity from inside his daydream of it. Freddy rises from the desk, triumphant, and tosses Danny another page. The poem's slow work, and requires a lot of fucking on Danny's part. When Freddy's about to get fucked, he wants to hear stories about the wars, minimally told: roadside bombs, mangled bodies, blood curdling in the heat. He wants Danny to evoke the orgy of death and destruction in a few sentences, while maintaining his stoic posture. These images will make their way into the poem.

At the rate of fire from all around, it would be just a matter of time before Danny was hit. Just a matter of time.

The risk of really speaking to himself is that Danny might become hysterical. Acknowledging the insanity and horror of his life or of the wars as real and without meaning might turn him into a woman. He hoped he would not be hit in the head and die. He thought maybe he could just lose an arm or a leg. He had seen men and women and children with their legs blown off. He scurried back the way he came and found shelter in an alcove with four other guys. Eric was a boy from Montana who had a kind of fat look about him, although he was in shape. Rosy-cheeked, milk-fed. Eric hated all of them, the Afghanis, but especially the skinny beggar boys, the ragged and skinny bruised boys, hustling and begging.

Danny asked his mother for a weight set when he was eleven or twelve. For Christmas. He lifted weights and masturbated on a foam pad in the moldy basement. At Christmas, there were cousins, older cousins who told him his mother was a whore.

They would drive around Kabul at high speeds, and once they destroyed an old man's cart. Eric would throw MRE bags full of shit and piss to the begging children as if they were bags of candy or food, just to see the looks on their faces.

Eric, a bad egg.

Mark was controlling two British Harriers fighter jets and they were tracking them and he popped red smoke so the pilots could differentiate the friendly from the enemy.

Where's Danny? Eric asked.

Danny had gone the other way and was wandering the perimeter of the abandoned town.

A town of the dead.

Usually, it was night. The curfew kept humans off the streets, holed up in their cold mud huts with kerosene lamps and young goats. Night. The daughter of Chaos, the lover of Darkness, the mother of Sleep and Death. The mother of Aether, Day, Doom, Fate, Blame, and Woe. That's according to Hesiod. In the poems of Orpheus it is Nyx herself, not Chaos, who is the first principle. She's chanting in a cave, with Cronus chained inside, drunk on honey and dreaming, while a nymph clashes her cymbals and beats her drum just outside, moving the cosmos in an ecstatic dance to the rhythm of Nyx's chants and prophecies.

Our mother, Night.

Logistical support to the base was a nightmare. Mostly helicopters dropping to a small zone outside the wire. A few jingle trucks would make the two-and-a-half-day drive from one of the larger bases, but they'd usually be ambushed or hijacked.

Abdur was a jingle driver and he spoke some English and he told Danny once that Danny was going the wrong way and that he should get back to the alcove, but that wasn't real. It couldn't be, because Abdur had been shot in the shoulder and drove into the compound with his blood everywhere and then he passed out.

He either died or he didn't. Danny avoided Eric, but he hung out with Corey, who seemed okay, and once he chatted with Calvin, who later became a kind of celebrity because he had murdered civilians out of spite and because he was caught.

It wasn't Eric, but Corey who ended up at Bagram.

Wandering the abandoned town, the town of the dead, without dying, which wasn't possible, he felt the presence of women and children behind mud walls without windows or doors.

An abandoned town is a space where things have happened and may happen again but are not happening now. Except Death and Night.

Death and Night are always happening. No kidding.

Why is Danny going back out there? A good question, the other Danny would say, from the alcove with Eric and Corey. Here, in America, he's got a girlfriend with rental units on the brain. She wants rental units, she wants to live on some stupid tenants' dime. Meanwhile, Danny lives for free with Freddy and makes his money fucking other guys for a website whose whole concept is straight guys fucking only for the money. As far as Danny can tell, he's the only one who's really straight.

Nobody was considered innocent and they were to open fire whenever they felt hostile intent or even the slightest discomfort. Any male of military age, anyone alive.

Most of the ammo was coming in by parachute to the drop zone but sometimes the parachute wouldn't open so the bundle would burn in.

A small boom in the distance and white smoke. An incoming missile. The drop zone was unprotected.

The only time when Freddy isn't either talking or writing is when he's about to get fucked. Freddy seems to believe that Danny is patriotic and believes he's fighting a just war. But *killing is one form of our wandering sadness*, Danny read in Rilke. Danny has the highest respect for the men who flew those planes into the towers, fellow members of the brotherhood. *Whatever has happened to us is pure in the radiant spirit.* It's a bloody adventure, a sacred path, and what team you join is as irrelevant as the concept of democracy for an old man crawling through the abandoned village with his entrails hanging out. Danny told Freddy about that one a couple of nights ago. In bed, Freddy wants to be shut up, to be forced past language, to be made to understand how hard the world is. An old man crawls across the poem with his entrails hanging out in Mayakovsky's Ouija board message, which begins the next stanza. You can always tell when it's Mayakovsky, he starts with the word *Listen*. This vector is interrupted by one of the twins, probably the evil one, digging through a bag of torture implements. It moves on to a discussion of techniques and tools of the Inquisition, such as the anal pear—a punishment for sodomites. Danny has an uneasy feeling that this discussion of torture will tie in directly to the "love of soldiers" vector. He's relieved when it is instead quickly interrupted by the Rimbaud-like androgyne, turning tricks in the shadows of an Arkansas truck stop. The little whore is insanely reclusive, ethereal, only glimpsed as the vision in the rearview mirrors of so many truckers. There are evil forces afoot, lurking around the edges of these last few stanzas, forces that want to capture the elfin trickster, expose him to the daylight. They're getting closer. They're about to solve the mystery, to stumble onto the disheartening truth. Demonic hands are reaching out to shackle the phantom boy-girl. But Danny is shipping back out to Afghanistan, an interruption that feels built into the structure of the poem. Probably then someone else will do the fucking. Danny will read the poem in its entirety when he comes back again, if he comes back—to find out what it all means.

2

SINCE DHOJI FIRST APPEARED at Raymond and Philip's door a decade ago, after sneaking out of Ricky's house with a suitcase and two babies, her ascent has been relentless. She's clawed her way up from Philip and Raymond's futon, first to a studio by the MacArthur BART and then to a Section 8 apartment in creaky, flag-waving Alameda. She's back in Oakland now in a three-bed-room house, all of it hers but the landlord's clutter underneath. Ricky, mean-while, has careened from one wreck to another. Wrecked trucks, a wrecked liver, wrecked sex dates, and a hand. He got careless with the skill saw, cut half a pinky off. Ricky, the American. Homeless half the time or shacked up with some woman. Shacked up with an old sugar daddy or camped out in his pickup truck. A tattoo of a demon from Bali inked across his neck.

In her ten-year competition with Ricky, all of the facts have lined up on Dhoji's side but one. Section 8 pays most of Dhoji's rent and her roommates pay the rest: her usual revolving door of freaks, a salve for her terminal bore-dom. She collects disability for her vaguely defined mental illness—can't con-centrate, can't *think* right—while working under the table as a nanny for a high-powered lawyer couple, Jackie and Yuki, who were, until faced with the daily presence of Dhoji in their home, vaguely entranced by the spiritual allure of Tibet. You smell like smoke, like cigarettes, Jackie is always complaining. Dhoji blames it on Ricky, her American ex-husband. Jackie hates him anyway. She blames it on the liquor store clerk, a refugee from Iraq.

At first after she tested positive, Dhoji was calling Philip and Raymond all the time, saying *My life is over* and *I'm going to die*, until they told her it was kind of insulting. They already had it, like fifteen more years. But Dhoji had to contend with her Tibetan friends, people who believed that only loose women got AIDS. But you are a loose woman, and they all know that, Philip said, who cares? Jamyang cried when she told him, but Nyima thought it was pretty goth to have an HIV+ mom. On the Internet, somebody threatened to kill her. Since then, Dhoji's dumped Nashawn for good and reconnected with a childhood boyfriend who's been living in Wisconsin. He's been talking about joining her here, in Oakland, where she's the reigning queen over an empire of Tibetan, Nepalese, and Bhutanese immigrants, lodgers and fellow travelers who intermingle with ex-boyfriends and other assorted monsters. Today the star of the show is Ann, her ex-husband's fuck.

I love Ricky's children more than I love my own, Ann announces to Ralph and to the room in general, and she gives Nyima a hug. Raymond is scolding Dhoji about her fried bread, telling her she's too impatient, she's rolling it out too thick. Her Bhutanese roommate, a quiet, gloomy young man, occasionally shuffles from room to room for no discernible reason. Tenzin, her more beloved roommate, a writing student at the New College, is asleep in one of the back rooms. Gompo, an ex-boyfriend, is watching *South Park* with Philip and Jamyang. Missy is in the backyard with Tony, grilling the meat. One of those dry, sunny winter days when California seems like it might really be a kind of paradise. Dhoji met Missy when they were working as nannies for neighboring families. Missy's boss, Tammy, wore her hair in a ponytail that would shoot out the back of a baseball cap, and then one day she noticed her daughter playing with herself in the tub. The boss, Tammy, thought that the only way a two-year-old girl could discover the pleasures of masturbation was from her African nanny, so she fired Missy. She accused Missy of strange African sex rites.

Raymond tears a cooling piece of Dhoji's fried bread in half to show Dhoji how doughy it is. Dhoji shrugs, smears some jelly on a different piece, and hands it to the little boy.

This is good one, she says. Taste just like donut.

Thank you, ma'am, says DJ. He consumes it slowly and symmetrically. He bites daintily around the edge, to form a slightly smaller circle of bread smeared with jelly and then he keeps going in a spiral toward the center.

Nyima is explaining to Raymond the difference between being emo and scene and goth. How did Dhoji end up with this American for a child? This baby, Dhoji used to pre-chew her bananas. Nyima *used to be* goth, she is saying, which is like thinking death is better than life, but now she's more emo, which is like: Who cares? Alive or dead, no difference either way.

Nyima takes DJ by the hand and sits him down at the kitchen table. She shows him her magic purple ink she uses to write out love spells and curses. She shows him the Barbie she decked out in black with skull necklaces back when she was into that sort of thing.

Gompo and Jamyang are cracking up at something on the television.

Back in India, Gompo saved Dhoji from heroin addiction, while she was in Delhi, waiting for Ricky to finalize his divorce in America. The chubby guy watching *South Park* might not seem like the romantic lead in anyone's story of salvation. But Dhoji had stopped believing Ricky would really ever come back to marry her. It would be 105 degrees in Delhi, with dying old men crawling along the curbs, hopelessly reaching their boney hands out toward young women passing by, or it would be 110 degrees later the same day and Dhoji would just want to do some heroin and become a kind of lizard or a stone, and not care anymore, or it would be 115 degrees and the corpses of the old men who had died in the meantime beside the curbs would start to stink. Dhoji fell in with some hustler girls and started robbing foreign tourists. When Gompo came along and took her away from that life, she believed she was in love. But then Ricky showed back up and she knew that she wanted out of India more than she cared about any man. After Dhoji left Ricky, when the kids were one and two, and she was struggling to get by, she would invoke Gompo's name like a magic incantation—any day he'd show up and give a repeat performance, save her from her life. Gompo finally negotiated a marriage with a girl who was already a US citizen, and he moved to the Bay Area, hoping to get back together with Dhoji on the side. By the time he showed up, older and fatter and married, she was over it. She wasn't a desperate junky girl in Delhi anymore, she was an American, a single mother, an emancipated woman. She'd grown tired of Tibetan men who viewed her as an easy woman and who made love like selfish children.

Nyima is painting DJ's toenails slowly and carefully. DJ's brother is out on the front porch, where the Nigerian is having a smoke. The nail polish smells like burning plastic.

When I was your age, Nyima is telling DJ, I saw something really freaky.

Really freaky?

Raymond wants to know why Ricky's girlfriend is here.

Ann is here hiding from Ricky, Dhoji says. They are fighting *again*.

I don't *care*, she says. But my kids like her, you know? Best to be friends.

Raymond peeks around the corner, where Ann has cornered Ralph on the couch. She's pretty, he says. And she seems bright. But if she's dating Ricky, there must be something wrong with her.

Dhoji gives Raymond a look with her eyebrows raised that means—Like me?

My mom had a miscarriage, Nyima is telling DJ, and the baby ended up in the toilet.

Ann is describing some huge house she owns in the hills, and all the money she made at some point in the past as a promoter—whatever that is. Grandiose schemes for making money are probably the bond that holds Ricky and Ann together, just as grandiose schemes for making money had been the bond that held Ricky and Dhoji together as long as they lasted, two hustlers who'd met, their story went, as they were hustling each other in India. Game recognize game, they said.

Most days now, Dhoji can avoid hating Ricky. Some days. Ricky, with his sad American childhood. Crazy mother, foster homes, sex for money and drugs. Americans always want to talk about what happened to them when they were kids. Fucked him up, no kidding. At first it was so strange, everyone hugging all the time. People who don't like each other, not for a minute. *Yeah, yeah, yeah* became her favorite English phrase. Heard it all before, Ricky.

It wasn't even my mom's baby, Nyima is telling DJ. These rich people were just paying her to have it for them. I guess the rich lady's womb wasn't any good, so they rented out my mom's. She had to take a lot of hormones. Probably why she got those polyps in her uterus.

Nyima shrugs.

It was your brother? DJ asks.

It was twins, Nyima says, and all bloody with these teeny little toes. Just like yours.

DJ's toenails are now outrageously blue.

All done, Nyima says. But you have to let it dry. You can't touch it, okay?

Raymond tells Dhoji that she can't cook anymore. She's been in America too long, she cooks like an American, lazy.

Remember when you lived in Richmond?

In Richmond, I had Zaher to clean up my house.

Nyima takes DJ's hand and leads him back into the living room. Ann makes a big show of hugging Nyima again and then she grabs DJ and puts him on her lap.

Whatever happened to Zaher? Raymond asks. Last time I saw him was on Telegraph Avenue. His hair was dyed blond and sticking out like he'd been electrocuted.

Dhoji drops some more bread into the grease.

I think he went to Rainbow Gathering, she says. And he never come back.

***

Ralph likes aggressive women, and so he's allowed Ann to paralyze him with the story of her life. In Indonesia, as a little girl, she was never sure if she was the slum child who had been switched with the princess by careless nurses, or if it was somehow the other way around. Her father was an incredibly wealthy man, apparently a real monster, and she was accustomed to having everything done for her by a maid. She would wander around the mansion (so vast there were rooms, maybe entire wings, she had never visited) sensing that it was haunted, haunted by the little princess who'd lived there before the operation.

Ann strokes DJ's hair as she tells the story, which seems to lull the boy into a kind of trance. Ann's mother was an educated, sophisticated, and beautiful woman, Ann tells them, and Ann had thought of her then as both mother and queen, there didn't seem to be anything strange about that, to have a queen as a mother—her mother had studied anthropology and most of the time it was just the two of them and about twenty servants. But the servants were mostly just ghosts, except for her nanny, Josefina, who disappeared while she was in the hospital and was replaced by a woman who seemed to be half asleep. This replacement would have been much more traumatic, Ann is sure, if it hadn't been explained to her as temporary, as a kind of fairy tale in which her beloved nanny's return was always just around the corner.

What Ann doesn't say: Her home was always an enormous tomb. The sort of mausoleum that the fantastically wealthy litter our sad little planet with, here and there, from a vague, psychotic compulsion that you either understand intuitively or you dismiss as simple narcissism or greed. What Ann doesn't say: A doll that wets itself, with eyes that are turquoise marbles. A jack-in-the-box, an unused room full of dusty furniture, a stuffed duck. Donald or Daffy, an American duck.

One night, Ann says, her mother woke her. The electric lights were off, only candles burning. Her mother helped her get dressed quickly, throwing some clothes over her pajamas, and insisted she stay perfectly quiet. It was a surprise, her mother said, and she didn't want anyone to hear. They crept out to a waiting car with their suitcases and drove away, and it was only then that her mother told her not to cry, but that they were leaving her father for good. On the way to the airport her father was transformed from a loving but stern stranger who spoiled her with gifts on the rare occasions that he came home, into a kind of demon, guilty of unspeakable crimes and capable of horrors she couldn't even dream of. Her former nanny was one of her father's spies.

Melvin and Hakeem come in from the front porch and land on cushions across from the couch.

For Ann, America was a descent into poverty and paranoia. She never saw her father or her former nanny again, although once or twice, in America, there were scares—her mother would declare that their father had found them, or that his arrival was imminent, and they would pack up again and drive away in the middle of some endless night, the night of Ann's childhood, and they would arrive in another identical American city. Her mother would get another job cleaning some American's house or taking care of some American's brat.

Ann gives DJ a squeeze and leans back into the sofa's mush, as if her story has ended or significantly paused. Ralph asks Hakeem how long he's been in America and what he's studying.

Five years and robotics.

I always wanted to fly planes, but America is not the best place now to be a Muslim pilot, he says. I am afraid to fall under investigation and they will discover that I went to Ogbmosho in the mountains, when I was young, for Islamic Athlete's summer camp, with other Islamic brothers and sisters.

Islamic Athlete's summer camp? asks Ralph.

It is mostly just obstacle courses and reading the Koran, Hakeem says. But it is, I believe, declared now a terrorist training camp.

Ralph isn't sure why Hakeem has just now become the most sexually desirable man he's ever met.

And so I have one more dream, Hakeem says, which is to create the Artificial Intelligence.

Ann starts up again, as if a button has been pressed. She tells Ralph that she isn't working, but has borrowed some money on her house to give her time to put together a *business plan*. With Ricky.

What's a business plan? asks Nyima.

Ann explains the concept in terms of an animated movie they recently watched together in which a lovable yet conniving and poverty-stricken princess hatched an elaborate plot to marry a prince and was able to cajole a talking sea tortoise into pawning a golden egg to finance the makeover she would need in order to enchant the prince.

Like a green-card marriage, suggests Nyima.

No, not the marriage part. It's more the *plan*. The *idea*. If you have a good plan, people will give you *money*.

Just then Felicia and Geordi arrive.

***

Felicia is wielding a magazine like a switchblade.

So there's this conversation in the latest *7x7*, she says to Philip, where Huey and Saphira Popper are bonding over child-rearing strategies.

Philip says, What are you doing with a copy of *7x7*?

I got it in the airport, Felicia says. What kind of boy Huey's age is even thinking about, you know, how to raise a child?

Melvin says, How old is Huey?

Supposedly, he's a little older than you.

I totally think about child raising, Melvin says, not because I wanna have some baby or something, but because that's how a species *evolves*. You know, the longer childhood is, the bigger the brain can be, because a little baby brain can only be so big and still, you know, get out of the pussy.

Nyima says that she cried when the old tortoise in the animated movie died.

That's not very emo, says Raymond.

Felicia shows Philip the photo shoot, with the Bay Area's powerhouse literary couple, Saphira Popper and her even more famous husband, Jacob Stratham, lounging around in their expensively furnished, yet tastefully disheveled living room.

So Huey doesn't appear?

No, says Felicia. He's simply "in conversation" with Saphira, by telephone.

Hakeem is explaining to Ralph that he lived in the camp rectory of Islamic mujahideen on the south side of Maiduguri, where they were training people to do battle for radical Islam.

I start to understand the difference between the radical Muslim fascist and Muslim true believers, he says.

I need to talk to you, Felicia tells Philip. I've got new information.

Okay.

I can't believe how easy it is to find out about people on the Internet, she says. You just plug in a phone number and out come names, addresses, family members, criminal records.

You've tracked Huey down.

Not yet, but I've got numbers he used in the nineties. *Hi, I'm trying to track down my old friend Huey, he used to use this number.* No luck so far, but there's one number that keeps going to voicemail for a guy named Mark Sassatelli. I have a feeling about that one.

Just then Tony and Missy come in from the back. Tony lifts DJ into his arms.

I love this little boy, he says. This little boy is coming to stay at my house, isn't that right?

Yes, Mr. Tony.

Dhoji brings out a plate of fried bread and some momos full of beef.

Missy is studying biology, Tony says to Geordi and Melvin, and she's been telling me about parasites and their elaborate life cycles as we grilled the meat.

Are parasites your specialty? Geordi asks.

No, naturally I want to be a lichenologist, Missy says. Lichen aren't actually parasites. They're symbiotic associations between a fungus and a photosynthetic partner, usually a cyanobacterium or a green alga.

Melvin says, No way.

According to Missy, lichen is a pioneer species. They transform mineral environments, life on land would scarcely be possible without them.

Hakeem is talking about a stoning he once witnessed.

Humans enjoy that sort of thing, he is saying. They like to gaze upon death, not just the end result, but the process. They like to feel themselves a part of that process.

A comforting illusion, as long as you aren't the one getting stoned.

Dhoji's quiet, gloomy Bhutanese roommate emerges from one room and enters another. The effect of this seemingly random action on the other guests and residents of this three-bedroom house near the MacArthur BART is subtle, but creates the vaguely intuited impression that they are all components of a larger machine or machines—the elaborate, intertwined parts of a music box or cuckoo clock. Hakeem moves from his cushion to the sofa, next to Ralph. Dhoji sets the plate, with just four momos remaining, on the table. If you see yourself as a component or a cog, a fair question is whether the machine's efficient functioning is really worth endorsing. Just because it's bigger than you, doesn't make it right. Different machines, of course, not just one. Different levels of organization, systems or cells overlapping, merged, working at cross-purposes, contributing to ever-shifting and always changing designs. DJ is trying to lick the blue nail polish off one of his toes, without much success. Gompo's cartoon ends, and although Gompo is just as interested in the commercials, Jamyang stands, newly restless, ready for the next entertainment. Ralph is now sandwiched in between Hakeem and Ann, both of whom tell stories about stern and erratic mothers and absent fathers. Missy tells Melvin that lichen forms like a kind of lace. After a volcanic eruption, lichen catches dust blown about by the wind. Eventually, mats of moss and sod form for grasses and other plants to grow on.

Melvin says that he's totally into volcanoes.

Outside, the sun is moving toward the west.

DJ is looking at Geordi with concern.

Mister, are you going to be okay?

Shortly after Hakeem's father's one visit (which was like the combination of a long punishment and a joke, he says), his mom left town for a better-paying job, leaving the kids with her mother. Hakeem was five. Instead of a job, she got remarried and rarely came back, even to visit.

Therefore, he says, I was angry most of the time as a child and played soccer and got in fights.

Dhoji and Missy gossip about their bosses, or in Missy's case, ex-boss. When Missy's boss discovered her daughter touching herself in the tub, she decided that Missy must be some kind of a witch. Nyima is still interested in witchcraft, she says, although she no longer tells anyone that she thinks of herself as a witch. You don't admit to those things at ten, not in her social circles. It's okay to find witchcraft interesting, amusing even, and to toy with a love spell or a curse occasionally, as long as it's treated like a kind of a joke.

Missy says that at her boarding school in Kenya, a bunch of students claimed the school had been invaded by ghosts and they tried to get the headmaster charged with witchcraft. But really he was just very strict and everybody hated him.

Did you ever see a ghost?

They say the home where I work now is haunted, Missy says.

Because she couldn't get another job working with children, she got a job at an old folks home in Hayward.

In America, nobody cares if you abuse or molest the old people, Tony says.

The other staff there are saying that they see people sometimes wandering at night, even when everyone is securely in their beds. Or sometimes the Assistance buzzer goes off to call us to empty rooms.

A punishment or a joke, Ann is saying. That's exactly it. But which is it—a punishment or a joke? Or does it shift constantly, back and forth, back and forth...

DJ taps on Nyima's shoulder and makes a funny face, then runs away.

Tony tells Missy and Dhoji that he used to work at an assisted living home, back in Illinois.

Those places are always haunted, he says.

There was this woman there, a Mrs. Quaid. Mrs. Quaid usually didn't understand where she was or who the people around her were. Mrs. Quaid often imagined that she was putting on a show.

Of course, we got along famously, Tony says, and she became my special charge.

Nyima races through the room and toward the back with DJ chasing behind her.

I'll zap you into a fish!

Felicia grabs Melvin.

So that's your little brother?

I'm watching him for my parents.

Your parents thought that was a good idea? The Mormons?

Melvin says, I left them a note.

You're a fish, you're a fish!

A note?

I mean, not a note. An agenda. We're trying to, you know, round out his education.

Are you watching him? I think he's headed out the back.

It's under control.

Hakeem is telling Ralph that his grandmother sent him to Islamic school on weekends to learn the basics: Fatiah, writing in Arabic, praying five times a day.

Mrs. Quaid usually thought one of the attendants, a girl named Tawana, was a singer and was always telling her that she had a beautiful voice. Of course I was the one with the beautiful voice, Tony says. Every time I sang for her, she fell into a kind of a trance, but she would have no memory of me or my voice the next time I saw her.

Hakeem is now saying that he's had three mystical experiences and it is these mystical experiences that showed him the possibility of a machine intelligence that could be open to social justice and compassion for all biological life.

Jamyang is explaining to Raymond that he isn't goth, not at all, but he only likes T-shirts with skulls on them, stuff like that.

Something really weird happened one day, when I went in to take Mrs. Quaid her lunch, Tony says.

Nyima collapses onto the sofa next to Felicia with a book.

What are you reading, sweetie?

It's a book about vampires, she says.

Nyima tells Felicia that the human girl loves the good vampire, but it's really hard to have a relationship when one person's immortal and the other one's not.

Yeah, tell me about it, says Felicia.

Are you an immortal, too?

No, not me. My husband. Geordi, she says, and she points him out.

He's standing next to Philip, looking slightly terrified. Looking like Geordi.

When you find out how it works out for them, Felicia says, let me know.

A voice is saying, The first mystical experience is during my seventh grade year after I read the mini Quran book from cover to cover, trying to treat the whole thing as a divinely inspired adventure novel.

Mrs. Quaid was wearing a beautiful necklace I hadn't ever seen before, a voice is saying, and a beautiful dress and slippers that looked like little bunnies and she was dancing around her room quite gracefully. She had the room to herself, because her roommate had recently died…

DJ's heart is thumping. Thumping, thumping, thumping. He stands as still as a statue.

Some of them are good and try to drink blood without killing too many people, a voice is saying, and some of them are just really bad and don't care.

In a few remarkable cases, a single lichen fungus can develop into two very different forms, another voice says.

Dreaming of a mind and then building it, a voice is saying. If AI is going to have this free will, then it must make use of fuzzy logic, ambiguous data, uncertainty. Approximate concepts.

A voice says, Wrong.

Everyone is talking. Everyone is standing or moving. It's like wandering through a forest.

A voice is saying, Do you think it's weird that ten- and eleven-year olds in our culture are like…*into* death?

The uppermost layer of interlaced fungal filaments is called the cortex, says a voice.

I have been dealing with a lot of personal issues and resentment carried over from my childhood, a voice says.

A voice says, So Mrs. Quaid took the beautiful stone and she put it into her mouth.

She swallows it? Just like that?

I am sort of craving for a wrong attention and those wrong attentions got me into few troubles.

In the moment between dreaming and waking, you hear them sometimes…

Beneath the upper cortex is an algal layer embedded in densely interwoven fungal hyphae.

I don't know what really happened to the jewel. But I told my manager, Clara.

Fingers of magma search for hidden weak places in their underground prison, another voice says.

I love my robotics courses but my favorite book I read was by an Islamic scholar named Hamza Yusuf called *Purification of Heart.*

But the very next day I went into Clara's office to check on something and she was wearing rubber gloves and she had a bedpan and I knew right away it was Mrs. Quaid's.

So she is looking for the jewel in this old lady's shit?

When one of these finds an unguarded path to the surface, the flaming magma escapes and blazes into the night sky.

I finally understand what I am seeking and my problem with my biological father.

Are you sleeping? I can't tell. Are you asleep or awake?

He was just a phantom, really. I found out he'd died a long time ago.

3

In Felicia's favorite Can Xue story, there are three characters, but maybe only two. A man and a woman, lovers. The story's full of time markers, but there's no way to make sense of them. The man also has a male companion, or maybe he isn't real, or maybe she isn't either. One of them says, I'm the puzzle inside the puzzle! One of them tells self-deceiving stories. He is an antenna that she has drawn and he belonged to the night. *The symbols on the walls were all alive.* There are ghosts involved, or wandering souls, or the story might have obscure meanings that have totally escaped her. *Two Unidentifiable Persons*. It ends with the nervous woman staring at the doorway. *She was waiting for the knock on the door.*

Raymond is in the kitchen rolling out a puff pastry dough. Geordi is skimming Huey's novel *Truckstop Tranny* for clues. Felicia and Philip and Tony and Melvin and Ralph are gathered around Philip's computer.

It's as if a bright wind has cleared Philip and Raymond's cottage of any previous thoughts, projects, obsessions, but for the mystery of Huey Beauregard. A door is opening, has opened. It seems reasonable to walk through that door. The activist Felicia lived with years ago taught her the compliance position. Hands on the head, just sitting. They would handcuff themselves together, all the activists, make a chain. I'm going to hurt you, the cop whispered in her ear, and he did, but he didn't leave any marks.

Ralph says, I swear I know her from somewhere. Or maybe I don't know her. But somebody does.

It's true, there's something oddly familiar about her face, this Trauma or Jezebel or Emma Jo or Slavenka. Not as if Felicia's met her somewhere—although it's possible. No, it's more like she recognizes the harsh rays that have baked her face into this scary mask.

Tony says, Maybe Trauma quit the band because she was too busy writing Huey's books.

Racer is bald and too skinny to seem mentally healthy, exactly, but her face is reasonable enough to suggest that she's found a category for her damage, drags it out only on special occasions. But Trauma. Always flouncing about in strange hats, leggings, and stripes—whorish and clowny. She looks like she's had too much plastic surgery, paid for by her mother. This name she's given herself, Trauma, it isn't just ironic, it isn't only punk.

Felicia's had the luxury of imagining Huey Beauregard as a "bad" person. A bad writer and a fake. This bad person was always a hideous little troll of some sort. Not a woman her own age with so many obvious psychological issues. *Hey, so you've been to clown school, too.*

In the kitchen, DJ is saying, What happened to that boy?

Maybe you're dying and you don't give a shit. You're lying in the hideous brightness, you've always been lying there, alone in the light. These longings you don't even understand, deep and impossible, they drive you wild. You'll do anything to make contact. To feel more or to feel less. The pain you live with is leading you toward the very edge of oblivion in the burning heat of the sun. You just don't care. The light that incinerates, the light that is so light it eventually has to dim. You're ready for anything. You call up a famous writer. *My name is Huey. I'm thirteen years old. Your book about murdering teenage boys meant so very very much to me, because I'm a teenage boy and sometimes I get into murder fantasies, too…*

***

In the kitchen, Raymond's lecturing somebody about the success with which we've made our victims disappear, but it takes a minute for Felicia to figure out who the "we" is. Not just the thousands of men and boys and women in Iraqi prisons and Afghani prisons and Guantanamo, and not just the ones being tortured at our behest by our allies in Egypt and Saudi Arabia, and not just the ones we've put *under the jail*, says Raymond, somewhere in Romania or Poland—but the ones hidden in plain sight, the thousands of dead and wounded civilians that everybody knows about, if they care to, but who've been buried under an avalanche of stories about surgical strikes and foiled terrorist plots, an avalanche of human interest stories about soldiers with babies back home, or gritty and determined female soldiers, stories about discharged gay linguists, stories about adrenaline junkies and heavy metal heads in the desert, the endless fucking stories about the death count of US soldiers, as if nobody else is real, Raymond says, and then Felicia tries to tune him out, it just exhausts her.

I keep that photo up there as a reminder that we don't live in reality, Raymond says.

Occasionally a phrase from Raymond's lecture breaks into her consciousness, he says something about fiery death raining down from the sky, he says something about pictures of handsome soldiers in Santa hats, he repeats the phrase *we don't live in reality* and then says *only that boy lives in reality* and he says *we'd have to see photos like this every single day to even pretend that we live somewhere in the slightest proximity to reality* and then she hears DJ say, Will they put the boy's legs back on?

Geordi reports that the descriptions of Arkansas and its truck stops in the novel contain no geographical markers and seem based on stories about Bill Clinton's childhood, movies starring Juliette Lewis, that memoir by May Thompson, or maybe that autobiographical novel *Floozy Outta Fletcher County* by Emmy Kay Perchkoff.

Has she ever even been to Arkansas?

She's nuts, that's clear. Cunning, manipulative, desperate. What kind of ride is she on? Who *is* this woman?

What about this Dr. Bailey, insists Tony. Is he a real doctor? Why don't we look him up?

Felicia says, Maybe he's the tall, charming man with good hair who picks up Huey's mail at the copy shop.

Geordi says he's had trouble following the plot, which involves a kind of gang warfare between pimps with silly Southern accents. *A Deep Dark Pain Called*

Mama is no more illuminating, although Mama's child-beating preacher boy-friend has one interesting line. *He has no name,* he says of the Huey character, *for whoever has a name is the creation of another.*

Wait a minute, says Felicia, clicking away at the computer. Is Dr. Bailey Dr. *Grover* Bailey? As in the poet?

Out in the kitchen there's a horrible clanging noise, as if Raymond has dropped the lid to an enormous pot.

Grover Bailey gave Raymond therapy, says Philip.

Raymond emerges from the kitchen, covered in flour, and snorts.

Mandatory therapy, he says.

Philip suggests they call Todd, who introduced Huey Beauregard at his first San Francisco reading so many years ago. Maybe Todd met the bandmates, maybe Todd knows their real names. Ralph suggests that they consult Jonny Taser, who went to work as a private investigator after he lost his outreach job. Philip suggests they consult Leon, who currently works as a psychic.

Felicia says, You're kidding, right?

He's been to the Philippines, Philip says. The psychic surgeons there plucked his eyeball out with, you know. Their spiritual powers.

They didn't pluck anybody's eyeball out, says Raymond. Ever.

Did you see the video? It's pretty convincing.

It isn't hard to fake a video.

I don't know, Philip says. I trust Leon. I mean I trust that he believes in what's happened to him, and he described seeing blood shoot across the room when they opened people up. With their fingers.

If they could really do that, if they could really cut people open with their fingers, then we'd know about it, Raymond says.

We do know about it.

But why aren't these doctors millionaires?

I don't know, says Philip. Maybe they are. Or maybe they're just, you know. Too spiritual to make money.

Felicia says, I'm not going to consult a psychic. We're nowhere near that desperate. We've got a lot of good leads here, but it would be great if somebody would talk to that private investigator.

Raymond is squinting at an image of Racer and Trauma straddling their guitars. As if he doesn't quite believe what he is seeing.

I know her, he says.

You know who?

The skinny one, says Raymond.

The skinny one.

I went to school with her. Her name is Connie Cohen.

Felicia gets a tingling sensation in her head at this point, a druggy feeling. The visceral sense of being "a detective" is combined with the inescapable conviction that "everything is connected," which would also mean, wouldn't it, that these two women, Racer and Trauma, are her destiny.

You went to school with her where?

AP Giannini Middle School and then Lowell High until I dropped out.

So she's the same age as you?

She'd be thirty-eight or thirty-nine.

The website for the band says she's twenty-seven.

That doesn't surprise me, Raymond says.

Do you know if she had a sister?

Sounds right, says Raymond. But I couldn't be sure. But Suzie would know.

Ralph says, Suzie, my sound technician?

Connie Cohen is friends with her sister. Actually, Suzie was going to tell me something funny about Connie Cohen the last time I saw her. At the porn shoot.

Felicia calls Mark Sassatelli's number again. It just rings and rings and then clicks over to voicemail.

Felicia's feeling disoriented, which is a way of feeling normal.

She discovers the real name of Connie's sister, Sarah. She discovers the names of former roommates of Connie and Sarah, and the real name of Connie's child. "Juno" is just her alias. She discovers that the only time they've ever done anything using their own names, it seems, is on an erotic audiotape from 1995. *Cybergasm*. She discovers that the editor of the erotic audiotape was a woman named Mimi Jones. Felicia and Philip did a reading with Mimi the very same year; they'd all been part of the same Generation X anthology.

Mimi was the slutty, sex-positive feminist, says Philip. And I was the gay. Who were you?

Felicia holds herself, as if she's cold and alone in the universe. But there are seven other people in the room.

Whatever you've lost along the way, doesn't matter.

She's never before noticed this particular painting on the wall. With an enormous hand in the foreground, and the figure of a tiny pregnant woman, preparing to push down a detonator, to set off dynamite. It doesn't look like anything she'd ever imagine Raymond and Philip owning, and yet it's strangely captivating. The promise of destruction that seems, for a moment, so very gratifying.

Let's go, she says. We need to talk to Suzie.

4

WHEN PHILIP WAS YOUNG, or younger at least, a hustler he met on Polk Street gave him a copy of his metaphysical treatise: MAGIC WORDS. Philip keeps the manuscript in a drawer with a variety of other texts he's acquired over the years, mostly from schizophrenics. Philip and Johnny would stand around on the same corner, and then one night Johnny invited him to sleep over. Johnny's bleak subterranean apartment was nicer than the room Philip was staying in, although it was almost empty. Johnny told Philip that he was leaving in a few days, for Hawaii. He told Philip he had a terminal illness, that he was going to Hawaii to die.

In everyone's life, there's a big, ugly, mean, fire-breathing dragon, his treatise begins. *His name is PROBLEM. Whether it's rainy or sunny, a good day is when PROBLEM is feeding on faraway fields. My intention is to slay him forever, using "Magic Words." P.S. A fractal is an infinite divisibility.*

Johnny's manuscript explains that every situation should be begun with a prime number; anything that ends with a nonprime, or worse, a false equation (a lie) will end in a knot. It includes a creation myth, and the statement that cats will be the next animal to evolve intelligence. It explains universal oneness, black holes, and love; all this Philip's gleaned with the most perfunctory skimming.

A few years after he spent the night with Johnny, Philip saw him on the street. The fact that Johnny was still alive seemed too embarrassing to mention. He let Johnny walk right on past, without saying a word.

***

They park on Polk Street, where the used bookstore used to be, to walk the two blocks up Nob Hill to Suzie's. It's all going to turn out fine, Philip's sure of it. It's like the investigation has already happened, and he's just going through the motions. DJ huffs and puffs in an exaggerated way, performing his exertion. When he lived in the Polk, Philip resented Nob Hill terribly, with its ghoulish cathedral on top. In five nearly vertical blocks, you could rise from the pissy alleys to the most expansive views and the priciest real estate in the city, long ago gobbled up by luxury hotels and the pope. The six of them arrive at Suzie's building effortlessly, however, as though some force was carrying them, a gentle wind.

The studio has been rearranged since Melvin was raped here. The furniture that had been shoved into the kitchen now fills up the space. The sofa, once at the center of a frenzy of lights and gawkers, is now poised discreetly against the wall, next to a coffee table and one delirious tulip in a blue vase. Felicia pulls up some images on Tony's laptop.

Yeah, that's them, Suzie says. Connie Cohen and her sister.

You know the sister's name?

Sarah.

And your sister told you…

Yeah, I mean normally I don't believe 90 percent of what comes out of Melinda's mouth, but she's real close to them. Has been. Last time I saw her, she was ranting about this scam the sisters were pulling. They'd invented this street kid, a writer, to help publicize their band.

Huey Beauregard.

Yeah.

Do you know where they live?

Yeah, up on Broderick, the Western Addition.

Supposedly it's a renovated squat.

What does that even mean? Philip says. Squats don't get renovated.

It's a Victorian flat, Suzie says. It's always been a Victorian flat. I was over there once, years ago, doing some sound work for them. For the band.

Briar Patch?

No, they were called something else then. Do Me Doggy, or something. Do Me Daddy, that's what it was. The two of them and Knute, Connie's boyfriend. Knute came from money, from Marin County, his father's a famous physicist.

A tall man, says Felicia. With nice hair?

Suzie shrugs.

His hair's okay.

So you were in their house? asks Philip.

Yeah, for a minute. This was maybe seven, eight years ago.

Supposedly, Huey would have been living there even then.

There weren't any child prostitutes sleeping on the futon when I was there.

Philip can picture it—a child prostitute, napping on the futon. Grimy and bedraggled, bruises on his little knees. A great distress enters the napping child's heart. All of the tree trunks have grown rotten. His mother is dead and his father is dead and for years he has been wandering through strange lands. Riddled with AIDS, splotched with it, marked and ruined; he weeps with his eyes in a dream. The San Francisco sky is divided into foggy gray wafers by the bars of the window, and the great exhaustion, the great sorrow, flows over him and through him as if he is floating on a flimsy raft down the river of time.

Melvin says, He's like…a wave.

You saw the whole house?

I saw enough. Sarah led me on this whole journey, like every corner of the flat, pretending to look for the money they owed me. Pretending to look for her checkbook. It was like that.

DJ is contemplating the tulip. Instead of touching it, he puckers his lips and exhales gently on the petals, as if it's a science experiment. He's figuring it out.

Connie's kind of a snot, but she's a reasonable person, Suzie says. But her sister. Wow.

And which one writes the books? Ralph asks.

Sarah. Sarah does everything, more or less, she's the brains, if you can call it that. The total nutcase. She's the one up on the phone all the time, I guarantee you that. I think Connie, you know, she's just along for the ride. And Knute. Didn't inherit his father's IQ, you know what I mean.

There's a doctor.

Yeah, the shrink. I don't remember exactly what that was about, but Melinda thought maybe Sarah was blackmailing him. I don't know.

Dr. Bailey.

Grover Bailey. The poet.

Could they have had a sexual relationship? The doctor and Huey?

Felicia has to remind them that *there is no boy*—so how would a middle-aged woman blackmail her gay therapist for a relationship with a nonexistent child?

Melvin suggests he could crack the case by seducing the boy, getting the boy naked and exposing that *there is no penis*.

Charles Scott said it was one of the sisters playing the part in public, says Felicia. But Connie Cohen looks nothing like the munchkin.

Does Sarah have another sister?

Not that I know of, says Suzie.

Tony suggests that Felicia contact her editor at *The Voice of Truth!* immediately.

We need to break the story before somebody else gets there, Tony says. How much longer could such an obvious charade go on?

It's been maybe ten years, so far. Eight or nine since Huey published his first story.

We'll have to prove it, he says. I mean you can't just say that Suzie's drug-addled sister told Suzie that they're really Huey Beauregard and the story matches up nicely with the version told by a drunken Los Angeles novelist who once wanted Felicia to abuse him.

Philip starts ticking off the other facts: Felicia was told that the photo on Huey's first book was a fake, Felicia was told that Huey offered this young writer she knows money to impersonate him on his book tour. Not to mention that Philip lived in the Polk in 1991 and '92 and never saw anybody who looked like Huey and not to mention that Raymond has been an outreach worker for ten years and has never seen that munchkin on the streets and not to mention that Howard has been constantly prowling for boys who look exactly like Huey for the past twenty years, blond boys with blindingly white asses for sale, and Howard has never seen any boy out there who looks anything like the munchkin.

You can't prove anything with an absence, says Tony.

The pictures in Waylon's archives are fake, too, says Felicia.

Can we quote you? Tony asks Suzie. Can we use you as a source?

Yeah, you can quote me, for what it's worth. But 99 percent of what I know is just what I heard from Melinda. I've been in the house just that once, and met them maybe just a couple of times before and after. Melinda knows the whole story inside out.

Then we have to talk to Melinda.

Suzie says, Easier said than done.

According to Suzie, Melinda was last seen by their mother, rapping on the window of the dress shop on Clement Street where their mother was working retail, to make a little extra holiday cash. According to Suzie, Melinda is known to hang out around 6th Street, around 16th and Mission, various obscure corners of the Tenderloin. Suzie once saw her sister begging for spare change in Noe Valley. She saw her made up like Uncle Sam in the Castro, poking people in the ass with a papier-mâché missile. She hangs out sometimes with this dealer named Jody around Hippie Hill—Jody's suffered some kind of brain trauma, a bicycle accident, Suzie thinks, and so he moves and talks very slow,

he can't really taste anything but sweets, there are long gaps in his conversations—you can't miss him. The last address she has for her sister is a room in
an SRO on Jones.

But I wouldn't go there, Suzie says.

Tony and Ralph are dispatched to the Good Vibrations on Polk, to procure
a copy of the erotic audiotape. With the kids in the back, Philip and Felicia
drive to the Western Addition, past the renovated squat. It's the upper flat in a
beautiful old Victorian, freshly painted blue and purple, like an ornate frosted
confection, one of the few left standing in the neighborhood.

Circle the block again, says Felicia. I think I saw someone in the window.

How can that boy be in a band if nobody's ever seen him? Melvin asks.

Supposedly, he writes the lyrics.

Philip says, Huey belongs to the realm of the invisible.

The realm of the unreal, Felicia says.

A lot of invisible things are real, Philip says. Particles, forces, ideas.

Huey is not one of those things, Felicia says. Let's not get all fuzzy-brained.
Sometimes invisibility is just a consequence of not really existing.

Philip parks and then walks back and forth a few times. On the sidewalk in
front of the neighboring house, someone has written in chalk *Every night screams
are heard*, with an arrow pointing at the house.

At Hippie Hill, in Golden Gate Park, a mishmash of tourists and regulars are
playing bongos, tossing Frisbees, selling weed. Hold my hand, Felicia tells DJ,
who seems enchanted by the bongos. None of the dealers who approach them
has any obvious brain trauma or speech difficulty and so Philip approaches a
sun-damaged gal with a hard face and a flowing skirt. I've got better stuff than
Jody, she tells him.

After some back and forth, she says to check in front of the McDonald's on
Haight Street. Jody's in love with some chick who's always spare-changing over
there, she says.

In front of the McDonald's, however, they are told by a guy Philip worked
with ten years ago, when the guy was an at-risk youth, that Jody has just left and
headed back to Hippie Hill.

We probably passed Jody on the way over, Felicia says. It was probably that
guy we passed in the tunnel who tried to sell us weed.

But when they get back to Hippie Hill, they recognize Jody immediately; he
looks like he's suffered some sort of brain trauma, like he was once athletic and

intelligent, but now can't entirely control his body or his speech or think very clearly, and he's sucking on hard candies. He's friendly until Philip tells him he's looking for Melinda.

No way, Jody says.

Philip says, Do I look like a cop?

Jody concedes that he does not. But, he says, all kinds of people have been looking for Melinda lately. Melinda's gotten herself into some serious trouble with the wrong people, he says. He speaks slowly and distinctly and shows no obvious emotional connection to his own words. I don't know if you're the wrong people or not, says Jody. No way do I know where she is. I haven't seen her in a long, long time.

Back in the car, Felicia says, You don't suppose that the wrong people Melinda's hiding from are Sarah and Connie, do you?

Philip can see that Felicia finds Sarah fascinating. An image in a distorted mirror, a damaged doppelgänger. Philip is already growing bored.

What do you call an at-risk youth who's all grown up? he asks.

An at-risk adult, Melvin offers.

That guy, says Felicia. The risk is over. It's all already happened.

Right.

Felicia tells Melvin that if he's going to come along on these missions, they're going to have to get a car seat for DJ.

Philip's not going to crash.

Right, but I can't afford to get a ticket either.

Haight Street is clogged, so Philip cuts over through Cole Valley. A black bird is viciously engaged with a bag of McDonald's trash in the middle of the four-way stop at Frederick and Cole. Traffic is politely stopped. Philip eases forward until he loses sight of the crow, he's just about on top of it. It jolts up and to the side, flapping its huge black wings in erratic circles around the car, as though deranged, with a mutilated bun hanging from its beak.

They proceed on, into the shadow of Mt. Sutro.

Melvin says, Never mind what I said before.

Which thing?

I was hungry and confused and I was desperate for…you know…a purpose.

Which thing that you said?

If you don't remember, that's fine.

Felicia is gazing out the window. DJ is singing a song about a train engine, as they begin climbing the 17th Street Hill. The view from the top is the Mission and Downtown, the East Bay hills in the distance, the pale, hazy sky.

She's just a bossy hustler, Sarah, he says. She doesn't have any secret powers.

I was kidding, Felicia says.

Kind of.

As they descend the hill, DJ actually squeals, like he's on a roller coaster. They pass through the Castro in silence. As they drive down 18th Street, Philip spots Bob Miller riding a bike around the fringes of Dolores Park. Philip honks, but Bob doesn't look, so he slams on the brakes, pulls over into the bus zone, and yells his name.

Jesus, says Felicia.

DJ says, Ow.

Bob's riding the sort of tweaker bike that Philip usually only sees around Polk Street, steered erratically by weird trollish white women of indeterminate age with mullets or hustlers past their prime who've just gotten an influx of cash from some nostalgic old daddy. The sorts of bikes that are bought for ten dollars on street corners of the Tenderloin and then lost, stolen, traded for drugs or cartons of orange juice, whatever, sucked into the whirlpool of repainted and patched together stolen bicycle parts. Reclaimed into the ever-regenerating universe of tweaker bikes, only to reappear in the most unlikely circumstance. Ridden erratically by a tiny drug dealer with a retro ponytail and spooky sunglasses or by a grotesquely tall drug user with pockmarked skin peddling bootleg CDs from China or maybe by one's best friend from elementary school, a graduate of Harvard Law School, Bob Miller, now circling Dolores Park.

I wanted to talk to you! Bob says.

I'm right here, says Philip, and gives him a hug. It's hard to tell if the hug is brittle or if it's just Bob's body.

Gosh, Phil, I'm real busy right now, Bob says. But we should get together. Did you try to call me? My phone got disconnected. But you can leave me a message, I'm using my friend's voicemail. Do you have something to write with?

Philip pats himself down—nothing. He jogs over to the car.

A pen anyone? Is there a little pencil there on the floor?

Felicia glowers and hands him an ink pen. When he hands Bob the pen, Bob looks at it with bewilderment.

Your number, says Philip.

Now Bob Miller pats himself down, searching for a scrap of paper. What emerges from one of his pockets is a crumpled-up orange flyer advertising a new kind of soup.

Bob, Philip says.

Philip's car is in the bus zone—that's like a zillion-dollar ticket. Bob hands him the paper with a kind of exaggerated flourish.

Let's touch base soon, he says, in what Philip imagines is his lingering "lawyer voice." He seems to have fewer teeth than the last time Philip saw him. He's riding away, along the gully where the MUNI train runs up the hill.

Back in the car, Felicia says, Who is that guy? A client of Raymond's or something?

Philip says, Remember I told you the story about the bridge?

He looks back at the gully where Bob vanished, as if he might see the tread marks he left in the grass. There was some real nothingness in Bob's hug, Philip thinks, something beyond mere terror.

I'm not used to the darkness, Melvin says.

Felicia doesn't seem to be listening much.

Yes, it's still getting dark so early, she says.

Right, says Melvin. That, too.

It's still early afternoon.

5

THE LAST TIME TONY HUNG OUT on Polk Street, Mark had just come from rugby practice. He was sweaty and wearing shorts, and they'd had a beer at one of these places that isn't even gay anymore.

We had a beer at a straight bar on Polk Street, he tells Ralph.

They're sitting in Tony's car out front of the Good Vibrations. Women in scarves carry flimsy plastic bags, a man in polka dots, crazy women in shorts and slickers and floppy hats.

This was like their fourth or fifth date. Tony told Mark the story of how he used to serve chocolates to Oprah, back when he was five hundred pounds and smoking crack in Chicago, and Mark told him embarrassing moments from his own past, fumbled speeches and fraternity hazing rituals, junior high bondage scenes, something like that. Tony was kind of drunk that night and they were joined by other drunks, who told other embarrassing stories, it's all blurred together in Tony's mind. The next day Mark flew off for New York, but not before they made concrete plans to get together again when he returned, not before Mark told Tony, I really like you, not before he said, I think we could really be something together. And then, on his flight back to San Francisco, those guys with box cutters took over the plane and slit the stewardess's throat and then supposedly the passengers rushed the cockpit, to save the president or whatever, and the plane crashed. Tony was too stunned to do anything. He fell into a kind of a dream for weeks perhaps or months. During that dream the ex-boyfriend popped out of the woodwork and claimed the role of the grieving widow, and as the public relations steamroller obliterated the actual person of Mark with the myth of a gay hero, in all the testimonials from John McCain and obituaries and Wikipedia entries the "ex" was left off and the former boyfriend became simply the boyfriend, *Mark is survived by his boyfriend of six years*, it would say, but Tony didn't care. Let them have the phantom. What Tony's life might have been with Mark was a different kind of phantom and it haunted Tony for a while and then it stopped haunting him and he moved on.

He presses *Cybergasm* into the CD player. It's a compilation of various performers, writers, and local erotic celebrities being naughty and sex-positive. For some reason there's an awful hardcore song mixed in by a band called Egregious Fuck. In their audio play, Sarah is a dominatrix who force-feminizes her butch lesbian lover after discovering her wearing her panties. She turns her into her little slut, while the butch, her sister Connie, protests. The incest issues aren't acknowledged, as the two of them are never identified as sisters, either in the audio play or in their bios.

It's like something Damien would do, Ralph says.

Damien and Troy, says Tony.

Ralph says, Whatever happened to Troy?

Whatever happened and happens, is happening. Across from the Good Vibrations, on the shady side of the street, a man goes into a mysterious doorway. Another one comes out. Two worlds, coming and going. Deep beneath the sea swim hideous creatures with eyeballs on stalks and razors for teeth. What kind of building is it, Tony can't tell, a residence or some unmarked business.

Tony says, Whatever happened to Damien?

Back at the house, Philip tosses the orange flyer with Bob's number into his drawer on top of Johnny's metaphysical treatise. Everyone has a cosmology these days. Why does he still have Johnny's in his possession? Underneath it is the thirty-page proof of the existence of God that Philip received from Roger, the crazy he had a crush on in Big Sur.

In high school Roger had spent a year as an exchange student in Finland, a sojourn he cited as evidence of the promise he'd once had, but as an adult, in Oregon, he'd had bad luck holding down jobs in woodworking shops. Co-workers were always threatening to shove a file up Roger's ass or throw acid in his face. He had that effect on certain men. It was the '80s; Philip was twenty-one. Underneath Roger's proof are several Xeroxed sheets of ramblings that a homeless guy in the Mission used to hand out on a regular basis. Orpheus and his dismemberment, a society of poets who rule the world. Philip isn't sure if that guy's still around or not.

When Raymond's Auntie Doll died, she left behind garbage bags full of her metaphysical ramblings from her own crazy years. The pages of Doll's notebooks are yellowed and smell of old nicotine. *The light ray will strike the gas and burn it up and therefore it can't travel and we most certainly will have our Electric City*, she wrote. Philip saved a few random notebooks, and they burned the rest. Some things are hard to just toss in the garbage. *You can't divide the universe against itself*, she wrote, and *We won't let your ass become the issue of the day*, as well as *Your funky ass bottomless pit does not extend through all eternity*, and she wrote that *After seventeen years a patent becomes a public domain*, and she wrote *And what you need to do is come out of the City of the United Nations, the City of Gas, Babylon and Confusion.*

None of the other texts he has shoved in his drawer compare in sheer physical beauty to the burnt pages of Amos's manuscript. It's like an Anselm Kiefer painting. Words careening around the charred nothingness at the center of every page.

Philip takes the flyer back out and dials Bob's number. A voice that identifies itself as "Larry Lou" invites him to leave a message, makes a few jokes, doesn't mention Bob. Larry Lou's tone is kind of histrionic, his cheerfulness forced, his wackiness probably clever only to men who haven't slept in several days. Philip doesn't leave a message.

Raymond is clanging around in the kitchen. Felicia's on her cell. Melvin is sprawled on the floor, ass up, contemplating the triple-beam scale. He might be contemplating the weight of the air itself or staring at his own reflection in the scale's mirror-like surfaces.

Philip calls Jonny Taser. Jonny Taser tells Philip that he does stake outs all the time, usually to catch cheating spouses. If he's lucky, they aren't cheating and so he never has to present anyone with solid evidence of their partner's indiscretions and even better—the stake out drags on, and Jonny receives five hundred a day plus expenses until the paranoid partner of the not-really-cheating spouse gratefully accepts that he or she was imagining the whole affair, and so Jonny has the funds to jump-start his next dramatic project. But usually they're cheating and it's two days, three days, tops.

So you're writing plays now?

I put on other people's plays, says Jonny Taser. I realized years ago that I wasn't really a writer.

I loved your stories, back when you were taking my workshop on Shotwell Street.

I might have actually enjoyed being a writer, Jonny Taser says, as long as I didn't actually have to *write*. Writing was just part of my aura back then, he says. You know: outreach worker/writer, guys loved it. I've always projected an atmosphere of genius, and the men who were attracted to me needed something concrete to anchor it in their minds, something more concrete than, you know, my personality.

So now it's private investigator/dramaturge?

I produce, says Jonny. I don't write, act, direct, or stage manage. I only produce. I scout for talent, I procure funds. I'm set to produce a major new work loosely inspired by the lives of Ted and Todd.

Loosely inspired?

You remember Maury?

Your old roommate. I know I met him, but for some reason I can't picture him.

Nobody ever could, says Jonny. He lived with me for most of the time that Todd did and for part of the time that Ted did. We loathed Maury then, laughed at him behind his back or right in his face, and we plotted ways to exclude him, or simply to create a general feeling of exclusion, says Jonny Taser, so that he would gradually realize he was unloved and unwanted and would spend as little time in the flat as possible. Youth is so cruel.

Wasn't that part of your aura, too? asks Philip. I mean didn't guys hang out with you who liked to be humiliated?

Jonny sighs. Philip's not sure how to interpret the sigh.

It wasn't our cruelty that drove Maury away finally, says Jonny Taser, but Ted's filthy habits. You know he wouldn't get up at night to use the bathroom? He used Tupperware containers instead. At first I thought he was just really, truly the laziest person I'd ever met. As time passed, and he didn't *empty* the containers, I realized he was one of the sickest. Funny, isn't it. Maury has fundamentally changed in a way nobody could have predicted, and has grown into a charming and insightful man, in his way—the author of my new play. But Ted!

We can't afford to pay you five hundred a day plus expenses, Philip says, but do you have any tips for us?

Even if this guy's just a transparent web of lies, shivering in a false wind, he still has to get paid. Follow the money, says Jonny Taser. Somebody has to cash those checks.

Mimi Jones remembers Sarah and Connie well, she tells Felicia. Connie wasn't so bad, but Sarah was a real nightmare to work with. Pushy and demanding and doing this whole prima donna routine, like she was the biggest star on the project. But who was she? She was nobody, nobody'd ever heard of her. She'd been on Jerry Springer once, as a phone sex worker, Mimi says, and thought that made her a bona fide celebrity. She actually sued me during production. It never made it to court, she was just trying to get what she wanted, which was something so trite—oh, I can't even think about it. It's infuriating. She's one of those people who's always suing, it's like intimacy for her. We'd talked about including a song by her band, but then nobody liked the song and it just didn't fit.

Briar Patch? says Felicia. Or Do Me Daddy?

No, it was just before they became Do Me Daddy. They were Egregious Fuck. The track is actually on the CD, because she claimed breach of contract, which was ridiculous, but it was easier just to give in. And she knew that, and I hated it, I hate giving in to bullies who know that they can get what they want simply by being crazier and more persistent and making trouble. But I had bigger battles to fight, real ones.

Was she overweight?

No, not at all, says Mimi, but she wore the clothes of the fat. Long flowing things, big tents of fabric that still managed to show off her cleavage. Like she'd been fat, like a month before, and hadn't gone out yet to buy herself a new wardrobe. I haven't seen her since, thank god. I just assumed she crawled back into oblivion. She could be sexy in a very sort of brash way, you know, and she wasn't completely without talent, but her sense of her own importance was so inflated she was just unbearable.

There's a pause and it sounds like Mimi's chewing on something, a carrot or a stick of celery.

You know who was friends with Sarah? Mimi says, continuing to crunch on whatever it is. At least they were always at the same parties. Rockin Rebecca.

Felicia doesn't know who that is.

She was like one of the first out dyke strippers, maybe the very first, in the '80s. She used to do this routine to that song "Rock Me Amadeus". She danced at the Mitchell Brothers, The Batbrick BurLEZk, Chez Badunkadunk...Later she got into the S&M scene and took the name *Dionisis Diabolique* and sometimes she was Beatrix Le James. I think she's still around, says Mimi. I ran into her two or three years ago, she didn't look so great, but, you know...she was alive.

Find Rebecca, says Mimi. I bet Rebecca can tell you some stories. I bet Rebecca's got the dirt.

Philip calls Jeremy Javits, his former agent. Jeremy had dismissed an early draft of Philip's demon possession book back in 1995, during the time Philip and Raymond were in Santa Barbara. They were already hitting bottom, Philip supposes, surrounded by beautiful architecture and sunshine and hostile rich people. Philip worked at the public library for minimum wage, Raymond massaged the old and the unusually shaped and sometimes Philip came along, they did sex shows or a four-handed massage, *with release* sometimes, it was easier that way, quicker and less strenuous, get them off and get them out, Philip all the while holding out hope for some small book deal or for the movie that was supposedly going to be made of his first novel, and then Philip had his run-in with the poet laureate of Carpinteria.

The conversation with Jeremy Javits is surprisingly warm, however. Jeremy took Huey on as a client in 1997, when Huey was still only seventeen, he tells Philip. Jeremy never met Huey in person, not once, too damaged everyone always said, painfully shy, his face covered with horrible oozing sores, scars from the cigarette burns he acquired from all of his fundamentalist relations, who were partial to using him as an ashtray. Once when he was visiting San Francisco, Jeremy was supposed to meet Huey but Huey canceled at the last minute, in the midst of a panic attack. Jeremy didn't much care for the work, he confesses to Philip now, but he was friends with Mary Stringer, who was championing Huey at the time. Jeremy had just sold Mary's book for a ridiculous sum to an editor she was having an affair with, and they were sure Huey's book would sell. In any case Mary Stringer had developed a bizarre, maternal, and yet oddly erotic, Jeremy says, relationship with the child, even more odd, he supposes, since she'd never met the boy either, but just chatted and chatted on the phone with him, talking him through a variety of panic attacks. Jeremy had never ever gotten sucked into that sort of relationship with a client before, he says, but

Huey had a real talent for drawing people in. There was one Thanksgiving, the last day he would see his aging mother alive, in fact, when he ended up ignoring his aging mother almost completely, Jeremy says sadly, because he spent most of the day talking Huey out of a suicide attempt.

Jeremy was honestly glad to be rid of Huey, he says, when, revealing his own truest instincts, Huey decided he'd found more suitable representation in Tristessa. Tristessa had promised to get him a better deal and to promote him more aggressively, which she did, Jeremy concedes, being the agent *du jour* for that sort of edgy and sensational writing just then, and honestly, Jeremy says, he was fed up and exhausted with all the nervous breakdowns, and endless, endless telephone conversations, the strange metamorphosis, he even says, that he was witnessing as Huey almost overnight seemed to morph from this shy, breathy, girly-sounding boy-child to this ambitious, name-dropping, megalomaniacal sociopath.

After a while Philip asks, So who did you make out the checks to?

A cousin, says Jeremy. Huey insisted he couldn't manage his own money, he was too much of a mess, so we always sent it to some Arkansas cousin who'd relocated to Mill Valley.

Mill Valley? Is his name Knute?

Yes, that sounds right. Hold on, I can tell you exactly, I have it in the records right here.

Felicia wanders out to the backyard to see if Geordi's there. It's only DJ, playing quietly with an astronaut and some mud.

Hello, Miss Felicia.

Hello, Mr. DJ. You know not to leave, don't you?

DJ just looks at her.

I mean don't go out the gate.

I know, DJ says. It's dangerous.

6

THE CIRCUS IS COMING TO TOWN, Tony tells them. Or rather, the circus has always already been in town, biding its time. Huey will have a reading. Well no, not exactly a reading: an event. Rock stars and literary giants shall be reading his work and photographs by the up-and-coming, super-edgy artist he's collaborated with for his forthcoming Drowning Man Press book shall be on display, photographs *inspired by the work of Huey Beauregard.*

Roland Warner, the publisher of Drowning Man Press, is a counterculture legend; he started out as a hippie student of abnormal psychology in Berkeley in the '60s, distributing limited editions of X-rated and druggie comics. He now distributes 15,000 titles a year as part of his million-dollar empire.

X-rated and druggie comics, says Melvin. That's like…

My brain, he's thinking, *or my brain in the future.*

Tony knows Roland from way back. He's like the only heterosexual opera queen in the world, Tony says.

Or maybe the brain of a future life form Melvin's doodled into being.

Roland lives in an old Victorian in the Lower Haight, and answers the door in a robe made of some kind of synthetic fur. Or is it real? His white, beardy thing is tied into a braid.

Nice to see you again, he says to Tony. You've brought a mob.

My colleagues, says Tony. Felicia, Philip, Geordi, Ralph, Melvin.

No pitchforks? No torches?

We come in peace.

Ah, peace.

Up the wooden stairs into a cavernous living room, where they are surrounded by life-size statues of that guy from *Star Trek,* human brains preserved in jars, pinball machines, and sideshow circus murals depicting headless women, creatures that are part human, part amphibian, and evil clowns. Melvin picks up a prosthetic leg stained with blood.

A memento from the set of *Blood Feast*, Roland says. The scene was a precisely accurate reinvention of a traditional bloodletting ritual. Blood, it seems, is the only symbol everyone interprets correctly.

He motions at DJ.

And what creature is this?

He's my brother, Melvin says.

I see. And how much do you want for him?

My brother's not for sale.

Nonsense. I'll trade you this perfectly preserved puppy fetus.

DJ hides behind Melvin's leg. Roland offers the jar, shrugs, and returns it to the fireplace mantel next to the brain.

The public is more and more bloodthirsty as every year goes by, says Roland. Don't you find that to be true? We're devolving. Savagery and mutilation. There must be a hunger, a deep hunger, something missing from our sanitized, liberal, safe little lives that only a good, bloody murder can sate.

Maybe, says Tony. But we're here to investigate one of the great mysteries of the age.

One wall of this room is lined with fun house mirrors, and Melvin slowly shifts along, with DJ still clutching his leg, watching himself turned into a variety of mutants.

You want to know about Huey, says Roland. You want to know if I've met him, if he's a real, living, breathing human being.

How did you know that?

In fact, I've had him to dinner in this very room, Roland says. He's broken bread with me here, at this very table. I've even had dinner at Huey's house, a more tastefully decorated flat, a renovated squat in the Western Addition.

Yes, we know all about Huey's renovated squat, says Philip. We're more interested in whether you ever saw this Huey person without the disguise.

Disguise?

The wigs, the fake beards.

What seems to be, in one of the wobbly mirrors, a future life form, sexy and sprouting wings, is really the reflection of a Bruce Lee doll.

But why think of it as a disguise? asks Roland. This is simply how Huey expresses his inner truth, his essence. In the same way that I choose to wear a robe made from the pelt of a young jackalope I once wrestled to the death.

We have reason to believe that Huey is not who claims to be, Tony says.

Right, says Roland. And who is?

What seems to be, in one of the mirrors, a ferocious angel, half skeleton and half mist, is just the reflection of a scary horse detached from its merry-go-round.

In your estimation, this person you had for dinner—was he male or was he female?

Categories are created by the bureaucrats, Roland says. Me, I was born a rebel. You always want to get outside the established framework. Once upon a time, that was underground comics. Now it's Huey Beauregard. The information context is always shifting, isn't it, so you have to pierce the veil…to see that thing, that place, that dream that the public is dreaming, but they don't quite know it yet. You have to show them that it's there.

So he wasn't either male or female? He was kind of intersexed or trans?

Who can tell in this town? asks Roland.

What seems to be the elongated ghost of a gay child, bound within the dungeon of biology and attached to Melvin like a Siamese twin, is just DJ, who won't let go of Melvin's leg.

Okay, says Felicia, but you've signed a contract for his new work. Perhaps you've paid him an advance. Does he sign his name *Huey Beauregard*? Do you make the checks out to Huey Beauregard? Or perhaps you make them out to his cousin Knute in Mill Valley.

Talk of money bores me, Roland says.

And so you know his roommates? Racer and Trauma?

We're like one big happy family.

With convergent financial interests.

I suppose. Publishing is that sort of business, isn't it?

Philip looks like he's going to puke.

Tell me about Trauma, says Felicia. Or Sarah or Emma Jo or whatever it is she calls herself for your little social visits.

Trauma? She's a bit boorish, honestly. Always chattering on, always trying to steal the stage. But that's why Huey has chosen her, you know. His light is so bright, his force, his talent, his energy. He has to hide among inferior creatures.

You actually believe that shit? asks Philip.

Huey is my friend. My dear friend.

And his voice. When you see him in person, does his voice match the voice that speaks to you on the phone?

I don't understand. Does it match?

From my understanding, he never seems to stop talking when he's on the phone. He never seems to stop talking in a girlish, whispery, overdone Southern accent. And yet in person he barely speaks at all, isn't that right?

What a story you're conjuring! He's a complicated boy or a boy-girl or a phantom or an angel. But he's very real.

At the end of the row of mirrors is a jail cell door. What seems to be, in the wobbly mirrors, a dark world of trembling and terror, could it actually be an ecstatic vision?

Either way, Melvin chooses not to move any closer to the jail cell door.

Trauma wrote the books, says Felicia. Sarah Cohen. We know that. Sarah talks on the phone. Whoever it is they drag along to your dinners is just some actor, some…dwarf.

How ugly your little game has become, says Roland. What an ugly little world you've chosen as your reality. Doesn't the dimness in there begin to… crush you?

We're just trying to get to the truth.

Ah, the truth. Seems to me your investigation is doomed to hit a brick wall.

Are you threatening us?

How melodramatic of you. Heavens no. I'm just using my higher faculties. I'm just looking at the path you've chosen and gazing into the future, describing how that path ends.

You're one creepy motherfucker.

Perhaps, but it's time for you to go. It's time for my massage.

He picks a little gold bell off the fireplace mantle and rings it. Almost instantaneously, some sort of masseuse emerges from a doorway that Melvin hadn't noticed, hidden by a velvet curtain. She's wearing a pushup bra and a towel around her hair—and bearing a massage table, which she quickly sets in place. A little suitcase full of potions.

In my youth, I was a student of experimental psychology, says Roland, as he sheds his robe and rolls his naked, pear-shaped body onto the massage table. A student of the human mind. In every age, they think they've got us figured out. But they haven't, have they? Which isn't to say human beings aren't predictable, God knows. The majority can be accurately located in space and time and psychological development, effectively *tracked* based only on—oh, I don't know. Their purchases, their votes, their trash. Their stuff. Mine mine mine. Gimmee gimmee gimmee.

He seems to lose his train of thought.

And the others?

The others? What others?

The illustrious minority that can't be so efficiently pinned down.

Oh, us, says Roland. We will forever elude you, I'm afraid. Good-bye now. Be careful on your way out.

He makes a shooing motion with his hand. The masseuse gets right into it with some painful-looking karate chops.

Yes, says Roland Turner. Yes, yes, yes.

The posse retreats back down the wooden stairs and clusters on the street below.

It's as if they've all seen the same person in a dream, but not the same dream and not the same person.

Wait. The answer is garbled or unclear. Inquire of the oracle once again.

The dreamer is interested in a series of adventures beyond the zone of physical extinction. Does this adventure make sense for you? Do you choose to join?

You think that time is not the issue. You think that for the new life, you must change yourself completely. Or maybe not.

Time and space are the same substance, a deranged zone where the psyche performs its shadows, its reservoir of psychic forces, its communicable diseases.

Don't say I didn't warn you.

7

OUTSIDE HUEY'S BIG EVENT for his Drowning Man Press book, Raymond will pass the time doing push-ups and reading the posters of missing animals and persons that are pasted onto every available surface of the city. A man Raymond's age named Jerry has been missing for over a year. "Jerry has a medical condition and needs medication. He has a scar on his shin, and a reddish-colored blemish on the center of his forehead." A thirteen-year-old girl with slick hair has been age-progressed to sixteen. Sometimes goes by Badass Tina or Baby Money or White Tina or Weasel Girl. One of the missing children will look vaguely familiar, kind of like DJ. But like an idealized version of DJ, more wholesome, more all-American, more butch and more white: the perfect child victim. *Stolen from Disneyland!* The identifying information for this perfectly bland missing child will have been covered up by a flyer for the event that will be, at the moment, just getting underway inside, where the audience will be atwitter with the possibility that the enigmatic Huey will make an appearance *in the flesh*, and so Raymond will stand watch outside the club, preferring not to run into Grover Bailey. He won't want to even glimpse the man who once gave him his mandatory therapy, perhaps imagining a secret life for Raymond that could be implied by a few disjointed phrases and images, inside, where the crowd will be working themselves into a kind of frenzy of adulation for their own perfect victim, now risen to unforeseeable heights of brilliance and possibly, perhaps, making an appearance *in the flesh*. Indeed, a taxi will pull up and out will step two of the scariest women Raymond has ever seen. Neither of these women hustling out on either side of a kind of munchkin will be the rail-thin Connie Cohen but one of them will surely be her sister, Sarah. The munchkin will be wrapped in a vast shawl, wearing a fake beard and a wig of long black hair straight off the set of *The Addams Family*.

Inside, Tony will study the photographs on the walls of naked or half-naked, semi-freaky, semi-pagan men. Young men posed in ways that suggest they spend their days and nights in dark alleys, parked cars, or lounging around on stained mattresses in the stinky rooms of SROs. Photographs *inspired by the life of Huey Beauregard*. Tony has met several of these models, or seen them around, over the years. They're from Connecticut suburbs, they went to Harvard or Brown, they're web designers, they live in houses overlooking the ocean.

Felicia will chat up an older woman who'll be selling CDs of Huey's band.

You his manager? Felicia will ask.

He's like my own child, she'll say.

Huey lives with me and my two daughters, the woman will confess, after babbling about the accomplishments of her children for several minutes, including their weight loss. The woman will be wearing some kind of fake hair herself, and a form-fitting shiny black one-piece outfit, an outfit many women in their sixties would let alone. I'm a performer, too, the mother of Sarah and Connie Cohen will admit. In a sense. Felicia will want to tell her that her daughter isn't overweight, but the older woman's lipstick will be too frightening. The woman will discuss ex-boyfriends who betrayed her, the blurry boundaries between performance and life, and money she's often found just lying in the streets, but Felicia's lack of enthusiasm for her biography will suddenly seem to get on her nerves. The show's about to start, the older woman will say, so you wanna buy something or not?

Philip will perch near Connie Cohen on the balcony, so that when the munchkin is, with a great commotion, escorted up to the balcony itself, with Sarah trailing behind, neither of them speaking to or even acknowledging a single member of the audience, not even brushing up against another person's flesh, Philip will be sitting just a few feet away, close enough to see the mole by Huey's lip. When some faded punk legend takes the stage, Sarah will call out *Goddess!* in a vaguely East European accent. Sarah's manner and outfit will suggest to the casual observer that she is not an American girl at all, but a refugee from the sex trade in a former Soviet republic. The faded punk legend will say a few words about Huey's brilliance, including *authentic, real, soulful,* and *fuckin profound.* The faded punk legend will begin reading one of Huey's stories somewhere in the middle and Philip won't be able to follow exactly—something about a middle school student getting rimmed by his tutor, and somehow a computer gets involved. A strange mishmash of tech language and spankings in the outhouse. *Demon Seed* meets *Deliverance?*

A voice will drone on, and then another. A demonic presence, Melvin's pretty sure. Photon-based or whatnot. Melvin will discern the demon's outlines in the mineral smoke that they'll pump out before the final performer, a drag queen, takes the stage. The indecipherable hum of the story she reads will create a lingering afterimage suggesting virtual entities both sexual and metaphysical. He'll doodle his impressions as future life forms in his notebook as the drag queen will read random passages and tell jokes he doesn't understand. Descriptions of the fog, of S&M dungeons. A timeless, ghostly light; the silver skeletons of extinct humans; bones of disappeared children form a lacework beneath the play space. Clear water emerges from a deep pit. You can change everything else, it's true, the buildings and faces and names, but not the deep pit inside you. Descriptions of beatings, whimpering, children cringing in fear. Something that sounds like *There's nothing here for you, just contaminated mud.*

Smoke from a cigarette burning in the darkened alley of a dream. Uh-oh, wait.

Not a dream.

He might as well give up: a sort of fiber or net, a dense web of associations and concepts *like a fence.* It's like not only are we trapped inside, but we trapped *ourselves.* Brainwashed and bewildered and *on fire.* The drag queen will tell more jokes he doesn't understand, but people will laugh, and then the drag queen will read some more, it will just go on and on and on, and Melvin won't be able to keep his eyes open. Exactly. He'll nod off and drift, as if forever, into some-body else's doomed little dream.

Outside, Raymond will finish his push-ups and wish he wasn't here. A po-lice car will be rolling down the alley toward him. He could have skipped this event entirely and watched a movie with DJ and Ralph. Only Ralph was wise enough to stay home, watching *Bride of the Gorilla*, starring Raymond Burr and Barbara Payton. Raymond and Barbara were close friends, it seems. Following the public scandal of her affair with former boxer and B-movie actor Tom Neal, who put Barbara's fiancé in a coma, the only acting job she could get was *Bride of the Gorilla*, with the help of Burr. It effectively ended her career. Within ten years she was working as a prostitute on Sunset Boulevard. The gorilla in the film was played by Burr himself, a brooding, orchid-raising homosexual in real life who, for his official biography, manufactured two fake wives and a fake child, all of whom he killed off. He claimed that they'd died in plane crashes or from incurable diseases.

8

BACK IN BERKELEY, over a late dinner after the reading, Geordi suggests that Huey's lack of features brings him close to the Mutazalite concept of God. As it turns out, Felicia tells him, as shadowy as he is, Huey does have several consistent attributes. Felicia says that Jane Dunlove interviewed Huey for *Poets & Writers* and told her that Huey was crazy for fried squid. Oh yes, Huey abso-lutely loves fried squid, the masochistic writer Farrah Alexander confirmed by phone later in the afternoon; she'd had lunch with Huey just a few months ago at Le Bistro Monique after having chatted with Huey on the phone for years, but at lunch Huey didn't say a word. *He's so damaged*, said Farrah. He just shoved those squid in his mouth while the unpleasant fat woman he's always dragging along behind him did all the talking. Jane Dunlove also told Felicia that Huey's "writing process" involves meditation on the kaballah, two hours of yoga, vast bowls of gummi bears, and *purity of intent*.

Geordi says that *purity of intent* sounds like a distinctly Mutazalite expression.

According to Todd, Felicia says, who helped set up Huey's first reading, nobody could fake the sort of crazy talk he heard from Huey. His graphic descriptions of the torments of hell awaiting him, where he would burn forever in searing agony as the victim of an unquenchable fire, surrounded by the hideous damned, were not something that could be invented as a kind of lark. He must have really been abused and molested by crazy fundamentalists in Arkansas, Todd said. He was subject to sudden and inexplicable eruptions of an almost cosmic fury directed at people named Skeeter or Drew—his mama's ex-boyfriends, Todd thought. Even the tarot cards showed a past, a present, and a future composed of such erratic zigzags that their owner had to be perched at the brink of insanity, Todd was convinced.

Geordi is drifting out of this conversation, wondering why he hasn't gotten any work done on his thesis lately.

According to Sylvester LaCarriere, however, Felicia says, Huey is a real genius, the sort of genius whose brilliance provokes odd eruptions of jealousy from less successful writers like Benton Archer and, he implied, Felicia herself. According to Saul Torstenson, Huey's erratic behavior makes perfect sense if you understand Huey's psychology *at all*, and all of this nonsense about him being somehow unreal is the fault of Armistead Maupin, whose trashy book about Huey has led all kinds of paranoid types, such as Felicia he implied, to imagine conspiracies instead of raw talent and a pure, wounded heart. When Felicia informed Saul that Armistead Maupin's book wasn't actually about Huey but about Anthony Godby Johnson, an imaginary boy with AIDS, beloved author of *Between a Rock and a Hard Place*, and that it is only the similarities between that verifiably fake child and Huey—such as the fact that they both claim to have suffered from delayed puberty and improperly formed genitalia because of the abuse they suffered as children—that has suggested any sort of conspiracy to the paranoiacs of the world, Saul admitted that he never actually read the book, and hung up on her.

Felicia pushes her plate away. She's barely touched her food.

God's *speech* was seen by the Mutazalites as holy but created, Geordi tells her, as opposed to the timeless document that predated God's creation of the universe. Mutazalite theologians argued that God's *speech* was worthy of critical attention. They developed a kind of speculative interpretation that then entered mainstream Islamic practice.

I don't get the fat thing, Felicia says, because you know I've seen her, Sarah isn't overweight, why does everybody keep calling her overweight?

Maybe she's always standing next to her anorexic sister, Geordi offers.

His wife disappears into the computer, while Geordi does the dishes. Her body is still there, hunched in front of the screen, when he goes to bed. He wakes later, still alone in the bed.

It's too late or far too early for Freddy to be calling Philip, but he is. I'm getting progressively deeper and deeper into hell, Freddy whispers.

The reception is bad and Freddy's voice blanks in and out.

Freddy says that after Danny left, he couldn't achieve any progress on his great work. Philip isn't sure if he actually said *my* great work or *the* great work.

I found a new one, he says. Army this time.

What happened to Danny?

Freddy says that Paul, the new one, lost a leg in the war. One of the wars, what did it matter which one? His wooden leg had gotten smashed the morning they met. His left leg was a rotting column—it sounds like Freddy says it's entwined with *syphilitic tropical-flower ropes*, but the blank spots are confusing. He's a monster, whispers Freddy, a god of sex and death.

There's a prolonged silence.

Freddy?

...regions of the mind which have also become regions of the earth, places where anything goes.

There's a pause that seems to be actual silence.

And do you have an interpretation? asks Philip.

Things have kind of moved beyond interpretation, says Freddy. I'm *inside* the war zone here.

Watch out for corpses and mangled bodies and scorched earth, Philip says.

The bottom line is that Freddy isn't sleeping. He's desperate for weed.

Not tonight, Philip says. I can be there around noon, no sooner.

Fine, fine, says Freddy. I'm not going anywhere.

Philip says, We need to talk about Huey Beauregard. I've got to tell you, we've confirmed some surprising facts. It might be a little shocking.

But Freddy has already hung up.

Felicia isn't sleeping. Some facts are still out there, she can sense them, the missing bricks in a structure. The "truth" or prison house for Sarah.

It's 3:17, the middle of the night, when the email arrives.

Ah hear yer tryin to do a story on me without even talking to me. That's totally uncool and ah'm just wonderin why yer pokin yer nose in mah business and what all yer up to. Ah'm here and ready to talk whenever. Huey.

Contact has been made. A haze has separated them, a kind of distorting substance rising like steam from the earth, but now. Now maybe they can really see each other. Was this the goal? Once, when Felicia was a girl, she wanted to have "fun." One couldn't have fun alone, but only in groups. She worked at making friends, joining in activities, making people laugh. Felicia, one of the gang. Yvette Signs worked at a pizza place, Linda Truman at an Italian restaurant called Toppers. They all had bosses, divorced men who flirted with them, men they ridiculed and made out with. *Toppers* were a variety of odd items that might be placed over a dish of pasta—French fries, olives, maybe even raisins. Felicia was probably in love with Yvette's name, more than Yvette. But for a long time now, intimacy with a luminous emptiness has been more compelling to Felicia than intimacy with other employees. She maybe could have just left the hazy substance in place.

Melvin wakes up in the middle of the night unsure where he is. For just a moment, he might be anywhere, anywhere new. A kind of darkness and solitude that he's approached but never entered, not until now. But then the shapes of Tony's living room come clear in the moonlight, the old mattress he's been sleeping on, the ornate ceiling curving overhead, and DJ sitting at the front window, looking out at the street. Just parked cars and some ugly, sculpted shrubs.

DJ is crying. In the moonlight, his brother seems lit from the inside. It's like his tears are liquid electricity overflowing from the breaking heart of reality.

The fact that *anything* exists is insane.

Melvin gives DJ a hug. Do you miss Mommy?

Yes. But that's not why I'm crying.

Why are you crying?

Because I'm sad.

Oh, says Melvin.

The ceiling of this room is so high above them, it's like it's in another dimension. Or like there is no limit, nothing to hold them in place.

Don't be sad. You don't need to be sad.

He puts DJ back to bed. DJ looks up at him, with a kind of blind hope or trust or revelation. Melvin supposes that his response to the sad child is just an adaptation—he's programmed to be charmed by his pouting face, so he won't starve him or beat him to death. The eye contact is giving him an oxytocin rush, for sure.

Why are *you* crying?

I'm not crying, silly, says Melvin.

He gives him a kiss.

You just rest. Everything will be okay. You'll see.

His brother nods off right away, but Melvin just sits there next to him for a minute.

It's insane. You *know* that.

He isn't talking to DJ anymore.

It's crazy. Why would you exist? Just for now. Not forever. Only for a while?

He gets up and goes to the window and looks out at the parked cars and the sculpted shrubs in the unreal light of the moon.

VI

To the right, the arc of the circle was bounded by a kind of retreat in the shape of an 8 which I understood constituted for the priest the Holy of Holies. To the left there was the Void: this is where the children stood.

— Antonin Artaud, *The Peyote Rite Among the Tarahumara*

1

As Philip's about to head over to Freddy's, Melvin and DJ show up at the door. DJ's looking a little worse for wear, grimy and bedraggled, his pants soaked through. On the Mission Street bus, coming over from the Excelsior, he wet his pants.

Yeah, I used to wet my pants, too, he reassures the boy. We all did, when we were little. Not a catastrophe. Just a minor accident. You didn't bring a change of clothes?

Forgot it, says Melvin.

DJ's looking around the room, as if he isn't being addressed, as if some other little boy has wet himself. He's wearing the same pirate T-shirt he was wearing yesterday. Actually, he seems to wear that shirt every day. Who doesn't love to sail forbidden seas and land on barbarous coasts? The soggy green slacks might be the same ones, too.

While DJ's in the tub, Philip walks down to Mission and picks up a new outfit at the Big Lots! The children's fashions and the toys are practically the same thing, pasted over with characters from the latest kiddie blockbuster or fast-food franchise.

In the car, on the way to Freddy's, Melvin tells Philip that everybody's into choking.

DJ is bouncing up and down on his seat in the back and talking to himself in rhymes.

Everybody? Even the girls?

Especially the girls

Where do you get your info? asks Philip.

Where does anybody get their info, says Melvin.

They have sex with each other, Philip says. People have sex. It's one of the things they do.

Melvin screws up his face, as if trying to make sense out of nonsense.

Or else they just look at other people doing it online, Philip says.

Okay, well, this guy we're visiting is into soldiers, right? What's that about?

It's kind of a tradition, gay men and soldiers, Philip says. Freddy's a sucker for that kind of thing, understanding himself within entrenched genealogical structures.

Entrenched genealogical structures, repeats Melvin. He seems to like the quasi-mystical sound of the phrase.

At Freddy's, Paul, the amputee, is shirtless and sweating, although he's sitting almost perfectly still. He's good looking, in a psycho-killer sort of way. He doesn't greet them, but acts like he's enmeshed in some more important business involving the remote. Clearly Paul is the one who's been dragging Freddy deeper and deeper into hell. There's something sadistic about the way he punches the buttons to change channels. Freddy signals Philip to join him in the kitchen. Philip carries DJ in with him—the kitchen seems safer. Freddy looks like he hasn't slept, ever.

I'm in over my head, he says.

Nervous laughter from the other room.

Philip tells him that they've discovered that Huey Beauregard is actually a middle-aged woman.

That's insane, you're insane, Freddy says, and he begins to weep.

A French press on the counter with the morning's leftover coffee still inside. A few dishes in the sink. The kitchen table a chaos of newspapers, books, papers. Is Freddy usually neater than this or messier? Is he breaking down?

Don't cry, DJ says.

Where did you get this child?

Maybe you should take a vacation, Philip says.

People do still have them, don't they, Freddy says.

Freddy and DJ stare at each other for a moment, intensely.

Greece, you love Greece, don't you? says Philip. Maybe you could use some alone time.

Freddy's laugh is chilling.

What other kind of time is there?

You know what they told Paul when he woke up, after his leg was blown off? Freddy whispers. The minister assured him that after he died, or when the world ended, whichever came first, his resurrected body in Christ would have all of its limbs. *Christ would transform his lowly body so that it would be like His glorious body.* Can you imagine?

If you don't feel safe, we could take a little walk.

Freddy shakes his head.

It's not like that, he says. It's not physical.

Freddy tells Philip he needs a favor. It's his twin brother. He needs weed.

You have a twin brother. What's he like?

Apparently his usual dealer had a sort of structure collapse on top of him.

Freddy embraces himself as if warding off a chill.

What are you working on these days? Philip asks.

Freddy gives a disturbing little laugh.

The eighth vector, he says.

Maybe...

Nothing's happening. I mean I'm not exactly writing.

Hey, Freddy, says Paul from the other room. You got a couple of bucks?

It's like I'm traveling farther and farther into that place, Freddy says. You know the place I mean. Where language doesn't matter except as...

Freddy sighs.

In the other room, the space between Paul and Melvin's bodies has decreased substantially. Let's go, kiddo, says Philip.

I'll catch up with you later, says Melvin. Can you like...watch DJ for me?

Freddy is tossing a few meager bills at Paul.

You sure?

Melvin stands and whispers in Philip's ear a hushed, relentless monologue summarizing the urgency of his need to do something, to experience something, something he doesn't name, but which is contingent on getting a beer or something with the psycho.

Philip's first impulse is to say simply, No. No, you cannot just wander off to your doom with this freak.

Come by later, okay? he says instead.

Yeah, sure, says Melvin.

So I guess we're just going to forget about a car seat, says Felicia.

Live free or die.

That's not funny.

Well sure, says Philip, but there's nothing I can do. Tony had to go to work and Melvin had an appointment, so I'm the babysitter.

What kind of an *appointment* did Melvin have?

Philip shrugs.

Stop at the Target, says Felicia. I'll pay for a car seat.

You're such a good person. You believe in safety and restraint.

It's not a metaphor. We could really have an accident.

Everything's a metaphor. Don't pretend that restraining a child in a special chair doesn't have larger implications.

DJ says, I didn't forget to use the bathroom.

Felicia says, Do you need to go again?

I don't think so.

She leads him inside her house, and Philip follows along. Geordi is at the dining room table, working on some elaborate chart with bubbles and arrows and Arabic words. He looks confused by Philip's presence, waves his hand in a way that seems more like a meager signal of distress than a greeting. While DJ is in the bathroom, Felicia says, I told Huey to give me his number, I'd give him a call.

Good, says Philip. We want to be in control here.

The Target is less than ten minutes away, but the adventure delays them over an hour. The store is vast, and while Felicia is searching for a car seat, Philip stocks up on cheap T-shirts and dishes from China. DJ knows where to find everything, as if he's been to this store many times. Once they get back out to the car, Philip looks at the items he's purchased as if he doesn't recognize them.

I think they brainwash you, he says. They pump in some kind of odorless gas.

Felicia says that conspiracy theories are usually a product of lazy thinking and a refusal to accept personal responsibility.

But it is kind of like being on drugs in there, she concedes. You have to channel your higher self or you'll be overtaken by your id.

As they drive across the bridge to the city, DJ creates a conversation between the bowls and salad plates. He seems to be turning them into some kind of family, but with blurry hierarchies and fluid gender identities. DJ calls one of the salad plates a little idiot.

Be nice, says Felicia.

DJ snaps his mouth shut, but gives the salad plate the meanest look Philip's ever seen on DJ's face.

After he parks the car by the SRO on Jones that Suzie told them they really didn't want to visit, Felicia says, I think we should both go up.

With DJ?

It'll make us seem less threatening. Like a family.

DJ waits patiently while Felicia unsnaps the belts that have been holding him in place. She takes his hand and then DJ reaches for Philip with his free hand and after a few steps he lifts up his feet and swings.

Since when are families less threatening?

After a few more steps he does it again, and then the buzzer doesn't work. A woman with her little boy comes out of the building and the boy gives DJ a dirty look, but the lady holds open the door for them and they all go inside. It's dark inside and smells of old nicotine and pesticides.

The elevator's broken, Felicia says.

They go up and up the stairs. Down a long hallway with a carpet full of strange textures and stains. They pass a scowling man wearing a towel and carrying a loofah sponge. Doors everywhere. But one of the doors is open and a person in a robe is smoking a cigarette on the bed. Everything is sagging.

Some slummy district in the shadow of the ziggurats, the person is saying.

He jabs the cigarette at DJ like he's going to poke him with it.

I'm not looking for the ignoramus. The ignoramus is looking for *me*.

He jumps to his feet.

Twisted amphibian seraph motherfucker. I saw what you…

Philip pulls him on past and the door slams behind them.

The woman they're visiting doesn't seem happy to see them either. She's dressed in a bathing suit and bones stick out of her emaciated belly. She's saying, If you know what's good for you, you'll leave it alone.

DJ says, Miss Felicia, I need to tell you a secret.

She's dead to me. Do you hear me? Dead.

Just a minute, DJ, says Felicia.

Melinda fucked over the wrong people, she says, and Philip says, Do you know two sisters named Sarah and Connie Cohen? and the woman says, Get the fuck out of here right now or I'm calling for help, get the fuck out of here or I'll kill you my fucking self, you hear me?

She slams shut the door.

Felicia looks frightened, but when they get back downstairs, she hugs DJ and asks if he's okay and DJ says, Yes, ma'am, we got out just in time.

They drive.

That was so disturbing, says Felicia.

She's just tweaking, says Philip. I don't think we should allow her confused thinking to influence our beliefs about reality.

He stops at a red light and reaches over to pat Felicia's shoulder.

The things she's talking about—it's just her own universe of anger and fear.

At Rockin Rebecca's building, Philip stays in the car with DJ. He can't make out what the crackly voice on the intercom says, but Felicia gets buzzed up and disappears into the complex. DJ wags one of the salad plates back and forth now and talks in a high-pitched, wicked voice. The salad plate is threatening to put a spell on the bowls, who protest, sometimes in deep, resolute voices and sometimes in squeaky, helpless voices that insist only DJ can save them. DJ tells the salad plate he'll break it into a zillion pieces. Philip says, You know not to break the dishes, right DJ, and DJ says, I know Mr. Philip. I'm only playing.

After a while, DJ tells Philip he needs to use the bathroom.

Can you wait?

I don't know.

Philip walks him down the street, looking for a place to go. There have never been public restrooms in this city. Because he is holding a child's hand, however, people smile at him. Slightly younger women even flirt with him. He has become Daddy. Even in San Francisco, Daddy is heterosexual. I'm Not Gay But My Five-Year-Old Is. He's never quite understood the appeal of Daddy—older heterosexual men, or the butch gays who mimic their stern, stoic ways. It's either lectures or silences in which you're supposed to imagine your own version of the lecture they are thinking. Why do these people assume he isn't a kidnapper? Just as he's about to whisk the boy behind a stern, dowdy hedge to do his business, a police car rolls past, a butch officer glowering behind her shades. DJ waves at the policewoman and even the gloomy officer smiles and waves back.

Uh-oh, says DJ.

What's wrong?

I don't want to get in trouble.

You're not in trouble.

When the police car disappears from sight, he stands guard and has DJ pee in the bushes. As they're returning to the car, Felicia emerges from the complex, looking stunned.

What did she have to say?

She didn't have anything to say, says Felicia. She's dead.

The air is still, the traffic is still. Nothing speaks.

DJ says, I always suspected this would happen.

One of her band members was in there, sobbing and going through her things, Felicia says. Rockin Rebecca died just three days ago. Suicide, says Felicia. Supposedly.

Not knowing: halted in perplexity at the brink of a dangerous abyss.

Rebecca played the drums, she wrote songs, says Felicia. Just like Huey.

Philip says, Supposedly?

She also wrote this novelette, says Felicia, and published it herself. They're going to sell copies to help with the expenses of the memorial service this afternoon.

You want to go to the service.

You can drop me off, she says. I'll take the BART back to Berkeley.

Philip gives her a hug.

Our two best sources have gone missing or dead, she says. What are we dealing with here?

Who's the conspiracy theorist now?

It only takes two people to conspire. Sarah, Connie, Knute, that's three. If Grover's in on it, we've got four. Roland Warner, five.

Yeah, but murder? And Charles Scott is a better source than either Rebecca or Melinda.

He would be if he'd put me in touch with Drew Malone, says Felicia. Otherwise it's just hearsay.

Drew Malone.

2

THE BAR HAS A CELTIC PAGAN-LIKE world-tree etched into the window and so Melvin thought it might be a kind of mystical place, the sort of place where a kind of revelation about the meaning of everything might finally coincide with the most intense orgasm of his life. In fact, it's just full of snooty people on the make. Ridiculous prices for drinks he's never heard of, but at least

Paul is buying. Someday Melvin might explore the world of people with ca-reer goals. Melvin has never met anyone who seems more like a sick rapist than Paul and would have thought that before the second beer he'd have been slammed against a wall in the bathroom and forced to endure things he really doesn't even want to. Two and a half beers in, and it's looking sketchy. It's loud enough that they have to lean toward each other, sloppy, and they still can't hear each other unless Paul's breath is right up in his ear. The hot breath and the heat coming off Paul's body and probably Paul's smell, it's all too much. Even though he can't pick out the actual Paul smell from underneath the co-logne he's wearing, Melvin believes that it's rendering him helpless, and this is the most soothing belief he's maybe ever held. The broody, barking noises Paul makes are just this sort of forceful assertion of Paul's belief in his right to own someone else's ass. He touches Melvin's leg.

...here are the incentives. Each referral you get, you get one-hundred dol-lars. Each referral that your referral gets, that's a twenty-dollar residual.

Melvin's committed himself to this path, so he doesn't want to pick at it too much or undo his own helplessness. The body wants what the body wants.

That's monthly income for the rest of your life, says Paul. Of course, noth-ing's really free in life.

Is Melvin attracted to men or to the sort of careless, selfish force that they inhabit so easily? They or whoever. He's working his way back toward his dis-covery that some things that seem to be related don't have to be. Men and mas-culinity. It's hard to figure out what his passion is exactly, without destroying it with his brain.

You refer three people, and those three people refer nine people. Once that happens, you qualify for a free $12,000 car for three years.

Melvin's not into penises. He doesn't want to touch another man's penis or suck on it or even look at it, he's clear about that. Probably then he isn't gay.

He doesn't like Paul, and yet he wants Paul to fuck him.

He is Questioning.

He never thought of it like that before, actually—not a word for what he isn't or isn't sure about, but for who he fundamentally is. *I am Questioning.*

Question: Would you please hold me down and force some or every ap-pendage into my ass?

It's actually $100 a month membership fee, but you get that $20 residual it takes away the five people and you got $80 profit a month.

I don't have any money, Melvin says. I mean, like zero.

Paul shrugs, like it doesn't matter to him.

I haven't done it yet, he says. What I'm gonna do is get as many people as I can get, and then join.

I won't have any money until I do my next porn, Melvin says.

Rape that straight ass, Melvin thinks. The idea of his own ass as something that has practically nothing to do with himself and as straight just adds to the sense of Paul's horrible and unstoppable force.

…chicks really go for you with your pretty-boy face, Paul is saying.

Yeah, it's all bi, Melvin says. There isn't as much money in straight porn.

Paul knows exactly what he wants and why they're together, but Melvin's still afraid that if he asks for it, Paul will hurt him, humiliate him, maybe punch him in the face. Is he that kind of closeted sicko or not? He leans in toward Melvin…

…pick up some bitch, and both of us fuck her…

…and practically falls on top of him, propping himself up with a hand on each one of Melvin's thighs.

Question: Would a rape feel like love even though I hate you?

My specialty is getting raped in the ass, Melvin says. That's where the real money is.

But the mention of money is a tactical error, because it takes Paul back to his sales pitch. Apparently if you get five referrals and each referral gets five referrals, you qualify for a $50,000 car.

Melvin says, Qualify?

So the thing is, you just have to borrow the initial $100 and there's really no risk, you just need to get your first referrals. You'd be doing yourself a favor and doing me a favor, too.

At this point, he brings up his missing leg in connection with an overly complicated monologue about all the kinds of work he can no longer do, like retail—where he'd have to stand around all day—and construction and porn and pro athlete and so on.

…at least I only lost the leg, but my buddy lost his life.

Paul rolls up the short leg of his pants, undoes his fake leg, and shows him the stump. Melvin rubs his hands over the scar tissue at the end. Melvin's dick is hard, like the hardest it's ever been. Whew, dizzy. He wonders what it would taste like, because the stump looks like it would taste like something really meaningful. Like the stump's taste would reveal aspects of the universe that he never suspected were crucial to its ongoing evolution. It's like the universe has evolved the leg, with its boring and obvious functions, into something that seems useless and not adaptive, but that is actually the prototype for a new, sexier body part.

I'm totally straight, but if you forced me to do something, Melvin says. Maybe with, you know. Your stump.

Did he really just say that? Paul just pretends he didn't hear or understand. He stiffens and leans backward, a sort of rejection, but he doesn't budge the stump that Melvin's fondling.

Question: Is love not even the point?

Jared: I've loved you since sixth grade, so probably not.

Paul's retreat from Melvin's words makes Melvin even hornier, dizzier, like all of this stuff in his head—all of this language, including Jared's voice—is a kind of false cloud that his brain secretes. He wants to get down on his knees before Paul, who he dislikes and finds ridiculous, with his corny ideas about how to be male, at the same time it's clear to him that Paul's a liar.

Even the idea of Paul's dead buddy is suspect. The idea of "buddies" in general. Culture is made of fronts. That's what culture is, he suspects: fake surfaces that pretend there's something underneath that isn't fake. Thinking of the rape of his own ass as "anal pleasure," however, allows Melvin to ignore all of the complicated and increasingly tiresome ideas of dominance, submission, alpha, beta, blah blah blah, in favor of the more basic concept of the nerve endings in his ass and their stimulation.

In fact, what if most of what he thinks about is just a kind of elaborate game orchestrated by his anal nerve endings to make it "okay."

Paul leans back into him, moving his lips like he's going to say something elaborate and sexual, and whispers right into his ear.

...see, there's two numbers. One you can listen to a twenty-four hour tape-recorded message. The other one is me, so that I can refer you.

Melvin needs a force and a will external to his own because he can't admit that his own asshole is more willful than his brain. What if what he tries *not* to think about is the engine or you could say the point of all his thoughts. Thoughts and culture are worthless and fake. Chalk lines around a dead body, but he can't remember when he had this thought before. The evolution of that concept in his own brain feels incredibly complex, becoming even more so, as if a kind of hologram that's understanding the cosmos is beginning to form itself right here and now, in Melvin's brain...But no, that isn't it—if they're pointing at what's not there or not being talked about...

...kind of dead in this place, Paul tells him.

The crowd has thinned out, it's true, and clustered into threesomes and foursomes that seem corporate and savvy. Savvy about things that aren't even slightly interesting. Money, dating, efficient ways to have fun. Being a little bit drunk is kind of like a contact high with something trembling and alive. Or the stump is like a hallucinogen. It's turned Melvin into an X-rated cartoon character with an empty speech balloon over his head. Melvin considers the evolution of anal pleasure.

Orangutans, rhesus monkeys, and bonobos have anal sex. Bonobos sometimes with red-tail monkeys. Orangutans with crab-eating macaques. Interspecies male-male buttfucking is more common than you would think. People do it with dogs and horses and sheep and probably with other species that haven't made it to video yet. Sex isn't just about reproduction or dominance but could also serve to strengthen social ties and alliance within the group. Feels good, why not? Evolution finds multiple uses for whatever. Example: the tongue, which is used for both tasting food and pronouncing words.

He finishes his third beer and cares even less.

Licking a pussy or an ice cream cone, both perfectly legitimate uses for the tongue, with all the evolutionary advantages that come from delicious nutrition and pleasing girls.

Melvin has always been a good-natured drunk, a funny and loving drunk, hasn't he? The sort of drunk that people like to take advantage of.

He has an idea for a future life form.

I'm not gay, Paul says.

Me either.

Words are used to mean their opposite, or not their opposite, but to sneak the possibility of doing something into the conversation. But it turns out Paul doesn't get what Melvin needs.

I'm not going to suck your dick just because you have a pretty face, Paul says. I'd have to have a whole lot of beers more for that.

Now *Melvin* stiffens, even though he doesn't stop touching the stump. Take that.

Why not get rid of the language centers in the brain, how about, pare down consciousness so that we've got just an orifice without self-consciousness but with about one hundred times more nerve endings. Pure fuck-joy into eternity. A kind of globe of flesh to house the orifice or even, maybe, more than one hole. No arms, legs, eyeballs, nada. It might even lack consciousness of death. Actually, without a brain, maybe it doesn't need to die at all.

But sight and sound and smell are related to sexual pleasure, so maybe we could retain the sense organs. He takes a deep breath, intoxicating himself with the smell of Paul that he's just sure is overwhelming him. Mmmmm.

How is the orifice going to find its mates if it can't get around? It needs to find something else that will prod it repeatedly. Self-prodding? Too narcissistic.

It can send out chemical signals or noises to attract the firm prodding members. But then how would it escape from predators? The orifice doesn't want to be eaten.

Okay, legs, what the hell, even arms. A voice. But no language, absolutely not. It just doesn't need to think so much. It can just *be*. It can just be getting *fucked*.

Melvin wonders if some of his pleasure is related to the way he thinks. It isn't just body-body. For example, Paul's rejection of him; the idea of Paul as a liar; the idea of a forceful event beyond language; the idea of himself as a bitch and helpless; words like rape, force, fuck, use, tool, stump. What if part of the pleasure comes from language and what if another part of the pleasure comes from the way that getting raped in the ass quiets the brain. If the brain is already quiet, there's not enough contrast.

So give it a brain, give it the words.

With the realization that his wandering orifice has evolved into a human being—and not just any human being, but himself—Melvin abandons that angle and gets back to work caressing the stump.

The $12,000 car is like brand new, it's a 2006, Paul is saying.

The stump is so much sexier than the person it's attached to. The stump is like a genius or designed by a genius so that some residual intelligence and cosmic perfection radiates from it, while the guy at the other end just blabs on about the residuals and how his mother didn't love him enough. Time is getting sloppy. Paul starts talking about "over there," which must be Iraq.

Melvin dated a girl when he was sixteen who made up a fake screen name and befriended him on the web as a boy who amazingly had all the same interests as he did. For a minute Melvin thought he'd found his best friend, but she was just using the facts she knew to try to catch him at something. Eventually she called him out for telling a lie—not to her, but to the friend she was pretending to be. It was like: If you'd lie to him, your good friend, how can I trust you? Freaky girl!

Not only is Paul not a rapist, they aren't compatible at all. He just likes to talk about himself. The little bits of code Paul lets out suggest that he's an oral bottom. Humiliated as a kid and a little bit nostalgic. And the harder he tries to prove it, the more it's obvious he's never been to Iraq. His stories are getting blurry and there's a hell of a lot more talk about farm implements than hand grenades. Paul starts weaving about and draping himself across strangers. With the realization that he won't be getting raped, it occurs to Melvin that maybe he's in big trouble.

Jared: Just because you aren't capable of love, it doesn't mean nobody else is.

True. But where's the evidence either way? Love exists or it doesn't.

Jared: You're fucking up your little brother's life with your kidnapping and your homophobia and everything else. You're reliving your own trauma through DJ. You obviously hate your own mother because she rejected you to marry Denny. You're in big trouble, buster.

It's not like he hadn't thought about that before. He'd even kind of, you know, planned for that possibility in some fuzzy way in his brain, but why does he have imaginary conversations in his head with Jared, of all people, whenever he starts to feel like he's done something wrong? Paul leans on Melvin now and "mistakenly" rubs against his crotch. Probably Paul just told Freddy some bullshit so he'd have a place to stay. Melvin can relate, but at some point it's gotta start fucking with your head. Paul turns away, starts going on to some stranger about some job he used to have at a shoe store. Melvin could play a soldier more convincingly than this guy.

3

IF FREDDY AND HIS TWIN aren't identical, they're just close enough to be freaky. Freaky, like actors capable of playing each other, body doubles who'd perform each other's nude scenes or dangerous stunts. Freaky in that their entire personalities then seem like costumes. Even freakier because they are "discordant" for sexual preference, as Franz Kallman would have said.

Freddy's twin looks like a reticent, bearded, heterosexual Freddy.

Franz Kallman was one of many evil scientists obsessed with homosexual twins. A scientist in the Nazi eugenics program in the '30s, Kallman studied under a certain Dr. Rüdin, coauthor of the 1933 Nazi sterilization law and author of *On the Role of Homosexuals in the Life Process of the Race.* According to Rüdin, that role was precisely zero. Kallman, a German Jew, fled Germany in 1936 and came to America. After the war, he began experimenting on twins.

In gay twin studies in the '50s, the straight one usually won at tennis, and considered the faggy one to be Mom's favorite, although they would grow up to be indistinguishable in photos, "strikingly similar, freckled young men" but "differing mildly in hairstyle (the homosexual's hairstyle is closer to a pompadour, while the heterosexual's is a kind of crew cut)." The homosexual twin couldn't stand to be alone in a room; he'd think there was something in the room he couldn't see, and just before puberty struck, he'd walk in his sleep. Wandering naked from room to room, dreaming. The straight would prefer jazz, snooker, darts, and motor bikes, while the queer would like classical music, pewter work, sewing, and cooking. Who did Mom love best? Who was weaker and sicker, moodier, and more depressed? Who was more cuddly, who was more naughty?

Although Freddy's twin has just as many books as Freddy, his apartment feels spare, emptied, pared down to the essentials. The twin pays Philip immediately and then scrutinizes the bag while Philip scans the numerous bookshelves in vain for some clue that these are the shelves of the Kathy Acker–torturing poetic genius of legend. DJ gets shy, clings to Philip's leg. Philip doesn't see a single book he's ever read.

So are you a writer, too? Philip asks. Freddy's twin shrugs.

Not anymore, he says. I'm a reader, really.

A far nobler pursuit, says Philip. Somebody has to be *listening*.

The twin just gazes at him.

I write only because I lack the moral sense to restrain myself, says Philip. You read poetry? Fiction?

Poetry, biography, history, some fiction, anthropology, says the twin, waving his hand at the shelves. Philip takes that as an invitation to continue his investigation more conspicuously. He finds only male poets and biographies of people he's never heard of. The men in these biographies have names suggestive of invention and industry, and the women have names suggestive of literary salons completely untainted with occult associations.

His walls, however, are covered with African masks.

The twin starts going on about some ancient culture. His sentences are so unadorned and seemingly fact-based that it takes a minute for Philip to realize that he's making a case for massive human sacrifice as an ecologically sustainable project. In times of drought, they simply couldn't feed all the people.

That reminds me of something the writer Kathy Acker once told me, says Philip.

The twin doesn't even register the remark as Philip makes up a Kathy Acker quote. Could Freddy's twin have forgotten this dead woman he so cavalierly tortured once upon a time? Philip thinks that if this twin was to shave off his beard, he could never convincingly argue for mass slaughter. It isn't that Freddy wouldn't take a similar position, but it would be ironic, pessimistic, unencumbered by moral posturing.

DJ lets go of Philip and slowly creeps toward the nearest wall, where a particularly hairy mask is glowering at them all.

The twin is standing with his arms folded now, as if their business is over and he's just politely waiting for Philip and the strange gay child to leave. His beard and his vaguely paternal joylessness bring up Philip's issues. Philip isn't especially interested in his own issues, but he knows he sometimes reacts irrationally in the presence of patriarchs. Philip would like to prove to this man that everything he esteems is revolting.

Can I ask you something?

Yes?

Do you know Huey Beauregard? He's a friend of your brother's.

The twin snorts, but not in a dismissive way.

Huey Beauregard, he says. Yes I do. Why do you ask?

I've discovered that Huey may not be exactly who he claims to be, Philip says. I'm concerned about Freddy, about how Freddy will deal with it.

DJ has stopped his slow crawl. The mask is a black disk that if you look at it long enough seems to be spinning.

How did you meet Huey? Philip asks. Your brother introduced you?

Huey contacted me. I replied.

A fan of your work?

He, too, was concerned about Freddy, the twin says.

Philip can't tell exactly how barbed this comment is.

He called you to talk about Freddy.

He imagined that my relationship with Freddy was causing my brother pain, the twin says. He imagined that we might be brought together, that he might be the catalyst for our rapprochement. This was some years ago already. Freddy and I live 2.9 miles away from each other, and yet I haven't seen my brother in person since 1994 when we happened to attend the same funeral, our father's. When we lost each other, long long ago, it simplified both of our lives significantly. We do, however, sometimes have occasion to speak by phone.

Like when you need weed.

Actually, that wasn't the primary business of our recent conversation, the twin says, but I mentioned my predicament and Freddy suggested you. He spoke highly of your product, your discretion and, believe it or not, your approach to the novel.

Philip can't quite believe it, actually.

So Huey's efforts were fruitless, Philip says. He was not the catalyst of your rapprochement.

He was not.

I spoke to Huey only a few times, the twin says. Once he figured out that the so-called "problem" of my relationship with my brother was far too complex for his own machinations, he apparently lost interest.

And you? Were you interested in Huey?

He drew me in, says the twin. He was skilled at making himself interesting, and yet I always had the impression that he was fishing for something, that he thought I might be useful. Whatever his needs are, however, they seem to be as vast and elaborate as my relationship with Freddy. I would be surprised, actually, if Huey was precisely who he claims to be.

Yeah, well, precisely, he's a forty-year-old woman named Sarah Cohen.

Interesting, says the twin.

But not surprising.

Surprising, yes. Not shocking.

DJ is still halted in perplexity at the brink of a dangerous abyss. He is whispering to the black disk. The ABCs are going to murder somebody, maybe his brother, because the ABCs are under a spell cast by the magic of fucking. No bad words, DJ says.

Philip says, I'm sorry, DJ, did I say something bad?

No, Mr. Philip, says DJ. It was somebody else.

The twin moves toward the door, signaling that the conversation is over.

I hear my brother's up for a MacArthur, the twin says. I guess the epic poem he's working on is being well received in all the right places.

He didn't mention it, says Philip. He seemed a little…stressed, to be honest. Not in the best shape.

The twin's face is impassive. He should apply for a Lannan-Jackson while he's at it, Philip says.

Freddy's twin laughs out loud.

To get a Lannan-Jackson you have to write about father-son bonding, says Freddy's twin. The poems are always full of men chopping wood and the smell of wood smoke.

DJ hurries over and takes Philip's hand, as if frightened he'll be left behind.

Wish my brother luck the next time you see him, says the twin.

After the door closes behind him, the noise of the deadbolt clicking into place, Philip stands in the hall for a minute, dumbfounded. *The poems are always full of men chopping wood and the smell of wood smoke.* What if Freddy's twin isn't heterosexual at all? What if his heart is a wandering flower? *Listen to the words of a dream.* What if nothing he's believed is actually true?

4

ROCKIN REBECCA'S MEMORIAL SERVICE is held at the mostly gay nondenominational church in the Castro. Felicia buys a copy of Rebecca's novelette and then stands in the back, by the snack table, watching to see if Sarah will show up. Hard, unripened, dark red strawberries surrounded by equally stone-like cantaloupe slices and then a tray of cheese and crackers. Probably the body was sent back to the Midwest, where Rebecca's Methodist minister father will bury her. This likelihood is suggested by the bio on the back of the novelette. There's a synopsis on the last page: It's an "enlightening, provocative, sexy and exciting look at the lives of exotic dancers." It involves money laundering, the Russian mob, angel entrance exams, abused women on killing sprees, the DEA, the premature release of lesbian killers from mental institutions. Eventually the gang of eight strippers discovers that what they are up against is antichrist incarnate, who has teamed up with the CIA to create a deadly strain of heroin. "At the climax, the girls suit up for the most deadly bachelor party they've ever attended."

It sounds like a Huey Beauregard plot, but with more concrete detail. Maybe Rebecca wrote the actual books and Sarah killed her because she knew too much. The bio mentions that Rebecca witnessed one of her strip club bosses get shot to death in the early '90s and that she has "chronicles of crazy stories that I draw from to create my fictional ones." After several tragedies "more specifically near-death experiences," she decided to more actively pursue fiction writing. The cover copy, written shortly before her "suicide," says she's currently working on the sequel.

The memorial service lasts over an hour. A video is shown of one of Rebecca's strip routines. The song "Rock Me Amadeus" is played. Several speakers tell stories of Rebecca's kindness, her innovative dancing, and the profound effect of her creative vision on the local S&M community. Several women and one man start sobbing while they speak.

The only time Felicia can remember her mother crying is when she was kneeling in a dark room in front of the television. Some soap opera or melodrama. Her mother didn't admit that she watched television; she would turn it on, just for some *background noise* while she cleaned up or cooked dinner. But then you would find her getting pulled in, closer and closer. Standing in the doorway to the TV room with her hand on her hip. Halfway between the doorway and the television, hunched over just slightly. Finally she'd be there on her knees, two or three feet away from the screen, tears running down her face in the dark.

Sarah doesn't show. "Rock Me Amadeus" is played again, and this time Felicia starts choking up. She steps outside and dials Mark Sassatelli's number.

He answers before the second ring.

Geordi is at home still, complicating his chart. He's looking at the evolution of verb forms. He's comparing forms through time.

Hours pass or maybe no time at all.

He can see this particular verb form mutating over hundreds of years, actually morphing before his eyes. The landline rings, probably Felicia, but he lets the machine get it, in case it's his mother. There's a pause and a strange crackling noise. It sounds as if machines are clicking into gear, transferring messages within an elaborate computerized grid.

Hello, Felicia, a voice says then. This is Huey Beauregard. Ah think we need to talk.

A pause during which something is squeaking, while a structure seems to be quietly and slowly crumbling into a fine powder in the background.

Ah emailed you the number to call. Ah'll be waitin for ya ta ring me.

The house is empty. Children shrieking in the neighboring complex. Is this it for Geordi? Is he going to die in this house?

He imagines himself screaming. He says it to himself: I'm going to scream.

He's going to break down; he's breaking down.

Geordi, Geordi, Geordi.

Why? What for? That voice has unleashed some horror. Or it's made the existence of a preexisting horror obvious. But maybe he's being overwrought. It's as though he has become two men at the same time, the sane Geordi, with a wife and a house and a thesis, and the lucid Geordi, who understands that his wife is barely here, a passenger he's settled in next to on a doomed plane ride, the house is a nifty little coffin with period details, and the thesis a flimsy excuse to search for the vibrating core of meaninglessness it'll be impossible to bear.

Two men: the crazy Geordi, who is locking up the house and rushing out to the street, and the deluded Geordi, who is happy to just sit there diagramming the evolution of verb forms.

He walks up to Shattuck and then down the broad avenue toward the downtown. Walking is good. You see nothing from a car. On foot you can really take stock of this thing, the material world, which it seems that Geordi has lost track of. What's it turned into, while he was busy with his thesis? What is actually *in* the world?

Rush hour is just beginning—it's getting dark. Cars rushing past, on their way somewhere, anywhere, many many cars. This is what people do; they drive cars. He walks past the Hungarian bakery, where a Mexican woman is mopping the floor. After that is a long fence with an ugly apartment thing behind it. A car lot. He walks past a fire station and an assisted living facility and another car lot. He walks past a furniture outlet, with the cheapest and ugliest furniture now actually out front on the sidewalk, as if it's spreading out from within, conquering the physical world. An acupuncture college, an appliance store, a fabric shop, a barber shop. This is what people do: They buy and sell furniture and appliances and fabric, they get their hair cut. And this, it seems, is enough. He walks past a chiropractor and a Mexican restaurant and Radio Shack and musical instruments, a Thai restaurant, a laundry, a chain selling picture frames certainly assembled in China or Haiti, and then he's standing in front of the Dollar Tree Store again. The front windows are full of Valentine's Day merchandise, way too early. Sad-looking roses and heart-shaped balloons. Some seem to be frogs, some monkeys. "I LOVE YOU!" "Everything is one dollar!" The Dollar Tree Store claims to sell fresh meat as well. "Wow! Item of the Week. Hardcover Book. Hurry! While Supplies Last!" In the picture on the poster is a stack of books by people Geordi's never heard of, except for Neil Gaiman. He steps into the store and the Hardcover Book Display is right there next to the cashiers. There are mysteries involving murderous faculty, history books by formerly disgraced Republican congressmen, memoirs by the mistreated spouses of halfway famous people. One copy of a dog-training book.

Mark Sassatelli doesn't remember Huey Beauregard's name, but he remembers Sarah Cohen. He seems to be fascinated by Sarah, in fact, although he hasn't seen her in many years. She was very charismatic, he keeps saying, very persuasive. He just loves to talk about Sarah.

Did you have a relationship of some sort with her?

Of some sort, he says.

A sexual relationship?

Not technically, he says.

He describes her as very artistic, very interesting, and very mysterious.

And persuasive, says Felicia. What did she persuade you to do?

Listen to what I'm going to tell you, Mark says. You shouldn't ever shy away from danger. This is what I learned from Sarah, during the time we spent together.

She was into risk-taking? She talked you into risky behavior?

For some reason he begins talking about the Korean gray hamster, which he describes as enormous and rat-like and, when standing on its hind legs, easy to mistake for a tiny person or a monkey. They live on the edges of human societies, emerging from complex burrows underground to steal what they can.

Sometimes the self just wanders, says Mark. Your thoughts and feelings just flow on and on, going nowhere, filling everything up with themselves. It doesn't matter what costumes you try on. There's no way—it isn't possible—to lose your own essential nature. It isn't possible. You're always yourself. You see what I'm saying?

Sarah taught you that, says Felicia. Are those the sorts of words she used?

She used so many different sorts of words, says Mark.

But Huey Beauregard used this number, says Felicia. He was a street kid, he was very close to Sarah. You sure you don't remember him?

Oh, right, says Mark. The Repo Man. I never actually met him.

Sarah used her *persuasive skills* to get Mark to let her use his voicemail system. People could leave messages for this kid, the Repo Man. They could leave messages on other lines for Sarah. Sarah was very good on the telephone. She was always doing different kinds of business, taking care of different kinds of business, always on the phone. She often spoke in different accents. A British accent, a Russian accent, a Swedish accent.

Did you ever hear her speaking in a Southern accent?

I can't remember. Maybe.

And why exactly was she talking in different voices? This was some kind of phone sex?

I think she was trying to purge herself of herself, says Mark. To purge herself of her own voice, her own language. She was trying to rid herself of her past, her childhood.

You seem to know Sarah very well.

I'm very sick, Mark tells her. But I believe I will soon be cured.

I'm sorry, says Felicia. I'm sorry, I'm just...a little confused. Sarah told you all of this?

I loved the stories she told and sometimes she wrote stories, too. Sarah made me believe that they would never end, that there would always be another chapter, and she would be there, telling me her stories.

These written stories. Do you remember any of the details?

They were very gritty, says Mark. There was a boy in one story, he was abandoned by his mother. At a Laundromat. It was so sad.

She showed you this story?

Yes, I read it, says Mark. She was taking a writing class. She wrote it for the class.

And she told you that she wrote it?

Of course she wrote it. It was so much *her* story. It was so *Sarah*.

Were you in love with her?

I wouldn't know.

Really? You wouldn't know. Are you still in love with her?

Our flow together eventually took on a different character. It was rather... terrifying, I guess you could say. And then I haven't seen her in a very long time.

Geordi walks on past a boarded-up business and past an Italian restaurant and past another car lot. A Blockbuster video store and more Thai, pizza, Staples business supplies. People eat and they purchase business supplies. They do business, they have business, they go about their business. This is what the world is. The UPS store and then a chain that sells used clothing, with windows full of headless mannequins dressed much more stylishly than Geordi. The headless women have necklaces. A light black jacket with flowered pants. A knitted cardigan over a sheer summery dress that shows off the headless mannequin's cleavage. A headless male mannequin has a T-shirt printed with an image of an elaborate ship, tucked into loose-fitting tan slacks. Another with tight reddish pants, a thin, squarish beige jacket, and a tie. Onward, into the downtown, past a CVS Pharmacy. An Indian place and a club with dancing and deejays and half-price drinks, the Shattuck Down Low. The United Artists Theater and then finally the beautiful green Art Deco Berkeley Central Library.

People read, apparently.

The bookstores are all way over across the wide avenue on the other side of the street. Some of them will soon be closing.

In the next block, yogurt and a Starbucks and the other theater, with the gutterpunks camped out in front with their clever spare change signs. And then Papa John's and a clock that doesn't tell the correct time and ice cream and Planet Juice and a video game store. And here he is in the plaza by the BART and he sits on a bench in front of a Site for Sore Eyes and a gelato store to rest.

It's bustling downtown. People stream in and out of the BART, they wait for buses, children ride past on skateboards. Wheelchairs roll along. They all seem insane, these people. Who are they? What do they do? Who pays them and for what? Some of them are students. Some of them might be his students, which is too terrifying to imagine.

The students are studying social sciences and engineering and biological sciences. Just a few are studying literature. The workers are computer specialists, professors, and managers, followed by scientists, lawyers, and media or communications workers, if they are men. Some engineers and office workers. A few mechanics and executives and business operations specialists. The women are managers and office workers, teachers and clerks and social workers. There are hardly any woodworkers or farmers or plumbers. Where do the plumbers live, if not in Berkeley? Why are there so many managers? Who are they managing?

We don't know how many sex workers and drug dealers there are. The largest employer in the city is supposedly the university, followed by the Lawrence Berkeley National Laboratory, the Alta Bates Medical Center, and the city of Berkeley itself. Bayer, the German chemical and pharmaceutical company, is next, and then more schools and hospitals and grocery stores.

But what exactly they do, what exactly they get paid to do, Geordi doesn't, for the most part, understand.

Some people don't have jobs and they are probably overrepresented in the downtown square. Killing time, low-cost entertainment. An oddly familiar mother type emerges from the eyeglasses chain, sporting oblong pink spectacles she has certainly just acquired. She looks directly at Geordi and then strides over in seconds.

Geordi, she says. How *are* you?

It's Urszula. It isn't just the new glasses. She's gained a little weight, which makes her seem calmer and more matronly. The glasses settle down her face a bit.

Geordi, she says. I have a question for you. I have been meaning to ask you this question. It is a little bit...how do you say? Delicate.

Geordi doesn't understand what she's saying. The word *delicate* only evokes that odd little boy. His face is as smooth and empty as an egg. It's a disaster waiting to happen.

I am looking for someone to marry my girlfriend, Urszula says.

Geordi says, But I'm already married.

Urszula knows that, she says. But Geordi maybe knows people. Geordi knows poets, gay people, people who need money. Not a lot of money, but some money. Urszula's girlfriend's visa has expired and there is no way she can go back to live in Poland now, not with the situation there. She cannot get a job at the university there, she cannot publish, it's ridiculous.

I'll ask around, Geordi says.

Urszula is just staring at him.

Is that why you took me on the picnic? Geordi asks.

Oh, Geordi, Urszula says. Don't be silly.

You think about it, she says. You let me know.

She doesn't leave.

How is your thesis? he asks.

It is always there, she says.

She shrugs.

A stream of people emerges from the underground. They carry shopping bags and backpacks. How do real people live?

You need a ride somewhere? Urszula asks. I can drop you off.

Real people, they do errands. They shop, they buy, they evaluate their purchases. They are happy when they think they got a good deal.

I still have some errands to run, Geordi says. But thank you.

5

Okay, this question is for you. What can you do when you realize you're not where you want to be?

For example, tigers once ranged widely across Asia: Turkey, Java, Siberia, Bali. But they've been eliminated from more than 90 percent of their historic range and there's maybe only 3,000 to 4,000 of them left in the wild. Just one hundred years ago, there were more like 100,000.

Fossils of tigers have been found from about 1.7 million years ago roaming the volcanic crust. Pretty soon, they'll only be in zoos.

Like Melvin, you know what a zoo is: an insane asylum for animals, animals you are driving insane. Melvin often dreams about tigers, although he's never seen one. In his dreams, there is nothing more electric and deadly. His dreams about tigers are usually dreams about his fear of death. He hasn't figured that out yet, but he will.

Once you separate life from death, existence from nonexistence, you've created a direction to travel and a distance to cross. This is time.

Time is a direction and a distance.

In time, you move from nonexistence to existence, and then back. It isn't far, your little journey. You can practically see the end just up ahead, can't you?

The clock is ticking. Yours, not mine. I'm *always* here, in my bed, in the forest or wherever. Always.

Do you believe me?

In any case, a new day: Melvin is in the basement of Philip and Raymond's house, with Ralph filming him. Melvin is earning some money. It isn't true that *time is money*. You can purchase another person's time with money and put him to work for you, but that's not exactly the same thing. For example, Melvin plays a pot farmer who gets stoned while tending his crop, making him so horny that he rips off his clothes and jacks off among the pot plants. *Stoner Boner*. Ralph gets bored with solo scenes, but they suit Melvin's talents.

Upstairs Melvin can hear his little brother singing some sort of nonsense song to himself. Upstairs, Felicia has left Huey a message from Philip and

Raymond's living room, and is awaiting his response. The phone rings and then a voice Melvin doesn't recognize is saying something that sounds like *a lame man dragging his hoof* and then somebody picks up. Holy shit! Melvin says and leaps to his feet. There was something moving, scurrying, over in the basement's dark corners. Ralph asks him what's going on. But Melvin's concentrating, listening, and trying to disentangle the threads.

A kind of whistling that might be the wind blowing through the cracks in the foundation of the old house. A dim muttering that might be Felicia's conversation. Underneath it a sort of silence that is too quiet. That is hiding a tiny cry for help, a cry of hunger or longing for mother. A mammalian need that is archaic and timeless. But maybe that's just the downward drifting traces of DJ's little song as he walks in some direction, farther and farther away.

Upstairs, Huey has returned Felicia's call. Geordi is sitting on the floor, bewildered. Felicia looks like she's being insulted or threatened, but then she laughs. Yes, Huey, you're right, she says.

Raymond is in the kitchen, working on strudel dough. It must be stretched until it is thin as parchment, until you can read through it. It's almost perfectly quiet, but for an occasional murmur from Felicia in the next room. That murmur has a tone similar to his father's poetry, he thinks. *I am rock dropped pond deep / upon the bottom of get-well quick* was one bit he liked and *Deep down, barnacle glutted pilot fish*, another Marianne Moore moment. Marianne Moore, Hart Crane, Gerard Manley Hopkins, his father's influences. Raymond appreciates the intricate off-rhythms of Marianne Moore, but Raymond never really *got* the Hart Crane thing. He could never understand those poems. Crane's mysterious disappearance into the Gulf of Mexico, on the other hand, is a kind of poem in itself, perhaps the exemplar of a twentieth-century poem. Its shameless confabulation of biography and legend and self-destruction. They are all dead now, all the old poets, the failures and the successful ones, too, buried or cremated or vanished under the waves, a suicide, we presume, lost at the bottom of the sea. All that remains, his father's *At noon, I am sand in the window glass of my abandoned house; tomorrow / pyrotechnics!* or Marianne Moore's *Though he is captive, / his mighty singing / says, satisfaction is a lowly / thing, how pure a thing is joy* or Hart Crane's *Insistently through sleep—a tide of voices— / They meet you listening midway in your dream.*

There's something exhausted about the murmur from Felicia in the next room, something failed, but lucid in its failure.

There's something so calming about it, Tony thinks. The presence of untruth in the middle of the afternoon. Felicia is wrestling with it, but there's nothing anyone can do to help her. The stars are not apparent. The whirring and clicking of the night sky, the oodles of collapsed ancient suns, supernovas and gas giants, the incomprehensible distances. In the nearer distance, wars and abominations. A dark cloud perhaps, choking some if not all of us. Nothing is visible of the grandeur circling this stage. A tiny stage, but a stage. Meaningless, a mere trifle. The only show in town.

Ralph emerges from the basement, unobtrusively flips open his video camera, and films Felicia. Her face, usually so dry, so reserved, has become a drama. Anguish then pleasure then confusion then relief then exasperation then something like fear. While that voice goes on and on and on. It never seems to stop.

It's a tangible darkness.

The tangle of language that Felicia has become enmeshed in, the breathy Southern accent relentlessly threatening, charming and cajoling her, a smoky vapor that keeps shifting out from underneath her, is somehow, despite the fact that Felicia is holding all the cards, the most frightening experience of her life. Why would that be? She is a rationalist after all, and doesn't believe that she's speaking to a demon or demon-possessed creature, doesn't believe that there's some dark energy in place, but only a strange, lonely woman who believes herself to be fat and who has, under whatever bizarre compulsion combined with simple greed and ambition, pretended to be an abused child for the past decade, speaking relentlessly in this same fake, breathy Southern accent. The voice wants to know where Felicia's coming from, if she's just jealous and motivated by cruelty and jealousy or if she has the characteristic so deeply important to Huey, *purity of intent*, like Dave Eggers, for example. Huey has one strict criteria for judging the presence of evil in the world, and that is if somebody speaks poorly of Dave Eggers, he knows that they are evil. Huey loves to stroll, secretly, in disguise of course, among the tutors and their charges, basking in the aura of benevolence and grace always emanating from 826 Valencia, because it does his heart a world of good to see such altruism in action, and maybe it would do Felicia's heart a world of good as well, giving something back. Huey wonders if Felicia aspires to selflessness and light, like Dave Eggers, or if maybe she has instead fallen under the sway of jealous writers like Benton Archer, who got angry when everywhere he went people wanted to ask him not about his own work, but about Huey's, and Benton couldn't handle it, he'd be reading from one of his many novels about the torture, murder, and rape of young boys and his audiences would just be like *Ho Hum* and during the Q and A they'd always say *but what about Huey, what's Huey really like, how did the earth spawn such a genius who could survive the most horrible circumstances and still write like an angel*, and although Huey believes that Benton once had purity of intent, whatever his critics may say about how he exploits children, how he's probably not the most reliable or truthful ally given his well known penchant for kiddie splatter porn, and although Huey knows him to be generous to a fault and a great influence, Benton lost himself, it seems to Huey, in the convoluted halls of his own petty ego. Huey hopes that Felicia isn't blinded by her own petty ego and its demands, he hopes that she can see the light of Huey's work, despite her own jealousy. Huey would like to know if Felicia does not truly love Huey's work, if Felicia was not deeply moved by Huey's books, as so many brilliant and like-minded souls have been deeply moved by the work, and he begins listing some of the people who are geniuses and who really *get* his work, an endless list of celebrities; from Madonna on down to the tall ex-junkie former girlfriend of grunge rock's most famous suicide; from the starlet and director daughter of the French horror auteur who'd been filming his daughter being murdered and raped since she was eight to the starlet and heavy metal groupie stepdaughter of the British fantasy auteur who divorced her mother and married his stepdaughter on her eighteenth birthday; from the cult film director of campy masterpieces starring obese drag queens and then big-budget extravaganzas that allow him to film all of Hollywood's most charming leading men in tea-bagging scenes on down to the art world darling photographer who became famous taking pictures of her pierced and tattooed and transgender friends who she then hired as servants once she'd made it to the top; from the Oscar-winning director who is rumored to have secretly married one or two of the biggest male stars in the business on down to the openly gay director whose art house success with films about junkies and hustlers propelled him on to doomed blockbusters starring those same male stars years after the Oscar-winning director had tossed them aside; from the depressed and obsessive-compulsive poet-wannabe lead singer of the post-grunge pop group that became famous for serially dating the tall ex-junkie former girlfriend of grunge rock's most famous suicide on down to the abused and manic-depressive poet-wannabe lead singer of the post-grunge pop group that became famous for performing in jock straps and goth makeup (although they weren't really goth at all, Huey adds, but a sort of inspirational *blend* of every successful style of music of the past twenty years); from the substance-abusing child star who turned her chaotic childhood of Academy Awards, orgies with hair dressers, and makeout sessions with nervous pedophile rock stars, and her young adulthood of crack arrests, poor career choices, and marriage to whiney tennis stars, into a best-selling autobiography on down to the substance-abusing star of a late '80s science fiction trilogy who turned her difficult post-trilogy life of drugs and poor career choices into a hit Broadway musical; from the *New York Times* best-selling memoirist who bravely abandoned the imprecise and showy realm of poetry to tell the gritty tale of her BB-gun-toting childhood in the shadow of East Texas oil refineries on down to the National Book Award-nominated former prostitute and masochist who turned her inverted contempt for *everything* into a compelling form of sexual satire; from the poet laureate of Carpinteria whose moving evocation of his difficult childhood in the shadow of his more famous older sibling, a child star who died in a tragic, freak boating accident in 1968, earned him a National Book Award nomination and made him the greater Santa Barbara area's best-selling poet *of all times* on down to the transgressive novelist whose love for tranny hookers was transformed into critically acclaimed if commercially unsuccessful novels about pre-Giuliani Times Square and earned him one of Belgium's most prestigious literary awards; from the Pulitzer Prize–winning memoirist whose tales of his abusive, alcoholic father stirred an entire movement of abused boy-children to come together and form an organization devoted to reclaiming their battered masculinity in the woods and deserts and other far-flung locales where they could pitch tents and build fires and just really truly express their wounded manhood on down to the unrecognized genius whose searingly honest tales of diaper fetishism had led him to a deep understanding of the wounded hearts, such as Huey's, that were struggling to illuminate the darkest corners of human existence with their brilliance; but maybe, Huey suggests, Felicia wasn't moved by Huey's work like all those stellar geniuses were, those wise souls who have, through the sheer force of their superior wills, thrust themselves onto the big stage, reached into the collective dream, and turned their own suffering into a kind of golden fluctuating energy field to inspire millions. Maybe Felicia is embittered, like the parents of those two substance-abusing stars who also bravely *spoke their truth* about their horrible childhoods, in the first case at the hands of the drug-addled star of several huge romantic comedies about rich lovers pretending to be poor and poor ones pretending to be rich, as well as a couple of Oscar-nominated melodramas about lovers dying of cancer or packing a particularly nasty tumor, and his first wife, most famous for her role as the folksy sheriff's girlfriend on a popular situation comedy from the '60s, and in the second case at the hands of one of Elizabeth Taylor's husbands and his first wife, the drug-addled star of several '50s musicals about nuns, mermaids, and car racing. Yes, maybe Felicia is embittered, too blinded by her own failures, which Huey knows all about, having looked her up on the Internet and found her remaindered books that nobody will even buy for a nickel on eBay. Huey has spoken to several people who seem to know Felicia personally, despite her phenomenal failure as a writer to capture anyone's imagination, because it seems to Huey she's been hovering around the edges of certain already marginal literary worlds just long enough that a few people have noticed her and know her to be seething with jealousy and resentment, embittered by her lack of success, but maybe they're wrong, Huey suggests, maybe she just hasn't yet found the way to let her light shine, the correct path, perhaps she does have *purity of intent* after all, and maybe she just needs to forget about her jealousy and resentments and *give*, to participate in the mutual succor of an artistic *community*, such as Huey's artistic community. The great pleasure for Huey, in becoming a master writer, has always been the mutual succor of other artists, a vast *community* he has formed with his readers, his thousands and thousands of loyal, moved, adoring readers, people who care about Huey, who would be so hurt by lies or trash talk about Huey, fans who are fed up with all the snarkiness, all the venom of popular culture, because let's face it, some of them aren't as enlightened as Huey is, Huey understands that identity is a fluid thing, Huey has always considered himself to be not an individual exactly, but a crossroads, an intermingling, yes, even a kind of *community* himself, and the books themselves are the result of input from so many different wise people, teachers, Saul Torstenson and Farrah Alexander and Mary Stringer and Brendan Pelt and Freddy Desmond and Sandra Holmes and Grover Bailey and Paul Chan Chuang Toledo Lin, the acclaimed author of the *New York Times* bestseller *Peking Man? Woman?* which meant a lot to Huey because of its examination of gender confusion from an Oriental perspective, and yes, Huey continues, even Benton Archer, despite Benton's jealousy and resentment, Huey will never speak ill of Benton, Benton did so much for him, taught him so much, it's just that *sometimes* when the student surpasses the teacher in artistic greatness, the teacher gets a little bit, understandably, muddled.

Huey, Felicia says. Do you know Rockin Rebecca?

You really get around, doncha? What kind of lies is Rebecca fillin up yer head with?

Not a single lie, says Felicia. She died several days ago. You didn't know?

The first time there has been silence on the line.

Ah'm sorry to hear that.

Another pause.

In any case, the dead are always still with us, Huey tells her.

In any case, Huey has always thought of himself as a sort of field of collective energies, a combination of all the energies of so many brilliant folks, and so anyway, what did Felicia think of Huey's work?

Felicia takes a deep breath.

She explains that the aspect of the work she found most interesting were those moments when exactly those issues of muddled identity were most highlighted. And so, for Felicia, the identity of the writer became a truly important subtext to the work, so that the fact that she believes she's speaking to a forty-year-old woman named Sarah Cohen she finds *fascinating*.

The creature on the other end launches another fusillade, in which it never actually denies what she is saying, and in fact almost seems to admit it, while reminding Felicia that there is a child involved, Trauma's child, a child that Huey considers to be his very own, a child who should in no way ever suffer for the way things have gone down, never be exposed and traumatized the way that Huey was exposed and traumatized so often as a child, and the vaporous words keep turning and shifting to the point that Felicia feels like there is a poisonous cloud of language choking her. The Southern accent, which has faded considerably during Huey's latter monologue, returns now with a vengeance. Ah would do most anything to protect my child, the creature says. So ah would request that you not take your decision on how to proceed lightly. An opossum that gets backed into a corner, she says, will let off a mighty powerful stink.

When, after two hours, Felicia manages to extricate herself and hang up the phone, Philip sees her visibly deflate. He takes her hand. She meets his eyes, but it's as if she doesn't really see anything. Come on, he says. And he leads her out, into the fresh air. They walk together in silence up Bernal Hill, into a grove of eucalyptus trees. I guess I get it now, she finally says. She says, It's like a shadow. It's like his words or her words or all the words are made of shadows.

Philip says, Well, sure.

It's like the earth is hopeless and doomed, he says.

It's like darkness has fallen upon it, she says.

He says, Glorious to behold.

6

My dear Felicia—

It was certainly great fun to hear that someone else knows the scoop on Huey Beauregard—however, as far as putting you in contact with Drew Malone, and further, soliciting from him the lurid details of the crimes his wife's god-daughters are perpetrating against literature, I must be explicit in my refus-al. Drew is a lifelong friend, who has been enduring a more than seasonal malaise. His constitution has been needlessly overtaxed by too many years ne-gotiating the *horror vacui* of our increasingly sociopathic artworld nexus, but Drew has no specially virulent *parti pris* against those women or their celebrity-worshipping parade—he views them as simply another gaudy carnival ride being hawked by particularly shrill barkers in the literary world's perennial geek show of vulgar mediocrities. Drew himself wrote two innovative story collections in the early '80s that were barely noticed in an increasingly myopic culture and quickly forgotten altogether as the literary world goose-stepped *avant* toward its current role as budget therapy for the guilt-addled bourgeois, and so he simply shares with me an entirely resigned nausea at the way literary personalities are manufactured in the era of Total Public Relations; I doubt if he could get any very satisfying thrill out of puncturing one particularly bloat-ed hot-air balloon that he happens to know about firsthand. I am not at all willing to put Drew, who is among other things a Buddhist and committed to abjuring this type of creative troublemaking, into the middle of an unpleasant *contretemps* with the untalented but relentless *femme fatales* he became entangled with through his own good manners as they pursued his attentions due to their unwavering belief, shared by so many of our media-saturated urchins, that literary fame can be achieved only with the collusion of some already estab-lished benefactor. They aren't wrong, of course. The current establishment for breeding authorial personae seems to have merged seamlessly with the culture of self-aggrandizement by-whatever-means-necessary in the lettristic matrices of postindustrial America. I'll admit I, too, would enjoy seeing this whole story splashed far and wide—not for any real literary reason, but only because one day when I phoned a friend who writes about fashion for the glossies to get Oliver Throckmorton's phone number, she was in the midst of a *tête-à-tête* with the elusive Huey, preparing for a huge spread, but phoned me back later to say that Huey was my biggest fan and insisted I attend a reading he was giving that evening at a place I forget the name of, but where, it turned out, there was a VIP room cordoned off as a way of asserting the majesty of Huey Beauregard, with the requisite five-hundred-pound darky standing behind the velvet rope, and where I was given a fair amount of difficult attitude and after finally being welcomed inside, found that my sister, who was up from Atlanta, was not being allowed in. Whereupon, over the shrill begging protests of Huey and some handler of his, my sister and I promptly exited the place, but not before I went up to anyone I recognized to announce that my BLACK SISTER had been excluded from the VIP room. The insane pretension of having a VIP room at a stupid little reading was, I suppose, merely hilarious, but not letting Alice inside when she was clearly with me wasn't funny at all, and from that moment Huey Beauregard ceased to exist for me altogether. He had not existed for me very much in the first place. Anyway, last year when Drew told me the story of the fat ghost writer and the sister she sends out in drag, it was with the understanding that I was free to repeat it, but only if I left him out of it as far as naming the source; telling you was a bit of a betrayal, actually, despite all the time that has passed, and I suppose I was carried away by the fact that I know this story to be true and almost no one I've ever told it to has believed me.

Drew is not a young man, he is in Iceland trying to recover from a host of chronic debilitating ailments, the last thing he needs is involvement in this kind of admittedly delicious scandal, and I promise you, even if I gave you his phone number, he wouldn't talk to you about any of this, so it's an entirely moot point—I am sorry that I'm unable to accommodate your request, but having long ago abandoned the practice of journalism in the conventional sense of confirming a story at all costs, I perhaps see this quite differently than you do. I would rather not alienate a friend by placing a reporter in his path, when that friend could vanish from the planet in a week or a month from now, after thirty years of pleasant and sustaining association, even if that means the fraud of Huey Beauregard continues its "transgressive" road show until, inevitably, all but a small deluded cadre lose interest in this bogus neuraesthenic and plagiarist. I don't mean to suggest that you are merely a journalist, only that you are operating as one in this situation and I learned long ago not to enter into complicity with anyone's journalistic enterprise. It invariably involves the betrayal of somebody, and while this is often useful for getting at the truth, it's not so useful in getting on with life with a good conscience. And though I still can relish the flavor of true, nasty gossip, the prospect doesn't really thrill me enough, either, to needlessly turn a lousy friend but reliable professional ally like Mary Stringer, a grudgingly supportive cunt like Saul Torstenson, or a seemingly harmless but vindictive and relentless monster like Brendan Pelt into bitter enemies. I don't hate Brendan, but he's too twined for me to much care what his inscription in the lives of his *poetes maudites* is; we did a panel together once and got along just great, and after that he was living in Hollywood for a while, and fell into a derangement of the senses with some child he was touting as the next Rimbaud, the boyfriend of some obscure Beat poet; well, Brendan was calling me constantly, informing me of his progress *vis-à-vis* the genius demon child and asking my advice. I just love it when people ask you to decipher the cryptic utterances of a teenager you've never met. This went on for the whole winter and into the spring, with yours truly asked to serve as translating priest to the ambitious teen's Delphic Oracle, but once Brendan finally "got" the boy in question (who, I heard later, he dumped within a few months for some constipated junkie who'd swaddle him in diapers in exchange for drug money), I never got another phone call from him—I mean never EVER got another call from him, which is why, during the many times I've been *en residence* in New York over the last ten years, I've never bothered to call Brendan on the phone.

Speaking of constipated junkies, Sylvester LeCarriere is a real piece of shit, in my estimation, and it wouldn't surprise me at all if he weren't in the Huey Beauregard story somewhere up to his ex-junkie eyeballs. You can take the junk out of the junkie but you can't take the junkie out of the junkie. I liked Sylvester a whole lot better when he was working the door at the Mudd Club than I ever did later on, tell you the truth. Talk about cold-blooded, the man hasn't got a single human gene, as far as I can tell. I will concede that Sylvester went to greater lengths than most publishers to promote my books and those of people like Monique, and I will always have to thank him for that, but the truth is that he was so slavishly devoted to Mary Stringer and Saul Torstenson and so privileged to buy into their own absurdly exalted idea of themselves that it was also, always, clear that he considered them "real" writers whereas his other authors were sort of, I dunno, SECONDARY. Secondary as I was, he arranged my tour with Mary Stringer at St. Martin's because I was far better known than Mary at the time and he knew his funny valentine would get infinitely more mileage out of touring with me than I would ever get from touring with her. All the same,

Mary and I did get along perfectly well, and I shouldn't put her down, if I were that abject over skanky sadistic drug addicts, I suppose I would treat my friends like shit all the time, too…

Funny you should mention Farrah: She's the person who "got me into" Huey's VIP room, and then told me there were too many people in there to let my sister in. The actual encounter with Huey was so creepy I wanted to get out of there anyway—such an obvious, obvious phony. Farrah is one of the most delusional and fame-hungry creatures I've ever run across and it wasn't much of a surprise that she was rubbing up against the legendary Huey Beauregard for good luck—I mean that metaphorically, as nobody was allowed to touch the little saint. If I blame anybody for this phenomenon, however, it's Cameron East, whom I've known since before the Oscar nominations and mega-million-dollar blockbusters, when he was peddling his little art house debut about horny street children at film festivals. I got him a producer and I introduced him to just about everybody who helped him out; years later, when I didn't know how to get in touch with Crispin Glover (with whom I'd appeared in several films, and whom I'd known since practically childhood, lived next to in Venice, etc.), I phoned Cameron for the number, and Cameron said, "Gee, I used to have it…" and I said, "Listen, you asshole, I introduced you to Crispin Glover, so go get the fucking number and stop playing me like I'm one of your suck-off sponges," and to my surprise, he obediently went and got the number. What I find lowering and *déclassé* about all these shabby publishing shenanigans is that they're invariably pulled on behalf of second- and third-rate people who, admittedly, are far likelier to find a constituency among a generation that has never read a book before glomming on to someone like Huey Beauregard, a generation that will never realize how thoroughly somebody else's work has been ineptly looted to throw some shitty piece of ephemeral fashion pablum together. What I'd like to be quoted saying is that the only convincing parts of Huey Beauregard's work were stolen from Eileen Myles, which I noticed right away. Tomorrow morning, by the way, I am supposed to go to a 10 a.m. screening for purposes of reviewing the film that's been made of Lawrence Kingdon Rush's tidy little horror of a novel, followed by the Technicolor version of AJ Weeks's *Dangerous Neighborhoods*, a grotesque parade of atrocious novels inappropriately splashed across the big screen, and all before lunchtime. *Dangerous Neighborhoods* must be the most misleading title anyone's come up with in years; the psychological dangers of growing up in wealthy Connecticut suburbs may be acute, but having grown up on a street where any unescorted child under the age of thirty was frequently assaulted by much more life-threatening circumstances than a frigid mother, I'd appreciate the title's irony a bit more, I suppose, if AJ hadn't played the role of poverty-stricken waif every time I met her, constantly whining that she had to take out student loans to complete her education at Yale, and if I didn't know that AJ pays her PR firm $16,000 a year to keep her name in the papers, with all the other allegedly famous people who shell out their trust funds to public relations firms out of panic and terror that they won't have their monstrosity pictured on the back page of *Interview* or some other monthly fishwrap on a regular basis.

Forgive me for bitching at random but I have come in for a great deal of unmerited animosity and malice from the so-called literary world for years, and for years, believe me, I ignored the explicit insult in being introduced, for example, by the author of *It's All Good*, at a political fund-raising event before the last election, as someone wrapped in a cloak of invisibility, as a writer *no one has ever seen*, which he claimed had been said to him by his voluminous mentor, Lana Myron, who was wearing some kind of outfit that seemed to have come from an airplane hangar. It was puffed up to make her look twice her actual size and seemed to get larger as she got to the podium to do her little tit-tup, as if it was specially designed to suck all of the oxygen out of that room, packed as it was with wheezing literary types, in order to inflate her own presence. No small feat in the midst of that crowd of allegedly famous people, rigorously pursuing their grants, promotions, and accolades by projecting their bland, pleasant personalities into every dark crevice and making goo-goo eyes at each other, hoping for some small crumb of glamour to accrue. Lana announced to this capacity crowd of Manhattanites, who had all met me many times, that *we have all been so inspired by Lawrence*. Ironically, I had no idea that this Lawrence asshole had even ever written a book—I thought he was merely another well-meaning and terminally disorganized member of Writers Against the War, the sponsor of this event, so I did not connect him with this ubiquitous decoration found beside bookstore cash registers for a period of several months, a book with a cover so implausibly ugly I couldn't imagine anyone buying it much less reading it. Well, I have had to dip into Lawrence Kingdon Rush in preparation for this screening—I've almost never in my life written anything simply to pay someone back for offending me, but unless this film turns out to be one of those Hollywood rescues of a lousy novel, I plan on tossing a little terror into LKR's existence when I review the thing. I mean he actually said, reading directly from the small bio note I'd been asked to provide, that I wrote for "a blog," as if every literate person in the room didn't know that the *Book Salon Book Review* had become the best weekly review in the country, and that Lawrence Kingdon Rush would have sucked off a plastic Santa Claus to have the regular reviewing job Tim Bloomberg provided me with there. Here is another unnecessary packet of forensic evidence demonstrating the cause of death for the corpse that is literary life in our era—*It's All Good* is a book you only need to read one page of to realize it was written to pander to the senescent generation of literati who've made careers pretending that profundity comes from shedding tears over the world's most celebrated horrors, which they have meanwhile transformed into kitsch. How this translates into the degeneration of literature into a branch of the self-help industry is fairly obvious. I have to say, the quotes on the front matter of *It's All Good*, which I bought last night and made the store clerk promise he would never tell anyone I'd acquired, had me in stitches: Just about every proper name (every "white male" proper name) that's made its reputation as a Voice for the Oppressed apparently bent over backward to hail this piece of shit not simply as a work of genius but the greatest story ever told.

In this connection, the event I mentioned by Writers Against the War was the kind of ghoul fest I always learn a lot from; it's the kind of snob event I avoid like the plague, and one of the reasons I don't live in New York, but I was doing a teaching gig at the New School that fall, and in this case, the organization had come to me asking if I'd write their auction catalog for free, because it's all about, you know, politics, and then when I saw the list of okay writers who'd been signed up for two programs of High-Class Readings that night and saw the name of a former intern of mine from the *Book Salon Book Review*, I promptly phoned Laura O'Malley, Tim's wife, who was doing publicity work for this thing, and told her if I was good enough to write their catalog I should fucking be good enough to be invited to read, something she instantly agreed with, as did Scott Ford, who put the readings together, and whom I honestly do believe would've asked me if his mind hadn't been elsewhere when he made the list, so I got folded into the program and gave the only reading in the first installment of this marathon that made anybody laugh, though certain others were turning themselves into pretzels to get just a giggle. In fact, I was immediately followed by Channing Wyeth, who read some earnest and delicate piece about daily life that to my horror sounded like a really, really bad impersonation of what I had just read. Well, guess which one of us gets the MacArthur Award. That's a little self-aggrandizing of me, so I apologize—what I'd started to say was that even though I hate those arriviste literary affairs, every once in a while I accept an invitation to one (I only that one time DEMANDED an invitation to one), just to observe the quotidian interactions of writers on the make, and in this connection, Channing Wyeth, I must say, provided a whole evening of mind-boggling entertainment—I have watched people kiss other people's asses, but I had never previously seen anyone do about fifteen in rapid succession—and, I realized, if I were the token Extremely Light Colored Negro *du jour* (I believe I was next in line for the title several years ago but was passed by in favor of another protégé of the voluminous Lana Byron) as Channing is the token Inoffensive and Funny Gay of the hour, I, too, might get away with brazenly hitting other people up for professorial recommendations, placement of stories in toney magazines, an intimate dinner in Harry's or somewhere else where we'd both be seen by everyone in the industry. Talk about it all being good! You get to a certain age and all of this becomes completely unimportant, or rather, as William Burroughs always used to tell me, *It's all just material,* but still, I think it's unfortunate that so many good writers we know aren't even allowed to have careers in this country, as they would in France or any other civilized culture; I don't mean "career" even in the sense of being famed or widely known but career in the sense of being able to make a living without having to get a teaching job, a newspaper or magazine job, or write screenplays. In France, even the most obscure writers have their complete works published in uniform editions and they stay in print for eternity, while here, since all the publishers are owned by movie studios and conglomerates, if you don't have a "big opening weekend," you've definitely flopped and can expect to find your book on the remainder table at Half Price Books.

And all of this is based on flimsy myth. Knopf even put "National Bestseller" across the top of that kid's novel *Delivery Boy,* I forget his name, he was Tristessa's nephew.

Well, I'm not saying anything you don't already know, I woke up on the living room floor surrounded by computer cables, and I suppose in order not to swallow a handful of klonopin and find my bed (**AND RISK MISSING THE SCREENING OF IT'S ALL GOOD!!!**), I thought it would be more fun to write to you. I did have great fun talking with you on the phone, and quite aside from that, it's always heartening to find out quickly that someone has a solid ethical sense, it being such a rare quality today. I myself am stupidly ethical enough that if this film turns out to be any good, I'll end up giving it a good review, even if every cell in my brain is crying out for revenge.

Best wishes,
Charles

7

THE CITY'S LEFT-LEANING FREE NEWSPAPER is located in a former industrial zone, now taken over by vast show houses filled with $3000 bidets. The conference room looks onto the backyard of a dingy apartment complex, where a young boy is attacking a bush with a plastic bat and cursing at it.

Something will break inside him or somewhere in space. He would like this.

Maybe it's just a trend, young humans decimating vegetation, taking out their anger on "nature." Can we still use that term without irony, I don't know.

Felicia's having a *déjà vu* regardless.

Felicia's meeting at *The Voice of Truth!* is with the editor, Kim Marconi; the arts editor, Landon Liu; and their star investigative journalist, BJ Lumpken, who's made his reputation writing about CIA torture planes. Kim and BJ are in agreement: Felicia just hasn't quite nailed it yet. The checks made out to Sarah's mother's corporation and to Connie's boyfriend Knute aren't enough. The copy store owner's identification of Knute as Huey Beauregard isn't enough. The story that Melinda told Suzie, Mark Sassatelli's report of Sarah speaking in strange accents and writing stories just like Huey's, the fake picture on the book cover, the boy who was asked to impersonate Huey in public already back in 2000, the fact that even their little girl is using a pseudonym, even Charles Scott's report, no good, she is told, unless she can find Melinda or get Charles Scott's old friend Drew Malone to go on the record.

Fine, she says, I can get more information. I've come this far after all.

But she has a bad feeling. It's something about the way Kim Marconi looks at her.

Down below, the vicious child has settled into a ritual pattern, eight whacks to the left, eight whacks to the right. Whack whack whack whack whack whack whack whack. Whack whack whack whack whack whack whack whack. In the midst of these magical alternations, he is granted access to his visions and dreams. Faces and architecture, for the most part.

I could stake out the house and identify the munchkin who plays Huey in public, Felicia says. I can keep searching for Melinda.

Great, says Kim. Just let me know how we can help. We're still behind you on this, 100 percent.

Landon Liu takes her aside, however, after the meeting.

You can do all of that, he says, but I'm afraid it won't matter. We were all pressing hard for the article—me and Zoe and Helena and Baby Ray. I don't know what's up with BJ, but…Apparently, Kim and the owner of the *Voice of Truth!*, Benny Henderson, are both good friends of Roland Warner.

It looks like Roland has used his influence to kill the story.

They'll string you along, Landon says, but almost certainly never publish the piece.

Huey Beauregard has won.

Ralph is pacing, talking into his tape recorder, like Joan Crawford in *Sudden Fear*. He's mapping out ideas for a new horror movie and having a dialogue with an imaginary critic, kind of like the dialogue between Jack Palance and Gloria Grahame that Joan's dictating machine would pick up as they plotted Joan's murder. Ralph sees the imaginary critic sometimes as the stern femme played by Jack Palance, sometimes as the cynical butch played by Gloria Grahame.

The campground restroom is a creepy little wooden shack full of spiders and occult graffiti, he says. Two stalls, with a hole in between, which has been plugged up with what seems like a combination of chewing gum and tissue.

That's ludicrous, says the imaginary critic. There's no glory holes in remote campsite restrooms.

The glory hole is really a hell mouth anyway, says Ralph.

There's a knock at the door.

Ralph's thinking about the scene in *Sudden Fear* in which Joan Crawford is hiding in the closet of the killer's apartment, and the closet door is cracked. The killer is out there and the little wind-up duck has been set in motion. The wind-up duck heads straight for the gap that leads into the darkness where Joan is hiding.

At the door, however, it's the police. Two of them: a stern femme and a cynical butch.

They have a warrant, and before he knows it, Ralph's been handcuffed, and they're reading him his rights. They're waving a postcard in his face, with some elves on it. They're demanding to know what he's done with Melvin and DJ. They start in with the good cop/bad cop routine.

The unemployed teacher who lives next door is watching from across the hall. People Ralph doesn't know have congregated by the stairway to see what's going on.

Darkness is Mind wrapped with restless Fire. Melvin's pretty sure about that one, at least. He suggests it as an opening voiceover booming into the darkness of the theater before the action begins. Tony lays out the most recent outline for his project across the kitchen table and jots Melvin's sentence in the margin. Melvin doesn't understand half of the squiggly lines and circles and arrows. Tony's original inspiration was to create a rock opera version of Philip K. Dick's *A Scanner Darkly*. But Hollywood long ago bought up the rights to everything that Dick ever wrote, he explains to Melvin. *Flow My Tears, the Policeman Said* would have been his second choice, but since he's intending the production to be an enormous success, there's no getting around the legal issues. Dick's creative property—like real estate, says Tony, shaking his head—is thoroughly owned, has been turned into a gated community—none of which will ever benefit the sad, dead man—but which must not either get in the way of Tony's vision. Of *our* vision, he corrects himself.

It remains only to take one of Dick's ideas, Tony says, and to modify it until it's unrecognizable, but maintaining the Dick spirit enough that his mad soul will still shine through. In Dick's novels people are always getting stuck in labyrinths composed of somebody else's subjectivity—somebody else's paranoia and trite obsessions—and that's the frame for Tony's opera. A space ship crashes, and because of some flaw in the collectively engineered state of suspended animation the crew has been kept in, in order to travel the light-years it would require to reach their destination, they find themselves imprisoned in the landscape of one crew member's unconscious. When they finally figure out how to escape, possibly by murdering the person whose mental landscape they're stuck inside—they only move on into another crew member's unconscious, a differently configured personal hell. In the opera there will be eight of them—a nice symmetrical figure for the opening dance number.

Tony thinks Melvin can be a huge star—this will be much bigger than Ralph's cute little crime movie. Melvin'll have to learn to sing and dance, but Tony's just the one to give him vocal lessons. Melvin just nods. No way. We'll try some sight-singing of Delibes, Tony says, and then you can repeat for me the tessitura and the chorus of the prelude of "The Flower Duet."

Maybe I could just be like an extra or something? Melvin suggests. A non-speaking part. Maybe naked.

Tony squints as if the vision is obscured but clarifying in the distance.

Rita Moreno! Tony says.

Melvin doesn't know who that is.

My god! says Tony. Emmy, Oscar, Tony, Grammy!

Tony's sure she'll want to be involved. She'll play the first crew member they get trapped inside, based on Tony's mother.

She's mad, you know, quite mad. My mother.

The trick will be to turn the stage into a suitably deformed and chilly landscape. Rita Moreno enthroned and creating her own chaotic forces—monsters with limitless appetites, bombers dressed in gowns, invasions of microscopic bugs, invisible armies of Nazi zombies that live beneath the sea—chaotic forces that she must endure, while ignoring everyone else around her, her own children, even as they are tortured and molested.

Everyone gets molested?

Usually, says Tony.

I'm not into torture.

The torture will be subtly conveyed through dance, Tony assures him.

The stage itself must become a labyrinth suggestive of Dick's search for meaning, filtered through his divorces, compulsive writing, séances, and suicide attempts. The pancreatitis and the burglaries. His mystical experience in February 1974 in which he realized that he was actually an early Christian being persecuted by the Romans. The beam of pink light that invaded his mind in March 1974, its benevolent voice competing over the next years with sometimes hostile voices from his radio that urged him to die.

Tony wonders, as an aside, if he has told Melvin about his own evil stepfather.

Tony's stepfather was a closeted cross-dresser. While Tony's mother was off at work during the afternoons, when Tony had just come home from school, he would masturbate in Tony's face. Over the years, Tony began to realize that during these scenes his stepfather would be wearing panties or a bra underneath his regular clothes or sometimes just some minor accessory of Tony's mother's, a scarf or a frilly blouse, or he'd be wearing just a dab of lipstick or of rouge.

Tony's stepfather reclined on the sofa in the living room, with *Hogan's Heroes* or *Gilligan's Island* playing on the TV and the sound turned up, the curtains drawn, although sometimes his stepfather would open the curtains just a little bit, which seemed to excite him even more, the danger of it perhaps, the idea of exposure, the idea of voyeurism and of hideous private scenes bleeding out into the neighborhood.

I was a beautiful and androgynous boy, Tony says, and so he hated me because, you know, he had his own issues.

DJ is playing with his remaining noodles, arranging them in geometrical
patterns.

Geometry, thinks Melvin. Should he know more about it? Melvin likes the
existence of geometry more than the specifics. He likes the word, not the discipline. When he tunes back into the conversation, Tony's talking about an
ex-boyfriend named Damien.

In the late '80s Damien ended up in Champaign, taking classes, dropping
out, and living with me, Tony says. I was in love with him, mad about him, but
in the beginning he withheld his affections. One night he didn't come home
and so I, of course, was a nervous wreck. He'd been arrested for disturbing the
peace and he finally called me and I went to the county jail and bailed him out.

He was filthy and fucked up, completely paranoid, Tony says. All he wanted
was a shower but he was afraid to go into the bathroom by himself, so we took
a shower together and I scrubbed him, because he was really just very dirty. We
gazed into each other's eyes for the longest time and it was then he told me how
beautiful I was and that I was his hero.

Nobody had ever said that to me before, says Tony, and I crumbled. I was
just so happy to be warm and loved. That's what turned out to be the essence of our relationship—I would save him and he'd tell me he loved me. But
Damien couldn't really love another human being, I would discover much later.
Only static from the radio.

One day we got stoned and drove to Indiana to visit Damien's brother Troy,
in the mental hospital, on our way to the Opera Barn for rehearsals, Tony says.
Troy had dealt with their unusual childhood even less well than Damien, to
put it mildly. We showed up, just like regular folks there to visit a relative, and
we went for a walk with Troy across the grounds, which were really quite drab.
Hedges and lawns and occasionally you'd happen on some lunatic just sitting
by himself behind a shrub. One of these people, however, engaged me in a
conversation about Jack Kerouac, who he thought was an underappreciated
genius, especially his early work and his late work, he told me, and he talked
about various philosophers he'd read. Oh, Nietzsche, Kierkegaard, the usual,
probably Hegel and Spinoza, probably Bergson and Alfred North Whitehead.
He was this kind of working-class philosopher, the type that can't get enough
of Nietzsche, even though Nietzsche was the sickest and most pathetic opera
queen of them all. His student in the crazy house, the working-class philosopher, would work in factories and sometimes sit in on classes at universities,

but he was opposed, he said, to the way that institutions dealt with knowledge. I wondered why he was in the asylum and he told me he'd checked himself in because he needed dental work done and he didn't have any sort of dental plan or insurance. He showed me his teeth and they were in fact quite rotten. If he spent a few weeks there, he told me, they'd work on his teeth and then he could check himself out whenever he wanted, since it was a state hospital and he'd committed himself. As long as he didn't get on the bad side of the doctors, he said, always a risk, because if they decided they hated you and wanted to punish you, they'd just sign a few papers and keep you there for good. Just as important, he said, was staying on the good side of the custodians and administrative personnel.

Meanwhile, Damien and Troy were having a private chat, which was mostly Troy talking about the vast conspiracy of evil he was enmeshed in.

It was going to be dinner soon, and we'd have to leave, Tony says.

Troy told us, and these were his exact words, that everyone there was being very mean and rude to him. If we hadn't have been so stoned, Tony says, I suppose we would have figured out that what he was describing was just, really, the basic fact of being in a mental hospital. We'd come to understand later why they were so mean to him, but at the time he made it sound so terribly sad and inappropriate and it just seemed so inhumane. So we kind of decided, more or less telepathically, to stage an escape. I mean it remained unspoken. I just pretended we needed something from the trunk, and the guard was right there watching, but then Troy jumped in the car and we sped away, with those awful hedges lining the road on either side.

We were totally freaked out at that point, Tony says. I'm talking major cop vibe. Kentucky was right there, across the Ohio River, so I suggested we should cross the state line. We took back roads, crisscrossing through fields and marshy areas with abandoned structures sticking up out of the water at places. In Kentucky we found a wooded area and stopped for some fresh air. But there was a family there or some kind of organization of adults and children that vaguely resembled a family, but that seemed somehow off, as if they were just impersonating a family, and they asked too many questions, the horrible little children. And so we didn't like them, and Troy complained how hungry he was, and we drove away. We had no cash. We'd been living on a gas credit card I got by forging my stepfather's signature. We ended up at a huge truck stop about one hundred miles down the road, where Troy ordered food nonstop and freak-vibed everyone in the restaurant. Troy had his little sex act down, where he played to anyone who would stare, which was everyone, always, because all he ever wore were leopard- or zebra-print spandex pants and a torn T-shirt off the shoulder. The waitress became overtly hostile and some of the other patrons began making suggestive or rude comments louder and louder, so we paid with the gas credit card and escaped into a strange night where we drove some more back roads and lost ourselves in the fog where the Ohio River runs into the Mississippi.

The next day we all showed up at the Opera Barn, back in Indiana, where I was to sing in *Madame Butterfly* and had also managed to get Damien a small part. We were to stay with a sixty-seven-year-old lady with dyed black hair and a house full of porcelain poodles. Her people were Eisenhower-lovers, you know, people who thrived on being *just folks*, travelers, and well-wishers. She was a good Christian woman and taking us in was a kind of Christian service—she thought she was working to save our souls just a bit. But Troy watched TV loudly all night in his leopard-print lycra and the next day the *grand dame* threw us out. But coming down the stairs shortly afterward, in a fit of rage, she broke her ankle. She later told me that the accident was God's punishment for being inhospitable.

No way, Melvin says, and Tony says, Yes, she wanted to make amends, but in the meantime we had nowhere to stay. That afternoon Brad showed up, my opera buddy from Champaign. He'd gotten me the gig and he was mortified at the presence of Troy and at our overly flamboyant self-presentation. But at rehearsal I sang like a god to purge my soul. The seventy-three-year-old lady playing Butterfly was so sweet—pink hair and so many wrinkles, with her husband always in tow. The poor little man never said a word. Her voice was wobbly in a kind of haunting way, like the voice of a child but strained through broken glass. I can still hear it.

The main characters in this story are all fags or old ladies, Tony says, the ruling class among opera types worldwide. And then there are these twelve teenage girls playing their parts in the extravagant pageant scene, and all the girls are squealing and freaked out about Troy, who's just constantly parading around in his sex-kittenish schizophrenic way, or circling the rehearsal like a crazed panther. And the girls' parents are there, too, none too happy, and the director of the whole Opera Barn scene is this eighty- or ninety-year-old matriarch who'd been doing this for thirty years. The orchestra is composed of skinny, sunburned high school students with their oboes and their clarinets. After the rehearsal, Brad shows us a place to camp. We smoke pot because everything just sucks. We smoke continually until the sun goes down, one of those incredibly beautiful and toxic sunsets of the modern era.

That was when Troy started coming on to Brad, Tony says. Brad ran around fluttering and waving his arms and declaring that he was not going to sleep with Troy and that this was all a travesty. Damien, driven insane with jealousy by this drama, began to chase Brad as well. With both brothers removing more and more of their clothes and following Brad around like lost puppies, I became despondent and ate all of the hot dogs. Brad, of course, was actually quite pleased.

Brad's at his worst in this story, I suppose, Tony says, although I'm not sure he ever gets better. His beautiful side did come out, however, when he got us to sing all those Beatles songs he loved so much and a few hymns. Troy was the ugliness, because he wasn't getting any sex or attention, and so nothing else mattered.

Brad locked himself inside his car that night because he said he was afraid of being corn-holed in his sleep. It must have been one hundred degrees that night and the sky was just this haze of humidity and the usual cloud that hangs over farm states. I used to think it was just the weather, but now of course, I realize that it's a toxic cloud composed of pesticide and fertilizer emissions and diesel fumes and it represents the layer of filth in our souls that separates us from the light of the stars. Brad actually did use that word, *corn-holed*. He was such a hick. To us he was merely beautiful at best, but he was fascinated by my voice and by Damien's body. Later, when we returned to Champaign, Damien and I both had sex with him.

But that night, with all of this free-floating lust forming its own little toxic haze over our camp circle, Damien kind of cold-shouldered me and passed out. I couldn't sleep. I heard Troy in my car and found him playing in the stage makeup. He'd made himself into a surreal female clown.

He came out of the car and kissed me. I got a hard-on immediately. Troy gave me a blow job and then we lay together in the backseat of the car. Before we fell asleep, he told me that he was different from other people. No kidding, I wanted to say. He said that he was a self-begotten, self-producing alien. To this day I have no idea what he was talking about. It's called schizophrenia, is what I was thinking. It's one of the possible results of being raised in a basement. I woke up early the next morning and quietly returned to my sleeping bag.

The next morning none of us spoke. We just quietly prepared ourselves and then drove to the rehearsal, Brad and Damien and I in Brad's car, with Troy still sleeping in mine.

Everyone was at the rehearsal, including the eighty-five- or ninety-year-old director and her Down syndrome daughter. The daughter was the real spirit of the opera. The rehearsal was frustrating—the twelve teenage girls kept missing their entrance and the director was losing her temper. Then Troy showed up, in lycra as usual, and planted himself next to the director and her daughter.

While the director was lecturing the little girls, Troy started coming on to the daughter, who began giggling hysterically.

The ninety- or maybe hundred-year-old director was trying to set the blocking for the opera, and Damien kept messing up his lines. Brad was cracking up and so the director interrupted everything to give us a speech about the need for dedication in the theater.

Just then the *grand dame* who'd kicked us out limped onto the scene. She had a large physical part in the production, that of Suzuki, Madame Butterfly's maid and confidante. Her broken ankle was news to the director and she just stared at the *grand dame* in stunned silence, the rest of us wallowing in our shame after her chastising speech. At that moment Troy calmly declared, *I've got Tony's cum in me.* This delighted the Down syndrome daughter, who turned the phrase into a mantra and danced around the production, repeating it over and over again. Everyone stared at me.

Damien was insanely jealous of his brother always being ogled in real time. But he said nothing. He said nothing for the entire four-hour drive back to Illinois with Troy in the backseat. He knew that I knew that he was holding everything back—it was a performance for my benefit.

That night he told Troy that Troy needed to get out. Troy would not go peacefully and so it turned into a fistfight between brothers. I sat and cried until Troy stomped off in a rage.

Where did he go? Not back to the mental institution, at least not immediately. Later, we would discover that he'd been to Florida and Nashville and New Mexico, although it was never possible to piece together the chronology, or to verify his stories. The parts about New Mexico seemed most vague, with his descriptions of the state sounding more like an alien landing pad or a hallucination based on Maya hieroglyphics. His stories about his time there resembled nothing more than a jumbled version of the plot of *Madame Butterfly.*

The actual performance at the Opera Barn was the next weekend and so Damien and I drove back through the muggy heat. Things were still tense between us. I'd watched him hold his private anger. He was showing me his strength, or maybe just his ideas about private and public space, and it wrecked him. Which is why we waited to make up at the Opera Barn in a celebration of the world, which is what opera is.

During the performance, Damien made a pathetic attempt to rise to his brother's heights by singing the line *May all be sons* as *May all be femmes.* Nobody noticed or at least nobody seemed to understand, except the hundred-and-whatever-year-old director, who was livid, of course.

To reward him, I led him out to the corn field during the "Un bel di" scene from the *Opera of the Night of Madame Butterfly*. A whole act where I had nothing to do. I was in a naval uniform and Damien was wearing a kimono and a large straw hat. The evening was perfect, a balmy eighty-two degrees, a little bit of heat fog and pickup trucks backed up around the Opera Barn like at a drive-in movie. Brad followed us out to the cornfield. Damien gave me a pouty look and ran away, but I chased him and caught him and kissed him passionately. Brad watched while Damien and I made love. He was always watching, he couldn't believe that we could act with such abandon.

Tony's story is interrupted by a knock at the door.

Two weeks after the performance, Tony tells Melvin as he gets up to answer the door, me and Brad and Damien left for California, making our way with the gas credit card. It wasn't so easy to eat out of convenience stores and truck stops—we couldn't eat just anything. Damien had been indoctrinated by his insane father with all of these very particular ideas about what foods were healthy and what foods were not. Later, Brad went on to become a great health fanatic himself, based on Damien's teachings.

At the door, it's just a canvasser raising money for some cause, although he looks more like a cop to Melvin than a political fund-raiser.

8

LEON'S APARTMENT IS NOTHING like Felicia pictured it. There are no mystical insignia, curtains embroidered with stars and moons, no candelabra, no crystal balls, no tinkly bells. The energy of the space is defined by the soothing indifference of the aquarium fish to any human life that isn't feeding them, and by the large-screen TV. A skinny woman named Thea with enormous teeth is reporting on a spa in Iceland where Hollywood types go to recover from their ailments. She speaks breathlessly of the magical rejuvenating properties of the sulfur baths, which have been intricately sketched, as no cameras are allowed inside the spa. No cameras, no phones, no computers, and certainly no reporters, which is why Thea is posed next to a volcano, with the front gate of the spa barely visible in the distance, waiting to catch a glimpse of one of the infamous patients coming or going.

Leon's had a bad time with Judge Judy, he tells her. He got picked for the television courts because of a dispute he had over a two-party check with a client for his psychic services. Hungry for the quirky and sensational, Judge Judy's people lied to him, misrepresented the show's judicial process, and left him defenseless in the face of Judge Judy's public humiliation. Judge Judy had no desire to get to the truth. The show was simply a setup for Judge Judy to berate whatever poor schmuck she decided would be most entertaining to use as a scapegoat. Fortunately, Leon's been able to save up enough money for another trip to the Philippines in the fall. He'll be visiting a town famous for its optimistic entities and its powerful atmosphere of spiritual transformation. He's picked up a lot of negative entities lately, not only during his brief sojourn through the entertainment industry and Judge Judy's courtroom, but also from some nearby dimensions that have been particularly agitated lately by all these torture memos floating around the halls of power.

Well, that's not good, says Felicia.

Caretaking his mother, meanwhile, has been another minefield of negative energies. His mother had an accident on the Golden Gate Bridge, according to Leon a kingdom of death ruled, on Earth, by a do-nothing cabal of bureaucrats who don't have the political will for the most basic safety measures, but ruled, on a different plane, by dark entities that feed off the chaos produced by the frequent, if random, collisions, living on the little bit of soul energy that is released whenever one car head-ons another.

Dark entities, says Felicia.

A more benevolent spiritual being, however, who's been visiting this plane to keep tabs on the traffic in and out of some hell mouths that have been recently excavated, has explained to Leon the way gravity works—it's not as simple as the missing particle the physicists are looking for, but a function of antimatter as much as matter, a collaborative effort across dimensions.

Now there's some practical knowledge, says Felicia.

Leon agrees. The higher beings are often so vague in their pronouncements. Kind of smug. Passive-aggressive even. And the dead—don't get him started on the dead. The dead are usually just so confused, mired in their own useless memories. He's so tired of the bleak hallucinations of the unhappy ghosts, the sad spirits chained to the bloody earth by their own desires, plotting to blow up the planet as if it was their own cosmic prison.

And yet it is the dead whose counsel Felicia has come seeking, specifically Rockin Rebecca, born Linda Briskie in a medium-sized Ohio town in 1963 to a Presbyterian minister. Leon takes Felicia's hands, mutes the TV, closes his eyes, and requests the presence of the dead stripper. Felicia's a little shocked by the speed and lack of protocol with which Leon crosses the membrane between this world and the spirit world. Leon falls silent, occasionally murmuring phrases she can't make out. She imagines other ways she could have spent this $60.

Leon squeezes her hand. It's real foggy where she's coming from, Leon says. She's really confused and I don't think she's accepted that she's dead yet. After another minute or two of murmuring, Leon's eyes pop open, and then they close again and a completely different voice speaks from Leon's mouth, confused and husky. Who is it? it asks. Who's there?

Felicia says, Rebecca?

Who is it? repeats the voice.

You don't know me, Felicia says. But I need to ask you some questions.

It's very windy, says the voice. I can't hear what you're saying.

Rebecca, I want to ask you about Sarah Cohen.

I can hear the wind, but I can't see it.

Rebecca, says Felicia, I need you to tell me how you died.

I don't know where you get off, says the voice. That was Alex. Alex died.

Felicia asks her where she's at.

It's all blowing away all the time, says the voice.

Sarah Cohen, says Felicia. Did Sarah have something to do with your accident?

That bitch, says the voice. There's a pause. She never paid me, says the voice.

I love my mother, says the voice. Will you help me find my mother? I hear her crying, but I just can't see, it's so damn windy.

Linda Briskie, says Felicia.

We never talked much, says the voice, but I always loved her. It was like we were two strangers traveling together for a while and we'd play games to pass the time, you know, and then I went one way and she went another. Just two strangers passing the time. I'm coming, Ma.

Linda, says Felicia.

I can hear you loud and clear, I'm coming…

Rebecca, Linda, do you know anything about Huey Beauregard?

What the fuck, says the voice. Who…

Leon's hands tremble and Felicia could swear she actually *hears* the wind, a strong gust of wind. The sort of wind that whistles through a rocky canyon at dusk from some cave or mysterious hole. A bright blue fish in Leon's aquarium darts erratically back and forth. A twisted smile forms on Leon's face and a different voice says, Ah thought ah told you…

Felicia lets out a little scream, drops Leon's hands, and jumps to her feet. Leon's eyes pop open and he stares at her for a moment as if regaining his bearings.

Very strange, says Leon. That wasn't Rebecca there at the end. I don't know what it was.

Okay, says Felicia.

She takes the money from her purse and presses it into his hand.

We can try again, Leon says. But usually with that kind of interference… it's best to wait.

No, says Felicia. Really, I should get going.

She hurries out, down the three flights of stairs, and back out into the gloomy winter light. She'll walk the ten blocks or so to the BART station, she decides. It's mostly downhill anyway.

She's at Market and Van Ness when Melvin calls.

It's all about the lichen, he tells her. A symbiotic pioneer species!

She tells him that she hit another dead end with Leon. She decides not to tell him about the voice at the end. Maybe there's some way to contact Drew Malone without going through Charles, she says, but she'd feel guilty about harassing a dying Buddhist.

Sounds like a plan, says Melvin, and she can tell that he's already moved on. He makes some noncommittal remarks and changes the subject back to lichen.

Doesn't it take like a hundred million years for the lichen to break down minerals into soil? she asks.

Time's an illusion, Melvin says. It's part of the hologram, and then he says, Hold on, there's someone at the door.

There's shouting in the background and strange popping noises and then she's cut off.

When she tries to call back, the call goes straight to voicemail.

Impatient, she boards the wrong BART train, figuring she'll transfer at West Oakland. But she doesn't get off at West Oakland or at Lake Merritt either and just keeps riding through squat, wasted towns to the end of the line. It's the sort of thing Geordi might do, she thinks. She's accepting horror, in a sense. Is that what he's up to? Or just taking inventory of what exists to remind himself how little interest he has in anything but books. At the end of the line, she stays on the train to come back the other way. Is she becoming "like" Geordi? Probably they're both just participating in one of a very limited set of behaviors you can choose to surprise yourself, to reject habits and obligations, to make the familiar seem strange. She gets off and wanders around a small city that seems to be an enormous strip mall. She pauses in front of a place called the Spa at Stacey Monroe's. Maybe she ought to have a beauty treatment.

It could be the beginning of a whole new life. She'll be pampered by women who are developing cancers from the nail polishes, polish removers, cuticle creams…She'll spend the afternoon in a kind of cheery dream, listening to the banter of the beauticians, listening to the other clients discuss whatever it is that women discuss in America these days. Felicia should call her mother, try to talk to her mother, try not to scream. Some sort of machinery will be humming inside the spa, the pleasant sound of forces beyond one's control, churning away. If there was ever a time for the life-world to rise up, wouldn't it be now, right this minute, right here in the parking lot to the Spa at Stacey Monroe's?

Step away from the child!

Tony steps away from the child.

The police charge in, knocking over several pieces of furniture, one of which falls directly onto the child. Melvin runs toward the back, an intuition or just an imitation of what fugitives do on shows. They've blocked the escape route, with their rifles and bulletproof vests. He puts his hands on his head.

Mr. Tony, I'm bleeding.

They cuff Melvin first, maybe because he weighs less, shove him out front. There are seven cars from various law enforcement agencies on the street outside, a man with a megaphone, and it looks like Ralph in the back of one of the cars, and in another—is that Hakeem?

Tony doesn't like being handcuffed and he doesn't find any of the cops even slightly charming. The public humiliation of being dragged outside in front of all the neighbors, however, is the sort of spectacle that he knows exactly how to perform. He was Jacopo once in *I due foscari*. Wrongfully accused he can do, martyr he can do. He decides that he'll never forgive Melvin. Fortunately they are shoved into the back of completely different police cars, while DJ is carried off beyond some barricade, where shrieking and applause break out.

It's evening before Felicia arrives back home and before she checks her messages. Philip's calling from the San Francisco County Jail. The glamour slammer, he says.

He tried to reach Bob Miller, the only lawyer he knows, but even Bob's voicemail line had been disconnected. There's nobody but the public defender.

According to the public defender, there's no real case against Tony or Ralph and they should both be out by morning. According to the public defender, however, the DA is working to establish her tough-on-crime credentials for a run for state office, and wants to charge Melvin with Kidnapping a Minor Relative. But without his mother and stepfather's cooperation, she's not going to get far. They didn't even visit Melvin in jail, but they want him to go free. At least his mom does, Philip says, and his father isn't going to fight.

Stepfather, says Felicia.

The DA will probably settle for misdemeanor Child Endangerment charges, Philip tells her, and he'll eventually get let off with time served and some community service, according to the public defender.

What about DJ?

He's gone. The mom and dad have already left town.

A long time ago, once, DJ was crying. It was a magical time. It's okay now, baby, says the woman's voice. He remembers something he heard once, and he believes that it's true. *Now's the perfect time for a beauty treatment.* He's falling asleep. It's okay now, says the woman's voice. We're taking you home. The woman, it's his mother. He knows that someday he must go far away. Or maybe he already has.

VII

Tomorrow will be the 22nd century.

—Nina Simone

1

JAIL IS NOTHING LIKE MELVIN imagined it, and yet it's somehow exactly like he always knew it would be. Okay, he decides, he can work with that. He's going to have to conquer Disgust. He's going to have to learn to be free within his mind and just deal with the nasty food.

After Disgust, you have to conquer Boredom. You have to mark it off each and every day, he is told by his cellie—a tranny, Miss Bronzi D'Marco—so as not to go insane. But another, more persuasive resident—probably already insane—assures him that the only way to experience this sort of time is to lose yourself in it altogether, to let time become space, enveloping you, smothering you, so that when something happens—a visit, a transfer, a release—it will be like an explosion, with space collapsing in on itself.

Time. There seems to be plenty of it.

There are no breaks, no spaces. A sticky gel that's endless.

Jail is still a metaphor for everything else, even as it's happening. Life isn't too short, that's another surprise. It lasts forever under the right conditions.

But really, nothing is ever a surprise here.

Miss Bronzi is in because she shot someone and then went shopping. Not the first time.

It's time for me to work on myself, she says. You know, unlearn the patterns.

She meditates a lot. She reads self-help books.

If it doesn't change your consciousness, she says, what's the point.

The public defender tells Melvin there's been some complications, but she doesn't explain them. She talks to him like she's planning a doomed military campaign and he's the brainless cannon fodder. They need to work the idea that Melvin has remorse and that he thought he was saving DJ, she says. His belief that DJ was being abused is crucial to their plea-bargain hopes, no matter how nonsensical. *Nonsensical*—that's the public defender's word. Her pants look like sweatpants and her jacket looks like an oven mitt. She likes to repeat things that Melvin supposedly told her. *You said "Denny was probably touching him and stuff." Why did you believe this?* Meanwhile, Melvin isn't raped, although there are several polite requests for a variety of activities he has no interest in, at least not yet.

Time isn't an illusion. It goes on and on. He remembers a phrase: the mystery of time.

Seems to me you're depressed, Bronzi tells him.

Depressed? I'm in jail.

Duh.

I mean...

Everybody's depressed in jail?

Or maybe...

Jail is like a manifestation of Depressive Illness?

Bronzi's face is sharp, etched. Distinct, with edges, as if she's been designed. Chiseled from amber.

But you have to move through it, she says.

She is totally masculine and totally feminine.

You have to make use of the time.

Maybe Melvin isn't as feminine as he ought to be. Maybe he isn't masculine enough either. Maybe he should develop both of his genders. Masculinity here is a surface: a hard, muscled chest with tattoos on it, even if sometimes it's kind of saggy. A wall that says Do Not Disturb. A place to hide where there isn't anywhere. But Bronzi's masculinity is like an *energy*. A *force*. Because her front is femininity, her masculine essence can be pure and intermingle promiscuously with her feminine essence.

Tick tock, tick tock.

The food: The peanut butter and jelly is not as disgusting as the hot pockets with cheese and tomato stuff. The vegan options tend to be less grody.

Bronzi isn't into Melvin. Not her type. Plus, she doesn't get involved with a cellie. Too domestic. Domesticated.

Why does it seem like he's been here before? What does prison resemble?

Plenty of time to think about…everything.

Everything that's dead and gone. *Happened*. The past, the nothing that's still here only as whatever he thinks about it.

When he was a kid, after the marriage, nobody talked about the past. Nobody talked about the future either—and they certainly weren't describing the present moment. Its lawns and chat rooms and snowy windshields. So what were they discussing? He can remember his mother saying, There's supposed to be something going on up at the mall. He can remember her saying, Your father doesn't like to hear about those things.

Which things? Which father?

Melvin knew nothing, not even where he came from. Mexico? Why does he believe that his mother escaped from a war? Did somebody once tell him that or did he imagine it? How else could they all have just ceased to exist—his mother's family. His supposed father's, too. *It's just you and me, baby boy.* That was before the marriage, all the time. Why he thinks of her as warm, even though she isn't warm, she only seems warm when she's standing next to Denny. Why does Melvin believe that his dead, crazy aunt, the supposed source or clue to everyone's bipolar disorder, a suicide that nobody ever met or talked about…

Did his mom and Denny have secret conversations? He can't imagine it. He just can't. They'd abandoned language together.

He remembers his mom saying, They have only themselves to blame.

This was moral instruction.

Why does he believe that his crazy aunt was raped and tortured by soldiers? What sort of war was going on in Mexico in the '80s?

Were they really happy together, Melvin and his mom, before the marriage, or just needy and poor? She was always having a battle with her roommates, one or more of whom might have been molesting Melvin, he just can't remember it. Somebody died on a bike. It was always snowing. The heat in the apartment smelled like burning toasters. Soggy mittens. Women with bleached hair gave Melvin wet kisses.

Snake skin. Boots and belts and a pair of pants once.

Why did Melvin take his brother anyway? Is he retarded? Is he full of rage? Does he really hate Denny or is it his mom?

She hasn't come to visit because she let him go a long time ago. First she let his childhood go. Only Jared talks about his past. Melvin needs gays and trannies to remember his past. Heterosexuality is a form of willful amnesia.

He likes watching people get raped on video, but he doesn't want to rape them.

Melvin will liberate every being someday. Including himself.

And yet no being will be liberated.

Remembering, that's one strategy. You could sit and think about everything that ever happened. But nothing did.

It's tiresome after a while. Tick tock.

Masturbating is good as long as it lasts, when he can get a minute alone.

He likes sex with girls fine. Guys not so much, although it's kind of more relaxing. Probably then he isn't gay. A lesbian with a strap-on or a tranny raping him would be just as good probably. A woman with a stump? He can't picture it. If it's a stump, it's gotta be a guy. A butch woman, an amputee. Okay. Sure. Why not?

Reading is a way to replace what happened to Melvin with what happened to other people. In the prison library, the books are full of passages underlined by the prisoners who went before. There's a whole special section of people writing from prison. Melvin's pretty sure when he links the underlined passages together it forms a secret message. A map.

Oscar Wilde: *But we who live in prison, and in whose lives there is no event but sorrow, have to measure time by throbs of pain, and the record of bitter moments.*

It hasn't even been a week.

Suffering is one very long moment. We cannot divide it by seasons. We can only record its moods, and chronicle their return.

This is the room: greenish and a bunk bed with bright blue mattresses and a silvery toilet and a thing that sticks out of the wall to hide the toilet, sort of, like that's privacy, and a narrow window that lets in some light from the other side. And the clothes, nobody looks good in this kind of orange. Bronzi comes as close as possible, because she does something to her hair to make it match.

With us time itself does not progress. It revolves. It seems to circle round one centre of pain. The paralyzing immobility of a life every circumstance of which is regulated after an unchangeable pattern, so that we eat and drink and lie down and pray, or kneel at least for prayer, according to the inflexible laws of an iron formula: this immobile quality, that makes each dreadful day in the very minutest detail like its brother, seems to communicate itself to those external forces, the very essence of whose existence is ceaseless change.

It's dark outside, Melvin supposes, sunset or some such, although he wouldn't know for sure.

It is always twilight in one's cell, as it is always twilight in one's heart.

And yet it isn't always twilight in Melvin's heart. Something tangled and intricate is happening within his mind. The slow or even permanent process of stifling a scream is actually constructing a system of roads within his mind.

He misses something. He's missing something. A new kind of hollow. He can't finger it.

The thing is how the inside changes the outside.

The outside—how grand, what a relief, its fog and motion, and yet.

And yet what is out there but people, at least that's how he used to see it. A person somewhere who can help him or touch him or make him see, a person he could sit with and watch everything explode.

But there are people inside too, plenty, and it's obvious that whatever they have to offer or vice versa is just making do.

They like to talk to Melvin. Despite their current circumstances, they believe they understand how the world works and how to make one's way through it. The key is to understand history, a guy named Bernard tells him. Forget the official history, the history they teach in school.

Melvin does his best. He listens for a while. Up close and personal, confined and multiplied, the mass of lives and stories is pretty crushing. It's just that—he doesn't want to be a snob—but he doesn't want to be one of them either. He doesn't want to imagine that the only difference between him and them is that it's his first time here and he's never coming back.

The other guys come and they go—most everybody in San Bruno's on their way someplace else, prison or parole. He doesn't want to be them, but he supposes he is them.

They believe in destiny and they believe in the exercise of free will.

Albertine Sarrazin escapes at the beginning of her book. *There are certain signs imperceptible to people who haven't done time: a way of talking without moving the lips while the eyes, to throw you off, express indifference or the opposite thing; the cigarette held in the crook of the palm, the waiting for night to act or just to talk, after the uneasy silence of the day.*

Outside she can't get around. Her ankle's a mess after jumping the wall, so she's hiding out in some room or eventually, too late, the hospital.

I'd been locked up too young to have seen much of anything, and I'd read a lot, dreamed and lost the thread.

Thank god he's got Bronzi in his cell and not some dumb guy. The guys insist on being recognized or else they're too used up to care.

Human beings. Overrated.

A person isn't the answer.

Meaning Melvin, a person, isn't the answer either. He must have always known this.

Wind—that's what's missing. A good breeze. A healthy gust. A fucking tornado.

A person isn't the answer but *God* doesn't follow from this thought either. A person, like Melvin, is born from a kind of darkness that probably wasn't so bad back *before* memory or irrelevant to memory's delusions and manipulations and the stories persons like to tell. A something that's maybe nothing before memory kicked in and a person's been hurled into a journey, doomed, moving relentlessly toward something beyond. Beyond love, hate, good, evil, motion, confinement—beyond existing.

He wonders if he's evil. If what he wants sexually is evil. That wouldn't be fair, unless everybody was sexually evil, meaning not really.

Every word is immense with hope and emptiness, there is no room for us on earth: either running away or jail, always, and always alone.

There's something he's believed, with the idea that everyone else does, too, since before he knew what he was believing: that you could be something other than alone. Probably he never felt alone until after the marriage, but actually. He can remember once, walking in the snow, toward home, and behind him was all the chatter of the school, with its raised hands and children moved here and there in line formations, and ahead of him was his mother and the roommate of the era, Debbie? He realized that there were two Melvins, the Melvin who colored and did math problems correctly in that school but who could never make sense of the story problems, and the Melvin who lived with his mother and they sat and watched their shows and ate that stuff with hamburger in it and spices. But here he was, no place, in between, only his thoughts to keep him company.

But later, unless he was drunk like that one time in ninth grade English when they were doing the Roman gods and goddesses and it all started to blur together, he was embarrassed to discover that nobody understood him and it was lonely, but he had come to believe that this was simply childhood and he would find some other person, someday, out there in the world, etc.

He's probably kind of believed that until now.

If other people aren't the answer, then it follows that sex isn't the answer either. No way.

It kind of has to be, doesn't it?

Villon, a thief, dead now for centuries:

You see us hang here, half a dozen who
Indulged the flesh in every liberty
Till it was pecked and rotted, as you see,
And these our bones to dust and ashes fall.

This would seem to be an answer to his question, but only partially so.

On the other hand, Boethius: *What are worldly goods but an emblem of death? For death comes for nothing else but that it may take away life. So also worldly goods come to the mind, in order that they may deprive of that which is dearest to it in the world; that is, when they depart from it.*

The Consolation of Philosophy isn't much of a consolation, it turns out, unless you're into the higher power, who remains surprisingly popular in prisons until now, despite its lack of care for a single inmate, as far as Melvin can see. The power Melvin's into isn't higher exactly. Isn't lower either.

The system of roads he's building with his stifled scream: it hobbles through an ugly, empty desert landscape of trash and scrub. Pointless cloverleafs circling outside a city that sprawls so much it's always evening.

Same silvery toilet and the same thing that shields it from view. Same peanut butter and jelly. Same ugly orange outfit. Another day hasn't even passed yet, but is crawling on its way.

He'd like to skip ahead. Nothing, bleah.

After lights out, things get pretty quiet. It's just the cherry end of one burning cigarette like a firefly in the dark. Somebody breaking the no smoking rule. And then from down the row somewhere, in the darkness, a voice starts speaking.

We understand now that every crisis is simply one more opportunity for *them*, the voice says.

It's a familiar voice, a rough voice, male, older, and lethargic.

They manage everything these days, not just us. Currencies, debts, ecosystems. Flows of weapons and medicines and communication. It's all being tracked and monitored.

The voice isn't preaching. It's simply reciting the facts, as if it's seen everything.

War isn't a distinct event, the voice says. It's an entire series of systems and relationships spread out across time and space. It's never been aimed at some imaginary victory. Winning and losing are irrelevant for them.

Miss Bronzi is just flipping through the pages of her fashion magazine, shining a little penlight over the glossy illustrations.

A constantly evolving system of total control.

Nobody responds to the voice or acknowledges it in any way.

They've turned everything into a form of therapy. Work, love, democracy. The sick, sad, self-absorbed little ego, plugging away. Adaptable, counseled, and medicated, situated in its cubicle or on its laptop.

Consume the events of your life, the voice drones on. Reproduce them and store them as "memories" of the "good times." Consume the time, the situations that your life is composed of. No more friendship—networking and self-improvement. Work on yourself as a *brand*. You can be more productive, a better "communicator." In a world in which nothing can ever actually happen.

The voice goes on like this and nobody ever mentions it. The next night and the next one, too.

Ever is a word that means endless time. The language is full of horrible words, once you start to pay attention.

Melvin looks around during the daylight to see if he can spot the prisoner who belongs to the voice. But maybe he doesn't really wanna know.

You attach a label to something and you kill it, Miss Bronzi tells him after lights out. You put another person or a situation or even, like, a magazine or a chair into this little mental box and it's a distortion of reality. The more you apply your little words, the more shallow and dead your reality is. You grow dead to the miraculous unfolding of being.

Miss Bronzi. How old is she? Nobody knows.

Me, I'm going to undo that habit, she says.

She's got her little penlight going and another fashion magazine, flipping the pages, slowly, precisely, as if she's luxuriating in the act.

Me, says Miss Bronzi, I just want to experience the miraculous unfolding of being.

Her penis is larger than Melvin's. She only identifies male for punitive purposes, as she prefers the men's jail to the women's. She gets around, here and there, but never gets caught, not for pleasure or for trade.

Melvin's dreams should be mentioned, considering how much time he spends sleeping. For a while, they are especially vivid, as if the boredom of waking life must be translated into an infinitely bizarre series of adventures and distorted horrors reflecting the daily life that sucks so much, and certain motifs repeat often enough that they are noticeable, even to Melvin, who has never been good at remembering his dreams, but wakes sometimes with the feeling that his heart hasn't yet broken, that it is just about to break.

The mystery of time.

Chester Himes is more consoling than Boethius. Even the title—*Yesterday Will Make You Cry*—is more consoling. *Jimmy turned over and looked at the ceiling. He couldn't get over the feeling that he was some one else. He couldn't be Jimmy Monroe, lying there on an upper bunk in a prison dormitory, looking at the low, flat ceiling.*

Soupy oatmeal in that prison, *the chalk settling in a white scum over the oatmeal with clear water on top.* Melvin has a few better options than the oatmeal here, which is more congealed. The place still smells of it.

There are many hazards in prison, but none greater than the hazard on friendship...

Lights out. Just enough for one more paragraph.

For weeks he and Walter had been nurturing a growing affection for each other. And then, just before dinner that day, the deputy's runner came with a transfer slip for Walter. Hacked off. No way to prepare for it, no way to brace himself against it. Just like walking down the street with a twin, and he steps off the curb and gets run over.

Melvin has never walked down the street with a twin, but it's like he has. Or like he's his own twin, or once was, one Melvin superimposed over the other, identical in every way except that one was full of rage and kidnapped his brother to hurt his mother and the other had already just let it go. That would be the twin the bus ran over.

Down the hall, the voice starts up again. Same tone, same lethargic recitation.

But wisdom isn't really the ability to adapt, it says. That's the slave-mind. Our inability to adapt, our unwillingness to adapt, are only problems from the point of view of the machine that's crushing us. The men and women who profit from the efficient functioning of that machine.

But the silences between the words that the voice is speaking, the pauses—they've changed a bit. The silence is deeper in them and the constant hum of whatever vague machinery churns away behind all of these cells and hallways and easily observable gathering spaces is more noticeable as a kind of hum, like the hum of a warm summer night. A real hot one with a breeze. Melvin can remember nights like that, before the marriage, before the air-conditioning. They clicked. They hummed. The heat was singing.

Melvin closes his eyes: dreams.

The recurring motifs include attempts at flight, occasionally successful, a place beyond the plains he's trying to get to, which in the dreams is called Kansas, the drowning of small creatures in moonlit lakes where somebody (sometimes Melvin) is rowing, an industrial area crisscrossed by train tracks and riddled with graffiti where Melvin is usually waiting to meet somebody (Jared or Jelena or a combination of Bronzi and DJ or a vague, unimaginable rapist) to spray-paint something or break a window or possibly even hop on board a train, rivers that need to be crossed by means of invisible ships or flimsy bridges, and the previously mentioned tiger dreams.

Saturday and Sunday are visiting days, Saturday by reservation and Sunday walk-in. Felicia comes some Saturdays, anybody else shows up on Sunday. Melvin discovers that what he wants to communicate is incommunicable. It's the way jail is a different way of ordering time and space but there are no words for it. America is an evil machine. Everybody knows that, right? It's also the place where demons are sleeping, the place where we live in their dreams, the place where the joke isn't funny, where the empire is disintegrating into indigestible cubes, where we try to eat them anyway. Not to mention that it's just like in the movies, and he's talking on a telephone, through glass.

Philip goes on about the rats that are running around his house now. At least two big ones, maybe a whole family. The landlady, who prosecutes war criminals for the UN, won't do a thing. The exterminator said the house isn't anywhere near up to code—put out some traps and some poison, but the rats will only come back.

Melvin says, Don't tell me. How long have I been in here?

Tell you or don't tell you?

Whisper it. Please.

Seventeen days.

What about Hakeem.

Hakeem?

Was it him in the other car?

The police deny knowing anything about him. We don't know his last name or where he lives. Do you know his last name or where he lives?

The Tenderloin, a big building. Hyde maybe or maybe Leavenworth.

He was studying robotics, right? Do you remember where he was going to school?

Or maybe it was Jones.

How little Melvin knows. People can't just disappear like that, can they? Can they or can't they?

Well, Bronzi tells him, it seems that section 412 of the Uniting and Strengthening America by Providing Appropriate Tools Required to Intercept and Obstruct Terrorism (H.R. 3162, the "USA PATRIOT Act") permits indefinite detention of immigrants and other noncitizens. Section 412 requires that immigrants "certified" by the Attorney General be charged within seven days with a criminal offense or an immigration violation but it doesn't have to be related to terrorism. However, immigrants you can't deport for terrorism, but maybe have an immigration status violation, like overstaying a visa, or whatever, could face indefinite detention if their country won't take them back. Detention would be allowed if the Attorney General says he has "reasonable grounds to believe" involvement in terrorism or whatever activity that poses a danger to national security, and detention could be indefinite if he says the individual threatens national security or the safety of the community or any person.

Any person? A kidnapped child?

Of course, says Bronzi. Our children are all in danger from Muslim men. Muslim men want to dress our boys up like girls, make them dance with bangles on, and rape them.

Muslim men…, Melvin says.

Hakeem.

You're being sarcastic? says Melvin.

Duh.

In bits and pieces Melvin has heard something like Bronzi's life. It's all about crazy times, good times and parties, empresses and duchesses. It's all happened in the Tenderloin and South of Market and only rarely International Boulevard in Oakland. There are a lot of handsome men, married men, truck drivers. There are hilarious fights and drugs and fashion. There are movie nights; Bronzi loves the movies.

Sonallah Ibrahim: *Torture: and since that time he feels that wherever he walks, whether he's coming in or going out, something will hit him, something will shock him. If someone surprises him, his muscles tense. He expects to be slapped or kicked.*

What does Melvin know about Egypt? Nothing, until now.

My sister came in and said, The city sewers are overflowing.

Moazzam Begg is a British Pakistani detained at Bagram, where he saw two prisoners beaten to death by American soldiers.

Then I couldn't see anything more as they put a cloth hood over my head. They pulled my hands behind my back, handcuffed me, and fastened flexicuffs (a disposable plastic shackling device) tightly around my ankles. I was physically picked up and carried into the vehicle, which they had parked in my driveway.

He ended up in Guantanamo for three years.

The Chinese character for confined or oppressed shows a tree completely encircled by walls.

Is Hakeem being punished somewhere for Melvin's crime?

Bronzi's favorite movie is called *Raw Deal*. Her favorite actress is called Claire Trevor. Claire Trevor springs her guy from prison, but later she knows something that her boyfriend doesn't know and the clock is ticking. It's her face and the clock, that's everything: They're in San Francisco, they're supposed to escape to South America, but there's another woman and the other woman's in trouble. Claire Trevor knows this but her boyfriend doesn't. Not yet.

If she tells him, he'll probably die. His love for Claire Trevor has already died. She can live a dream with a man who's always dreaming or live in reality with a man she's set free to die. The clock is ticking.

Who are you, when you're all by yourself?

It occurs to Melvin one day, in the middle of eternity, as he's skimming *Prison Memoirs of an Anarchist* by Alexander Beckman, that despite everything Bronzi tells him about her life, he knows nothing of her childhood. It's like she popped up on the streets of the Tenderloin one day fully grown and popping black market estrogen.

I like to feel *full*, Bronzi says.

But where did you grow up?

Bronzi sighs and gives him a theatrically tragic look.

Evergreen. Her father ran a fish and chips place. Her father was from a small region of rocks and sand that was claimed by two countries but neither one really wanted. India and Pakistan. Her mother was from Manila. When she was eleven, her father first got ill, had dizzy spells. He fainted, got headaches, his vision would get all blurry, and he could barely work. The hot grease, the bright lights. They struggled for several years that way until somebody finally figure out that he had a tooth infection.

They took the tooth out and he felt twenty years younger, he said. Two months later he left the family for good.

I loved my father more than anything, Bronzi tells him. My mother and I, we never got along.

Evergreen?

San Jose. Eastside.

You never saw him again?

I saw him.

Bronzi's father—was he a Muslim?

She grew up with maps of London. At the fish and chips place, where she would sleep in the storage room on a little shelf while her parents were working. Or do her homework. The London subway. The British flag. Everybody asked if she was from London. Nobody had ever been to London, it was just about the fish and chips.

The subway map was a map of her dreams. She went for a long weekend once. There was a special on flights, she flew to London, and she wasn't dressed for it. She didn't have any plans, she didn't know where to go or what to do.

And then what.

Unshaped fears, the more terrifying because vague, fill my heart. In vain I seek to drown my riotous thoughts by reading and exercise.

The prisoners used to sculpt their bodies into elaborate armor, so they got rid of the weights they used to have in prison.

Too much flab around these days, Bronzi tells him.

How old is Bronzi? Is she an immortal?

I had then such a peculiar idea of prison: I thought I would be sitting on the floor in a gruesome, black hole, with my hands and feet chained to the wall; and the worms would crawl over me, and slowly devour my face and my eyes, and I so helpless, chained to the wall.

Melvin gets transferred to San Bruno, driven in a van. The hazard on friendship—no more Bronzi. Outside for a minute, in between one jail and the other. It all flows out there, it's like a movie where every image is always being transformed into the next darkness full of the imagination. But once in a while you sink into the depths of awareness—in the pursuit of liberty or for some other reason he can't remember, it's like you have to reject all that stuff that's just fine and kind of boring and so you have to think up new ways to act. Because once you sink into that place, you can really see the usual dimension from the *outside*. You can see how it isn't working.

At San Bruno everything is the same except the architecture and the faces. The cells are more decrepit and lined up in rows like you see in the movies. The toilet's grodier. The food, more or less the same. The library's not so good. His cellie here is a guy named Jesse, but he likes to be called Lakota Dawn, owing to his Native American roots. Some granny or great-granny. He's older, almost twenty-two, and his deal is assault. His mom's boyfriend beat her up and so he handled it. Second strike, first was robbery, something like that. Lakota Dawn pretends he can't remember. He was a juvenile, he says. Long time ago.

This is my last visit for sure, Lakota Dawn informs him. Lakota's on anti-anxiety meds that keep him pretty unfazed. One more strike and I move in for good, he says.

The prisoners here believe in surprisingly rigid ethical codes. They believe in the active pursuit of liberty. A guy named Johannes keeps trying to recruit him into various moneymaking projects once they get out.

I'm not really into crime, Melvin explains.

Then what's this all about, says Johannes.

Victim of circumstance, says Melvin. More or less an accident.

Accident, says Johannes dismissively.

The DNA testing got me, a guy named Billy tells him. My brother got into his own mischief and then they tested him and found a half-match. So you see, if it wasn't I was born into such a fuck-up family, I would have never been caught.

They believe in the hope of a liberating catastrophe, despite the guards' instructions. In case of catastrophe, Melvin is told, the guards' instructions are to lock inmates in their cells and abandon the prison.

Melvin misses Miss Bronzi and he misses the voice from the darkness. He designs a future form of life that's super slippery, evanescent, able to detach every part of itself and then regroup: gaseous and tentacled, the ultimate escape artist.

Victor Serge: *They used to escape from the Bastille. They used to escape from Noumea, in spite of the ocean fraught with squalls. They still escape from Guiana, across the virgin forest. No one escapes from the model jail.*

Modern prisons are imperfectible, since they are perfect. There is nothing left but to destroy them.

In the absence of Bronzi, spoken language has dissolved. Chimps, not chips. Or either way, no difference: zoos, cages, life forms, disgusting food. His mother, his stepfather, his dead Mexican daddy.

Jimmy Santiago Baca: *I'd been in plenty of cells, but the Yuma County Jail cell beat them all with its horrid smell.*

More lumpy oatmeal. The human community, the species, life on earth: *Every time someone in another cell flushed the toilet, particles of sewage bubbled up from the commode and puddled on the floor.*

Doodles: alleys and walls. Written language needs to become a crazy masculine feminine essence: it needs to ejaculate flowers.

I deciphered the graffiti on walls and checked the six-by-nine cell for a way to escape.

Jimmy Santiago Baca's reading a highlighted textbook, the simple story of a man and his pond. Reality kind of morphs as Melvin sees himself in jail reading about a man in jail reading about a man and his pond. The pond—is it a jail for a fish?

Melvin starts to write Bronzi a letter, but it doesn't go well.

It doesn't help that you have to assume the pig men will read it.

Lakota reads Stephen King novels and sometimes, while Melvin's engrossed in a book—Nawal Sa'dawi's *Memoirs from the Women's Prison*, for example—Lakota masturbates.

On the ceiling was an electric light staring like a strangled, bulging eye…Faces concealed beneath niqaabs—all-enveloping face-veils with small holes through which I could perceive the steady gaze of human eyes.

Had I fallen to the bottom of a well? Or sprung on to another planet? Or returned to the age of slaves and harems? Or was this a dream?

A women's prison is a dream in a different way than a men's prison: Time is the dream, but not a dream, not yet. Someday.

The spasms of Lakota's face and his whole body when he cums are like an electric shock.

Time is no longer time. Time and the wall have merged into one. The air is motionless. Nothing moves around me except the cockroaches and rats, as I lie on a thin rubber mattress which gives off the odour of old urine, my empty handbag placed under my head, still wearing the white dress and shoes in which I left the house.

The clothes in which Melvin "left the house" are apparently in storage somewhere and will be returned to him someday that isn't even imaginable. And yet he imagines it every day. A Che Guevara T-shirt and the leisure wear that Jared gave him so much hell about. Skulls and dollar bills. Once, on drugs, he realized that his clothing was a message, but not one he'd given much thought.

The air is motionless here, too. Motionless air pervades every crack in a stifled universe that is dying.

Inside the cell, it is just a living hush. Medicated. Death and masculinity. What hope is there?

In prison, I learned what I had not learned in the College of Medicine. The gecko had crawled over my body and nothing had happened to me. Cockroaches had run over me and nothing had happened. I had lived with a fear of these small innocent beings that move with a marvelous grace in the night, searching for sustenance in the garbage and the wall cracks, and my fear now dispelled. I finally became capable of a deep and healing sleep as these creatures danced around me, causing me no harm.

Melvin draws beings who have evolved beyond physical and even psychic forms of confinement—beings impossible to confine because they are so essentially free. Even a photon can be confined, within a diamond, for example. Or a black hole, obviously. But at the quantum level, it might still be free within other dimensions. He draws predators who have evolved the most sublime pleasures to offer their prey before they consume them. He draws prey who have evolved mechanisms to experience their own consumption as a sublime pleasure and to survive the whole process as the chrysalis for an even more evolved life form.

Time is passing without Melvin, the world's time, out there. The winter is turning into spring.

Felicia's pitched her story to a major magazine. Real money, real support. And she's discovered where her missing source is hiding—Felicia just keeps talking and Melvin's thinking: Is that all it was? All that spinning and whirling? Everybody's just out there murdering time and ignoring the implications of liberty.

Human speech is a luxury, the human face—the greatest sadness.

He asks Felicia to bring him books. Books written by imprisoned people.

Is that really all you want to read about?

It isn't the reading so much I'm into. It's the same texture a lot of times as my life.

That's what I'm saying.

Escapist entertainment, we have plenty of that.

It isn't necessarily a bad thing, she says.

I have a project. I skim a lot. I skip almost everything—I like to skip almost everything, it helps me…to prepare…to imagine that I *can* do that. Skip ahead.

Are asylums okay or just prisons?

Asylums are fine.

Philip's not as calm, he's found a new place to live.

Me, too, says Melvin.

Philip says, What's the public defender say?

Melvin says, I'm practicing my remorse.

Philip says, Good boy. Use your acting skills.

Philip tells Melvin that he was awestruck by the new landlady, even on the phone. She invited him and Raymond out to meet her in her Daly City home, before he had even seen the rental house. She was a little bit crazy, Philip had realized from their telephone conservations, but then so was he. There were special circumstances. The current tenants, who had been like children to her, could no longer pay the rent, and were, at least technically, being evicted. But there were no bad feelings, Mrs. H. explained, and so Philip and Raymond drove out to Daly City one evening to meet her. Her husband was gruff, but not unfriendly, and his English wasn't great, but he showed them a blueprint of the house. Mrs. H. was the obvious star of the show, a former glamour queen back in the Philippines, long long ago. Her house was full of froufrou, Christmas lights and statues of saints, weird ceramic doodads, and a permanent Christmas tree. There were pictures of her obviously gay son prominently on display, as if it was part of the sales pitch, and she seemed to hint, in her initial conversation, of her special relationship to gay men. Her husband brought out the blueprints to the house, for reasons which Philip didn't entirely understand, although he wanted to explain that there was a gap, but Philip wasn't sure if it was a gap between the house and the one next door or between the house proper and the in-law unit or between the living space and a parallel universe, and even now that he's moving in, Philip isn't sure what Mr. H. was talking about, but it didn't really matter. While they were scrutinizing the blueprints, her son strutted through the living room shirtless, in a way that Philip was convinced his mother had arranged.

After the deliberations of the blueprint, Mrs. H. set them down in her living room surrounded by doll-like things and blinking lights and enormous armoires, put her hands in her lap, and sang to them girlishly, *Getting to know you…*

That was how it began—with a brief musical number—but then they were there for hours, unable to extricate themselves, and Mrs. H. told them her story. For Mrs. H. there was only one story, which she had told many, many times.

Mrs. H had worked in an office building in downtown San Francisco. Long ago, a jealous lover had shown up at the office with a box of long-stem roses. Whose jealous lover didn't really matter, one of the employees, no one Mrs. H. knew. But he didn't really have long-stem roses in that box, it was an assault rifle. Mrs. H. and the others with her in the office heard shots, they couldn't tell if they came from above or from below, they seemed to come from all around. They immediately climbed under their desks. Mrs. H. said that she experienced a different kind of time there, under the desk. Mrs. H. said, Have you heard this phrase, *My life passed in front of my eyes?* Well, she said, it wasn't exactly like that—it wasn't like her actual life passed in front of her eyes, but that every life she could have lived passed in front of her eyes, every moment expanded and contained within it every other moment, every possible moment, and you'd think it would be spectacular, she said, but it was really kind of awful, and she shuddered and wouldn't discuss it anymore. The shots continued, in any case, and came closer. Her boss tiptoed to the door and peeked out, then gasped and warned them to run. A shot rang out and he crumpled to the floor. The suddenness and the slowness of it, while everyone leapt to their feet and began scrambling away, was like a continuation of the moment she'd lived huddled under the desk. Mrs. H. followed the rest of the employees to the stairwell. They went down; Mrs. H. went up.

Why up? Melvin asks.

Philip says that sometimes the less obvious route is the best. Sometimes just doing the opposite of what everyone else is doing is the key. Mrs. H. credited her survival to luck, but Philip credits her genius and her destiny. The shooter followed the others down and shot them all. Mrs. H crouched waiting, in the stairwell up above. She heard it all. The shots, the screams.

There was a settlement for the survivors, she told them, but she wouldn't take any of the money. She was superstitious about that.

Visiting hours are over.

During the next week, while Melvin's waiting for Felicia's books, there's Horst Bienek. A book without underlinings, a book that hasn't been passed from prisoner to prisoner, would be worthless the way that language would be for the last person on earth.

Melvin is the last person on earth, but this isn't Earth. Earth is over and exists only in his memory. Nothing out there deserves to be called reality from in here and nothing in here deserves to be called what is real either.

Waiting. Waiting isn't living, but then again, it is.

...suddenly I wished they would come and torture me, for I wanted to scream, but nobody came, I remained alone, alone in the cell, alone in the white foamy darkness...

But language wouldn't be worthless, as the last person on earth, because you can do things besides communicate with it. You can think with it, right?

Language is social, but sometimes it's all alone.

Melvin's mother loved him more than anything. She sang to him at night and read to him and hugged him and kissed him, like all the time. He was her best friend, her everything, and they were all anybody had, each other, and then she traded that in, his childhood, for a house and a husband. Was she trying to give Melvin a better life? Was she sacrificing herself for Melvin's future? Did she say that to him once? *A better life*. Did she grow to hate him because she'd sacrificed herself for a future that was already doomed?

When was it? The moment when Melvin figured out he didn't have to do it. Whatever it was they wanted him to do. Go to BYU or something. He had the grades, but Denny didn't really care, had already written him off.

DJ was the investment, the future.

Hakeem once described his father's visit as a punishment and a joke.

Hakeem is locked up somewhere. Nobody knows where. Hakeem is forced to sleep inside a coffin, to sleep in icy water, Hakeem is submerged under cold water again and again, unable to breathe. Confined in tiny spaces, alone. Sexual and religious humiliation. Where is Osama bin Laden? Where is Osama bin Laden? Where is Osama bin laden? Hakeem is threatened with vicious dogs. Hakeem has a bag over his head. He isn't allowed to sleep. Can't sleep, can't sleep, until the world is just a messy vicious horror—all meaning has dissolved. He's hallucinating, and in his hallucination the world is a potato and the potato is rotting. Hungry, so hungry he would eat a rotten potato. Thirsty, the only water he sees is the water they shove his head into. Sleep deprivation. Where is Osama bin Laden? They tell him they'll rape his mother. Him, too, of course. Stress positions, prolonged stress positions. He's given enemas and put in diapers and flown to black sites all over the globe, black sites, the globe is a potato with little black sites sprouting all over. Hakeem is bound to a declined board, feet raised and head slightly below the feet. Material is wrapped over Hakeem's face, and water is poured over him, asphyxiating him. Hakeem is left to stand naked in a cell kept near fifty degrees while being regularly doused with cold water in order to increase the rate at which heat is lost from the body. Hakeem is forced to stand, handcuffed and with his feet shackled to an eyebolt in the floor or wall for more than forty hours, causing his weight to be placed on just one or two muscles. Eventually, after excruciating pain, this leads to muscle failure. A hard, open-handed slap is delivered to Hakeem's abdomen, and to his face. And another. And another. Hakeem is draped with the Israeli flag and interrogated for eighteen hours under strobe lights. Hakeem is forced to wear a bra, and fed rectally. Hakeem is left bound on the floor in icy water. Hakeem is beaten so hard he dies from internal bleeding—he is beaten to death. Captured on video, but the video is destroyed and nobody ever hears of Hakeem again, and the country *moves on.*

Remembering and forgetting, two lousy options.

The prisoner had been chained by the wrists to the top of his cell for four days.

The prisoner is forced to dig bottle caps out of shit buckets.

Felicia brings Melvin books by Jean Genet, the Marquis de Sade, Antonin Artaud, Leonora Carrington, Anna Kavan, Breyten Breytenbach. How would you get a name like that?

She brings books by Janet Frame, Unica Zurn, Emma Santos, Isaac Babel, Alexander Solzhenitsyn, Émile Zola, Nelson Algren, Thomas De Quincey, and Celia Abad.

Melvin isn't even sure where San Bruno is at. Is it a real place or is it just a broken-down oasis in another dimension. Time is passing without him out there, the news of the day. The spring is turning to summer and people are leaving the state or the country or whatnot.

Tony shows up one Sunday early, aglow with the idea of the future. He has a new boyfriend and a job offer from some vast cable network that's seeking new ways to branch out into Internet music sharing. Tony's mapping out his next ascent: a triumphant return to New York, no more opera singer Tony, those horrible divas can kiss his ass. Out of the chrysalis of his previous incarnation shall emerge the King of Content, the visionary of web-based music.

Once you're out of here, you can come see me in New York, Tony says.

Melvin can't quite process the sentence.

Melvin gives him a present—he's drawn a picture of Tony singing opera in another dimension. It's a cyborg Tony, a Tony who's evolved—he's technologically enhanced, luminous and telepathic, signaled by thought bubbles that move in and out of the permeable membrane of his skull. He lives off of energy from the sun.

After Visiting Hours, Melvin sinks back into eternity, where he is just hungry enough to eat a small portion of the food without Disgust and then he thinks, well, at least Disgust was something. At least Disgust has a relationship to time, which is more than he can say for anything else around here.

And yet it is here in prison that he really knows that he will die.

There are so many people left who should die before he does. A whole world full of old people. Will he still be around to watch his mother die and Denny and Tony and Felicia and Philip and Geordi and Raymond and Ralph? Even his crazy ex is two months older.

When he was a kid, his mom would take him to this slide. It was rickety and maybe three stories high, and you'd go down it into a cold, murky lake. Probably illegal now. The ladder was the scariest part, especially as you got toward the top and realized that you were next in line.

Once, sitting in the darkness after lights out, there's no sound but Lakota's measured breathing as he drifts off into sleep, but then the voice starts up, somewhere over to the left.

From inside we can sense America more exactly, it says. Its organic nervous system replaced by a machine that dispenses decorative food and pills and weapons to form robots shuttled along paths instead of conscious beings.

Different prison, same voice from the darkness.

Every insurrection is a part of the same insurrection, the voice says. One insurrection spread out across space and time like music. Every insurrection shares a rhythm, a kind of vibration. Feel it. Feel it coming, feel it inside you, not someday, but right now.

The return of the voice proves to Melvin that every prison is the same prison. Every prison is different. That's what they call a koan, Bronzi would have told him.

Felicia's books have underlinings, too, faint little pencil markings most of the time, but sometimes bright and blue. For this to work, for these underlinings to exist as a part of the secret message, he has to either pretend that Felicia is a prisoner in her own way or to believe in magic.

There is no love here, nor hate, nor any point where feeling accumulates. In this nameless place nothing appears animate, nothing is close, nothing is real…

…prisons behind which sleeps, dreams, swears, and spits a race of murderers…

The room is as dark as a box lined with black velvet that someone has dropped into a frozen well.

I soon found myself a prisoner in a sanitarium full of nuns.

Feeble, enfettered creatures destined solely for our pleasures…

I knew that Christ was dead and done for, and that I had to take His place, because the Trinity, minus a woman and microscopic knowledge, had become dry and incomplete.

In short: shudder, tremble, anticipate, obey—and with all that, if you are not very fortunate, perhaps you will not be completely miserable.

God does not exist, he withdraws, gets the fuck on out and leaves the cops to keep an eye on things.

The weird gloomy fringe of the void surging up after the flash.

For the operation does not consist of sacrificing one's ego as a poet at the moment one is alienated from everybody, but it consists of letting oneself be penetrated and raped by collective consciousness in such a way, that one is no longer in one's own body anything but a slave to the ideas and reactions of all others.

…dreams like light imprisoned in bright mineral caves; hot, heavy dreams; ice-age dreams; dreams like machines in the head.

Though it may be wretched when seen from within, it is then poetic, if you are willing to agree that poetry is the break (or rather the meeting at the breaking point) between the visible and the invisible.

He set a ship and a crime adrift.

My writing bounces off the walls, the maze of words which become alleys, like sentences, the loops which are closed circuits and present no exit, these themselves constitute the walls of my confinement.

Like those barracks which in the morning are open to all the winds, which you think are empty and pure when they are swarming with dangerous males sprawled promiscuously on their beds.

I have seen machines fighting a lot but only infinitely far behind them have I seen the men who directed them.

And so, on the surface of daily life, consciousness forms beings and bodies that one can see gathering and colliding in the atmosphere, to distinguish their personalities.

I write my own castle and it becomes a frightening discovery: it is unbalancing something very deeply embedded in yourself when you in reality construct, through your scribblings, your own mirror.

…empty theaters, deserted prisons, machinery at rest, deserts…

I believed I was being put through purifying tortures so that I might attain Absolute Knowledge, at which point I could live Down Below.

Because in this mirror you write hair by hair and pore by pore your own face, and you don't like what you see.

My thoughts have become strands of weeds, of no special colour, slowly undulating in colourless water.

I was not greatly inconvenienced by the filth.

But it is important to know that you are nothing. And to search without stopping, be you awake or withdrawn into the wakefulness of sleep, for the hairline cracks, for the gaps and the

unexpected moments of deep breathing, for the space which is created by alleys and by walls…
prepare yourself for the interstices of freedom.

2

THERE'S ONE OF SONYA BRAVA'S STORIES out of *Muchacha Was a Sex Monster*—
Felicia's favorite—where a middle-class Mexican-American woman goes to
Cuba and has constant sex with a poor Cuban philosophy student. The story
is Sonya at her least narrative. It's all just descriptions of sex and philosophical
discourse. It sounds awful, but Sonya made it work. In Sonya's hands it became
more than just softcore porn and Foucault.

The flight to Iceland is like a dream, something dreamt by another species. The
music of the Icelandic language, percolating through the airport, is something
she remembers from a life she never lived. The transparent bird is flying again,
surrounded by haze and the eerie light that might germinate aliens. Her own
ghost is descending toward the Reykjavik Airport.

She arrives at night, but of course, the sun is still hovering there at the horizon.
She knew this would be true, and yet she can't say that she really believed it. She
collapses into her motel and dreams about the room she is in. In the dream, she
does a web search for the phrase *soul asylum*. The results are confusing, however,
and have nothing to do with the band she used to listen to with JJ, her ex.

She's looking for evidence and that search has distracted herself, certainly, from
various habits of thought and emotion, various ways of being that she confuses
with herself. The object of the quest probably doesn't matter, she knows that.

The trip out to the spa is briny and flat and glacial, but melting. Her job is to investigate a mystery whose solution is irrelevant.

The spa is tucked next to a volcanic landscape, active and geothermal, just a quarter mile from the town. We keep our guests safe from visitors and other toxic intrusions, the brochure states, and so she'd imagined it would be more fortified, more separate from the surrounding neighborhood. All the borders are indistinct, however. The doors are not guarded, but an incredibly tall woman in gauzy white emerges from behind a Japanese screen and greets her warmly. The woman performs sincerity graciously; she doesn't make Felicia feel like a cheap tourist, even though she's staying only for one day in the least expensive room in the Stein Steinarr Wing, but accepts the payment discreetly and makes a fluttering gesture that summons a particular blond boy, twelve or thirteen, who emerges from nowhere to show her to her room.

The spa is fairly incredible. It is made of organic materials primarily, and yet it is gleaming white around every curve, clean and ordered. The rooms give out onto little gardens, surprising nooks of vegetation, random steam baths. Above the entrance to her own curving hallway is a wooden plaque identifying this as The Stein Steinarr Wing for Disenfranchised Experimental Writers, with lines by Steinarr underneath, translated into several languages:

Time is like the water,
and the water is cold and deep
like my own consciousness.

And time is like a picture,
which is painted of water,
half of it by me.

And time and the water
flow trackless to extinction
into my own consciousness.

It is in one of the random steam baths that she finds an old man stewing, eyes closed, who she immediately knows is Drew Malone. He looks like a soggy piece of parchment. He looks dead, but not quite. He looks just like she would imagine a dying Buddhist to look, easing across the boundary to nonbeing in a tepid sulfur bath.

Drew, she says. Drew Malone.

The eyes don't pop open. They open more gradually than would seem possible for such a tiny action. They gaze at her for a moment and then they close again.

Have you read my novels?

No, not yet.

Not yet, I like that. Well, nobody has, pretty much. Not yet.

She tells him about Pontormo. About Pontormo's unfinished mural. He doesn't open his eyes, but she can see that he is listening.

I used to consider myself an Ontic Structural Realist, he tells her. I probably still would, if I cared enough to consider my self. Tell me. What do you want from me?

I want you to tell me about Connie and Sarah Cohen. I want you to tell me about their relationship to Huey Beauregard.

Is that all?

What is an Ontic Structural Realist? What does an Ontic Structural Realist believe?

Neither matter nor energy is essential. It's relationships and qualities. You must be a writer, too, yes?

I have the credentials they required, Felicia says. To be placed in the Stein Steinarr Wing.

Playing games with language—what a quaint diversion, he says. But you're young, you've got some life left in you. Perhaps you find it urgent business. Disenfranchisement and all.

I'm not sure, she says. I try to pretend, at least, that it's a form of urgent business.

The process of externalizing our thoughts, our dreams, our desires, says Drew. It seemed like a good idea, I suppose. A screen is like a bloody little membrane, don't you think. Smeared with our guts, but at the same time almost painless.

You make films, says Felicia.

Made films.

His first screenplay was one of the existential road movies from the '70s. Nameless racers live on the road. Wagers against death, fabricated life histories, western landscapes. A cult film. He made a movie about the manic, delusional American who used military force to become the president of Nicaragua in the 1850s. He made a movie in which Keanu Reeves played the Buddha.

Walk with me this evening, says Drew. The volcano at dusk, there's nothing like it. And I'll tell you all about Huey Beauregard.

There's a Leonora Carrington story or maybe it's Luisa Valenzuela or even Alice fucking Munro—in any case, Felicia's favorite—where a woman leaves her home for a long weekend, and when she returns, the house has shifted, in imperceptible ways. Everything looks exactly the same. But something has changed.

She's a very *troubled* girl, Sarah Cohen. The other adjectives that Drew uses to describe her mental state include *perturbed, uneven, restless, searching*, and *unhinged*. The volcano at dusk. Trenches fracture the earth, because the crust is being stretched.

What is Sarah thinking? Who *is* she?

In the Middle Ages, Europeans considered this a gateway to hell, Drew says.

Vapor steams out of cracks and fissures. Chemical residue: red, charcoal gray, blue, green, yellow. Iron oxide, iron sulphide, nickeline salts, copper sulphate, sulphur. Drew is pale, white. Shaggy white hair, cracked flesh. He resembles a dead tree, ancient parchment, a wisp of vapor. He still has a body. We still have bodies.

He met them through Knute, Connie's boyfriend. Knute is his wife's godson, his wife is friends with Knute's father. The physicist. An old farmhouse in Bolinas, a long weekend, it all came out. Sarah wanted to tell him everything, wanted to impress him. Her success as a writer. It's not the sister, it's the baby girl, Sarah's baby girl they send out in disguise to play the part. She's thirteen, maybe fourteen years old.

What kind of parent dresses up their teenage daughter as an abused and molested boy?

Well, says Drew. Yes.

There's a resemblance to the other case, Anthony Godby Johnson. She explains to Drew: a different set of gay writers leading to a different set of celebrities. Same childhood of incredible abuse. Same stories of delayed puberty and mutant genitalia, because of the abuse. The insane woman in New Jersey who orchestrated it all.

Yes, I remember, says Drew. That wasn't them, but they knew about it. They studied her methods, the New Jersey woman. Improved on them, covered their tracks.

The evolution of the form, says Felicia.

The doctor, they do that by telephone. Apparently he actually believes that he's been giving telephone therapy to a troubled young boy for the past ten years.

How is this possible? How does he get paid?

Well, says Drew. Yes. I don't know.

Bright green moss over black lava. The unreal light of dusk deepening the colors. Unreal. Unreal, unreal. Are the colors not real? Oh yes, things exist. Whispers, echoes, vapor. Clouds, pink around the edges.

It isn't that we're alone or not alone. Alone, what does that even mean? Who is speaking? Who is listening?

A complicated case, Drew says. There's something about her. It's like she's so deluded that she's enlightened. So evil that she's good. She doesn't get it, not really, I don't think. The depth of what she's doing. She's made everything so fake and lived that fakeness in a way that it's like a path…it's like…

Steam rises from the darkening sea. Felicia doesn't even know the name of this sea.

She does have a sense of humor, says Drew. She can be quite funny. Charming.

You're the first person I've heard say that, Felicia says. Except one guy who was probably in love with her. Everybody else seems to find her annoying. They all love Huey. Huey is a genius, an empath, and then there's this pushy woman he drags along with him, wherever he goes.

A history of eruptions and black volcanic sand washed to the sea by streams of glacial meltwater. The earth: scarred and pitted. Frothing, steaming, catastrophic.

It must be very painful, she says. You seduce people with your words, you talk to them intimately on the phone, you make them love you. And then they can't see you, they treat you like some idiot, like trash. They love this image, this thing that isn't real, but that you've created.

It's like Kim Novak in *Vertigo*, Drew says. It's like Jimmy Stewart's love for Kim Novak.

It's like Kim Novak's love for Jimmy Stewart, says Felicia.

They cross a patch of earth that seems to be solidified foam. It's crunchy and black and leads to a ridge, looking down on an icy blue pool of water that is steaming.

I suppose that's why I could find her charming, says Drew.

She wasn't playing a role with you.

She was playing a different role. She was playing herself.

He stops walking.

You get the idea, he says. It's strange and rare. It belongs to us. It's just like us.

Honestly, says Drew, I barely know her.

3

Philip has his father drop him at the hospital directly from the airport. He doesn't want Bob Miller to be dead before he even gets there. The waiting room outside Intensive Care is big enough for a wedding, a class reunion, a valedictory address—and yet Philip feels miniaturized, a new specimen tossed into a muffled vivarium. Bob could easily already have died, while Philip was flying over Nevada or western Colorado, while he was changing planes in Denver. It takes Philip a stunned moment in this vast self-enclosed universe of television screens and upholstered chairs to spot Bob's contingent. There's Bob's mother Dottie, tinier and whiter-haired than seems possible. There's Dave, Bob's debate partner from high school, and then a handful of people Philip doesn't know, including a guy who looks like a shorter, wider, and slightly younger version of Bob. Bob's long lost half-brother, now up from Tampa, with his wife. There are several of Bob's ex-girlfriends. One of them, Evie, lived in Philip's dorm. Philip dropped acid with Janine when he was twenty; now she's a respectable mother of three.

Dottie hugs Philip as if he is her own long-lost child and sobs. And yet, since Philip got the call, Bob's stabilized. They've got him on dialysis and he's been lucid, more or less. But nobody's supposed to see him right now, nobody but family, he needs his rest. But Phil has come all the way from California, Dottie says. I'm taking you in, you're family, my gosh, I've known you since you were five years old.

Philip realizes that in the intervening years he's come to think of Dottie even as a kind of joke. The PTA mom who raised her husband's mistress's child as her own, who dated closeted gay men after the divorce. Her anxieties about what the neighbors might think had helped to mold Bob into a weird, obsequious pretzel. But Philip remembers now how much he'd loved her as a child, this tiny Republican with her owls and her cookies. She'd always organized the best slumber parties. She'd taken all of the boys, Bob and his friends, out to her parents' farm, where they played hide-and-seek in the hayloft and told ghost stories. Somebody was always coming back to life in those stories, some child who'd died in an industrial accident; the parents had been granted three wishes and wished, quite naturally, for money—not thinking that it would come in the form of an insurance settlement for their gruesomely mangled dead boy. For their second wish they wanted their child back, alive.

He *does* come back, the climax of the story. His footsteps draw closer, more the sound of something dragging along the earth than actual footsteps. A hush then and the sound of heavy breathing. He's knocking at the door.

Bob, too, looks like he's already died, but changed his mind.

My gosh, he says, Phil Yoder! Why, you didn't come all the way out here just to see *me*, did you?

Just to see little old you.

It's a struggle for Bob to talk. I'm just so short of breath, he keeps saying. His eyes roll around in his head, his speech is tangled. Philip checks the labels on the IV bags.

After Dottie's left them alone, he asks Bob if he knows what meds he's on. Bob shrugs.

You know how many T-cells you have?

Bob shrugs again.

Oh, three or four.

Normal range would be something like 500 to 1500. It used to be that anything under 200 got you an AIDS diagnosis; Raymond's got down to six.

You didn't know you were positive?

Bob shrugs a third time. Hovering near death hasn't damaged his sense of comic timing.

Knew, didn't know, he says.

Philip tells Bob that he'd forgotten Evie and Janine even existed.

That's understandable, Bob says. Me, too.

There's so much Philip's forgotten.

I don't keep very good track of my past, Philip says. It's good I have you to keep track of it for me.

Bob had always seemed like the more reasonable of the two of them. It was Philip, wasn't it, who imagined the worlds where they played, in the woods next to Bob Miller's house, leading down into the drainage ditch, or at the Howard Johnson's Motor Lodge, after Bob's house burned down, or at the abandoned brick factory, with its crumbling structures and pits full of concrete rubble, twisted iron bars, and half-shattered windows. Philip had transformed these everyday landscapes into games and into places of mystery. Bob had gladly followed wherever Philip would take him. Philip led Bob into the unreal and maybe Bob got stuck there, disappeared there, a somnambular world of gay orgies and crystal meth.

It doesn't matter what Philip believes about the path through the bottom, he decides. If there is a path, that's the only one left. It's the only map worth dreaming of, he supposes: the map that charts a path through the bottom.

Dottie returns with the latest arrival from the East Coast, another one of Bob's ex-girlfriends. Cindy Myers—Philip had a play date with her when he was five. Out in the waiting room, there are more debaters and college roommates, more ex-girlfriends, who still live in town or live in the next state over. None of Bob's former boyfriends are here. None of the hundreds or thousands of men he tricked with in Paris, Los Angeles, or Oakland.

Maybe everybody feels as wavy, jet-lagged, under water, as Philip does.

They've all heard so much about each other. From Bob.

Bob's half-brother Chad was raised by his mother for the first two years of his life, he tells Philip, until she killed herself.

Unlike Bob, says Philip, who only knew her as the lady with the green hair.

If that was even her, says Chad.

Philip remembers how fervent Bob had been, talking about his two mothers, his slutty suicidal biological mother, his saintly real mother Dottie, their mystical connection in Bob's mind with Marilyn Monroe or Doris Day.

Bob's dad had a lot of mistresses, Chad's wife Inna says quietly. Maybe that was his mom and maybe it was another fake blonde.

Inna's from California, too, at least that's where she grew up.

Used to be a logging town, she says. Now it's a prison town.

Chad has no actual memories of his mother. He was raised by her parents at times and by his father and his father's new wife at others. He got into trouble as a teenager, was sent to a home in Texas for a while. He'd known about his mysterious half-brother Bob since he was a little boy. He can remember the day his grandmother first asked him if he wanted to meet his half-brother. He was sitting on the back porch of a house they lived in for a while in Indiana looking out at the trash that was blowing across a vacant lot across the street. His grandmother was wearing a Christmas sweater that she wore even on summer evenings, it made him uncomfortable just to look at her. Drove everybody nuts. Chad had just been suspended from his junior high again. His grandma was probably only trying to help. At the time he just thought of this mysterious half-brother as someone perfectly normal and well adjusted they were throwing in his face. Then six years ago, he got a letter from Bob.

At the next table over, the people from Bob's debate circles are discussing somebody they all knew, back in the day, who's just gotten a job with the Bush administration, as a mouthpiece for torture policies.

Eventually Philip goes home, to eat and to sleep. He needs to be there early the next morning to talk to the doctors; nobody else in Bob's ever-enlarging contingent knows anything about AIDS, and he's not sure the doctors do either.

The next day, the kidney specialist sashays into the waiting room like a celebrity and suggests Bob could actually make it through. There's about eight different things going wrong, he says. But there's no reason that any one of those eight things isn't fixable. The infectious disease specialist pops up later. She talks a good game about HIV and immune reconstitution syndrome, but Philip can tell she's learned it all from books.

When Raymond was sick, everything made him nauseous, the food, the car, the trips to the hospital that never solved anything. Every day there was less of him there, and nobody had any answers. He'd get headaches if he lay flat on his back, so they moved the mattress into the living room, which seemed to help. The bedroom had come to seem like a torture chamber. One morning Raymond was jabbering away, but it wasn't making much sense: the dirty nurse, the evacuation, the dirty war. Philip was delirious with lack of sleep himself, cooking some Cream of Wheat in the kitchen. Maybe Raymond could eat a spoonful or two. Raymond stopped talking, and for a moment it was a relief, a relief from that tortured voice explicating its torment and confusion, until he took the food in and saw that Raymond had lost consciousness. Philip shook him. He didn't wake up and in that moment time expanded or slowed down or sped up, it's always like that, isn't it.

Why is that, do you know?

Something popped, a series of little explosions, and something passed before Philip's eyes. It was one of the worst moments, maybe the worst.

And Raymond passed over, but then he came back. They saved him. The infectious disease specialist in San Francisco had seen hundreds of cases like

Raymond, back in the day. He knew how to monitor his progress, how to ease him back from the abyss. That doctor had seen a lot of people die, but he'd also seen people survive.

Sometimes when you start antivirals and the immune system bounces back, underlying infections go haywire, for reasons nobody yet understands. Sometimes it's the cure that kills you. Philip suspects that's what's happening with Bob.

Bob is resting most of the time, but Philip chats with him briefly. They talk about politics; Bob's interested in the presidential campaign, Hillary and Obama. Which one of them might really end the wars? Eventually Philip tells Bob that he needs to go home and get some dinner, but promises to come back that evening. What he actually needs is a nap. Dottie walks with Philip toward the exit. She grips Philip's hand with surprising force.

It was back in April that Bob finally came home, she tells him. She hadn't seen him in over a year and she knew that things hadn't been going well, and she knew about the drugs, some of it at least. He didn't tell her everything, she knows that, but he told her many things. But he was still a good boy, wasn't he?

Of course, says Philip. He was still a good boy.

He was caught up in that court case back in San Francisco, Dottie says. Caught in the wrong place at the wrong time, in some sleazy drug dealer's apartment when the police came in. He'd already let his license to practice law expire at that point, and then he couldn't sit for the bar in California until he cleared all that up. But he could sit for the bar in Iowa after just a short wait, at least that's what they thought. I needed some help with some things and he could do some volunteer work and study for the bar, that was the plan. Get himself together.

Bob took a train most of the way across country, she says, because he wanted to stop and visit his cousins in Kansas. Or maybe he needed some time in between the life he was living back there and the life he was coming back to, I don't know. He caught a plane for the last leg, though, from Kansas City. The flight wasn't so much money, Dottie assures Philip, and you know, I wasn't up to drive all the way down there to pick him up. The train doesn't come through town and the bus would have been almost as much as the plane, isn't that crazy? So he flew, she says. I'm not sure how he got from the train station in Kansas City to the airport, she says, but he got there somehow and then he flew.

She went to the airport to pick him up, she says, and she was a little bit late because of the traffic, and when she got there, she didn't see him. There were some women who looked like soldiers' wives, says Dottie. She's not sure why she thought that, but there were three of them together, and Dottie was just sure from looking at them that their husbands had been off at war. And there was a young man with a little boy who was holding on to the man's leg, and a young woman with her identical twin, and then this little old man sitting in one of the hard plastic chairs. An older woman showed up and left with the twins, and a young woman came out of the restroom and took the man and his little boy and so then it was just the soldiers' wives and the old man kind of hunched over in his chair. He was so skinny and wrinkled and balding. He didn't have any teeth. And I looked at him and looked at him again, Dottie says. I swear I didn't recognize him, and he just sat there without looking up. This little old man waiting for his mother to come and take him home.

That afternoon, Philip sleeps in his childhood bed and dreams.

Things don't go well in the dream. Some crumbling structure is where he lives, where everybody lives. There's no more patching it up. The corpse's hair has been dyed to make it seem a little livelier, but everything is drifting away to the north. Toward Canada and the Northwest Territories. A small unrecognizable group of people, like characters from a poorly remembered film, need to escape from the planet to a small nearby planet whose destruction is less imminent. Destroying a planet destroys all of its ghosts as well, so that it isn't just the living who are going to die, but the dead. Philip's in a little space pod, waiting for blast-off with these few strangers and the reinvigorated corpse, whose dyed hair has grown at a phenomenal rate or who's wearing a wig. The little pod is headed toward the small nearby planet—the planet is just a cartoon really, barely big enough for the pod to land on—and the only difference between its destruction and the earth's is a matter of hours. The destruction will be absolute.

Philip wakes up at 7:30 in the evening, feeling hollow again, doomed and disoriented. He eats a sandwich and returns to the hospital, putting on his cheeriest face.

They tried to call him—Dottie wanted to talk to him before they took off the life support, *Call Philip, Philip will know if it's the right thing to do*, she kept saying, according to Dave—Bob's systems were collapsing, his organs failing. Bob started to get really freaked out and he was clearly in a lot of pain, but they gave him more morphine and he quieted down. He's not conscious anymore and he never will be again.

And so Philip discovers that he must have already said good-bye. And here is Dottie, hugging him, and finally now, breaking down. And here he is, reassuring her that she did the right thing, the only thing there was to do.

He was a good boy, wasn't he? she asks again.

And yet Bob isn't exactly dead yet and so there is still the technical business of his dying that they all must wait for. There's a lot of weeping and hugging with strangers and with people that Philip barely knows. Before long the hospital's minister comes in to offer her nondenominational support to the grieving family. She's a mannish dyke, and she hovers in the waiting room, apparently with no greater spiritual emergency to take her away. There's an awkward moment of prayer around the dying body.

I suggest we project an outward flow of open, alert attention without wanting, the minister says. Just be present.

She clasps the hands of those on either side of her, Dottie and Inna.

I guess there's supposed to be someone up there in charge of this whole thing, Dottie tells the minister. But I don't know. None of it makes too much sense to me.

She drops the minister's hand and leans over her son's body.

When you get to heaven, Dottie says to Bob, tell your father what I think of him.

People take turns around the deathbed late into the night, watching Bob's troubled final breaths. At some nameless hour of the morning or night, Philip finally gets a last minute alone with Bob's shriveled, toothless form. He strokes Bob's thinning hair and is joined by a vague figure from Bob's past, and from his own, Janine.

For some reason, Janine starts telling him about the birth of her most recent child. Six months into the pregnancy, something went wrong. It's like she's describing a scene from a horror movie. There's blood everywhere. There are strange tissues in clumps on the hospital floor. A weird, life-threatening growth in her womb, a super-rare condition that gets all the doctors in a frenzy. She's just bleeding all over everything: the crisp white paper on the examining table, a magazine article about Gwyneth Paltrow, the nurses. The doctors in her small Illinois town decide to fly her to Chicago in a helicopter—she remembers being lifted into the sky with the chopper blades twirling and gasping overhead—that sound was drowning out everything, it was so loud—and all around her, the sky. They're giving her oxygen and huddling around her, all these faces. Who were they? She felt so deeply connected to them, two or three of them, she wasn't quite sure, hovering around her in the sky, but she doesn't think she ever saw them again. Once she got to the hospital in Chicago, there were others who took over. She never thought to ask what happened to the ones from the helicopter, what their names were. She'd lost so much blood, everything got confused. She was kept in the Chicago hospital for weeks, until it was time for the actual birth. It was too dangerous, they said, for her to be anywhere else, until that baby was out of there. That's how they put it—as if he was stuck in a cage, as if she was stuck along with him. She was so medicated for the actual birth, there was just this gap in time and then she felt like the site of a battle. But the baby was fine. There was all that blood, but the baby was fine. Janine seems slightly stunned, as if she's reciting a story she's memorized, but she doesn't know why. Philip squeezes her hand.

He kisses Bob on the forehead and says good-bye and goes out to the waiting room to tell Dottie that he's going home to bed.

Philip isn't thinking clearly. Somehow he takes a wrong turn or gets off the elevator on the wrong floor and finds himself in a long, deserted hallway with no exits, perhaps in the hospital basement. The doors that line the hallway are all locked, so he forges on.

Once, in 1986, Philip picked up a hitchhiker on his motorcycle. His name was Billy or Bernie or Doug, and this was in Colorado. Philip had picked him up because he was shirtless and from a distance he looked pretty good, but then up close he didn't look good at all. He convinced Philip to take him back to the small mountain town he came from—it was just off the highway anyway, along the Colorado River. He'd been chased out of town by his family or the town authorities, or maybe it was the same thing. They dropped in on his grand-mother, who set them down on upholstered chairs covered in plastic, folded her hands in her lap, and chatted awhile, just catching up, until she made a phone call and they had to get out of there quick. Then they went to the supermarket and Billy or Bernie or Doug shoplifted some meat and beer. Philip told him he'd need to drop him off somewhere, he had to head back to Boulder. They stopped at a rest stop just outside of town, at Doug or Bernie's request, a rest stop overlooking the river, snaking through the canyon with the railroad tracks running along beside. The key to Philip's motorcycle disappeared. It wasn't in the ignition or any of his pockets or on the asphalt by the motorcycle—it had vanished into thin air. Soon it would be dark. There was nothing to do but spend the night at that rest stop, Billy or Bernie or Doug suggested, and build a fire, grill the meat. They could sleep right here over the river, which was stunning and romantic in a slightly contrived way. They drank the beers, and as it got cold, the hitchhiker started groping Philip. He just needed some warmth, he kept saying, just a little warmth. In the morning, the key magically reappeared in the ignition.

The hospital hallway ends at a T intersection, and in the distance, down the corridor to the left, Philip can make out an Exit sign.

Once, a man whose name Philip doesn't remember and whose name he might not ever have known, paid Philip to go with him back to his bleak little room in an SRO. He had AIDS dementia, Philip's pretty sure, and he raved and ranted. He, too, just wanted a little warmth. He just wanted to be held, he said, and he curled up on the fetid, spongy carpet of his tiny room, no bigger than a walk-in closet. A little warmth was just about the only thing Philip had to offer at that point in his life. They didn't do anything sexual, but Philip barely held him either. The guy mostly just ranted as if Philip wasn't even there, as if he was arguing with his own ghost. He had those crazy kind of eyes that would never focus on you, that would dart erratically here and there as if he was being witnessed and persecuted by hordes of invisible faces, as if he was in turn witnessing and persecuting the legion of invisibles—all of the living and all of the dead—but eventually he fell asleep or passed out or something, clutching a wad of cash in his hand. Several hundred dollars, he'd probably just cashed his SSI check. Philip didn't take it all, only the amount that he'd been promised. *I was still young then*, thinks Philip. By that point he had gotten over his youthful practice of imagining himself as a good person. He didn't think of himself as bad or wicked; it just didn't seem to matter so much what stories you told yourself about being nice.

Philip's not sure how to think about Bob now. He knows that his story of Bob isn't Bob. What Bob was for Bob is pretty murky, but Philip would like to imagine it.

Maybe Bob got so far gone into his meth and his orgies that he'd demystified sex completely. Maybe he stopped being a victim of sex or worshipping the people he wanted, instead of the places sex could take him. Maybe it wasn't about other people, or even himself. Maybe he couldn't bear his own face, or could bear it only intermittently. Maybe it felt good, and nothing else really did.

The hallway slopes down, farther and farther, as if it's tunneling under the river. The atmosphere is cool and increasingly moist. The hallway levels out, makes a few abrupt turns, until it begins ascending again, and as it ascends, it brightens and the corridors become less austere, with carpeting and potted plants and abstract paintings, but still not a soul to be seen. More and more of these potted plants fill up vestibules to nowhere until it seems as if he is wandering into a forest. He hits the hallway's end and a door marked *Botanical Gardens*.

It's green and humid inside. The vegetation is thick and quickly evolves from the sort of shade-loving bromeliads that fill up dentists' offices to actual trees.

Oak trees, actually, and they're covered with lichen. A small child sits alongside the path vrooming a jagged piece of metal and a toy jeep.

Hello, says Philip. Are you lost?

The child shakes its head. It might be a boy.

Is your mom or dad here?

The child stands and takes Philip's hand. Come, it says. I'll show you.

The paved path evaporates into a narrow, well-trodden dirt trail through even thicker vegetation. It would be easy enough to get lost. The *Exit* sign is still visible behind them, dimly glowing. My friend is just up ahead, says the child.

Your friend.

Haven't I been here before? asks the child.

Funny, Philip says. I was just going to say the same thing.

Philip stops. Maybe once as a child. The vegetation clearly thins out in a spot up ahead, but there's something odd. It looks like a large bed. The child is beaming up at him with a smile that Philip can't imagine, even as he's looking at it. He releases the child's hand.

The heart has to present itself alone before nothingness.

It has to beat alone in the darkness.

And then...

Why are you crying? asks the child.

I'm very tired, Philip says.

Something is ruffling around in the bed or whatever. Philip isn't sure why he imagines it's a kind of hog or wild boar. He is terrified for a moment, but then he lets his terror go, along with the child. Something has been let go, or maybe everything.

You better go on ahead. Tell your friend to keep a better watch on you, okay?

You don't want to come along?

Not tonight, says Philip.

The child skips ahead. But his hand is still sticking out at his side, as if he's still holding Philip's hand or as if he's holding the hand of a shadow. Or as if he's a spastic little fairy accompanied by a dark smudge, his future perhaps, which disappears along with the child into the trees.

4

IT'S LATE AFTERNOON, and Geordi is viciously blotting out paragraphs of his thesis with a black marker, when his aunt calls. Geordi's granny is in the hospital. The neighbor girl found her.

Geordi leaves his thesis behind, throws a few things in a bag, some clothes, some weed, *The 8-Fold Garden of Space and Time*, the notebook from the tent, and drives straight toward Bakersfield.

Around Livermore he gets mired in rush-hour traffic.

It always startles him, the obvious fact that there are too many people. Too many roads, too many cars, too much heat. Something is about to happen. His body won't be able to withstand it. Just past the merger with 5 South he has to pull off the road at a rest stop. It's a memorial rest stop for Larry somebody. Even after he shuts off the car, everything is still vibrating. Something happened, something happened. Everything is vibrating and the truckers are driving much too fast. There's a field of young almond trees in the distance across the highway, perfectly uniform, hundreds of trees exactly the same. Beyond that is the shimmering blue ribbon of the aqueduct, carrying water from the north to the parched Central Valley. None of these trees should grow here, not really.

When he was a boy, the aqueduct seemed like a magical swimming pool that went on and on forever. If they were driving past it, it meant they were leaving and going somewhere else.

It's that point in the summer evening when the day has been going on forever and there has always been too much light. But eventually it will be dark, he knows, and so he gets back on the road and drives the stretch of 5 that he's driven over and over again, north to south or south to north, past Patterson and past Andersen's Split Pea Restaurant and past the endless feeding lot of cows north of Coalinga. When he is on this road, he's always been on this road. But of course, after several lifetimes, he reaches Buttonwillow and turns off for Bakersfield.

In Bakersfield it is the same summer evening that it has always been. In the hospital, he sits by his grandmother's side, waiting for her to speak. Get some rest, his aunt tells him, we all need some rest. Nothing's going to change tonight.

Change means death.

It is the same evening it has always been. You know that.

Geordi will spend his night in the hospital room. Every few hours, when his grandmother's IV is low, a machine will start beeping. Hours will pass or days or weeks or eternity will collapse in on itself and he'll have an email from his wife. What kind of parent dresses up their teenage daughter as an abused and molested boy? she asks.

The parking lot of the hospital will be black and flaming asphalt like the lava from the volcanoes of his granny's hometown. What kind of parent, what kind of parent. The words fall apart early one morning, right after his grandmother has died. What kind of parent. Kind of what parent. Kind parent of what.

The same old searing emptiness above, impossible to imagine even when it's there.

It's easy to have a breakdown. You just wait for a good excuse, and then you do it. He'll drive south and then he'll head east on 40 and drive across the Mojave shimmering like a reanimated fossil and past the Edwards Air Force Base, homicidal metal shrieking through the sky.

Geordi hates men today, all men.

He'll avoid Barstow, even though he should probably fill up the tank. That woman might find him, that woman from the Grapevine, and then he would die. He'll cut south instead and drive on past Palm Springs and Indio, the walled resorts and trashy shimmer, and at Indio he'll cut south past the Salton Sea.

The beaches are covered with dead fish and dead fish are bobbing in the water and it all smells like dead fish. There are housey structures and other signs of occupation but not a human in sight. Eerie. Animals in a cage of light, an amazing cage. Eerie eerie eerie. The only time he felt stranger than this he cannot remember.

He'll cut east on I-8.

He used to play with this bossy girl. She was older than Geordi and lived in the neighborhood and she was obsessed with this group, the Only Ones. One of those strange temporary friendships from childhood that nobody calls friendship. She didn't want to mother him exactly. It was more like he was a captive audience. She'd sit him down on the floor in her bedroom and play that song for him over and over. "Why Don't You Kill Yourself?" Her bedroom was dark, the curtains always shut, and it smelled like wet dog. Sometimes she was so nice to him and then sometimes she was cruel.

Just east of Yuma, he runs into a checkpoint. A queue of traffic sprawls across several lanes, and as each car approaches the checkpoint, a guy in a uniform with a vicious-looking dog on a leash lets the dog approach the car and then steps back, approaches and steps back, and sometimes the dog barks wildly, as if it's enraged, driven mad with excitement, and those cars that enrage the dog are directed to pull over to a special area.

Geordi understands what's happening just as he reaches the checkpoint.

The mad snarling thing lunges at him, barking wildly, as if enraged.

The guy in uniform directs Geordi to pull over to the side.

He parks next to the car of a young, faded, hippie-ish couple, already emptying their pockets and answering questions.

The Border Patrol guy is smug. He asks Geordi for permission to search his car and explains to Geordi the total power he has to do whatever he wants, whatever Geordi says.

It will go better for Geordi if he gives permission, the agent says, and if he's completely honest and tells the agent exactly what drugs he has in the car and where the drugs are.

No, he doesn't want Geordi to give him the drugs, Geordi just needs to step out of the car and stand to the side.

The dog jumps on Geordi and sniffs him at the orders of the smug agent and he's asked to empty his pockets, while the dog jumps into the car slobbering and sniffing everywhere.

Geordi makes eye contact with the hippie-ish woman, suggesting some sort of solidarity. Or maybe suggesting that they've witnessed each other, in case somebody goes missing.

Mammatus clouds in the distance. Gray to pale blue, a cartoon of cells and tissues and fingerprints in the sky. It isn't clear what the threat is of the storm that produced them. A moist and unstable middle or upper level in the atmosphere over a dry layer.

The agent asks Geordi if he's an American citizen and if he can prove it.

Geordi is seething with a rage so incandescent that it startles him that the agent smiles in an almost jocular way, once he's established Geordi's citizenship and found the weed exactly where Geordi told him it would be, and it startles Geordi that the agent doesn't seem to understand that Geordi wants to urinate on his corpse.

Geordi is led to a decrepit little holding cell they've built by the side of the road and he is locked up there, alone, while they prepare the paperwork he'll need to sign. What is the central topic of prison writing, Geordi wonders.

They're taking their time. They've got all the time in the world; they own the time.

Narrative is time.

They were sailing at night, beneath a sky streaked with heat lightning, down a river full of alligators.

The waiting is over; hence the idea of revolution.

This journey is named the journey through the land of the dead.

Eventually Geordi's given a citation and told that he'll need to return to Yuma for his court date in two months. No way. No way is he ever coming back to this state, this country, no way. He heads back to Yuma. He pulls over in a parking lot behind a McDonald's, and he's trembling. The notebook sits on the front seat beside him, filled with empty pages. *The Coming Revolution of the Lifeworld Against the Tyrants of Space and Time.*

Geordi, my dear, all writing is prison writing. Don't you remember? The storm is already here, it will never arrive. The air is still and trembling. He knows the two legible sentences by heart. *Come on, let's run away, into the desert, with the icy stars and the emptiness of space overhead, where the incessant wind will obliterate any trace of our footsteps in the shifting sands. And they will never find us.* He closes his eyes and drifts toward sleep with the evening sun on his face. It's as if he's entering another world, along with his grandmother. The passing away of his childhood and every connection to it, the passing away of his memory, of his connection to the earth itself. He knows that he can never come back, never. It isn't like *he's* sobbing, because there's nothing left of Geordi.

It is written that each one of us must one day go far away.

Past the place where the mountains come together, past the place guarded by a watchful serpent, past the green lizard, you cross the eight deserts, over the eight hills; you travel to the place of the obsidian-bladed winds.

The rationale for Geordi's breakdown is more difficult to maintain through the complicated process of crossing the border and then afterward, driving farther and farther into the Mexican night. The voices of his sisters, of his mother, of that bossy girl with the record player berating him. There's only one voice he wants to hear, that's the problem. He turns on the car radio to fill his head with her radio shows and all those voices speaking as if in a kind of trance.

5

RAYMOND WAKES UP IN THE MIDDLE of the night with the rats chewing and rustling out there in the dark. Everything is packed into boxes, ready to go. He gets up to ride his bike until daylight, out through the cold and drug-addled streets of the Mission and beyond into the colder and practically deserted streets of the Avenues. Out past the scary Catholic university where his father went to school and into the Richmond District Avenues, where it's just Raymond and an occasional cop car and the ghostly blurs that keep pace with him for a moment before veering off toward the trees of Golden Gate Park. Maybe he should outreach to one of the jogging anorexics, asking her about her history of drug use and sex. Sexual contacts—none. No men, no women, no trannies, no oral, no anal, no oral/anal, no "other." Only one orifice, used strictly for binging and purging. But then why is she a client? She has sex with her husband every few months, whenever he starts insisting she see a psychiatrist. The husband visits prostitutes, she is certain, and surely doesn't use condoms, maybe even shoots drugs with them. Thus, her risk factor. She's had chlamydia and has hepatitis, either B or C, she's not sure. Evidence of mental confusion. She speaks only in non sequiturs, she tells many lies. Her stories become more and more elaborate and nonsensical, as if she is in a prolonged faint—*as if while she is standing there talking, she is simultaneously fainting, or blowing away in the wind.* But now, in reality, one of the ghostly blurs stops, jogging in place, and moves its mouth, waves its arms, Raymond, it is saying, hey Raymond. Raymond has to suppress a gasp when he finally recognizes Judy, his old tennis partner Roy's wife.

Judith's training for a marathon. Raymond tells her they'll be moving and he'll call Roy to give him the new address. They have nothing much to say, and Judith is raring to go.

It's only after riding farther out toward the ocean and then veering into the park itself that he remembers a dinner he cooked for Roy and Judith once, deep-fried sand dabs, okra, and roasted little red potatoes with sesame seeds, maybe a dozen years ago, when Judith was still plump and kind of dykey, before she became an overachieving and boyish psychotherapist. Roy has always loved to eat and had feasted on the deep-fried sand dabs, okra, and roasted little red potatoes with sesame seeds. Raymond had been feeding him since they started playing tennis together, just after the years when Raymond was a troubled teen and committed to a variety of sick institutions, where other troubled teens would wake him up in the middle of the night and mutter to him about the blackening, the devastation, the cloud of death swallowing up the planet and its plants and animals and people, and when he saw practically nobody he wasn't related to, when his only other tennis partners besides Roy were the children of the cult who lived in a camper shell next to the Ashby tennis courts in Berkeley. Ra and his boys wouldn't eat pork but they'd stuff their faces with the cheapest sugary pies every morning. He rides out past Spreckels Lake now and past the sad bison in their paddock and then back east and south, toward the AIDS Memorial Grove, until he remembers that already, back in 1994 or 1995, Judith had barely touched her deep-fried sand dabs, okra, and roasted little red potatoes with sesame seeds. Poor Judith, Raymond thinks, as he pedals past the cruisy restroom. The city is now lightening around the edges. Poor Judith. He imagines some troubled child coming in to tell Judith his or her problems—delusional parents and bizarre sexual fantasies, the side effects of antidepressants, suicidal thoughts, the usual things—and she's good, Raymond's sure that Judith is empathetic, nurturing, a great listener, but every week the child comes in and there's less of Judith there, every week Judith's more and more fervent in her desire to save the troubled child, the kind of fervency that only comes when you're starving your body's cells. Becoming a kind of skeleton, an immaterial, fleshless automaton—that's one possible descent, admirable perhaps in its extreme response to the question of how to be a human, how to live ethically within the food chain, within the orgy of slavery and consumption, within the permanent war economy, the answer Judy is giving and all the jogging anorexics, barely at all, that's how you live, barely present, barely here, one foot in this world and one in the next, like in the last story Raymond ever wrote, at the high school that he'd been assigned to after Lowell didn't work out, College Park High, where he was housed with other dropouts, teenage mothers, juvenile delinquents, and retards, in classrooms presided over by the most rickety, the most jaded, the most bottom-of-the-barrel adults, adults who would sleep through their own algebra classes, adults who would set the kids up with educational board games during learning skills classes and then skip out for parts unknown, adults who expected absolutely nothing from their students but that they allow the day to pass more or less without dramatic incident, although occasionally a young fresh-faced recruit would wander in, trying to do something for these kids, to save them, like the young woman who presided over his English class, although it wasn't called English at College Park High. It was called language learning, and one day the fresh-faced young woman read a story Raymond had written, the last story he ever wrote, the last he ever will, which was like a little myth about a boy who had to fast and live off berries and nuts and climb a mountain as part of his coming-of-age ritual and he made it to the top of the mountain, but he was so hungry he couldn't keep himself together anymore, and he turned into a little triangle of light and fell off the mountain and died. The language learning teacher told him it was great. But, she said, did you really write this or did you copy it from somewhere? Raymond was insulted. He said, Yeah, I wrote it, but didn't explain to the teacher that he hadn't always been surrounded by the dropouts, teenage mothers, juvenile delinquents, and retards at College Park High, but had been a pupil at Lowell, the most illustrious high school in the city.

Barely present, barely here, one foot in this world and one in the next. Deep underneath the earth, with the bones, like his grandmother's bones, like Ricky J and Louie's bones, like Bob Miller's already decaying corpse, or with the ashes, lost among the waves of the Pacific Ocean, like his father's ashes, feeding some sort of cadaverous fish. One foot with the ghosts, the nonexistent, the eternal nothingness, and one foot right here in creepy and unsatisfying reality, a way of being he himself is horrifically familiar with, not only because of his experiments, like the boy in the story, with fasting, during his days at College Park High, when he went for five days without eating once, until he was dizzy all the time and he couldn't sleep, *go get food*, his body was telling him, *do not sleep, do not dream*, and then more recently of course he acquired that nasty case of cryptococcal meningitis and lost fifty pounds, not because he was aiming for some sort of monkish enlightenment and not because he thought his body contained too much matter, not because he didn't want to eat but because he couldn't, he was nauseous, he'd vomit his food, and nobody could figure out exactly why. It was so retro. Nobody got those nasty AIDS illnesses anymore, he thinks as he veers north so as not to arrive at the AIDS Memorial Grove after all, and heads instead toward the botanical garden and then the Haight, remembering how his head would scream with pain while he was wasting away as Philip watched and tried to make him Cream of Wheat or some other bland slop that might not make him ill, until the morning that Raymond was sitting up in the bed, trying to explain something to Philip, something that was barely making sense inside his own head, but was deeply important, even crucial. What was in his head after all? What did he consist of then? It's all just a blur of pain and nightmares and sweat. And then he just kind of drifted away, toward nothingness, oblivion. He let go. It felt good to let go, it was all okay. Good-bye, good-bye. He was on his way. What is the self when the dream is ending? What is the self when the dream is over? What is the future, what is time, it's nothing, it's nothing, it's nothing. And yet from somewhere far away, in a time frame that had no referents, the paramedics were shouting his name *Raymond wake up, Raymond, Raymond* and clapping their hands the way his grandmother used to clap when she wanted to startle him from his overly complex and dramatic thought processes, when she wanted him to be practical, when she wanted him to *stop all that foolishness*, and then the paramedics were strapping him onto their gurney and he was being whisked away to the hospital, as if, he thinks now, dying was what his grandmother had always meant by *all that foolishness* and the boring, practical business of daily life was the only alternative she knew. He rides over the 17th Street hill and descends into the Castro, with the sun just coming up, and the marquee of the Castro Theatre advertising a sing-along version of *West Side Story* and he stops outside the kiosk next door that sells magazines, not open yet, but in the window is the face of Huey Beauregard on the cover of *7x7*, trapped not only behind glass but behind its silly little mask. It doesn't seem quite real, although he isn't sure what "it" is exactly, that doesn't seem quite real, not just Huey or the magazine or the gaudy surfaces of the Castro Theatre and the Victorians that rise up into the hills like a fabulous façade, not just the fact of time itself, the strange passing of the years, but not exactly "everything" either, which would just be lazy thinking, but something, certainly, central to life and to death, something doesn't seem real, and he'll wonder then if his own descent was in fact the most spectacular descent, the lowest anyone he knows has gone and then returned, the deepest into the grave.

6

AMOS IS WAITING FOR PHILIP at the barricades with the full outfit: hat, suspenders, blue shirt. He looks different, but almost the same.

It's July and so Iowa is squashed and sultry, shimmering with humidity.

They drive together, mostly in silence, several hours south, toward the lake where Amos's mother killed herself. On the way, they stop at an abandoned house on top of a hill. An ugly prefab box plopped in the middle of nowhere, overlooking a small highway. Amos's stepfather used to rent the place, and the garage beside it sits wide open, still stuffed full of the stepfather's trash, which he's abandoned here. Pamphlets and tracts, mostly of a religious nature, but also touting various nutritional supplements. Brochures detailing the prophecies of Nostradamus. Elaborate plans for a new community with bomb shelters, schools, radio stations, purified water, and organic gardens. Old board games and bicycles, books of photographs, and cracked mirrors.

She kept a diary, Amos says. Lots of diaries.

Philip lets him poke around. After ten minutes or so, he finds just one notebook. August through October 1991, the year before Amos was born. Amos doesn't read it, but he holds it tight as they continue south to the lake.

They arrive at dusk, with a sky full of ominous clouds, purple in the fading light.

They stand on a bridge overlooking the spot where she drove in.

It's not a beautiful lake. It's dammed, and dead tree branches and even a few odd structures from before they flooded the plain stick out like the woody or rusted arms of a drowning woman.

There are some pretty cliffs nearby. Still.

It certainly feels haunted. It certainly feels apocalyptic and Amish. Philip can see himself and he can see Amos reflected in the murky, rippling water below, two wavy, dark figures without faces or histories.

They talk more during the drive back, through the muggy night.

Do you ever see that boy? Philip asks. The shooter's son?

We used to do things sometimes, Amos says.

Do things?

You know, Amos says.

This was before the shooting or after?

Amos shrugs.

Can't keep track of all of that, he says.

But Philip doesn't think that Amos has told him yet everything he knows.

Did you ever hear of Nico? Amos asks.

Nico? Who sang with the Velvet Underground?

Amos has never heard of the Velvet Underground, but yes, it seems that's the Nico he means. The woman who sang "Wrap Your Troubles in Dreams."

My mother was like her, Amos says.

Like Nico?

His mother was shunned by her family and ended up the wife and prisoner of a man with a dark nature. But now maybe she's at peace. Or maybe not at peace, but at least...

Philip has a bad feeling.

My oldest friend just died, he tells Amos. That's why I'm here. The memorial service is the day after tomorrow, and then I'll go back.

Amos smiles in a dreamy way and then makes a sad face and then he shrugs.

Amos is satisfied with his life among the Amish, he tells Philip. It isn't necessary to be happy, he doesn't think. He doesn't write anymore or play his guitar.

Was the shooter's son there that night? asks Philip.

It gets confused, says Amos. You don't need to sort it out.

Did he kill himself? Was he wearing...a wedding dress?

I don't know, says Amos. You can look it up on the Internet if you want to.

No, says Philip.

I forgave him, Amos says, but I didn't love him. I tried to take him to the other side, but it must not be enough.

I think it is, says Philip. I think it's enough.

But he isn't sure what the other side is even the other side *of*, and why anyone would want to get there.

I have your manuscript with me, Philip says. I saved it from the fire. You can have it if you want it.

No, thank you, says Amos.

But if Philip wants to do something with it, he says, that's fine.

Amos rests his head on the window. He's still clutching his mother's journal.

Pretty soon, he's softly snoring. He doesn't wake until they turn off the highway, just a few miles from his grandfather's farm.

Bob's old neighborhood is bright and shady and empty, although the sound of unseen power tools and lawn mowers creates a buzzing and ticking that is like the ambient noise of suffocation. Bob's house is at the end of the street, tucked in next to the little patch of woods that descends toward a soggy drainage ditch.

Philip and Dave and Bob's brother and Inna and Dottie are meeting here with some old friend of Bob's father, who'll be delivering the eulogy. They are to share stories about Bob, to help create a complex portrait for this family friend, who only knew him, after all, as an adult knows a child. The chalk line around a dead body, thinks Philip. Should he tell this man the story of the bridge?

Dottie shows Philip around the house. About ten years ago she built a little sunroom in the back, overlooking the woods.

Where are your owls? asks Philip.

Dottie says that after the fire, she never really got back into the owl thing.

Philip's ideas about Dottie are ridiculously out of date. Still, Philip knows that every time he comes back to visit his family in Iowa now, he'll visit Dottie, who won't leave her house much. He knows that she'll cry every time he shows up at her door and that every time she will ask him the same question. He was a good boy, wasn't he?

They're seated. The family friend remembers Dottie helping Bob with his math problems in the back of the car when he was five. Bob's brother tells a story about Bob driving them around the East Bay, all enthusiastic about showing them the Oakland Museum, but getting lost. All of this buildup and they finally find it just before closing. It wasn't much of a museum anyway, Bob's brother says, but Bob, he made it seem like the greatest thing ever. Nobody was a more enthusiastic tour guide than Bob. Dave tells a story about the trip the debate team took in high school to New York and how Bob insisted they see a Broadway show and how they ended up seeing *Little Johnny Jones*, starring Donny Osmond.

The family friend keeps talking about Bob's wasted potential and his dark side. This is code for the meth and the orgies. It becomes clear to Philip that despite the family friend's obsession with Bob's dark side, the word AIDS is not going to be mentioned at any time, nor is it going to be publicly acknowledged that Bob was gay—*Little Johnny Jones* will be as close as it gets. He remembers how angry that would have made him back in 1992, but in 2007, it just seems surreal.

You know, one of the things I really loved about Bob, Inna says, was how he could find something fascinating about everywhere. That year we went out to California for the holidays and he showed us around Oakland, but then he came with us to the little town I grew up in, in the mountains, to celebrate Christmas with my family. It used to be a logging town, and now we have three prisons, a federal and two state, and you know I hated it all the time I was growing up there and I just wanted to leave. But Bob, you know, it could be the most wretched place in the world and he could get you to see the beauty there. Or well, almost, she says. It was like, the weird little details of those lives, he'd totally get into it. There's this little museum in my town and I'd been there probably just once, when I was a little girl, and hated every minute of it, you know, but Bob insisted. It kind of memorialized the pioneer forefathers and glorified the logging industry and told funny stories about the natives who'd still hung around after most of them had been killed off, but some of their baskets were on display and they were really beautiful. It was just one room full of weird stuff, really, the museum. Sunkist crates, because Sunkist, the orange company, they owned the logging company, too. They chopped down the trees to make the crates to ship their fruit. And Bob found this weird little doll they had on display, it was the creepiest little man, and it had belonged to this old character from like the 1920s or the '30s called Dad Popcorn, who sold popcorn on the streets of the town. The doll was a part of his popcorn machine, it turned the kernels and kept them from burning, I guess. But then once, in the '30s, his machine blew up and injured two little girls. I guess Dad Popcorn never recovered from that, Inna says, and she looks around the circle of listeners as if she is looking there for some explanation herself. Then she falls quiet.

Back in San Francisco, in their new place, all that's left are the dreams. Philip has dreams in which Bob doesn't seem to realize that he's dead, and it's Philip's job to break the news to him. Dreams in which Bob seems to be finally getting his financial affairs together, now that he's dead. A dream in which Philip's seeing Bob for the last time, before Bob heads to Europe—but then they both realize that he'll never come back from Europe, and Philip tells Bob maybe he'll come see him there, in Europe, and in the dream he tells Bob he loves him and he begins to cry. It's the evening after that particular dream, with the wind blowing like crazy from the west, that he makes the phone call to Bob's ex, the Southern belle Dwight, to tell him the news.

Dwight is grateful to Philip for the call. They talk only briefly, but in that short time Dwight tells Philip about the time that Bob gave him that fat lip.

Things were already getting bad between them, and then Bob caught Dwight in a lie. Bob kept bringing it up over and over again and he said, Just tell me the truth, I just want to be able to trust that you're telling the truth, it doesn't matter, and so finally Dwight told him the truth. And Bob hit him. And then he started throwing things and then he started choking Dwight. I thought I was going to die, Dwight says. In that moment I really thought he was going to choke me and I was going to die and it seemed incredibly stupid. I mean my whole life, my life with Bob—it all seemed incredibly stupid, if this was how I was going to die. His face was just inches from mine and his teeth were huge, he was acting like he was going to bite me, bite my head off.

Philip says, So he still had his teeth then.

It was like I wasn't looking at a human being anymore, Dwight says. He was just this monster, just these teeth and this rage. That kind of rage, I mean I guess I'd glimpsed it before, sure, but it had never seemed quite real. I mean here it was so out of proportion to anything I'd actually done is what I thought. Sex, who cares? But he was squeezing my neck and I was gasping for breath and it was like I could see all the way down his throat. You never really think about a person's throat, Dwight says. The inside of a person's body. I just mean all this stuff on the surface…People's faces and conversations and the hours of the day. It was like I was just there forever with Bob choking me and threatening to kill me and like looking at his teeth and his gums. It was like I'd always been there, like that. He was demanding that I tell him everything I'd ever done. He said *Tell me the truth or I'll kill you*. And I told him the truth, which was nothing, really, and eventually he calmed down, and we lay down without either of us really sleeping and then later I started getting ready to leave him, Dwight says. A month later, I was gone.

7

MELVIN THOUGHT HE'D HAVE a chance to argue his case, to reconcile the official events of history with his own version, but nobody's in court. Felicia has gone "abroad," and Philip had to go back home for some emergency, the public defender tells him. They enter the plea of Guilty of Child Endangerment and Melvin is sentenced to time served plus two hundred hours of community service and he's free.

Time served, over five months.

Outside again, in the city, it all comes rushing back. Maybe murdering time and squandering liberty isn't such a bad thing after all. He wanders around just looking at everything and flowing through the streets. Since the Cambrian, not a single new phylum has evolved. No new body plans. Same old same old. But there still seem to be plenty of outlandish surfaces. Melvin has no place to sleep.

At Philip and Raymond's cottage, a woman answers the door. Would you like to rent it? she asks. Come in and take a look. Emptied of its things, except for two chairs, the apartment is too metaphorical. Then again, what does that even mean?

I'm a little overstimulated right now, says Melvin.

Back downtown in the Tenderloin, a squat little drug dealer man is calling to him. Hey, bubba. Melvin ignores him, but stops to look at some books that are laid out for sale on the sidewalk, along with tattered clothes and rip-off DVDs, the refugee products from last year's or last decade's fashion bins, the trickle down of what somebody thought we'd buy more of than we actually did, the excess that has filtered down to the street, being sold for fifty cents to support a drug habit. *The Poisonwood Bible* by Barbara Kingsolver and *Hollywood Heartbreak* by Laurie Jacobson and *Before and After the Wedding: Exploring Intimacy in Marriage* by Grace H. Ketterman and *Beyond Eden* by Catherine Coulter and *Othello* by William Shakespeare and some kids' book called *Sabertooths and the Ice Age*. He picks up *The Nexus Factor* by Dr. Carson J. Tryon, which looks like a combination science fiction and diet book. He picks up *In Search of the Neanderthals* because he can identify with that. Extinction, melancholy, musical brains. Hey baby, says the squat little drug dealer man, and Melvin turns to see if he's really still talking to him. You know me, the man says in a weird raspy accent, and he opens wide to reveal a mouth full of crack rocks. No thanks, says Melvin, and the man keeps strolling. For the longest time Melvin's been confused as to whether sex is a trick pointing to a realization of the void or vice versa. He's looking for one thing, he always finds the other. Does the strange little man recognize the toughness Melvin acquired in jail, that little extra swagger? *The Entities* by Philip Yoder. No way. Only fifty cents and the book has even been signed in the front, *To Rick with love and respect*. He flips it open and catches a sentence that's been underlined, by Rick most likely. *Used to be so thick with trees you'd never know the Great Highway was on one side and the soccer field on the other.* Exactly. It's like Melvin's path is through a dark forest in the process of being clear-cut and on one side is the road to heaven and on the other some stupid game that's all about humiliating and murdering the losers. Melvin would rather be still flailing about in the decimated stand of trees than wandered onto either the Great Highway or the soccer field. Maybe he's finally figured sex out. One disappointment after another into eternity, because it's really just a sign pointing toward a ghostly fantasy. The world? In Philip's book it says, *It was already dark when I went into the forest.* Exactly. Melvin walks down toward Civic Center. It's like these people speak a million different languages, hip-hop or Honduran or something he doesn't know what the fuck anybody's talking about sometimes. Uncharted territories where everybody's strange. Someday the mutations might matter, we'll sort it out among ourselves. At Civic Center he breathes deep and sits in the sunshine and lets it all wash away. Some guy with a guitar and a wool cap claims to be working on several songs, rock and roll, he keeps saying, but when he plays, it's inaudible. Like it's so quiet nobody can even hear him. This stoned guy cracks up. This girl shoves a video camera in Melvin's face. Tell me your name and where you're from and have you ever stayed in a shelter, she says. She's making a documentary. He explains his unpleasant experiences in the past and his philosophy of freedom and mystical connections. The girl is a little bit underwhelmed, she has a different agenda: how smelly and crowded and horrible shelters are is the news she's trying to convey and he's veering off message, but her boyfriend, who's handsome but with crooked teeth, says he thinks Melvin could be the documentary's star. Melvin believes in being represented. An image shining its light long after the flesh has been battered and bruised and suffered and passed away. The fog, just a weird little wisp of it, passes over the sun. In the changed light he sees that he's just surrounded by weird biological forms. One has scarred elbows and carries a skateboard. What he means is that the mind is in the forms, but not only. It's like a science experiment with no rules. A dark forest, like in the book. Experiencing pleasure makes people look kind of animal and dumb. He laughs, looking animal and dumb. He wonders if it's his desire that has trapped him in this world. Awesome. Disappoint me some more! Some pop song is floating through the air, a horrible but catchy refrain that will someday make him cry. The girl and the boyfriend are going to this party at Elijah's and Bruno's and Melvin finds himself going along. He should call somebody, but then he ends up alone with the girl and she just starts talking about how much her boyfriend lies to her all the time. What does he got to lie about? His story just keeps changing all the time. One of the skills Melvin developed in jail is making his face look like it sort of cares what another person's saying even when he doesn't. He tries it out now.

But on the street in the Haight, in front of the house with the party, he runs into his ex.

You still have your scarf!

Yeah, so what?

I just mean you haven't lost it.

She has a black eye, a smaller bruise on her cheek. She seems flimsy and endangered.

I'm not materialistic. It's my favorite scarf.

I know you're not. Are you still…

What?

Oh, you know…

Crazy?

No, no, I mean doing your stuff.

I don't wanna talk about it.

Although Melvin's come to believe that the fog loves him in its way, this respite is okay, too.

Things have been difficult, she says.

Yeah, tell me about it.

She had this boyfriend for a while. Didn't work out.

I have problems, she says. She taps her head with her finger.

Did your boyfriend do that to you? he asks.

She shakes her head.

He wouldn't ever care that much, she says.

Care.

I know, she says. Like I said, she says, and she taps her head again.

What about you? she asks.

Well, you probably know about the whole kidnapping thing.

What?

It was all over the news, wasn't it?

Kidnapping? Were you kidnapped?

No, no, says Melvin. You mean you really don't know?

A group of people lit up with glowing crap descend from the party, suffocating their conversation for a moment, shoving past them and moving on.

Oh, well, I was in jail for a while.

She's looking at him like he's talking nonsense. Or like: Who's she even talking to?

Never mind.

You look like you're about to pass out, she says.

Hmmm, I don't think so.

I better get going.

Oh okay.

I'll see you around, she says.

She turns to go.

Jelena, he says.

What is it?

He doesn't know.

I don't know, he says.

Once she's gone, and he's alone on the street in front of a party he'd rather not return to, he misses Bronzi and he even misses Lakota. His cellies. Maybe it was only when he was forced to, that he could really relate to another person. Weird. Eventually Melvin crashes and then gets lost, has adventures, and the days pass by. A lot of the adventures are crappy and boring. He has disappointing sex with people he doesn't particularly like or who don't particularly like him. He wanders around the city and does some drugs and and and starts to feel lonely when he realizes that he's not in a movie and nobody's watching except the spirit world and maybe they don't care either. But he can't shake the feeling that it's all leading to something magical. When that doesn't pan out, he isn't happy, but the feeling passes. Pretty much. Melvin loses himself and walks until he's exhausted and avoids the street and the building where Hakeem used to live, and ends up smoking crack with some vampires and then crashing on some stranger's floor. More days go by. A lot of them and he loses his lucky hat and he loses the copy of Philip's book he bought for fifty cents, and he finds a book of spent matches on the sidewalk and then another one, as if somebody was walking along lighting whole books of matches and then tossing them just to watch them burn, and he follows the used books of matches down the sidewalk and finds himself one day back in front of that supposedly mystical bar with the paganish world-tree on the window but knows better than to fall for that trick again. But why not stop over at Freddy's, he thinks, and share some insights with Paul. Every person is a possible door, that's lesson one, but you can never tell which one of you is going to walk through who, which one's the door, he means, and which one walking through. There's more to life than thinking about your bad childhood and thinking you're cool because you're the type of guy who could kill a person, that's lesson two, but will Paul be ready to hear it? Humans have paved the way for an explosion of new snakes and rodents, for example. In the future, snakes and rodents in every possible color. Different habits, different forms, filling every niche you can imagine.

8

THE STREET IS EMPTY outside Sarah's apartment. The night wears a billion shapes in the darkness. The darkness under a layer of fog obliterating starlight and the waning moon.

It's often the middle of the night.

You are no stranger to that empty feeling. The chill and the despair. Somewhere, outside in the darkness, Sarah's future bridegroom is creeping relentlessly toward her. Sarah suspects that evil has been defeated—for now. The angry mob. And yet Huey has abandoned her. His little broken sighs, little panting sounds, the tender shade of crimson of Huey's cheeks, his parted lips, which grow moist when he is having phone sex with older writers. They're still calling for him, the older writers, but she lets it go to voicemail. Destroy my little boy's ass, my tender cheeks, wreck me mercilessly, Huey would beg them. Everyone still lives in terror of Huey's rage. *I'll never let them smack me around again, I'll get them while they're sleeping, I have to strike first*. Huey was there at Joni's birth. Just before and that's where it began. A voice calling out of the vast dark. When the voice called again, she sat up and waited for this discarded tissue of a boy dragging empty feelings along behind him. Huey explained that Sarah was being taken to the hospital to be put to death. That made perfect sense. She was stripped and marked and maybe slapped under the frozen gaze of evil nurses. She screamed the entire time. When the masked surgeon arrived and found his pregnant patient thrashing and shrieking, he was furious. She was always somehow still trapped in that room in terror: the masked man's rage, voices going back and forth overhead, a horrible light drives itself into her brain, and then the world goes black and she is sucked up into darkness and nothingness.

Later, Huey gave orders through her from the hospital bed. Just wait, he said. Become an inanimate thing—an ashtray or a lump in the mattress, he insisted, and lose your awareness of time's passing. Escape your phantasmic existence; I'll handle the rest.

Huey desired nothing more than to slice and stab fathers and faggots and doctors and fill the white room with blood.

Sarah has finished her midnight correspondence—a hundred e-mails to old supporters and newfound friends—and now it is time to be quiet and to listen. I know who you are, Sarah says to herself. But where is the road? She peeks out the blinds.

The street is empty. You are no stranger to the feeling. Perhaps you have seen this empty street in a dream.

Outsiders can't live by conventional moralities, can they?

She awoke tonight from the strangest dream. She could read the chalk writing and it all seemed to follow a sort of thread but the meaning disappeared as soon as it had been grasped. She lost interest. The invisible radio was everywhere. The river started rising and some helicopters were dropping care packages. The masters were whipping the crowd into a frenzy. The losers would be annihilated. She was lost in the crowd in the streets of some pathetic village among people who looked so much like herself it should have been disturbing. She was almost there, in heaven's VIP room. She saw a fig tree once that was a million years old.

Huey could be so mean. Sarah's such a bitch, he used to say, on the phone. What the fuck? Sarah gives a little laugh. It's her crazy laugh, a kind of indulgence she allows herself, as if somebody is listening in. And yet all they were ever doing was spreading love.

For a moment, it is quiet here. For a moment, it's absolutely still. For the first time, maybe in forever, there isn't any voice. Your permanent companion, speaking from a flawed place in your heart, has gone silent. Connie is out running. Sarah's daughter is fast asleep and dreaming, dreaming of somebody or something else since Huey has left her as Huey has left Sarah and how will Joni go on into the future alone, how will she learn to be merely a self?

But *something*. Something injured and new. Don't be afraid, says Sarah. I'm listening. Just a little squeak. Like the sound of the machinery inside a mouse. Genetically engineered robot parts for the rodents. How cute. How delightful! The little voice is coming from that mutinous darkness where the little ones are forced to hide. Come out, says Sarah. Come out! It's indecipherable, the little squeaking voice. But it's getting clearer and it's getting louder. Hello? says Sarah. Who is it? I can hear you? To her wonder and delight, the voice introduces itself. It tells her its name.

VIII

It is a "Night Sea Crossing" across a mesocratic nebula propelled by "perfect emptiness." One is then unflinchingly sustained as if giving oneself up for dead. One releases one's image, of what one's shadow has accomplished at a previous time, so one casts less weight than a lepton.
—Will Alexander, *Sunrise in Armageddon*

1

DHOJI'S BEEN DRINKING when she calls with the news. After an endless series of phone calls with the old boyfriend in Wisconsin, he decided to come live with her. He's been here for two days.

So how is he? asks Philip. Is he *aga*?

Don't say that, Dhoji says. We've known each other since we are kids.

So what? says Philip.

I have a surprise, Dhoji says.

If you're pregnant, I'm done with you.

Don't say that, says Dhoji. And another thing, she says. I am going to India.

She consulted some *puja* guy in San Jose. He told her she was sick in the blood. No kidding, says Philip. But she didn't say anything to him about HIV, but still—he knew. Anyway, she has to do three things. One is hang this scroll and two is burn these candles...

Was three give the *puja* guy some money?

He says I have to go to India, says Dhoji.

So just go, says Philip. But don't go because the *puja* guy told you to.

I am a little bit drunk, Dhoji says.

Philip sits down on a box full of cookbooks he has yet to unpack. Tonight, the wind is rocking the whole house.

Why are you drinking? he asks. You never get drunk anymore.

Tonight I am feeling like I don't care, Dhoji says.

You're drinking so that you can be numb enough to have sex with your new boyfriend, Philip says.

Fuck you, Dhoji says. You know me too well.

I am going to hang up now, she says.

But I didn't tell you my surprise, she says.

Her old roommate Zaher found Ricky on the Internet and Ricky gave him Dhoji's number and now here he is. He wants to see Raymond and Philip. Maybe tomorrow?

I haven't seen Zaher in ten years, says Philip.

She is going to school at Berkeley, says Dhoji.

Dhoji, don't call Zaher *she*, says Philip.

No, no, no, says Dhoji. She told me to call him that.

Dhoji says that it isn't ten years, not yet. She says it *has* been *over* ten years since she's been to India. I think I have to go back now, she says. Or I will forget who I am.

The next day Dhoji drops Zaher off, along with a couple of Tibetan scrolls Philip and Raymond are supposed to hang. For your new house, says Dhoji, and then speeds away. Zaher looks the same, almost. Maybe he's fifty-six, maybe he's thirty-two. His chest is shaved and his head is shaved and his scarves are flamboyant and his cologne is overpowering.

Philip serves tea. Raymond is still examining the scrolls. A green-skinned goddess floats above the earth, enveloped in stylized vegetation. The background is blue, but the fringes are every color of the rainbow.

It's kind of ugly, says Raymond. Kind of cheap and tacky looking.

She gave me one, too, says Zaher. I think it's supposed to save me from AIDS.

Raymond rolls it up and shoves it in an open box. They sit on the porch with their tea and apple pie.

So, says Philip after a few preliminaries. What have you been doing for the past ten years?

Zaher's story at first lacks clear markers. There's a Rainbow Gathering somewhere shortly after he leaves the Bay Area, and then, he says, he just kept going. Going where? Mostly around the Pacific Northwest, sleeping in his car or here and there. The last time we saw you was in Berkeley on Telegraph Avenue, says Raymond. He gives Philip a look. Zaher had looked that day like he'd just emerged from a wind tunnel. He'd looked crispy. Crackling with quantum energy. Zaher's not sure when he left *exactly*, but he knows that in December 1999 he's still in the Bay Area waiting for all the computers to crash. Then come the cramped basements, the vans full of musicians, the freezing tents in Canadian National Parks, and strip searches at the Canadian border. forty-eight-hour dance parties and ecstasy. Wonderful. In Spokane he meets a man who claims to be Jesus and for some reason stays with him. He ends up living in Olympia for two or three years with a straight guy who's into meth. Zaher runs a catering business there—he's the best worker in the world on speed, he tells them. Which comes first, Olympia or Spokane? Zaher shrugs. Speed is the worst, says Philip. Oh, it is the world that is the worst, says Zaher. Sometimes you have to make it a dream. His journey is a vast expanse with gaps that suggest endless speed binges and sleepless nights in more filthy hippie vans. The lights of the aurora borealis. Wonderful. There are several unconsummated love affairs with straight men and "side trips" out East. In DC, Zaher's whorish sister has turned all prim and proper since she got married. She was the only one of Zaher's three brothers and five sisters he could even have a civil conversation with and now she just wants him to go away because he knows her too well. Her husband isn't having it either—he wants the sexy party girl he married, not some old wife in a head scarf. What did she do with all of those beautiful, sexy dresses, Zaher wants to know. I've never quite understood the allure of respectability, says Philip. Zaher shrugs. Maybe her last abortion drove her crazy, he says. But the second afternoon he's there, he finds her secret stash. He takes just two dresses, a red one and a blue one. Blue is Zaher's color, he says, but men love him in red. Wonderful. But then there are screaming matches, broken dishes, she kicks Zaher out, and then in the South the heat is unbearable. Zaher's in a car with these two straight guys who are just traveling and the asphalt is always burning. The guys he's with are watching golf on the motel TV which is like a form of hypnotism. That's when he first suspects that they've taken a wrong turn. But the guys he's with are just these sort of happy guys, they love to sightsee and jump off of high places and swim naked, and they want to show him this amazing place, they tell him, in the next state over. Wonderful. Zaher is just sitting in the backseat all the time and they are all stoned and they drive him through some lovely countryside with very tall trees on either side, with feathery leaves, so the road is like a tunnel, it's like they are moving in slow motion, because it's so hot and the breeze is so slight that the rustling of the feathery leaves is almost imperceptible, and the road lasts forever, but finally at the end of the tunnel is a rotting sign that says *Psychiatric Hospital*. For a moment it seems to Zaher that he's a patient or maybe a nurse, but he's forgotten which it is, but the straight guys are just grinning at him and at each other like the sign that says *Psychiatric Hospital* is the most clever joke ever. It's a B&B, says one of the straight guys, but it used to be a mental institution. Isn't that crazy?

The B&B is run by a couple, these two perky gay men who renovate old buildings and prune the grounds and plant extravagant but overly manicured plants with enormous flowers that smell sweet and rotten and they've gotten into all of the guidebooks by turning this old asylum into a themed Bed-and-Breakfast. They serve the coffee in the morning in these decrepit tin cups that the prisoners used and the beds have straps on the sides that once tied the patients down while they received their electroshock therapy. Eventually the two straight guys go on their way, but Zaher stays behind in the B&B, working for the gay couple, scrubbing. Scrubbing dishes and toilets, bathtubs and sidewalks, walls and floors. He isn't sure how long this lasts, *exactly*. It's a strange time for me, says Zaher. The B&B is haunted. Lost memories float down the hallways. He has the most horrible dreams, sometimes his own dreams, about his childhood in Rabat, all the horror of those years in his father's house, his three brothers and his five sisters, and Zaher shudders, but sometimes he has dreams that are not his own dreams—somebody else's dreams pass through him. Madwomen with knives lunge from dark doorways and dismembered bodies shudder in rhythm to music from beneath the earth and airplanes crash into rooftop swimming pools and always the electricity. Lightning flashes that electrocute children wandering across empty golf courses where their mothers have disappeared. Sea creatures that kill scuba divers with their whip-like tails. Lightbulbs that crackle alive with a sick yellowish phosphorescence in the middle of the night and then shatter. He is always asleep and dreaming about electricity and then he is awake and scrubbing the halls and the bathroom with bleach in the middle of the afternoon with the horrible humming sound of those Southern insects. The shadows in that house are too dark. Things move around in those shadows. Something is being born in those shadows.

Were you doing drugs? Raymond asks. Zaher shrugs. We choose our own reality at every moment, he says. Still, as the days pass in that B&B with all the perky tourists who come and lounge around in the humidity on their way somewhere else, like maybe Nashville or New Orleans or the Carolina coast, he scrubs the floor and the walls with bleach and the wallpaper starts to disintegrate under the force of his fervent scrubbing and he discovers strange doodles behind the wallpaper. Skulls and eviscerated babies and male figures with their dicks cut off and stylized blood droplets gushing from the holes and female figures stabbed in their pussies and male figures with burning hot irons shoved up their assholes and evil fanged monsters surging upward from the depths of the ocean with cavernous mouths and eyeballs hanging on antennae and rats with blazing eyes and squids with too many tentacles and foul-smelling corpses and bodies splattered on the pavement after having jumped off high places and strange carnival creatures with organs in the wrong places and clown makeup on prostitutes and whore makeup on clowns and enormous screaming vaginas and winged phalluses perforated with earth-to-air missiles and haunted houses burning into eternity and bleeding hearts and faces with the eyes X'd out and the mouths taped shut and bodies hanging from nooses with huge erections and cellar doors with warty hands emerging clutching hand grenades and painful carnival roller coaster rides composed of murder machines and robot hearts and shimmering bronze body scales composed of metal and flesh and infinite labyrinths of mineshafts populated by blind devouring creatures with no skin and scurrying genitalia and the severed limbs of mutilated psychopaths crawling through the tunnels, and when Zaher shows them to the perky couple who run the B&B, they giggle and they're like, This is precious! And they rename that bedroom the Charlotte Perkins Gilman Room and jack up the price $40. But still Zaher wakes in the middle of the night to screaming and moaning sounds and the muffled grunts of someone being suffocated with a pillow and he wanders the halls through deep pools of shadow and something's trying to speak to him. I think it is a dead girl, he says. The perky gays tell him it doesn't make any sense—this was a mental institution, there weren't any children around. The little girl is being asphyxiated, he is sure of it. Constantly, over and over again—the girl is being smothered. We choose our own reality at every moment, Zaher repeats, but I have to get out of there. He makes his way to San Diego—an affair with a banjo-playing hermaphrodite in Colorado, a rave at Joshua Tree—and gets a job in a hostel there in San Diego in the Gaslamp District. His room at the hostel is a little oven with a buzzing industrial fan outside his window and the mushy little mattress is like a torture device, but they don't care that he doesn't have a green card. Australians spraying their underarms and the loud snoring men in slippers, but one day he gets a ride up the coast to the Torrey Pines, some of the only Torrey Pines in the world and just south of the Torrey Pines and the Torrey Pine golf course is a cruisy parking lot, the most beautiful cruisy parking lot in the world, where he meets this man who wants to be his boyfriend. Wonderful. The lover is a local and a history student and he loves San Diego and he loves to show Zaher the sights and so on their first date he takes him to the Macy's department store and they push the button on the elevator for the basement and nothing happens. The boyfriend laughs and explains to Zaher that now the basement is only used as storage and they've walled over the Down escalator on the ground floor, which is guarded by three headless male mannequins, and he shows them to Zaher, the three headless male mannequins standing guard over the wall where once it was possible to descend into that basement, and he explains that in the early '70s the basement there was the location of a men's restroom that served as a meeting place for gay men. In 1974, the cops conducted a sting operation and arrested forty men within the course of one week. They arrested several doctors, teachers and college students, a chief deputy county assessor, two hair stylists, a truck driver, a mail carrier, an unemployed salesman, an optician, a busboy, a fence builder, an assembler, a cook, a quality inspector, a hospital orderly and one very high-ranking Republican official, a gynecologist and for-mer chair of the California Republican Party. Their names were printed in the paper and then rednecks began calling these men and trying to bring them to Jesus at three in the morning or else they'd describe to the accused men's teen-age daughters in graphic detail the acts they were accused of committing, and so several of the men filed lawsuits claiming invasion of privacy and false arrest and they actually won. Zaher and his new boyfriend spend their afternoons visiting other overlooked pieces of San Diego's history, or driving toward the border and gazing out at the hills above Tijuana under strange, hazy skies, or strolling around Balboa Park without ever getting too close to the zoo, because caged animals give him the creeps, Zaher says, but then one day the boyfriend takes him for a special weekend in the country to this town in the mountains that is famous for its apple pies. Wonderful. He can't stop talking about how delicious the apple pies are and how incredible the town is, but then they get there and it's just like 1,000 tourists crammed into a square block of this town. The tourists, who look oddly hypnotized, are overflowing out of pie shops and shops that sell things made of yarn and stuffed rag dolls and pieces of ma-chinery from one hundred years ago. Anything that is "old-fashioned," Zaher says, and Zaher doesn't get it, he thinks that Americans just love to declare that something is fun so that they can cram as many people into the same space as possible, he thinks that Americans love to be shoved up against each other, he thinks maybe it is the wide-open spaces of the American desert that make Americans long for asphyxiation. And the pie was okay, but it wasn't like this, he says as he takes the last bite of Raymond's pie, which he says is exquisite. But his boyfriend is just in love with this little apple pie town and Zaher isn't able to feign enthusiasm for the experience, which just feels fundamentally fake, unlike the journey to the Macy's to see the walled-over entrance to the basement. At least something once happened there, something horrible that has left its trace. That's what history is, something horrible that left its trace, and the attempt to ignore that history is so much more poignant than some sort of cheesy memorial, some sort of transformation of an entire town and its people into a folksy museum. It isn't right, it is a form of oppression, Zaher says, and so on the weekend in the country it becomes apparent to both Zaher and his new boyfriend that the relationship isn't going to work and so it's back to the mushy mattress at the hostel.

A few months later Zaher moves to the sister hostel in Hollywood to start attending community college and he finds out he has AIDS. That's what they say, at least, says Zaher and this comment is followed by a tangential debate between Philip and Zaher about the "theory," as Zaher puts it, that HIV causes AIDS, and about the "crackpot," as Philip calls him, Peter Duesberg. Zaher says, Did you see the movie? and Philip says, I read the book like fifteen years ago and Zaher starts talking about how self-hatred and homophobia destroy people's immune systems and Philip says that only African dictators take Duesberg seriously anymore and Zaher says that nobody has ever actually *seen* the virus and Philip says that while it's certainly true that pretty much everything has a psychosomatic component, you can't have actually lived in the middle of this community and watched the way people bounce back under combination therapy and not believe that HIV somehow causes AIDS, and Zaher stands up and says, That's the placebo effect, people believe and they become healthy again, and Philip says, They've had placebos for a long time and they never worked before, and Zaher points out that what is killing people now is liver failure from all those drugs, and they go back and forth like this for a while. I've just seen too many people die because of their own denial, says Philip in conclusion. Zaher concedes that despite his belief that he doesn't have HIV anymore and that he has chosen that reality as his reality among the infinite number of realities he could choose at any moment, he has still been taking the meds anyway and he gets his bloodwork done regularly anyway. In any case, Zaher managed to take his classes in LA and get enough credits to transfer to UC Berkeley, where he says he will go to school for his BA in political science and for his master's and his PhD. He will keep taking classes until they kick him out, he says. He also managed to become a US citizen and to get on disability. Wonderful. Fuck Morocco, he says and he shudders again. With the exception of his formerly slutty and now virtuous sister, he hasn't spoken to his five brothers or his three sisters in eight or nine years. A few months ago his stepbrother called up, out of the blue. Zaher found out that his mother has been dead now for six years. Why didn't you talk to her? Raymond asks. Zaher shrugs.

Raymond and Philip hadn't known anything about Zaher's family. They'd known so little about each other back in the day. They usually only saw each other in the context of chaotic gatherings at Ricky and Dhoji's house in Richmond, where Zaher was living rent-free in exchange for housekeeping duties. The kids were just babies and into everything and Dhoji would be cooking huge dinners and people would be constantly in and out, Ricky's old sugar daddies and a handful of scandalous Tibetans and Ricky's old friends whose wives he'd eventually sleep with. Zaher would be vacuuming and scrubbing and Ricky would always be scheming to make money, and Philip would be asking Ricky questions about his life. He was working on the book about Ricky and Dhoji that was supposed to make everyone a lot of money, so Ricky was always talking about going AWOL from the army, about his relationship when he was sixteen with the medical marijuana guru that he blackmailed for the money to go to India, and about the meat he and Dhoji smuggled from West Bengal to Uttar Pradesh.

I didn't even realize you were a writer, Zaher tells Philip now.

Philip thinks for a moment that he should give Zaher a copy of *The Limping Man* but then he remembers that he made Zaher a minor character, and he can't remember exactly what he said about him. He didn't even bother to change his name. Did he use the word *flamboyant*? Did he use the word *scary*?

Raymond wants to know when and how Zaher left Morocco. Before America, he was in Italy. When was this? Zaher shrugs. How did he get there from Morocco? Magic, says Zaher. In Palermo, he says, the young men's hairstyles are very androgynous. Bobs and curls and barettes. Wonderful, says Zaher. But life for immigrants is terrible there, Africans and Indians. We live separately, we are treated like animals or else we are just invisible. For me, America is better, says Zaher. Everything is so old there. Like Morocco. It is beautiful but it's haunted. Nothing is possible. Everywhere you turn it's the Virgin Mary. There's a mural in some old church from 1200 or 1300, *The Triumph of Death*. Wonderful. These toothy skeletal horses of doom, but it's the dissolution of the paint itself, the weird stylized clouds and sky with patches altogether gone, replaced by sheer time-worn texture that is so beautiful he could cry. That dissolving sky, still full of light—he couldn't take his eyes off it. You see this theme everywhere in Europe, *The Triumph of Death*. Naples has the thickest haze of smog over it he's ever seen, and he takes a dip in the bay and finds himself covered in this foul, sticky film that he can't get off. He gets an eye infection and he ends up on Ischia, an Italian island completely colonized by Germans. He works at a hostel there but the fifty-nine-year-old Germans all bring their cars over on the ferry and they just drive in endless circles around that depressing little island, where Zaher ran into some trouble with the authorities and barely escaped, and then once, back in Naples, he was being chased down the street by an old prostitute who was wearing only one shoe. Why? Zaher shrugs. In Rome, he works at a hostel and scrubs the floors with bleach. Barcelona is like a frat party with French mimes. Philip's not sure if that's a criticism or if Zaher thought it was wonderful, but then Zaher says that Joan Miró is overrated. His final word on Europe. Instead he describes the aurora borealis.

Haunted, Zaher says. The sky is haunted, it is magic, it is alive. Wonderful. You have to see it like a woman sees it. You have to see it like a little girl wandering for days and nights through the snow, he says. The planet is haunted, Zaher says. He says, I think when you encounter ghosts, they can only show you a mirror. I think the aurora borealis is a kind of a ghost and a mirror of the planet and that we are made of color and light. *Zaher*, he says, means pure, beautiful, shining being. I believe that when you see a ghost, you can only see yourself.

Like that little girl in the B&B, he says. The ghost girl who was strangled and trying to speak.

Maybe it was really only me.

2

GLORIA CARRERA'S ANSWERING machine light is blinking when she gets home, just after dawn. She hates that.

Really, she's just been gone overnight. She slept in the forest.

She didn't die there.

Now that Tony has flown off to New York. Now that he's left her house again, she can breathe.

She doesn't much care. Out in the forest, she mingled with the earth.

She fixes herself some sandwiches. Enough for lunch for the rest of the week. The absence of hope isn't a novel feeling.

It's an adult feeling. Her child, with all of his plans for the future.

She sits at the table with the sandwiches and flips through a brochure. *Aztlan Evolving: Chicanismo Meets the Virtual World*. That History of Sciences monster from Michigan will surely be there. She likes to wander the neighborhood around the Zócalo in any case. All the crumpled-up beggar women and their trollish children sticking out their filthy hands. Filthy and plaintive. She never gives them anything and that calms her.

Not to accept responsibility. Why did she let that History of Sciences monster eat her pussy back in 1997? At a conference on *Reproductive Control and Heteronormative Dystopias*, of all things.

She's always been a good liar, but not to herself.

The light is still blinking. She discovers that she has eaten all the sandwiches. She's never done such a thing in her life. It's the sort of thing that Tony used to do.

He wanted her attention, even then. He'd come home from school in the middle of the afternoon and only her second husband would be there, watching his shows. He was working the night shift if he was working at all.

What really happened when she was asleep, she didn't know or especially care. It was her house, even then.

Tony always says he's going to help her organize her life, but all he leaves is a mess.

And that new boyfriend of his, he's addicted to interactive computer games.

She doesn't care for the movie that Tony left behind, even if it is hypnotic.

Is the final revenge real or a fantasy? When did Scorpion acquire those supernatural powers? The way she floats is beautiful. The way she's relentless and inescapable.

For a long time as a girl she'd dreamed of marrying a priest.

Priests in Cincinnati are still allowed to shake children's hands, pat them on the back, and give them high-fives. They can still look at children with longing.

Once, she was driving down a road in Texas. All by herself, crossing the country to start a new chapter of her life. A small plane, like a crop duster, kept crisscrossing the road.

There was nobody else anywhere. Just the land. She should have been frightened, but she wasn't. She couldn't see his face. For a long time afterward she liked to pretend that it was a woman. There must have been some scrub, some stones, some barbed wire fences to keep in theoretical cattle.

There weren't any animals at all. There are still all those boxes of books in the basement. Liquidize your assets, Tony kept saying. But he didn't carry a single box upstairs for her.

Hundreds of copies of Sonya Brava's short story collection. Hundreds of copies of Lucrecia Mendocino's feminist science fiction about cloning. Clones are repugnant, but in the novel they aren't. Gloria has given her life to books, but what have they done for her in return? Her basement is just stuffed full of caged dreams. Hundreds of copies of *Leyendas del Barrio*. Linda, she knew how to listen. She had a little respect. Linda was like a time traveler and the stories were like the landscape of Gloria's own childhood.

Long ago and far away. Everything covered by dust. Her father in that goddamn rocking chair.

There are boxes full of Jenny's book of poetry about cough syrup rappers. Boxes full of Donna's hybrid book *Voodoo Rising*, in which human consciousness is in and for itself irrelevant. The old gods, the colonized gods re-emerge as ideograms, splotches of graffiti, streams of language. They might contain vast spaces or very small ones.

The book isn't fiction or poetry or anything like that and is almost incomprehensible. And yet Gloria loves it more than she ever loved her own father. And maybe more than Mama, too.

There are boxes of that poetry book by that dead girl, what was her name? Arrows made of bones rain down from the sky.

Tony, she wanted to say. *You are not the one.*

There was only ever one.

She checks several times that the door is locked then tries to think about that one in order to help her sleep off all that food, but that one is nothing but a blurry colorless montage—like all of her memories. Still, she would like to cry a little. But she can't. She has no reason to.

3

TED ALWAYS NEEDS JUST a little bump, not much, to get through the night shift. He needs to transform the night shift into the Penny Arcade Peep Show. Each booth an ancient film flickering a cryptic charade he both watches and acts in a luminous language of embodied symbol systems forever. He's still feeling the bump as he emerges from the basement of the Nob Hill Theatre's video arcade into an oddly cheery morning—is it Saturday again? The fog is burning off already. Down the hill to the Internet café.

He never uses his own picture anymore in his sex work ads—too many scammers were stealing his identity, too many sadistic clients with an axe to grind started flagging his ads. He uses pictures that look like himself *anyway*, no biggie; he finds them on porn sites, or Craigslist ads in other cities. He hasn't been getting as much mileage with the twink (Bobby) or the ex-con (Scorpion) lately. The jock (Brad) is a little too generic, he's become convinced. He could find a picture with some football equipment in it or give him a cast and a broken leg or a chipped tooth and a hockey mask perhaps. Ted feels that with the war going more and more poorly, the mood just isn't right for the Marine (Josh), and he stopped trying to pass as Latino (Hector)—they always wanted him to talk dirty in Spanish, and there he'd be grunting phrases from junior high Spanish class while they sucked his dick: *Te gusta el windsurfing? Tienes el equipo?* He advertises as an exotic Afghani (Omar) sometimes, but most compelling are the twins (Matt and Zack). He'll show up alone with the excuse that Zack's girlfriend dragged him away or that Matt got called by their agent at the last minute for a sports equipment commercial. Once, the same guy even called him back afterward, desperate for the incestuous two-man show. Ted pretended he'd never met the guy before, or rather, *Zack* explained that Matt had just been in a motorcycle crash and was in the Emergency Room, but he'd insisted that Zack go on without him, he'd told Zack how great the client was and how important it was for Zack to please him for the both of them. It was frighteningly addictive. Ted wanted to go back to that man over and over again, forever, alternating between Matt and Zack, the wounded twin and the healthy twin, the stoic twin and the demonstrative twin, the butch gay and the bi-curious, the good and the not good or the evil and the less evil or the wounded and the not demonstrative or the gay and the evil, but it all became so confusing sometimes during the night shift at the video arcade when the screens were flashing from this booth or the other, this boy and that boy young ghosts blurred faces a blazing twisted shrubbery a maze of tentacles and animal skeletons.

Afterward, Zack or Matt hit that guy up for another twenty, to help cover the Emergency Room visit, since Matt or Zack wasn't insured. But that was a long time ago. Ted supposes the johns all talk to each other now, on the Internet.

The radio in the café is playing this old song, *Baby we can do it, take the time, do it right, we can do it baby, do it tonight…*

There's one identity he hasn't pulled out in a long time, but maybe it's time. (Jake) is an eighteen-year-old Amish kid fresh off the farm and needing to be shown the ropes by a big-city daddy. Ted found a picture of a good-looking Amish kid on the Web after that schoolhouse shooting, decked out with his suspenders and hat. He posts a picture of a buffed naked chest next to it—he figures with an Amish boy you don't show ass or cock.

Once, his ex-boyfriend, the Beat poet, dressed Ted up in a skeleton costume. He wanted to be fucked by Death in the carnival of flesh. Ted could see himself in the mirror and it was totally hot. They were both on something, Ted's pretty sure, although maybe not the same thing. And the old poet started laughing hysterically while Ted was fucking him, The face of Death is the face of *energy*, he kept saying, or maybe he said *entropy*, or maybe he just thought it because maybe Ted, as Death, could read his mind, and silver arrows made of bones were raining down from the sky.

The response to the ad is quick, some old queen in the Castro.

On the MUNI train Ted maps out a scene for his novel in his head—the baby unicorn descends into the subway system of a vast intergalactic interdimensional City where everything is for sale and dangerous figures congregate from every corner of the many universes. Ted nods off, and the scenes of the novel are *almost* perfectly mapped out, he can *almost* grasp the whole in a language of images forever slipping away figures *congregate from every corner* many laughing hysterically. The descriptions of scenes are a secret code about Ted's life and everybody else's he's passing through many dimensions and configurations *an unknown language on shifting screens read once before the dawn of time silvery letters a wisp of smoke fade into scenes from a long time ago* flashing at the last-minute motorcycle crash sadistic clients with axe to grind started: *Te gusta el* cast and broken leg chipped tooth always transform the night shift into phrases from *windsurfing? el* agent *can do it baby, do a long* bump emerges from the basement fog burning empty ass shot or cock shot—ex-sky can't think of maps scene for the skeleton costume to be fucked by Death in the novel in his head fucking him face of Death face of screens flashing caught in tendrils animal skeletons more and more evil on the Internet to punish the time, *take your time*, do himself in the mirror an eighteen-year-old kid fresh off the wording never his own anymore—too many laughing hysterically last-minute figures *congregate from every corner*—

Ted wakes up just in time for his stop. Slaps himself once, to jar himself into the present time configuration. He's surrounded by wooden people, filing off the train with their weekend recreation faces on.

You look different than in your picture, is the first thing the john tells him.

Ja, people always tell me I look better in person, says Ted.

The john waves him to take a seat.

So whatta you wanna do here? asks Ted.

The john says, Take off your shirt.

Ted hopes the john doesn't see him rolling his eyes. But with his shirt off, the john says, That's not you in the picture.

What do you mean? says Ted. Of course it's me.

Different body, says the john. Different face. Bait and switch is bad business practice, honey. You'll get reported to the Better Business Bureau.

I don't know what you're talking about, says Ted. It's me. A couple of years ago, sure, but it's me.

I was more tan then, he says. My hair was a little bit different.

Now the john rolls his eyes.

Listen, I'm willing to work with you here. I came all the way up here, you just want a massage?

You're not Amish, says the john. And if you're not a good decade and a half past eighteen, then I'm the good witch of the North.

I didn't come up here to be berated by a schizophrenic, says Ted. If you want me to leave, you need to give me forty bucks for my cab fare to come all the way over here.

Ted closes his eyes for a moment, and imagines that the powers of his mind might lead him to victory.

I've seen you tweaking around this neighborhood for years, says the john. In fact, I think you may have been part of this AIDS benefit show I set up back in 1995—weren't you friends with that kid who used to date Allen Ginsberg? Didn't you go-go dance together at the Detour or something?

The john gets up and goes into the kitchen. Ted looks around for something small enough to shove into his pocket, but the john's back in a flash. He gives Ted a Tupperware bowl full of some weird macaroni salad.

Just take this and go, says the john. You can sell the plastic container for a buck after you eat the food. It's good for you, it has fresh organic vegetables in it, out of my own garden.

Ted stands and musters his most aggrieved look.

This just isn't right, he says.

The john makes a shooing motion with his hand.

Let's not turn things ugly, he says. That route doesn't end well for you, I promise.

Ted struts to the door, slams it behind him. Cheap cunt! he yells as he goes down the steps. He sure got the best of that guy, that guy's neighbors will be talking about him for days. On the way back to Castro Street he samples the macaroni salad. It's better than it looks. It's actually delicious. Another fact he weaves into the story of his triumphant morning, the story of the power he wields as he makes his way through the world, the story he is always telling himself: the inevitability of his ascent toward status and toward grace.

4

HOWARD CRIES FOR THE HUNDREDTH TIME as he watches the big scene of Frank Capra's final film, *Pocketful of Miracles*. And what's wrong with being a sentimental old man? He always cries when bad people in movies do good things. When they find that spark of virtue in themselves and sacrifice something for America or for their families or just people in general. It always gets to him when the gangsters in this movie finally escort the bride and the groom to the waterfront for the sake of Bette Davis. Bette Davis is really an old bum named Apple Annie, but not even her daughter, Ann-Margret, knows that. Ann-Margret was sent off to a fancy school in Europe long ago, where she met this

Spanish royalty she's marrying, and nobody knows that her mother is just some loser who sells apples on the street. The film revolves around the elaborate and heartwarming deception in which Bette Davis is made out to be a *grande dame* by the gangsters, a ruse which draws in the mayor and the governor and eventually everybody in the whole city is in on the touching scheme to make the aristocrats and Apple Annie's own daughter believe that Apple Annie is a wealthy socialite, not some worthless piece of street trash. When Ann-Margret and her aristocratic husband and his father Count So-and-so sail off for Europe, none the wiser, it renews Howard's faith in human decency.

He calls Philip up, but nobody answers, so he leaves a rambling message on the machine, his preferred method of communication in any case, about how cynical Philip is and how it just isn't right. It leads to great unhappiness, he tells him. Unlike you, he says, I am a proud humanist, and then he starts to explain the plot of *Pocketful of Miracles* and to sing one of the musical numbers and has almost finished before the answering machine cuts him off. He gets dressed, wrapping his legs in paper towels under his baggy jeans and putting on a hat against the October wind and goes out for a walk down Polk Street. Every day he is lighter and lighter, it's like magic. He's down to 240 pounds, because almost every day he walks.

When he was in the hospital, maybe a week or two into the stay, after his little incident, the suicidal event, as somebody called it, he found himself sobbing on the phone to somebody, maybe Philip. He was repeating over and over again *I am nothing and I have nothing, I am nothing and I have nothing, just the way they wanted it*... "They" were his parents, of course. He actually referred to his mother as *that bitch who gave birth to me*. But by the time he'd left that hospital, the other patients in the ward were leaving notes about "that nice tall man" and he'd become beloved, spreading sunshine wherever he went, whether with the story of the time he kissed Judy Garland or the rendition of "Over the Rainbow" he performed while having a painful procedure done on an infected boil. He isn't nothing, he realized then. They did their best, but he's not.

He passes the video arcade, the check-cashing place, the liquor store, and waits to cross Post. The other week Cameron also brought Howard to tears. Cameron made it through the first twenty-one days of his treatment program and called to thank Howard for everything. It wasn't that much that Howard did for him, but he offered him encouragement when he saw him on the street, paid him a few dollars to clean his room sometimes. Now that Cameron's clean, he's taken him under his wing, feeds him breakfast most days, or pays Cameron to do his laundry. When Cameron disappeared with his laundry, Howard feared the worst—that he'd taken the quarters and sold the dirty underwear and relapsed. He didn't care about the underwear, it was just that he wanted to be able to trust Cameron, or he at least wanted Cameron to be able to feel that he was trusted. And then yesterday Cameron showed up, the laundry clean and folded perfectly. He'd been picked up on a warrant, but he'd carried those clothes with him to jail and back.

Howard crosses the street, passes the bar on the corner that used to be gay, passes the other check-cashing place, the smoke shop, the cell phone guy, passes the bar that used to be a hustler bar, *Reflections*. He stops at the corner of Polk and Sutter, waits for the light to change. For many years now Howard has told himself that the one crime a person must not commit, the one crime that is really against the rules, is suicide. Someone's waiting on the other side to send you back, or deliver you to some even more horrific fate—lifetimes that just get bleaker and bleaker, until you can finally make it through without pulling the plug. A suicidal event, they said, when he took all those pills. Maybe, but Howard doesn't really think so. It's just like any trapped or caged animal. You get stuck in this place and you just can't be there anymore, so you do everything to bust out, whatever it takes. It's part of the mammal brain probably, so that even the most enlightened mammals, the ones who get as enlightened as you can get within the confines of a mammal brain—you start to think bashing out of here is built into the program. You start to think that if you lay waste to yourself and whatever's around you, you'll get to move on, go somewhere else.

Ramon is semiconscious on the sidewalk, enough to give Howard a little wave. Howard first met Ramon maybe ten years ago. He's lost his teeth and looks like a horrid old troll, but can't be more than thirty. He was just nineteen when Howard met him and took him home one night out of the rain.

Howard walks on past the café with the chairs out front. He does what he can as the years go by. Buys a boy a sandwich, pays a boy to carry his groceries home from the store, tries to instill some small work ethic or sense of decency in them that might actually help them make their way in the world.

The years are rarely kind to them. From their own perspectives they must always see themselves in motion. So much frantic activity must seem like it's taking them somewhere. For Howard, they are not even a group or demographic, but a kind of substance. A resource sharing the same trajectory as the air, the water, the soil—slowly, steadily depleted, contaminated, eroded. Howard was in love with John for a while. Years, even. In and out of prison, on and off speed, cruising around on some bike he'd lose right away, back and forth between the few square blocks around Polk Street and Hawaii, where his sugar daddy lived. Howard became friends with Otis, the sugar daddy. They both did what they could to help John, as he made ridiculous plans to marry a variety of junky girls with armfuls of babies, to start businesses, to get jobs or live with Otis forever. Hawaii always drove John crazy, it was like all of his reference points had been taken away. What could he do with the sea, the sky? Always he'd come back, complaining loudly. Stomping around, making stupid threats. No impulse control and not a shred of empathy. Then, after one too many ugly scenes, Howard cut him off. A few years later Otis cut him off, too. Otis, who would have left him his entire fortune when he died.

Just past Bush, Howard runs into Spider, Terry's drug-dealing partner. For years, Howard knew Spider as Ervin, and then one day, suddenly, he'd reinvented himself. It's one thing to turn into Spider when you're nineteen or twenty, but not very plausible when you're pushing forty. Sure, everybody went along with it, everyone called him Spider, but there was always a skeptical hesitation. Hi Spider, says Howard.

Did you hear about Terry? Spider asks.

Terry's been dead for a month. According to Spider, it was hell for his few closest friends. Terry wanted everything to be a secret. All those times he said he was going on trips, he was really in and out of the hospital. Then, at the end, Terry's family showed up. According to Spider, none of what Terry said about them was true. They hadn't disowned Terry. They never told Terry not to come home for Christmas. They didn't seem to have a problem with his sexuality at all.

Don't believe everything the family tells you, says Howard. Something seems to have rattled Spider and he hurries off down the street. Howard strolls past the construction site where the hustlers used to hang out, soon to be home to a megachurch complex with shops and condos and *hope*. He catches a glimpse of some guy ducking into Frank Norris Alley, could be Jamie. Jamie still lived with his mother in Daly City when Howard first met him. He always made promises he wouldn't keep, because he hated to be touched. He'd get thin as a rail, then disappear and come back so fat Howard wouldn't recognize him—like the heavier twin of the feral youth he'd known and fondled. Within days he'd be a skeleton again.

Ruben, that was a long time ago. He looked like a cartoon. Byron still pops up once in a while, but he's lost his teeth, too. Philip, he was different, just passing through. Like Darren, who came from a wealthy family. And Trent, who claimed that he'd been hired by several movie stars and star athletes. Whether he was delusional or just lying, he vanished within a month.

Howard's known Terry for years and all this time it was the same refrain: the horrible family, the family that couldn't love, the toxic Indiana farm. I am nothing and I have nothing, he remembers. If he had died young, he can't imagine the lies his parents would have told, the lies his sisters would have told. He walks on as Polk Street slopes down toward the Bay.

With Freddy out of the country, Freddy's twin feels incredibly calm.

He digs through his drawers, through his sheaves of unpublished poems, for an appropriately textured and creamy piece of paper. His penmanship has always been exquisite.

My dearest brother,

I imagine that the Muslim world suits you because although it is a complete mystery to me I believe it to be deeply layered. If anyone can appreciate the ways that the past exists in intricate patterns visible in physical space, it is my twin. Every action reverberates backward and forward. I find it exhausting, honestly. Perhaps you needed me to be perfect and perfectly good only so that you could despise me later on when I disappointed you. You set us both up, knowing that I would be unable to bear your hatred. The inevitable separation would prove to you what you always wanted to believe anyway and would give you carte blanche to form your own individual identity. In Aztec culture, children born on one of the five unlucky days would generally be called Useless Person or, if a girl, the feminine of this. The concept of destiny for the Aztecs was kind of overbearing. Why this one and not the other? Why pretend? Individuality is always a form of evil, one that suits you better than it suits me. I don't resent you as you believe I must because you got to have all the fun or even because of Mother's attitude toward your wickedness.

Now you're very far away with your soldiers and their murderous ways. How dark of you. Which of us is enamored of catastrophe? Which of us thinks it's all or it's nothing? The difference between us is that I know it's my role to have my heart broken, the reason that I'm here. Don't mistake masochism for virtue or think that my will to suffer makes me special. I can hear you now—you're confusing your own persona with mine. As if that wasn't always the point. I'm sorry, I'm doing it again. I can't help myself. If I were an abstract principle, it wouldn't be one I'd care to harness to history. Wouldn't that be an unrelenting series of disasters? We used to imagine, didn't we, that we were born to a race of monsters but that we were somehow different. A different species: angels or Martians or human beings. What you look forward to is already here, my dear brother. Look around. Didn't we need to create a kind of nightmare to escape into? Yours has become larger than mine, I suppose, which is largely confined to books. Funny that I've never felt closer to you or more free—more my own self at the same time deeply, perhaps only in my own mind, a part of you.

Love, Gus

PS. You dream of vengeance, I'm sure. Please forgive me even if what I did to you, to both of us, eons ago—it may as well have been the dawn of time—even if it's unforgivable.

He folds the letter carefully so that it is perfectly creased. He has no stamp for the envelope, but then he has no address either. He moistens the adhesive, seals it, and heads out.

He walks up Polk Street, imagining he'll find a mailbox. They still exist, don't they? The few blocks before the business district are deserted, but for the strangest man who is walking toward him, all bundled up, like a serial killer. Paper towels stick out of his pants.

Excuse me, says Gus.

He hands Howard the letter and quickly walks away.

Howard opens the letter carefully, in case he'll want to reclose it afterward. The part that gets to him is where it says, *The difference between us is that I know it's my role to have my heart broken, the reason that I'm here.* Somehow, it makes him think of Billy; Billy, with his gap-toothed grin and his freckles. When Howard got out the belt, Billy's eyes lit up. Howard gave Billy such a beating and Billy just wanted more. Billy didn't give a shit about bruises. He had the most beautiful, almost translucent skin. Howard let it out then, for once, almost all of it. When he was done, he was spent, really, and a kind of calm descended on the two of them. Billy gave him the sweetest, most spontaneous hug he's ever been hugged. I love you, Billy said, and Howard knew that in that moment, he really meant it.

5

THE TOWN'S NAME IS NAHUATL for "place with an abundance of sand." The volcano looms above it. It's pretty at first but then you kind of just forget about it. When Geordi was an undergrad in Boston, a city he decided was the most racist city in America, he read *Pedro Paramo*. There was no resemblance between the rhetoric in his Latin American literature class and on the streets of Boston. He went to another planet every Tuesday and Thursday for an hour and twenty-five minutes and then he returned to the dorm room where he was tormented by a guy named Connor, his clueless, sadistic roommate. Every day, waiting in the mud. Connor didn't think it was righteous or authentic that Geordi had spent his childhood picking peaches, he thought it was a joke.

Geordi tries out a little café off the main square. The clientele is tourists here for the weekly market or to climb the volcano, and a few solitary Mexican men. Geordi's served his coffee by a skinny boy in a white shirt, and then the owner, a gringa, pops up behind the counter. Her hair is blond and severely damaged. Her skin is damaged, too. Next thing he knows, she's sitting next to him.

I love men with scars, she tells him. I won't beat around the bush, I guess you could say it's my thing. I'm sure you've met women like me before. I could talk about when it started and probably even why, but we're a little too adult for that, don't you think?

She looks like she's about sixty, but she might be ten years younger. It might just be that she's been in the sun too much.

More men with scars in Mexico, she says. I'm talking, you know, per capita. Oh, Nicaragua, the Congo, Afghanistan, but me, I'm not really a risk-taker. The men, you guys, that's as far as it goes. I mean I've lived a life, that's for sure.

She says, You guys—you don't want my pity. You carry your scars with a certain pride and you want somebody who understands that, who understands that it has nothing to do with feeling sorry about your own suffering. It's a "whatever doesn't kill us makes us stronger" sort of thing, isn't it?

Geordi says nothing. It's so easy to be another person's fantasy—to inhabit their dream and make it flesh—and it barely requires a sacrifice. Only of language, and what kind of sacrifice is that?

Cut with a bottle, right? she says. She reaches out and runs her finger along the raised bumpy zigzag across his face. It has that unmistakable look of jagged glass, she says. A razor or a knife couldn't give you that sort of keloid pattern you've got going, honey. She squints at him as if appraising a painting. You don't have any other scars, she says. You don't need any. Just the one. Every scar tells a story, she says. You've had that scar since you were young—probably sixteen, seventeen. Got jumped walking through the wrong neighborhood, maybe in a bar, you were talking to the wrong girl. Just a kid, waiting for something to happen, surrounded by blood.

The solitary man at the next table over doesn't even look at them, but he has scars up and down his forearms. Not suicide scars, Geordi doesn't think.

I can look at a bullet scar and tell you the make and model of the gun, she says, the time of day it was fired, I can tell what kind of person did the shooting. More or less.

Geordi imagines himself saying, It was the greatest day of my life, but I don't remember. He imagines himself saying, I learned on that day that life is a dream and that the dream is real. Instead, he touches his face.

I lived in LA for a while, the woman says. Me, I've lived all over, but a lot of that decade, you know, just forget it. But things were looking up in the '80s, she says. My boyfriend was this big-time dealer, we had this house in Malibu. Huge, tacky as hell, but whatever, I mean you had the ocean right out there and at night you could hear it. I slept like a baby in that house. I never slept as well as I did in that big ugly house. Made me complacent, I guess. I thought about death too much. Technically I *always* owned the house, because my boyfriend didn't want any of his assets in his own name. He knew what he was doing, at least I thought so. But then one day he left for a weekend trip and he didn't come back. April 1985. Waiting, waiting. When he was two days late, I knew that was it. It wasn't legal trouble, I knew that much, it wasn't like he was lying low. We had systems developed for such occasions, clandestine methods of communication. He was dead and I was pregnant and completely alone. I was thirty-three years old, I thought I was an old lady then. Funny, isn't it, how ready we are to think that this is it, the end of the story. To imagine that whatever has happened is the ultimate deal. Whatever. Do you have any idea how long ago all of that was? Everything happened so long ago. Life is short, everyone says. Blink of an eye. Not mine, honey. I thought I'd woken up from a dream in that house to find myself completely alone and that was pretty much true. All those Malibu people, all of Darin's people, I hated them. All of them. I didn't have any real friends, that was clear. I didn't have too many illusions. One possibility, a very real possibility, was that bad people would come after me. I'd settled into a pit, and then one day three men showed up. I served them snacks and drinks. They wouldn't remove their shades, until finally they did. We just chatted about this and that. Optical illusions and recipes, I think. Chilled soups, fruit salads, that kind of thing. And then they got up and left and I never saw them again.

I didn't run. I aborted the baby, Jesus, didn't think twice. And I sold all the drugs in the house to friends of Darin and then one day the drugs were all gone and the money was all gone and it was just me and that house worth like a gazillion dollars. And that fucking empty, beautiful Malibu sky.

She reaches out to Geordi, runs her finger over the scar tissue on his face again.

It's been a long ride. Guess I fell asleep a few times. But it's like a job, you know. Sometimes you want a day off.

He's heard this voice before.

I'm awake now, she says.

She seems to be trembling just a bit.

Long ride, baby.

She gets up, opens the blinds to let the harsh light flood the room, sits back down.

Every sky has a different story, too, she says. The story of your Mexican sky is that man is a sacrifice. It's a sky for the ruthless gods. Most any desert sky, that's the story. Never enough rain, so they want your blood. Now your Paris sky, your San Francisco sky. Bogota maybe. The Big Island.

Like I told you, she says, I've been around.

I sold the house, she says. I wasn't stupid. I knew what a girl has to do to take care of herself in this world. I invested the money, not all of it, but most. It's kept me going. Kept me moving for a while. Landed here. The volcano, you know, it leaves scars in the earth like the scars that fire can leave on a man's flesh.

Studies show that women want to sleep with scarred men but not marry them, she says. I guess women are supposed to want men who live less danger-ous lives to raise their children.

I don't believe anything too much, she says.

The young waiter is sitting behind the bar, flipping through a comic book of some sort. He leans his head back then, and closes his eyes as if he's thinking very hard and Geordi sees that he has a scar like a gash across his neck.

He loves the villains, she says. He understands them at a very deep level. There's this glamorous shadow, kind of a Mexican version of Batman's Joker. His desire isn't really to destroy everything around him. It's not like he hates everything, it's just he wants to be free and so he's been driven insane because he can't figure out how to be free.

He's young still, she says. He'll learn better. You, you don't need that kind of illusion, she says. You'll stay here with me, I imagine. Choosing to stay in the place you belong is still a kind of freedom, even if it lasts forever.

All of the men sitting by themselves—each one of them has a prominent scar.

Geordi's sister insisted on an open casket at his father's funeral.

His father had no eyes, because the birds had eaten them. They'd put some glass ones in, although they'd closed the lids so that it looked like he was only resting.

All those peaches, all those years. His father worked and worked and barely said a word.

As if he was never really here.

6

IN MARRAKECH, MELVIN AND FREDDY sit around the Djemaa el Fnaa with this old Spanish writer, Juan Goytisolo. Freddy and the writer speak in Spanish or sometimes French mixed with English and so Melvin just sits there watching people scald themselves for money. He knows what Jared would say—funny, isn't it, how everywhere you go, you end up with gay men. Next to their table, somebody's drinking gasoline and then breathing some half-assed flame. Nobody's been saved. Not once, no matter what they say. That makes Melvin feel better. Mr. Goytisolo tells a story in English about Che Guevara. Melvin supposes it must be for his benefit, since he's wearing the shirt. Mr. Goytisolo met Che at the Cuban embassy in Algeria. Upon discovering one of Virgilio

Piñera's books on the shelf, Che hurled it against the wall and shouted, *How dare you have in our embassy a book by this foul faggot!* Juan Goytisolo is Spain's greatest living writer, Freddy declares back at the hotel. Melvin won't mention that he actually read *Landscapes After the Battle.* It doesn't seem like a very soldierly habit, despite the title. The presence of such genius has made Freddy horny, so Melvin gets out his sketchbook. They're not really compatible, but if Melvin lies on his back, he can sketch future life forms while Freddy sucks his dick. It's not that hard to be another person's fantasy. It's probably easier than trying to make somebody else your own—a rapist or what-have-you. I wouldn't have pegged you as a soldier, Freddy said when Melvin showed up at his door, looking for Paul. Melvin visits the pages of soldiers in Iraq once in a while and throws Freddy a detail, something gruesome and appalling. Freddy seems to enjoy the fact that Melvin doesn't much like to be touched and he gives him lectures about the military-industrial complex that Eisenhower warned about. That's who killed the Kennedys, he explains. I thought the gays killed Kennedy, Melvin says. He saw the movie with Joe Pesci in a powdered wig, pinching Tommy Lee Jones's nipples—Tommy Lee was painted gold—and saying, *You're mine, Mary.* You shouldn't rely on Oliver Stone for your history, Freddy tells him. Kevin Bacon was wearing a powdered wig, too. He was the one who told Kevin Costner that he didn't understand anything because he'd never been fucked in the ass.

The only time Freddy seems to get even slightly suspicious is when Melvin tells him he's vegetarian. He can't believe that somebody who'd join the Marines wouldn't eat a bloody steak, but Melvin refuses to talk about it, like he's been so traumatized by all the ribbing he got from his buddies. Now, everywhere they go, Freddy's saying *No Meat Juice* in French but Melvin thinks his French must be crap because they always just cook it in chicken juice instead. Freddy can go on for ten minutes explaining *No Fucking Meat Juice* but it's always the same. Melvin is left picking at the uncontaminated couscous and apricot pieces and getting bread from the market afterward and figs.

Even Freddy gets bored with how impossible the wide avenues of Marrakech are and they take the train back to Casablanca. There are weird little houses built along the tracks, and then the tracks run through dusty ravines full of garbage. Freddy says that if the US government didn't actually plan the 9/11 attacks, they *at the least* let them happen. You just look at who profited, says Freddy. Follow the money. Melvin could care less. In his little corner of the universe, the money mostly belongs to Freddy. The sun drifts behind a solitary cloud and Melvin can see his reflection in the window glass. He grimaces just a little, to look more like the professional killer that he's supposed to be. Freddy says, Your whole life is just in the service of an evil machinery that's only about killing and only about death.

So why are you even with me? asks Melvin.

Freddy looks at him then as if he's enchanted.

Because nothing's more beautiful than deadly force, Freddy says.

Freddy talks then about his mentor, some great poet that Melvin can't remember. Somehow he taught both Freddy and his brother everything they know, but the way Freddy tells it, it sounds like the plot to *Star Wars*. The old poet was in favor of peaceful troublemaking, Freddy explains. Rolling blackouts, clown costumes, disrupting daily commutes. Shutting down power grids and industry. Terror without violence. Peace within, chaos without. He was willing to risk everything for chaos: let a thousand horrible flowers develop in the nightmare markets.

Cool, says Melvin. Can we visit him?

Only in a K-hole, says Freddy.

You mean he's transdimensional?

He's dead, says Freddy. Just dead.

Thirty-five years he's been dead. Freddy was only nineteen. Later, Freddy fell in love with an anarchist, but the anarchist died, too.

So why aren't you in love with an anarchist now? asks Melvin. The question seems to confuse Freddy. Freddy looks like he's drifting off to sleep, but then he keeps talking, quietly, in a way that Melvin's never heard him talk before—not as if he's lecturing to a moron or a deaf person, but the voice is so quiet. It's like he's talking to the only person he ever loved.

There used to be a free library in Berkeley, he says. In the old McKinley building. There weren't any rules about returning books, he says. But if you could, you were supposed to exchange, you know, a book for a book. Moe's had donated all these books, I think Cody's gave some, too. Inside every book, the librarians had stamped or pasted the image of a grain stalk from a fifteenth or sixteenth century woodcutting. I loved those little grain stalks, and I still own several books with those insignia inside. The first time I went to the library, I discovered Valéry. I discovered Sor Juana de la Cruz there and Villon. I kept going back for the books, but then I started wandering down into the basement, where they had a kind of free store. It was positively medieval down there, like something out of Poe, but everybody liked to hang out there, young people from all over the country. There's something about a basement or maybe any sort of shadowy environment, with dark corners and crevices, that lends itself to a peculiar honesty, or at least to a convincing simulation of honesty. Everybody wanted to confess or to release themselves from their own stories, I suppose, to compare horrors. Most of them had been out on the road. I was far too timid of a boy to ever do anything like that, but I loved to sit down there and listen to them talk. Some of them had been jailed in horrid little towns and fined for all the money they had, which was never much, and then dumped back out by the highway with nothing. Many of the women had been abused or even raped. The country they had all wandered through was made to seem like an insane, criminally insane even, outpost or byway or repository of some ancient curse. One boy said that he'd been reviled in the streets, he actually used that word, *reviled*, and he'd been pelted with rotten fruits and vegetables, and then others chimed in, so many had been pelted with rotten produce, cabbages and bananas and tomatoes, it made one wonder, really, at what sort of society this might be, it made me wonder about the relationship between small-town people and food, I don't know.

The landscape out the window is flat and every shade of brown. Tiny people make their way through it in the distance, on foot.

Although many of the stories were terrible and terrifying like that, Freddy continues, there had developed a particular attitude among the boys and the girls, a kind of ironic acceptance that there was nothing out of the ordinary in their stories. They didn't seem bitter or enraged, not ever. They didn't even seem especially melancholy, in the way that would seem appropriate to a life of constant change and continual loss, although I imagine that came later, as it did for so many of us. After we discovered that everything wasn't really possible. Or we discovered that everything *was* possible, but that we ourselves would never experience it. It would only be later, I suppose, after watching so many of our friends die or go crazy, that we'd understand the melancholy was always there, nourishing itself on our stories, even then, when we were young.

The strange desert out the window is like a mirage of discarded plastic water bottles. The wind never stops blowing the trash across the planet.

Back then, says Freddy, it was just hopeful and exciting. Young people had deserted the towns and cities they came from en masse, Freddy says, and were attempting to build another kind of community on the road or in the temporary rest stops, like that basement beneath the free library. It was understood, or seemed to be understood by all of us or most of us that there was a different kind of war going on. Maybe it's just youth, or maybe it was the drugs, but I don't think so. It was like all of these walls had come down for a moment and you could see space as it really is, infinite, indivisible, terrible. You could sleep with anybody and often it was just awful but then sometimes it wasn't, and the awful experiences didn't seem so bad, that's just how it was. You could open up to anyone or you could make it all up. We'd grown up and, quite rightly, demanded the world. That's where I first met the anarchist, although it was several years before we got together, before I realized I was in love with him.

What we were battling was monstrous, certainly, says Freddy, although maybe not exactly in the way we believed. We thought we were the Life Force waging war against the Death Machine. I guess it isn't as easy to separate the two as we might have believed. We were actually doing battle for poetry, or for consciousness, which is exactly the same thing. It's a battle that never ends, and we seem to be losing more and more ground. Every parent in America only wants its children to be safe and successful, it seems. They watch them every minute, don't they? Even the liberals and the gays. Especially the liberals and the gays. They attach tracking devices to their teenagers, if they're young enough they even leash them. It's all on video and it's dreadful.

So why aren't you in love with an anarchist now? asks Melvin.

Freddy looks over at him, but as if he's already dreaming, and then his eyes close, and before Melvin knows it, he's fast asleep. You should still be in love with an anarchist, Melvin says. I could be an anarchist, he says.

It never really occurred to Melvin before that old people used to be…young. That fact alone seems like it should alter him somehow, but he isn't sure it's working out that way. By the time Freddy wakes up, this Moroccan guy has convinced Melvin with his impeccable English to buy a lot of hash from him once they get to Casablanca. He describes himself as a teacher and a world traveler to Freddy and Freddy's very friendly but Freddy suggests he come by their hotel later that evening and tells him where they'll be staying, but then they go to a completely different place. In Morocco you never buy drugs on a train, Freddy instructs Melvin. You buy them from the staff of the hotel.

They stay in this bizarre optical illusion of a room in Meknes. It was designed in the '70s, Freddy explains. Then they go to Fez where little boys are always trying to massage them or guide them or sell them some rugs and Melvin thinks it's weird to be as poor as he is but everyone thinks he's full of money and wants to get it all the time and then they move on to this dreary little seaside town where everything smells like gas and the beaches are littered with garbage and then back up through the mountains on a bus late at night through the mist and it seems like the bus is about ready to drive off the cliff over and over again and Melvin's about to get sick and this woman sprays him with perfume and that just makes it worse and he throws up in a paper bag. Night falls and the bus churns on through the mountains and the fog. Strangers step out of dark corners and trees in the little foggy roadside stops and try to sell them pounds of marijuana. In Chefchaouen, the buildings are all kind of bluish and someone in the market offers opium flowers and Melvin's excited, having read De Quincey, but he doesn't tell Freddy that, he just says that he read online that on opium time would last forever and Freddy says, How dreadful that would be, but then he says, You mustn't believe everything you read, would you like to try? That evening they drink opium tea and just lie around in the bed and time doesn't last forever although it does move pretty slow, but for Melvin it's all about the cartoons, he just closes his eyes and sees the most excellent and detailed cartoons full of intricately drawn life forms with squiggly heads and landscapes and forms keep morphing and then Melvin sees himself as a little cartoon that's devouring everything in sight and becoming a city named Melvin and then a whole country and the world, and he cracks up 'cuz it's so silly it's just hilarious, it's like the stupidest and fakest part of himself, that part that has a name and wants its name to encompass everything and he thinks, *Is this what people want?* And he thinks, Is this what some stupid part of me wants, too?

In the morning he has a headache. Back on a train to somewhere, another shady guy insinuates himself into their cabin and tries to sell them drugs and Freddy's all polite and tells him where they'll be staying in Tangier, but then they go to a completely different hotel again, where Freddy buys the hash from the staff. The hotel's supposed to be grand, but it's just a bunch of Germans sitting out on the patio with Coke bottles. The ocean or the bay or whatever it is, is right there and it smells. *The Sheltering Sky* was filmed here, Freddy explains. One of the worst movies ever made of an excellent book.

One day Freddy goes out to see some supposedly amazing gardens. I'll just stay here, Melvin says. I don't feel so great. Alone in the hotel room, he smokes and looks at Freddy's books. *Voluptuous Panic: The Erotic World of Weimar Berlin* and *A Science for the Soul: Occultism and the Genesis of the German Modern*. He looks through Freddy's suitcase and reads his diary, which doesn't mention Melvin once, at least not by name. A lot of pronouns. "He" does all kinds of things. *His acceptance of this separation between sexuality and being was an invention of hell.* Is he talking about Melvin? He finds some index cards with quotes written on them. *If you realize that all things change, there is nothing you will try to hold onto. If you are not afraid of dying, there is nothing you cannot achieve.* Lao Tzu. *Oh, and there's Night, there's Night, when wind full of cosmic space feeds on our faces: for whom would she not remain, longed for, mild disenchantress, painfully there for the lonely heart to achieve?* Rainer Maria Rilke. *Tread the earth gently, for it will soon be your grave.* al-Hasam al-Basri. *The perplexing incident just over, before the john / stood the wall filled with base graffiti, / and from the other side of the hole in the middle of the wall, a glaring / parched eye was looking in.* Takahashi Mutsuo.

Tangier is a throbbing insect hieroglyph out the window.

Melvin's been ready for his epiphany, but maybe what actually exists is better. Something has to change. Partially it's the way he talks up all that soldier bullshit all the time. Has he really turned himself into a dream of Death? As it turns out, for the most part, Melvin doesn't want to be a slave and he doesn't want to own one either. He doesn't want slaves in the background either, slaves that he can't see, working for his benefit.

He gathers his things, his passport and money and so on, because you never know. The way he's feeling is that maybe he's never coming back. He takes the notecards, too.

Free and alive in the city, it's just hilarious. The city's putrid but amazing. It's hot, but nobody wears shorts here except for the ragged little boys who chase him for several blocks demanding money or sweets. There are only boys here, it seems, and men with facial hair, and nothing in between. The head scarves, on the other hand, are outrageous. A whole world that could care less about him and his ideas going about its business. Buying, selling, a lot of worthless crap, but some of it's fruit, and some of it's beautiful and wooden. The squiggly language resembles something he saw once, in the sidewalk, on drugs. People give him hard looks all over the place, men, women, little kids, not mean looks, just like *Hey, I'd do it with you* looks. Terror without violence, he thinks. Peace within, chaos without. He just flows through the city, losing his way. Melvin stops in front of this handsome guy who's selling tissues. Instead of one of his legs, it's a stump. Looks like maybe he's been tortured or escaped from a dungeon. Melvin points at the tissues like he might buy one. The guy's staring at Melvin like he can't believe his good fortune. Melvin just starts laughing. The guy starts laughing, too. Melvin points at himself and then back and it's crazy. *Beyond reproach*, Melvin thinks. That's what he wants to be. Exactly. It's the *Beyond* part that mostly does it for him. The guy fastens a stick to his stump and they walk through the city together, saying things that nobody understands, smiling and shrugging at each other until Melvin sees a sign and they go inside and Melvin gets a room. A room of my own, Melvin thinks. It's up a winding stairway, at the very top of the tower. Halfway up, Melvin picks up his new friend and carries him. He barely weighs a thing.

It's a shabby little room but the light that comes in through the diaphanous curtains is beautiful, almost golden.

The handsome guy sits on the bed and looks at Melvin's notecards with interest. Melvin's like: I'm *not* a dream of Death. Then again, he's not like *the opposite* of a dream of Death either. Without the clothes, the guy's body is even more of a mess. Who tortured him? The genitalia are out of the question.

The light in this room is sure golden. Maybe it's already dusk out there.

Melvin lies back and the guy slowly, real slow, sticks his stump in his ass.

Jesus fuck.

Melvin cums right away.

No question is being answered. There is nothing to understand.

The guy doesn't stop and that's cool. The stump goes in, the stump goes out. In and out, like breathing.

He always wanted a revelation that would coincide with a really strong orgasm. But now that the orgasm's over, and the stump is still going in and out, the torture victim begins telling him his story in a language Melvin can't understand. Cries from the street float in, laughter sometimes, the sound of grief.

If Melvin was a goddess, the material aspect of existence, with eight fluctuating limbs, a freakish vibrating animality, a radiant pallor, making and unmaking...Like maybe he's just partly a dream of Death and the other part...a dream about strange interminglings?

Before she married the Mormon, Melvin's mom would sit on his bed at night and sing to him. In prison, Melvin had a dream once early in the morning, just before he woke up, and it was that Madonna song his mom used to sing. A voice was singing, *Now I believe that dreams come true...Cuz you came when I wished for you...This just can't be coincidence...The only way that this makes sense...*

It wasn't his mom's voice and it wasn't Madonna's voice either. The voice sang, *Oooh, you're an angel.* She sang, *Oooh, you're an angel. In disguise—I can see it in your eyes.*

When he woke up for real, tears were streaming down his face.

If Melvin were responsible for dreaming of Time, a history, a story, what would the point of the story be? In this room with the light that never seems to change.

It's tricky, without interfering with the motion of the stump, but he twists forward and kisses the guy and the guy kisses him back and Melvin wonders if maybe in the Arab world they aren't as sexually confused as in America. Or maybe it's just because he can't speak the language.

7

Alone with the mist. Alone with the evolving forms, the erosion. Alone with vapor and stars, the idea of stars, with the idea of atoms and time and nothingness. Alone with a mind so packed full of language and people, memories and ghosts, that it's like her mind is a crowd and Felicia isn't alone. But she is. Alone with the lichen spattered on volcanic rock, with ice, with blue and orange and blue. Alone with the idea of blue. Here at the end, nothing is settled. Everything's in flux.

When she got married, Felicia's decision to take Geordi's last name was fraught with difficulties. She'd published under her own name and didn't want to lose those readers; she was a feminist; most important, she distrusted her own enthusiasm for having a Mexican last name. It was during Felicia's deliberations that Sherry Mbeki came to town and told her that she'd married her second, African husband for two reasons—out of friendship, to get him American citizenship, and because she wanted his last name: Mbeki. An African-American lesbian taking on her African husband's last name was in no way equivalent to her own situation, but it was all the permission Felicia needed. She kept her original name for writing but used Geordi's for official documents.

Her fifth day in Iceland, Felicia dyes her hair black. She stands forever looking at herself in the hotel mirror, as if she's Kim Novak in *Vertigo*. A trashy brunette from Salina, Kansas, who's transformed herself into the icy blond aristocrat of Jimmy Stewart's dreams, and now, after the fake murder of the dream girl, has transformed herself back. She wants Jimmy Stewart to love her for herself, but he just wants to transform her into the fake woman he remembers.

With her Mexican name on her passport and her black hair, she imagines she can travel un-American and almost incognito. She reads and she walks, which she's pretty sure is most of what she's ever wanted to do.

***

Things can't exhaust themselves, the *I Ching* says. But maybe she has exhausted herself, maybe things need to move beyond her. Or maybe they already have.

There's a store on the corner and she buys herself a pack of cigarettes.

She hasn't smoked cigarettes since she was twenty-three or twenty-four. She wants fire. Is she angry? Angry at what has become of everything. Angry at the dreamer of this dream. Probably at Geordi, but that's just a mask, she's pretty sure, over a deep core of smoldering cosmic rage. *Thus, I am able to feel the very root of life, with all its inhospitable workings*, as Will Alexander's narrator said. Frenetic, torrential, pyrocrystalline. Felicia walks as if burning and sits and drinks coffee with milk at a café near the sea. In the warmth of the sun, she writes, but not much. She isn't ready yet. She's listening.

She is rereading a story from *Autobiography of My Dreams* when she is interrupted by a strange creature wrapped up in scarves, like a mummy. The creature, as Felicia thinks of me, is of indeterminate gender, although clearly dressed as a woman. Excuse me, I say in a heavily accented English. I couldn't help but notice your reading material.

I'm listening to music, but remove my earbuds.

Are you a fan of Celia Abad? Felicia asks.

I laugh. I guess you could say so, I say.

May I sit? I ask.

Of course, says Felicia. *Please*.

There's something very masculine about my features. Felicia wonders if I'm an old drag queen or TG.

When I was still a very young girl, I say, I became quite interested in death. I'd discovered that death frightened me. The fear of death made me weak, I thought. I didn't want to be weak. I wanted to be a writer. I didn't realize, even there, in Manila, that there are far more frightening things than oblivion. I hadn't yet watched anyone die.

You're from Manila? asks Felicia.

She doesn't think I look even slightly Filipina.

My dear, I say. I want to introduce myself. I am Celia Abad.

Felicia's first impulse is to laugh, but as a foreigner she's developed a certain veneer of politeness.

I know, I say. You think I withered away in that asylum where Oliver left me in the '80s. It's what everyone believes.

Felicia is shocked less at the idea that I could actually be Celia Abad—which isn't even plausible—than at the fact that she's met somebody in Reykjavik familiar enough with the life history of an obscure Filipina surrealist to even tell the lie in a somewhat coherent way.

And what brought you to Iceland? asks Felicia.

I hate the heat, I say. Connecticut made me want to die, the summers there.

I shiver and Felicia looks carefully at the lined face behind my shades. I could even be eighty, she supposes, but wouldn't Celia be over a hundred if she was still alive?

She asks me if I remember Waylon McClatchy.

My memory isn't what it used to be, I say, and it was never much.

I read some letters you wrote him, Felicia says.

Yes, I used to write letters, but I gave that up.

Felicia tells me that Waylon's dead, she's not sure why.

You must be my biggest fan, I say.

I just might be, Felicia says.

It isn't often that I meet one of my readers anymore. I'd like to invite you to lunch on my boat.

Probably it's all a weird scam or a setup, Felicia thinks; she's going to be robbed of an organ, kidnapped and held for ransom, murdered for a snuff film. But those scenarios wouldn't make any more sense than the ludicrous idea that this light-skinned old drag queen or butch woman in Iceland is actually Celia Abad.

Of course, says Felicia. It would be an honor.

I rise, surprisingly agile, and reach out my hand.

Then come, I say. Let's walk together.

The boat is anchored in the shallow, incredibly green sea. The water is warm as a bathtub. As we walk up the short ramp, a man emerges onto the deck, about Felicia's age. He's dressed in the formal attire of a servant from some bygone era. He nods to Felicia and takes my arm, leads me to the enormous bed that is somehow perched there on the deck, where he helps me get settled, covering me with blankets, and helping me with my bonnet. Thank you, my dear, I say. I do fear I've caught a chill. The wind has picked up, as if there might be a storm coming someday. The sky is hazy and the summer air is surprisingly cool. The servant disappears below deck and Felicia sits in one of the deck chairs by the bed, leaning toward me so as to better hear what I say. Felicia thinks that maybe she actually has met an insane, wealthy old drag queen who believes himself to be Celia Abad. The more terrifying possibilities don't yet occur to her. The servant brings us out a tray with tiny little triangular sandwiches and tea and then disappears. Within a few moments, Felicia realizes that the boat has been untied and that we are slowly drifting out to sea.

As a young girl, I tell her, I tried to embrace the idea of my own oblivion. I discovered that it was possible to not care. About life or about death. I found that this was a very interesting state from which to write.

It is a difficult state. You forget, after a while. It isn't the same thing to watch other people die as it is to practice your own death.

I loved my little sister Eme more than anything, do you know that? We would play together for hours when we were girls and I would tell her stories. I would tell her my dreams as if they were real events that took place while we were sleeping and I would tell her stories I'd read in books as if they were about us. And then when I was older, I left the country and I went all over the world with my husband and I didn't speak with her or receive letters from her but everything I was doing and thinking, I would imagine telling Eme about and so they became real, these things I was doing. My life became real and my dreams became real and they were no different one from the other. That is just how I would tell it to Eme.

Years later, I discovered that Eme died shortly after I left the country. Nobody told me. They were afraid I'd die of grief. She was beaten and murdered by her boyfriend. Later, he went into politics.

When I was a girl once, my father took us to the carnival, I say.

In Manila? asks Felicia.

I suppose so, I tell her. We followed a road that climbed steeply toward the edge of the city. Only with the sun at its peak in the sky, in the wilting oppression of the heat, the dazzling silence of noon, did I feel uneasy, hearing the shouts of small children echoing up from the city, which was now below us. A cloud of blue butterflies rose from the shrubs at the side of the road and Eme squealed, for she had been told that when you see a blue butterfly, you are really seeing an angel. Angels prefer the squalor of cities, somebody had told her, I can't remember if it was something I passed on or maybe it was only my mother. My mother wasn't with us that day. She was washing her hair with a very fragrant kind of powder that she mixed up herself. It was only my father and Eme and me. A procession of villagers passed us on the road from the opposite direction, carrying a coffin. There was a brief pause, as if the procession was over, but then came a group of mourners, featuring one old woman who was shrieking and ranting and sobbing so loudly it was shocking that we hadn't heard her until we'd passed the bend and she came into view. Her tirade contained only verbs and adjectives, I remember it clearly. She didn't use nouns at all. It was as if she was being drained of something, as if something was being forced out of her—after she'd passed us, the noise of her grieving just kind of withered away. It was—well, it was mostly like she'd been possessed by a force of some sort, a force that doesn't really belong in our little corner of space. The road was dusty and the sun was like a horrible pulsing eyeball in the sky.

It was late in the day by the time we arrived at the carnival. At the carnival, I discovered an incredible alien intelligence, hiding within a flesh so convoluted, so textured, yet so flexible. It was being humiliated and enslaved. It spoke to me telepathically. It told me the story of its enslavement and humiliation. What other story did it have to tell? It had a kind of ancestral memory of freedom, but that memory had just become a kind of myth that the enslaved elephant hadn't yet found a use for. There was, too, a peculiar feeling, a feeling of profound and inexplicable horror concerning *myself*. I told Eme the elephant's story and she began to weep. My father promised us sweets and meat and we moved along. After that he took us on the rides. I wasn't interested in any of them anymore. The painful robot rides, the collective hallucinations, the funhouse of mirrors, or even the haunted house, where the dead would come back and mingle with the living in terror and ecstasy. I wasn't interested in the freak show, where all the mutants were displayed, the miniatures and the rest. If things only made sense when everybody was separated, named, caged, and revealed, I wanted no part of it. I have never been interested in revelation. The Tunnel of Love was the worst of all. There was a hideous descent through a sticky and sentient darkness, and a babel of voices utterly alien to all that I knew of life and the body and the world. What a strange fantasy, I thought. An intimate darkness in which to hide something only exciting as vital sin. It left me cold and yet deeply aware, as if I was awake and dreaming at the same time. Dormant sense organs seemed to waken within me, bringing me knowledge I had no use for, of pits and voids crawling with conscious forms and leading even further, to places where no light had ever shone. So that's what they mean by the Tunnel of Love, I thought. This was the evening I first achieved my ideal state. Oblivion no longer frightened me and I knew then that I had nothing to lose, and I didn't care. It was just a few years later that I met my husband, when I was fifteen.

Eventually I forgot that I didn't care and I lived my life, although I sometimes wrote as if I didn't care. But in fact I did care. I cared about my success as a writer, I cared about my literary reputation, trivial things that have nothing to do with writing as if one has already died. I believe that it is important to write as a ghost might and to care as little about living as a ghost cares.

I didn't live an especially happy life, or a good one. I don't know what either of those things would mean. I left my sister when I was a child, and I've been alone ever since. I get no satisfaction from looking back over the things I've finished. It's nice that you like my books, I guess, but you don't matter to me either. I am no longer in a mental institution, that is important. That is the best thing.

For a while now, however, I've not cared about the future at all. All I have is the pleasure of the sun on my face and the pleasure I get from hearing my own voice drone on into the afternoon to some stranger or another. To you, my dear. My biggest fan. Really, of course, I am only talking to myself. But it's nice to pretend.

The heart has to present itself alone before nothingness, I say. It has to beat alone in the darkness. And then…

And then it must keep on. Keep on beating. I don't know why. I don't know, but it must.

We have drifted quite far out into the sea. The city seems to be still visible in the distance, but then it seems to waver, and Felicia catches a glimpse of what might be the coast in a different direction, before it, too, shimmers and seems to vanish. She looks around, completely at a loss as to which direction leads to land. The sky is so hazy, she can't even tell where the sun is. There's maybe an island visible sporadically on the misty horizon. The only sound is the quiet murmur of tiny waves lapping against the boat and my heavy breathing. I've put my earbuds back in and Felicia imagines that I've fallen asleep. She walks from one end of the deck to the other, trying to get her bearings. The water is startling and green and shallow; it looks to be only a few feet deep. Might just be an optical illusion created by the amazing clarity of the water, but the breeze has become quite cool. She climbs down the ladder to the lower deck to find the "servant," but there isn't anyone there. She does find a windbreaker, however, puts it on, and returns to the deck.

She can see an object that looks nothing like she's ever imagined an anchor would look, and yet is still, clearly, an anchor, keeping us rooted in place.

The sea is perfectly still. She walks from one end of the boat to the other, scanning the glassy surface for some sign of the servant out there, swimming or diving or whatever. Whoever it is who steered the boat this far must surely still be nearby.

The sea is quite beautiful, if not at all inviting.

***

After a while she sits back down in her deck chair to wait. Even if she's not sure what she's waiting for. My earbuds are off again and Felicia puts them in, to listen. It's the Velvet Underground, with Nico singing. Felicia listens to the song all the way through and then sits back down to wait some more.

Felicia isn't sure how much time has passed when I begin talking again. You could die, I say. But where would you go?

I tell her that complete shamelessness is treated in some quarters as proof of genuine liberation from simple *manners*, of all things. The way people walk down the street licking their ice cream cones like cats, I say. But I was telling you about that beautiful young man who escaped from his seducer's apartment, I say. I describe a maze-like structure of staircases and closed doors.

Something cold smacks against Felicia's forehead, an icy raindrop. I continue my strange story, which is about this beautiful young man and his perpetual mutation. There's no clear pattern in the story. It isn't really a story at all, but just descriptions of moments in time that seem to flash into my mind and then vanish, as if I was still back there in the middle of my false history, my delusional life, telling my dreams to my little sister. It's like the tracks of some fugitive, glimpsed from a train window, disappearing into the forest. And then I begin humming that Nico song. "I'll Be Your Mirror." Felicia is struck again. A few light flakes of snow are falling from the hazy sky. The snow sizzles as it hits the warm green sea, a sea like pale green glass.

You can look deep inside it. What will it show you?

The water reflects, but it reflects only the hazy sky. It reflects only the flakes drifting down.

For a moment it seems that Felicia can see land in every distance, as if she's floating in the crater of a volcano. But it isn't land, she can see that now, only mist. But maybe there are islands. Maybe any direction would take her someplace.

A new character crosses the deserted plain, I say, and disappears, limping toward a kind of...

I trail off. Only the sound of my wheezing remains, as if I've suddenly fallen into a deep sleep. As close to death as one can be, Felicia imagines, and still be alive. The sky brightens for a moment, as if on fire, as if the sun might peek out from the haze. Felicia settles back into her chair. In her windbreaker she feels like some kind of security guard. After a while, she steps over and peers down at my face wrapped up in all of those blankets and shawls. Trying to see if I'm still breathing. The sea out there is almost perfectly still.

8

THE MAN'S VOICE IS SAYING, Why is he putting toys down his pants? Why is there a little man in his butt?

It's just a toy, the woman's voice says. Maybe he's hiding it.

DJ refuses to open his eyes, even as he is picked up off the bed, and then dropped again. The little man is blue and handsome and thinking very hard. He's irresistible.

What did they do to him in California? the man's voice asks.

DJ won't open his eyes and he won't cry and so his dad just keeps spanking and spanking until his mom says his dad's name and then his father starts sobbing and his mother holds him. Later, she holds DJ.

It's his hypersexuality, he hears his dad saying in the kitchen. It's a symptom of his gosh darn bipolar disorder. It's in his gosh darn genes.

Later, when DJ goes to school, the children on the playground are cracking open. The school is enormous and the children are imprisoned and somebody is making them sing in rhymes. On the other side of the street is a vacant lot covered with weeds that blow in the breeze as far as the eye can see. Everything is impossibly vast and bright and the world itself is glossy and smooth. Later, when he's inside the yard, he stands at the fence. Everything outside of the school seems alive and real and moving about, but inside it's just a humming machine. After recess, he is sitting at his desk and the teacher is saying things but he can't make any sense of them. That's when he wets his pants. He can feel it running down his legs and then forming a puddle at his feet. How big the puddle is. DJ, what has happened? his teacher asks, and she gasps, and the children start shrieking in horror. She sends DJ to the nurse and the nurse calls his mother. He's burning up with fever.

He dreams of a barn burning bright with white electricity. It is smooth and shining.

His father believes that he was turned into an ungodly mess. When he was kidnapped.

His mother loves him efficiently and nonchalantly. Your brother won't come around here anymore, she tells him. The word *kidnapped* has come to seem like a magic incantation, a key to everything wonderful and strange that will ever happen.

His mother tucks him into the bed. A hundred and four degrees, she says and she looks worried. A kind of fairy tale missing the most important pieces. He learned a secret he can't remember anymore. A big man who was always singing and a nice woman with hair and a house. The times get all mixed up. What has happened and what is happening and what will happen for the rest of his life. His mother is sitting on his bed, holding his hand and singing a song he's never heard before. *Now I believe that dreams come true…Cuz you came when I wished for you…This just can't be coincidence…The only way that this makes sense…*

I used to sing this song, she says.

He doesn't know why she is whispering.

Only for him.

She begins weeping.

I'm sorry. I'm sorry, baby.

From the depths of his fever, he can see that it's a performance, and that it isn't for him. It's for somebody who isn't here, or for herself. Either way, it won't do anybody any good.

Please forgive me, she says, and she is sobbing.

Somewhere, outside, his father is incinerating the little blue astronaut man and the stench of burning plastic declares the murder to the neighbors. Dizzy and choking and burning alive! DJ will leave his body. The pools of ignorance and fear only appear solid, like congealed, painful layers of energy, from down below. In fact, everything is moving colors. The revolution of the life-world has been ongoing, it is just beginning, it will never end.

When DJ is ten, he'll discover Melvin's abandoned page on some old social networking site and it will open a hole in space and time. A picture of Melvin making goofy face and a quote from some band that nobody listens to anymore.

A few months later, DJ will find a Christmas card he doesn't remember ever seeing before packed in the bottom of a box of old pictures. *I'll see you soon and we'll have lots of fun I promise* and then it looks like he wrote XOXOXO but scribbled it out. And then *Love, your only brother.*

DJ will look up the return address on Google Maps, with street view and overhead view, hoping to see a tiny Melvin looking out a window or lounging around the backyard.

He'll search Melvin's name and he'll discover *Roost*. He won't mention it to his parents. DJ will have his friend Emma order a copy. When it finally arrives, he'll be disappointed to find that there aren't any pictures of Melvin. Only the things that surrounded him.

He'll discover *Tinky Winky Rising 2*, described as a "gaysploitation" film. The director's website will lead DJ to two porns Melvin starred in, using the name *Johnny Nitro Cruz*.

The porn he won't get his hands on until he's almost fifteen, just a few months before he runs away from home. He'll meet a married man on the Web and they'll rendezvous at a local park and the man will drive him around in his car and he'll go to Secrets, the Adult Bookstore, for DJ, to buy a copy of *Bi Force*. Right there on the shelf between *Bi Enigma* and *Bi Night*. The first time he'll watch it will be in the company of the married man, in a motel room, seeing his brother get raped by a man and woman who dump him by the side of the road, with the married man egging them on. Yeah, fuck that little boy-pussy, he'll say. He'll have the married man order him a copy of *Stoner Boner* off the Web. It will take weeks for it to arrive, or at least the married man will claim that it isn't there yet. The married man lies about most things, DJ has learned, and DJ really only forgives him his personality when he's naked in bed. He'll keep suggesting that DJ isn't nearly as grateful as he ought to be for all the trouble and the risk he's putting the married man through.

At night, in the den, in the basement, DJ will watch Melvin's six-minute scene over and over again, all by himself. With the sound turned down completely.

Later he will pack his bag and Emma will take him to the bus station.

How can you just leave? People are crazy out there.

But he's been there before. Anyone can do it, you just have to go. This is like the worst place in the world.

I know, she'll say. Just watch out for yourself.

He'll fall asleep on the bus and dream about a forest of oak trees with tiny skeletons hanging in the trees.

He'll get off the bus in Reno and it's like he's done this a thousand times before. He's always been getting off the path in some strange wasteland, through all of human history, and walking through the empty downtown, by the river, where kids his age, kids who live here, are huddled, plotting something. But they don't speak the same language anymore, do they—he's moved beyond them, he's an adult, he's all of history. He's off the bus.

He has stepped out of his childhood—finally—and he is alone in the night. He's done this millions of times and will do it a million more. But now, here, DJ, he's alone in a way—tonight—that can never be undone. In Reno he has become himself. A ghost haunting himself. An outcast and a thief alone until the end of time. Same old story.

Because Reno is so familiar, like a joke he's grown up inside, except for all the lights, it's like something's wrong with his perception. He's left one place and arrived in the same. But there's the Five Star Saloon. He'll hang out across the street and give the men who come out hard stares. A guy in a cowboy hat will take him back to his hotel room, high in one of the casinos. To the north, there's a building lit up with warm green lights. This is DJ's disappearance. To the south there's a building lit up with pink lights, so beautiful. This is his heart. Beyond that, in every direction are the moments and just slightly higher dark clouds. The cowboy, too, lies about everything, DJ figures out, a few hours into the adventure, and so the words are just this sound, the babble of the river that rushes through the middle of the town, a few blocks away, dividing into two and coming back together again.

Stay awhile. Why not?

The cowboy awakes sometimes in the middle of the bright and dehydrated days and makes his way down to the casino. DJ goes for walks. Down Virginia toward the pink building, unlit during the day. The city is empty and glaring, a few stragglers rolling their luggage down the avenues or riding their bicycles erratically in pursuit of something.

You all right? asks one shirtless zombie.

Yes? Maybe? The trees are the same. Pale skeletons and some pines. The clouds are the same. Bright taffy close overhead. Vicious quarreling birds. The people in Reno seem poorly programmed. The clouds get angrier late in the day as he trudges back up Virginia, past a closed bookstore. Do people read? Even the gay men here drive big old trucks. Where do our instructions come from? Who are we thinking for? Can you share a dream?

Why would you want to?

One afternoon alone in the room he'll put *Stoner Boner* on the cowboy's laptop. Meanwhile, the desert will go on forever. Flat land with scrub on it. Lichen pale green and orange on purple rocks out there. Isn't that so? The mountains all around. The sun going down to the west and rain clouds so still with their dark trails in the distance like they have a message for him. He'll close the blinds and in his reflection in the glass he'll see his own face with the little scar on his forehead from when the police burst in to save him.

What do the vapor trails dream about? What is the old man saying to the boy?

He has touched himself here and descended into himself until the bottom fell out and he must believe that if you go deep enough into that dream—Reno, say, a numbed and desolate hallucination—you touch everyone who has ever dreamed, you touch them there, uselessly, hopelessly, there, where the bottom's fallen out.

It doesn't do you any good, but it's a vision. And it's yours.

Later, he'll leave the guy a note and just go. Back at the bus station he'll play Silent Scope, a game with a big-sighted gun, you can't see anything except through the scope. Given a choice of Story Mode, Shooting Range Mode, and Time Attack Mode, he'll choose the story. Do Not Shoot Innocent Bystanders! He's supposed to save the president, who's in a bunker somewhere. He'll think he hears his name being called on the intercom, but it won't be real.

Back on the bus.

Approaching San Francisco, all these strange windmills on the hills that gave him nightmares a long time ago, he's pretty sure. Nightmares about birds. And then he's crossing the bridge. A bright new bridge with palm trees, but the old ruined bridge will still be hulking next to it, an iron dinosaur. One side of the decrepit structure has been completely dismantled, so it's like an industrial island haunting the bay.

The function of a bridge is to take you from one side to the other. What is the function of a ruined bridge?

Maybe it's an island in time.

He'll have the name of the woman who wrote the magazine article and the director's name. Probably he'll just walk the streets in San Francisco, and he'll run out of money, and he'll stay at youth shelters, and he'll lose all hope.

As the bus comes into the city, he'll realize that now his life is beginning. That anything can happen, and he'll be free.

Acknowledgments

This novel first developed from my interest in the stories that surrounded me during a particular time, in a particular place. The goal was always to make a structure and a space that could contain voices other than my own. Nonetheless, it is a work of fiction and it is mine. While some of the stories are distorted versions of stories I've been told or have read, the characters are not meant to represent real people, even if they share the names of real people or have written the same sentences as real people.

Along with the stories I have been told, the stories I overheard, and the stories I received from the atmosphere, I am indebted to many written sources, foremost among them *The Opera Barn*, an unproduced screenplay by Opera Joe and Ralph Dickinson, and the testimony of Anonymous, "The agony of the years after," pp. 306–15 in Jonathan Katz's *Gay American History*. Other sources include *Malcontent in Cambridge*, an essay on Maria Komornicka by Izabela Filipiak; *Means of Intelligibility*, David Larsen's PhD thesis; *Pontormo's Diary*, translated by Rosemary Mayer; the journals of my grandmother, Leah Beachy; the *Chicago Review* issue "New Polish Writing"; the *I Ching*; *I Ching: Walking Your Path, Creating Your Future* by Hilary Barrett; *Writers in Prison* by Ioan Davies; *Kabbalah: A Very Short Introduction* by Joseph Dan; The Invisible Committee, *The Coming Insurrection*; *Arabesque: Narrative Structure and the Aesthetics of Repetition in 1001 Nights* by Sandra Naddaff; "A Philosophical Approach to Artificial Intelligence and

Islamic Values" by Ali A.Z. from *IIUM Engineering Journal*, Vol. 12, No. 6, 2011; the journals of Vera T. Scott; and *Aztec Thought and Culture: A Study of The Nahuatl Mind* by Miguel Leon-Portilla.

There are many sentences and phrases from other writers clearly quoted within the text, but there are sentences that I've appropriated as well, for my own transformative purposes, without clearly sourcing them, including sentences or phrases by Clarice Lispector, Kathy Acker, Mutsuo Takahashi, Jean Genet, H. P. Lovecraft, Boyd McDonald, Mohammed Ahmed Abdul Wali, Yusuf Sharouni, the *Apocryphon of John*, Mohammed Khudayyir, Ibrahim al-Kouni, The Invisible Committee, Heriberto Yepez, Gloria Anzaldua, Mustafa Mutabaruka, Juan José Saer, Dante, Henry Corbin, Miral al-Tawahy, John Yau, the *I Ching*, Marie Redonnet, the *Sophia of Jesus Christ*, Roland Omnes, WG Sebald, the *Paraphrase of Shem*, the Marquis de Sade, and Leon Kass.

I would like to thank Matt Roberson, Dan Waterman, and everyone else at FC2 and the University of Alabama Press. Also: Johnny Ray and Kelly, Opera Joe, David, David L, and Ralph. Also: all of you, living or dead, whose stories have somehow partially ended up in these pages. If you're reading this, you probably know who you are. Thank you for letting me listen.